The Price Of Freedom?
A Gallant Gesture.

It is 1918. As the German and Austrian empires are crumbling before the victorious armies of the allied powers, Captain Harry Phillips, British prisoner of war is offered his freedom by his German captors. To secure it he must smuggle out of Rumania a beautiful young princess whose pro-German sentiments have made her a target of socialist revolutionaries on the prowl through middle Europe.

Phillips agrees. And finds himself involved in a breathless, perilous chase across war-torn Europe with a woman too courageous to deplore, too resourceful to disregard, too beautiful to resist—and too far above him to love . . .

Flight From Bucharest

R. T. STEVENS

In My Enemy's Arms

(original title:
Flight from Bucharest)

WARNER BOOKS

A Warner Communications Company

Original title: *Flight from Bucharest*

WARNER BOOKS EDITION

Copyright © 1977 by Souvenir Press Ltd.
All rights reserved.

This Warner Books Edition is published by arrangement with
Doubleday & Company, Inc., New York, N.Y. 10017

Cover art by Walter Wyles

Warner Books, Inc., 75 Rockefeller Plaza, New York, N.Y. 10019

Ⓦ A Warner Communications Company

Printed in the United States of America

First Printing: September, 1980

10 9 8 7 6 5 4 3 2 1

In My
Enemy's Arms

One

On a day in October 1918, when the Austrian and German Empires were on their cataclysmic slide into oblivion, the atmosphere in the German-occupied hospital on the north side of Bucharest was orderly and quiet.

Captain Harry Phillips limped along a corridor in his faded woollen dressing-gown, his armed German escort behind him. Other walking patients glanced briefly at him or studiously ignored him. He was the acorn in the bag of nuts. They were German, he was British. They were casualties of the battles now raging in Serbia, where the revitalised Serbian Army, supported by British and French divisions, had the Austrians and Germans in escalating retreat. Harry was a casualty of bad luck.

Somewhere in the hospital he heard a gramophone scratchily playing Beethoven's Moonlight Sonata. A nurse, watching his approach, opened a door in the corridor for him. He thanked her in English. She was German, as all the nurses were, but he did not speak her language. Classroom French was his only linguistic achievement, but he had at least managed to improve on the spoken word during his service in France.

The nurse pointed to the grounds outside and said, "The Herr Major."

"Thank you," he said again. She was polite but did not smile. He understood. She could see defeat staring her country in the face, a defeat so humiliating that the position of Kaiser Wilhelm himself in the balance.

He walked through the lobby, using his stick, and out into the grounds. The turf was autumn green, the day bright but fresh. He was thankful for the warmth of the hospital dressing-gown. His escort marched solidly at his back. A lean figure in the tailored field-grey of a German officer awaited him. The armed escort was dismissed by the gesture of a gloved hand. Harry came to a stop.

"Good morning, Herr Captain," said Major Carlsen, a man of thirty-five.

"Good morning, Major." Harry was twenty-seven.

"Shall we sit?" The English was easy, fluent.

"Thanks."

They were both pleasantly civilised. They seated themselves on a bench. The leaves lay thick in sheltered corners, elsewhere they lifted, rustled and skittered in the breeze. Harry wondered what Major Carlsen was after, he did not think this was a mere social call.

He considered himself a little unlucky to be in German hands, although he had no complaints about the hospital. The Allies had begun their Balkan offensive in September, from Salonika. They had quickly put the Bulgarians out of the war, then driven into Serbia, which had been under Austrian occupation since 1915. The Austrian and German divisions were pushed steadily back, but in one determined counter-attack the Austrians cut out some forward British batteries. Harry was among the prisoners taken. Sent north to an Austrian prisoner-of-war camp, he escaped on the way and began a hazardous trek back through enemy-occupied country in the hope of rejoining his unit.

He had almost broken through the southern-most German lines when he bumped into one of their patrols. In the dusk of evening a young German soldier, nervously reactive to shadows, fired first and enquired later. Harry, a bullet in his thigh, was recaptured muttering and swearing. He was sent for treatment to the Queen Constanza Hospital on the north side of Bucharest. The hospital had been taken over by the Germans, the conquerors of Rumania. He was interrogated by a very correct but very courteous German officer, Major Carlsen, who congratulated him on his initiative and commiserated with his bad luck.

The German doctors and nurses accorded him the same attention they gave their own wounded and were as courteous as Major Carlsen, who visited him a couple of times. He was fit, his wound was not serious and it healed rapidly. They gave him a stick to help him with the therapeutic exercise of walking about. They did not want to keep him too long. His presence was slightly embarrassing.

"You wished to see me?" said Harry.

"Yes. A cigarette?" Major Carlsen offered his case. Harry took a long white tube with a gold-coloured tip to it. They both lit up. The cigarettes had the strong aroma and distinctive flavour of Balkan tobacco. "You are considerably improved, Captain Phillips."

"Considerably," said Harry. "The treatment and attention have been first-class."

"It was not a complicated matter, I believe, merely a small hole in your leg."

"Oh, nothing at all," said Harry.

"You are a very fit man."

"Am I? Perhaps. The war, of course, hasn't been quite as uncomfortable for the gunners as for the infantry." But he did look fit, considering his hospitalization. He had no surplus flesh, his dark eyes were clear and alert, and his five-eleven frame was vigorous. True, his auburn-brown hair needed trimming, but it was thick and healthy. The German barber had offered his services but having seen how he cropped the German officers, Harry ducked the operation that would have made him look like an egg. He managed, by being very persuasive, to get one of the nurses to use her scissors on him. She had snipped his tufts quite professionally and Harry left it at that.

"You will be discharged in a day or so," said Major Carlsen, removing his cigarette and watching the smoke curl before the wind whisked it.

"I've been expecting that."

"There is a camp near Bistrita." Bistrita was in Hungary.

"Is it comfortable there?"

"I doubt it, circumstances being what they are," said the Major, "but it may be educational. You will meet Russians, Serbians, Poles, French and a few British, I think."

"Very educational," said Harry, "and very crowded, I imagine. However, circumstances being as you say, I may not be there too long."

Major Carlsen's impassiveness cracked a little. Harry discerned a momentary flicker of sadness, an acknowledgement of coming defeat.

"No, perhaps not too long at all, Captain. Indeed, if you prefer, it can be avoided altogether."

"I don't suppose you mean I can stay here," said Harry, "I'm rather an embarrassment, naturally."

"Yes. Those who feel a sense of defeat can't communicate with those who wear an air of victory. And you do represent to us a nation whose declaration of war was unnecessary and unjustified."

"I hope," said Harry, "that we're not going to argue about who started it and whose fault it was." He smiled. "We shall end up fighting."

"Those arguments are for the politicians," said Major Carlsen, his grey eyes observing the caped progress of a hurrying nurse across the grass. "We are the tools they use to resolve their more intractable differences. But you may be sure they will take no blame for the war. That will be laid at the doors of others. No, I did not mean you could stay here. I meant you might be allowed to make your own way back to your country."

Harry blew a startled smoke ring. It was picked up by the breeze and carried flirtatiously away.

"Will you say that again, Major?" he said.

"It would not be impossible for you to get to Trieste, and from there to France or Italy, do you think?" It was said in a pleasant, enquiring way.

"You'll turn me loose?" Harry was skeptical. "From here to Trieste it's your territory. I'd be damned lucky to get halfway."

"Oh, I don't know." Major Carlsen sounded casually English. "I'd say your ingenuity would carry you farther than that."

"I've nothing to lose, I suppose," said Harry, "but there's a catch somewhere, isn't there?"

"There's a little more to it, yes," said the Major. "You'll need papers. You speak French, I think?"

"Fairly well. It wouldn't deceive the French, but it wouldn't have to, I imagine."

"I thought the role of a White Russian would do admirably. They are known to speak French."

Harry regarded the German with curiosity. Major Carlsen's eyes did not waver. He seemed like a man sitting in calm judgement of his own suggestion.

"Pardon me for not falling over myself, Major," said Harry, "but I'm wondering why you should do this for me, provide me with fake Russian papers and send me on my way."

"Because in return," said the Major, "I

thought you might do something for me. I thought you might agree to having a travelling companion."

"Oh? You don't propose coming, do you?" Harry allowed himself a moment of humor. Major Carlsen did not smile.

"That is a joke?" he said.

"Just a light aside," said Harry.

"In defeat we can try to joke amongst ourselves, perhaps. It's a little more difficult to joke with others."

"You concede defeat?" Harry was interested. He knew nothing of the pessimism rife within the German High Command. "But you're still fighting."

Major Carlsen did not sound bitter as he said, "Yes, I myself concede defeat. There comes a time when hope must give way to reality. Germany will have to sue for peace within the next month or so." He managed a light rider. "But we gave you a good run, Captain Phillips, a good long run."

"Too damned long," admitted Harry, who had fought in France, Mesopotamia and in the present Salonika campaign. "Who am I to be saddled with on my wandering journey of hope?"

"I'll come to that in a moment," said the Major, "but first have I your word as a British officer that whatever you decide you will not speak of our conversation to anyone? I can assure you it's not a matter that will affect the course of the war. It does not even concern the war. It is purely a question of giving help to someone who desperately needs it."

"You have my word," said Harry, not disliking the German.

Major Carlsen waited until two patients and a nurse had gone by before going on.

"Captain Phillips," he said, "this is not only a bad time for Europe and its peoples, it's a bad time for kings and emperors. The end for many of them is coming. They will be the first scapegoats for the politicians. The Tsar of Russia and his family have already been found guilty and executed. Soon others will be condemned, some because they have been all-powerful or not powerful enough, some for being incompetent or merely patriotic. And some for simply being sons or daughters of the mighty. Do you know Princess Irena of Moldavia?"

"Moldavia? Is that a principality?"

"It was until it became part of Rumania about sixty years ago. Do you know the Princess?"

"Personally?" Harry was a little ironic. "No. I've never moved in exalted circles."

"I was not expecting you to claim personal acquaintance, of course," said Major Carlsen with the flicker of a smile. "I meant, have you heard of her?"

"I've probably heard or read of all of them in my time, without it meaning anything to me." Harry was not an avid devourer of court circulars but he read his newspapers. "One European princess is much the same as another as far as I'm concerned."

The October sun slid behind a grey cloud and the fresh day suddenly became colder.

"Princess Irena isn't quite the same as

14

others," said Major Carlsen, "her temperament and character are highly distinctive."

"I don't know what that means in a princess," said Harry, "but in a woman it can mean regular fireworks."

"It means in Princess Irena a woman of intelligence and spirit."

"Then I'm pleased for her," said Harry dryly.

"She is distantly related to King Ferdinand of Rumania, whose Queen is the granddaughter of Queen Victoria."

"Yes?" For some reason, thought Harry, the Major had been doing a little homework.

"Yes." Major Carlsen was definite. "Princess Irena remained here when we occupied Rumania. King Ferdinand and Queen Marie accompanied their Government to Jassy. The Princess has always been pro-German and was against Rumania going to war with us. Now certain Rumanian Socialists and extremists wish to try her for treason. She has frequently spoken out for Germany and is among those being blamed for many things."

"Well, for God's sake," said Harry, "speaking out on behalf of a country which conquered her own wasn't the most sensible thing to do, was it?"

"All of us hold opinions, Captain, but not all of us are brave enough to continue holding them and speaking them irrespective of circumstances."

"Where did you learn your English?" asked Harry.

"At Oxford," said Major Carlsen, "I spent three years there. Captain Phillips, Princess Irena is still in Bucharest. But when Germany has to sue for peace and leave Rumania, she will no longer be under our protection. She will not be safe in her own country, despite all that King Ferdinand might do for her."

"Then send her to Germany," said Harry.

"That is what she wishes, but that is what is denied her. We have been forbidden to help her in that way. Apparently, she would be an embarrassment to the Emperor. He himself is not too safe now, since he will have to take all the blame for the war. His ministers have advised against giving Princess Irena sanctuary. Her presence would be very unwelcome to them."

Harry drew his dressing-gown tighter around his pyjamaed legs.

"That doesn't make sense," he said, "not in view of her sympathy for Germany."

"I think it's a little chilly for you, Captain," said the Major politely.

"Yes," said Harry, "can we do a turn around the grounds?"

"You can manage that?" said the Major, looking at Harry's stick.

"No trouble at all and I'm supposed to do more walking than sitting. The bullet hit bone. Walking fends off atrophy, I believe."

They began to walk, keeping to the paths. There were few other patients about.

"Our ministers require the best possible atmosphere to prevail if they are forced to seek an armistice," said the Major, "and the Princess is notoriously against anything but a continuation of the war. She believes the survival of Germany and Austria absolutely necessary to save Europe from the disaster of Socialism. And she has said so."

"I see," said Harry, "she's pro-German and anti-Socialist. That's consistent, I think."

"All the same she's being denied entry into Germany. They think she will influence the Kaiser and induce in him a mood of obstinacy that could lead Germany into civil war. No, I am not exaggerating."

"I should think she's got problems enough in her own country," said Harry, "without wanting to get involved with Germany's."

"That's a good, sound black-and-white comment, Captain," said Major Carlsen, "but a little too easy to make, if you'll forgive me." The sun came out again, sharply outlining the thinning branches of trees. "Princess Irena is Rumanian first, but has blood ties with almost every European country. In some matters she insists her chief loyalty is to her beliefs and her conscience. She has consistently attacked the policies of the Allies which, she says, will reduce Europe to anarchy. So it's as difficult for her to find refuge in France or England as elsewhere. In your own country several of your politicians have been asking whether certain people in high places are arranging to receive her in England. They have said the British people would not tolerate it, any more than they would tolerate the arrival of Kaiser Wilhelm. However, she cannot stay here. Each day becomes more dangerous for her. Her enemies mean to arrest her, condemn her and shoot her."

"As a traveling companion," said Harry, "she sounds like dynamite with the fuse lit. And where would I take her if nobody wants her?"

"She is headstrong, Captain," said Major Carlsen, "but she is worth saving. This is agreeable to you, walking and talking?"

"Oh, agreeable enough," said Harry, "but leading to the improbable, I feel."

"Wars happen and armies engage," said the Major. "Men blow each other to pieces or shoot each other to death. To sight a rifle for the purpose of killing someone is either an instinctive act of self-preservation or a premeditated act of aggrandisement. However, in the main we have not been so uncivilised as to involve women."

"Except in wars where they have been considered part of the plunder."

"An irrelevance, Captain in these enlightened days," said the Major. "Would you take a woman out and shoot her?"

"The French shot Mata Hari and you shot Nurse Cavell," said Harry, "but no, I'm not in favor of shooting women. Is this really likely to happen to Princess Irena?"

"It will happen the moment Germany withdraws her troops from Rumania."

"But won't the Austrians or Hungarians give her protection?"

"Out of the question." The Major, hands clasping his short cane behind his back, was dismissive. "In Austria or Hungary she would be delivered into the hands of Socialists, who would then hand her over to the Rumanian extremists. I am hoping you will try to get her to England, away from the Balkans altogether and safe from the long arms of people determined to execute her. I confess to you, Captain, that I admire her, and I have told her I will do what I can for her."

"You want me to get her to England?" Harry did not fancy that. "Ye gods, what a hope. And even if I did manage it, she won't be received, she'll be deported back to Rumania."

Major Carlsen thought deeply before commenting on that. Then he said, "Not, perhaps, if she were the wife of a decorated British officer, a man of proven courage. Politicians are capable of things you and I would not consider for a moment. But even the most cynical of them would not stand up and ask for the wife of one of the country's heroes to be taken from him and turned over to people obviously intent on shooting her."

"Hold on," said Harry. He stopped on the leaf-strewn path. He was decidedly curious. "I think I've followed you up till now. Now I think I'm falling behind. Is she married to a British officer?"

"She's married to no one."

"Oh, by God," said Harry.

"Yes," said Major Carlsen impassively, "I think you have caught up."

"I still think you'd better put it in plain words."

Major Carlsen said in his courteous way, "Captain Phillips, would you consider giving Princess Irena your care and protection by marrying her?"

Two

A nurse came up and said something to Major Carlsen. He nodded and thanked her. She hesitated, her curiosity aroused by the indefinable, by the strange quiet existing between the politely formal German Major and the handsome, resolute British officer. Pointedly, Major Carlsen thanked her again. She flushed slightly and hurried away.

"There's some coffee available, apparently," said the Major, "we can have it in a private room."

The private room was someone's small office on the second floor. The coffee was on the desk. The Major poured it. It was not remarkable coffee but it was hot. Harry sipped his with his mind on Elisabeth. Calm, unflappable, her approach to this flight of German fantasy would be endearingly analytical. He thought about the whimsical smile she had given him when, on his last home leave a year ago, he asked her to marry him.

What was it she had said?

"You're being very gallant, Harry."

"I'm being positive, I hope. Give me your answer, won't you?"

"Yes. Of course yes. You know there's never been anyone else."

There never had been for either of them. They had known each other, lived close to each other, for years. He knew no other girl he would rather be married to than Elisabeth. He could not keep her poised on the edge of uncertainty forever just because of the war. They would be married immediately it was over. Their families were delighted with the engagement, especially as they had been waiting in hope for quite some time. Elisabeth wrote him charming letters on his return to the front, telling him in each one to take particular care of himself.

"I must say I'm flattered by your confidence in me, Major," he said, "and absolutely bowled over by the Princess's willingness, especially as she's never met me. But it's impossible, of course, you must realise that."

"It's fanciful," said the Major, "but not impossible. The Princess feels that as a British officer you must also be a gentleman, and that therefore it's not necessary to meet you in order to approve or disapprove of you."

"Oh?" Harry was slightly amused.

"It would put you at risk if you gave her

22

your help and protection. I should not wish to deceive you about that."

"Major, I'm not free to even consider it." Harry was firm, decisive. "I'm engaged to a young lady in England, I've contracted to marry her at the end of the war."

Major Carlsen did not seem ruffled or discouraged.

"That's a complication," he conceded, "but not an insurmountable obstacle. Your marriage to Princess Irena will be annulled as soon as it's tactically and reasonably convenient. The annulment would be on the most unquestionable of grounds, which would make it automatic."

"I see," said Harry dryly. The war had made him a little irreverent about proprieties and niceties. "You mean—?"

"Precisely," said Major Carlsen with distinct nicety. "It could be arranged without any publicity after you had spent a little time together in England and any fuss had died down. With luck you might get her into England simply as your wife and without her true identity coming to light at all. Then there would be no headlines and no fuss of any kind. Your fiancée must be considered, of course, but I am sure she is a sympathetic and intelligent woman. If so, she would understand all you had done for Princess Irena and even admire you for it."

"A very nice thought, Major," said Harry, sitting on the edge of the desk, "but I can't see any woman in a light as angelic as that. We're sometimes inclined to ask of women things we'd never ask of ourselves. And I really can't see myself in the role of Galahad, in any case."

All the same, he was intrigued, he was interested, and not completely sure he couldn't be persuaded.

Perhaps Major Carlsen sensed this. He said, "You may have seen newspaper pictures of Princess Irena?"

"I don't know, I may have," said Harry.

"Let me show you something that does her more justice than a newspaper picture, Herr Captain." Major Carlsen reached into his pocket, took out a wallet and extracted a postcard-sized photograph. It was a sepia print, a formal portrait of a young woman of about twenty-one, but with her expression soft and pensive. Her head was slightly turned to show the graceful line of her neck, a tiara adorned dark hair glossy and beautifully dressed, and she wore ear-rings to match the glittering tiara. Her shoulders were bare, her dark lashes long and thick. She was quite lovely. Harry, impressed, smiled wryly. He could not imagine how he would cope with a marriage of convenience to a woman as royal and as beautiful as this. Nor could he picture Elisabeth receiving the news with joy or falling into raptures of admiration for his gallantry. That was too much to ask of any fiancée.

He looked up from his absorbing study of the portrait and caught on the Major's face an expression that was almost tender. It told him that the German's concern for the Princess was not based on sympathy alone.

"Well?" said the Major.

"Frankly," said Harry, "I don't think she stands a chance."

"Captain?" The Major raised his eyebrows.

"I mean," said Harry, "that with those looks she'll be recognized on every street corner. I wouldn't even get her out of Bucharest."

"Most men might not. I think you would. You are a man of courage and initiative. And you would receive some necessary co-operation."

"Look here," said Harry, "I've got to have time to think it over."

"There isn't too much."

"I'm sorry about that, but you have sprung it on me. And I'd better meet her, don't you think? I appreciate her confidence in me as a gentleman, but I think we need to see each other before any decision is made. I've spent four years firing high explosive at you and the Turks, and it's probably taken some of the polish off me. I wouldn't want the Princess to think she's getting Little Lord Fauntleroy."

"Captain Phillips," said Major Carlsen, carefully putting the photograph away, "I will arrange for her to visit the hospital this afternoon. That will arouse no suspicion among those who are watching her, for she visits many hospitals."

"I'd better have a fresh shave," said Harry, wondering why the devil he was suddenly halfway to taking on the impossible.

Perhaps it was the photograph.

Perhaps it was that the only alternative was a prisoner-of-war camp. That loomed as unbearably depressing and damned dull.

He was called from the ward later that day. He was taken up to the same small office on the second floor. He knocked. Major Carlsen's voice invited him in. He went in.

She was there, the young woman of the photograph, standing at the window with the Major. She turned. She wore a long silver-grey coat trimmed with fur and a matching hat and veil. She put up the veil. Her features were smooth, healthy, her brown eyes inquisitive and alive. She was unarguably lovely, her color giving her warmth, her hair glossily rich below her hat. But she was cool in her self-possession. He glimpsed teeth immaculately white between her slightly parted lips. She was as curious about Harry as he was about her, and Major Carlsen momentarily delayed the formal introductions.

Harry, lean from campaigns in Flanders and the deserts of Mesopotamia, looked taller than his five feet eleven. In her grey shoes she stood only a few inches shorter. He saw her, aside from her physical beauty, as a problem, a challenge, a rarity. She saw him as a man who might be an invaluable asset or an incalculable liability. She also saw him as a personable British officer whose hospital dressing-gown gave him an air of casual charm. His dark eyes were speculative, quizzical.

He smiled. Her response was immediate, a smile of animation and warmth. Major Carlsen coughed.

"Your Highness, may I present Captain Harry Phillips? Captain Phillips, Her Highness, Princess Irena of Moldavia."

Harry bowed. He supposed that was the right thing to do. She acknowledged the courtesy by extending her hand. He took it. He supposed

26

the next thing to do was to kiss it. He bent his head and put his lips lightly to her fingertips.

"So you are Captain Phillips," she said in English touched with the soft accent of the Balkans. "You are the officer Major Carlsen has told me about. Thank you for wishing to meet me." She had so much charm that Harry wondered how the devil she could upset anyone, politically or otherwise. Well, she was a woman of course. One could never tell which way the most delightful of them would jump.

"I was interested, naturally," he said.

"I am glad you were," she smiled, brown eyes soft as they met his.

They were measuring each other, taking stock of whether there were any warts plainly impossible to live with.

"We are establishing a rapport? Good," said the Major.

"I'm in trouble with some people," said Irena.

"So I'm told," said Harry, repressing a desire to suggest she may have brought it on herself. She was regarding him without guile, without any hint of guilt, yet he thought there was an air of appeal beneath her calm. Harry, having spent most of his four years of war out of touch with women, had decided that the longer he was away from them the more worthwhile their role in life seemed. Their sense of logic might be a trifle suspect, their tantrums inexplicable, but when one was thinking about them in pools of icy, muddy rain the creatures made a better reason for living than anything else. Princess Irena, for all her high-born status, was vulnerable, her call for help irresistible. There would be nothing about the adventure itself Elisabeth would disapprove of, and the marriage certificate would be torn up at the right time. It would be the relationship that Elisabeth would have suspicions about.

"You are thinking me over?" said Irena in a way that was enchanting.

"I'm thinking how crazy it is," said Harry.

"I shall be a problem, I know," she said with a rueful smile, "but I promise not to be a nuisance as well. Major Carlsen has told me about your fiancée. I should not make the slightest difficulty about that, it is too important to you. I should explain to her how gallant you had been and we would arrange for the annulment to be as quick as possible."

"That's very important, yes," said Harry, "but how can I guarantee I'll ever get you to England?"

"You would be willing to try?" She was softly earnest.

Harry looked hard at her. She was a warmly regal elegance. Quixotic generosity tilted at the windmill of commonsense and for once the windmill fell over.

"Yes, I'll try, Your Highness," he said.

Her eyes became bright, grateful.

"Thank you, you are very gallant, Captain Phillips."

"I think I'm also slightly off my head," said Harry.

"Perhaps we all are," said Irena, "but sometimes doing the crazy thing is the only answer, isn't it?"

"Sometimes," said Harry with a smile, "it leads straight to suicide."

Her laugh was slightly emotional. Major Carlsen's watchful impassivity was softened by relief. They said goodbye to Harry, the Major promising he would return later for a further talk. Harry stood at the window and watched them go. There were three open German cars in the drive. Major Carlsen and Irena took the center car. The others were full of German soldiers, sitting with rifles upright between their knees. That, thought Harry, had to be a sign of the danger the Princess faced in her own capital. The cars moved off, Harry came to. He shook his head at his impulsive idiocy.

He wondered if he'd have said yes had the Princess not been so lovely. The advantage women of beauty held over their plainer sisters was typical of the utter unfairness of life.

Major Carlsen was back that evening and again they met in the small office. The German spread a map over the tidied desk.

"First," he said, "I am asked by the Princess to tell you how grateful she is. She is also very impressed."

"After a meeting as brief as that? I must say," said Harry a trifle caustically, "that I marvel at your willingness to entrust her regal personage to me. You really know nothing about me. At the first sign of trouble I may hand her over to those who want her."

"Would you do that, Herr Captain?"

"No. But how can you know I wouldn't?"

Sometimes, Captain Phillips, it isn't necessary to have known a man all his life to decide whether he is a better risk than others."

"It's a risk right enough. Look here," said Harry plainly, "don't make it more difficult for me by trying to convince me I can perform miracles. I can't. I can do my best, but I'm not Jesus Christ and I'm not Hercules. Be logical about our chances and stop making me feel that you think I'm infallible."

"I shall simply put my trust in your courage and initiative," said Major Carlsen firmly. "There shouldn't be too much difficulty getting you and the Princess to Belgrade." He put his finger to the map, tracing the line from Bucharest to Belgrade. "You will go by train, you will leave her house with her in the evening and travel to the station as a German officer, since the curfew puts restrictions on civilians."

"German officer?" Harry could not see the sense of that. "I don't speak a word of German."

"You won't need to." The Major was crisp, clinical. "We will have your throat bandaged as if you have been wounded there. The Princess will do your talking for you. She will be travelling as an Austrian woman not restricted by the curfew."

"When will this be?"

"Two evenings from now. You will be even fitter then and it is as much time as we can give you. Once you are out of the city proper and on the train it will be safe for you to change into the civilian clothes I shall get for you. With these you will assume the identity of a White Russian acting as an agent for the German Army Headquarters in Belgrade. I will see you're supplied with the necessary papers. It will be too risky on the train to maintain your pose as a German officer, even with a bandaged throat, for it will be full of troops. As a White Russian you will get by with your French."

"You sound remarkably confident," said Harry, "I feel remarkably nervous."

The Major reflected, not for the first time, on the quality of his man. He was aware of the British habit of underplaying their hand, of the tendency of other peoples to be taken in by this. There was a slight smile on Captain Phillips' face, but his eyes were as cool as the devil, the line of his mouth and chin firm.

"I am more confident about you than I am about other things," said the Major. "Plans can go wrong, events take an unexpected turn, but as long as the man in charge is equal to the need for improvisation all will be well. A great general is not one who can make plans but who has the courage, if necessary, to tear them up."

"Major," said Harry, "you're the general in this case, you're making the plans, but I think I'm the one who may be faced with the responsibility of tearing them up."

"Perhaps," said the Major. He went on to suggest that once in Belgrade, Harry should go into hiding with the Princess and wait until the Allied advance forced the Austrians and Germans to evacuate the city. That should only be a matter of days if the Serbian, British and French operations continued to be conducted as aggressively as they were at the moment. Then Harry could come out of hiding, wearing his own uniform, and make his way with the Princess across Croatia to Trieste, which would be a most suitable take-off point for Italy or France. It would not be easy. The Princess's enemies would be looking for her the moment they realized she was no longer in Bucharest, and there would probably be a certain amount of civil disorder when the Austrians and Germans began their withdrawal from Serbia. That would not make things easy for anyone but as a British officer Harry would have some standing, some immunity. The extremists and their agents would look for the Princess to be travelling as a peasant or a refugee, anything but what she was. They would not, however, suspect the wife of a British officer to be Irena of Moldavia.

"That wouldn't stop some of them recognizing her," said Harry.

"True," agreed the Major, "but she will dress modestly and look as inconspicuous as possible. A little care and thought will be needed."

"Officially," said Harry, "once you've let me go my way I'd be expected to rejoin my unit, providing that was reasonably possible."

"And if it weren't?"

"Then it would be my duty to try to get back to my country."

"You will stretch a point?" said the Major.

"I suppose I must," said Harry, "or it all falls down from the start. I could, I imagine, simply wait for the first British troops to arrive in Belgrade and then hand myself and the Princess over to them."

"Do you think that a good idea?" asked the Major sharply.

"No," said Harry frankly. "I should be posted

back to my regiment and she, as my wife, would be billeted somewhere. Somewhere fairly decent, of course, but not, from your point of view, very satisfactory."

"I think we are approaching a point of fine understanding, Captain. It would not be satisfactory at all. She would inevitably be discovered. She must be taken out of the Balkans, out of Europe to England. They will probably be after her all the way. Your problem, when Germany and Austria have sued for peace, will not be with us but with the kind of people who rise to temporary power in towns and villages. There'll be Socialists in some places, ambitious Bolsheviks in others, all demanding the heads of those they consider guilty of crimes against the people. It will last until new law and order is established. You will need steady nerves at times."

"Really?" Harry was slightly caustic again. "Frankly, I think my nerves will be jumping about all the time."

"But you will go through with it?" said the Major.

"You say she's worth saving. Perhaps she is. I can only do my best. If I succeed my only concern will be with the quick annulment of this marriage. My fiancée is the best of persons. She too is worth something. When I see her I don't want to be humming and hahing about things, I want to be positive."

"You may reassure yourself about that." Major Carlsen allowed himself a slight smile. "It isn't likely that Her Highness will develop a romantic attachment, she will keep her feet on the ground, as you say."

"I hope so," said Harry, "as I don't think

you can rely on every woman to do exactly what men expect her to. Perhaps princesses are different."

"You're cynical about women?" said the Major with a lift of an eyebrow.

"Not at all. They're delightful." Harry smiled. "I haven't seen enough of them recently, in the social sense. But I like to be a realist about them. Then one can avoid what I'd call shots in the dark."

"Captain Phillips," said the Major severely, "Princess Irena is not likely to wish to remain married to a commoner."

"Well, damn good," said Harry fervently.

"Is that realistic enough for you?"

Harry laughed. Major Carlsen smiled. It was a slightly sad smile.

"What else do I need to know?" asked Harry.

"You might care to hear in confidence that certain high personages in your country will be grateful if you manage to arrive safely with Her Highness, but naturally they will not allow their feelings to be made public."

"With her pro-German background, very naturally."

"Until recently," said the Major, "she has refused to believe she was in any real danger from people she has only contempt for. She believes it now because they have been watching her for weeks. They watch her house. They pass to and fro. They watch her when she goes out, they watch to ensure she returns. They slip the curfew to watch her. They make no move but they are always around, day and night. They will arrest her as soon as we Germans go. I am able to see she has adequate protection here in Bucharest and that is all I can do. I could not, for instance, take her to Belgrade myself. I should not get the necessary permission. But if I did our Socialist friends would probably think I was going to take her all the way to Germany, and as likely as not would arrange for a bomb to greet her in Belgrade. I am hopeful, however, that with your help we can get her out of her house at night and on the way to Belgrade without bringing the pack down on you."

"I don't like the sound of that word," said Harry.

"What am I achieving, Captain, with all this talk?"

"You're making me nervous," said Harry.

The Major, obviously considering that a satisfactory condition, said, "Good, it will give you eyes in the back of your head. By the way, don't look for any help from the Serbians in Belgrade. They would do what they could for you as an escaping British prisoner, they would not lift a finger to help the Princess. Almost certainly they would turn her over to Rumanian extremists here."

"You know," said Harry thoughtfully, "with your knowledge of all the political and military implications, you'd make a better protector and guide than I would. Isn't it possible your immediate superior would turn a blind eye if you went off with her to Trieste? I think you'd manage to keep her out of bombing range."

Major Carlsen began to draw on his gloves.

"My orders, Captain Phillips," he said, "are

such that I could do nothing of the kind without being placed under arrest on arrival in Belgrade. You as an escaping prisoner of war have much more latitude. May I arrange for you to be brought to her house in two days' time?"

"I should like to think that we're not gambling with her life," said Harry.

"Her life will be worth nothing if she stays here. She will either be tried and executed, or simply executed. Do you wish to reconsider?"

"No, damn it, I've lit the gas under the pot," said Harry, "and it's up to me now to stay with it. Otherwise the porridge will burn. But is it absolutely necessary to marry her?"

"She will not be able to get into England except as your wife. She will be safe there, she will know what to do. I'm afraid you get little out of it, Captain, except your freedom in advance. And that, at times, may be an uncomfortable freedom."

"Allow me to say," said Harry dryly, "that you have a very distinctive way of spreading light and cheer."

"I am glad I am not the instrument of gloom," said Major Carlsen gravely.

Three

Major Carlsen put in his promised reappearance two days later, in the evening. He brought with him the uniform of a German infantry colonel.

"In this," he said, "you will be able to enter the Princess's house without suspicion. She frequently entertains German officers."

"I'm not surprised," said Harry, "that she's in trouble with her people."

"She entertains us, she does not collaborate, she has never given us a single piece of information." The Major was stiff in his defense of Irena. "The house will be watched as usual but no one will stop us. They haven't yet reached the point of being arrogant, of making demands on us. But they are aware of the Allies' advances and they may get bolder any moment. We must have you away with her this evening. The train leaves the station at Chitila, north of Bucharest, just before midnight. It will be mainly carrying troops."

The uniform was an excellent fit. It turned Harry into a coolly handsome German officer and had Major Carlsen smiling faintly.

"You realize what will happen if I'm caught by your people wearing this?" said Harry.

"Normally, you would be shot."

"I'd prefer to avoid that."

"Show them the papers you'll find in the suit of civilian clothes. They establish you as an agent working for us."

"Yes, a White Russian agent."

Harry was not regretting his decision, but the uniform did seem to signify a point of no return and he felt he must be quite definitely off his head. He was a man, however, to whom adventure appealed. His father was a bank manager but he had chosen farming as his own career. During breaks from his job as an assistant farm manager he had climbed the Matterhorn, helped to crew a clipper and joined an archaeological dig in France.

He thought about Elisabeth again, and her possible reactions. He smiled a little, he frowned a little. Major Carlsen asked him if he was having second thoughts.

"Mixed ones," said Harry. At least his wound was no real problem. The bandages could come off tomorrow. He took up a parcel containing his own uniform and accompanied Major Carlsen out of the hospital. They passed a doctor, a nurse, an orderly. They were acknowledged but without second glances. Outside it was dark and fairly cold. There were few lights. They were on the northern fringe of Bucharest. A staff car took them to Princess Irena's house. With the city under curfew from dusk until dawn, German patrols were active most nights, but on this night the area through which the car passed seemed innocuously quiet.

The house, in a long street, was large and square. Harry saw no one about but could well believe there were eyes on his back as he went up the stones steps with the Major. The German rang the bell. It was answered by a housemaid dressed in dark blue and crisp white front. She bobbed politely to the Major. He stepped into the hall, Harry following. The maid closed the door, led them through the entrance hall into a larger hall and up a wide, carpeted staircase. On the spacious landing she knocked at a door. A woman's voice responded. The maid opened the door, stood aside and the visitors went in.

A small candlelit chandelier illuminated the room. There were shelves full of books, armchairs in a half-circle round a fire in which wood sparked, an Oriental carpet with a fringe and an atmosphere that invited quiet and cosy with-drawal from a world in the final throes of Armageddon.

Irena rose up from a chair. Her dark chest-nut hair glinted richly under the light, her brown eyes were warm from the fire and her face glowed a little from its heat. A dress of deep green silk swathed her figure. The shortage of dress materials in wartime, as well as new atti-tudes to style, had cast from women the volum-inous drapery of Edwardian fashions. Harry, who could remember the play and rustle of satin and lace petticoats, and the mystique of frills and furbelows, nevertheless liked the simplicity of the modern styles. Irena's dress enhanced slender waist and rounded bosom.

He executed a little bow but resisted the impulse to click his heels as she eyed his German uniform, for her expression was cool, as if she disliked this kind of imposture.

"Good evening, Captain Phillips," she said. Her English was as fluent as the Major's, her soft accent appealing. She did not offer her hand. Major Carlsen glanced at her, obviously asking for a continuation of the rapport established two days ago. She gave the faintest of shrugs, she smiled philosophically and extended her hand. Harry took it, lightly pressed her fingers and relinquished them.

"You must forgive the way I look, Your Highness," he said with just a suspicion of irony. His front as a German officer was something she and Major Carlsen had undoubtedly cooked up between them.

"It's of no consequence," she said regally.

Since it was, he thought that remark absurd. He suspected she was in a slightly overwrought state. It was natural. For all her engaging friendliness during their first meeting she had to have some doubts, and she could not be entirely rapturous about a plan which placed her under the protection of a virtual stranger and nominally into his arms. He was an Allied officer and although her country had entered the war on the side of the Allies, it seemed she considered this to have been a mistake. Incurably pro-German she was bound to dislike the necesity of turning to a British officer for help and she perhaps believed her sense of obligation would come to feel like a hairshirt. But he liked her pride and the way she held herself. The Germany she admired so much was tottering and her life was in danger. It was not the best time to expect joy and warmth from her.

"I'm jumpy," he said, "are you?"

Her smile this time was soft, real.

"Forgive me," she said, "I let my own nerves show for a moment." She turned to indicate a bottle of wine and some glasses on a small, inlaid table. "Will you please do the honors, Major Carlsen?"

The Major poured red wine.

"Your Highness," he said and she took the glass he offered. She looked at Harry as he accepted his.

"It's a little gesture, you see," she said. "Please, shall we drink to being three friends? That is better than drinking to war and to not being friends. That is almost over, the war. We three must lead the way to reconciliation, yes? So, my friends?"

"My friends," said the Major, straight-backed.

Very touching, thought Harry. Brown eyes were warming him, charming him. She was striking, beautiful. He felt the weight of his coming responsibilities. Well, they were a challenge. So was she. So was Major Carlsen.

"My friends," he said.

They drank. The Major looked at his watch. Irena smiled again.

"Shall we be married, Captain Phillips?" she asked.

"That seems to be a very necessary part of the plan," said Harry.

"Yes," said Irena, "but I promise, it will not be a complication for you when we reach England. I shall not forget you have your fiancée to consider, I shall be no trouble, I shall live quietly in London until people become sane again and I can return here. Until then, where else can I go but England?"

"I've no idea," said Harry, "I'm not au fait with Balkan politics and I can't keep up sometimes with our own. But as long as you do keep quiet when you get to England, that should help you stay out of trouble there."

"Oh, you are thinking I'll say things there because I've said things here?" She was a little quick off the mark. "You believe people should not say what they think?"

"I believe personages should be discreet." He offered that as a friendly suggestion.

"Personages? Personages?" She was ready to be royally mettlesome.

"Princesses in high places," said Harry, finishing his wine.

"Really?" Now she was a little fiery. "Sometimes to be discreet is to be hypocritical, Captain Phillips. Shall we be married or not?"

"Your Highness." Major Carlsen sounded a soothing note.

Harry smiled. Perhaps she was indiscreet, but she was also fearless and honest. One could not object too much to that.

"I am sorry," she said, liking his smile, "per-

42

haps I'm a little on edge, yes? I do not get married every day, you see."

"Neither do I," said Harry.

"Or run for my life," she said ruefully.

That appealed to him. He agreed with Major Carlsen. She was worth saving, worth a little trouble and even the complication of a marriage of convenience. It was still a crazy venture but not as much as it had seemed at first.

"Father Jacobus is ready?" enquired the Major.

"I think so," she said.

"And you two?" Asked of both of them it offered Harry his last chance to draw back.

"Are we?" she said to Harry.

"I'm told it doesn't actually hurt," said Harry.

Irena laughed.

"At least, I don't think Captain Phillips is going to be dull, Major Carlsen," she said.

"We are asking a little more of him than that," said the Major.

They were married by Father Jacobus. Sonya Irena Helene Magda Ananescu of Moldavia to Harry Gordon Phillips of Amblestoke, Hampshire, England. It did not take long. Major Carlsen was in attendance and so was the maid who had appeared earlier. Father Jacobus took a small glass of wine before discreetly vanishing and the maid returned to her duties. The Major consulted his watch again.

"You must leave in ten minutes," he said. "A cab will be waiting, Her Highness knows where, and our curfew patrols have orders to let it through. You wish to say goodbye to your staff?" he said to Irena. She nodded. "Please, no longer than ten minutes, Your Highness."

"I shall not be long," she said and left the room.

The Major produced a bandage, Harry undid the collar of his uniform and the bandage was wound and fastened around his neck like a white stock. Final details were explained to him. His British uniform and the civilian clothes were in a case, the uniform pressed flat under a false bottom. Her Highness would also be taking one case. She understood it was impracticable to take more. She would be posing as an Austrian woman from the Tyrol, lately widowed and on her way home from Bucharest.

"All in black, you mean?" said Harry. "Isn't that rather too obvious and too conspicuous a disguise?"

"Not in Central Europe, Captain, and certainly not among Austrian and German women."

Harry was to dispose of his German uniform as he could. The civilian clothes contained the faked Russian identity document, together with papers signifying he was a courier for the Germans. Naturally, he was not committed to any rigid course of action except that of getting Her Highness to England, and each step would most likely be governed by circumstances and expediency. For the moment he was Colonel Rupert Wagner.

"Wagner is good enough, I think, Captain? It has a musical ring to it?"

"Has it?" said Harry. "I thought Wagner went in for thunder and lightning."

Major Carlsen indulged in one of his rare smiles. He rationed himself strictly.

"Your Russian name will be Sergius Rokossky."

"My problem," said Harry, "will be with making up my mind who I am from day to day."

"I think you will manage," said the Major calmly. "Be careful as soon as you reach Belgrade. Once her enemies find the Princess has gone the news will travel fast."

"I'd be obliged," said Harry, "if you'd keep them in the dark."

"I shall do what I can, but they will know eventually. It's even possible the news will come from inside this house. Princess Irena's servants all seem loyal, but who knows how deeply politics can penetrate domestic loyalty? That is the most contemptible facet of politics. It undermines the most devoted human relationships. I am glad, for all my faults, that I am a soldier."

"I rather enjoy bringing in a good harvest myself," said Harry on a practical note.

He and Irena were to leave by the back door, through the gardens and over the wall into the gardens of the house behind the Princess's. From there they would make for the adjacent street. A cab would be waiting for them a few minutes walk away. It would take them to the station at Chitila. On the train they were not to know each other, for if they were seen as a pair at the outset they would be looked for as a pair from then on.

Harry said, "Major, because of language difficulties, I don't know if I conveyed adequate thanks to your hospital staff. Will you please thank them for me?"

"I shall be happy to. It has been an ugly war, Captain, and a destructive one for my country. But Germany will rise again."

Harry grimaced.

"I rather wish you hadn't said that, Major."

"Germany must rise. It will. There are errors to rectify."

Harry shook his head. Irena came back. She wore a black hat and full veil, with a black coat. She looked like a young widow in mourning. Harry hoped it wasn't an omen.

"Come," said the Major. They went down the rear staircase. The house was solemnly quiet. At the end of a ground floor passage was a bolted door. A large case stood on the floor. Irena looked at Harry. He perceived a faint smile and a new call for help through the veil. He was carrying his own case. He picked up hers as well. The Major unbolted the door and quietly opened it.

"Wait," said Harry. He put down his case and lowered the wick of the oil lamp fixed to the passage wall. "Not much sense in lighting up our departure," he muttered. Carrying the cases he followed Irena and Major Carlsen out of the house and along a path winding through the dark gardens until they reached a high brick wall. The Major moved silently, lifting a ladder and placing it against the wall. Ivy covered the better part of the brickwork.

The Major whispered his goodbye to Irena. "You are the bravest of women. Auf wiedersehen." He kissed her gloved fingers.

"And you, I shall not forget you," she whispered.

He said to Harry, "You must take good care of her."

"I'll do my best," said Harry. His nerves were beginning to jump about and he didn't feel he could safely promise to leap over the moon with her. He rather felt the Major was in love with her. Where that would get him with Her Highness was probably nowhere, whatever her own feelings were.

"Goodbye, Captain Phillips. Perhaps we shall meet again."

"A civilized thought, Major. Goodbye."

They did not salute. Briefly, they shook hands. Harry went up the ladder and Major Carlsen hefted up the cases to him as he sat astride the ivy-topped wall. He dropped each case to the soft earth on the other side. The night was comfortingly dark and quite moonless. Perfect for cloaks and daggers, he thought. Irena mounted the ladder. He helped her to sit on the wall. She seemed quite cool. Silk stockings glimmered in the night as her coat and dress rucked. He lowered himself and dropped lightly. His thigh twinged just a little. Irena let her legs dangle, let her body go and came plummeting down into his arms. That was damn well done, he thought. No fuss at all. He set her on her feet. She was warm, rounded, her coated bosom just brushing his chest. He groped for the cases, picked them up, one in each hand, and looked around. The solid block of the other house loomed ahead of them, rising square above the gardens. He saw a faint glow at one heavily-curtained window. There were no other lights. Irena began to lead the way over a wide, paved path. He followed. She walked carefully to mute the click of her heels. His tingling nerves kept the cold out.

She still seemed cool, she did not hurry. But the tension was there, mutual and communicative. The night enclosed them and muffled them. They reached another path which led them around the side of the house to a wooden gate. It was bolted. Both bolts were stiff. Harry put the cases down and took the strain off the bolts by pulling on the gate handle. Irena drew them carefully back. She opened the gate as Harry took up the cases again. The gate led to the street. She waited, putting a finger to her mouth and looking back into the solid darkness. A light flashed once, twice.

"That's to say everything is quiet," she whispered.

Not very brilliant, thought Harry, and not very conclusive, either. It might be all quiet outside the Princess's house but how the devil could the Major know whether this other street was clear? Any black-bearded Reds who wanted to keep Princess Irena penned up to await the day of judgement weren't going to watch only her front door. They would watch all possible exits. The flash of a signalling torch could kindle a prowling Red eye.

Irena turned into the street, going left. There were no street lamps. Some curtained windows masked domestic lights, that was all. Bucharest seemed in dark, silent abeyance between occupation and deliverance. Harry walked with only a slight limp beside his black-clad companion. He would have preferred her to dye her hair rather than put on widow's weeds. Despite what Major Carlsen had said, he could think of no disguise more obvious. He could only hope that the Major's fears concerning the Princess's enemies were the exaggerated fears of a man in love.

No one stepped out of dark places to accost them or question them. The curfew seemed to have closed the city down for the night. Irena crossed the street and entered another. Harry was warm from the weight of the cases and the tension. With eyes adjusting to the darkness he saw the outline of a horse-drawn cab not far away. Irena did not quicken her deliberate pace and they walked without haste to the cab. The driver was there, up on his seat. He looked down, his face mistily pale under his hat. He did not get down to offer help. Harry tossed the cases in. He gave Irena a hand and she boarded. He got in after her.

On the other side of the cab a man appeared. His hat was pulled low, the collar of his jacket turned up against the cold. He opened the door and Irena drew a quick breath and squeezed herself back into the dimness of the interior. The man was bearded. Harry thought by God, there had to be whiskers.

Whiskers spoke to Irena.

"Well met, I think, Your Absconding Highness." Harry did not understand the language. Irena's response came muffledly from behind her veil, drawn down under her chin to completely cover her face.

"You are mistaken. Go away." Whatever

bitter disappointment she felt was muffled too.

"Who is your fine military friend since he is not the Major?" The man was pleased with himself. He leaned in, smiling, his right hand deep in his jacket pocket, his left resting on the open door. Harry did not need to ask what the dialogue was all about.

"Go away, please," said Irena, veil moving against her mouth.

The man discerned the mourning black of her clothes. "You've suffered a bereavement? Tck, tck. You're going to the funeral, of course. How sad. My friend," he said, turning to Harry, "who are you? Her Highness's butler or Major Carlsen's influential uncle from Berlin?"

Harry ignored the fact that his bandaged throat was supposed to signify damaged vocal chords. He did not know what Whiskers had said, the moment was one for improvisation, so he put his hand to his ear and barked, "What, what?" He was belligerent.

"What, what?" The man repeated the words in an amused fashion. He looked more closely at Harry, who sat opposite Irena. "What, what?" he said again. The repetition enlightened him. He searched for some foreign words. "English? You are English?"

"Espionage," said Harry curtly.

"Espionage? What is that?" Whiskers asked the question carefully, as if not so sure of himself.

"Good God," said Harry, "I'm working for the Allies, your friends. This is Magda, my comfort, my help and my decoding mistress."

Irena smothered a little gasp at this outrageous statement. The man chuckled.

"That is good," he said, "very good. But not good enough. Take her back, my friend. You understand? Yes? Go back. Tck, tck, a waiting cab in times like these. Not good, eh? Not clever." He shook his head at the stupidity of it.

Yes, that was another mistake, thought Harry. A waiting cab within any reasonable distance of the Princess's house was bound to attract attention and invite questions. He wondered who was sitting up in the driver's seat.

"No, it isn't good," he said, "I have to go into the city and you're holding me up."

"Ah, so? I am in the way? Of course." Whiskers chuckled again. "But she will get out, your Magda, your comfort. It is strange you are English, strange. Ah, I see. They have sent you for her. Not possible. She belongs to us. I, Nicchi Michalides, tell you so. No, do not use that," he said nodding at Harry's holstered German revolver, "it would be silly." His hand was still in his jacket pocket. "Very silly."

"Oh, get in," said Harry, "you're damned untidy there. Where the devil do you want us to drive to?"

"That is better," said Michalides. "Yes, I will come with you."

He boarded the cab. Few people board any vehicle with one hand pocketed, and the withdrawal of the hand was instinctive, automatic. It gave Harry, in an atmosphere stiff with tension, the only moment of opportunity he could expect. He thrust his boot between Michalides's legs. The man began to tumble, a curse on his lips. Harry hit him with a gloved right fist smack in the back of his neck. Michalides pitched and sprawled. He opened his mouth to gasp, to shout, but Harry, following up, was on him, kneeling on him, grinding his face into the floor of the cab, Irena staring wide-eyed. Quickly he extracted the stubby revolver from the man's pocket. He chose the spot, measured the distance, weighed up the necessary force and thumped Michalides behind the right ear with the revolver butt. The spitting Rumanian jerked and slumped.

It wasn't good. Harry knew it wasn't. It was the worst start possible.

"Damn," he muttered. Irena, a little appalled, thought the atmosphere had not improved. Momentarily they had won themselves respite, but the street, quiet again, now seemed redolent of dark treachery and violent murder. They would not hesitate to assassinate her if they thought she might get away.

Harry got out. The driver was getting down. Harry, as conscious of the atmosphere as Irena, could take no chances. He pushed the revolver into the man's coat-covered stomach. The man said something. Harry called softly to Irena. She put her head out, looking in her darkly-veiled Balkan mystique so much the integral part of it all. Harry asked her what the man was saying.

"Something I could not repeat," she said.

"Is he a friend of ours or his?"

Irena spoke to the man. His response was hissing, angry. Irena translated it to Harry in plain but acceptable language. The man was not the driver and he was wanting to know what had been done to Michalides.

"Tell him," said Harry, "that Michalides hit

his head. Tell him to pull him out and do something for him. We'll leave. Tell him we're going into the city but don't be too obvious about it or he'll know we're not going there at all."

Irena, her veil as efficacious at night as a mask, spoke to the man again. He pushed the gun away from his stomach with the gesture of a man conceding the advantage for the moment, and he leaned into the cab and pulled out the inert Michalides. He spat in disgust. Irena looked up and down the dark street, shivering a little. She felt as if every shadow must disgorge its anarchist. Harry closed the door on her, looked at the man kneeling beside the now groaning Michalides and heaved himself quickly up into the ledged driving seat, his feet jammed against the angled board. He shook the horse awake and drove off. The man waved a fist after them.

Harry reached behind and knocked on the cab roof. The little flap opened.

"Which way to the city proper?" he asked.

He was terse. She understood that and said, "Straight on for a while. But it's Chitila we want and we should take the first left turn."

"Yes, but let's look as if we really are going into the city. Can we turn off later for Chitila?"

It would lengthen their journey, she said, but it could be done. So Harry drove straight on for the moment. He wondered about German patrols. Major Carlsen had said this would be no problem, that the patrols had orders to let this particular cab through. The only danger was that they might become curious or suspicious because it was now being driven by someone who looked like a German colonel. Well, he had to chance it.

They were lucky, they met no patrols. And when they did turn off for Chitila it was not long before the urban areas began to seem darkly aloof and disinterested. Development thinned out as they reached the main road that would take them north-west, Irena calling instructions from time to time.

Driving at a small trot, they left Bucharest behind and at a little after eleven o'clock reached Chitila without incident. They left the cab in a street, the horse with its head in a sparse bag of oats. They walked to the station, where the train was due in forty minutes. Chitila seemed as much in limbo as Bucharest, as most of Rumania. Elsewhere disintegration proceeded apace. To the east Bessarabia was in chaos, at the mercy of roving bands of Russian deserters, Balkan bandits, scavenging Bolsheviks and mercenaries of every kind. To the west and north-west, the proud but ungainly Empire of the Habsburgs was falling apart. In Serbia the Austrian and German garrisons were breaking and retreating as the Serbian, British and French offensive gained momentum. Only Rumania, sleeping under the imposed aegis of its German conquerors, seemed untroubled by the thunder of guns or the anarchy born of disorder. It was a deceptive quietness. But it well suited Harry at this time. There were no massive troop movements to contend with, no columns of field-grey blocking every road to every station, no questions to be answered. At least, not until the station came into view. Here the German soldiers were thick on the ground.

"That looks like trouble," he said. Irena

glanced at him. He had done well so far. But the incident with Michalides had been frightening and she new he was as tense as she was. She must not let him down. "I'm a colonel," he said and stopped. She stopped with him. "I can't be seen carrying my own luggage, I'm damn sure I can't. Wait. Call one of those men when we get nearer."

He gave orders very coolly, she thought, as if he had already decided that however important her escape was her status meant nothing.

"I'm to shout?" she said as they went on.

"Can Princesses shout? I don't think they're trained to, are they? No, just call."

Trained to? How absurd he was. She glanced at him again. He looked very commanding as a German colonel.

"They're looking," said Harry, "no need to call. We'll signal one over. You speak to him."

"Of course. He is to carry the luggage."

They halted. Harry signalled. A soldier detached himself from his comrades and approached. He saluted. Harry returned it. He touched his bandaged throat and indicated Irena. The soldier clicked his heels. Irena said to him, "This luggage. Please take it for the Herr Colonel. It is impossible here, he has had to carry it himself. No one to help, no one to call on, no cabs. But at least there are good soldiers. Thank you." The infantryman hoisted the cases and they followed him into the station and on to the platform.

The station was as dark as everything else. Four years ago Armageddon had opened, as usual, with color and song and light. It was coming to its end, as usual, in pallid depression and darkness. There might be a brief flash of rejoicing among the nations claiming to have won, but it would be very brief.

While Harry paced the platform in soldierly fashion, Irena sat on the cases, a dark figure of veiled and unapproachable mourning. Harry, stern and reflective in his pacing, hoped he looked just as unapproachable himself. She was not easily going to give herself away, he thought. She had kept her head with Michalides and her pose now as a widow of sadness was touchingly convincing. She sat in quiet, withdrawn isolation and men in field-grey, awaiting the train, did not intrude on her. Something about her affected Harry. He had been given an uncomfortable job in trying to get her to England, and he had a feeling he was completely wrong in principle in helping a pro-German princess to escape justice, suspect though that justice was. But as he slowly paced, as he looked at her, at her air of dark mourning, it seemed as if she were inwardly weeping for what she was about to lose. Her country.

All men, all women, love their own country, he thought, whatever the faults, the wrongs, the shortcomings. Those who praised other countries at the expense of their own, those who deserted their own countries, were called renegades.

She was not a renegade, but she would be called that sometimes when she was in her enforced exile. Harry felt for her as she sat so quietly on this chilly station platform. He could not go and talk to her. He was supposed to be unable to talk. And possibly, at this moment, she wanted no one to try.

The train did not come in at the stated time. Irena suddenly got up and as she approached Harry he saw that her face was pale behind her veil.

"I am suffering," she said, "I am cowardly with nerves."

"So am I," he said in a sympathetic murmur.

"You do not look nervous."

"But I am," he said. There was no one near enough to hear his whisper, but talking was something that could be seen as well as heard.

"The train is late," she said and went to an official to complain. If that was her way of fighting cowardice it was worth remembering, thought Harry.

To the official she explained she had just lost her husband in the fighting in Serbia. Was she now to lose her right to see him buried because of a train that should be here but wasn't? The official was a "dear me" man, who could absorb this kind of punishment all day and often did. He was sorry she had lost her husband and even sorrier to inform her that in these days it was even possible the railway had lost a train. He was grief-sticken to think she might miss her husband's funeral, but then he himself had missed seeing his own mother buried, not because of a lost train but because she had been blown up by bombs dropped on Belgrade at the beginning of the war and not even a shoe button had been found.

Irena rejoined Harry and told him, with the glimpse of a smile, that the official was a most diverting man, that she felt much better. Harry, standing immaculate guard over the luggage, appreciated her restored morale. The station became noisy as contingents of soldiers formed and massed. A number of Wehrmacht Military Police appeared, led by an NCO. They marched crisply to the end of the platform and stood at ease without losing their smartness. They looked as if the night itself could not hide from eyes as alert and well-trained as theirs. Irena was the only civilian on the platform, the only woman. The well-trained eyes regarded her. And the colonel she was with. Harry, becoming aware of the survey, stood with his feet apart, hands behind his back, clasping his stick, and returned the survey with martial severity.

"Oh, that is very good," whispered Irena in some delight, "you will make them shuffle their feet in a moment."

Some began to do just that. The NCO barked at them. Even when standing at ease soldiers should not look untidy or behave sloppily. Harry kept his stern gaze fixed on them.

"No one is going to dare to approach you," said Irena.

He turned so that no one would see he was talking.

"Look here," he whispered, "you realize the apple cart's already upset, don't you? The whiskery gentleman—Michalides, I think he said?—is on to us. They know who to look for now. A German colonel and a widow."

"Yes, I understand," she said.

"It was a damned bad start, I thought."

"Forgive me," she said quietly, "but there's to be no swearing or blasphemy. You can explain things at all times without that, for you have the benefit of a language extensive and descriptive."

Four years in the Army had taught him the sharp, brutal distinction between an acceptable adjective and a blasphemous one. He smiled a little.

"Yes, quite so," he said, still speaking in a murmur. "Do you mind if I say we'll have to discount your title and status? It has to be put aside, you know. And eventually you'd better call me Harry."

A slight flush showed behind the veil.

"Certainly not," she said, "I would never descend to a specious familiarity."

"And I'll try to call you Irena."

"You are not to engage in familiarity of any kind, sir."

That, he thought, was delicious. He teased her as he said, "Sometime in the near future it may be necessary or expedient for me to kiss you."

"How dare you!"

"Or for you to kiss me."

"Never!"

They were having their dialogue in whispers. His were light, hers indignant.

"When you get on the train," he said, "go straight to the toilet and change that hat and coat for anything else you've got in your case."

"Major Carlsen's instructions—"

"His instructions included leaving nothing to chance. That means we have to act according to circumstances at times, not to the plan. Since we've been spotted we're vulnerable as we are now. So will you please change your clothes? I have to change mine. After that we aren't to know each other. You have your ticket?"

"Yes." She was newly flushed. "Captain Phillips—"

"I'm Colonel Wagner at the moment."

"Oh, puffle." It came through her veil in an exasperated way.

"Puffle?" He wondered if his light attempts to take her mind off the sadness of exile were doing any good.

"Perhaps it's piffle, I cannot remember exactly, not when I'm so nervous." She took a breath and steadied herself. "I was going to argue with you, but no, I will do as you wish because of what you are doing for me. I am sure it's going to be very dangerous for you. We must not have little words about things, must we?"

She propounded commonsense with charm and appeal.

"No, of course not," he said, "you must excuse my nerves."

"You had no nerves when you dealt with that man Michalides." She went on in a quick, cautious voice, "There's an officer coming, he looks as if he is going to speak to you."

Harry came to attention, saluted her by touching the peak of his cap with his stick, then turned and resumed his pacing of the platform. A German infantry captain, who had almost reached his elbow, now found himself being passed. He saluted. Harry returned it without really looking at the man and strode on. The officer looked after him, then at Irena, all in black. His heels came together and he gave a stiff little bow of sympathy.

"If you'll forgive me," said Irena in her effortless German, "I shouldn't bother him if I were you. Poor man, he was wounded in the neck and is still hardly able to speak."

"Bad luck, that," said the German, "but he seemed to be the senior officer around here and I wanted some information on priorities. I've got a company to get aboard, the transport officer doesn't seem to be available and I thought the Herr Colonel—I'm sorry, it isn't your problem." He smiled, saluted and went off. That was a little close, she thought. Captain Phillips would not have understood a word, but even accepting he was unable to speak he would have been expected to shake or nod his head or make a few intelligent gestures.

He paced his way back. They heard the train then. Within a few minutes it came lumbering in. Shuddering and hissing, it was enormously long and it was armored. Fiery sparks blew about as the engine passed them. The faces of the driver and fireman were hot, sweaty and sooty, and white teeth gleamed between red lips. The train was carrying troops and guns, the latter lashed on the flat freight cars with soldiers sitting around them, caps jammed down on their heads, greatcoat collars turned up. Wagons, with doors half open to admit air, disclosed their complements of men. A series of passenger coaches drew up as the train came to a noisy, clanging halt.

Irena went aboard. With her ticket she had a special pass. Harry pushed her case in. She took it, wincing a little at its weight, and made her way along the corridor. German officers were gazing out of compartment windows. Harry stepped smartly up and in, carrying his case. He remained in the corridor. The troops were piling into the wagons. Irena had disappeared. The train blew steam impatiently and was away as soon as the last soldier was off the platform. An official waved his lamp, brakes unclamped and the engine powered slowly forward. The coaches jerked and the movement piled Irena into a heap in the confined space of the toilet. She mentally recorded what she might say to Captain Phillips about that.

The huge iron wheels strained, the long monster plucked itself from the deadness of its own weight and surged forward out of the station. Harry at the door of the coach saw a man burst on to the platform. The official restrained him, shaking his head and wagging his finger. The man pushed him aside but had lost his chance to reach any of the coaches. The wagons were passing him, the train already picking up speed. Harry, carried into darkness, missed whatever happened next but suspected the official was being harried with questions. He had been unable to clearly distinguish the man but felt sure it was Michalides, curfew or no curfew.

He stood by the door for a while, the train clamoring into the night. At the other end of the corridor Irena appeared. She had changed into a costume the color of gingernut brown, with a cream blouse and a brown hat. To the hat was attached a brown half-veil, masking her eyes. Her case sagged heavily from her hand. Ignoring Harry she slid back a compartment door. Four German officers in comfortable occupation looked up at her, then rose as one man, clicked their heels as one and lifted her case to the rack as one.

"Thank you, gentlemen," said Irena in their own language. Harry passed by, going on to the toilet to make his own change.

"Fraulein, how good of you to join us," said a young lieutenant, moving to allow Irena a corner seat. "You're going to Belgrade?"

"Yes." She was charming, demure. "Are things very desperate there? I do so want to be in time to see someone special."

"Of course, of course." Empires might be tottering but not in the presence of such an attractive young woman as this. "It's not as desperate as that. We are re-grouping and—"

"Never mind about that, Schmidt," said another lieutenant, not so young and not quite so affable.

They talked to her, glad to have her company, although Lieutenant Gruhner, the more formal officer, did not talk as much as he listened. Finally he said to her, "You're not German, are you?" He had perhaps detected the slightest of flaws in her accent.

"I'm from the Austrian Tyrol," said Irena.

"Ah." The women of the Tyrol were the healthiest, shapeliest and most hospitable. This one was also extremely lovely. However, there were few civilians on this train. Those who were had their passes. "You have your papers and your pass, fraulein?"

"Now look here, Gruhner," protested another officer.

"I have them," said Irena and opened up her handbag. She took out her papers. The pass was in order, the papers faked. She handed them over. Gruhner glanced briefly through them, already satisfied by her unhesitating response. He handed them back. Her heart was beating a little quickly but she looked quite cool.

"Thank you, fraulein," he said.

The compartment door slid back. Harry put his head in. He wore a suit of dark grey over a black jersey with a high neck. A dark blue cap with a peak sat on his head. He had the appearance of a seaman. Gruhner frowned up at him.

"This is reserved," he said.

Harry looked enquiring but uncomprehending. He mumbled something. He came in and put his case on the rack. Gruhner's frown deepened. Harry sat down in the corner seat opposite Irena. He cleared his throat as if nervous. He decided he was, in fact, very nervous.

"Who are you?" asked Gruhner.

"I don't think he understands German," said Irena. She tried Italian. Harry shook his head. She tried French. In that language Harry informed her he was a Russian, a refugee from the Bolsheviks.

"Your papers," said Gruhner, who knew French.

Harry produced them. Gruhner examined them with interest. They named their owner as Sergius Ilyich Rokossky and included the information that he was attached on special duties to the German Headquarters in Belgrade. Gruhner returned them. Harry smiled agreeably and his nerves settled down a little.

The passengers relaxed, easing their limbs. The train would not reach Belgrade until midday tomorrow. It ate slowly into the night, snaking and winding, pulling and jerking, ascending and descending. It denied the comfort necessary for sleep. Heads lolled, eyes closed. Heads snapped, eyes opened. Tiredness seduced Irena, she sat back and cuddled herself. Harry sat upright, looking blankly Russian. The Germans dozed fitfully and Irena twisted and turned.

They crossed the Hungarian border without stopping and pulled into Vrsaac when the sun was up. There the majority of the German troops got off and guns began to be unloaded. Gruhner and his companions rose stiffly to their feet. They said goodbye to Irena and left the compartment. Emptied of field-grey it suddenly seemed spacious.

"Heavenly," said Irena, stretching her legs. Harry disposed himself along the seat and closed his eyes. He seemed to fall into instant sleep and she could hardly believe it. "Well," she breathed almost indignantly, "for one who is supposed to be living on his nerves, that's too good to be true."

Outside the noise was deafening, the morning air echoing to shuddering thuds and gigantic clangs as the guns were craned off the freight cars. Irena got to her feet and slid back the door.

"I should stay here if I were you." Harry's eyes were open, his voice sleepy but insistent.

"I'm going to see if there's coffee somewhere."

"No, don't show yourself," he said. She threw him a look that was slightly haughty. "Your Highness, you're too noticeable in daylight."

"Not more so than any other person."

That was hardly true. She was decidedly noticeable, slender and striking despite her night of comfort.

"You should not look so attractive," he said, "someone will give you a second glance and recognize you."

Her faint blush surprised him. He would have thought her used to compliments and flattery.

"Oh," she said, she herself not sure whether it was a compliment more than a warning or the other way about. "Perhaps you are right." She sat down again. "But I am dying for coffee or some refreshment, there is nothing on the train. This is what a war does, you see, it even makes it difficult to get a little coffee."

Harry sighed. The sleepless night had been a strain on limbs and nerves, and he thought he might have snatched five minutes rest before the train moved off again. Five minutes would be something. But the soft warm voice going on about coffee was impossible to ignore. He got up. Brown eyes smiled at him from under lifted veil.

"Are you going to show yourself?" she asked.

"I'm going to see if I can find anything."

"If you find nothing you aren't to worry, please," she said, "it is the thought that is remembered."

Princesses, he supposed, were brought up so well that irritability after a sleepless night was something they simply did not indulge in. And if they wanted coffee they beguiled it out of one.

"You must be very tired," he said.

"Oh, I think we have both survived very well, yes?" she said.

"I won't be long," he said, leaving the compartment.

The train stood long, solid and hissing as he put his head out of the coach door and surveyed prospects. Both ends of the platform seethed with field-grey. It was clear adjacent the passenger coaches. He got out and walked into the station building. There, refreshment was available and a number of German officers were drinking out of the crested china cups of the Hungarian State Railway. No civilians were in sight and Harry thought the station was probably temporarily out of bounds to all but the military. A woman behind the buffet looked at him. He sensed he was out of place. He saw Lieutenant Gruhner eyeing him. Harry approached and spoke in French.

"I'm asked to give you the lady's compliments, M'sieu Lieutenant, and to enquire if I may take her some coffee. There is nothing on the train."

Gruhner nodded briefly, then waved a casual hand.

"You may take her some," he said. He caught the eye of woman behind the buffet and pointed to Harry. She nodded.

Harry walked across to the buffet, indicated the orderly array of cups and held up two fingers. He smiled. She smiled back. As she poured the dark brown liquid he saw some fat-looking stone bottles. He peered at the labels. The bottles contained the local brandy, given many certificates of merit. She gave him the cups of coffee. He pointed to the brandy. She put a bottle on the counter. Major Carlsen had supplied him with money and he paid in German marks. She smiled, she was buxom and beaming. He could see no food. He pointed to his mouth, then his stomach. She responded with a comment that was all Dutch to him. He said in French that he did not comprehend, that he was asking for food. He opened his mouth wide to show how yawningly empty it was and that made her giggle, as if she found the cavernous vista entertaining. Magically she produced two dark bread rolls and some fat olives from the depths of a large, square biscuit tin. Harry nodded in appreciation and paid for them. She wrapped them in paper, he put them into his left pocket, the bottle into his right. He smiled his thanks, the Hungarian woman beamed, and he carried the coffee back to the train, which had stopped hissing and was standing in huge, elongated apathy.

Irena greeted the coffee with warm cries of ecstasy.

"Oh, how wonderful!" She was even more rapturous when he unwrapped the rolls and olives, and when he showed her the brandy and suggested it would add welcome body to the coffee she was quite overcome, assuring him he was the most admirable husband Major Carlsen could have found for her.

"Cupboard love," said Harry.

Her knowledge of English did not run to an understanding of its colloquialisms and its peculiar sayings. His mention of love startled her.

"Please?" she said and again he saw the slight pink creeping.

"Oh, it's just a saying," he said, "but you must put what you've just told me into writing and I'll show it to Elisabeth."

"Elisabeth?"

"My fiancée. On second thoughts, no, perhaps you'd better not. It's liable to be misconstrued."

"It was only a joke," said Irena.

"I know," said Harry.

They sat and enjoyed their small, simple repast. Harry suggested a dash of brandy in the coffee and Irena declared it the best thing that could have happened to this particular coffee. Outside the noise gradually abated. The guns were off, the troops beginning to move.

"I hope we aren't simply going to be left here," said Irena. It was a comment, not an impatience, and Harry was impressed. He supposed she was completely divorced from her normal environment, which he imagined was one of comfort, elegance and sophistication, and she was literally a refugee on the run from extremists. But she was taking everything very coolly, even cheerfully. She represented a problem to him, certainly. It was a help to feel she was not going to lack character or courage.

"Oh, we'll move eventually," he said, and that coincided with an influx of new troops. They were Austrian. They surged on to the platform and climbed into the wagons, their officers invading the passenger coaches. Three entered the compartment occupied by Irena and Harry. They looked tired and drawn, too tired even to take much notice of Irena. Silently they stretched their legs, sat back and closed their eyes. Harry had a feeling they had been marching through the night.

Fifteen minutes later the train at last began the final stage of its journey to Belgrade. It stopped again, but briefly, at the Serbian frontier to let customs officials aboard, and then went on. The customs men went through the train perfunctorily. Troop trains were not normally their province unless there were special circumstances. When the compartment door slid back and the officials looked in, Harry wondered if there were special circumstances. The officials paid no attention to the Austrians, they looked at Irena, then at him.

"You have passes?" was the question.

They produced them. Irena looked cool but felt terribly apprehensive. Captain Phillips, his case. The German uniform would be in it. For all the fact that his papers proclaimed him an agent for the Germans, that colonel's uniform would be so suspect, for he could not speak German. He was only one spin of fortune's wheel away from inquisition and capture. And did they shoot as spies enemy soldiers who were caught in civilian clothes? She had a terrible feeling they did.

The passes were handed back. Now they would want to see the papers. But no. The officials simply said, "Thank you," and left it at that. The door closed and they went on their way.

Irena glanced across at Harry. She thought he gave her the faintest of winks.

When the train drew into Belgrade's main station, they sat still, waiting until the three Austrian officers had left. Then she said on a sudden rush of relieved breath, "Oh, I thought if those customs men examined your case everything would be lost."

"You were thinking of that uniform?" he smiled. "No, I bundled it all up and dropped it out of the coach door window as soon as I'd changed."

"I wish you had said, I should not have been so near heart failure then."

"I'm sorry, I thought you'd have guessed," he said as he watched soldiers streaming along the platform.

"Well, I did not," she said, a little frosty because of his casualness, "I am not a mind reader, Captain Phillips. I think it is better that you tell me what you do, not leave me to guess."

"I'm sorry," he said again. He supposed she was bound to have her moments of haughtiness. "I believe Major Carlsen gave you the address of the place where we're to hide up in Belgrade."

"Yes," she said. She had memorized it and told him what it was. He wrote it down on a piece of paper the rolls had been wrapped in. He lifted the cases from the racks.

"We'll go separately," he said. "If any of the comrades here have received word about last night they'll be looking for a woman in black—"

"A woman in black?" She was definitely haughty.

"A lady in black." He conceded his mistake. "With a German colonel. Or at last they'll look for a lady and a man together. So go by yourself. I'll follow on with the cases."

"Go by myself?" She obviously considered this a complete dereliction of his responsibility.

71

Behind the veil her eyes were at their coolest. "I am to be caught and carried off by my enemies?"

"I hope not," he said, "since they won't be able to drag you off kicking and screaming through crowded streets."

"Captain Phillips, I do not kick and scream, I am not a gypsy." She was very high on her horse.

"Well, look here, you must if they are waiting for you and do try to carry you off. But I don't think they will. They'll simply follow you. Watch for that. There's a cathedral here, isn't there? So if you think you're being followed don't go to the address, go to the cathedral, go inside. If you're not at the address when I get there I'll come to the cathedral myself and we'll work out a way of slipping them."

"Very well."

She left the train. Harry followed a minute or so later.

The station was a massive echo of sound. Contingents of Austrian and German troops imparted urgency to the atmosphere of crisis. Field-marshal von Mackensen, in charge of this theatre of war, was having to make up his mind whether to evacuate the Serbian capital or defend it. But the German High Command was in no position to send him fresh divisions, and the Austrians, who had done so much to help hold back the Russians and the Italians, were now in a state of acute and tired depression. Their Empire was about to collapse and it showed.

Two men, swarthy and keen-eyed, dressed in dark blue serge suits and flat caps, stood at the entrance to the station. But they were not interested in those who were going in, they were scanning everyone coming out. They were there in response to a telephone call from comrades in Bucharest and were looking for a man and a woman. The woman would be wearing black, the man might be in the uniform of a German officer but he was English and therefore likely in his English cunning to have changed into civilian clothes. It was to be assumed that the royalists in London had sent him.

"English, eh?" muttered one man. "What do the English look like, Palichek?"

"I don't know," said Palichek, "except that I've heard they consider themselves on speaking terms with God."

"What are we looking for, then? An angel? Gabriel?" The first man, called Dimitroff, was heavily sarcastic.

"No, no," said Palichek, "simply a man looking superior to everyone else, I should think, with a woman in black. The Princess."

"Well, I may not recognize a man like that, but I'd know her anywhere. She'll have her nose in the air."

But Irena, in her brown costume and hat with its half-veil, came out of the station with other travellers and in company with an elderly lady whom she had enquiringly approached and who had promised to direct her to the cathedral. They were chatting as they passed under the noses of the two Serbian comrades. Palichek and Dimitroff gave them scarcely a glance.

Harry, lumbered with the cases but not with a lack of caution, was doing some scanning himself. The crowded station was too much of a bedlam and a bustle for anyone to successfully engage in a little private detective work. People looking for other people would almost certainly post someone at the platform exit and someone at the station exit. He scanned the latter, for she had only been a seething mass at the platform exit. Outside there was room for a man to stand and watch the people emerging. He saw two men in caps. His nerves tingled. They might be waiting for friends or relatives but somehow he did not think so. In any case he could lose nothing by being cautious. He found a boy in a huge peaked cap, a boy with bright eager eyes wanting to earn a tip. He showed him the address on the piece of paper and said, "Cab? Carriage?" The boy screwed up his forehead. "Taxi?" ventured Harry.

"Ah, taxi, taxi," said the boy happily at this universal word. He nodded. Harry nodded too. He took the hospital stick which had been strapped to his case, showed the boy the promise of a German banknote and gave him the bags. The boy put the smaller case on his capped head, carried the larger and made his way to the exit. He returned in a few minutes, smiling and beckoning, and Harry, using the stick, a gift from the hospital, hobbled after him like a man crippled. The boy led him out of the station to a waiting horse-drawn cab, both nag and vehicle of ancient lineage. Several people were fighting over it. The boy pushed his way through them, Harry limping at his heels. He gave the boy the banknote, received breathless thanks, then hefted himself into the cab with a show of awkwardness and the cabbie, with a whistle to his horse, took off.

As the vehicle moved away Palichek and Dimitroff stared after it.

"No, not English," said Palichek.

"You're saying that or meaning it?" said Dimitroff.

"A cripple," said Palichek.

"You think?"

"I think? What do you think?"

"I think about people when they're running from something," said Dimitroff, "they all pretend to be cripples."

"But there was no woman in black with him, no woman at all. Look some more."

"We should have been at the platform," said Dimitroff moodily as they resumed their survey.

"No, no, there's no platform indication about troop trains, we should not have known which one to wait at," said Palichek, "and we should have lost them at the start. There, look, what about the woman with that man?"

Dimitroff eyed a woman in black on the arm of a stout man.

"Fifty if she's a day," he said disgustedly, "and nothing was said about the Englishman being fat."

Four

Harry felt fairly satisfied but not completely.
Michalides might have been able to arrange for
Belgrade station to be watched and those two
men might have been his comradely eyes. They
had given the cab a hard, enquiring look as it left
the station precinct, but they had made no move.
He felt fair satisfaction was as much as he could
allow himself, considering everything.

The cab moved slowly through the traffic.
The streets seemed full of hurry and urgency.
The atmosphere was heady, the undercurrents
could be felt. The people and the city itself were
excited, expectant, the Austrians and Germans in
a mood of dangerous bitterness. A year ago, with
Russia virtually out of the war, the Central Powers had pulled back scores of divisions from the

Eastern Front to strengthen their armies else-where. It had seemed then to the Serbians that it would be years, if ever, before their capital could hope to see the back of its conquerors. Now, suddenly, the Allies had taken command of the war, and the Central Powers were splitting and cracking. Their withdrawal from Belgrade looked so certain that it was difficult for the citizens to hide their elation.

The Austrians and Germans were still very much in evidence, but not in the same way as before. They were not drinking in the cafes or monopolizing the pavements as they had been since 1916. They were, in fact, no longer at play. They were patrolling the city in platoons, they were assembling in their barracks or massing around their headquarters. Or flying about in staff cars. The Serbians kept out of their way. There was no sense in provoking troops about to depart.

Harry was impressed by the wide streets and the imaginativeness of some of the architec-ture. He saw, from the cab window, the ancient citadel that stood high on the cliff overlooking the meeting-place of the two rivers, the Sava and the Danube. The citadel had once been known as the White Castle, from which Belgrade took its name, but age had long since turned it into a mellow russet-maroon.

The cabbie, a Turk—there were Turks in every Balkan town or city—gave way unfailingly to the gliding, clanging trams. His old vehicle creaked loudly as it carried Harry to a modest residential area and stopped outside an apart-ment block which looked massively Victorian.

There was some argument, not unhappy, and conducted mainly in sign language before Harry was able to understand how much the fare was compared with how much the Turk would accept. There were also a few incomprehensible words from the Turk about German marks being offered. He took them when Harry added another, and he also agreed to carry the bags up for a little more. They went up four flights of stone stairs, the concierge in his cubby hole on the ground floor taking no notice. The cabbie deposited the cases on the landing outside a door numbered 44 and left Harry to it.

Harry knocked. No answer. He could see no bell. He knocked again. Silence. He grimaced. He thought about the cathedral. Then he tried the handle. It was free of the lock. He opened the door and put his head in. The door opened straight on to the living-room. The furniture was practical. He brought the cases in and closed the door.

"Anyone home?"

No answer.

Damn it, he thought. A worried feeling took over. Either he was at the wrong address or something had happened to the Princess. He crossed the living-room and cautiously opened a door. She was there, resting on a bed and sound asleep, shoes off and ankles peeping amid the white froth of petticoats. He smiled. She looked blissfully dreamless, her breathing deep and even.

"Delightful," he murmured, "but naughty Princess for leaving the door unlocked. The ugly frog might have got you."

He realized how tired he was himself. The train journey had been nerve-racking and exhausting. Hunger added to the attack on his system. He explored the apartment, first locking the door. The place was about as commodious as a small bachelor flat, with one bedroom, the living-room, an adequate kitchen and a tiny bathroom with what Harry thought must be the prototype of the world's first geyser. He tried it, lighting the gas jets. Within seconds the whole contraption began to shake and thunder. It sounded like the prophet's warning of the coming apocalypse. He turned on the water spout. The thunder changed to a frightening, vibrating rumble, water gurgled menacingly, then spurted hot, steaming and the color of weak cocoa. He let it run but removed himself from a possible explosion. He found a linen cupboard which contained some sheets and blankets and, yes, a towel. But decidedly not a bath towel.

He explored the kitchen cupboards for food. Nothing. The flat was clean but empty of everything except its plain furniture and its minimal amenities. The geyser made a noise like a small, hostile eruption and thudded into silence. He listened to discover whether it had woken up Princess Irena. He heard no sound and went into the bathroom to examine the geyser. The gas had failed. A thin layer of brown water covered the bottom of the bath. He saw the coin meter, its slot a thin hungry maw. He took coins from his pocket and tried them. One went in and the gas hissed. He turned it off. He would need to find a decent-sized towel before he could take a bath.

The apartment door rattled to a sudden knocking.

His nerves re-awakened. He walked very quietly to the door, his hand around Michalides's revolver in his jacket pocket.

The door rattled again.

He opened it.

Two German soldiers, one of them a sergeant, looked at him. The other, a private, carried a square, brown-paper parcel tied with string.

"Ah?" said Harry casually.

"Herr Rokossky?" said the sergeant.

"Oui," said Harry, then remembered there was one German word he knew. "Ja," he said.

The sergeant gestured to the private, who thrust the parcel into Harry's arms. He accepted it, his smile masking his distrust of it. They nodded, turned, tramped along the landing with a smart slam of booted feet and descended the stairs. Harry closed the door, took the parcel into the kitchen and unwrapped it gingerly. There were various ways of delivering a bomb. But it contained tinned food, including condensed milk. There was also a packet of tea.

"Tea, by God," he said. The thought of a steaming cup pulled at him, but heavy eyelids suggested sleep was a more immediate need. He went into the living-room, sank into an armchair, put his feet up on another one, and thought satisfyingly about it. Tea. It was there to hand. He would have ten minutes in the chair and then make a cup.

He fell asleep.

It was dark when he woke up. Stiffly he felt

his way to the door and searched for the light switch. There wasn't one. He struck a match. He saw two gas brackets above the mantelpiece. They were mantled. He lit them. The mantles glowed white. He drew the curtains to cover the window. He looked at his watch. It was ten o'clock. He'd slept for hours. There was still no sound from the bedroom. He boiled a kettle of water on the big, cumbersome gas stove and made tea. He found thick china cups and saucers. He knocked on the bedroom door and looked in. There was sufficient infiltration of light from the living-room to reveal that she was still on the bed. He coughed. She turned, opening sleepy eyes. From the shadows she looked up at him in vague, brown-eyed dreaminess.

"Tea, Your Highness?" he suggested.

"Tea?" She was not fully awake.

"Hot from the pot. Well, from the kettle, actually. I couldn't find a pot. In Belgrade, don't they make tea in pots? Perhaps they don't make tea."

Sleepily she smiled. It was a gracious one. She sat up. She had unpinned her hair and it was loose, spilling around her. He thought her about twenty-one, but in the shadowy half-light she looked younger.

"You are saying there is tea?" she said.

"Yes. Just made. So if you'd like to risk it? I mean what it's like I haven't the foggiest. Don't get up, I'll bring it."

"No, I'll come," she said, "I'm so thirsty I will risk anything." She slipped her feet from the bed and into her shoes. She stood up, shook her head, flung back her dark hair and gathered it at the nape of her neck so that it hung thickly fan-wise over her back. She fastened it with a narrow tortoiseshell clip. It made her look soft and unsophisticated. She followed him into the kitchen.

He filled both cups, the hot liquid running golden-brown from the iron kettle. She shuddered very delicately when he pierced the tin of condensed milk and she saw the thick liquid ooze.

"There are no lemons?" she asked.

"So sorry, no lemons or sugar," said Harry, "just some tinned manna."

"I will drink mine as it is, then. You aren't going to put that stuff in yours, are you?"

"Well, I prefer cow's milk, of course, but I've been making do with condensed in the Army. One can't always find a cow."

She wrinkled her nose a little at that remark, then positively winced as he upended the tin over his cup and let the liquid run in. It spread like a creamy-brown sludge and when he stirred the mixture with a spoon it was not so much tea in her eyes as a concoction quite undrinkable. He seemed to enjoy it. He looked refreshed and vigorous, but she wondered if he was not poisoning himself.

"How can you? It must be hideous." She was delicately revolted.

"Hideous? My dear Princess—"

"Captain Phillips." Quick to remark familiarity, she interrupted him coldly. "You will please not address me like that."

He did not seem to think he had been seriously at fault, and he looked quizzically at her

83

over his cup. She considered him at least guilty of condescension.

"I meant nothing," he said. "I was going to say that tea comes in various ways, and individual taste has a lot to do with it."

"In any case," she said, keeping to what she felt was the more relevant point, "it is wiser not to call me Princess or Highness. I thought we had agreed on that. What are all these tins?"

"Food, I think," he said. None of the tins was labelled. Some showed a little rust. "I opened one. It's a mixture of meat and vegetables. We call it MacConachies. It makes a fairly decent change from bully beef. I rather suspect they've come with the compliments of Major Carlsen, who somehow managed to get the German Army to deliver them."

"Well, he is thoughtful about such things and very competent," she said, sipping her tea, "and it is like him to arrange some food supply for us. One must concede the Germans to be the most thorough of people."

"I'm not in a position to argue about it," said Harry, "we've been fighting them on and off for four years."

"Yes, and see what a dreadful mess it has made of Europe."

"I'd prefer it if we didn't become involved in these kind of arguments," said Harry.

"Who is arguing? I am only saying," she said. Her attitude of slight regal omnipotence was offset by the soft informal look of her hair. "Shall we take our tea in the other room?"

"Yes, of course," he said. He might have realized she was not used to drinking tea standing up in a kitchen. In the living-room she sat composedly, sipping the beverage. She decided that having been a little on her dignity she could now be gracious, and so she said that her tea, even without lemon, was very refreshing, and he was to be congratulated on being able to prepare a pot.

"I assure you, there's nothing to it," he said.

"You are too modest," she said, "I know I should find the process of making tea in a pot confusing and complicated."

"You'll manage," said Harry, "it's simplicity itself, except that you'll have to make it in the kettle. And the tinned food only needs putting into a saucepan and heating."

Her brown eyes opened wide, her dark eyebrows lifted.

"Captain Phillips, I am to prepare meals for us?"

"Well, I confess to being a very rough and ready cook myself," he said. He looked at the glowing gas mantles, he said, "Ah—um—and a woman's touch, you know, Mrs. Phillips?"

She sat up straight.

"Don't be impertinent," she said.

"Hmm," said Harry thoughtfully. It was difficult to know exactly how to address her and what footing to try for. "I think we should agree on a little informality, don't you?"

"That was not a little informality," she said, and he thought perhaps she might feel slightly vulnerable and that when they were alone she wished to establish an atmosphere of propriety. The immediate fact was that they were sharing this small apartment. She was probably sensitive about it. It was the last thing a young woman of her status would be used to. On the other hand, she was more responsible for the situation than he was.

"I'll see what I can do in the kitchen," he said, "you must be very hungry. I know I am."

She came impulsively out of her frigidity to say, "Oh, I am silly. You must forgive me, but I am quite unused to this sort of thing."

"So am I," said Harry.

She flushed. It made him wonder if, despite her little bouts of hautiness, she was not a little shy. They might be in this apartment for days. He had to consider her modesty. And she was stunningly attractive. He had to ignore that. In her eyes, according to Major Carlsen, he was a British officer and therefore a gentleman. She expected him to be understanding and gallant. He gave her a reassuring smile.

"Captain Phillips," she said, "you must not let me be ridiculous. We must be informal, of course we must. You should call me Irena especially when it's necessary for the sake of appearances."

"It's not necessary here. While we're in Belgrade it's not even wise."

"Oh," she said, "you mean my name. No, of course. You must call me Sonya, then. Sonya is my first name, not Irena. But Irena has always been used. It is agreed, then, we must not stand on ceremony. That is right, not stand on ceremony?"

"Perfectly right."

"Good," she said. "We have our part to play, yes?"

"Including looking married when the time comes?" smiled Harry. "Well, that wedding was chiefly designed for getting you into England," he said, "but since it's not a bad idea to be prepared for the opposition, and since they're looking for a widow I suppose we could try to fox them by presenting them with a picture farthest from widowhood. What I mean is, you could try looking like a bride."

She was amused by that but just a little suspicious too.

"I'm to go about in a wedding gown?" she said.

"I don't know where we could get you a wedding gown," said Harry, "but we could try for the next best thing. Why not go around wearing a few shy blushes?"

"Captain Phillips?"

"With a very nice dress, of course," he added.

"Oh, you have a very disconcerting sense of humor," she said, but she put her hand over her mouth to smother a peal of laughter. Then she said, quite demurely, "Thank you for the dress, now I am sure we shall get used to each other."

"I'll get something to eat," he said. He got up and moved towards the kitchen.

"Wait," she said, "was it difficult for you, getting away from the station this afternoon? I was quite clever myself, I thought." She told him how she had left in company with a woman and walked some way with her and then, when she was sure no one was following her, she had made her way to the apartment.

"That was better than clever," said Harry, "that was simple and damned original."

"Very original will do, thank you."

"Yes, quite so. I did the obvious rather than the ingenious. I realized afterwards it could only have drawn attention." He explained how he had left the station and his suspicions of the two men he had seen.

"Do you think they might have been looking for us?" She was more interested than perturbed, he thought. She had been dismayed when Michalides appeared last night but she hadn't panicked. Lots of pluck about her.

"I'm not sure," he said, "they had a good look at me, yes, but they stayed where they were." He remembered something. "Just when the train pulled out from Chitila last night I think our friend Michalides turned up. He was too late to join us but I daresay he had a good idea we were aboard, especially as I don't suppose he missed that cab."

"Are you sure it was him? There was the curfew, you know."

"I think Comrade Michalides would work his way round that."

"And I think you are thinking very well for us, Captain Phillips."

"I'll heat the food," he said.

She joined him in the kitchen and looked on with interest as he dealt with the complexities of preparing a meal. She seemed piquantly charmed by the coming together of food, saucepan and lighted gas.

"Well, you see," she said, "one is taught codes and ethics and proper behavior, one is not always taught practical things."

Harry stirred the mixture of meat, vegetables and gravy with a spoon. The aroma made her feel faint with hunger.

"I suppose saying the right thing at the right time and doing the proper thing at all times is more important to queens and princesses than knowing how to cook," he said. "But this isn't cooking, this is only heating food already prepared for the pot."

"All the same," she said graciously, "you are very versatile and much more useful than I am."

"Charming of you to say so, Your Highness, but on the other hand you would always be a better princess than I would. Ah, I think we're quite hotted up." The stew was steaming, the gravy bubbling. "Shall we see if we can eat it?"

They could. They ate at the table in the living-room. They did not expect to dine sumptuously while in Belgrade, for the food shortage was as acute here as everywhere else in Europe, and the meat and vegetable mix was as good as they were likely to get. Irena said it was really very nice, especially when one was so hungry.

"Do you know," said Harry, chewing reminiscently, as if the stew was an old friend, "damned if I don't think this is our Mac-Conachies. Part of some captured British supplies."

"How considerate," said Irena warmly.

"Considerate?"

"Of Major Carlsen," she said. "Well, what could be more so than returning some of your own food to you?"

"I won't commit myself on that," said Harry,

"but I will say that a really considerate man would have included a bottle of wine."

"One should be thankful for what is provided," she said primly, "one shouldn't ask for a banquet, not in these times. But a little wine would have been nice."

"Ah, that reminds me," said Harry, remembering the brandy. They drank a little of it at the end of the meal. It produced a warm and friendly glow. The atmosphere between them became more natural. Irena held out her empty glass. Harry peered into her eyes and detected a glimmer of well-being. "I think not, Princess," he said.

She smiled.

"You are quite right, I simply cannot drink brandy. Champagne is better, isn't it?"

"For some people," said Harry. "May I ask, where are your family?"

"My family? My parents, you mean?"

"Yes. Where are they?"

Her eyes dropped to regard her glass.

"You are talking of Prince Paul and Princess Alexandra of Moldavia?" she said a little sadly. "He was assassinated in Bulgaria ten years ago, she died two years later. You did not know?"

"I'm sorry," he said contritely, "but I didn't know, I was at an agricultural college ten years ago."

"It's a blissful and oblivious time when one is growing up, isn't it?" She was still a little sad. "Well, it has been a long day, Captain Phillips."

"Yes," he said, "a long night and a long day. Oh, one thing. It would be wiser, when you're ever alone here, to keep the door locked."

"Naturally," she said.

He did not point out she had earlier left it unlocked. He did not want her getting on her high horse again. They separated for the night on their friendly note. They did not discuss the one bedroom and who was to occupy it. The bed and the room were naturally hers. She slept soundly. Harry blanketed himself up on the living-room floor, using a cushion as a pillow. The floor was not as uncomfortable as other resting-places he had experienced during the war. He thought about things for a while. He thought about Princess Irena and the menace of Michalides. He thought about Elisabeth. He drifted off with his thoughts confused.

Next morning he suggested he should go out to see if he could buy some fresh food to go with the tinned stuff, and also a bottle of wine.

"Yes, I will come too," said Irena.

"Wouldn't it be wiser if you stayed here?"

She put on her cool look.

"I shall suffocate," she said, "I must have some fresh air."

That was natural, but Harry wasn't sure whether it was wise.

"I suppose we must run a few risks," he said.

"We'll go in thirty minutes," she said.

"I'm ready now."

"Well, I am not." It was not said perversely or argumentatively. He accepted she was merely stating her case. As a Princess, as a young lady, as a woman, she was simply not prepared to go out until she was satisfied with herself. She confirmed this by saying, "One does not merely throw a coat on, you know."

"Quite so," said Harry agreeably, "I'll give

you half-an-hour, then. But I assume you're not going to make yourself recognizable?"

"I thought," she said coolly, "that the idea was to look as if I had just been married."

"Well, you have as it happens, haven't you?" he smiled.

"I have not forgotten," she said. She pointed out that in half-an-hour there would be more people about, making it easier for them to lose themselves.

He was mildly surprised when she was ready precisely at the agreed time. She came out wearing a warm, plain coat over a dress. A headscarf covered her hair. It gave her a peasant look. It was a look that was not out of keeping with his commonplace grey suit and black jersey. They walked to the center of the city, which was buzzing. There were rumors that the Austrians and Germans were grouping to the west of the capital, which had to mean they were contemplating a definite withdrawal from Belgrade. Their forces engaged in trying to stem the Allied advance were also retreating to points west of the capital.

Irena said, "Let us find a cafe. I know the best one. I am dying for some coffee." They had only had tea for breakfast. They might get a little something to eat at the cafe.

Nicchi Michalides sat down, nodding brusquely to the two men who had been waiting at the riverside cafe for him. He was dark, bearded, thickset and quietly formidable.

"Well, comrades?" He opened on a fairly cordial note, although he knew from their faces that they had failed him.

"They weren't on the train," said Palichek.

"Or they got off before Belgrade," said Dimitroff.

"You think so?" said Michalides, scratching his black beard.

"It's a possibility," said Palichek.

"You were diligent and thorough?"

"That is a question, Comrade Michalides, which you don't need to ask," said Dimitroff.

"Well, they were coming to Belgrade, you may rely on that," said Michalides. "Would you say it was impossible for them to have slipped by you?"

"I'd say so, yes, if they were on that troop train," said Palichek.

"At least, almost impossible, I'd say," said Dimitroff.

"So?"

"One could not easily miss her," said Palichek, "but an Englishman? Who knows how to pick out that kind of a man? I tell you, I've read about the English. Saxons, Normans, Danes, Vikings, what does a mixture like that make them look like now?"

Michalides dismissed that with a brusque gesture of his hand.

"You saw no German colonel with a woman in black?" he said.

"There were so many women in black, there always are," said Dimitroff, "but none came out with any German officer."

Michalides thought for a moment or two.

"He changed his clothes, of course," he said. "The obvious thing to do once he got away from us." He rubbed a spot behind his right ear. The swelling was still tender. He bore Harry no real malice for that, it was being outwitted that rankled. "He's a slippery customer, that one. You're sure you saw no one like him, no one who might have been him?"

"The description we received wasn't very detailed," said Palichek.

"Comrade," said Michalides, "I only saw him in the dark."

"Ah, there are always the little problems," said Dimitroff.

They sipped brandy, with water added. The day was grey and cold.

"But the Princess," said Michalides, "there were no problems concerning her appearance. You know what she looks like."

Palichek shrugged. "We still didn't see her," he said.

Dimitroff came out of a thoughtful moment to say, "But we did see a man who hobbled and a boy who carried two cases for him."

"Two cases?" A little light glinted in Michalides's dark eyes. "Yes, there were two. You spoke to him?"

"For myself," said Dimitroff, "I thought what reason did we have for speaking to him? And there were idiots in the way, arguing about the cab. But there was something about him that took my eye. What it was I don't know, and I wouldn't swear he looked like an Englishman."

"What does an Englishman look like to you?" asked Michalides patiently.

"When they arrive with our Serbian Army, we shall see," said Dimitroff.

"I'm not dealing with fools, am I?" said Michalides not so patiently.

"That's not very friendly, comrade," said Palichek. His was a hurt protest, not an angry one. Comrade Michalides had a reputation and an influence that extended well beyond his own province of Bucharest.

"Then find the boy," said the Rumanian, "and find the cab driver. Ask about the man. You saw how he was dressed?" They described Harry's clothes and Michalides nodded. "That at least is something," he said. "Comrades, where the Englishman is, there she is too. I've been promised help by your party secretary."

"We are the answer to your cry, comrade," said Dimitroff.

"Then do this for me, you'll know where to look," said Michalides. "Find the boy and the cab driver and ask questions. Ask the driver where he took this man who hobbled. And be quick. I shall be at Grocca's house. They mustn't slip us again. The Princess isn't here to enjoy herself. She'll be out of Belgrade as soon as it suits her. Well, it won't suit me if she's already flown. It won't suit any of our comrades."

Palichek mumbled something and Dimitroff pulled on his ear, but they got up and went.

Five

The cafe near the cathedral was fairly crowded but they could talk. They sat at a table inside. At an outside table they felt they would be too exposed.

"What are you thinking about?" asked Irena as they drank hot brown liquid said to be coffee. Harry was thoughtfully watching people passing by outside.

"That I don't like sitting around. I'd just as soon chance a train to Trieste today."

"But you would be at risk all the time," protested Irena, "there are Germans on all the trains. Who knows what they would do to you if they caught you? I should feel terrible. We must wait until the Serbians and British get here, then we should only have Socialists to worry about. I am not going to let you get shot. The Germans are in the mood for that and it's natural now that they feel they are losing the war. They are conquerors by nature and to give way to the Serbians is a bitter pill to them."

"Oh, damn bad luck and all that," said Harry.

"You do not like them of course."

"Not quite like you do," he said.

"Well, you have done enough conquering in your time," she said.

"I have?"

"The English," she said coolly. "It is permissible for you to go out conquering but as soon as other people try it you are standing on rooftops and shouting how disgraceful. The Germans wish to take nothing from you but all the same you fight them, and it is going to benefit no one but the Bolsheviks. Yes, you will see."

"Look here," said Harry, "I don't know any Germans personally. They may all be quite delightful, and they obviously are to you, but they've been firing damn great shells at my battery for years and all I've felt is a desire to fire back. I don't think we ought to argue about these things, not when we should be trying to get on with each other."

The slight pink flush that was becoming familiar tinted her cheeks. She seemed to alternate between coolness and confusion.

"There, now you are being cross," she said, "and I was only speaking an opinion."

"I'm not being cross," he said, "I'm only sitting around. I think I'll go and buy some wool and learn to knit. One must do something."

She stared, then laughed.

"Oh, you are quite amusing sometimes," she said. She looked at her watch. "Yes, you can do something, you can go and shop now, yes? See, I've written down what you might be able to get, you can go into shops and show it." She took a piece of paper from her handbag and pushed it across to him. "There, that is bread," she said, indicating the first word. "And that is fish. You aren't likely to get any meat. That is fruit, that is lemons. You will see what wine you can get. I will stay here, it's better not to be together all the time."

She couldn't cook, thought Harry, and she probably couldn't shop, either. However, that wasn't her fault, that was royal conditioning. He smiled good-temperedly, and glad to have something to do he took the list and rose to his feet.

"I'm not sure how long I'll be," he said.

"It will take a little time, but I will wait," she said. Her dark red scarf, tied under her chin, had slipped back a little over her head to reveal a wave of glossy chestnut hair. She looked up at him. He seemed quite confident about things. "Please be careful," she said.

"You're more at risk in Belgrade than I am," he said, "so stay here under cover and don't wander away."

At his firmness she flushed again. He smiled to show her he was only being fatherly and left the cafe.

The food shops were sparsely stocked. There were queues at most of them, queues which were more animated than usual. It did not seem so bad now, all this daily searching and patient waiting for the necessities of life when things would soon be much better. Harry found himself having to join more than one line of talkative people. He worked his way through the list, obtaining a small amount of bread, some strips of dried fish, even some pears and olives, all with the help of his piece of paper and some sign language which bemused shopkeepers before it enlightened them. It fascinated many of the female onlookers. Women glanced at each other, smiled or giggled, and wondered was his wife ill that he had to do his own shopping. They supposed he was married, he was too personable not to have a wife. He had been a soldier, of course, he had the look.

"Ah," said one woman to her friend, "and there's my Chernik doing nothing all day but clean boots."

"Well, that's his trade," said her friend, "he's a fine bootblack and a good spitter."

"There's no one who can spit on a German boot better," said the woman proudly. "But," she confessed, "at everything else he's the world's first incompetent."

"Everything?" said her friend.

"That's between you and me, of course."

"Of course. Yet you have six children."

"Even then he hardly moved a muscle. Woman's work is never done, my dear."

They watched Harry leave the shop with two bottles of wine and some wrinkled green beans. He caught their glances and winked at them. They blushed to their roots and turned away to giggle breathlessly. With his purchases in a large brown paper bag, he made his way back to Irena. He had been well over an hour. He hoped Irena had not lost patience. He would not put it past her to let the lure of shop windows drag her out of hiding.

When he was some thirty yards from the cafe he saw a man come out, a man in a dark grey coat and hat and brisk in his movements. He walked quickly to the edge of the pavement, sized up the slow-moving traffic and crossed the street as if in command of every vehicle.

It was Major Carlsen.

Harry blinked and said, "Damn me," under his breath. He watched the German, in mufti, merging with people on the other side of the street. He wondered what his mother would think of this development. She liked a good story, well-defined heroes and murky villains. She could not stand what she called the lack of body in Virginia Woolf's plots and characters, nor did she hold with heroes and heroines being burdened with strange social attitudes. Princess Irena, seeking to escape anarchists and assassins, would appeal to her as the perfect heroine, as long as she did not become tiresomely political, while the mysterious metamorphosis of Major Carlsen, the symbol of devious German militarism, into a mere civilian, would be considered utterly intriguing. She would probably tell him to follow the man. It was a thought. But there was Irena. If she was still in the cafe she would certainly have been talking to the Major. Was that why she had gone there, to meet him? Ah, an assignation with her love? Harry smiled to himself. It was interesting all the same. She had preferred to stay there rather than to go shopping. Was this a thickening plot?

He went into the cafe. She was still there. She smiled in welcome when she saw him.

"Oh, you've not been long at all," she said.

"Almost too quick?" said Harry. "But I've been over an hour." He put the bag containing the meager provisions on the table. He sat down. The flat, leather-covered seat of the chair was warm. "Well?" he said and waited.

"What have you bought?" she asked. She leaned and opened the carrier. She peered into it. "Oh, how well you've done. But what do we do with these?" She brought out a green bean.

"Cook them and eat them."

"Naturally, I did not think one smoked them." She seemed quite vivacious. She and the Major must be in love. She had obviously met him and talked to him, and it had left her looking pleased with life. "Are we to have a banquet or are we to make all this last?"

"It won't last long, there really isn't very much," he said. Then, after a pause, "Well, young lady?"

She glanced up from her inspection of the wine he had bought, lifting long dark lashes to regard him in innocent enquiry. Then she frowned a little at the way he had addressed her. Then she smiled.

"I'm hungry," she said, "shall we go back to the apartment and have a meal?" He looked at the table. There had been two used cups when he left her. Now there were four. "Oh, yes, there was nothing to do but drink more coffee while I was waiting," she said.

102

"What did Major Carlsen want?" he asked.

"Major Carlsen?" She was so natural in her surprise that one had to place her on the side of the angels. "Oh, yes, Major Carlsen."

"Yes." He was curious, very curious.

"I was so surprised," she said. A waiter came up. She shook her head. Harry asked for coffee.

"Go on," he said.

"I had no idea," she said.

"Go on," he said.

"Why do you keep saying that?"

"Because I'm waiting for you to say something."

"I simply looked up and there he was," said Irena, "and he was so pleased we were safely here. He knew we had been seen—"

"I should damn well think we couldn't have been missed the way he was flashing light signals."

Irena put her nose in the air.

"Really, Captain Phillips, there's no need to be bad-tempered."

"Oh, it's just my simple inquisitiveness," he said. "May I ask what he's doing in Belgrade disguised as a man about town?"

"It's something to do with orders, I suppose," she said, "he did not discuss it with me. He has been very kind, very understanding, but we have never talked about confidential military matters. After all, I am Rumanian."

"Really? I'm glad to hear it. How did he know you were here?"

"But we are supposed to be here, that was the arrangement." She was quite composed.

"I mean in this cafe," said Harry, looking her in the eye.

"He was passing and saw me in here." She smiled as if it was all very simple and reasonable. "Naturally, he came in. He was delighted about things. We drank coffee together. It's rather awful, isn't it?" Harry had just been served and was trying it for flavor. "He told me to tell you how well you had done, because of course I told him about everything that had happened."

"I'm flattered," said Harry, "but I'm not impressed. We didn't do at all well. We were spotted in the first place, but that was no surprise considering how our departure was advertised. And if your extremist friends are as dedicated as Major Carlsen says they are, then they're going to be on our tail, if they're not already."

"Major Carlsen said that doesn't matter as long as we are all right now and as long as we stay in hiding."

"I'm glad he's not worried, because I am," said Harry, "and the fact that we're all right at the moment, and not actually on the guillotine, is only half to his credit."

"I hope," said Irena, at her coolest, "that you are not going to turn out to be a rather beastly person."

"Well, I do have some little failings," said Harry, "but I really feel more curious than beastly at this point. What's so odd is why Major Carlsen didn't bring you to Belgrade himself. It would have been easy for him, and he must have known he was going to be here soon after us."

"Why must he?" Irena was in protest.

"Everyone in uniform is rushing about because of the fighting in the south and I expect he never knows what his next orders might be. Do you think that having seen me he shouldn't have spoken to me? Even though the war is going so badly for Germany he was most concerned about us and so relieved to know that nothing had happened to us."

"He might consider Michalides counts for nothing. I don't."

"Really, you are not very grateful," said Irena.

"Grateful?"

"Major Carlsen did let you go instead of sending you to a prisoner-of-war camp."

"Well, if that doesn't beat duck-shooting," said Harry. She wasn't quite sure what that meant but sensed it was a reflection of his astonishment and had the grace to blush a little.

"Oh, I am sorry," she said, "but I wish you would not be so—so—" She puzzled over the right English word.

"Carping?" suggested Harry.

"No. Grumpy. Yes, that is right, isn't it? Grumpy?"

He restrained a smile. He could not see how in their situation he could talk with anything but frankness. She being more used to flattery and hand-kissing, no doubt, was not going to take kindly to too much frankness.

"Grumpy will do," he said, "and I expect everything will sort itself out. Shall we go and do some cooking?"

They got up. The cafe was full of talkers, all immersed, and the one face that was turned their way was like a bright, round beacon. Harry, immediately aware of it, looked into the alert eyes of youth and experience. They belonged to a boy in a huge peaked cap who stood at the door. The boy glanced over his shoulder at the street, then back at Harry. He looked as if he considered something was up.

"He wants you," said Irena.

The boy sidled in, keeping his eye on the nearest waiter. The waiter, however, was engrossed, exchanging rumors with customers about which way the Austrians were going to run. The boy reached Harry.

"M'sieu," he whispered. Like all impecunious hopefuls who piratically competed with porters at railway stations, he had picked up words from many different tongues. Yesterday he had heard Harry produce one or two French words. "M'sieu?"

In French Harry tried the helpful but noncommittal response of, "My aunt is in the garden."

The boy looked foxed for a moment, then grinned. The limping man, who had been very generous yesterday, was saying he could understand French. Perhaps he would be generous again. It was surprising what people would pay for information that had no meaning to others.

"M'sieu," he whispered dramatically, "they are asking questions."

"They?" Harry was interested but cautious.

"Two men, m'sieu." The boy went on in limited French to explain how he had had his ear twisted by these men who wanted to know all about the man with the stick. A man who hobbled. Not liking the pain inflicted he had only said he carried the man's bags to a cab. He knew he was not likely to be paid for any of the information, so why should he tell them where the man was going?

"No, with your ear hurting," smiled Harry, "why should you? Have you been following me?"

"M'sieu?" The boy's bright eyes were clear. "I see you in here, so I tell you what perhaps you like to know."

"There," murmured Irena, "he saw you just as Major Carlsen saw me."

"Someone's asking questions," said Harry. To the boy he said, "That was all you told him, that you carried my cases to the cab?"

The boy said that was all the men deserved for twisting his ear. Harry gave him the welcome tip. It was received with an engaging smile. Expectancy had been satisfied. One soon got to learn who were the generous people and who were only ear-twisters. He sidled towards the door. The waiter spotted him at last and moved, aiming a cuff at him to help him on his way through the door. It missed by a yard.

"We'd better go," said Harry.

"In a cab, perhaps?" said Irena.

It was impossible. Every moving vehicle was full. It was not only the Austrian and German troops who were preparing to leave Belgrade. Numbers of officials and civilians who had collaborated with the occupying powers were also trying to get away. They did not want to be around when their protectors had gone. In the eyes of Rumanian patriots, Princess Irena was in this category.

The atmosphere was electric. Irena and Harry walked swiftly, Harry bothered by no more than a twinge or two in his leg. From time to time he turned to look for an available cab. He felt impeded on the pavements. People were moving slowly, watching the traffic, or clustering in talkative knots. Only the Turkish citizens seemed unaffected by events. The men in their blue jackets, white trousers and red fezzes, followed by their veiled women, accepted that all things were the will of Allah, and their calm eyes said so.

Harry obtained a cab at last. The driver took them only because their address was on the way to the stables. He had been working night and day for the past week and now he was going to sleep for two days and so was his horse. He dropped his passengers off at the apartment block. The area was quiet, the street itself very quiet except for the sound of the departing cab as Irena entered the block. Harry, on edge again, stood listening.

"What are you waiting for?" called Irena.

"It's my nerves," he said. He heard more clearly then what his ears had faintly picked up a moment ago. Breaking into the lessening sound of one cab was the rhythmic creaking and clip-clop of another. Harry took a step forward. Away down the street an ancient vehicle was advancing, rolling along with a sway, and with old springs shuddering. Harry knew it. He ran to the entrance. "Quick!" Irena did not argue, she raced up the stone flights with him. He noticed with relief that the resident caretaker, the concierge, was not around. That meant the man would be unable to answer questions. They reached the fourth floor, unlocked the apartment door, burst in. Harry put the bag of groceries in the kitchen, ran into the bedroom, opened up the wardrobe and flung all Irena's clothes back into her case. "You must go to the top flight and stay there," he said. "Take everything that belongs to you."

She pulled open drawers in the tallboy, swept undergarments into the case, threw in brushes, combs, hand-mirror and everything else.

"Your uniform!" she cried. His British khaki hung there in the wardrobe.

"Leave it," he said, "it'll prove to Michalides that I am a British officer, if he is paying a call on us. They found the cab driver, damn it, of course! Can you manage that case?"

He took it out for her, thrust it into her arms. She gasped. But she went up the remaining flights of stairs with it. She disappeared. He waited until the sound of her footsteps ceased, then closed the door, took his own case from the living-room into the bedroom and put it in the wardrobe. He looked around the apartment, checking quickly.

Someone knocked on the door. Unless he answered they would prowl around the block, inside and out, up and down. And they would wait.

He answered.

Michalides smiled, white teeth gleaming amid his black beard. Behind him were Palichek and Dimitroff.

"Ah," said Michalides. He sounded amiable but his eyes were glinting.

"M'sieu?" enquired Harry.

"What, French today, my friend?" said Michalides. "First you are German, next English, now French. That is good, very good."

"Who are you?" Harry peered into the whiskers. "Oh, it's you," he said casually. "Well, you'd better come in, I suppose."

This slightly disconcerted Michalides. He had expected anything but an invitation, and his foot had been thrust forward to prevent the door being closed. Harry, however, was now opening it wider and standing politely aside.

"You may bring your friends in with you," he said.

They all entered. Michalides looked around. Palichek and Dimitroff looked at Harry.

"He is English?" said Palichek.

"Who'd have known? It shows how cunning they are," said Dimitroff.

"Gentlemen?" said Harry.

"My friends are saying you look the same as other people," said Michalides, eyes darting.

"What did they think, that I'd only have one eye?" said Harry.

Michalides caressed his beard. He smiled in a way that made him look genially willing to come to terms. Harry was not deceived.

"It was a lesson for both of us, our first meeting," said the Rumanian. "Each thought too little of the other. You left me with a sore head and a setback. That was my lesson. But I am here, you see. I am not easily put off. That is your lesson."

"Accept my apologies for being rough," said Harry, "but I had to get to Belgrade."

Michalides gently adjusted his wide-brimmed black hat. It was a hat which was sinisterly traditional among anarchists. The flat caps of the two Serbians were indicative of followers who had yet to climb the heights to greatness.

"One accepts the blows as well as the blessings of life," said Michalides. "Of course, I do have a proverb. It says that a man who sets fire to his neighbor's house will have his own fall in on him."

"Oh, we say what's sauce for the goose is sauce for the gander."

"Ah?" Michalides, hands in his jacket pockets, began to wander about.

"Have you come to pull my house in on me?" asked Harry.

Michalides waved that aside. "Not important. Justice is important."

"I know, my dear chap," said Harry, "it's only the condemned man who argues about it."

"Where is she?" asked Michalides abruptly.

"I'm sorry?" Harry looked mystified.

"The woman, the royal swan with the long neck, where is she?"

"I'm afraid I'm riddled with ignorance," said Harry. "Who are you talking about?"

Michalides showed a glimmer of white teeth. He was a man who had learned to contain his temper and to use his patience and persistence, so that when the right moment was reached he could strike with a great deal of self-satisfaction. One showed one's teeth but one did not bite precipitately. Undisciplined hunger could lead one into biting off the wrong head. The Englishman was cool enough, but so he would be. He had already shown his mettle. But undoubtedly the Princess was here. She had to be. She was the one he, Michalides, had come for. And he would take her and escort her to the house of Serbian comrades, where she would receive civilized comfort but be held until the war was over and trials began. Then she would be sent back to Rumania for her own trial.

Michalides nodded to his friends. Palichek and Dimitroff searched the bedroom, investigated the kitchen and tried the bathroom. The blanks they drew nettled them. They returned to the living-room on the verge of bad temper. Michalides, seeing their faces, took off his hat, carefully brushed the nap with the sleeve of his jacket, and put it on again.

"Comrades?" he said.

They shrugged and spread their hands. Michalides searched the bedroom for himself. He did not make much noise. He was quietly systematic. He came out carrying the jacket of Harry's uniform.

"So? What is this?" he asked.

"Mine," said Harry, "I told you I'm a British officer. I'm on a mission. And I'm waiting now for the British to arrive with the Serbians. That's all I can say. Except that we're on the same side."

"Are we?" Michalides pursed his full lips. He thought. Light came. "Ah, yes, we talked about it before. Your Government sent you for her."

"What you're talking about I didn't know then and I don't know now," said Harry. "I don't even know why I let you in here, except to apologize for hitting you over the head. But that sort of thing sometimes can't be helped."

"Naturally, you must lie about her," said Michalides, "but, my friend, Princess Irena was with you when we first met. You came from her house with her. Your mission is to take her from us. Yes? Come, if as you say we are on the same side, you can say so."

"Who the devil is Princess Irena?" Harry sounded irritable.

"Come," said Michalides again, "I am not a fool."

Palichek and Dimitroff, understanding not a word of English, shifted about impatiently.

"If you care to check," said Harry, "you'll find I was captured after we began our advance from Salonika. I escaped, got a bullet in my leg and was treated at the Queen Constanza Hospital in Bucharest. I met a German officer, Major Carlsen."

"Your mission was to get a bullet in your leg?" Michalides was ironical.

"No, to make contact with certain people in Belgrade. I can't discuss it, or the ways and means. However, the bullet in the leg spoiled things for a while. Then Major Carlsen suggested there was little point in sending me off to a prison camp since he considered the war nearly over. Rather a civilized man, the Major. There aren't many of them around."

"Only a mirror reflects the true face of each man," said Michalides sententiously, "only in a mirror does a fox see himself. What a fox is Major Carlsen. And you are his first cousin."

"My dear chap," said Harry, "he offered me a ticket to Belgrade. Nothing could have suited me better. I was asked only a small favor in return. That of escorting a young lady recently widowed. I agreed. I parted from her at Belgrade station."

"That is good, that is very good," said Michalides. "So, you are given your freedom, a German uniform, a ticket and a widow. Tck, tck."

"She was a distressed soul, poor woman, and rather mournful company," said Harry reflectively, "I thought Major Carlsen quite decent about it all. But there are occasions when a unique camaraderie arises between friend and foe, which makes up in an odd way for all the other occasions when we're shooting at each other."

"Do you take me for an idiot?" Michalides was insulted. "I ask you again, where is Princess Irena of Moldavia?"

"Good God, is that it?" said Harry. "Is that what you're trying to tell me, that the lady was no widow but a princess? Not that it means much to me, I've never heard of any Princess Irena."

"My friend," said Michalides, "you are making me tremble. Do you understand?" He stuck a thick forefinger into Harry's chest. Harry removed it and picked up his uniform jacket which Michalides had thrown on to a chair. Palichek sucked his teeth and Dimitroff cleaned out an ear.

"Mr. Michalides," said Harry, "please look carefully at this jacket. It was tailored to fit me, not some mountain goat. It signifies I'm commissioned to serve my King and country. My country has a long arm. I'm not concerned with your problems, with the whereabouts of some person you say is Princess Irena of Moldavia, and you should not concern yourself in any way with me. In any way. Now, do *you* understand?"

Michalides, his cold eyes at variance with his smile, shrugged.

"You have made a point," he said. "May I ask who you are?"

"Phillips. Harry Phillips. Captain." He pointed to the three pips.

"Captain?"

"Quite so."

"One can be reasonable," said the Rumanian, "and I am very reasonable. I will tell you, no, I do not concern myself with you. Only with the Princess. So you see, tell me where she is and you and I will be good friends. It is right, we are on the same side. Against Germans and against traitors, yes?"

"I still can't help you with the Princess," said Harry. "What do you want her for, what has she done?"

"She loves Germans," said Michalides.

"Unwise at the moment, perhaps, but hardly a crime, and when the war's over what will it matter?"

"It will matter to us." Michalides stroked his beard again. Softly he said, "Where is the other case?"

Damn, thought Harry. He had slipped up there. But then this kind of thing was new to him.

"What other case? I've only one, and that was given to me by Major Carlsen."

"Yes, there is only one here," said Michalides, "but at the station you had two. A boy carried them to a cab for you. The other one, you have eaten it?"

Harry laughed heartily and thought rapidly.

"Well, I must say," he said, "you are a suspicious chap. The other case was hers, the lady I escorted as far as Belgrade station. So of course it isn't here. She wasn't only in a distressed state, she was unhappy about all kinds of things, it seemed. Perhaps she is the person you want, I don't know. She asked me to look after the case for a few hours and to take it to a cafe for her in the evening. Well, damn it, whoever she is, could I say no? Would you refuse a young widow with tears in her eyes?"

"Ah, the tears of a young widow are sadder than the cries of a lost lamb," said Michalides. "You took the case? To which cafe?"

"The one almost opposite the cathedral, there's a white cross over the door. I met her there, gave it to her, we parted and that's all. You realize, do you, that in answering all these questions I'm being very accommodating?"

"I am not sure, Captain, if you are answering questions or merely talking," said Michalides. "I am thinking you are a great one for talking."

"Well, I've got time to spare for that," said Harry, "while I'm waiting for the advance British forces to arrive. However, I don't want to be drawn into what I think is a local political matter. I don't care for that at all, and my superiors would be against it. Your Princess is probably on her way to somewhere else by now. I've time to spare, as I said, but I think you're wasting yours."

"Tell me about the cafe again," said Michalides.

Harry repeated what he had said about the cafe with a white cross over its door. Michalides spoke to Dimitroff. Dimitroff answered, nodded. Palichek, who had wandered into the kitchen, came out again. He was not so sour-faced. He was grinning. Harry felt a little alarm bell ring in his mind. It was smothered by relief when the man brought a bottle of wine out from behind his back.

"It's been a thirsty morning, Comrade Michalides," said Palichek.

Dimitroff brightened and said, "It's not much to ask of your English friend, a glass of his wine."

"He's not my friend," said Michalides, "he's like a woman with all his devious talk."

Harry, guessing the wine was the subject, said, "Do they want a drink? Tell them to help themselves."

"Bring it with you," said Michalides to the Serbians, "we're going to the White Cross cafe." To Harry he said, "Well, we shall do some looking and ask some more questions. We shall find her."

"I can't wish you luck, I'm impartial," said Harry. Politely he saw them out. Michalides looked around the landing and at the upward flight of stairs. He glanced back at Harry, standing in the open doorway. He smiled and went up the stairs, to the fifth floor and the sixth, the last. They heard his footsteps on the stone flights. Harry waited for a cry, a scuffle. He knew for certain now that Major Carlsen was right. These men wanted the Princess, and badly. He slipped his hand into this jacket pocket. The revolver was still there. He could not let them take her. Michalides would cheerfully hang her.

There was silence at the top. Palichek fiddled with the bottle of wine. Dimitroff leaned against the wall. Footsteps sounded again. Michalides came down. He looked at Harry, gave him a cold-eyed smile and took Palichek and Dimitroff down to the street with him. Harry went quietly to the head of the stairs and heard them cross the tiled hall. Was the cab still there? He went to the landing window which overlooked the street. They were getting into the cab. He waited until it drove off, then ran to the top floor, taking the stairs two at a time. The top floor landing was deserted, the doors of each apartment closed. Irena had gone, and her case.

Six

Somewhere, faintly, Harry heard a child crying.
The apartment block was solidly built and closed
doors shut out most of the ordinary sounds of life
and living. The silence left by Irena's disappearance was an uneasy one. He disliked it intensely.
Where the devil was she? Obviously, she had not
been here when Michalides had come nosing up.
Had she decided the landing was too exposed?
If so, and she had gone creeping down to the
street, she had taken a terrible risk. She could not
have known whether Michalides had a man
waiting.

The child cried again. Had that panicked
her, a child's cry and the thought that a door
would open and someone see her ask her questions? No, she would think quickly and act

coolly, he was sure. The fire escape. He paced across the landing and looked out of a cold, high doorway at the iron staircase. He saw one or two people walking down below, he did not see Irena.

An apartment door opened. He turned, closing the fire exit. A woman was looking at him. She shut the door. It opened again a few seconds later and there was Irena, her hopeful smile asking if everything was all right. The woman appeared beside her and regarded Harry with feminine interest. Irena turned to her.

"See, he's here. Now I've no more worries. But I'm sure this was the apartment number he gave me. Love makes some men get little things wrong. You've been so kind. Thank you."

She pulled out her large case, slithering it along the floor. The woman remained there, intrigued, wondering how a young married couple would reunite after having lost each other. Harry did not understand what Irena had said, but her look of simulated relief and pleasure gave him a clue. She was a resourceful young woman.

In French he said ecstatically, "Sonya! My love!" He swept her into his arms and kissed her resoundingly on both cheeks. She had not expected him to play up as demonstratively as that, and the vibrations that ran through her body were of indignation and shock. The woman smiled to see that the war had not spoiled love for some people, then closed the door. Irena, face burning, retreated in hot confusion from Harry's arms. He picked up her case and they went down to their apartment. Inside it she faced up to him.

"How dared you!" she said.

"Please, not now, Your Highness."

"Not now? What do you mean?" The inference she drew turned her pinker. "You are a cad, sir!"

"No, it was all for the benefit of the lady upstairs. I'm right, aren't I, in thinking you knocked on her door and told her you were looking for your husband? And that she invited you in to hear your story?"

"Yes. But even so—"

"You can tell me later." He was brisk, urgent, treating her sensitivity as an irrelevance. "They're on to us. You must go. Leave your case, I'll pack as many of your things into mine as I can. Leave by the rear exit on the ground floor, you can get through to the adjacent street from there. For God's sake be careful. They've gone off in that cab but they won't go far. Michalides will give me just enough time to make me think he's going to the cafe in the cathedral square, then he'll be back, hoping to catch you here. He's convinced you're around. And the least he'll do is have someone watch this place."

Irena looked haughtily obstinate.

"We are staying here," she said, "Major Carlsen—"

"Oh, you'd rather wait for Belgrade to be relieved, would you? I doubt if it'll be like Mafeking night for you. They'll pick you up before then. I might be able to stall them for a while but I can't shoot their heads off. We'll leave tonight. Go to the station, find out if there's a train leaving for Trieste this evening and if so, get tickets. I'll meet you there just after dark."

"But that is not the plan!" She pulled her

headscarf off and flung her hair about in a spasm of temperament.

"I know it isn't," he said, "and you must know that the original plan, such as it is, has fallen down dead. Now there's no plan at all. We've just got to cut and run for it."

She calmed down and said in her cool way, "Major Carlsen said we were to wait here until the war was over, bcause then it would be safer and easier for us to get to Trieste. I don't think we should run just because those men have found you. They have not found me."

"My dear young lady—"

"You are forgetting yourself, Captain Phillips."

"Your Highness," he said firmly, "wayward princesses are out of place at the moment."

"Oh!" She stamped her foot.

"Listen, please. They aren't idiots, they'll be back. Now despite my lack of qualifications for this job and my limitations as a lord chamberlain or grand vizier or royal paperweight—"

"Oh!"

"—I'm going to get you to Trieste, and then to England, even if I have to launch you on a raft."

"You are a bully, sir! Do you hear! A bully!"

"Yes, but I happen to agree with Major Carlsen now," he said, "I think you're worth saving from the hangmen of Michalides. But can we be more agreeable about the ways and means?"

Irena stared at him, at his dark, uncompromising eyes and at his expression, which was almost grim. Her hot resentment melted. Her lashes drooped as angry eyes softened.

"May I put on a hat and veil?" she asked quietly. He opened up her case. She found her brown hat, with its half-veil. She put it on. He frowned a little because she looked so chastened by his bullying, so vulnerable to a man like Michalides. His frown was at himself. "Please," she said, "will you make sure that whatever else you leave behind you will pack my brown costume?"

"Yes," he said.

"I will stay and pack the things I want if you like."

"No. You must go. Please."

"There are some things—" She pinked.

"Yes, I understand." He knew she would want him to include as much fresh underwear as could be managed.

"I'll try to get something to eat at a cafe," she said.

"I'm sorry," said Harry, "I know how hungry you must be again, but I'll bring some of the food we've got here. Wait." He fetched two of the pears and gave them to her. She put one into her handbag and bit into the other without ceremony. It was a crisp, hard fruit. "Good," he said, "eat them on the way." He opened the door for her. She looked at the pear in her gloved hand.

"You will meet me later?" she said.

"Of course. Keep yourself out of sight and watch for me soon after dark."

"I know you will come," she said, "but I shan't go on any train until you do arrive. You will remember my brown costume, please? I must have that."

"Yes," he said. She left quietly. He followed her down, watched her leave the building by a rear exit, then he slipped out through the front door. He looked around but saw no sign of the men or the cab and sped back upstairs.

Irena's case had to be got out of sight. If Michalides did return he had to be let in again. Harry sensed he had a certain immunity in the eyes of the Rumanian, but only as long as Michalides remained a little unsure of his ground. Once he was convinced of Harry's complete involvement with the Princess, that immunity would cease to exist. Politics were more important to men like Michalides than the war—when he spoke of which side people were on, he had politics in mind, not armies. Well, the man had rummaged around and searched the bedroom himself, and had found nothing he could associate with the presence of Irena. If he came back it would be in the hope of bursting in on her.

The case. There was only one place for it. Under the bed. They would have already looked there. If they came back and there was no sign of her, they would not rummage around again. He must chance that they wouldn't. He took the case in and shoved it under the bed, tightly up against the wall, where it was darkest. In the kitchen he turned the beans out of the bag and into a bowl. He put some water into a saucepan. He poured himself a measure of brandy. Then, with his jacket off and the sleeves of his jersey rolled up, he simply waited. He nipped off the tops and stripped the spines of a couple of beans as an afterthought, putting them into the saucepan.

He felt Michalides had swallowed nothing of his story. He had lied on a first-class note—well, one either performed well or not at all—but Michalides had not been convinced. He would not have checked the upper landings otherwise. And if he intended to return the knock would happen any moment now.

It came five minutes later. Harry lit a low gas under the saucepan and answered the summons with a peeling knife in his hand. Michalides had only one man with him this time. The other one, obviously, would be holding a watching brief downstairs. Michalides looked ready for trouble.

"Oh, damn it," said Harry in reasonable exasperation, "what the devil is it this time?" In his right hand the blade of the peeling knife glinted.

"What is that for?" The Rumanian's voice was soft.

"Beans," said Harry, "I'm trying to get myself a meal."

"Excuse." Michalides thrust the door back and brushed by, Dimitroff on his heels. Harry shut the door, called Michalides a time-wasting idiot and returned to the kitchen. Michalides flashed in after him like a black shadow and caught him using the knife on the beans. He plopped each one into the saucepan of water. Michalides looked almost outraged. Dimitroff appeared at his shoulder.

"You're wasting your time, you know," said Harry shortly.

"I am not satisfied," said Michalides.

"Neither am I," said Harry, "you're turning

this place into a railway station." He took a sip of the brandy he had poured himself. Michalides turned abruptly, shouldered past Dimitroff and strode through the living-room to the bedroom. Dimitroff put his head into the bathroom, into cupboards, then joined Michalides in the bedroom. Harry finished preparing his beans, listening to the sound of their voices. Carrying his brandy he sauntered casually in on them after a while. They had opened up the wardrobe again and this time had stripped off the bedclothes, which lay in a tumbled heap on the floor beside the bed. That could be a help, thought Harry. It restricted the view under the bed. Michalides looked the picture of black frustration.

"Good God," said Harry irritably, "what the devil are you doing now? Do you think I've got her sewn up in the mattress? Or perhaps in a sack under the bed?"

Michalides showed his teeth. They were grinding.

"I am not satisfied, I tell you," he said.

"That's damned obvious," said Harry. He took a mouthful of brandy. He sensed the menace of the Rumanian's henchman standing close by, the temptation Michalides felt to try more primitive methods of persuasion. "If you wreck the place you'll pay for it, I tell you that. I'll be in the kitchen when you've come to your senses. There's some brandy if you want it. You're having a tiring day. So am I."

It worked. They followed him into the kitchen. He pointed to the brandy bottle. Dimitroff was not a man to worry about losing face. He helped himself. He poured some for Michalides. Michalides took it, scowled at it and tossed it down his throat. Harry put salt in the beans. The water was steaming.

"What's he doing, drowning them in hot water?" asked Dimitroff.

Michalides, giving himself time to think, put the question to Harry.

"I don't like oily beans, I like them cooked clean and slightly salted," said Harry. "Look here, if you're convinced your elusive Princess is still in Belgrade, why don't you try the cathedral? Royal personages are known to be very devout and you can be very devout in a cathedral and keep your face hidden at the same time. After all, it was in that cafe near the cathedral where I last saw her."

"Talk," said Michalides and ground his teeth. "I have never heard any talk which said as little as yours. No, I am still not satisfied. She is here somewhere." He walked out. Dimitroff finished his brandy and went after him. Harry heard the apartment door close. He went to the door and stood with his ear against it. He caught the faint sounds the two men made. They were going up and down flights, searching, looking. He heard the hollow sound of a fire exit door slam. He had thought about putting the case somewhere out on that iron staircase. He stayed at the door, listening, until finally he heard them descending to the ground floor. Then he returned to the kitchen.

The beans simmered and cooked. He ate them with a piece of dark bread, which tasted of chaff. He hoped Irena would forgive him for having this minor meal. He ate one of the hard pears for dessert. He saved the wine and the rest of the food. He retrieved her case from beneath the bed and opened it up. A tumbled array of clothes looked up at him.

"Something has to be sacrificed for the cause," he said. His own case was smaller. His British uniform must go in, plus his razor and toothbrush. The rest of the space had to take what it could of her things. She had the clothes she was wearing. He would include her brown costume, as promised, and as many of her undergarments as possible. With her royal background she might endure the prospect of only one change of outer clothes, but would consider life an outrage if she did not have a sufficiency of fresh underwear. He packed his uniform first, then her undergarments en masse, thus avoiding the delicate responsibility of having to make a selection of what she might consider the utter necessities and the do-withouts. He stowed in all her toilet articles. Lastly he put in her costume.

Yet there was always the possibility that he might have to get rid of the case and all its contents in an emergency. If he was going to have literally to run for it the case would have to be dumped. She had been very insistent about her costume, the brown one. He wondered why. He was having to leave dresses and another costume behind, but had to take the brown jacket and skirt, with the cream blouse. He thought about it. It came to him that she was wearing no jewellery. That was wise. But as she was going into exile it was also improvident. What was she going to live on unless she had funds salted away somewhere?

He took the costume out. He examined it.

He ran his fingers over the closely-woven material. Around the hem of the skirt he felt the presence of hard, small stones. With a sharp-pointed kitchen knife he carefully snipped some of the neat stitching. A minute later a tiny cataract of brilliance spilled into his hand, forming a small pyramid that flashed with iridescent light. Fifty matching diamonds at least, fifty.

"Ye gods," he said.

He wrapped them carefully in one of her tiny, lace-edged handkerchiefs, then sat down to think about Michalides. He had no doubt the apartment block was being watched. One man at least would be lurking somewhere around. Michalides himself was probably on his way to that cafe. He would get no satisfaction, but he would ask his questions, be suspicious of every answer, roam about and ask again. Then sooner or later he would be back here.

Harry knew he could not leave before dusk. If he were spotted, and with his case, there would be no more politeness, no more patient probing. They would have the case off him, open it, see her clothes and know for sure that he knew where she was. Therefore, if he were spotted, he would have to run for it before they laid hands on him. That was when the case would have to be dumped. "Ye gods," he said again. If he hadn't examined her costume he would have been in danger of dumping a fortune. The thought made him take another look at the costume, and at the clothes he was leaving behind. He found nothing more. He re-packed the costume. He pushed in the wine, the brandy and the small amount of wrapped food.

At the first sign of dusk he went out on to the landing and peered through the window into the street below. He knew why it was so quiet. Almost everyone was in the city center, unable to keep away from the hub of news, rumor and excitement.

If Michalides had a man on watch he wasn't visible from the window.

When darkness swam to submerge dusk Harry left the apartment. Going down the flights a man and a woman passed him on their way up. They were both talking at once. They glanced at him and went on talking and ascending. He continued quietly down. On the ground floor the single economic light in the hall scarcely fingered him as he skirted it and faded into the darkness by the rear door. Cautiously he opened it, staying close to the wall. He looked and listened. Somewhere he thought he could smell cooking. The quadrangle at the rear of the block, its paved surface slightly crumbling, was dark. He counted himself invisible against the wall. He put the case down, reached into his pocket and drew out a paper-wrapped ball of bean strips. He tossed it upwards and outwards. It fell into the quadrangle with a small rustling noise. The sound drew an immediate and perceptible reaction. Harry heard the soft slither of feet. A torch suddenly beamed, sweeping to and fro as Harry closed the rear door. It picked up nothing, it rushed back on itself and was swallowed by its source. Darkness reclaimed the quadrangle and its gate, the gate through which Irena would have gone earlier, but which was denied to Harry now.

He left by the front entrance. His emergence was fast and in socked feet, his tied boots around his neck. He turned eastward, away from the city center, carrying the case in his arms and against his chest, camouflaging it. There were no street lights and in the cold darkness his deep grey suit, black jersey and peaked cap made of him a moving shadow. But Dimitroff, inconspicuously posted on the west side of the block, was sharp of eye and adjusted of vision. He came out from cover and began to walk in long-striding pursuit, signalling to Palichek with a low whistle as he did so. Harry, silent in his socks, heard him before he whistled, heard him the moment he moved, and immediately vaulted the yard-high wall fronting the house next to the block. He stretched himself flat on the ground beside it, the case pushed out in front of him. He lay in the chill well of darkness, grateful for the wartime fuel shortage which denied all but essential light to a city.

He heard the man go by. He waited as he caught the sound of another man, a man running, who passed by quickly. Harry did not wait for a second chance, a better chance, or a longer interval. He was over the low wall at once, speeding silently back past the apartment block and going westward. He ran, softly padding, risking his socked feet as he kept close to the line of houses, the case swinging heavily in his hand. If he trod on a stone it would be murder. But he ran faster. He stopped abruptly at the sound of people ahead. He turned and flitted across the street, avoiding them. He heard them pass. He went on, entered a street on his right and began to run once more. He stopped again after a few minutes and put his boots on. Then he strode on quickly, making for the railway station. How long he had before Michalides decided he was on his way out of Belgrade he did not know.

In a little while he was in streets that were crowded. Shop fronts showed a few lights. To the Serbians the excitement was of the kind that kept a tongue buzzing or grew like a knot in the stomach. They were watching their conquerors departing. Down the main street they came, battalions of German troops, marching in long columns. At the head of each company rode the officer commanding.

Harry had to stop. He could not cross until the columns had passed by. His impatience was of an eruptive quality. Princess Irena had been alone for hours and God knows who might have recognized her if she had been wandering about. She would be waiting for him now, looking for him. He stood on the pavement, hemmed in by the people of Belgrade, and the Germans, their faces expressionless, came marching through. Momentarily, Harry's impatience was mitigated by the drama of the spectacle.

They marched down the Balkanska with precision, still governed by years of incomparable discipline. They were great-coated, their rifles slung. Beneath their steel helmets their eyes were like dark shadows. They marched in faultless step, each battalion going by in companies, and towards the west. As soldiers, thought Harry, they had no superiors. Their officers rode looking straight ahead, aloof to the citizens of Belgrade and to the implications of their retreat from this

Serbian capital. They had helped the Austrians to capture it and hold it. It could be held no longer.

The people became silent. It was a silence that was impressive, that was almost a tribute to the soldiers of Kaiser Wilhelm. The Germans did not look like defeated men, they were not departing like defeated men, and no Serbian with any sense would spit at even the most insignificant of them. The company machine-gunners would execute a streetful of people in return.

A number of policemen lined the route of the march, but except for the steady, rhythmic tramp of booted feet it was a silent and completely undemonstrative event on both sides. Harry looked on with emotions of his own. In one way or another he had been up against men of this kind for four years. He knew what they were like. More or less, they were all like Major Carlsen.

There was a break as the rearguard of a column passed him. Horse-drawn transport was following on, but fifty yards away. He heard the sound most familiar to him, that of rolling gun carriages. There were no policemen to hold him back and he slipped across the road while it was clear. The station was not far and he reached it without incident. After the quietness the noise here was deafening. Standing trains were letting off steam and most of the platforms seemed to be choked with Austrian or German troops. Not every soldier was marching. Civilians were besieging booking offices and station officials. Hundreds of people had been slipping out of the city for days. This evening it looked as if hundreds more had decided to follow. Serbian women who married Austrian or German soldiers were waving papers at clerks, officials and even porters, demanding their right to a place on a train.

Harry thought the prospects of getting to Trieste must be pretty slim. He thought the prospects of making the journey by road even slimmer. Transport of any kind would be at a premium, many of the roads would be swarming, and he frankly did not fancy the wildness of Croatia, or some of its more medieval reception committees, except from the security of the railroad. The greater part of the journey to Trieste would be through the country of the Croats, and although it was under the administration of Austria, the crumbling nature of the Habsburg Empire now was an encouragement to Croatian insurgents and irregulars.

He detached himself from the worst of the press. Irena had to be able to see him. He prepared himself for the possibility of having to search for her, feeling that after all these hours she might have engaged herself in a tête-à-tête situation with someone simply to relieve her boredom. There were times when nothing could hold a woman back from a companionable dialogue.

As he scoured the eastern side of the station with slightly anxious eyes a gloved hand touched his arm.

"Thank goodness," said a soft, warm voice, "I've been looking for you until my eyes hurt."

He felt immensely relieved to see her. His responsibility to get her safely to England was not a risky adventure any more, it was, because of Michalides, something that had become a compulsive necessity. There she was in her brown hat, half-veil and dark coat, looking quite cool and lovely against the shuffling, surging background of the noisy station. He drew her into the entrance of a closed station shop.

"I couldn't leave before dark," he said, "Michalides and his men had their noses all over the place."

"They came back?"

"Yes. And then they were prowling about."

"But you have given them the slip?" She was earnest.

"I hope so."

"You are very clever," she said. Then came a soft rush of words. "Oh, I'm so glad you're here, it's been hours, and I did not like feeling so alone after being so well protected."

"Well, I swore all those oaths," smiled Harry, "so I had to get here. Otherwise you'd have thought me an advertisement for hot air."

"Oh? What is an advertisement for hot air?" She was sure it was amusing, she wished to be amused. It had been such a long wait, such a relief to see him in the end. She did not want to be responsible for something terrible happening to him.

"Oh, hot air just means talking for the sake of it," said Harry. "You haven't said, is there a train to Trieste?"

"Yes. It's supposed to leave in an hour. I have tickets. Do you know, I have been quite clever again, I think. I have been hiding myself in the office of the senior Austrian transport officer here. He was very charming but a little curious. I think perhaps he felt my face was familiar in some way." She did not look as if that had worried her. She laughed a little, her mood reflecting her relief. Her qualities of courage and resilience, her charm, her vulnerability and her little lapses into hauteur, were growing on him. She looked warm and alive at this moment. "You are listening?" she said.

"Of course. About how clever you've been."

"Yes? It was, don't you think, to keep out of the way in the railway offices with the Austrians? And although the officer thought my face was familiar, he did not hold it against me. So we have tickets, you see, and he will see that we have seats too."

"Well done," said Harry.

"Yes?" She was pleased. She looked at the case he held. "Oh, that is smaller than I thought it was, but you have most of my clothes in it?"

"I'm sorry, no," he said, "I managed all your undergarments but—"

"But my clothes, my brown costume!" She was agitated. "You have never dared to leave me with only the things I stand up in!"

"I put your costume in," he said.

"Oh," she said and sighed with new relief.

"And these," he said. In the recess of the shop entrance they were apart from the mob and he pulled a small knotted handkerchief from his pocket. It was one of her own and the knot was tight and secure. He handed it to her. She felt the small shifting heap of stones it contained. Her eyes widened and she flushed.

"Captain Phillips—"

"I felt you were worried about that costume," he said, "and as I might have had to get rid of the case I thought I'd better investigate. They were sewn into the skirt hem, they're all there, as far as I know, fifty-two of them. Is that the right number?"

"Yes," she said, closing her gloved hand over the tiny bundle.

"You must keep them with you, don't sew them back unless you're going to wear the costume permanently. You never know when we might have to run for it and leave everything behind. Are there any other stones?"

She did not know what to say for a moment.

"Oh, I'm sorry," she said, "I should have trusted you and told you about them. But I was not to know you would be as intelligent as that, was I? I've not always heard the most flattering things about British officers. You are quite a pleasant surprise."

"Really?" Under his peaked blue cap Harry raised his eyebrows. "I never apply generalizations to individuals myself. If I did I'd never have taken this job on."

"Please?" She wanted clarification.

"Well, I've always heard that Balkan princesses spend most of their time screaming their heads off and scratching their maids into shreds. I thought this simply couldn't be true of all of them and it isn't."

"I should think not," said Irena hotly, "it's a shameful lie, an odious slander and it isn't true of any of them."

"Are there any other stones?" asked Harry again.

"Yes." She put the knotted handkerchief

deep into her handbag. "But not in any of my other clothes, only some sewn into the hem of this coat I have on. And I have one or two pearls in a little pot of face cream in my handbag. They—"

"I'm only concerned to know I left none behind," said Harry.

"But I am concerned to tell you what I have," she said, a little distressed. "They are all I've brought, everything else I've had to leave."

"I don't think you'll be poor," said Harry and smiled. "Have you had something to eat?"

"Yes, I went to that cafe where we had coffee this morning, they were serving riblja corba and there was a little bread to eat with it. Something is wrong?" She was aware that he wasn't looking at all pleased with her. "Oh, you're wondering about riblja corba? That is only fish soup, it isn't dangerous—"

"You went wandering about, and to that cafe of all places? When? How long ago?" The station was a hubbub of sound and movement. Harry was oblivious of it.

"About an hour," said Irena, "but what does it matter? Why are you looking so fierce?"

"Why? Why?" Harry wondered almost helplessly if she knew what she was saying. Her casual indifference to the threat posed by Michalides would have been admirable if it hadn't been suicidal. She knew flight from her enemies was necessary, but apparently she wasn't going to realize just how necessary until they were standing her up against the wall on a cold dawn. "Were you trying to walk into their arms?" he asked. "Didn't I tell you Michalides would be going to that cafe?"

"You did say something but not quite that," she said. She became cool, as she always did when he was treating her like this. "I wish you would not speak to me as if I were ten years old."

He wanted to tell her not to behave as if she were, but he didn't. He knew he would sound arrogant and presumptuous, and he probably would be. She was not an ordinary young woman. In her position the cold hard facts of life would be kept from her. Now she was out in the cold hard world. No one could expect her to behave as ordinary people would.

"I'm sorry," he said, "but I didn't have time to give you the full story, although I thought I did say enough to make you understand you weren't to go wandering about, you were to stay here."

"I was not wandering about, I went to find something to eat."

"Yes. All right," he said. "Anyway, it's done now, and obviously you didn't see Michalides. But I wonder if he saw you?"

"Of course not." Her eyes flashed at him through her veil. "He would have dragged me off if he had."

"Yes, if he could have got away with it. Well, we can't be sure he didn't spot you and follow you." Harry regarded her with a little severity. "You do realize that, don't you?"

"Oh, you are an old fuss," said Irena. Then she smiled. "I suppose you are right, but are you sure we must leave? It's going to be crowded on the train and whether it will ever get to Trieste no one knows. Really, I should not at all mind taking the risk of staying here for a few days longer and leaving when things are quieter."

Harry surveyed the teeming station. The roar of steam and the din of sound rose like shock waves to rebound from the vaulted roof.

"Things aren't going to get quieter for weeks," he said, "and if we stay here a mountain of trouble will fall on you. We must catch that train."

She hesitated, then gave the slightest of shrugs.

"Very well. You are in command, Captain Phillips."

"Look here, I don't mean to be bumptious," said Harry.

"What is bumptious? You are very firm, that's all. Firmness is necessary with funny Balkan princesses, isn't it? I should not think much of you if you dithered and dallied. That is right, dithered and dallied?"

"Nearly right. You should say dillied, not dithered."

"Well, nearly right is quite good, isn't it?" She was smiling again. "Shall we see if the train is in?"

"Idiots," said Michalides, and not for the first time. His mood was blacker than his beard. It was cold outside the apartment block and they had already spent a chilly time on the fourth floor trying to break into the vacated flat.

"I protest," said Palichek.

"I share his protest," said Dimitroff, "and you have done all the talking, you have sown all the seed. Now you blame us for a barren harvest."

"But to let him get away when there were two of you, what could have been more idiotic?" said Michalides coldly.

"Bad luck is an impartial pest," said Palichek, "it attacks the wise as well as the foolish. It's no good using hard words, comrade. You did no better than we did, going all the way to that cafe and finding nothing."

"That was a stone that couldn't be left unturned," said Michalides. "But a moment, my friends, before we quarrel. Let me think." He did think. He was capable of very clinical analyses. He came to a conclusion with a gleam in his eye. "Of course! He has run, and in running he's confirmed what we all suspect."

"What do we all suspect?" asked Dimitroff, hands in his pockets and his jacket collar turned up.

"Why, that Irena of Moldavia, the she-puppet of the Kaiser, is running with him. Ah, that slippery fox. Why else did he go? To get to her before we did. To go off with her. To cheat us of her. We were making life too uncomfortable for him, we were getting too close to her. He'll not come back here. He's acting for others, my friends. He'll get her out of Belgrade, take her to England and deposit her in the comforting laps of the royal family there. Ah, these cursed royals, thinking more of each other than their countries. It's burglary, I tell you. They're robbing the Rumanian people of their right to hang her."

"If we catch her," said Palichek, "we Serbians will be proud to hang her for you. No one can say we're given to fiddling about when there's a people's account to be squared."

"Ah, the flames of justice," said Dimitroff.

"No, that might cause unnecessary dissatisfaction," said Michalides. "We Rumanians are a jealous people and like to square our own accounts."

"It's good to know you're not too jealous to allow us to help," said Dimitroff with his tongue in his cheek.

"Believe me," said Michalides generously, "we couldn't do without it." He said nothing about their lack of imagination. They were Serbian gift horses and he had to make the best use of them he could. "Now, my friends, our slippery pair won't go back to Bucharest, that's certain. They'll head west, with the retreating Germans. Our talkative Englishman will risk the Germans rather than us. You may rely on it, he's been ordered to help our plump royal partridge escape us, and if I know her she's already twisting him around her little finger."

"I'd not call her plump," said Palichek, "not from her pictures."

"From her pictures," said Dimitroff, "I'd say she was so so." And he used his hands to describe a rounded figure and a slender waist.

"Well, she'll hang as good as the plump ones and dance better than most," said Michalides. "No more time must be lost. Get your friends to watch every road and every train. They'll try to get out of Belgrade tonight or, at the latest, tomorrow. Trains are difficult, but he'll use that slippery talk of his and she'll use her sugary smile. Every station must be visited."

"This is work for our comrades," said Palichek, "but many of them have their own pigeons to trap, their own business to see to. We are after our own traitors, Comrade Michalides. It's not possible to find enough of our friends to watch every road and every station."

"We shall lose her!" Michalides, about to jump into the cab that had been standing by, turned fiercely on the Serbians. His beard bristled.

"No, we shall get her," said Dimitroff, "there'll be enough of us, comrade. We have friends who'll be glad to stay up all night looking for her. I know someone who could find a lost leaf in an autumn forest."

"Ah, that's what makes good comrades of some friends," said Michalides as they settled themselves in the swaying cab.

"We're all ready to serve," said Palichek. He produced, in the most natural way, a long-bladed knife with a finely-tapered point. He caressed it. "If there is trouble in bringing her back, comrade?"

"Naturally, she must not be spoiled," said Michalides, "but you may slice him up if it's necessary. Forgive me for raising my voice a moment ago, but we Rumanians are a serious people in matters of this kind."

"We Serbians don't joke much, either," said Dimitroff.

Seven

There was only one passenger coach available to civilians on the Trieste train. The other two coaches were for German officers. The rest of the train was made up of freight cars and wagons, carrying German troops, stores, horses and guns. Harry and Irena were in a compartment managing to seat ten. As she had suspected, the journey was not going to be one of comfort and joy. She resigned herself to it without complaint, however, which Harry thought both sensible and advisable. An uncomfortable train ride was preferable to the uncompromising finality of losing her lovely head.

As railway officials channelled privileged ticket-holders into the right coach and right compartments, Irena sat in squashed contact with a window. Next to her was a large man with a hot body and a worried frown. Troubled by the circumstances which were forcing him to leave Belgrade, he sat brooding and overweight, his right side compressing Irena, his left burdening his small wife. Irena's eyes sought Harry's in appeal. Discomfort was one thing, smothering was another. Harry saw her crushed look. It was not what she was used to at all. He smiled a little. Irena could hardly believe it. He was laughing at the way she was being squeezed to death? She flashed a withering look. He leaned forward from his seat opposite her and tapped the man on the knee. The man gave a start of heavy flesh and his jowls quivered. His little wife stared anxiously.

"Ja?" he said.

Irena took it up.

"Do you mind if places are changed?" she said. An irresistible smile followed.

"Changed?" The large man had other things on his mind.

"Please, everyone stand," said Irena as if she had been rearranging crowded train compartments all her life, and nine people rose to their feet, including Harry, who wanted to laugh at her audacity. She herself remained seated. The door slid back at that moment, an official said, "There, this is the best I can do for you," and a girl appeared. She had a mass of black hair, a breathless, eager look, and was dressed in a warm woollen costume of dark red with a matching hat.

"Go away, we are full!" cried the large man's wife.

But the girl was like a quick cat among

shuffling pigeons. She was darting while others were trying, for no reason at all, to change seats. Irena seized Harry's wrist and jerked him down beside her.

"Where is your initiative?" she hissed in French.

"I rarely use it on mere social occasions," murmured Harry.

The girl had whipped into the seat he had vacated opposite Irena, and other people, quickly recovering from their moment of induced hypnosis, were falling back into theirs. This alleviated the confusion but did not cure it completely. The little wife was kicking and scratching on behalf of her large husband, who was doing his slow, bear-like best for her and his ponderous best for himself. No one said a word, muttered exclamations of incomprehension were as far as anyone went. It was all over quite soon, a brief Slavonic dance which never achieved rhythm. It left the large man seatless. The cause of the dance, Irena, had not moved at all. She now sat with a cool, pleased look on her face. Harry next to her was far more acceptable than the big man, far less overwhelming. The latter now loomed enormously out of place, and was embarrassed as well as worried. His wife sighed in sympathy for him. There was simply nowhere he could sit, it was impossible to make room for his bulk. He mumbled, accepted defeat, slid back the door and took up a position in the corridor.

"He'll be better there," said his wife sagely, "he can walk up and down. He has all his worries."

Other passengers nodded. Everyone had

their worries, including three young Serbian women married to Austrian soldiers. They were going to Zagreb and then north to Austria. There were two hard-faced men who had policed Belgrade for the Austrians and wished to put as much distance as possible between themselves and Serbia. And there was a quiet-looking man who used his eyes more than his tongue.

"It's a bad time," said one of the Serbian women, and they all began to talk then, the women. Women have an exceptional ability to communicate. It is often better, as poets of old imply, not to silence a woman with kisses but to let her talk on until man's love and woman's conversation achieve a confluence, flowing and uninterrupted.

Harry thought about it and smiled, then let it go over his head. He sat back. A gloved hand slid inside his arm.

"This is much better," whispered Irena, "I should have suffocated or caught fire with that stout man next to me."

"Well, you've very successfully resolved that problem," said Harry. He could not afford to play any role but the accepted one with Irena. Anything not strictly related to the object of the exercise was to be avoided. Not that he was likely to fall in love with her. Princesses who had haughty moods would make errand boys of any men senseless enough to fall in love with them. And he wanted to have an absolutely straightforward story to tell Elisabeth. Elisabeth deserved straightforwardness. "I wonder if we'll get to Trieste?" he murmured. The train, full of noises, thumps and bangs, seemed in no hurry even to start.

"Oh, nothing is easier to you," she said a little coolly, for she was quite aware of his lack of response to her friendliness, "you would get a three-legged elephant to the top of Everest as long as it didn't argue with you."

Harry wondered if a three-legged elephant would be any more manageable than a highly individualistic princess. He did not put the question but the thought of doing so made him smile.

"You beast," she whispered, "you have just thought of something horrid to say."

"No, I've just thought I shan't feel comfortable until this train has taken us out of Belgrade. I feel it's standing around waiting for our friends to jump aboard. We're doing the obvious thing, being aboard ourselves."

"Well, it is your idea," she said. They were whispering in French.

The girl in the dark red costume and woollen hat was giving Harry shy, quick glances. Irena did not miss this or the fact that the girl had decided Harry was the one with whom she would most like to converse. Was he the best-looking? She glanced at the other men, then at Harry in profile. He had a good profile, firm mouth and thick lashes for a man. Irena felt a strange little tug at her heart. The girl was waiting to pounce, to engage him. Breathless, eager girls, once they pounced and attached themselves to a man, clung like rustling ivy. Irena's gloved hand was still inside Harry's arm and she kept it there to discourage any outside overtures.

They could not afford to pick up unshakeable acquaintances.

Suddenly whistles shrilled. The loaded train vibrated and began to pull slowly out of the station. At which the girl said excitedly to Harry, "Are we going, do you think?" She spoke in Serbo-Croatian, which sounded like garbled Greek to him. The silent man looked across at her, mildly disgusted that anyone could ask so unnecessary a question.

Harry said, "Pardon, mademoiselle?"

"Oh, you are French?" Leaning forward, whispering the words in French, she invited his confidential response. A Slav, she seemed like all of them to have a natural interest in anything remotely conspiratorial or out of the ordinary. A Frenchman on a train full of German soldiers was very out of the ordinary.

Harry leaned forward too and just as earnestly whispered, "I am Russian."

"Russian?" She breathed in little intakes. "Oh, you have been through the fire of revolution and felt its heat? It was awesome?"

"Hot," whispered Harry in confidence, while Irena from behind her veil eyed the girl extremely coolly. "And noisy. People running about, and everyone shouting and shooting night and day. One could not get to sleep."

"Oh?" The girl seemed a trifle perplexed, as if a mundane complaint instead of a great revelation would hardly make sense to anybody. Then she became very shy and confused, for no one else was saying a word now, all eyes were on her and this resolute-looking Russian. She sat back. Irena applied a pinch to Harry's arm, it was a warning not to get involved with an obvious chatterbox. The girl, aware that everyone was looking and waiting for more, said breathlessly, "Well, he's a Russian, think of it."

"A Bolshevik?" gasped the little wife, turning pale.

"You are a Bolshevik?" the girl asked Harry.

"Certainly not." Irena interrupted coldly. "He's a friend of some relatives of mine in Galicia. Do you think a friend of relatives of mine would be a Bolshevik?"

"Oh, no," said the girl. "He's not a Bolshevik," she informed the little wife. There were sighs. Things were bad enough as it was without the problem posed by the presence of a Russian Red. The girl remarked that she had heard the worst Bolsheviks ate babies.

"Not their own?" cried the little wife, eyes dilated.

"Oh, no," said the girl reassuringly, "it would only be aristocratic ones."

"Rubbish," said the mostly silent man.

"It's not rubbish," said the girl.

Contemptuously the man said, "What are you saying, that the aristocratic ones taste better!" He turned away, obviously impatient of the foolishness of people.

Arguments began, arguments about the character of Bolsheviks, about their aims and whether any political party had the right to take a people into civil war. The girl leaned forward to talk to Harry again.

"They're discussing Russian revolutionaries," she said with an air of intimacy.

"Not a peaceful subject, mademoiselle," said Harry.

Irena was icy. The girl was blatantly making up to Harry, her shy eagerness a foil for her boldness. An utter minx, thought Irena. The girl smiled at her. Irena responded with a glint of white teeth. The three Serbian women resumed their own kind of conversation. The quiet man's slightly moody eyes contemplated them with dislike. The train rattled, running slowly out of the western environs of Belgrade to feel its way into the night. The girl said she was glad it was making up its mind.

Irena glanced at Harry again. He seemed relaxed, a half-smile on his face as the girl fed him trivial comments. It was obvious to Irena that the creature was dying to become his best friend. The world was growing up but surely it would never be proper for an unchaperoned girl on a train to behave with anything but modesty.

The coaches and wagons gathered momentum behind the engine, couplings rattled and wheels bit firmly as the train stretched to run at speed. It passed over the last series of points and steamed into the dark mouth of night. It entered Croatia-Slovenia, annexed by the Habsburg Empire decades ago. The three Serbian women were visibly relaxed, glad to feel they were well on their way and leaving the mounting hostility of relatives in Belgrade, for in marrying Austrian soldiers they had committed the unforgivable social sin. They chattered freely. The two ex-policemen smoked and disappeared behind the clouds they emitted, the little woman made fluttering signals to her husband outside the door and the quiet man behaved himself, closing his eyes to rest in peace.

No one expected the train to stop at St. Pazova, only at Zagreb. But it did stop, pulling up with a smooth application of the brakes and the sound of metal yielding to stern compulsion. Waiting to board were about fifty German soldiers, an officer and, it seemed, several black-clad peasant women. Harry leaned and peered. Under the light of makeshift oil lamps the soldiers began to move, gestured on by the officer. He was immaculate in greatcoat and cap. He was a man easy to recognize, despite the inadequacy of the station lamps. He was Major Carlsen. Harry looked at Irena, sitting next to the window. She had seen the Major too. She met Harry's glance, gave him the faintest of smiles and a little shrug. Behind the veil her eyes were darkly brown.

The German soldiers boarded. Major Carlsen waited by the door of the second coach. The peasant women edged nervously and anxiously forward. The Major turned and with a gesture of finely-edged mockery bowed slightly to indicate they should precede him. They rushed past him, his presence and his manner agitating and confusing them, and climbed up into the coach. Harry got up and went into the corridor. There were several people sitting on their belongings. The large man was sitting on the floor, still brooding. Major Carlsen entered the corridor from the other coach, wrinkling his nose a little at the earthy odor of the peasant women preceding him. He was ushering them forward. They were all in thick black dresses, black headscarves covered their hair and their black boots were tarnished and streaked with the dried grey earth of their fields. They looked confused and lost, the more so when confronted with the obstacle of people. Major Carlsen called to them and they stopped their rustling, crowded advance. He slid back the door of the first compartment, occupied by a senior Austrian railway official who was dining alone and in comfort on a bottle of wine and a precious piece of cold sausage.

Harry, at his end of the corridor, heard the Major say something, then he saw him turn to the peasant women, who looked from behind a little like elongated crows with broad beams. The Major's courtesy was still edged with a subtle shade of mockery as he gestured them into the compartment. They sidled in awkwardly, six of them, eyes lowered, simple women whose existence was governed by the basic tenets of survival. They filled the compartment, they overflowed as they sat with their clothes voluminously occupying space their bodies did not require. The Austrian official, discomfited and disgusted, took his wine and sausage and beat a retreat under the uncompromising grey eyes of Major Carlsen. The Major bowed to the women, closed the door and turned his attention on the people littering the corridor. He saw Harry then. The two observed each other from the opposite ends of the corridor. The Major stared in surprise and cold disapproval. He moved, stopping to ask abrupt questions of the human obstacles. Answers came nervously, were received expressionlessly. He reached Harry as the train gathered speed again. He glanced into the compartment before speaking. He saw Irena. She made no sign.

"Who are you?" He asked the question of Harry in German.

Harry, understanding it was for local consumption, asked in French what was required of him. The large man had got up and was trying bulkily to make little of himself.

"Your papers." The Major's French was crisp. Harry produced his documents and the Major inspected them. "Come with me," he said. Harry followed him back down the swaying corridor, stepping over legs. The Major passed the compartment full of black-clad peasant women and went through to the next coach. Two German soldiers stood outside the first compartment. They saluted the Major and stepped aside. He slid back the door and entered. Harry walked in after him. The Major closed the door. He turned to Harry.

"Are you disobeying orders, Captain Phillips?"

"Orders?"

"You understand me, I think." The Major was frowning, dissatisfied. "What are you doing here?"

"Going to Trieste," said Harry, "it's pressure of circumstances. And look here, I'd like to know what you're up to, Major. I've had the devil of a job getting as far as this, and it seems to me you could have done just as well with no bother at all. Damn it, you were in Belgrade this morning taking coffee with your problem Princess—"

"You will oblige me, Captain, by not referring to Her Highness in your music hall terms."

"I can't not call her a problem," said Harry.

"You were in mufti, by the way. Is there anything you think you should tell me?"

"Sit down," said the Major. They both sat. "Yes, I saw Her Highness and naturally I spoke to her. The fact that I was not in uniform was merely to do with confidential orders I received. They did not concern you or Her Highness. You must remember I was able to control events only up to a certain point, I told you that you were more of a free agent than I was. It was impossible because of that for me to accompany Princess Irena to Belgrade or anywhere else. I'm on my way to Zagreb now because of new orders and our meeting on this train is a coincidence."

"But very fortuitous," said Harry, watching his man with interest, "you can take her over now, can't you?"

"Impossible," said the Major flatly, "and outside the terms of our agreement. Are you forgetting those terms? You are on your honor, I think, to look after the Princess and get her to England. I could not accomplish that. May I now point out that you were advised to stay in Belgrade!"

"I was also advised to use my initiative," said Harry. The compartment shook a little as the train rattled and swayed. "A man called Michalides and a couple of his comrades were squeezing us in Belgrade. Do you know Michalides?"

The Major's eyes flickered. "I know him," he said.

"He traced us to that apartment, he was on to us from the moment we left you." Harry was as crisp as the Major. "That was rather too obvious, that waiting cab, wasn't it? Michalides was waiting with it. But you know all about that, the

Princess told you when you spoke to her at the cafe this morning."

"I was not aware they had traced you to the apartment." Major Carlsen showed a faint line of worry.

"No, that happened later."

"I am concerned. This man Michalides, he saw her there?"

"No. We knew he was on his way and I had her out of the place before he arrived."

"Captain Phillips," said the Major with relief, "it is good to know you can make your moves quickly."

"You make yours mysteriously," said Harry.

"No." The Major shook his head. "My moves are entirely governed by the decisions of my superiors. We agreed you might have to act according to developments. Had you remained undiscovered in Belgrade you could have waited until we had evacuated Serbia and withdrawn from Croatia. Then you could have travelled to Trieste. Instead you are travelling with our troops all round you and that is dangerous, Captain. The slightest suspicion that you aren't what you claim to be and they will shoot you. I should regret that."

"No more than I would," said Harry.

"However, the Princess's one chance is still with you," said Major Carlsen emphatically, "therefore kindly remain alive. She is taking things well?"

"Remarkably well. She's the coolest young lady I've ever met. I suppose she's conditioned to present a calm royal front whatever the circumstances. Even so, she's still remarkable. Personally, when I'm in a blue funk I want to go and lie down.".

Major Carlsen smiled.

"I think you will survive," he said.

"Will I? I had to face up to Michalides and two of his cutthroats in that apartment, and I've a feeling they were measuring my neck for the same rope they're saving for her. I told Michalides I knew nothing about her. He knew I was lying. We had to get out. That's why we're here."

"We must hope," said the Major, "that you've left him foxed."

"Let's hope he's not on this train," said Harry, "because I'm damn sure he isn't foxed. All we've done is to slip him for the time being."

"I still have confidence in you," said Major Carlsen, "and so, I'm sure, has Her Royal Highness."

"I haven't lost her yet," said Harry, "but there's still time. Tell me, who are all those women who came on the train with you?"

"Unfortunately," said the Major, "they were foolish enough to appear on the roads in their market cart, and the roads are full of our troops, who are short of transport and food. The carts contained fruit and vegetables. Everything was commandeered. It's a conventional necessity of war. The women came wailing to the station hours ago, not wishing to walk many miles home. I did what I could for them, as you saw. I even gave them seats which some of my men should have had. I hope, when you reach England, you will feel able to tell your newspapers that not all Germans cook peasant women and eat them."

"Oh, glad to, Major," said Harry. "Are they going all the way to Zagreb?"

"No. We shall stop at Vrycho. You had better rejoin Her Highness. I will do what I can to look after you while I'm on the train, but my orders take me only as far as Zagreb. Now that you are on the train I advise you to stay on it."

They stood up. Harry said, "I wonder why the devil I let you get me into this?"

The Major said, "In times like these, Captain Phillips, would you really prefer to be sitting on your backside? No. Please give my felicitations to Her Highness."

When Harry returned to the compartment everyone began asking questions, except Irena. Irena knew she could not get the right answers until they were alone. And the quiet man dourly asked only for a little peace.

The girl in dark red was eager to know what had happened.

"It was all because I'm a Russian," explained Harry in his correct French, "and the German officer wanted to know whether I was a good one or a bad one."

"He thought perhaps you were a bad one, a Bolshevik?" she asked excitedly.

Harry laughed and shook his head, and the girl informed the other passengers that he had safely survived severe interrogation.

Irena wondered if the age of naivety was not for a girl the sweetest and most satisfying. The innocence and faith and hope of youth filled one's life with perfect images, everything was beautiful or could be made beautiful. When one was twenty-one, as she was, one had grown up and could no longer run barefooted through the grass and dance in the dew. There was decorum to be considered. And at sixteen one did not mind wet feet as one minded them at twenty-one.

She sighed. Really, she had accomplished nothing beyond her climb out of blissful adolescence. Except that she had met Major Helmut Carlsen, an ingenious and fearless German officer, and Captain Harry Phillips of the British Army, in the strangest possible circumstances. She did not think that Major Carlsen had ever suffered the awkwardness of boyish adolescence, and Captain Phillips had come of age long ago as far as attitudes were concerned, she thought. But he wasn't cynical, even though he had fought in this terrible war. It was making so many other people very cynical and intolerant, willing to listen to no views which did not coincide with their own. She thought Captain Phillips still had faith in some things, even if only in the ridiculousness of people. Of course, he was as masculine as most men, thinking that making women do as they were told was the same thing as protecting them. She must not let him speak to her as if she were not a princess. That would never do. It would make Major Carlsen frown.

It was frustrating not to be able to talk to him about the Major, but nothing serious could have come up between him and the German or he would have communicated a warning note of some kind to her.

The night passed slowly, the train chugging over its iron road, surmounting gorge and river and snaking around the hills of Slavonia. People brought out what food they had. The little wife went out to join her worried husband in the corridor. Harry extracted the food he had packed. It wasn't much. Too hungry to ration the small amount, he and Irena finished it up. They drank wine from the bottle, then passed it round.

Heads began to nod. The steamed-up windows hid the night. The dour man went to sleep. The Serbian women dozed off. Irena's head tipped slowly sideways and came to rest on Harry's shoulder. A small tired sigh escaped her. She moved and cuddled his arm, tucking herself close, and drifted into a series of catnaps. The girl in the dark red suit smiled a little enviously, closed her eyes and relaxed. The petite wife shared the discomfort of the corridor for a while with her husband, then sneaked back into the compartment to leave him wondering what had gone wrong with his life when he had been such a good servant to the Austrian authorities in Belgrade.

Dawn came greyly, fingering the windows uncertainly until the shadows left by night had cleared from the sky and slipped from the clouds. The train was steaming through the wild and rugged terrain of Croatia. The valleys, the gorges and the heights created a spectacular extravagance of nature in its most bizarre mood. Neither road nor track could be seen, neither sheep nor goats.

Passengers got up to exercise stiff limbs in the corridors. The train began to slow down. It was moving over the tracked road cut from the face of the hill, which rose on the left and sloped down on the right. Climbing the long gentle gradient it did not take long to come to a stop.

The contact of buffers between coaches and wagons produced a harsh grinding ripple of noise that startled the silence of the thickly-wooded slopes. Hollow echoes rolled around the cloudy sky. Steam hissed.

Harry wondered if the stop was to allow the peasant women to alight, but it was hardly likely in country as wild as this. Major Carlsen had mentioned a place called Vrycho. This wasn't Vrycho, this was nowhere. God had made it and then forgotten it. To the right, on the other side of the green and brown canyon hills rose bleakly forbidding. The quietness, the lack of any sound apart from the hiss of steam, was uncanny.

"Why are we stopping?" The girl who liked to ask questions and exchange glances made the enquiry of Harry. Really, thought Irena, why doesn't she ask me? I am as wise about it as he is.

"Yes, why, I wonder?" said Harry.

"I am Nadia," said the girl, smiling. The moody man came to and gave her a look which plainly told her there had been far more earth-shattering news items than that during the course of history.

"I'm Sergius," said Harry, "and my friend is Helga." That was the name, Helga Strasser, which Major Carlsen had given to her in her faked Austrian documents.

The girl seemed enchanted. Irena smiled. The train stayed locked to the hillside.

"If you'll excuse us," said Irena, "Sergius and I will go and find out what is happening."

"I'll go with him if you like," offered the girl, "there's no need for you to trouble."

"It's no trouble," said Irena sweetly, "and

162

you must rest, you look tired. One can have a bad night on trains." She got up, saying to Harry, "Let's go and ask some questions." They left the compartment, the quiet man looking as if peace would never happen unless people stopped walking and talking.

The train was a motionless, grey-coated centipede of iron, the slopes thick with trees and bush that never stirred. Irena thought the moment justified a call on Major Carlsen, and since Harry thought that if anyone knew the reason for stopping at such a spot as this it would be the German, he accompanied her along the corridor. It wasn't easy. They had to step over huddled bodies, Irena not wanting to ask tired people to move. She whispered to Harry.

"That girl, don't encourage her, she's the kind one never gets rid of."

"I know," he said, "but it might be useful to make a few friends here and there."

Major Carlsen appeared, frowning. He looked into the compartment housing the peasant women, then glanced up to see Irena and Harry. He turned abruptly and returned to the next coach. The two German soldiers were still policing the corridor. The Major held back the door of his compartment, nodded to Irena and Harry and joined them as they went in and sat down. He gave Irena a courteous but formal smile, as much as he would concede in acknowledgement of her under these circumstances.

"What's holding us up?" asked Harry.

"I've sent some men forward to find out," said the Major. He peered through the window at the tree-infested slopes that rose on the left of the train. It was then that hidden rifles opened up. The unchallengeable silence broke. Whining bullets began to pepper the coaches and wagons. Lead thudded into woodwork, smashed through glass and smacked against steel. Windows splintered and shattered. Women shrieked. In every compartment passengers flung themselves to the floor or threw themselves into the corridor, which overlooked the descent to the foothills. Irena heard Harry shout and she tumbled from her seat and went to ground with him, Major Carlsen flat beside her.

"We're ambushed," said the Major in cold fury. The enfilading rifle fire lessened and he cautiously lifted his head. He saw some of them, dark figures flitting from tree to tree, moving downwards.

"Who the devil would ambush us?" asked Harry, taking a look for himself.

"Croatian irregulars, brigands and thieves," said Major Carlsen. "The beginning of our retreat from Serbia is one of the moments they've been waiting for." He ducked down as bullets whistled and struck the outside coachwork with sharp coughs. "They're after whatever they can get, booty, ammunition, weapons and lives. Any lives. Everyone on this train is expendable, Captain. Everyone. And the train itself, they will ransom it or blow it up."

"You mentioned nothing like this," said Harry grimly.

"A hazard of the times, Captain. You should have stayed in Belgrade."

"We had our own hazards there—look out!" Harry pushed Irena down as the corner window smashed and splinters rained. Two soldiers appeared, thrusting back the door and crouching low. Bullets were screaming into and through the train. One man spoke to Major Carlsen. They had been investigating up front. The engine was unattended, driver and fireman missing. There was no obstacle on the line, no track damage. It looked as if driver and fireman had simply brought the train to a stop and vanished.

"Frightened off or damn well bought off," said the Major, having explained to Harry.

Harry did not like the sound of the rifle fire as it reached a crescendo. It was not the sound of a few rifles but hundreds. He heard the rumbling sound of heavy wagon doors sliding back, followed by the consoling sound of German troops returning the fire. German officers, trapped in compartments farther down, were shouting orders. Major Carlsen's small complement of troops in this second passenger coach were clearing glass from smashed windows and poking rifles through. But the sweep of bullets, constant now from the hillside, made it risky for a defender to show even the top of his head.

"They're up to something," said Harry.

"Thank you for that information," said the Major, his sarcasm coldly savage.

"It's a hackneyed old tactic," said Harry, "but with enough fire power it always works. They're using a ton of ammunition to pin us down. I think that means a piece of sly old trickery is in the offing. What? I think they're after the engine. They'll uncouple it and immobilize us."

"Without a driver we are immobilized," said the Major.

"Then somebody please do something," said Irena, hating the noisy impact of bullets and her proximity to the dusty floor. "Major Carlsen, you must do something."

"Yes, I know that," said the Major grimly.

"Go and see," said Irena, then shuddered as coachwork was gouged and splintered, bullets ripping into the train from end to end.

"I'll go," said Harry, "I was once seconded to the Royal Engineers. I can handle a locomotive. But I'll need someone to shovel coal for me. And I think we'll have to hurry."

Major Carlsen scrambled from the compartment, Harry after him. Irena turned.

"Stay down," said Harry.

"On this filthy floor? Never," she said bravely. She thought the noise hideous as the three of them scrambled along the corridor, almost on all fours.

"Go back," ordered Harry.

Breathless, shaken by the murderous hostility of the constant rifle fire, she gasped, "What does it matter?"

"Leave her with me," said the Major brusquely, "take two of my men." He slid open a compartment door. The peasant women lay in black, shapeless heaps on the floor. The Major went in, flinging himself face down over a seat. He called to a soldier, who tossed his rifle in. The Major caught it. He nodded to Harry, he spoke to two of his men. Irena crouched outside the compartment. German troops appeared, pounding down the corridors, thudding an accompaniment to the whining, pulverising din of bullets. They hurled themselves into compartments and over seats, over huddled passengers, and sighted rifles through shattered windows. Harry kicked, crouched and struggled his way down the corridor.

From the side of the hill, from the trees, the Croats kept up their rain of fire. A man slithered out from behind a tree and came hurtling down the slope. His arm swept back and he flung the stick grenade as he bounded. It came flying and twisting, exploding as it bounced off the roof of the coach. A German sighted. Unhurriedly he picked out the man, now scrambling for cover. He fired twice in rapid succession. The man jerked from the impact of the second bullet and fell back, sliding and tumbling until he plunged into the embrace of a bush. Shots came screaming from his comrades in angry reprisal.

The peasant women were moaning and praying, Major Carlsen was firing and barking orders with every shot. At Harry's heels were two soldiers, one of whom passed him a rifle. He worked his way towards the front of the train. As he passed his own compartment the silent man lifted his head from the floor and looked at him, his expression indicative of his complete disgust with life and people. Harry, ape-like in his crouching advance, went on. The train vibrated with noise, screams mingling with the smack of Croatian bullets and the unequivocal crack of German rifle fire. The subtly confusing sound of muffled lead entering upholstery induced cries and prayers as reverberations rushed through the train like hollow hammerings. The

Croatians kept the Germans penned in the wagons and lying flat on the freight cars. Another man chanced his arm, emerging from shelter to leap down the slopes and to hurl a grenade. Of the German stick variety, it arced high and fell fast, exploding against the side of a half-open wagon door. Smoke and fragmented metal split and polluted the air.

Harry emerged from the front coach on the far side. He shot back up again as a rifle spat from a point in advance of the engine. A number of men were weaving their way down the line towards the locomotive and it did not need a psychic genius to pronounce on their intentions. The Germans might have a substitute driver available. Therefore, take away the engine and the immobilized train became a sitting duck.

Harry turned to the two Germans, efficient-looking professionals. Well, for once, he and they were on the same side. He leaned out of the open coach door and pointed. The soldiers leaned out with him and saw the Croats. There were six of them, all carrying rifles and wearing bandoliers of Croatian insurgents. They were advancing along the track, which curved in from the right. There was a seventh man by the side of the track acting as look-out and sniper. He had already had a crack at Harry.

"I'll have to make a dash for it," said Harry, "can you keep me covered?" He was too pent-up, too involved with the highly problematical, to think or speak in any language but his own. The Germans looked stumped.

"He's asking you to give him protection so that he can get to the engine," said a calm, soft voice. Irena was there, speaking in German. "He will drive the train then. Your officer says he's not to get shot as that would be no help to anyone."

Harry gave her a look that was grim but admiring. The Germans, impressed by her composure, nodded and moved. One took up a sitting position in the open doorway, the other leaned. Their line of fire was helped by the long bend in the track ahead, which would keep the advancing Croats in view until they were close to the engine. They were coming on cautiously. The look-out man was clearly visible, down on his stomach by the side of the rail. Harry got ready to go and the sitting German opened up. The moving Croats scattered, plunging face down and digging in with teeth and feet. The sniper squinted along his rifle, but a German bullet smacked into a sleeper close by and he dug in too. Harry leapt from the coach and hared towards the engine, the leaning German opening fire now while his comrade reloaded.

The Croats saw Harry and slid their rifles forward. The second German emptied his magazine at them. Harry received cover just long enough to reach the footplate and scramble up. The look-out man had an instant to achieve something. He fired. His bullet pinged against smoke-grimed steel a fraction of a second too late to do more than scorch the cloth of Harry's jacket. He was in the cab, the engine bulk protecting him.

All hell was erupting on his left, the hillside alive with a drumming cannonade of rifle fire, the streams of lead rattling against the train, the returning fire of the Germans from coaches and wagons smacking into hill and trees. The clouds, dark grey now, dulled the scene but enhanced the tiny flashes of fire.

Through the thick glass of the cab window Harry saw the Croats flat on the track some fifty yards away. He heard the whip and crack of bullets from the two Germans, but the Croats were squirming to the left, removing themselves from the line of fire. The look-out, too exposed now, made a dash for cover. A bullet took him in the leg and he pitched beside the track. Harry knew his two Germans could not show themselves on the left side of the train, they would be shot to pieces from the hill. He ran his eyes over the engine controls, over smeared brass and steel. The cab was hot, the fire rumbling. He looked up, saw the six Croats moving well to the left of the track. He leaned out, drew a bead on the foremost man and squeezed the trigger. The rifle cracked, the stock jerking against his shoulder and the sound creating a small, booming echo around the cab. The leading Croat pulled up with a crazy flip of his hips, rolled like a drunk and fell twitching. The others, with cover, fell flat on their faces again.

Harry, re-sighting, heard someone on the footplate to his right. He swung around. Irena stared at the glinting rifle barrel with eyes enormous.

"My God," hissed Harry, "are you mad?"

She came up into the cab and pushed the rifle aside.

"Mad? I? What a thing to say when you were about to blow my head off." She was a little pale but very self-possessed. "Give me the

170

rifle. You are to drive the engine and get the train moving."

Her veil was turned up. He agreed, it did not seem important to hide her face now. Her eyes were dark with obstinacy, her mouth cool but set. The two Germans were still doing their best but the grounded Croats were wriggling closer. They would not stay grounded for long. Whoever was directing the ambush would do something to help them. Insurgents lodged in trees were already turning more attention on the leading coach. Irena put her hand on the rifle.

"Get down," said Harry, appalled at her presence. The Croats would blast the engine to Kingdom Come, with her in it, rather than give it up. "Get down, for God's sake."

"No, we are sheltered here," she said, "and if they do try to hit us they are just as likely to hit their own men. Please, do be practical." She took the rifle from him. The hills threw back the rattling, cracking cacophony of war. "I can use this, I am not quite helpless. Please start the engine and leave me to do the shooting." She moved to the footplate, rested the rifle over iron and sighted it on the men making ground in quick, surging darts. She fired. They plunged flat.

Harry studied the controls again in sweating urgency. The steam was hissing at a reduced rate.

"How the devil does it all work?" he muttered.

Irena, watching the Croats inching forward, said in shock, "You are saying it's a mystery to you?"

"I took a ride once when I was a boy. Well,

damn it, someone has to have a go at it now, it's our only chance. I know there's a valve somewhere and I think the fire's going dead. Ah, what's this?" He pulled out the damper and the fire glowed and leapt into flame. It was a wood-burner. "Now I'll burst the damn boiler, I suppose." He fiddled with a brass wheel. He muttered fiercely. Irena closed her ears to his muttering and prayed for a miracle. Bullets began to fly around the engine, pinging and ringing as they struck iron. But she kept her eyes on the Croats. One of the German soldiers appeared, down on the track, using a huge wheel as cover. He fired. She fired. The Croats flattened again but came on, wriggling forward and always farther to the left. Soon she and the German would not be able to see them.

Aware that the engine was coming under fire, Major Carlsen sent more men forward, ordering them to give what cover they could to the man trying to get the train moving. It had to be moved, for there were four or five hundred insurgents in those wooded slopes and they were pressing their attack insistently and savagely. They surged downwards in little rushes, from one belt of trees to the next, in ones and twos, in little groups, coming closer. They had a few grenades, and periodically one rose in a high lob to pitch at an open wagon door, which was promptly slammed shut by the Germans. The explosions as the grenades bounced off the massive sides were shuddering. The threat they posed, together with the sustained rifle fire, bottled the Germans up. Nevertheless, their return fire, spitting from smashed coach windows and half-open wagons, contained the ambush to some extent. The Croats suffered casualties. Dead and wounded lay around trees.

Major Carlsen, icy in his fury, used his borrowed rifle with telling precision, while on the floor the peasant women were moaning, grumbling.

"Mother of God, what of my little ones?" groaned a frightened soul.

"Your little ones aren't here," said a calmer woman, "you're in enough trouble without inventing more."

In her position on the footplate Irena felt like a woman deceived as Harry muttered and fiddled. What was he doing there at all if he couldn't drive the thing? And what was she doing here with him? She squeezed the trigger of the German rifle in a spasm of disgust. The bullet ricocheted off the rail into the arm of a Croat. That, she thought, was not bad for a shot aimed in temper, and hitting a man's arm was better than killing him.

The fire was eating up its fuel. The tender was loaded with logs and there was a supply at the rear of the cab. Harry, imprecations hissing between his teeth, found the brake wheel. That was something. Bullets screamed thick and fast, smacking into steel and rushing overhead. The Croats in front of the train were so close now, getting cover from the hillside, and from the right side of the engine Irena knew the iron monster was about to block them from view. She fired her last round. The German crouching beside the wheel flung himself forward beside the track.

"Reload!" shouted Harry, wrenching at the brake wheel. Nothing had happened in response to his manipulation of other controls.

"What with?" she shouted back.

The other German was out of the coach. He climbed into the cab and dropped ammunition on the floor. Irena crouched and reloaded while he took on the closing Croats from the exposed side of the engine. Three of them were wounded, four were coming on. The covering fire from the hillside bit into the air around them and one lifted himself from his worming position and shook his fist at the slopes. Harry saw a stick grenade hanging from the belt of the German soldier. He tapped him on the shoulder and pointed. The man said, "Ach!" He grounded his rifle, slipped the grenade free, set the pin and stepped back to lob it over the engine. Whistling bullets rushed. He was struck in the leg. He fell, so did his grenade. Harry went into mad action, ducking and diving to retrieve the live stick bomb. He seized it and swung it loopingly upwards over the roof of the cab. It dropped, keeling and twisting, hitting the earth on the side of the track and bursting like an obscenely giant flower with a red heart and pitted grey-black petals. Shrapnel sprayed. The four Croats, scrambling forward, lunged for the protection of mother earth. The explosion swept them and left one jerking and another shuddering and bloody.

"Oh, this is terrible," gasped Irena.

"It isn't yet, it could be," panted Harry and chanced his arm. The hissing steam shrieked. He had found the valve. There was the vibrating sensation of an engine throbbing and alive. Irena turned. He looked at her, the faintest glimmer of hope in his eyes. He manipulated the valve, it did things with the power of the steam. The Croats on the hillside were closer, a swarming barrage of men slipping from cover to cover. The Germans on the train maintained a steady fire and on one flat freight car they were trying to mount a machine-gun. Bullets slammed around them and into them.

Irena wondered how long it would be before she and Major Carlsen and Captain Phillips and everyone else on the train were all dead.

She jerked and slewed as the engine suddenly lurched. She gasped. Harry was beginning to smile, his hand on a brass wheel. From the cab floor the wounded German said something. He was obviously living in hope too. Engine wheels began to turn.

"Oh, Harry!" Irena was ecstatic. "Oh, you wonderful man!"

"Wait," said Harry, his fixed grin a little fiendish. The engine howled, jerked in tremenrous outrage under the hand of a novice, then pulled and strained. Germans crouching behind wheels far down the train sprang to their feet as they felt the vibrations of iron movement. The wheels were turning, slowly, slowly, hideous skids and clashes taking place as Harry manipulated the throttle. The enormous driving power of steam was awesome.

"God," he said suddenly. Those Croats, staggering up from the grenade explosion, would be aboard as soon as he drew level with them, and there were others scrambling down the hillside, ignoring the German bullets as they raced towards the slipping, shuddering engine. Harry found the reverse lever. He flung everything to the wind. Brakes were off, wheels in reverse, and the throttle open wide as the Croats charged. The whole train screamed, clanged, boomed and buffeted, but it began to run back down the track. Irena saw the running insurgents recede. From death in close-up they changed to faraway faces of frustration. She sprang up from where she had been clinging and found the shelter of the cab. She laughed in exhilaration.

"We are going, going!" she cried.

"I hope we can stop," said Harry.

The train thundered back down the gradient in unchecked reverse, the Croats on the hillside pouring fire after it, but it was quickly out of range. It rushed backwards round a long bend, swaying and lurching, and the wounded German skidded over the cab floor. Harry stuck out a leg and brought him to a halt. He apologized in French for his abominable driving.

"Wunderbar," said the German, happy despite his wound.

"We're going rather fast," said Irena unsteadily as she clung to the rail.

"Well, that'll get us back to a new starting point in nice quick time," said Harry hopefully.

"You are not going to drive us all back through that ambush again?"

"There's no other way to get to Zagreb," said Harry. He eased the throttle and felt a little surge of triumph as the revolutions decreased. The gradient became kinder as the hill receded and the speed decreased as wagons led a rumbling, rolling way on to a long straight track. "We'll have to work up a fast run and charge like a column of tigers," said Harry.

"Don't be silly," said Irena.

The wounded German, a little cloudy with pain, wondered what language these two were using. He would like to have heard what the remarkable woman and the seamanlike man were saying to each other.

"Do you think," said Harry, leaning over the side but keeping his hand on the throttle, "that you could put some coal on the fire? Well, wood, actually."

"I will surprise you," said Irena. She took the long iron bar and opened up the fire. The German, sitting with his back against the pile of logs, guessed what was wanted. He began to hand the split timber to Irena. She took the logs one at a time and fed the fire. Harry began gradually to close the throttle, looking back down the line. The train was running at a controllable speed and he felt things could have been a lot worse. They had one wounded leg between them. The other German had scrambled safely back into the leading coach. One wounded leg was damned hard luck on the sufferer but not bad under the circumstances.

He began his tug on the brake wheel. Immediately everything shrieked in iron protest.

"I'm not as good as I thought," he muttered. He eased the brakes, the juddering and shrieking ceased and with the throttle closed he let the train glide.

"You are very good," said Irena, who had heard his mutter. She was looking at him with a faint smile, her brown eyes bright with admiration. "Yes, very good."

"I think we'll save the compliments until we've made our charge."

"Don't be silly," she said again.

"All the same," said Harry, the wind tugging at him as he leaned out to watch the gliding train, "you deserve an unqualified vote of thanks. You're the coolest young lady. When we stop you can take a well-earned rest. We'll transfer you to the care of Major Carlsen and I'll get someone else to help me up here."

"You will not." She was proudly decisive. "That is a fine thing, thanking me one moment and trying to get rid of me the next. Do you think I will be useless?"

"Far from it, but—"

"Then I am not going to be ordered about. You have done enough of that. I am going to be your fireman."

"It's a brave thought, but you're not," said Harry. The train was slowing. Hills on both sides opened out in rugged color as the track began to ascend into a green and brown landscape. Spots of chill rain began to fall. "You know you're not," he added.

"You are like all men," she said, "you wish to have all the fun."

"I'm not thinking of having fun," said Harry, "I'm thinking it might get rather noisy again and you're too valuable to be put at more risk. And too nice."

She looked at him. He was speculating on the finer points of brake manipulation. He was a little sooty. She supposed she might be too. She hoped not.

"Harry, please let me stay," she said, "I shall be as safe here as in the compartment. Safer if I'm with you. I could not have a better protector."

"Oh, look here," said Harry, "I can't deliberately put you in the firing line."

"Then I shall volunteer. That is right, volunteer? We shall charge them together."

Harry said something about demon princesses.

"We'll see," he said, "but I don't think Major Carlsen is going to approve. Wouldn't you rather join him for a while?"

"That is not the point." She was cool, obstinate. "I am going to do what I wish for once and not be ordered about."

"I didn't hear that," said Harry. "Well, let's try the brakes again and see if we can stop this thing without breaking it in half."

She came out of haughtiness then and laughed. She was in a state of high excitement. War was terrible, killing unforgivable, but because the wrong kind of men took up the wrong kind of positions and Governments were so unyielding, war and killing became inevitable. But sometimes even in war something splendid happened, something exhilarating and pulse-quickening, and for a moment it made the war seem like the heroic background to glorious adventure. Harry would not really take the train back again, would he? Major Carlsen would never allow him to. There was too much at stake.

Harry braked. The engine juddered, the train pulled at it then seemed to squeeze and strain through the cold, moist air, to concertina, to unfold and concertina again. Noisy shocks ran from the locomotive to the farthest wagon and back again. The wounded German braced himself against the timber stack, Irena hung on and Harry looked as if he was grinning. When the jarring violence abated and the monster stood quite still, Irena said, "I think you should be decorated, even if only for not breaking it in half."

"You too deserve meritorious mention," said Harry, letting steam escape, "and I might just put it to the King of Rumania that you be made a railway admiral first-class."

"I hope the uniform will be ravishing," said Irena, and bent to speak to the German soldier, whose hands were tight around his wounded leg. His trousers were wet with blood. But he was quite cheerful.

German troops hastened down the track and climbed into the cab. They clapped Harry on the back. They carried the wounded man away. Major Carlsen arrived, spoke to a couple of officers standing by the track and then swung himself up. He waited until all troops and officers had gone before speaking. Then he saluted Harry and said, "Thank you, Captain. Well played. May I say that?" His smile was almost warm. "It was the thing to say at Oxford."

"Frankly, Major," said Harry, "it was all a gigantic fluke. I—"

"He is going to be overbearingly modest," said Irena, straightening her hat, "he is going to tell you something quite unnecessary and ridiculous. I am going to tell you it wasn't a fluke, it was splendid, a miracle."

"Same thing," said Harry.

"Major Carlsen," she said, "are there many people hurt?"

"There are a few casualties among the troops," he said, "and some passengers are hurt. But no, not many."

"Everyone else is all right?" She was quietly anxious.

"Everyone," he said, "you need not worry. Our only problem now is to make a decision. If we stay as we are we take the risk of being attacked again, if we go forward we take the same risk. But all units aboard have been ordered to reach Zagreb and unless we can get those orders changed—"

"But, Major Carlsen," said Irena, her immaculate look not what it had been, "it is not quite like that now. Captain Phillips says we are going to take the train on again, that we are going to mix up an immense amount of steam and charge on to Zagreb like galloping tigers."

"It can be done?" said Major Carlsen.

"Well, as you say, we can't stay here," said Harry, "and it's just as easy to go forward as backwards. Easy needs to be qualified, of course. And we want to get Her Highness to Trieste, not run her all the way back to Belgrade."

"You can see about Trieste when you reach Zagreb," said the Major.

"Major Carlsen, you will let him do it?" said Irena, the air cold and fresh in her face.

"I would prefer to go on myself," he said.

"But the risk," said Irena.

"We will all take the same risk together," said Major Carlsen. "Captain Phillips, I'll send you two men and take Princess Irena back into the train."

"That is not necessary," said Irena firmly. In her hat, which had turned smoky, and her coat, which was patterned with smuts, she looked as if she was not unused to stoking fires. Her face was slightly smudged. Neither man dared to mention it. "I am to be the fireman. Captain Phillips and I can manage very well on our own."

"I think she'd better go with you, Major," said Harry, hefting wood into the fire.

"I am staying here," said Irena, "I wish to correct the strange idea Captain Phillips has that women are weak and helpless and men should have all the fun. I should also like to say he has protected me very well, and I am extremely grateful, but he is to stop giving me orders."

"Good God," said Harry, watching sparks burst and fly as he threw in a split log.

"I think Her Highness will be as safe inside this cab as anywhere," said Major Carlsen.

"Rubbish," said Harry. Irena stared fiercely at him.

"He is very trying," she said to the Major.

"One grenade will blow both of us and the cab to bits," said Harry.

"You see?" said Irena to the Major. "The way he speaks you would think I was a peasant."

The Major regarded her keenly, his grey eyes taking in her pride, her determination and her look of smudged wear and tear. She lifted her chin and turned away. He saw the faint blush that mantled her in the grey, cloudy light.

"The Croats may have dispersed by now," he said, "and if you really feel the train can be taken on, Captain, then take it on. The two of you may as well stay together. Separated, you are no help to each other. When you reach Zagreb you will have to change trains. They will not let this one continue. We have some wounded aboard and the sooner you can make your run the better. Do you say you can manage? You can have some help if you wish."

"Two men could ride the tender," said Harry, "they'd be near enough to us then to give us any necessary help."

"But not near enough to overhear you." The Major's smile was his bleak one. "Yes, it must be difficult, always having to be careful what you say and what language to use." He looked at the countryside, wild and gloomy under the lowering clouds, then turned his eyes on the red, roaring fire Harry was building. "You are ready?" he said.

"Almost," said Harry, "but I'd still feel happier if you took charge of Her Highness for the time being."

"Oh!" She stamped her foot.

"I think we'll need to be running at thirty," Harry went on, "at that speed we should run through them if they're still there. That means we'll have to rush at the gradient like runaway elephants—"

"Tigers," said Irena.

"Yes." Harry wiped oil and soot from his hands with a rag. "If we lose too much speed when we start climbing and the Croats are still

183

around, we'll have to run into reverse again. Will you explain that to everyone, Major?"

"I will," said Major Carlsen, "and we shall do our part, I assure you. I am happy to leave you to do yours." He descended to the track. He called up. "Will you remember to stop at Vrycho? It's about five miles on and those women are to be put off there."

"I can't guarantee I can coincide the train with the station," muttered Harry.

"What?" The Major cupped his ear.

"He is muttering," said Irena, looking down from the cab, "but he will do as you wish."

The Major returned to his coach. He sent up two men to ride on the tender. They ensconced themselves firmly amid the piled timber. The fire was roaring. Harry, aware of the vibrations of power, let steam escape. It blew fiercely and frighteningly.

"It's all right?" asked Irena a little uncertainly.

"It's what they call a good head, I hope," said Harry. He knew he was walking in the dark, but circumstances being what they were he thought he might as well run as walk. He couldn't see himself driving the train in reverse all the way back to civilization without either cannoning into some other wandering iron monster or piling his train into a heap because of some unseen hazard. He put his trust in luck, in the feeling that the Croats would have gone, and he released the brakes and reached for the throttle.

"It is all right, isn't it?" said Irena, as conscious as Harry of heat and power.

"Confidentially," he said, "I think there's a

chance that through sheer ignorance we can burst the boiler. I mean, exactly what is a good head of steam? See that gauge? I think it indicates the temperature. What's the danger mark, that fat-looking line? I don't know. Well, let's try hitting the thing for six."

He opened the throttle and the engine jerked and pulled, the wheels gripped and turned, and the train followed. Familiar bangs and clangs smote their ears. Irena laughed a little hysterically. Harry gave the engine more throttle, the pistons responded and the locomotive bore down the track in chugging mastery.

"Oh, how wonderful," cried Irena.

It was hot in the cab, although cold outside it. She took off her coat. Her gloved hands pushed her veil farther up and left smudges on her forehead.

"Keep your eye on the fire," said Harry. It was a roarer at the moment, devouring the timber, and Irena kept it roaring, bringing the fuel log by log and plunging the timber in. Harry opened the throttle wider still and the engine began to thump and thunder. The heat of the fire turned Irena a flushed pink. The train gathered speed, running fast over the long level stretch, Harry hazarding all on the first two miles of their return to the place of ambush. He had to use those two miles to achieve the speed he thought necessary to carry the train up the gradient at a pace that would see them safely through. Men in short bursts could run at fifteen miles an hour. If the Croats were still there they would either have blocked the line or be waiting to blow the engine off the track with grenades tossed into the cab. He knew nothing about the capacity of a locomotive on an upward gradient, except that he did not think he had ever seen one racing when it was climbing. Not that the approaching gradient was steep, it was kindness itself. If they did not drop below a speed of twenty-five he thought they would get through any new ambush.

The fire was a blazing furnace. Irena had fed it to its limit. They had a boiling head of steam. If anything blew up he felt neither of them would know very much about it. That gauge was pulsating. And she was amazing. He had never envisaged her in this kind of role. Few princesses would care to stagger about pitching heavy logs into the redhot fire of a pounding locomotive cab.

"There," she panted, and used the long iron bar to close the fire. She was covered with tiny grey smuts of wood ash.

"Well done, Princess," he said.

She laughed excitedly, holding on as she leaned outwards to look at what was ahead of them. The cold air rushed bitingly into her face, plucked at her hat and almost dislodged it. The hatpin held it. She put a hand to it, the wind taking her breath. The dully-gleaming rails ran at them and were swallowed by the ravenous iron wheels, track and bush and landscape hurtled at them and swept past. On the left the line of hills began to close in, and somewhere ahead was the point where the track had been cut out of the hillside. She drew back into the shelter of the cab, out of the wind, her face tingling.

There was a bend in the distance. Harry,

peering through the thick glass look-out window, saw it. They were thundering at it. God, he thought, we'll run straight off the line. He throttled down and opened the steam outlet. It rushed white and noisy into the moist air. Heat and vibrations enveloped them. The train pounded on, vast and weighty, its small front guiding wheels grinding against the rails as the bend swooped towards them. The engine lurched, ploughed on, the whole train screaming, rocking and clattering. The Germans lodged in the timber pile clung grimly. Irena staggered, Harry flung an arm around her waist and held her until she found purchase. Her teeth clenched as the engine seemed to keel, careering into the long line of the bend, its gigantic volition threatening to tear it from the rails. The wheels shrieked, the iron monster shuddered and Irena prayed. The wheels gripped, touched down and ran true, the locomotive steaming powerfully on and pulling swaying coaches and wagons with it.

They cleared the bend. The track ran straight again, Harry opened up and they hammered on towards the gentle ascent. The hill rose on their left, dropped away on their right. Harry gave the engine more throttle and the vibrations turned into a thumping, frightening protest of straining power.

"Go, old lady, go," he breathed.

They were powering their way up to the scene of the ambush, the train a roar of steam and smoke. The ascent burdened the engine with the deadening weight of coaches, cars and wagons. It began to lose speed. And the Croats were still there, with their dead and wounded. The hillside, dark under the grey sky, flickered with a hundred tiny flashes of light as rifles opened up. They had heard the train coming. The bullets began to whack and whistle. Train windows already smashed suffered disintegration, and flying lead played its deadly tattoo on the iron. The Germans high on the tender flattened themselves. Those stationed in coaches and wagons opened up a retaliatory fire.

Harry glimpsed men slithering and sliding down the hill ahead. Bullets whined through the open end of the cab. Irena pressed herself tightly under cover close to Harry. Harry muttered something about hell and the devil and flung the throttle wide open. He waited for the blinding cataclysm of an engine blowing up, but instead pistons thumped and the fire roared. The train charged on, running on boiling, hissing steam, and Irena in wild exhilaration pulled on a cord and the whistle shrieked. Dust, smoke and vapor burst into the air. Harry watched the track, straining to sight obstacle or opposition. It was the two Germans, flat on the tender, who saw the Croats surging beside the line a little way on, stick grenades in their hands. They dug in over the timber and opened fire. It warned Harry, he brought Irena closer to him. The Croats tumbled under the rapid fire and the locomotive, pulling and straining, roared up to them. The ascent was draining it of power and Harry sweated at the loss of speed. A man lobbed, the grenade thumped over the cab floor and he kicked it wildly out over the footplate. It exploded seconds later as the tender passed it, flame and shrapnel fierily kissing a wheel.

Croats reeled back from the charging train, which thumped and belched on as the two Germans emptied their magazines. The hillside flashes increased to give the effect of insurgency suffering the fiery frustrations of rage. The train ran on with the useless crack of bullets signalling its escape and departure. Harry looked back, gesturing his thanks to the two soldiers. They gave him the international thumbs-up response.

Irena, free of apprehension, laughed aloud. They were clear. They had done it. They had made the charge and sustained it.

"Oh, Harry!" Her eyes were shining. She flung her arms around him and hugged him.

"Steady, old girl," he said, watching the jerking temperature gauge.

"Old? Who is old? What a cheek!"

"No, no, not meant like that," said Harry, "it's just a bit of quaint English."

"It is hardly quaint." But she was laughing and just a little pink from her demonstrative impulse. She had never known such excitement, such splendid endeavor. "Oh, you did it," she said happily, "how marvellous."

"We all did it," said Harry, wiping sweat away. They were running on level track again. He pushed back his peaked cap and wiped at more sweat. He eased the power, feeling safer on steadier revolutions. He did not want to careen around any other bends.

"What a game old galloper," he said, patting smeared brass. "Sorry if we were a little rough, old thing. It's our nerves."

"Oh, no one is going to complain about your nerves," said Irena.

"Or yours," said Harry. "You have my warmest admiration, Princess."

"How kind," she said.

"Put some more wood on the fire," said Harry.

He was sooty. He peered at her as she laughed. She was flushed and she looked lovely through her soot. She had dancing lights in her brown eyes.

They both laughed. They felt bravely free and triumphant.

Eight

Vrycho was a halt. What for and why Harry had no idea. The countryside looked as uninhabitable as ever, although not so hilly. He could see no village, no signs of cultivation. He applied the brakes tentatively, turning the wheel slowly, realizing here was an art in itself. But despite his care the engine wheels took their incurable umbrage and grinding shudders of protest ran the length of the train. He did not have the heart to ask more of it than it was prepared to give to an unknown hand. He let it take its time to pull up. Hissing, grinding, the train ran slowly on past the halt and came to a stop with its tail looking back at the landing point.

Harry leaned out of the cab. He saw the six peasant women descending to the side of the track. It was a long way down for them. They accomplished it by sitting on the step of the open coach door, dangling their legs and launching themselves. The ubiquitous Major Carlsen, enigmatic to the last, was there to help them. He stood while each woman launched herself down into his arms.

"Good God," said Harry, "never thought him that kind of ladies' man."

The women formed into a tight little cluster of shapeless black. Seeing Harry they bobbed and smiled at him. Harry gave them a wave. Major Carlsen, a bottle having magically appeared in his hand, walked up to the cab.

"Captain Phillips, I'm honored to have discovered you," he said. "I will," he added with a slightly bleak smile, "take some of the credit in that having discovered you I made the right decision about you. This is from the women, with their thanks. It was something that escaped being commandeered." He held up a bottle of rough white wine. Harry bent and took it with a smile, giving the women another wave. They giggled. Irena appeared at his elbow. Major Carlsen blinked at her sootiness.

"Himmel," he breathed.

"What is wrong?" asked Irena. "We have done well, haven't we? So what is wrong?"

The Major climbed up into the cab. The Germans on the tender watched, as much interested in the bottle of wine as the conversation they could not hear. The Major murmured his next words.

"Your Highness, everything is very much better than it was."

It seemed as if he did not dare to look her in the eye. She turned to Harry.

"Captain Phillips," she demanded, "what is wrong?"

"Do you see me?" said Harry, while the locomotive stood and steam rose.

His face was streaked and smudged, his hands dirty and oily. She looked at her gloves. They were disgraceful. She looked at her dress. It was deplorable. Awful truth began to dawn. The heady excitement which had lifted her out of the realms of convention, which had sustained her in her hour of glorious endeavor, sank to cold zero. Her handbag was tucked into a corner of the cab with her coat. She picked it up, took out a mirror and looked into it. Her gasp was like a tragic moan. Her face was covered with smuts.

"That is me?" Her eyes regarded her reflection in glazed horror. "That is me? Oh! I am disgusting!"

"You are not," said Major Carlsen, "you are brave and beautiful. I salute you." He took her gloved hand and raised it to his lips.

"She's also a very good fireman," said Harry.

"I am filthy," she cried in despair.

"It's very honest filth, you know," said Harry, trying not to smile. "But go back into the train and Major Carlsen will—"

"No." She rose above despair. The damage was done. She was hideous and it was as much his fault as anybody's. Therefore he would have to put up with her state. Moreover, she was not going to be robbed of completing the adventure. "After all, I am no more filthy than you. And nobody at Zagreb will recognize me now. They will think I am a woman who sweeps roads. That is something, isn't it? And you need not look at me while you are driving."

"Very well," said Harry gravely.

"Captain Phillips," said Major Carlsen, keeping his face just as straight, "I think that after all this you will have no trouble reaching Trieste. I shall expect to hear sometime in the future that you have Her Highness safely in England. I have your address and when the war is over I hope to be able to land in England myself, to call on Her Highness and to see you."

"I don't like the way you make it all sound simple," said Harry, "it's shooting an arrow at providence."

"I am very confident, Captain. I am also grateful." The Major saluted them both, then descended to the track. Irena leaned from the cab, watched him in his progress and gave Harry the all clear.

Harry handed her the bottle of wine. The cork was loose. She pulled it out and drank thirstily from the bottle. The wine was new. It stimulated her, took the edge off her mortification. Harry had several mouthfuls, then put the cork back and tossed the bottle up to the Germans on the tender. They received it gratefully.

Irena, resigned to the fact that she could not look any worse, fed the fire and Harry drove the train on to Zagreb. His abysmal ignorance of railway systems was hardly conducive to bliss and all he could do was to keep the speed controllable. He could at least rely on the fact that the train was expected, that the line would accordingly be clear. But as the comparative simplicity of the track began to spawn a complexity of urban tracks, he wondered whether it wouldn't be wiser to stop and to get out and walk. How the devil could he successfully take the train into a main station like Zagreb?

Irena, reading his thoughts, said, "It is going to be difficult?"

"I don't know, I suppose we could end up with a collection of old iron and a badly mangled station," said Harry. He caressed the engine with a tender, cautious hand. "But look here, I don't see why we shouldn't try to make a go of it. They might make a fuss of us then. The Austrian authorities aren't going to be small-minded about two people who brought home a train for them. And not just the train but people and troops. Which reminds me, what am I doing, saving German troops? I could be court-martialled."

"What is wrong with saving German troops? They have helped to save us, haven't they?" Irena was slightly militant.

"My dear girl—"

"Don't call me that!" Again came that stamp of her foot. "First you say I am old, now you say I am not grown up."

"It's my careless English," said Harry, watching the multiple tracks as the train clattered over points. "Nothing meant, I assure you." He looked at her. She had her chin in the air. "Well, what do you say, Princess, shall we risk Zagreb? We don't want to walk from here to Trieste, do we? Let's take our iron maiden in. Why not? In return, we won't ask for any decorations, only a comfortable first-class compartment on a train to Trieste."

Irena turned forgiving brown eyes on him. She glowed.

"Oh, yes, let us do it, let us steam beautifully into Zagreb."

"Do you mind if we creep in? I think it'll be safer. We can't really expect to be beautiful, we're too knocked about. And I don't know what the devil is going to happen if we meet a train coming the other way. Keep your eye open for signals."

"What do I look for?" she asked.

"Oh, ups and downs," said Harry. He had the engine chugging comfortably, the coaches and wagons winding steadily along behind it. "I think you stop if it's down. But they must be expecting us. We're hours late and I suppose all the points are being attended to. We'll just—"

"Harry, a train!" she screamed.

They saw it, majestically steaming towards them in the rain-cloudy light. It seemed magnificently capable of tossing them aside and Harry thought of the irresistible force running smack into an extremely movable object, except that he knew they weren't as movable as that. Their train was steaming slowly, the oncoming locomotive running fast.

"It's on the other line," he said.

It was. From out of the bewildering array of shining steel rails it sheered past them and the air vibrated to the impact of its going. They went on, the system beginning to look like an impossible confusion of rails and points. They rattled as points channelled them from one track to the next. Signals stood like an array of tall, slender sentinels. As far as Harry could see or guess, none commanded him to stop. He crept on. Irena clutched his arm as the leading wheels forked. She saw men in signal boxes staring down at her, and at smashed and splintered coach windows. Harry took out his khaki silk handkerchief and gave it to her. She cleaned the worst of the soot from her face.

He shut off power and let the train glide under the impetus of its own weight. He put his hand on the brake wheel.

She saw the station ahead.

"There, you will do it, Harry," she said, but prayed a little under her breath.

"I hope there are no buffers," said Harry, "just a clear line. What a fool if I end up in the street."

"Oh, a buffer or two will be nothing," she said, "you will only give them a kiss."

He began to apply the brakes. They slowly clamped and the gliding train groaned. It crept in frictioned resistance into Zagreb station. They saw the crowds, uniformed officials, Austrian officers and gaping railwaymen. Irena stood by the footplate, watching the platform and smiling in proud delight as Harry brought their game old iron maiden to a shuddering stop beneath the high station roof.

He wiped his hands. He smiled at her, liking her for her aptitude, her courage, her soot.

"Thank you, Your Highness," he said. She made a little face at him for such formality at such a triumphant moment.

The noise of the station was deafening. But

it was almost comforting after the noise of violent ambush. Irena's smudged look yielded to her feeling of victory and she smiled in pleasure of their shared achievement. As bemused and astonished officials converged on the engine she laughed a little breathlessly.

"Oh, it was nothing," she said, "I would do it again anytime."

"Would you?"

"With you I would."

The train was besieged. German officers were calling for ambulances to hospitalize wounded men. Passengers began to exchange excited comments with people on the platform. Two station officials, gold-braided, clambered up into the cab. A slim, slightly stooping Austrian Army officer of middle age also ventured up. They stared at Harry, looked in astonishment at Irena, and broke into incredulous speech, but all at once.

"Please, gentlemen," said Irena, and when they had quieted down she began to explain in her fluent German. She was very descriptive concerning their arrival at the point of ambush and how the driver and the fireman had vanished.

"Vanished?" One official did not know how that shameful fact could be put down in the report.

"Yes. However," said Irena comfortingly, "with exemplary courage, a Russian friend of mine—"

"Russian? Russian?"

"Yes. Sergius Rokossky." Irena cordially drew their attention to the exemplary one, who smiled modestly and wondered what the devil she was telling them. "I am Austrian, he's a

White Russian. Now, the driver and the fireman having deserted the train—"

"What scoundrels." The official shook his head sadly and a seething mass of people on the platform stared and chattered excitedly.

"Please, let her proceed," said the Austrian officer, his astonishment giving way to intrigued interest. A colonel, he was the senior transport officer of the area. He was involved now in the shattering consequences of the grand failure of the Habsburg Empire, at his wits' end to find transport for the retreating divisions of Austria and Germany. But for a brief moment, this young woman and her male companion, and the implications of their presence in this cab, made Colonel Oscar Gebert forget the harrowing hours. They were quite dirty, both of them, but he thought them singularly impressive.

"Everyone was ducking or lying down," continued Irena, "and the firing made it terribly difficult for anyone to get up to the engine. But as my friend Sergius was the only one who thought he could drive it, he did what he could and I gave him a little help." She smiled demurely, hoping no one would be ungallant enough to think her sootiness was more distracting than her story. "What else could we do but get the train moving? We had no choice but to brave the rigors and the dangers for the sake of the soldiers and passengers on board."

"Fraulein, it was brave indeed," said one of the officials.

"Oh, it was nothing, nothing," said Irena. The officials and Colonel Gebert were fascinated, quite unable to leave the cab until they had heard all. Harry looked on, all too aware of Irena's occupation of the stage without understanding a word she said. He smiled at her gestures, the way she used her eyes, the life and animation she conveyed. She described the trials and terrors of the ambush with slightly more than poetic license, so intent was she on making Harry's part loom larger than a mere basket of eggs. She told how he had run the train in reverse while under heavy fire and the magnificence of his charge to freedom. She had been more than happy to act as his fireman and she did not think she had been altogether hopeless at the job. Her listeners were both impressed and enchanted. The officials were also expressively grateful, for there was no asset more valuable these days than rolling stock. The train was damaged, but it had been saved.

The platform meanwhile hummed with excitement. Passengers were helped from bullet-scarred coaches and the German troops vacated the wagons with their wounded. Two of their officers pushed their way through the mob to climb into the cab, where they saluted Irena and Harry and congratulated them. They spoke to the Austrian officer, Colonel Gebert. It was a pity, thought Irena, that Harry could not understand German, for he would feel very flattered at what was being said. How very funny if the Germans and Austrians decided to decorate him, if he returned to England wearing a German medal.

The two railway officials, while enthralled, did not know how it could all be translated into a cogent report for there had been phrases from the charming woman like ". . . and then my gallant Russian friend burst into the bend like a rocket so that for unimaginable seconds we hung over bottomless space with our wings folded." As for her sooty state, they were distressed for her. She had been so courageous. It was a deplorable indication of the railway's fall from grace, but then everything had suffered so much from this terrible war.

Harry, while getting an honorable mention, understood none of it. But as long as Irena was making a good case for them, he did not mind. All they wanted was a decently comfortable passage to Trieste. He was cooling down now. The nerve-racking encounter with the unpleasant and the unknown had been prolonged. He felt hungry, thirsty, dirty and tired.

"Is it possible to get a meal somewhere?" he asked Irena in French.

"Oh, that would be heaven, I am starving myself," she said.

Colonel Gebert introduced himself. French, the language of diplomacy, culture and intrigue, was the second tongue of most European countries.

"Allow me, please," he said, "I am Colonel Gebert, senior officer here. We owe you much more than a meal."

"Perhaps a bath and some comfortable rooms? We are so dirty," said Irena.

"Please, come with me," said the middle-aged Austrian.

They accompanied him down to the platform. Stretchers had appeared and wounded troops and civilians were let through the buzzing throng. Harry clapped a hand to his head.

"The case," he said.

"Oh," said Irena. She knew his British uniform was carefully packed in that case. It could be important to them at a stage in the immediate future, it represented a dangerous unmasking of his identity if discovered before then. It was a risk to have brought it at all.

They investigated, Colonel Gebert assuring them he would wait. Outside the passenger coach, with its every window smashed, was the girl in the dark red suit. She saw them and almost rushed at them in breathless wonder and admiration.

"Oh, how brave, m'sieu," she cried to Harry, "it was magnificent, everyone says so."

"Thank you, mademoiselle," said Harry, lightly fending off what looked like the promise of a heartfelt cuddle from the adoring girl, "but I rather think I jerked everything about a little too much for your comfort. Never mind. Has the compartment been emptied? My case was there."

"Your case, m'sieu?" Nadia was eager to help. "It was brown and so big?" She used her hands. The little group was being bustled a bit by a cosmopolitan crowd wanting to see the man and woman rumored to have rescued a train from rebels and robbers. Nadia took no notice, she was proud and happy to concentrate on what she knew about Harry's case. Yes, she thought it was still in the compartment but she was sorry to say everyone had used it to help ward off bullets, especially that man who had sat in a corner glowering at people. Harry remembered the man, quiet and rather moody. "See, there he is," said Nadia, pointing.

The man was standing aside from the bustle, leaning against a wall, his hands in his pockets. He still looked dourly disapproving of humanity, and as he met Harry's eye he gave a shrug as if to say he did not know why Harry had bothered.

"Yes, I see him," said Harry, "but it's my case I want."

And the case, as Nadia had said, was still in the compartment. On the seat. Someone went in for it and handed it out to Harry through the gaping window. The leather strap that had been around it was gone, it was pitted front and back, and the lid gaped at one end where a catch had broken.

Colonel Gebert came up and regretfully said, "Hm."

"Full of bullets. Oh, sacre bleu," said Harry with Gallic realism. But it could not be helped, he said, and he thanked the girl, Nadia, for her kindness. Then he and Irena went through the station with Colonel Gebert. Nadia looked after them and sighed.

Zagreb was not buzzing in the same way as Belgrade. It had known Austrian administration for many years, and while its Croatian citizens were aggressive in their demands for independence the solid German and Magyar minorities, who formed the greater part of the aristocracy, knew they had no future in any kind of independent Croatia. Feelings in Zagreb were therefore polarized. They were triumphantly overt on one side, defiant but pessimistic on the other. The Austrian authorities, lacking now a directive of strength and purpose from Vienna, were beginning to feel they were standing on a castle of sand which was slipping from under them with every new setback.

It did not strain the resources of Colonel Gebert, however, to have rooms made available for Irena and Harry in the private building backing on to the ornate station hotel. The building, owned by the railway, was used for receptions and conferences. The Colonel also saw to the question of having food prepared for the guests. He forgot the mountainous worries of his work for the moment. It was a time for temporarily putting despondency aside and doing something for two young people whom he thought were among those a little out of the ordinary. She said she was Helga Strasser from the Tyrol, he said he was Sergius Rokossky, a White Russian from Petrograd. Perhaps this was so, perhaps not. At this stage of the declining war it did not matter. They were courageous young people.

The Austrian, full of the charm and courtesy of a bygone age, even assured Irena that since her clothes had been ruined he would arrange for his wife to do something about this. Irena, the sound of a running bath beautiful in her ears, said he was extremely kind but he was not to bother his wife. Because of the war they had enough worries of their own. And she had a costume she could wear.

"Very well," said Colonel Gebert, "but tomorrow, Fraulein Strasser, you may draw on railway funds to buy what you wish from the shops. I will see to that. Perhaps I should tell you, however, that because of things being so bad the shops aren't offering an abundance of fashions."

"Oh, anything will do," she said, "and this is not really the time to dress as if one were going to a concert or ball."

He seemed in gentle agreement with that. She thanked him for his thoughtfulness, his generosity, and when he had gone she knocked on the communicating door. Harry opened it. He was wearing only his trousers and vest. He still looked sooty. She could hear his own bath running.

"Oh, I'm sorry," she said and turned away in modesty.

"I'm not actually undressed," said Harry. She was quite pink and he thought that rather sweet. He had once looked up from a naked bathe in a French river to see a group of French housewives staring fascinatedly and without a blush between them.

"I was simply going to ask how you were feeling now," she said, "and to tell you that Colonel Gebert will arrange for me to buy some clothes at the railway's expense. That is kind, isn't it?"

"No more than you deserve," said Harry. What a strange girl she was. She resolutely refused to turn her head. She was either shy or prim. She would, as a princess, certainly be correct. Even so, they were not living in Victorian times. Edward and Alexandra had brought the whole world out of its laced-up Puritanism. "You've washed your face," he said.

"Of course I have," she said, "and now I am going to take a bath."

"What I mean," said Harry from the discreet

side of the open door, "is that you took a risk, didn't you, in showing an utterly clean and uncovered face to an Austrian officer who may be familiar with royal countenances?"

"Oh, how silly," she said but looked a little guilty. "Are you saying I must go about with soot all over me?"

"Well, it was a good disguise," said Harry, "and not unappealing."

She took a quick glance. He was laughing.

"Oh, that isn't a bit funny! Go away, you beast." She turned and shut the door on him. She heard him give a cry of pain. Aghast she pulled the door open again. He was standing there with his hand over his nose. "Oh, I have hurt you?" she said in distress. He uncovered his nose. It was quite unmarked.

"I think you missed, Your Highness," he said, "but it was fearfully close."

"Idiot!" she cried. She would not be treated so lightly, as if she had become part of a circus. She slammed the door.

But when she was in the bath she began to laugh. The bath, sheer heaven, was conducive to divine well-being and put her into a mood where she was able to forgive all men for their imperfections, including Harry.

The case had been unpacked. There actually were bullets in it. But she was able to put on clean and untouched undergarments after her bath, and that was heaven too. She had hung up her brown costume. It was all she had to wear in the way of outer garments, that and her cream blouse which Harry had had the sense to include. A spent bullet fell from the blouse when she unfolded it. The lead had left a tiny mark but fortunately the costume jacket hid it. She had washed her hair and it was still damp as she braided it. She finished with a crown of rich chestnut that gleamed.

A meal was served to them in a small, private dining-room. They were ravenous and Irena delightedly plunged a large ladle into a miniature cauldron that was placed on the table. It steamed. Harry sniffed adventurously.

"Fish stew," he said.

"Oh, a little better than that," she said, "it's brodetto. Fish ragout."

"Yes, I said that, fish stew. Well, anything outside of a crust is a banquet to a starving man." He let her fill his plate. He thought she looked better than refreshed from her bath and make-up. Her hair was superb, her eyes clear and healthy and quite absorbed in seeing that she had given him enough. He tried the dish. "Delicious," he said.

"Yes?" she said.

"Yes."

She helped herself. He thought her aptitude for survival quite admirable. Life neither frightened her nor intimidated her. She had no maid, no lady-in-waiting, and had not once complained about the lack of either.

She was enjoying herself, eating her meal with relish and no fine or finicky airs. They were given a bottle of wine from the vineyards of Slovenia, a clear and exhilarating Ljutomer Reisling. She drank that with relish too.

"I'm ashamed," she said a little later. "Look, we have eaten it all."

"Your Highness," said Harry, who thought that from time to time she did not object to the right form of address, "you don't think we were supposed to save some, do you?"

"Do you think we were?" Irena looked as if she was sure they had deprived other hungry people. "Oh, how awful."

A man in a blue, sleeveless jacket, black trousers and red waist sash, came in and ventured a glance at the pot. It was empty. He smiled delightedly.

"It was good?" he said.

"Oh, delicious," said Irena.

He asked if they wanted anything else. Irena translated this to Harry. Harry rather suspected the generous dish of fish ragout had strained the thin wartime resources of the larder and it was a pleasure, therefore, to truthfully declare he wanted nothing more. Neither did Irena, except for coffee. Could they have coffee? It was brought to them and was as near to genuine coffee as any they had had for some time.

"You know," said Harry, "you haven't said a word about Major Carlsen."

"Oh, should I have done?" She did not sound worried. "But why?"

Harry leaned back, looking thoughtfully at a large oil painting on the wall behind her. It depicted a standing group of magnificently attired railway officials.

"He didn't appear when we got here," said Harry. "Odd, don't you think? I thought he'd be the first to show himself. In his more Machiavellian pose, of course."

Her flush was instant and marked.

"What do you wish me to say to that?" she said, sitting up straight-backed and defiant.

"I simply said—"

"Well, I will tell you what I will say." Her defiance became cold hostility. "That Major Carlsen is a gentleman. That you are odious."

"You're misjudging me," said Harry. He understood why she was so sensitive about the Major. They held each other in mutual affection and regard. "Why didn't he show up, I wonder?"

"You forget how late the train was," said Irena icily, "and that he doesn't have the time we do. We can come to these rooms and have a bath and a meal. We can take time to talk. Do you think, with the days so critical for the Germans, that Major Carlsen can step airily off a train, saunter about, say hello and wave goodbye as if he had no worry in the world except us?"

"The days are critical for everyone, including Rumania," said Harry. He looked cleanly admonishing. His suit and jersey had been taken away while he was in the bath and returned dry-cleaned an hour later.

"How dare you say it like that!" Irena stared fiercely at him. "Do you suppose I am not concerned about my country? I am as much concerned as you are about yours. But I am not blindly prejudiced."

"Prejudiced?" He was quite calm, thinking it all a storm in a teacup. This did her no good at all. They were quarrelling and therefore he simply had no right not to be as passionate about it as she was.

"Yes, that is what I said. You are fighting the Germans, so of course they must all be hateful or sinister or Machi—Macha—" She was groping because of hot resentment.

"Machiavellian." He helped her out. "Which means devious."

She left hot resentment behind and became coldly furious.

"You are speaking of my grandmother, sir!"

"Your grandmother was Machiavellian?" he said interestedly.

Oh, the cool beast!

"How dare you!" she flamed.

"You mean she was German? Mmm," said Harry.

"I see! You are saying I am sinister and devious because I have some German blood?"

"I'm not saying anything of the sort."

"But you are looking down your nose!"

He laughed. She regarded him freezingly. He coughed. She was quite different from Elisabeth. Elisabeth was fair and tranquil. Princess Irena was dark and sensitive.

"Your Highness, you're really getting worked up about nothing at all," he said.

"I am not! Major Carlsen is a fine man. And that is what this is all about." She bent her head over her coffee.

"Well, I'm sorry if I wonder about him sometimes. By the way, I think someone opened our case. The strap was gone and the catches had been forced."

"Oh," she said, calming down.

"Nothing had been taken, as far as I could see."

"But your uniform, if someone saw that—?"

"No that was in the false bottom," he said.

"The case had certainly been used to stop bullets. I found six or seven."

"You missed one. It was in my blouse." She looked at him a little hesitantly. He smiled. "Oh, I am sorry," she said, "we should not quarrel, should we?"

"Have we quarrelled? I don't think so."

"You will think me very ungracious, you are taking such risks for me. Oh, I am sorry," she said again.

"I think you very courageous," he said.

"Oh, it was splendid today, wasn't it?"

"Frightening?" he suggested.

"Terrifying. But splendid all the same. Perhaps," she said, "someone thought there were valuables to steal in the case. Yes, I think so. I have been keeping all the jewels close to me."

There was a knock. A door opened and Colonel Gebert looked in.

"Ah, that is good," he smiled. He came in and enquired if the food had been to their satisfaction. Irena assured him it had.

"Will you have some coffee with us, Colonel?" Harry asked the question in French. Colonel Gebert said he would. He was happy to sit down with them for a while. He apologized for the quality of the coffee and became a little sad about so many things not being as they had in the past. He spoke of the war rushing to a finish of tragic proportions, politically and economically. What was to happen to Austria and her Empire he did not know. It was falling apart, thought Harry, but did not say so.

Colonel Gebert recounted how he had lived for many years in Zagreb, as an officer in the

211

Austrian garrison. It was a city which over a long period had acquired a look of Viennese charm, with its own nucleus of intellectuals, artists, writers, and poets. It was perhaps considered a backwater by the more sophisticated European capitals, but Colonel Gebert was sure that people could live as graciously in Zagreb as anywhere. It had prospered under the protection of Imperial Austria. Now there were incredible rumors that the Emperor Charles was being forced to abdicate, of the Empire being piecemealed. What good would that do?

"No good at all," declared Irena, "and those who are thinking of doing such an insensible thing aren't thinking of tomorrow."

Colonel Gebert said, "One doesn't tell children they must look after themselves, one doesn't remove from them the wisdom and protection of their parents and leave them to fend for themselves. Let us hope that if the Allies win this war they won't be shortsighted enough to create a number of little nations. These would only be swallowed up eventually by a power far less benevolent than Austria." He looked sad, introspective, then said, "But there's still hope for the future when there are young people like you around. Is there anything more we can do for you?"

"There's one small favor," said Harry, "we want to get to Trieste. Is there a train tomorrow?"

"Perhaps the day after tomorrow we may only be able to shrug our shoulders," said the Colonel, "but tomorrow there will still be trains, even if they don't arrive or depart at stated times. And Trieste, you say? Yes. But no one these days seems to want to stay in one place. Everyone is either going somewhere or returning from somewhere, infected merely by the mood of a moment or the rumor of the day. Some are in a state of constant panic, others are uneasy and others either running from trouble or looking for it. There are so many different nationalities, so many minorities. You wish to go to Trieste. What I am trying to say, my young friends, is that you will probably find a thousand others who wish to go at the same time."

"In other words," said Harry, "all trains to Trieste are crowded."

"All trains to anywhere are crowded."

"We were hoping for a quiet ride this time," said Harry.

"It isn't possible to have a reserved compartment?" said Irena. "No, of course not, that is a little selfish, isn't it?"

"If that's all you're asking for after all you have done today," smiled Colonel Gebert, "that is remarkably modest. For you, one must attempt the impossible. No, one must achieve it. My dear young lady, you remind me of prouder days. Have I seen you before, on some grand occasion?"

Harry felt his nerves quicken. But Irena was equal to the moment.

"Oh," she said lightly, "on any grand occasion I should only have been one more face among thousands, Colonel Gebert."

"I should not put it quite like that myself," said the Colonel, quite taken by her looks and her vitality. "Well, if it's Trieste you want there's a train timed to leave at noon tomorrow. I will see that you are accommodated. Perhaps you will meet me in my station office at eleven-thirty. But then there are the clothes you wish to shop for. Please call on me earlier concerning funds."

"Oh, that isn't—"

"I insist," smiled the Colonel, "and the railway board will insist. Now, if you'll excuse me, I must go home to my wife. It has been good to meet you both and to talk to you."

In Belgrade, Dimitroff took the telephone call from his comrade in Zagreb. He listened carefully to what was said. It was necessary to communicate the exact details to Comrade Michalides, who had a critical mind and cold eyes.

"Amazing," he murmured, "and you're sure the man is the Englishman?"

"From your description, I have no doubt. Also, he has a British Army uniform hidden in his case. I was able to open it when everyone else had left the compartment."

"Ah, what fine eyes you have," said Dimitroff warmly, "I knew you would use them, comrade. He was with the woman all the time?"

"They were inseparable. One must admire them for their work."

"It was merely concern for their own shifty lives," said Dimitroff, "and what a liar the Englishman is. He's told our friend Michalides a hundred different fairy stories. But you have your finger on him now and her too. She is the person Comrade Michalides is looking for?"

"I've never seen her in her parasitical trappings, comrade, but yes, she has all the characteristics, together with a fine nose she puts in the air at times."

"That's something they're born with," said Dimitroff. "Now, you're sure you know where they are?"

"I am sure."

"Good. But watch them, they're slippery, both of them. Wait now, let me talk to Comrade Michalides." Dimitroff talked to the Rumanian and came back. "Listen, here is what you must do. First, go to see our friends in Zagreb."

"I can't do that and also keep watch."

"They're nesting for the moment, aren't they? Michalides says they won't make a fresh move until morning. So. Listen, Comrade Jovanovic."

Dimitroff outlined the plan.

Nine

At breakfast the next morning in the same private room Irena told Harry he must see that nothing made her feel more destitute than having to go about in worn rags.

"Rags?" He concealed his amusement, passing a hand over his mouth. She was wearing her gingernut-brown costume, which he thought very stylish. Almost too stylish. "But that costume?"

"I have worn this three times already," she said.

"But you're not on a royal tour," he said.

"I am not going to turn into a gypsy," she said. Therefore she would go to the shops and buy new clothes. Also a few other things and a new case.

Harry demurred. Her dress and coat had

overnight been cleaned and were as good as new. He did not feel the need for either of them to encumber themselves with further clothes.

"But, Harry, please," she said, "we aren't having to run from those men now, we have lost them."

He was a little uneasy. Not on account of what the frustrated Michalides might be up to, but because he was unable to resist her. They were still on the run and unnecessary luggage was an encumbering luxury. He ought to put his foot down. He had tried that once or twice. She did not like it. He felt less inclined to now.

"Please buy only what you really need," he said abruptly, "and make sure the case is small, not enormous. I'm not even certain it's wise for you to go shopping."

"But I'm not to shop alone, am I? You are coming, aren't you?" She was fresh and lovely after her night's sleep and quite vivid with color.

"Yes, I'd better," he said, "I can keep an eye on quantity then."

She laughed.

"You are going to behave like a husband? Oh, dear." She cast her lashes demurely. Witch, he thought. "Harry, why are you looking so Russian this morning?"

"I had no shaving soap, it's hard to get here, I suppose," he said, rubbing his bristly chin. "But I made signs and I think there'll be something in my room now. I hope it'll lather."

"No," she said, "I meant you were looking pokey-faced."

"Poker-faced."

"Yes, I said that." She laughed again. She

was vivacious this morning. "Well, while you are shaving I'll go down to the station and see Colonel Gebert. He will insist on giving me funds and I have no local money."

"I think he wishes well of you. I'll meet you in his office as soon as I've shaved." He looked hard at her. "Put your hat and veil on."

She put her nose up a little.

"But they are so sooty," she said.

"Put them on all the same," said Harry.

Her brown eyes were challenging.

"I wish you would not—"

"I'm sorry," he said, "I sometimes forget who you are. I shouldn't give you orders. Forgive me."

"Oh, no, I don't want you to be always thinking of that," she said, "it's so different now. We are friends now, aren't we?"

"Companions in distress," he smiled. "I'm escaping Germans, you're escaping Michalides. Would you put your hat and veil on, please?"

"Yes, of course," she said.

"Why didn't you have them cleaned with your other things?"

"Because all the jewels are inside my hat. I have very cleverly sewn them inside the lining."

"Well played," said Harry. "Your Highness, I should hate to lose you now to Michalides."

Her dark lashes flickered, a faint flush warmed her face.

Harry left the building as soon as he had shaved. He made his way to the railway transport officer's enclave. The station was full, the tide of people enveloping porters, officials and platforms. Harry spotted Colonel Gebert outside his office, talking to a German captain. He waited until the German had saluted and gone, then approached the Colonel.

"Colonel Gebert?"

"Ah, good morning," said the Colonel warmly.

"Is my friend Helga in your office?"

"Not as far as I'm aware."

"But she's been to see you?"

"Not this morning, not yet."

Harry's built-in alarm bell was touched off. Irena had knocked on his door five minutes ago to tell him she was on her way down.

"She's not the kind of person to lose herself in a station," said Harry.

"No, I'm sure she isn't." Colonel Gebert spoke on a pleasant conversational note. He had no reason to feel Harry's concern. "Well, she has stopped somewhere amongst all these restless people." A corporal came out from the office and spoke to him. The Colonel nodded. "Excuse me, please," he said to Harry and went into his office to deal with one more impossible worry.

Harry stood anxiously surveying the crowded station, seeing faces move like heads on a round-about. His alarm increased. She was so infernally cool, so casual about the dangers she ran. He could well imagine her fearlessly speaking up for the Germans she admired no matter who was listening. Or strolling blithely around looking into the station shops. Harry turned a little grim. Wait until she condescended to appear. Highness or not, there would be things to say to her.

But he knew he was not convincing himself. She was not strolling around. She was cool, she was not thoughtless or stupid. If she had walked into the waiting arms of her enemies, what chance would he have of getting her back? Without any knowledge of the country, with his ignorance of any of the Balkan languages and his further ignorance of their hot-tempered politics, he would be like a blind cockerel in a den of foxes.

Perhaps for some reason she had gone back to her room? The hope of that was like a rush of light. Hurriedly he returned to the building. She was not there.

"Damn everything," he muttered. "God, it's my own fault, I should never have let her out of my sight."

He went back to the transport officer. Colonel Gebert was in evidence again and curtailed a conversation he was having with one of his staff to spare Harry some time.

"You have found her?" he asked.

"No. Colonel Gebert, I'm worried."

The courteous Austrian looked at him. Harry was dark and grim.

"Come into my office," said Colonel Gebert. Harry went with him through a room full of desks, papers, telephones and military personnel, and into the Colonel's own sanctum. "We may get interruptions, but let us do the best we can. M'sieu Rokossky, why are you worried?"

Harry considered his position carefully. Helpful and considerate though the Austrian was, he would not be overjoyed to find Sergius Rokossky was actually an escaping British officer.

Since the British were as much responsible as any of the Allies for the impending collapse of the Austrian Empire, Colonel Gebert was more likely to become coldly correct. And highly suspicious of Helga Strasser.

Phrasing his French with care, Harry said, "The fact is, Colonel Gebert, I am running from the Bolsheviks and Fraulein Strasser is running from the International Socialists." He did not know if there was such an organization but it sounded credible enough. And perhaps disagreeable enough to the aristocratic Austrian Army officer.

Colonel Gebert rubbed his chin. The lines under his eyes signified harassment, weariness, but there was a smile on his mouth. He did not seem surprised.

"You are political creatures, you and Fraulein Strasser? Agents, perhaps?"

"There's only one conclusive way of fighting battles, Colonel, there are various ways of fighting political systems."

"Bolshevism and Socialism, yes," said the Colonel, "these are our new enemies. The difficulty is in persuading people to see it." He regarded Harry shrewdly. "I'm not sure what you are or who Fraulein Strasser really is, but I do know you saved an ambushed train and everyone on it. My world, I think, is finished. My wife and I will only have our memories to live on soon. But your world is about to begin and you and Fraulein Strasser will be needed in it to fight for it. I will ask only two questions. Do you assure me that Fraulein Strasser's enemies are these

Socialists? And if she has disappeared are they the people most likely to be holding her?"

"Yes," said Harry, "and I further assure you they will have her head if they can. She wished to go shopping, to see you first, and I was to meet her here. I know her. The only reason why she would not be here would be because she'd been taken."

"Well, we still administer Zagreb," said the Colonel, "and we know where the political extremists are to be found, the ones who would shoot their own mothers if they got in their way. They are unusually quiet at the moment. They are waiting for Austria to sue for peace. They will be very noisy then. But today there are things we can still do. Let us go straight to the most likely point, a house in Javoga Square." He picked up a telephone, asked for a number, was connected and spoke rapidly to someone at the other end. He replaced the receiver. "Come, my Russian friend," he said.

"Colonel Gebert, do you have time for this?"

"No," said the Colonel, "but I have even less time for extremists and anarchists, and I do have an admiration for your colleague, a most remarkable and lovely young lady. It would be a pity not to spare a little time for her."

Harry recognized a man coming to terms with his feelings, not with facts. Colonel Gebert preferred to help rather than ask questions. Questions might produce the wrong answers. Harry judged his man to be in his middle fifties, but he was neither dilatory in his decisions nor slow in his actions. Five minutes later he had Harry motoring with him through the district north of the station. Harry thought the place looked mellow, charming. They passed the King Tomislav monument and the Academy of Science and Art, founded by Bishop Strossmayer, long-living champion of Croatian independence and therefore a slight thorn in the side of the Emperor Franz Josef and a misguided man in the eyes of Colonel Gebert.

Harry, however, was far too tense to take on the role of a normal sightseer. He was savage with himself, he knew he had slipped up in letting her leave the building by herself. He could not believe that Colonel Gebert would merely drive up to some house and have her handed over to him. It could not be as simple as that. And the Colonel did not know the value of the hostage, did not know it was Princess Irena of Moldavia the extremists were holding, if she was indeed in their hands.

The car pulled up at the end of a street, just before a large square. The center of the square was a green garden, slightly neglected because with the gathering crisis the authorities could not get the ordinary things done in the usual way. Colonel Gebert, who had said nothing during the drive, possibly because of the ears of the corporal at the wheel, alighted and took Harry with him. Few people took much notice of them. Austrian troops here were not under the same pressure as those in Belgrade, threatened by the advancing Allies, and they maintained a numerically strong if tactically uneasy command of Zagreb.

Colonel Gebert looked across the square from the street corner. On the far side a man in a hat and coat put his hands into his coat pockets.

"This way," said the Colonel and turned around to lead Harry down a paved walk running adjacent to the near side of the square. The houses on this side of the square backed on to the walk. There were neat, painted tradesmen's doors let into the high boundary wall that ran ͟he length of the walk. Three men ambling over the flagstones approached as the Colonel stopped outside a dark green door. It was latched but not locked. He opened it and went through with Harry, the three men following. They were in the paved garden of a house. Shrubs and fruit trees grew in round beds, which were overgrown with weeds, and moss crept along cracks in the paving.

"Bolsheviks and Socialists," murmured the Colonel, "leave gardening to the people. It's a fine point, M'sieu Rokossky, but a true one. This will do," he added and took up a waiting position by some shrubs. They all waited there, the shrubs and the wintry-looking trees camouflaging their presence. It was a dull, moist November day, with the fallen leaves of autumn looking dead and wet. The windows of the three-story house seemed just as dead. Steps led down to the garden from the ground floor and up to it from the basement. There was no sign of life.

In the square another plainclothes man climbed the front steps of the house and knocked on the door. It was opened after a minute or two by a balding man. The policeman pushed him back and immediately other men, loitering nearby, rushed up the steps and surged into the house, where they began a thorough search. One man went to a back window, showed himself and signalled.

"Well, we shall see now," said Colonel Gebert. He was quite restrained, quite calm, but he was aware that Harry was tense with acute worry and he hoped very much that the raid would be successful. But no one emerged from the back of the house, there was no sudden flight of men from the basement. Except for the man who had answered the door, and his wife, the house was empty. Colonel Gebert and Harry went in. They walked from room to room while a second search was made. Harry felt there was nothing here but the transient echoes of people who had slipped away. The balding man and his wife knew nothing of any woman. He walked back to the car with Colonel Gebert, his mood fierce, his anxiety mounting. The man in charge of the plainclothes police detachment walked with them, talking to the Colonel.

The Colonel said to Harry after a while, "Is it possible you were so closely watched by the agents of these people that they might have known you were in contact with me?"

"Very possible," said Harry.

"Then, my friend, it's also possible they would not have taken her to that house. That house is their daily rendezvous, where they talk about putting one half of the world to death. We know this house and they are aware we know."

"I see," said Harry. They paused at the car. "Wherever they've taken her, they'll keep her until a man called Michalides comes to collect her, which will probably be when the war is over and power lies in different hands."

"The police will do all they can," said the Colonel, "but I must get back to my office. I am so sorry. We can at least check again whether she's returned to her room. There may be that chance. Will you come back with me?"

Every instinct told Harry she would not be in her room.

"I must do some walking, some thinking." he said.

He plunged into the city, its unfamiliarity a complication and an obstacle. His anger with himself and his fear for her made it difficult to think. He was desperately worried not only by his failure but by the possibility that she was already being carried miles away, in a cab, a cart or even a car. She was not just a problem figure to him now, she was someone who had become very real and close.

He thought. He racked his brains, but every thought led nowhere. It was not long after ten, the day was young. There were queues at shops. He walked, he looked, he worried. A familiarity reached into his sub-conscious realm as he waited to cross a street, as his introspective eyes took in passers-by on the other side. It was a dark red costume that obtruded itself, and its familiarity clarified into recognition. He knew its wearer, the girl Nadia. She was hurrying and she did not look like the naive, breathless girl of the train. She was purposeful in her walk.

It was curiosity which captured Harry first, then a wondering suspicion. He remembered her entry into the compartment and how the official had shown her in, although the man must have known all the seats were taken. He had not left her in the corridor with other unlucky passengers. Either she had heavily tipped him or he had known her. In the compartment the occupants would have been expected to squeeze up to make room for a slim pretty girl. The farcical musical chairs being played at that precise moment had fortuitously offered her a vacancy, but no genuinely eager-to-please girl would have been brazen enough to take it in the way she did. And there had been her eyes, innocently bright, watching him and Irena.

His curiosity and suspicion melted into hope and he thought he saw a forlorn chance. He could not pass it by. He crossed the street and followed her. It was not a lonely and obvious furrow he ploughed, however, for the city was alive with people coming, going or wandering. For the busy pavements he was both grateful and uneasy. Grateful because he was one of many at her back, uneasy because among so many people ahead he might lose her.

She went across a square and turned right down a narrow street. He followed at a distance of about forty yards. She stopped midway down the street, looked into a shop window. Harry drew back into a doorway. He emerged after a few moments and saw her entering the shop. He walked quickly on, stopped and examined the shop window himself. It was a tobacconists. Through the window the shop looked small and dark. He saw a counter but no proprietor, no customer. He counted to five to steady his nerves and went in. A little bell rang as he opened and closed the door. He saw a bead curtain on the customer side of the counter. Through an open door on the counter side a stout woman appeared. Harry looked at the shelves. He pointed to some cigarettes in lurid packets on an upper shelf.

"Kaj?" she said. What?

He pointed again and in French said, "Cigarettes, if you please."

Heavily and grumblingly she began to climb a little ladder. The shadow of a man darkened the dusty shop window. Harry made up his mind. There was nothing to lose except the stout woman's goodwill which, because of her climb, was minimal already. He shot quickly through the bead curtain and found himself in a passage. At the end was a half-open door. He heard the voices of men, they came like an angry buzz. He heard the lighter tones of the girl who called herself Nadia. He slipped his hand into his jacket pocket. The feel of the revolver he had taken from Michalides on that first night was comforting.

From the shop the woman was calling in hoarse indignation. Harry sped quietly along the passage and into the room. There were three men and the girl. His pulses raced as he also saw Irena. She was sitting on a chair, the men were talking angrily to her and Nadia was arguing with everybody. They all had their backs to him except Irena. She did not seem frightened, but she was pale, her hands pressed to her to shut out the sound of the threats and insults. She saw Harry. Her blood rushed, her paleness submerged beneath the glad, surging tide and her eyes came to warm, beautiful life for the briefest moment before filling with alarm for him.

The men turned. The girl turned.

"Ah, the brave one," she said, "how good to see you, m'sieu. It's better to treat with both of you. There are questions, you see."

"I hope I'm not going to be a disappointment to you, mademoiselle," said Harry, his French a little rushed because of his nerves. He brought out the revolver.

"Stand still, please."

But one of the men moved fast. He pushed Nadia hard in the back and she tumbled and pitched at Harry. The man came at Harry from behind the lurching girl and smashed a clenched fist down on the gun. Harry let his arm go with the weapon, keeping hold of it, and as Nadia fell on her knees and the man closed with him he brought up his right knee and made crippling contact with a highly susceptible stomach. The other men rushed, Irena held back a scream and looked wildly round for a weapon. Quick footsteps sounded in the passage and suddenly the room was swarming with plainclothes men. They swooped and the room became a bedlam of kicks, curses, armlocks and arrests.

Irena, up from her chair, stood spellbound, staring at Harry out of dizzy and joyful eyes, warm blood suffusing her.

"Are you all right?" he asked, pocketing the revolver.

"Harry?" Because of emotion it was all she could say and the room was still so noisy.

"Have they hurt you?" He was intensely relieved.

"Oh, no, and I am quite all right now." Her color would not go. She wanted to kiss him.

Oh, how wonderful that he had found her. The police were cuffing and subduing their still resistant captives. Nadia was spitting like a robbed young tigress. She was bundled out with her comrades, all of them advised they were under arrest for abducting a citizen of Austria.

"Austria, Austria? You are fools," she cried, but it made no difference. The orders of the police were to hold them all for twenty-four hours and allow them to communicate with no one.

Irena and Harry were escorted back to the railway station, where Colonel Gebert was delighted to see them. He had asked the police to keep track of Harry, confessing that he felt Monsieur Rokossky had his own undisclosable methods of finding things out, but that for his own good police protection had never been far away. Irena and Harry were both warmly grateful for this piece of foresight. The arrival of the plainclothes men had resolved a very tricky situation in their favor.

"But I had no methods of any kind," said Harry, "only an immense piece of luck." He recounted how his feelings and suspicions concerning the girl, Nadia, had led him to Fraulein Strasser.

"My friends at Police Headquarters have already telephoned to give me the names of the four people involved," said the Colonel. "The girl's full name is Nadia Jovanovic. Does that mean anything to you?"

"Nothing," said Harry. "Except for Michalides they've all only been faces to me. But then," he went on casually, "in this business one's adversaries are often anonymous figures until the moment of truth arrives."

"Really?" The Colonel nodded as if he understood that that was something not open to general discussion. He informed them they would not be required to stay in Zagreb, the matter would be settled quietly and Nadia Jovanovic packed off back to Belgrade. Therefore they still had time to catch the noon train, especially if it did not quite leave at noon.

"But I have still not been to the shops," protested Irena.

"My dear young lady," said the Colonel, shaking his head and shuffling papers about on his desk.

"It's one thing to be remarkable," said Harry severely, "it's another thing to be careless."

Irena made a little face. She had not been careless, she said, she had simply been carried off by ruffians. She told the Colonel what she had already told Harry. She had been stopped by that two-faced girl when she left the building. Three men had appeared, all with nasty-looking knives, and she had been bundled into a waiting cab right outside the building. She had been taken to that shop and held in the unpleasant room. They had threatened her with all kinds of things, none of them very comforting.

"That is the way of people whose god is dark politics," said Colonel Gebert. "You are lucky to have escaped them, Fraulein Strasser. And you, M'sieu Rokossky, have a very fine aptitude for your work, whatever it is."

Irena said, "Colonel Gebert, we—"

"No, my dear young lady, I wish to hear no

232

more." His smile was tactful. "I wish to remain satisfied with things as they are. Might I suggest you find some coffee and food, then meet me again in thirty minutes? You will not miss the train."

Harry took her quietly but firmly back to her room. He followed her in and closed the door. Irena turned, glowing and alive, glad they were alone at last and she could tell him how wonderful he had been in rescuing her. Their eyes met and held, hers were brown and big and warm, his dark and withdrawn. She felt a little shock that he looked grim rather than glad.

"Your Highness—"

"Oh, no," she said in protest at such formality.

"I want you to know I'm not forgetting your position," said Harry stiffly, "but now that I'm able to talk to you without others listening, I'm going to give you an order, whether you dislike it or not. You—"

"Oh, what are you saying?" She was distressed. "Why are you so cold when you have just done something wonderful? You are trying not to let me thank you. I thought you could never find me and when you did, when you came into that room, I was so happy—oh, I was a little afraid too—"

"It was my responsibility to find you."

"Your responsibility?" Irena felt frozen.

"Yes." Harry was forcing himself to be brutal. The intensity of his relief at her rescue had made him realize he was developing feelings that could escalate to an impossible level unless he re-established the impersonality of their original relationship. "I am telling you, Your Highness, I am insisting, that you are not to go wandering about again."

She was pale with shock.

"What are you doing, why are you like this? What have I done?" She had never been so distressed. "I was not wandering about, I was going straight to Colonel Gebert."

"That was a mistake that was almost fatal. You should have waited for me."

Aghast, she wanted to weep. Instead, she drew fiercely on her pride. She flung up her head.

"Then it was a mistake by both of us," she retorted, "you did not tell me to wait."

"I know I didn't." He turned, he faced the window. "I was an infernal idiot. I'm so damned angry with myself for letting you take risks. I should have known Michalides wasn't going to be fooled as easily as that. My God, I thought he'd got you for good."

How intense he was, how dark. She stared bitterly at him, then her warm blood began to rush again. He was not angry with her, only with himself. She desperately did not want him to be angry with her, but she did not like him being so terribly angry with himself. Not when his arrival in that room had made her so giddy with happy relief.

"Please, Harry," she said.

He looked at her so strangely, almost as if seeing her for the first time. He was silent, she was distressed. The moment was emotional. She dropped her eyes, her heart beating a little painfully.

"I'm sorry," said Harry. He found it impossible to sustain brutality. Her distress made him wince. "I really had no right to talk to you like that. But I'd hate to have Michalides drag you back to Rumania. So shall we decide not to make any more mistakes? Frankly, I wouldn't like to have to look Major Carlsen in the face and tell him I'd lost you."

She had turned her back. She was unfastening her coat. He helped her off with it. She removed her hat. Those men had been irritated by its little veil and had ripped it off. They had not ripped the hat, thank goodness. She turned it over in her hands, looking at it but not really seeing it. She had wanted to thank Harry, to show him her gratitude, but he did not want her to be demonstrative.

She heard him say, "Your Highness?"

That was it. He did not think she was entitled to be demonstrative, to be an ordinary woman.

She said muffledly, "I understand. But you are being unfair to yourself. How could you have known that that dreadful girl was an agent for Michalides? You have done so much for me already. Perhaps it was a mistake for me to be on my own, but we are allowed one mistake, aren't we?"

"I think we've made more than one, but we've been lucky, we've survived them. We can't take any more chances."

How formal he was, how polite, how logical. The adventure, which had been so dangerous but so exhilarating, had suddenly become a matter for cold commonsense.

She turned to look at him, spots of color tinting her cheeks.

"Captain Phillips," she said, "we knew it was going to be difficult, but we are ahead of them now, aren't we? It was something special, your work this morning and getting them locked up. I may say that, may I? You do not realize how depressed I was, how unhappy, and they were shouting at me—"

"Yes, why were they shouting at you?" asked Harry, thinking about it. "They had you, all they needed to do was to keep you quietly out of sight until Michalides was able to come and collect you. So why were they shouting and looking so annoyed when they should have been feeling pleased with themselves?"

Irena went to the dressing-table and began to tidy her hair. It was easier to talk in this changed atmosphere when she was doing something.

"Oh, they were very pleased," she said, "but they are naturally abusive people and dislike me for all kinds of reasons, and so of course they had to shout and use dreadful language. Oh, and yes, they were angry because I would say nothing about you. That girl did not come in the cab herself, she stayed to find out what you would do. She came later, just before you did and told the men you had gone somewhere with Colonel Gebert, which made them more abusive. They wanted to know why you had gone with him, but I knew nothing and said nothing."

"But what interest would they have in me once they had you?"

"I think perhaps they knew you were not

the kind of man who would simply sit and do nothing," she said, "and they were right, weren't they? I am glad they were."

Harry was thoughtful. He remembered the rifled case.

"Tell me," he said, "are those diamonds and your other jewels anything to do with all this?"

"Oh, how silly," she said, "of course not."

"Are you sure? Jewels of that value do bring their own troubles."

That upset her. Did he think it was the jewels he was being asked to protect? She became as cold as he had been a few moments ago.

"Thank you, Captain Phillips, for being so frank. It is always better to know exactly where one stands. I realize I am a problem to you and my jewels a trouble. What shall I do to make it easier for you? Throw myself or the diamonds out of the window? Myself, of course. The diamonds are much more manageable."

"Stop talking nonsense," said Harry.

"I'm not talking nonsense." She whirled round on him. It was better, yes, it was better to be like this. It did not embarrass him as her desire to be grateful did. "I am quite serious, Captain Phillips. But as I am rather a coward perhaps you would help me by opening the window for me and giving me a push?"

He laughed. That was better for him too.

"Shall we see if we can find coffee and some food?" he said.

"I am too upset," she said frostily.

"That's understandable after what you've been through this morning," he said, "but I must contradict you on one thing. You are not a

237

coward. You are a princess. Major Carlsen is proud of you. So am I."

She stared wide-eyed at him. She was back on the rack of emotion.

"Harry? Oh, I know I'm a little trouble to you, and there is Elisabeth to think about, but I am not quite a disaster, am I?"

"Not yet," said Harry.

They got some coffee and a little food, during which she was quiet. When they had finished they collected their things, vacated their rooms and went to find Colonel Gebert. He was in his office, immersed in the insoluble problems created by the news that the Austrian forces were withdrawing completely from the Balkans. He would have to find transport for all those who reached Zagreb. But he insisted on escorting Irena and Harry to the Trieste train. He took them to a compartment not only reserved for them but guarded by a soldier from his staff.

"You should not be disturbed," he said, "the man has orders to this effect and will be going all the way to Trieste."

"How do we begin to thank you?" said Harry. He felt guilty at his deception of this courtly Austrian, but also he felt that if the Colonel did find out he had helped an escaping British officer and a Rumanian princess, he would accept that it could not then be undone. Colonel Gebert was a man who would be philosophical about a *fait accompli* and the fortunes of war. Harry hoped he would have something more than his memories to live on when his more gracious world had disappeared.

"You've been so very kind," said Irena, giving the Colonel her hand. He gallantly kissed her fingertips.

"Kind? I've been very intrigued," he said, "and I shall always find it difficult to believe you are just a young lady from the Tyrol." He turned to Harry and said something that sounded extremely foreign and incomprehensible.

"Pardon?" said Harry, asking for enlightenment.

"Young man, whoever you are, I've just said goodbye to you in Russian," said the Colonel and pressed a slip of paper into Harry's hand. He smiled, he turned in the doorway of the compartment on his way out. "By the way, trains run on steam. To make steam you need water. You arrived here with not more than a few litres in the boiler. It was very narrowly timed and typical of a man who takes risks. There's something in each of you two which makes for a compatible partnership in all that you do. When the war is over live in peace and with courage. I hope you will not have to wait too long before the train is on the move. Meanwhile, I must go and attend to the impossible again. Goodbye."

When he had gone Irena looked hard out of the window, her eyes moist. Harry, his back against the closed compartment door, unfolded the slip of paper the Colonel had given him. He said, "You know, with a man like that one wonders what all the shooting has been about and why. And I don't think he ever believed I was Russian."

"He is the kindest of men," said Irena muffledly.

"A friend," said Harry. He read what was scribbled on the slip.

"Yes."

"It's confusing my loyalties, you know."

"Then it is making you think." She sounded upset, accusing, her eyes on the platform scenes. "Perhaps that is good for you. Perhaps it will make you understand that only the Bolsheviks will get anything out of the war. People like Colonel Gebert will lose everything."

"You'd like me to join the Austrians and fight the Bolsheviks? I'm sorry, I can't do that." He was calm, unaffected and that upset her more.

"I'm not asking you to," she said, "I'm only thinking how nice Colonel Gebert is. You are only thinking of winning the war so that England can tell the rest of us what to do and what not to do. Well, England will see what happens when she tries to tell the Russian Bolsheviks what to do. She will find then that she has been fighting the wrong people."

"I see. Those are your politics, are they?"

"Those are my feelings," she said, her face still averted.

"Well, damn me," said Harry. He stared at her. She did not care to return his look, it seemed. "Thank you for that observation, Ma'am. But at the moment, before I can return to blowing the enemy to bits, I'm committed to getting you to England. You might now prefer Colonel Gebert to do the job, but since I've given my word to Major Carlsen you'll have to continue putting up with me."

240

"Yes, it's a nuisance for you, isn't it?" she said.

"Look here, I can't stand this," said Harry, "what the devil is happening?"

"Nothing," she said in a suppressed voice, "I am just upset that is all."

"I see." He didn't see. He was aware of his own feelings. He was not sure of hers or precisely why she was upset. He looked again at the slip of paper. It contained the address of the Austrian-Lloyd Steam Navigation Company of Trieste, and a name, Josef Halder.

"Look at that," he said in a matter-of-fact way to ease the atmosphere, and he passed the slip to her. She bent her head, hiding her eyes, and after a little while managed to read it. "Colonel Gebert passed it to me," said Harry.

"What does it mean?" she asked.

"That he suspected our reason for wanting to get to Trieste may have something to do with arranging a sea passage to somewhere. After all, would you go to Trieste in order to get back to the Austrian Tyrol? He must have thought about that. Now he's indicating that if we want to go to sea we should call at these offices in Trieste and ask for a Josef Halder. Do you think perhaps that he did recognize you?"

"No, how could he?" Irena was recovering.

"How? Your pictures and your person."

"Do you think so? Well, perhaps," she said. "He was so very helpful, wasn't he? And he did not like Bolsheviks." She drew a breath and said with a little air of formality, "Please sit down, Captain Phillips. There is all this room, it isn't necessary for you to stand."

He sat down opposite her. He needed to re-orientate his feelings, to complete his mission on a detached and impersonal basis. But there was this new and highly disturbing awareness of her. She had removed her coat. She sat in her good-looking brown costume and the brown hat she had managed to clean. The veil was missing, and her protected eyes looked as if they had just been softly washed in their absorbed study of the platform. She had so much charm, so much swift life.

The fact was, she was extraordinarily lovely.

He realized how damned difficult the rest of the journey was going to be.

There were the usual masses of people in the station, some there to say goodbye to others, some in search of others and some who, in the depression of the moment, wanted nothing to do with anybody. Croats, Slovenes, Austrians, Hungarians and Germans mingled, separated, pushed and shouted. Irena at the compartment window was a striking visibility.

"Where's your veil?" asked Harry.

"Somewhere in that room," said Irena, "they tore it off. But we are quite safe now."

"Are we?" he said.

"I mean," she said a little confusedly, "I mean we are at least safer, aren't we? It is going to be much more difficult for Michalides to trace us with his friends here locked up."

"I'd like to think so," said Harry.

"You know, I've only the things I've been travelling in and you have only what you are wearing. Does it matter about trying to hide our faces when our clothes are so familiar to people who are looking for us?"

"They're familiar to Michalides and his friends, Ma'am," said Harry, "but I was thinking that any member of the public in these regions might recognize you. I admit I wouldn't have known who you were myself, but you're very recognizable in most of the Balkan countries, aren't you?"

"Oh, not really to many people," she said.

"But perhaps it's a good idea to get some different clothes," he said, "we'll see what there is for you in Trieste."

"Yes," she said.

"Are all these people looking for trains?" he said as she turned her eyes on the platform again.

"Perhaps they aren't sure what they are looking for." She cast a quick glance at him, her nerves and emotions betrayed by the sweeping cast of her lashes as he returned her glance.

"No, perhaps they aren't," he said.

She felt so upset. Things were not the same between them. He was keeping himself at such a distance and she had said such unfair things to him. Something had happened between them, it had happened when he had swept into that room to deliver her from political ruffians and make her dizzy with joy, and when she had wanted to thank him and he would not let her. Now he was being terribly polite and it hurt. He was even calling her Ma'am. It was making her live on emotions far too finely balanced. She wished the train would start. They would be able to be natural again when it did, when there was movement and scenery and Trieste lay ahead. It had always been easy to talk to him, even when he had been making a little fun of her or ordering her about.

The silence too much for her, she said lightly, "When we are on our way, I do think Michalides will give up, really."

"Give up?" Harry was astonished. "Don't you realize that when he receives nothing but a blank silence from his friends here, he's going to arrange for some new frenzy of activity?"

She was quite glad in a way to be able to say, "Well, there's no need to scowl at me."

"I'm not." He wasn't. "But Michalides is a hungry bloodhound, not a fat cat, and if you think he and his friends are ready to let you go now, what was Major Carlsen making all the fuss about in the first place?"

Oh, that is better, she thought. He is back to bullying me and worrying about me. Anything was preferable to having him silent or polite.

"Oh, you are right, of course." She managed a smile. "I think my escape this morning has gone to my head a little. See, I will do everything you say from now on, I promise."

Those eyes of hers. So hugely bewitching, thought Harry. They could charm the boots off Hindenburg. No wonder the Germans thought she might induce a mood of defiance in their ambivalent Kaiser.

"Just let's do everything the safe way," he said.

"Yes," she said. "Please, I am sorry I said silly things just now."

"No," he said with the glimmer of a smile, "you must speak your opinions. They're very illuminating, Ma'am, I assure you."

"Captain Phillips, please don't call me that."

"Queen Victoria accepted it as appropriate," he said.

"I am not Queen Victoria."

"If you were, I'd be frightened to death," he said.

"Please, we are friends, aren't we?" She was making an effort, finding the strain unbearable when everything only a few hours ago had been wonderful. "It's nice that we have the compartment to ourselves and can talk. Tell me about Elisabeth."

It came out impulsively. Compulsively. Elisabeth was far more important now than she had been. Before she had been a shadowy factor, meaning something to Harry but not to her. Now it was necessary to know all about her, for Harry to talk and not be withdrawn and formal.

"Elisabeth?" he said, while the train stood and the people outside got in each other's way.

"Yes. Your fiancée. You have not forgotten her, have you?"

He thought about Elisabeth. She was as fair and honeyed as Irena was dark and vivid. His mind's eye pictured her in portrait, investing her with the soft, serene beauty of Gladys Cooper in those postcard photographs soldiers put up on the walls of their trench dugouts. He had known Elisabeth for twelve years, ever since his father, a bank manager, had taken charge of a branch in a Hampshire market town. He was fifteen then, Elisabeth twelve. She lived close by and followed him about, having a calming influence on his boyish recklessness. He liked to scrump apples. She would never let him take more than

245

they could eat, say two for her and three for him. They had become the closest and most affectionate of friends through the years. To be friends as well as lovers was to promise the best of marital relationships.

"Elisabeth is really much too good for me," he said.

"Is she? You are being too modest, aren't you? Is she pretty?"

Harry smiled.

"She's a woman," he said. "Girls are pretty. Women are lovely. There's a difference, isn't there, when they come of age?"

She knew he did not simply mean when they became twenty-one.

"She will be so glad when the war is over," she said.

"She'll be wondering at this moment what the devil's happened to me," said Harry, "I'll have been posted missing weeks ago."

"Perhaps, if she had come of age in an imaginative way and is very lovely," said Irena, "she will decide to marry someone else."

"Imaginative way? I would be too dull for her, you mean?"

"Oh, no!" She was shocked at his inferring she meant that. "Oh, you are not at all dull. I meant she will attract men whom she can see each day—oh, I am saying quite the wrong things. No one who is engaged to you would marry anyone else."

"Oh?" said Harry with a smile.

Doors slammed then. Whistles blew, officials took command of the platform and the crowds drew back. The train began to move. It was not much after noon. Colonel Gebert, thought Harry, would be pleased about a train almost leaving on time when the Empire was in such chaos.

Ten

Trieste. It had been governed by Austria since
1382 when it placed itself under the aegis of
Leopold III and secured protection against the
aggressive ambitions of the Venetians. But it was
a city Austria had never been able to separate
from its extrovert Italian origins and the more
Austrianised its façade became the more rampant
grew its underlying florid Latin exhibitionism.

Austria, claiming it an integral part of her
dominion, pursued an uneasy relationship with
the Italian community during the war for the
simple reason that Italy herself was on the Allied
side.

The evening was dark, the wind from the
Adriatic cold and damp, as Irena and Harry
emerged from the station. But the seaport's win-

try chill crackled with the overtones of Austria's imminent plunge into the abyss. The Emperor Charles was conducting independent peace negotiations with the Allies and Austria was within twenty-four hours of her Armistice Day. The Italian irredentists of Trieste were celebrating in advance. Carrying burning torches they were dancing and cavorting in the steep, narrow streets of the old town and conducting a noisy prelude to the act of separatism.

Harry was not inclined to be drawn into these premature festivities and he supposed Irena's pro-German outlook was hardly likely to make her want to dance. He suggested they go immediately to the steamship company, find Josef Halder and make enquiries of him. If the offices were closed they would have to look for accommodation and try again in the morning. Irena wondered if that was not hurrying things, but said that as she had promised to be amenable she could not very well be otherwise now, could she?

"Not without being a disappointment to both of us," said Harry. He put his hand under her elbow as roistering Italians surged by. His touch made her impulsively responsive. She put her arm through his.

Her speech was just as impulsive. She said, "Oh, you aren't angry with me any more, are you?"

He was a little astonished. They had left the memory of that scene behind them hours ago.

"I know I sometimes sound as if I'm giving orders," he said, "but I'm not allowed to be angry with one of your high state."

"Please don't sound as if you are making a speech," she said.

She kept her arm through his. The streets were cold and dark in places, bursting into torch-lit tides of revelry elsewhere or bringing rowdy running students out of junctions, and it was natural for Harry to give her his arm and for her to take it. She was close to his side. He felt her warmth. He tried to think of Elisabeth waiting at home for him. He smiled wryly at himself. A woman who was waiting was a far more logical comfort to have on one's mind than a woman who was a princess.

Some shops were open. So were the offices of the Austrian-Lloyd Steam Navigation Company, which looked besieged. There were queues and clamor, people desperate for passage on ships which either did not exist or were block-aded in, but which might exist or might be free to sail because of the news. Harry forced his way through with Irena and spoke to the first harassed shipping clerk he saw.

He asked in French if he could see Josef Halder.

The clerk, unresponsive, said in German, "What is it you want?" Harry let Irena answer, telling her to mention Colonel Gebert.

So she said, "Do you know Colonel Gebert of Zagreb?"

"No," said the clerk, preparing to shuffle off. He had had a thousand people all asking questions he could not answer.

"Herr Halder does," she said, "please fetch him."

"Impossible, impossible, do you think liners are suddenly sailing?"

"Please," said Irena with her loveliest smile, "please will you fetch Herr Halder?"

He could not resist that smile. He disappeared. He returned a few minutes later.

"Come with me, please," he said and they followed him through a maze of corridors. They met Josef Halder in an old office that looked as weatherbeaten as he did, with his white hair and thin, nuggety-brown face. His white moustache was tipped with brown from cigarette smoke, his hair tufted above his ears like white wings.

"We are closing in a moment," he said, lifting a large watch from his waistcoat pocket and consulting it. "You are friends of Colonel Gebert?"

"We count him as one of our best and kindest friends," said Irena.

Harry was not going to be able to follow the German conversation, but he laid the slip of paper on the desk. It had been signed by the Colonel.

"Humph," said Herr Halder, eyeing it suspiciously.

"The Herr Colonel wishes you to put us on a boat," said Irena.

"Boat? Boat?" Josef Halder looked at her in comical disgust. Then at Harry, who in his blue peaked cap and black jersey did not seem unlike a seaman. "Do you mean a rowing-boat?"

"I mean something that puts to sea," said Irena.

"Something?" Herr Halder was gravely. "A ship, perhaps?"

"What is the difference?"

"I would not put to sea in a boat myself, but then I am a cautious man. Where is it you wish to go?"

"Where do we wish to go?" asked Irena of Harry in French.

"To the nearest Italian port," said Harry.

"Ah, he's French?" said Herr Halder ominously.

"I am a White Russian," said Harry, producing his papers.

"And you, fraulein?"

"I am Austrian," said Irena.

"So," said Herr Halder, curling one of his tufts, "he's a White Russian and you are Austrian, and of course you both have identification documents and all you want is passage to Italy. No doubt for the purpose of seeing Hungarian relatives who are unfortunately dying but who don't mind passing into the merciful hands of God as long as they first see you and exchange a few last words with him. Are you married?"

"Colonel Gebert did not ask that question, why should you?" said Irena.

"Because you have come to coax a favor from me, because ten thousand other people are trying to do the same," he said. "They all want a passage to somewhere, anywhere, as long as it resembles the Garden of Eden. Day and night I'm accosted, bullied, cajoled, seduced and battered by people I've never seen before and never will again. And what rogues, vagabonds and miscreants most of them are, looking over their shoulders the whole time and not a respectable relationship among any of them or a single truthful eye. It would be a welcome change to look into the face of truth and virtue again."

"Herr Halder!" Irena was biting, frosty. "Really, you must count yourself lucky that my Russian friend doesn't understand you or he would certainly have the fiercest words with you. How dare you suggest that I'm not virtuous and he isn't truthful?" Her brown eyes were scolding. "The fact that we may not be married today doesn't mean we shall not be married tomorrow."

Herr Halder caressed his moustache, his deepset eyes thoughtful beneath his shaggy white brows.

Harry said, "What's going on?"

"He's concerned that we're not respectable," said Irena.

"Name of a name," said Harry with teeth-grinding effect.

"I've told him," said Irena, "that though we may not be married now we may be tomorrow."

"Quite right," said Harry.

"There, you see," said Irena to the hard-headed company manager, "my friend has just pledged himself to me in the most respectable fashion."

"Humph," said Josef Halder. He searched among some papers on his desk and found a note he had scribbled. "You are lucky. Colonel Gebert has spoken to me on the telephone. Otherwise I'd have you arrested."

"He has taken the trouble to telephone? Why, then," said Irena, "are you conducting such an unfriendly interview with us?"

"Ah, we all have our ways of discovering what people are like. My good friend Colonel

Gebert said you were not quite like other miserable people who came hammering on my door." He chuckled. "You have a laudable tongue, young lady, and your Russian friend is a saviour of trains, I believe." He turned over more papers. He peered at one. "Well, go to the Porto Franco at midnight, to the gates. A man will meet you there. A Captain Sabata. He'll take you to Italy." He chuckled again. "But not in a rowing-boat. It will cost you money."

"How much?" said Irena.

Josef Halder turned his peering eyes on her. "Captain Sabata will tell you that. Do you imagine that I wish to make myself rich in such a way? The Austrians may go, the Italians may come, but I am interested only in the sea and ships. Men will never make of the sea what they have made of the land, and every ship afloat sails only on sufferance."

"You are a good man, Herr Halder," said Irena. She informed Harry of the arrangement, adding that if they were to leave at midnight she would like to find time to buy some new clothes.

"Agreed," said Harry, "but the important thing is to leave."

"Yes," she said. He was thinking of Elisabeth, of course, who did not know what had happened to him. "My friend is very grateful," she said to Herr Halder, "and immensely in your debt for arranging things so quickly."

"Ah, the Russians, they are very intense," said Herr Halder, "and with them such things as going to Italy for the sake of love are a matter of life and death."

Deeply the pink suffused Irena's face.

"Now what has he said?" asked Harry.

"Nothing," she said.

They shook hands with Josef Halder, thanked him and said goodbye. Like Colonel Gebert, Josef Halder wondered why when so many other events were far more important, far more doom-laden, he had chosen to give time and help to these two young people. Perhaps because he saw in them hope for the aftermath, perhaps because he felt they were inseparably committed to life and adventure, and each other.

Shops in the Italian quarter were open, cafes were full. There was not much to sell in the shops, not much to serve in the cafes, but who wanted to close when the war was coming to its end and the future was going to be Italian? Trieste would return to the warm embrace of Italy, for the Allies had promised it would. And one could celebrate on a feast of words and orations, while adding water to the wine to make more of it.

Irena and Harry sat in a cafe. The coffee was awful and Irena could not understand why the fish they were eating, baked in sauce, did not taste fresh. It smelled, she said, like a trawler's deck drying in the sun.

"Eat it up," said Harry.

He was more relaxed. He was not terribly, awfully distant any more. They were able to talk again.

"Eat, eat it up, my child," she murmured, "or your guardian and protector will stand you in a corner."

"Then we'll see if there's a dress shop open," said Harry.

"Oh, I have your permission? You will let me shop?"

"You've been a good girl this evening," said Harry, "you deserve a small treat."

"Oh, Harry, you beast to tease me so." It was a little burst of delicious reaction because he was smiling again, teasing her again. She knew she must be very careful all the same, they both had to be careful in their own ways.

But as they looked at each other they laughed.

They went in and out of shops. There was nothing, simply nothing, Irena said. It was bad enough the war costing so many lives and forcing people into near starvation, without taking away from women the means to dress decently. No, she was not getting things out of proportion, she insisted. Anyone who had studied the effects of war on the civilian populations would know it was the morale of women which was of the greatest importance in helping nations to survive.

"But what we've seen so far seemed decent enough to me," said Harry.

"Something which covers one is adequate, it is not necessarily decent. It must have some style or one might as well go around in sacks."

"Quite so," said Harry tolerantly as they avoided fervent Italians wanting to embrace them, "but something adequate, warm and practical would really be a better buy than a silk morning dress."

"Practical? Are you crazy? I would rather die."

"I now understand," said Harry, "why when they put the princess into a bed of twelve mattresses she couldn't sleep because there was a pea under the bottom one."

"How ridiculous," said Irena. She laughed in the cold night air. "How funny," she said.

People surged over the cobbles and a girl linked her arm with Harry's and a man helped himself to Irena's hand. In loud and amorous Italian they issued invitations to love and excitement.

"Parley-vous Français?" said Harry.

"Oui," said the young Latin lady.

"Good," said Harry, "I'm trying to find a shop where my wife can buy a decent dress. By decent I mean something to make her mouth water. Comprendre, mademoiselle?"

"Ah, you're the right kind of husband to have in times like these," she said. "M'sieu, go to Merlini's. Even now they're still able to dress the very best people, though not every week. It's for the celebrations you wish your wife to dress well?"

"Yes," said Harry, "but even on ordinary occasions she wouldn't be seen dead in anything practical."

"Such a good principle," said the girl. She instructed Harry on the location of Merlini's, then she and the man disengaged themselves and went to look for people more interested in amour than fashions. Harry explained to Irena about Merlini's.

"I heard everything, thank you," said Irena,

"including the revelation that you are an exceptional husband and I am an impractical wife."

They found their way to Merlini's, which did not look much on the outside but was very elegant inside. There were no creations on view, only some imposing chairs of blue and gilt selectively residing on a blue carpet. And a madame, who did not seem very accommodating at first. Merlini's did not specialize in receiving customers who came in company with someone who looked like a seaman and carried a battered case only good for housing bombs. Irena, cool and gracious, put matters right with the information that her companion was an eccentric acquaintance of Victor.

"Victor?"

"Who else?" said Irena, sweetly urbane and convincing.

"The Italian K—"

"Hush," said Irena.

Madame was not completely taken but she was amused. And this was how many of the best people did behave, as if they were slightly off their heads. She called an assistant and from the coffers of fashion buried unseen beyond the salon came dresses and coats. Irena wanted one dress and one coat, nothing more, she said. Harry hoped she was not deceiving herself.

As far as dresses were concerned there were no silks. Silk was tragically unobtainable. Irena went into a room and tried on a selection of dresses in other materials. That selection was of three only. Each dress was exquisitely styled and stitched, and to her delight one in speckled grey and white, so unusual, suited her beautifully. At least, she thought so. So did Madame, who would never let any client leave the shop with a Merlini creation that did not. No one else's opinion was needed. However, perhaps Harry should see she was not wasting her money.

"I think perhaps my eccentric friend might like to see it?" she suggested. Madame's opinion, which she did not voice, was that husbands allowed price to prejudice them but men friends did not. She preceded Irena back into the shop and presented her to Harry with a flourish. He took in the sweeping, slenderizing lines of the dress and the willowy look it gave her. She wore a quite shy smile with it and the faintest flush. "What do you think?" she asked shyly.

Harry thought it enchanting.

"Is it warm?" he said. He could have said much more. He knew it was better not to.

Irena, bitterly disappointed at such unimaginative response, said, "Warm? Warm? Oh, Philistine!" She swept back into the dressing-room to try on coats. She settled on a long, waisted black one with a white fur collar. She insisted out of sheer heartburning that Harry see her in this too. He thought it made her look like a warm winter princess.

"Excellent," he said, "that should keep the cold out."

She could not bear it. She swept up to him and whispered fiercely, "You are supposed to tell me how it makes me look, not how it will resist the weather!"

"It makes you look like a princess," said Harry as lightly as he could manage, but that made up for everything and her eyes shone.

Madame stood aside in smiling satisfaction, judging their whispers to be romantic. It was a good time to be romantic, with Italy and Italians looking in the face of oncoming victory. Irena, her feet taken from under her because of what he had said, wanted to hug him for being so nice. Harry, caught by feelings he knew he should guard against, wondered whether Her Highness should be kissed courteously for being what she was or generously for being so beautiful.

"I shall now buy a new hat," said Irena a little breathlessly. Madame said they did not sell hats as separates and there was only one she could offer, which was that belonging to the coat, a black-and-white one. It was quite perfect, so much so that Harry took only one brief look at sheer enchantment and then studiously regarded the carpet to bring himself back into the realm of commonsense. Irena went back into the dressing-room to change, to pay for her purchases and have them packed in a large cardboard box.

Harry waited. A woman came in, a woman wearing furs, who was so obviously aristocratic that naturally she thought Harry, in his seaman's black jersey and dark grey suit, was someone who carried furniture about. She looked around, faintly surprised that a furniture man should be in sole occupation of the salon. Madame emerged with Irena, Irena carrying a long white, gilt-lettered box. The woman stared, Irena caught her stare. The woman smiled in delight and gushed.

"Sonya Irena! I—"

"You are mistaken," said Irena and walked

aloofly by, leaving the shop in company with
Harry.

"What was that all about?" asked Harry in
the street.

"Nothing important," said Irena.

"She recognized you," said Harry.

"It's nothing to worry about."

"Yes, it is."

"It is not! And we had better hurry."

"There's plenty of time," said Harry. "She
did recognize you. Well, it was bound to happen
sooner or later, I suppose. Who was she?"

"Oh, some insignificant countess," said Irena,
"and who would think that after four years of
war she would walk around in all those ostenta-
tious furs?"

"She'll gossip about you all over Trieste. The
sooner we get away the better."

"Yes, I have just said that." She was a little
agitated. "Did you buy a veil?"

"No."

"Hmm," said Harry.

"Please don't hmm," she said. He was carrying the case. He took the long box from her and
put it under his arm. She thanked him. He was
silent, thinking about her vulnerability. She said
in a small voice, "Harry, please don't be cross
again. I will not need a veil once we are in Italy,
we can both be ourselves."

"I'm not cross," he said, "but even in Italy
there may be comrades willing to do Michalides'
work for him. Comrades throw bombs, you
know."

"You are still worrying about me," she said.

"Yes," he said.

They got away from the increasing night revelry, away from singing and dancing Italians and out of the damp cold, whiling away the next hour or so in a cafe illuminated by tall candles. Harry drank brandy and Irena drank wine. The place was crowded and warm.

"Do you really think we shall be able to get on a ship?" asked Irena.

"You're not thinking of a P and O liner, are you?" he smiled.

"P and O? What is that?" She was wearing her plain coat and brown hat again. He did not think she looked any less attractive.

"A shipping line, very well thought of in my country."

"Oh, yes, I think I know." She smiled. She was happy that they were so companionable again. "They have ships that go sailing into the sun and are also very well thought of for honeymoons, yes?"

"If you're rich," said Harry.

"And if there's no war. Yes, that would be nice, do you think?"

"Oh, very nice," he said casually. "Well, perhaps you'll meet an exiled Russian Highness and try it with him." Irena winced. "And unless the war is over when we get back I shan't have time to go anywhere with Elisabeth, I'll have to return to my regiment."

"But Major Carlsen said the war is bound to be over soon."

Harry wondered if she needed a Bible when she had Major Carlsen. That correct, persuasive German had landed him with more than the original problem. He looked at Irena, at her earnest, brown-eyed beguilement. She was always earnest when she was quoting Major Carlsen.

"The war looks like being over for Austria, perhaps, but Germany is a different kettle of fish. In spite of Major Carlsen."

"Yes, you are right, of course. You are always right." She was sweetly stinging. "You are quite an oracle."

"Well, you can get Major Carlsen to wrap me in plaster after the war, turn me into a monument and mount me on a piece of marble somewhere in Ancient Greece."

"I would like to know what I have done," she said a little bitterly, "you have been grumpy on and off with me all day."

"Grumpy again? Where did you get hold of that word?"

"Isn't it right, grumpy? Oh, is it gruffy?"

He couldn't help himself, despite the necessity of keeping at arm's length. He laughed. She felt relieved. But she simply wasn't going to be able to stand it if he continued to say things that made her feel he didn't like her.

"I'm sorry, did I sound grumpy?" he said. "It must be things on my mind. You put up with me very well."

"Oh, I have a temperament quite angelic, you know," she said.

"Have you?"

"No," she confessed.

He laughed again. The cafe was cosy because of all the people there, everyone cheerful because the war was nearly over. Irena was looking at him from under her lashes. He thought her resilience as endearing as her courage. She was going into exile because people considered she had been too pro-German. It was not going to be easy for her, whether she stayed in England or went elsewhere. She was facing the loneliness and bitterness of exile, but she was not crying, she was not complaining. She had just bought herself some brave and beautiful new clothes.

He supposed that in new clothes young women like Princess Irena could face up to all kinds of disasters.

How the devil could one supply a purely impersonal service to a woman like that?

Eleven

They arrived at the harbor of Porto Franco just
before midnight. It was black, it was chilly, and
the Adriatic looked menacing. The gates to the
shipping berths were locked and guarded. They
waited, growing cold. It was a little after midnight when a short, tubby man in a thick coat
and peaked cap loomed up out of the damp darkness. He had eyes like a cat and came straight to
them.

"You're Herr Halder's friends?" He spoke in
German.

"Yes," said Irena.

"Good. This way." He took them away from
the gates, round a corner and into an empty
warehouse. Harry, carrying the case and the box,
was aware of the easy target he made in the cold,

unfamiliar surroundings, but he did not think Josef Halder a man who rubbed shoulders with assassins.

Captain Sabata lit an oil lamp, lifted it and showed his prospective passengers his honest face, which was round, bristly and amiable.

"I am Captain Sabata," he said.

"Do you speak English?" asked Harry.

Captain Sabata could but did not ask why that language was preferred. He stated in so many words that he was in business to help those who needed it and could help defray the overheads. He was the soul of Italian amiability and his round, fat smiles induced refugees to pay up with much less heartbreak than if he had been a stony-faced bargainer. He had been running the gauntlet in his fishing smack for many months now, ferrying people from Trieste to Italy under the noses of the Austrian Navy, which never ventured very far because of British and French warships. The war, yes, that made things difficult and expensive, but when one was in business for the good of people one had to take risks.

It was understood, was it, that he could not afford to do it out of pity or sympathy alone?

Harry said it was completely understood.

Where did they want to go? To any port in Italy? Well, he could put them ashore wherever they liked as long as it was close to Chioggia, south of Venice. It would be costly but not prohibitive. That was understood too?

Harry said it was and wondered how much he and Irena could produce between them.

How much was it understood? Captain Sabata's lamplit smile was a beam of encouragement. Harry had a little money left, he pooled what he had with Irena's residue of German banknotes. Captain Sabata took them, flipped through them and handed them back with a fat smile. He was sorry, excessively so, but there was some paper money which he did not regard as a good investment. Perhaps English pounds? No? What could be done then?

Irena asked him to compose himself for a moment. She vanished into shadows. She came back and showed the Captain two shining, lustrous pearls. His sigh was an exhalation of happy relief for all of them. However, they would permit him? He took the pearls, examined them under the lamp, tried them between his teeth and then said with the utmost cordiality that when understanding was mutual between people nothing less than mutual satisfaction came of it. No more need be said. They could come fishing with him.

"We're to go now?" said Irena.

"But yes, signorina, sure we go now. What is it you think, that with Captain Pietro Sabata you stand around?"

Harry was glad to move. The warehouse seemed full of rustles and whispers. That could be because of rats. But Michalides had pressed so close on them that it was difficult to believe they would simply walk out of this place and on to Captain Sabata's smack without hindrance.

They followed the Italian through the warehouse. He unbolted a door and they stepped out on to the dockside. Irena shivered a little because of the cold sea wind. It was so quiet that they heard the soft slap of water against moored vessels. Captain Sabata's vessel, the sloop *Antonia*, was a dark mass of masts and tackle, hugging the jetty as if loath to be parted from its solid, landrooted security. Two crew members, awaiting the Captain, helped Irena aboard. Below, in the low-ceilinged quarters, she and Harry found the Captain was not doing business with them alone. There were at least twenty people, men, women and children, crammed into a space designed for six. They were on the bunks, around the clamped table and on the floor. They were quiet but anxious, patient but impatient. A sigh went up as Irena and Harry descended into their midst to take up what little space was left.

The old tub coughed, the engine dully hammered, and the *Antonia* reluctantly divorced itself from its berth. With chugging heaviness it nosed towards the harbor mouth. The wind was cold but light as Captain Sabata put to sea with other vessels of the Trieste fishing fleet, but when they veered south for the fishing grounds he kept to a south-west course. The crew doused the lights.

It was cramped, uncomfortable and dark for the passengers, all of whom had their own reasons for risking the trip. The silence was compulsive as if each of them was listening for the sounds of pursuit. It was tense for nearly an hour, when any coastguard cutter or naval launch, lurking around to pounce on just such a runner as Captain Sabata, might have made an interception and blinded the *Antonia* with light. But nothing happened and there was a perceptible relaxing of nerves and bodies, although they had hours of chugging progress still in front of them.

It rained. They heard it pattering insistently on the deck, but no one mentioned it, no one talked about anything, and the few children who snuggled close to parents did not raise a sound. It seemed that everyone had secrets to keep.

Irena and Harry sat on the floor, backs against a lower bunk. They were silent too, Irena with her arm in his and close to his warmth. She did not think Harry minded this, it was just her natural need for feeling secure, and she hoped Elisabeth would not mind, either. He was probably thinking of Elisabeth. In these crowded quarters, in this silence, only one's mind could be busy.

A swell developed. The *Antonia*, known as a drunk, was a roller, a wallower, and several people, including two children, were sick. Included in the price, however, were basins. Everything began to smell, but no one complained, and the seasick sufferers did their groaning in the basins.

Harry thought that Italy should see the beginning of the easiest and safest part of the journey. It was an Allied country. All they had to look out for in making their way to France and through France were the comrades Michalides might be in touch with. Harry had no idea whether the Socialist ramifications were as internationally widespread as Major Carlsen had implied. If they were he supposed an extremist French comrade would be as hostile to Princess Irena as a Rumanian one. He was sure of one thing. Michalides did not want to lose her.

He felt her move. Her head came to rest on

his shoulder. She was actually composed enough, even on this wallowing old tub, to close her eyes and sleep. She had taken off her hat and her soft hair caressed his cheek. As the *Antonia* slugged a rolling way through the heavy sea to Chioggia, Irena achieved a modest series of catnaps, as she had on the train to Belgrade.

Apart from the seasickness among some, the crossing was uneventful. An hour before dawn, with the *Antonia* standing well off from the Italian coastline, the passengers were rowed to a beach south of the island of Chioggia. Captain Sabata said a round, smiling goodbye to them. Having cheerfully skinned most of them he invited all of them to come back when the war was over.

There was a long walk, a trudge, ahead. Irena and Harry made light of it and that afternoon reached Padua by train. There Irena begged the comfort and rest of an hotel for a day or two. Padua of ancient fame was beguiling, and Italy, although torn, bewildered and impoverished by the war, was in a state of sudden headiness. Austria had this day concluded an armistice with her. The Habsburg Empire had collapsed and the picturesque city of Padua was as delighted as the rest of the country. Women, resuscitating the best that they had in their depleted wardrobes, were out wearing feathers and boas and hats and colors again. And everybody was kissing everybody else.

"Hotel?" said Harry. "Hm."

"Oh, hm, hm," said Irena.

"Your papers. Austrian. Perhaps it won't

272

matter now. I think the Austrians are probably being kissed too."

"Oh, I no longer need those papers," she said, "I'm myself again. Sonya Irena and so on. And so are you." She laughed as they walked. "Also, we are married, yes? There is the marriage certificate which I have. I have kept it very carefully hidden. We are supposed to be husband and wife from now on, aren't we?"

"I thought the idea was that we weren't supposed to be that at all, that it was merely an arrangement to get you safely into England."

"I am only saying," she said calmly as they crossed the Piazza dei Signori, "that if anyone makes a fuss about who I am, or if I'm required to answer fussy questions, I shall simply point out I'm your wife. As you are a British officer who has just made a marvellous and heroic escape no one will wish to make things uncomfortable for us then, do you think?"

It simply wasn't possible to resist her. Harry smiled. The day was dull and wet but Irena was delightfully indifferent to it. She was responsive to life, to people, and rain or sunshine were only important inasfar as they governed what she should wear. Rain could not depress her.

"Well, we'll look for an hotel," said Harry, "and then I must see if there's a British consulate here. I'd better show myself if there is."

They managed to get a cab. They asked to be driven to a good hotel. The cabbie looked at Irena and said he would take them to the Victor Emmanuel. Bowling choppily along through the wet but festive streets it gave Irena the opportunity to delve into a tiny pocket in her handbag.

"There, you see?" she said and showed him a gold wedding ring. She took off her glove and slipped the ring on. "It is necessary to wear it now, isn't it?"

"I suppose so," said Harry. He remembered the ritual of the ring at the ceremony in her Bucharest house. She had removed it after finishing her role as a widow. Now it was on her finger again and she was viewing it with rather a wry smile. Harry wrestled with unreality and found it rather an unsatisfactory contest.

The Victor Emmanuel Hotel was imposing. Harry in his crumpled suit and common jersey was obviously not the greatest catch the establishment had made, but Irena, for all her signs of travel and travail, was obviously not just somebody who had come in out of the rain. At the reception desk English was spoken. Harry asked for two adjoining rooms.

"Or a suite," said Irena, with visions of lots of space and a huge bath. "My husband is Captain Harry Phillips, it is no good giving us something pokey."

Ah? They looked at Harry's clothes. Well, there was a family suite available but—

The but concerned Harry's workmanlike look and their combined luggage of a small, shabby case and a long cardboard box. The clerk and the manager eyed both items unenthusiastically. Irena did not bother with the clerk. She looked the manager up and down. He recognized then the air of a personage. Personages mattered. It was persons one discouraged. The luggage, such as it was, was taken up.

The suite was commodious. It included a

large sitting-room and two bedrooms, one bed-room with its separate dressing-room. They would not be thrown together too closely, but an awareness of the unconventional and imprudent existed the moment they took up occupation. Irena thought back to the small apartment in Belgrade. Circumstances and necessity had been the only conscious factors there. No sensitive, personal aspects had disturbed the common-sense nature of the situation. Belgrade had been a practical stepping-stone. Zagreb should have been another. But it hadn't been. Something had happened there.

And Padua was going to be so trying to her emotions.

Harry took his bath first so to lose no time in presenting himself to the nearest British authori-ties. He shaved while the bath filled. Irena came knocking at the door.

"Harry? Excuse me, please." She sounded worried.

"What it it?" he called, turning off the loudly rushing bath taps.

"What am I to wear this evening?"

He looked at his half-shaven face in the steamy mirror.

"Good God," he said in amazement. Was it possible that a woman who was also a princess could be so pricelessly feminine? "What?" he called, thinking he might have misheard her.

"Harry, I have nothing to wear." She sound-ed worse than worried.

He swept the razor over the unshaven half, rinsed off lather and dabbed his chin with a towel. He opened the door. There she was, looking sincerely desperate and lovely.

"What do you mean?" he said.

"Mean? Is it possible you can accept my going down to dinner looking as if I am dressed for afternoon tea?"

"I'm not sure whether hotels still serve dressy dinners, or if they even serve dinners. Look here," said Harry firmly, "we've been through all this. In any case, what's the point of dressing up and looking like Your Highness? Please, Your Highness, I entreat your wisdom and your sense of caution. Put on the dress you bought last night in Trieste."

Irena staggered around in despair.

"Are you crazy? That dress is simply something to wear, it's not an evening gown. Harry, it's their armistice today, everyone will dress like heaven tonight. If I wore that dress to dinner I should look like an old maid."

"Good," said Harry.

"Good?" Irena could not believe her ears. "Good?"

"Yes, good," he said with straight-faced candor. "After all, in my clothes I look like Captain Sabata's second mate. I think you should do your best to look like a second mate's wife. I daresay you could adjust the old maid look a little. That would fill in the picture very well for outsiders and lurking comrades. Looking like a princess simply won't do, Ma'am."

"Oh, how terrible you are," she cried, "you are condemning me to death by slow mortification."

"If they do serve dinner," said Harry, "we can have it up here."

"But we shall miss all the excitement," she cried.

"Is it exciting for you?" he asked in curiosity. "Are you pleased, then, that the Austrians have surrendered? That doesn't help your German friends, does it?"

"Oh!" From whimsically pleading an indulgence she leapt into angry resentment of injustice. "That is too much! Now I know what I have done, I have said things! Because you are helping me escape and putting me in your debt, I must say nothing, I must not have opinions and I must think the same as you do about my friends!"

"Your German friends?"

"Yes! Yes!" She stood up to him, proud, bitter, fuming. "I have German friends and Austrain friends, I have Swiss friends, Italian friends and Hungarian friends, and what has happened to most of them I don't know! But I am glad of one thing, I have never had any English friends! I would not want any! I am sure they are all like you! Odious!"

"Your Highness, nothing will have happened to your Swiss friends. They've been wise enough to stay out of the war."

"Oh!" She was outraged. "You are doing this deliberately, and I know why! Yes! You wish to be rid of me! I am a trouble, a nuisance, and you have had enough. So you are making it impossible for me to continue with you. Well, I will go, then!"

She stormed away. He went after her. She

began to throw things into the long cardboard box. In seconds it was madly overflowing.

"I'm sorry, I can't let you do that," he said.

"Go away!"

"I've a promise I must keep."

"You can discuss that with Major Carlsen." Her bitterness was cold now. "I hope he is old-fashioned enough to call you out and run you through. Please go away." She turned on him as firmly he took things out of her hands, out of the box, and put them aside. "I don't need your services or want them."

"I'm sorry," said Harry grimly, "but that is irrelevant. The arrangement is a matter of honor. I shall get you to England whether you need my services or not. And please don't think, because I'm curious about you and ask questions, that I'm trying to insult you. You must not be so sensitive. Please, put those things away. I'm not going to let you leave."

She was breathing hard, her face flushed, her eyes big.

"You would dare to stop me, to lay your hands on me?"

Harry's expression was regretful but resolute.

"Yes," he said, "I would have to commit the unforgivable, Your Highness, even if only to save you running headlong into the arms of your enemies."

She stared, her flush deepening.

"You would seize me, bundle me about, throw me down?" she gasped.

"It would be a matter of my honor and your

safety," he said gravely, "but I should actually tie you up."

"Tie me up?" She looked incredulous. "Tie me up?"

"Only if it were unavoidable," said Harry.

"Oh, I cannot believe it," she gasped, "you are a monster in disguise."

"Will you promise to behave?"

"Never! Never!" She turned and ran. She darted from the bedroom and through the living-room. As she reached the door Harry caught her, lifted her and carried her. She did not scream, but she kicked furiously, legs a shining flurry amid a cloud of white petticoat lace, and she beat at him with clenched fists. "Monster, monster! Put me down!"

"I warned you," said Harry and carried her back to her room and spilled her on to the bed. She lay there, staring up at him out of enormous, outraged brown eyes, her breathing fast and agitated. "I must have my bath," he said, "and you must calm down."

Speechless she watched him take the key from the inside of the door lock and transfer it to the outside. He closed the door and she heard the key turn. He had locked her in. He had laid his hands on her, thrown her about and locked her in. She sat up, gave one tight little scream, then fell back again. Oh, how magnificent. No man would do such desperate things as he had, taking hold of her, bundling her about, making dire threats and actually locking her in, unless his deepest concern was for her. She lay there in exhilaration.

It was forty minutes before the door was

unlocked. This was followed by a knock. She made no response. She watched the door. It opened a little and Harry put his head in.

"Your Highness?"

"Yes?"

He came in.

"I must apologize, Your Highness," he said, "but all the same I meant what I said."

"Oh," she said as she saw him. He was in khaki. His tailored uniform fitted him so well. He should have had it pressed because of the creases but the warmth of his body would ease them out. He looked so impressive to her susceptible eyes that her thoughts flew again to an evening gown. She must have one, she must be complementary to him at dinner tonight. "Oh, how splendid you look," she said impulsively.

"I don't want to lock you in—"

"Oh, Harry, we are so silly, aren't we?" she said.

He thought that was the least of it. She was still lying on her bed, and in her cream blouse and brown skirt, with ankles and lace peeping, much more of an endearing young woman than a troublesome princess. He had elected for an attitude of restraint. In her vulnerability, in her smile that was asking for a restoration of harmony, she was a bewitching threat to his good intentions.

"It's the strain," he said, "and I should remember it's much more of a strain for you. I'm used to roughing it a bit. All the same—"

"Yes, I understand, it is a matter of honor," she said swiftly. She slipped from the bed and came up to him. "You need not lock me in, I shall not run away, I promise." Almost shyly she said, "How could I manage on my own and without you now?"

"Well, we'll manage it together," said Harry.

"Oh, you are very good to me," she said. Since he had laid hands on her a short while ago this made him smile. "But you must not have the wrong impressions about my loyalties," she went on, "I am a Rumanian and I love my country. I simply meant to say I was glad the war is nearly over for everyone, not just for the Italians. I was silly to be so angry with you, but never did I think you would be so angry with me as to throw me about."

"Ah," said Harry, not sure of his depth. "Unforgivable," he said.

"Oh, I do forgive you," she said graciously, "but there is still this terrible problem about what I am to wear tonight. Harry, please, the waiters, the *maître d'hôtel*, they will never believe it if I appear at dinner in a day dress. They will not come near us. I must go out and buy a gown."

"I'd rather you didn't," said Harry, "and we agreed you shouldn't."

"Very well." Irena drew herself up. There was a way out but she would keep it to herself. "You are awfully stern with me sometimes."

"I know," said Harry, "but most monsters are tyrannical. I'm going to look for the consulate now. You'll stay here until I get back?"

She said yes, she said she would not go out, she would take her bath and perhaps try to get her hair done in the hotel salon. He was not to hurry on her account but on the other hand he was not to be too long. Her smile and her manner were so engagingly warm and open that he wondered if she was up to something.

When he had gone she sat down at the dressing-table. She looked into the mirror. She mused on an emotional problem becoming more insoluble by the hour.

"Elisabeth," she said, "I'm sure you're very nice but I do wish you would marry someone else. You're very lucky that life is so uncomplicated for you, that you only have to sit and wait for him." She smiled ruefully. "And he is in a hurry to get home to you."

She requested the manager to come up five minutes later. He, visibly impressed by her looks and charm, quite understood her desire to celebrate Italy's armistice with Austria by acquiring a creation. He would have Signor Carletti of Padua's leading fashion house call on her. To be frank, it was the only fashion house because of the shortage of materials, but Signor Carletti would not disappoint her. As for the celebrations, she might care to know that at the University they would be dancing until dawn.

She did care to know. Dancing. How wonderful.

Signor Carletti arrived with a model, a dresser and an array of gowns. Considering the ravages of war and the gargantuan appetite the warring nations had developed for all raw materials, Signor Carletti had triumphed superbly over his difficulties. There were actually silks. Irena did not ask where they had come from. She had an entirely delicious time simply looking, followed by a rapturous moment of purchase. Signor Carletti departed in a state of artistic fulfilment, leaving Irena certain that to look, to consider, to decide and to buy beautified one's soul when it happened after four terrible years of war.

She would have her hair done later. She suddenly felt tired. The crossing on the *Antonia* had been as exhausting as other stages of their journey. She would rest for a while before having a bath. She slipped off her shoes and lay on the bed. The feeling of drowsy pleasure was immediate. She closed her eyes. Harry would be back soon. Could it be true that he had actually laid hands on her and thrown her about? If Major Carlsen had seen it happen he would almost certainly have shot Harry. He would not have understood.

She slept.

It was dark when she woke up. The winter had drawn its cold night veil over the ancient city. She felt dreamy but refreshed. She turned. There was a lamp on the bedside table. Where was the switch? She reached, then stiffened as she heard a noise. Not from inside the bedroom. Outside it. It was like a slither, a shuffle, and with it a faint clicking.

Harry? She found the light and flicked the little brass knob. The lamp glowed. The red velvet curtains hung darkly. The clock said ten to six.

"Harry?" She called tentatively. She got up and went to the door. "Harry?" She realized she was frightened. How silly. There was no need to be. She heard the noise again, like someone trying to slide open a badly-fitting window. Her heart began to hammer. She opened the door quietly and looked into the darkness of the sitting-room. She listened with goose-pimples icily searing her skin. Harry's room, opposite hers, showed no light. Even so, she called his name again.

The response was a little rushing slither of sound, as if someone had rapidly moved. She froze, a sensation of exquisitely cold and rarefied air attacking her back. She simply stopped breathing. The deadly silence which ensued seemed to scream at her. The service bell, the light. The light. She forced herself to feel for the light switch on the wall beside the bedroom door. The polished brass plate with its knob slid smoothly under her fingers. She clicked on the ceiling light of the bedroom. It transmitted life to the bedroom, gave light to part of the sitting-room. Outside the November wind blew in a sudden gust and rattled a swinging sign. The bathroom door, ajar, quivered and slammed. Irena jumped, screamed and stood paralyzed. The bathroom door, it had been closed when Harry had gone, hadn't it?

Again came that slither of sound. It plucked like a sharp, tearing bow at the frayed strings of her nerves.

"Who is there? Who is there?"

She rushed into the sitting-room, switched on the light. Where was the bell? No, the door, the door. She must get out. Blindly she found the door and reached for the white enamelled knob. Before she could touch it the door opened. The scream that was locked in her throat leapt free, only to choke on itself as she saw Harry. The strangled sound shocked him.

"What's wrong?"

"Harry—oh!" She flung herself into his arms and clung. The warmth of his body and the reassurance of his presence equalled the rapture of the awakener who realizes horror has only been a nightmare.

"What's wrong?" he asked again. She was trembling violently.

"There's someone in the bathroom," she gasped against his shoulder.

"In the bathroom?" He was dubious about a cry of warning that seemed to carry a hint of farce with it. But he was very aware of her frightened state and she was not a young woman who lost her nerve easily. He was also aware of her slender, rounded warmth, the pressure of a quivering body seeking security. Had Michalides traced her already? "Are you sure we're invaded?" he asked quietly.

"Yes. There is someone there. I heard him."

"Well, we'd better have a look," said Harry.

"Are you crazy?" She lifted her head. "Get the manager, call the staff. You don't have to go in there yourself."

"Somehow," said Harry, "I don't think anyone would pick a bathroom to hide in and I'm sure Michalides' Italian comrades aren't on to you yet." He put her gently aside and walked to the bathroom. Irena shivered at his recklessness. As Harry opened the bathroom door she heard the sound again, a slither and a clicking. Harry heard it too. He went in. The bathroom was empty. But he saw the small window he himself had left latched wide to clear the steam. The curtain on its line of small brass rings was moving, the wind tugging it. He called Irena, he showed her the moving curtain. The rings slithered and clicked over the rail. "Is that what you heard?" he asked.

"Oh," she said and became pink with mortification. Imagination had played its unkind trick and shattered her customary coolness. Harry was smiling. Her facile mind laid rescuing fingers of quick thought on her, plucking her from total demoralization. "Oh," she said, "who would have believed anyone would have climbed out of a window as small as that?"

"And then fallen three floors to the ground without cracking his head," said Harry.

"Incredible," said Irena, full of beautiful relief and rich absurdity. "But of course you have heard of a proverb of ours. Those who leap with courage draw kindness from the earth."

"No, I haven't heard of it," said Harry, "I think it's not so much a proverb as a piece of quick thinking."

"He must have been a very thin man," said Irena, shamelessly avoiding the question posed by the comment. They returned to the sitting-room. "Why were you away so long? See what happens when you go wandering about, some strange man finds his way in and nearly stabs me to death."

"Your Highness—"

"You know there's no need to call me that."

"Yes, quite so." Harry was guarded. She had taken the pins out of her hair before lying down and her spilling hair, dancing softly around her, made her look so young. He took his eyes away from enchantment. "Was I a long time? Perhaps I was." He took off his peaked khaki cap and tossed it on to a chair. "But there's no consulate here, so I took a taxicab to Venice. It's not far. Now I've answered all the questions and re-established my identity. I received an advance, otherwise I couldn't have paid the cab off. I'm expected to rejoin my regiment as soon as possible. I'll rejoin it via England. We leave here tomorrow."

"Tomorrow?" She did not seem rapturous.

"The sooner the better for both of us," he said, "and I imagine you won't feel really safe until you get to somewhere like America."

"America? I am not going to America."

"But it's a nice long way from Michalides and they look after princesses there. You'll like New York. It was built for princesses. Young ones, anyway." He was taking the conversation along lightly, casually, and Irena was stiffening, and they were heading for another clash of nerves. "I went there for a short spell when I was at college. It's what they call dynamic and it's made for the young and the free. And there aren't any anarchists."

"Really? How very informative. What do you have in mind now, tying me up and putting me on a ship to New York? Thank you," said Irena with her nose in the air, "but I am going to England." With just a slight note of regal triumph she added, "It is a matter of honor, you remember, to get me there."

"Oh, I thought America worth a mention," he said.

"Well, you have mentioned it, so now it is done with. But must we leave here tomorrow?" England and his reunion with Elisabeth seemed alarmingly close, so did the awfulness of being on her own.

"You must remember I'm still on active service," he said.

"But it's so nice here," she said, "and you are entitled to a few days rest. It's unfair you should have to go tomorrow."

"It can't be all that nice," said Harry, "not with thin men slipping in and out of the bathroom window with knives between their teeth."

"Sometimes, you know, you are quite horrid," said Irena. He laughed. He was apt to laugh a lot with her and she did not know why just lately he had taken to being so stiff or stern or distant. But he was laughing now and she seized the chance to ask him to take her after dinner to Padua University, where there would be dancing until dawn. The University was the foundation of Padua's history and culture. They ought not to miss the chance to go there and she dearly wanted to dance until dawn herself.

"But are you really in the mood with the Central Powers collapsing?" he said.

"Oh, we are not to argue about that again, are we?" she said. "Are you happy to know that no one will really win except the Bolsheviks? Germany would have kept them out of Europe, but now, you will see, they will swarm all over it."

"I see," he said, "what you really mean is that you're anti-Bolshevik."

"So should everyone be who has any sense," said Irena.

"We must find a platform for you in Hyde

Park," smiled Harry, "at a place called Speakers Corner."

"Oh, I would speak, yes," she said defiantly. "Harry, please let us go to the dance. The manager will arrange it for us. I have been good, haven't I? I stayed in while you were out. Oh, I would so like to dance."

He could not resist her.

But he did say, "Won't it be risky if the nobs are there?"

"Nobs?"

"Ducal personages and so on."

"Oh, no, I have never mixed with the dukes of Padua and it's to be masked and very festive, but all very informal, to celebrate peace."

"All right," said Harry. He wondered how it had come about that this young woman of exalted position allowed him to lay down the rules. He supposed it was because he bullied her so much.

"Do you mean it? We can go?" She was not sure if he did mean it. But he did. "Oh, how nice you are to me," she said, and the faint flush came to pink her face. "To dance will be fun, won't it?"

"It'll be a nice change from boats and trains," he said, "but for heaven's sake, don't go wandering about dancing with furtive villains. Make do with dukes or doges."

"I'm not going to dance with anybody but—" She stopped, she blushed vividly. "I mean, you must approve my partners for me, of course. You will let me know if you wish to dance with me yourself, I should not want to go off with dukes all the time if you did not care all the time to go off with their ladies."

"Hmm," said Harry, working thoughtfully

on that one. He wondered what dancing with her would do to his dangerously heady state. For his own sake and Elisabeth's it would be better to stand in a corner and keep his eye on Irena. Elisabeth drew a man into a context of calm. Irena, so colorful, was far more disturbing. "When I'm not a soldier I'm a farmer," he said, "and I'm not the world's best performer at a ball."

"It isn't a ball, it's a masked frolic," said Irena, "and I'm not a very good dancer myself, I have an imperfect sense of timing. So we will be two dunces together and will suit each other very well. Yes?" She was almost shy again in the flicker of her lashes, the hesitancy of her smile. He nodded. "Well, now I shall have my bath," she said, "then have my hair done, then have our meal sent up and then I shall dress. We need not go down to dinner, after all. I have spoken to the manager. Oh, and he will send up masks for us."

"Great overworked pumpkins," said Harry helplessly, "how long is all that going to take? I'm starving."

He was so like a man, quite unable to understand how she would enjoy every moment of all the time it would take to make herself look beautiful. He did not even understand it would be for him. She had a wrench of conscience, for she knew she was beginning to fight Elisabeth. She simply could not help herself.

She had her bath. Then she went down to the hairdressing salon and returned an enormous time later with her crowning glory a rich chestnut brilliance. It made Harry look away, it made him study a painting of Venice on the wall. Their meal was served. The Victor Emmanuel was still managing to excel in its preparation of food without being able to disguise that quantity was limited. So was the menu. It did not matter. Irena and Harry enjoyed what they had. It was ten o'clock when Irena retired to her room once more to dress for the festive frolic. The manager sent up masks, a black one for Harry, a silver and red one for Irena.

She made her entrance as coolly as she could, saying casually, "I am ready now, Harry," as she came out of her room. Harry turned in his chair. He had been thinking, but not about what she was going to wear. He had vaguely supposed she would wear something nice, like the dress she had bought in Trieste. He was quite unprepared for her visionary effect. She shimmered. She was gowned in silky white with gold brocade. It rounded her figure and sheathed her hips, it gave her a regal richness. It had a collar, turned up and studded with tiny gold stars. It had flowing sleeves. From beneath the hem peeped gold and silver slippers. She wore no jewellery except a ring and the gold wedding band.

Harry blinked. She laughed a little nervously and said, "A Signor Carletti from a dress shop came, and this was the best he could do for me. There's a shortage of things because of the war, you know. Do you think because of the war I should not be gowned like this? But there is the armistice between Italy and Austria to celebrate, isn't there?"

"Oh, good God," said Harry.

"What is wrong?" Irena's nerves showed a little. "Doesn't it suit me? Is it gaudy?"

"Tell me," said Harry, "is this how you look when you're entertaining crown princes?"

"No," said Irena, "it's how I look when I am celebrating an armistice with you."

"I'm overwhelmed," said Harry.

"That is a compliment?" Her eyes danced. "Well, I think you are quite nice too."

They took a cab to the University. Padua had the lights of peace on, even though no armistice had yet been signed with Germany. The university hall was an ageless wonder and tonight was alive with color, revelry and music. With a feeling for the appropriate an Italian military band had been engaged to play. In uniforms of red and blue, and their brass instruments gleaming, the soldier musicians produced music full of martial melody through which ran the infectious panache of Italian nuances.

The youth and the men and women of Padua, masked and dressed in anything that had individuality and color, danced and galloped as if at the birth of a new and beautiful world. The students were bizarre in what they wore, nerveless in all they did. Irena and Harry stood watching for a while, Irena's eyes big and brilliant through her mask, her foot tapping. It was so exciting, so colorful in its gay pageantry after so much somber death. They were so lucky, she and Harry, they were alive.

A man, slim and dark and playful, leapt clear of the swirling mass of dancers and alighted at the feet of the radiant Irena.

"Enchantress! Goddess! Diana! Venus! Fly to the stars with me, I am Hermes!"

"Alas, I am totally engaged to Jupiter," said

292

Irena. She said to Harry, "He says he is Hermes, but I think he's a little drunk and it was never Hermes who was drunk, was it? It was someone else, yes?"

"Bacchus," said Harry. "But I think he means well and is obviously taken with you. So dance with him if you wish, I'll keep an eye on you."

"Oh, you beast," she whispered, "I am not going to be pulled around by an intoxicated Bacchus."

"What are you saying, O heavenly body?" cried the smitten young man.

"That I can't fly away with you, signor."

"Ah," said the young man woundedly, "that's how it always is with Venus. Mortal men can never get near her. But be warned, I may descend more purposefully on you and carry you off to my garret and my gramophone."

"I'll turn you into a cheese if you do," said Irena. She whispered again to Harry. "What are you doing? You are letting him accost me."

Harry resigned himself to a night of emotional turmoil. He took her hand, and they became part of the riotous mass of dancers, part of the joy and exhilaration of peace.

She had lied. She danced vivaciously, rhythmically, headily. She was so warm, so vibrant, so intensely committed to revelry. It was as if she was snatching all she could from life before the loneliness of exile enclosed her. She swam, she floated, she spun. Vitality, eager and extravagant, poured into her and from her. Her teeth glimmered between her breathless, parted lips, her eyes shone through her mask. She was superbly gowned and it made her feel like a queen. Eyes were on her, a hundred eyes, her silver and red mask hiding her identity but not her vivid appeal. Harry in his British khaki was acclaimed like a conquistador from time to time, couples breaking apart to lift their hands high and applaud him as he danced by with Irena. She laughed at that.

"That is nice, isn't it? They would not be like that with Major Carlsen."

Wondering about her feelings for the handsome Major, Harry said, "Well, he has others who love him, I suppose."

"Oh, yes," laughed Irena.

There were speeches and orations in between dances, and periodically intrigued and animated men swarmed around Irena like magnetized galaxies. They sought with Latin verve to separate her from Harry, to discover who she was and whirl her away. Harry, always conscious of who she was and what she was, adroitly contrived to pluck her free of every imbroglio before the outrageous Italians could outmaneuver him. One was not to know how dangerous some of the more radical students might be if they recognized her. After what happened in Zagreb, he did not want to let her run the faintest risk.

So periodically he rescued her from gallants who wanted to carry her off.

"Harry, what is the matter with them? Are all of them drunk?"

"Not really, dear Princess. Dazzled, I think. You've made yourself the belle of the ball."

She was having the loveliest time, being with him and dancing with him. She colored at being called dear Princess. She said lightly, "Well, I am lucky you are keeping your head. I should have been torn to pieces if you had not stood up to them. Isn't it wonderful to dance? I haven't done so for ages, you know."

He took the hint and they went in a crazy, flying polka, the music of the military band racing the dancers into a gallop. Joyfully, Irena went hand-in-hand with him, then into his arms, and away with him. She knew he had been too modest about his accomplishments.

She was breathless at the end of that. They withdrew from the hall to find a seat in a corridor, and Harry brought her a tall glass of sparkling white wine.

"Oh, how good," she said. Excitement had made her more vivid. He took his eyes off her. He leaned back and looked at the brown stone of the vaulted corridor. "What are you thinking?" she asked.

"I don't often dance with princesses," he said.

"Nor I with English farmers," she said, then gave a little gasp of dismay as she realized how awful that must sound and she hadn't meant it to be awful at all. "Oh, I mean—"

"No, you're right," said Harry, "few English farmers must have come knocking on your castle door. I count my luck exceptional. Actually, I was thinking of Elisabeth. I have to."

Irena looked into her glass.

"Do you mean because you are here, because you are dancing and she is waiting and wondering?"

"Well, yes, that and because I'm going to

have to explain things, because I'm going to arrive on her doorstep with a wife."

"But you will give her the reason for that," said Irena, "it was all discussed by us. She will understand. Oh, I have made things very complicated for you, haven't I?"

"Yes," he said unequivocally. It took some of the life from her expressive eyes. She did not realize he was answering a question much more comprehensive than the one she had asked.

But they danced again. Irena said he had lied about his ability, he was very good. At which Harry said she had lied too, but whereas he had done so out of natural modesty he was surprised that with her impeccable upbringing she could lie at all.

"But sometimes it simply isn't possible to tell the truth," she said, "and I wish that when you were being so nice to me you would not be so horrid as well."

That made him laugh, which in turn made her wish there was no Elisabeth.

She intrigued an Italian officer. Through his mask his eyes watched her, followed her. Once or twice he seemed tempted to approach her but held back, perhaps because he did not want to compete with so many others.

He spoke to his companion, a young woman. "Do you know who that lady is?"

The young woman was not exactly enchanted by the question. She had a natural disinclination to share any interest he had in other women.

"I have no idea, except that she is making quite an exhibition of herself."

"No, she only seems to be enjoying herself, it's the young men who are exhibitionist."

"If you are terribly interested in her—?"

"I'm curious, that's all. I feel I either know her or have seen her before."

"Well, everyone says there are few women you aren't on some terms with, Alberto."

"Everyone is you, silly girl. Come, dance with me and stop looking put out."

But a little later his eyes were drawn to Irena again. She had come off the floor with her escort, a British officer, and she was laughing, her white teeth sparkling between her warm lips, her eyes animated through her mask.

"I do know her, at least I think I do."

"I am thrilled for you," said his companion, then went into a huff as he excused himself and approached Irena. He nodded politely to Harry, and Harry thought him different from the rest. He was more sophisticated, more self-assured and, perhaps, more of a danger.

"Signorina?" he said and bowed to Irena. Irena glanced at Harry, giving him a rather rueful smile. One could tell when it was not going to be easy to discourage an advance.

"Signore?" she murmured. The Italian's eyes glinted. He did know her.

"Alberto of Brabanti at your service," he said with a smile.

Irena stiffened and a flush deepened her coloring. Harry sighed a little. Someone had recognized her, despite her mask. That had been on the cards all along. They had been lucky up to now.

"Signore?" said Irena again.

"I'm not mistaken, am I?" said the Count of Brabanti. The conversation was in Italian, one more language that was all Greek to Harry.

Irena, recovering, said lightly, "You wish to dance? Of course. I shall be happy to." She turned to Harry and murmured in French, "You will excuse me?"

"Certainly," said Harry.

He watched her enter the whirl of movement with the Italian. He did not think she would panic. She was a resourceful princess.

Irena was still a little flushed as she danced, her eyes coyly averted. The Count looked at her, happy to have resolved his perplexity about her.

"How unexpected, how delightful," he said.

"Signore?" she murmured innocently.

"Come," he said, "we know each other, confess it."

"Do we? The advantage is yours."

"The luck is mine. I swear, despite that mask, that you've grown even more beautiful. How long is it since we last saw each other? Four years? Yes. It was at Castle Elau on the Danube. A magnificent house party. Do you remember?"

"Castle Elau on the Danube? Where is that?" Irena was coolly enquiring.

"Sonya Irena, it is I, Alberto, who holds you. Alberto, your most devoted one."

"Alberto? Oh, Alberto—yes, of course." Her eyes simulated surprised recognition. "Please forgive me, but four years is a long time, and your mask, your uniform—"

"It's been far too long," said the Count, smiling. "We were so young, I was so earnest, you were so haughty."

"Never," said Irena, "I'm not made that way."

"Oh, you were always devilishly on your mettle."

"Not as devilishly as you were on yours," she said.

She made light conversation with him, but began to let her eyes run all ways in search of Harry, who would be watching her every move. She sighted him and he was not watching her at all. He had been seized by a gloriously shapely creature in red, who was dancing with him. The gloriously shapely creature was shamelessly close to him. Irena burned. Oh, how dared he be so—so—yes, irresponsible. Why, for all he knew, anything might be happening to her. Alberto of Brabanti might be someone in the pay of the Socialists, ready to sweep her back into the fatal embrace of Michalides, instead of a charming Italian count whom she had known before the war.

If Harry was making up to that woman—

"This is enchanting, to have found you again," Alberto was saying. "But the last I heard you were trapped in Rumania and having to endure hordes of German conquerors. How did you get out?"

"It wasn't easy, but I'm here now," she said.

"Mysteriously so," said the Count. He ran on. He was a smooth, polished dancer, an effortless talker, and his conversation flowed in easy confluence with his physical rhythm. Irena circled in his arms but the exhilaration was not the same. He was only one more of many young men who had danced attendance on her because at seventeen and eighteen she had been called Rumania's loveliest flower. But he had recognized her. Harry would be angry with her. He would adopt his bullying "I-told-you-so" attitude or be frowningly dark and hideously English, making her feel he would be only too glad to see the back of her.

"You still haven't told me how you did get out," said Alberto.

"Oh, it's very secretive," said Irena, "and yes, darkly political."

"Darkly political?"

"You know how it is."

"No, I don't."

"Where is my escort? Can you see him?"

"He's closely engaged," said the Count. "Sonya Irena, you're being very mysterious. Why is it darkly political and how did you escape the Germans?"

"Who is closely engaged?" Irena, following Alberto's rhythmic flights, glimpsed Harry. The shameless configuration of red was so close to him that she quivered in outrage. Oh, he was horrid to dance like that with such a woman. Had he forgotten he was supposed to be taking care of her? "Oh, how indecent," she breathed.

"What is that?" Alberto peered at her, observing the warmth in her face, the heat in her eyes. "Tell me, Sonya Irena, tell me your story."

She was on dangerous ground. Alberto had always had a charming persistence.

"Oh, it's far too long," she said, leaning back against his arm as he deftly flighted her to escape the exuberance of other couples, "I will tell you when I next see you."

"But tomorrow I must be in Rome."

"How lovely," she said and meant it.

"It isn't lovely to be in Rome when I've just found you here in Padua. Who is your escort, the British officer?"

"Oh, he is all part of it being political and secretive," she murmured conspiratorially, "and there are others who have managed to get away."

"Others? King Ferdinand? Queen Marie?"

"Hush," said Irena. She was a little breathless, Count Alberto so tireless. And she was shocked to see that Harry was now actually seated beside that creature who looked like a hothouse bloom with her gown a scarlet undulation over her white bosom. Oh, she thought, I am in terrible trouble with my emotions.

The music stopped. Alberto released her, took her gloved right hand and raised it to his lips.

"Sonya Irena, that was delightful because it was so unexpected. Now, let me take you back to the man who is all part of this dark, political secretiveness."

"No, there's no need. Thank you, Alberto."

Count Alberto insisted. She was not a shop girl, he said. And even a shop girl would not be left on the floor. He took her hand again, drew it through his arm, looked around and saw Harry. Harry was on his feet, parting from the flamboyant figure in red.

"Please, Alberto," she said, "say nothing at all to Captain Phillips. He's absurdly fierce about the secrecy of everything. We are really not supposed to be here, we couldn't have come had it not been masked."

"It's devilishly mysterious," smiled the Count. He returned her to Harry. "Thank you, Captain," he said, "it was a great pleasure."

"Pardon?" Harry groped for an interpretation of the Italian words.

"Count Brabanti is saying he's enchanted with me," said Irena in English.

"Indeed, yes," said Alberto, "and I am also intrigued. Take care of her, Captain. She is priceless. She—"

"Thank you, Alberto," said Irena, "we will meet again in Rome, perhaps."

"We must," smiled Alberto, "we have much to make up for." He looked as if he would like to have lingered, but he knew that his erstwhile companion would be spitting a little now and he was also aware that Irena's escort did not seem disposed to take a further back seat. He said goodbye, kissing Irena's fingertips extravagantly.

When he had gone Irena smoothed her gloves and busied herself looking at each slimly-sheathed finger.

"Hm," said Harry, "is it serious?"

"Serious?" It was not a bit serious now that she had avoided the brink, unless he meant the extent of her relationship with the Count. "He's just an old friend."

"Hm," said Harry again.

"Oh, you are not jealous, are you?" she said, and immediately could have bitten her tongue out for being so stupid. Oh, what an idiotic thing to have said. He would think her utterly childish. "I mean, it does not really matter that I danced with him, does it?"

Harry, pokerfaced, said, "What I meant was

is it serious that he recognized you? Is he going to talk about your being here and is someone likely to throw a bomb at you before we leave?"

"Harry, of course not," she said. Dancers were galloping to music that raced. "Nothing like that will happen. Alberto will be very discreet, I told him to say nothing." Before he could become cuttingly English she changed the subject. "Harry, really, that woman was very vulgar."

"Which woman?"

"The one in the red gown."

"In? She was halfway out of it," said Harry.

Irena blushed for him. But he was laughing. Not out loud, but laughing all the same. Sometimes his sense of humor made her feel in delicious rapport with him, sometimes it made her want to bite. Now it made her feel weak and yielding.

She would not dance with anyone else at all, although she was still frequently besieged. In a little extravaganza of emotional sentiment she made the evening an occasion for memories bitter-sweet. It was stupid, but eventually she would have only the memories, she knew that. She was very sad when they left at last, before the unmasking took place. Back at the hotel she was not sleepy, she still felt so alive, and in the sitting-room of the suite she whirled around before sinking into a chair.

"Oh, it was so good," she said, "I have never enjoyed myself so much."

"I'm sure that's not true," said Harry, who saw the necessity of keeping his feet on the ground.

"But think of Michalides, think of all we

have been through," she said in soft earnestness, "and then think of tonight. Harry, you weren't bored, were you?"

"Bored?" He looked down at her. His eyes, dark and intense, made her heart beat a little painfully. She wished he would kiss her. But he had never stepped outside his role as her help and protector, except that he had managed to call her dear Princess tonight. That had been something.

"What is wrong, I am dishevelled?" she said unsteadily.

"No. You look very lovely. And I wasn't bored. Goodnight, Your Highness."

She did not want to be left, not after being called lovely.

"You are not going to bed, are you?" she said. "They will send up some coffee if we ask and you can talk to me. I'm not at all tired."

"We're off tomorrow—no, today," he said soberly.

"Yes, I know." She knew he was thinking of Elisabeth again. A sudden little rush of jealousy shocked her. For a moment or so it attacked her quite fiercely. She drew a breath, calmed herself. "Yes, you have to go home to Elisabeth. But you aren't the only one who has to think of someone else."

She meant Major Carlsen, thought Harry.

"You've an understanding with him?" he said ironically.

"Of course." She sat up proudly. She hoped he would not ask who the man was. She would have to lie. "Do you think I am not as eligible as your Elisabeth?"

"I think you very eligible, Your Highness."

If that was a compliment, it was said very brusquely. But the evening had been so lovely and she did not want it to be spoiled. So she smiled, shook her head at him and said, "Harry, it is true, you really are a farmer? That is what you will do when the war is over, farming?"

"What I hope to do is buy a small farm of my own. I assisted in the management of a large one before the war." He smiled at a thought he had just had. "I must go to my father's temple and ask for a loan. My father's temple is a bank."

"Oh, I could—" She stopped in time. She knew she could not offer him money, that he would never take it from her. "I think I should like to have a farm," she said.

"No, that's not for princesses," he said.

"You think I could not work hard at it?" she said a little proudly.

"Farming is nothing to do with good intentions," said Harry. "No, you'll set up court for Rumanian exiles somewhere, I expect."

"That would be chasing shadows," she said, "and is for others, perhaps, not for me." She stood up. "Oh, I will go to bed, then. That is what you wish. But I have had a wonderful time, yes. Really I have. Thank you, Harry."

"I'm not complaining, you know," he said and his smile was affectionate. "Goodnight."

She put her hand lightly on his arm.

"Goodnight, dear guardian, I am so much in your debt."

Their eyes compulsively held.

"Even though I bundle you about?" he said whimsically.

"Even though you do," she said. And the kiss was there, unenacted but there. In her eyes.

He lay awake for a while. Irena, who thought she would be unable to sleep, sank into beautiful dreams almost at once.

Twelve

They left Padua the next day. Their journey from there to France and through France was slow and tiring, full of delays and minor inconveniences. It took them a week to reach Dieppe. In other respects it was troublefree, although Harry was constantly looking over his shoulder. Irena seemed quite without qualms and stood up to him when he firmly requested she buy herself a veil.

"No. We are quite safe now. And veils make me look old."

"What does that matter?"

"Nothing to you," she retorted, "but everything to me."

"Anyway, you're wrong. They don't make you look old. You wear a veil very elegantly. We may be quite safe but we'll not take chances, not when we've come so far."

"I am to buy a veil, then?"

"Yes."

"I will not." She was as highly-strung as a thoroughbred.

"Princess Irena—Ma'am—"

"Oh!" More than anything she hated him calling her Ma'am. And they were always so close to edginess, to emotional clashes. The nearer they got to England the worse became the tension between them. "I will not!" she repeated.

"I insist."

"No!"

"Then I beg you," said Harry and gave her a smile, "I ask you. I think you charming in a veil. Perhaps it's rather Edwardian but there are still some Edwardian things worth keeping, especially those relating to elegance. Will you buy a veil, Your Highness?"

"Oh!" It was almost a wail. "Oh, I wish you would not call me that!"

He knew he should not but he said gently, "My dear Sonya Irena, shall we go to a shop?"

She went with him, her eyes alarmingly moist.

She wore the new veil. Harry felt a little happier for her. He still looked over his shoulder, but if Michalides had friends, comrades or agents in France, none showed up.

They arrived in Dieppe tired but very fit. Irena thought Harry looked as lean and hungry as Shakespeare's Cassius, and she pictured Elisabeth falling radiantly into his arms.

The moment of nerve-racking confrontation

with authority came when they crossed to New-
haven on the day of the general armistice, when
the flags were out and the church bells ringing,
when the day was dry but pale with winter.
Irena, in her waisted black coat and new hat,
elegance and composure hiding her anxieties,
stepped ashore as coolly as if she already belonged. But oh, the questions, the straight-faced
intransigence of uniformed officials, the suspicious scrutiny of the marriage certificate by one,
two and even three of them, each passing it
around as if it were as suspect as a dubious banknote. And Harry was looking grimmer and grimmer, quite tall and quite magnificent.

Where was her passport?

At which Harry said in a grinding voice that
Rumanians having to run from Germans don't
stop to apply for passports.

Oh, she had never had a passport?

Harry said there'd been a war on. Perhaps
they hadn't heard?

He had married her in Bucharest? How did
that come about?

Harry said he had been a hospitalized
prisoner-of-war and she had been a ministering
angel who had brought him flowers, at which
Irena, for all her hidden anxieties, wanted to gasp
with delight. But the immigration officers did not
seem amused.

"Well, sir—"

"Never mind that," said Harry ferociously,
"do you see this lady?"

"Yes, sir."

"Well, this lady is my wife. Fetch my M.P.
I'll wait. We'll both wait."

How superb, thought Irena. Oh, dear heaven, how was she going to manage without him, without having him there to laugh at her?

The officials scrutinized the marriage certificate again, they scrutinized Irena again. In her black coat with its white fur collar and the matching black-and-white hat, she was worth a second look. She smiled tenderly into inquisitive, interrogative eyes. Her smile, her clear brown eyes, combined with Harry's muttering ferocity, created the longed-for rapport. The possibility of being anything but cordial in the face of such a combination was coughed away.

"Welcome to Britain, Mrs. Phillips."

It was with a feeling of climactic giddiness that she discovered in the customs shed that she was not required to open a single piece of luggage. Customs men looked at her, looked at Harry and his uniform, and said, "Your wife, sir?"

Harry said, "Yes, I found her on the other side of Salonika. She wasn't doing anything else at the time so I married her."

They slapped cheerful chalk marks on the luggage. And she and Harry walked out of the shed to the waiting London train. They had done it.

"Well, here you are, then," said Harry. "Now you simply live quietly incognito for a while. Is that the idea?"

"Yes," she said. "Thank you, Harry, you have been quite marvellous. Isn't it nice to hear the bells ringing?"

"Someone must have known royalty was arriving," said Harry.

The train took them to London and they deposited their luggage at Victoria Station for the moment. She was fascinated as they emerged from the station and she saw the festooned buildings and flag-waving crowds. They had seen Padua on Italy's armistice day with Austria and to be in London on Britain's day of peace and victory was another excitement. They queued for a cab so that they could drive to the Strand, where Harry thought she might like to see the celebratory spirit of the West End.

The Strand was choked. They left the cab before they arrived there. Buses were almost at a standstill, their open top decks packed with people up on their feet, showing the flag and singing *Tipperary*. On the pavements and in the roads people swung along arm-in-arm, hats tipped and voices hoarse. Army khaki and Navy blue threaded through the pattern of color. The day, overcast but dry, was itself shot with color.

They moved towards Trafalgar Square, Irena keeping close to Harry because of the crush and, she thought, the imminence of a frightening riot.

"Harry, so many people! Is everyone in England here?"

"Haven't you ever been to London?" asked Harry.

"Never," she said.

"Not to your distant relatives at Buckingham Palace?"

"Oh, they are very distant," she said, "and I'm not on their guest list. Harry, look, those women are trying to take off the policemen's helmets."

"All jolly fun," said Harry, "nobody will get shot."

As they struggled through the crowds Harry was repeatedly seized, hugged and kissed by women with hats askew and hairpins dislodged. He explained to the slightly overcome Irena that the women were a bit tiddly and would kiss anybody.

"What is tiddly?" she said.

"A little drunk."

"I should like to get a bit tiddly, then," she said.

"And kiss anybody?"

"No, not anybody," she said with a faint smile.

On the edge of Trafalgar Square she herself was embraced by an American doughboy. It startled her, made her blush crimson. Harry laughed. Then he was almost swept away from her by a group of khaki-uniformed Waacs, who knew that on Armistice Day they could get away with any breach of discipline providing no guns were fired. The Waacs, on the prowl for forbidden fruit, were happy with their capture.

"Come on sir, come on, dance around Nelson with us. I'm Cecily."

"Don't have anything to do with her, sir, she eats even sergeant-majors, and I'm Freda."

"Come on, sir, come on, oh do!"

It was a wonderful day. Harry kissed them all. Some clung tightly to get more than their dues. Irena was shocked. Certain that if they made away with him she would never get him back, she stamped her foot.

"Let go of him!" she cried. They were pulling him all ways, utterly delighted with his kisses, and Harry did not seem disposed to resist the partitioning. He was laughing. "Harry, stop this!"

"Hello, ducky," said a rich, ripe voice, and a large sailor gathered her into an expansively fond embrace and kissed her with gusty, naval goodwill, then gave her another for luck. Irena's hat went awry and she sucked in astonished breath. "God bless yer, love, even my Aunt Mabel would like you and mostly she can't stand no one except her parrot," he said and pinched her bottom. Irena shrieked, jumped and blushed to the roots of her hair, all composure gone.

"Harry," she gasped, "save me!"

Harry was roaring with laughter. The sailor had passed on in search of similar beauty. There was a lot of it out and about today. Irena looked utterly incredulous. Harry rescued himself from the adventurous Waacs and moved to her side, cautioning her against her predilection for careless wandering. Irena drew herself up, straightened her hat and delivered her pink-faced riposte.

"What do you mean? It was nothing to do with me, I am not responsible for the outrageous behavior of others, and you did not tell me English people were like this. Oh, you are a fine one to shake your finger at me when you are kissing every woman you see and leaving me in danger of being trampled to death!"

She was delicious. He could have told her she was in much more danger of being kissed to death.

"Come along," he said and steered her firmly through people massing by Northumberland Avenue. He put his arm around her. It was protective, only that, but it made her quiver a little. And it was very upsetting that he could kiss those girls so amorously and not kiss her at all.

A linked line of soldiers, sailors and young women spilled from pavement to road, singing and dancing, the girls with legs kicking and petticoats whipping.

"What are they doing?" asked Irena.

"It's a ritual enactment of tribal joy called 'Knees Up, Mother Brown'," said Harry.

"It is very—oh!" Irena went hot as in seemingly abandoned vulgarity the young women revealed undergarments that one simply did not reveal. And Harry was looking. And laughing again. "It is not a bit nice," she said.

"Don't the Rumanian girls dance like that at harvest time?" said Harry.

"Well, I do not," said Irena.

Harry, slightly intoxicated by the uninhibited gaiety of the day, and quite entranced by discovering that Her Cool Royal Highness was really deliciously shy about some things, said, "I wish you would, this is just the occasion for it."

"Oh, you are terrible," she said and went resolutely on. Harry took her arm. "You would wish me to kick my legs about with everybody looking?"

"No, not everybody," said Harry. He was laughing so much. And then she was laughing too.

"It is nice, isn't it?" she said.

"What is?"

"Oh, to be just a little bit naughty sometimes," she said in a rush, "but only for—I mean—"

"Yes, I know," said Harry and felt very tender because she was blushing again. They watched other revellers for a while, with Nelson turning his blind eye far above, and then they made their way to the War Office. Harry did not want to waste time or opportunity. He would report to the top and let the best red tape sort it out.

Inside the building the air of celebration was more polished, more disciplined, and it took Harry quite a while to break through it. Eventually, however, he was taken to see a Colonel Smithers. He took Irena with him. She was quite willing to accompany him anywhere, to darkest Africa even, but she did not say so. She did, however, ask him not to disclose her identity. Harry did not want to provoke loud and pompous reaction in Parliament and said the last thing he had in mind was disclosure. She was not to worry, he said.

Colonel Smithers was an extremely decent type and charmed to meet Irena. He peered keenly at her. She smiled. He listened to Harry, asked questions, requested him to fill in a form, congratulated him on his escape, even if it had come a bit late, and on his gallant venture into matrimony when things had hardly looked as good for orange blossom as they did now. Altogether he obviously considered Harry had got far more out of the war than most. Irena could not quite understand why he did not wring Harry's hand, clap him on the shoulder and decorate him there and then. But Colonel Smithers, of course, could not be expected to see through

315

the limited details Harry gave him of his escape. Only she knew of the blood-tingling magnificence of their charge through that ambush. That was something Harry had to keep to himself. Otherwise Colonel Smithers would want to know why he hadn't handed the train and its complement of German troops to those Croatian insurgents.

There was a fairly friendly humming and hemming as Colonel Smithers wondered exactly what to do about the matter. It being Armistice Day he felt there was no immediate urgency to do anything except decently celebrate. The location of Harry's regiment must be looked into. Meanwhile, Harry could take indefinite leave and wait to hear.

Harry did not quarrel with that.

"And then there's your wife." Colonel Smithers smiled at Irena. "I hardly think it's been a honeymoon since you slipped out of Bucharest, what? Have to arrange the adjustment of your pay. Did we get the date of the marriage? Good. Well, highly commendable effort, Captain. Highly."

When they were on their way out of the building Irena murmured, "Do you think he meant your escape was highly commendable or your marriage?"

"I think he meant you were quite the best part of it all," said Harry. "I'll probably get a different reaction from my regimental colonel. He'll want to know why I didn't try getting back to my battery instead of gallivanting across Europe with a wife whom I married without his permission. His mind works rather like a pair of crossed swords. On the other hand, I'm not a regular officer, I only hold a wartime commission. Now, let me see," he went on matter-of-factly as they emerged into Whitehall, "I'd better catch a train home tonight, but first do you think we might dine together if we can get a table at the Trocadero or the Criterion or some other place fairly decent and lit up? No, before that I must find you an hotel. Let's try the Northumberland, it isn't far."

Irena, paling, said disbelievingly, "An hotel?"

He drew her aside from the thumping surge of people, sheltering her against the wall of the building.

"I assume this is where we go our separate ways," he said, "we have to do that some time."

She looked as if she had been struck in the face.

"You mean now?" she said numbly. "You are going home and leaving me here in a strange hotel?"

He was unable to explain why this was so necessary and what it would do to him. His one chance of saving the relationship he had with Elisabeth was to break with Irena now. If his association with Irena went longer he knew he would be totally unable to do justice to any marriage with Elisabeth. He would be hopelessly in love with a personage, and personages might dance with farmers, they would never marry them.

"I thought," he said, "that you intended to stay in London once we reached England. You're safe now and you have your own plans, I imagine. Perhaps you also have some way of letting Major Carlsen know you're safe, I think he wants to know. I presume you and I have to meet again when the question of the annulment comes up, but I did think we might have dinner together before we say goodbye. You know, don't you, that I am proud of you, that it's been a privilege to be with you. You do know that?"

She was pale, incredulous, stricken. London in eruptive revelry was not exciting now, it was a noise that beat at her. She could not look at him. Instead her eyes were on the choked traffic, the blur of people and waving flags.

"Captain Phillips?" Her voice in a strange way did not seem to belong to her. "You are going to leave me in London? Here, by myself?"

He did not think that that in itself was a great problem to her. She walked into hotels as if they belonged to her. And she had a way with her, a way that charmed people into serving her and helping her, and she had courage and aptitude. London was confusing to her now. She could have it at her feet by tomorrow.

"Isn't that best?" he said.

"I don't understand." Her brown eyes, frozen, were fixed on nothing. "What have I done? Is it that you don't like me? We—we were supposed to stay together until the annulment."

"Were we?" He could not precisely remember when that was arranged. He was torn by her stricken look but governed by the necessity for commonsense and by all he owed Elisabeth. "I'd assumed you would be in London, at least for a while." He held off pressure from a new surge of people. He tried to do what he could for Elisabeth and his peace of mind in the gentlest way possible. "Elisabeth will accept my story, I hope, but I'm not really sure she would accept the necessity of you and I living together. I've a small house in a Hampshire village which is hardly suitable for a platonic relationship, even in the eyes of the most charitable people, and it's less than suitable for Your Highness. What do you think it would do to a straightforward annulment if I took you there? It's better, surely, that we don't live together."

"An annulment is only affected if—" She swallowed. "If we had loved each other."

"I know that isn't likely to happen, but—"

"I see." She had expected the break to come eventually, but not now, not today when they had only just arrived, now at a moment when everyone else was celebrating. It was shattering. She had only her pride with which to face up to him. She spoke quietly, as oblivious as he was to the waving flags. "I do understand about you and Elisabeth. I will go to the hotel and get someone to collect my luggage from the station." She was very proud but so pale, and he felt sick with himself because in his insistence on commonsense he knew he had hurt her. She had been so unafraid, so stimulating in adversity, so endearing in her little moments of temper. She had stoked the fire and held off the throat-cutting bandits of Croatia. "Yes, you must go home at once, of course you must," she said. "I am sorry if I did not see that just now, but it has been so—so—"

"Yes, I know," he said, wondering if he

would ever forget how bravely beautiful she had looked through her soot.

"It was all so splendid, so magnificent. Everything." She was drawing on every reserve of desperate pride. "We will say goodbye now? That would be better. I have your address, I will write to you about the annulment."

He found it unendurable. He had known it was going to be difficult. It was far worse than that. Here, in Whitehall, with processions of people hampering real communication, parting from her was impossible.

"Oh, damn and blast," he said, "I'm making such a mess of this."

She put out a gloved hand. "How am I to thank you, how am I ever to thank you?" she said.

"We did it together," said Harry. He did not take her hand. "Oh, hell," he said. She winced. "Well, how the devil can we say goodbye here, in the street? It's not so much that I feel I'm leaving you alone. You're not a penniless nobody, you've got distant relatives at the Palace and personages in high places who are supposed to be worried about you. And failing their hospitality there's the Ritz. You'd fit into a suite there as naturally as any royalty. But that's not the point, is it, I'm damned if it is."

"I don't wish you to get angry or to swear," she said, "I'm sure I shall be quite safe from anarchists, if that's what you are thinking about."

"No, I'm not thinking about anarchists at all. You should be safe enough in London." He muttered under his breath. "Look here," he said.

"I do not want to be a worry to you," she said.

"Well, you are. Look here," he said again, "the war's over, everyone's having a high old time and you don't deserve to be left out of it." He took her by the arm and moved her back into the entrance to the War Office, where they would not be jostled and inhibited by the thickening crowds. "Would you like to spend a few days in London with me? We could both wind down a little."

"Wind down?" A faint ray of hope brightened her.

"Relax. Forget all the tensions and simply celebrate. I'm not sure we both don't deserve a few days off. I'll say nothing to Elisabeth or my parents about being back yet. I can't leave you to cope with Armistice Day on your own, I owe you more than that."

"Harry, you owe me nothing, it is I who—"

"I owe you for being on that train with me, for using that rifle, for other things. On the other hand, you've had to put up with me for quite a while now, and you may not want too much more of me. It's just that—"

"Harry!" She was distressed. "Oh, how could you even think that!"

"Well, look here, then, shall we celebrate for a couple of days? Then we can talk about your future again."

"We will stay at the hotel together?"

He rubbed his chin. Her eyes were big, ready to brim if she lost control of herself.

"Not quite together, as we were in Padua," he said, "not now we've arrived. We have to be careful about these things now, don't we, in view of the annulment? We must get separate rooms."

"Yes, of course. Oh, I'm sorry, I've made such a fuss, haven't I?"

"No, not at all." Harry finally reduced the dialogue to an easy conversational level. "Now you're sure you'll like this, a couple of days seeing London with me?"

"Oh, yes," she said gratefully, "it will give me time to get used to it. It is very foreign to me, you see."

"Yes, that's a point," said Harry matter-of-factly. "Well, we'll see how we go."

"Yes," she said, managing to sound quietly restrained. He did not know what an effort it was for her not to be demonstrative in her relief. It was easy for him. Distaste for showing one's emotions was born in the English. She wondered if English babies cried like other babies when they came into the world. They probably did not dare to. To be demonstrative, to show blissful relief that he was not going to leave her yet, would never do. And it would make things worse. She said, "Thank you, Harry, it will be nice to celebrate."

They managed to get rooms at the Northumberland. From her window Irena looked down into the Avenue and saw flags flying in a thousand hands. There were so many different uniforms, Allied as well as British. The passage of countless people strung across the width of the street merged with the tides sweeping into Trafalgar Square. The noise was tumultuous, it affected one's blood. The windows of buildings were open and filled with the heads of people.

Beer bottles spouted foam from one window as tops were twisted off. There was a heady deliriousness about the mood of the people. They sang and they danced. Irena thought of Rumania, its conquest and its passive resilience under German occupation. She thought of Major Carlsen. At the moment he would be bitterly aware of an outcome he had at one time never envisaged.

It hardly seemed possible that his great nation, for so long Europe's greatest military power, lay broken in defeat, that the Kaiser Wilhelm had lost his throne, his Empire and his people. Major Carlsen would need all his nerve and courage to live with the fact that Germany, which had promised so much, lay in greater ruins than any other country.

Irena sighed. But she watched fascinated from the hotel window, opening it wider to look and to listen. How bright the celebrations made the grey November day. The clouds swept low over the capital, running before a light wind, scattering a few drops of rain which counted for nothing as the people surged and danced through streets and avenues to mass in Trafalgar Square or to force their way through to Piccadilly Circus. No one had ever told her that the British danced in their streets on occasions like this one, that the girls and women of London kicked up their legs and showed their petticoats, that they lost their hats and hairpins, that their hair ran free and wild and that they behaved like laughing gypsys.

And there were even some American soldiers, with their boy scout hats and their wide shoulders, picking up girls and throwing them high and throwing their hats up after the screaming girls and catching both on the way down. And there was so much kissing. All this time, all the way from Bucharest, and she had not been kissed once, except by a large sailor she had not even been introduced to. She had been harried and carried and bullied, but not once had she been kissed. Not even today, when it was his victory day. Naturally, there was Elisabeth, but surely—

"Oh, I am so stupid!" she cried out loud.

What with the emotional impact of the people, the soldiers, the victory, and Harry, the hot tears pricked her eyes as she stood at the window. Someone saw her, someone able to distinguish her vivid beauty even from the street below, but not her tears, and he called, a soldier of the King's Own Light Infantry, a man of Flanders.

"Come down, love, come down!"

She laughed at him through her tears and she waved and he waved back, a young and thin-faced veteran of the trenches, in his peaked khaki cap and his uniform of blue, the uniform of the convalescent wounded. His left sleeve was empty but his eyes were full, enraptured by the vision of a beautiful young woman laughing down at him from the hotel window.

"Come down, sweetie, come down!"

She could not hear him above the noisy exultation, but she saw his empty sleeve and the smile eager and encouraging on his face, and extravagantly, still crying, she blew him kisses with both hands. He kissed her back in the same way, but with one hand, then was swept along and away by the flowing mass of revellers.

It was so emotional, all these people singing and dancing because the war was over and won. Here in London they surged through the streets, they rode on the open tops of crawling buses. Yet in Berlin, Irena couldn't help remembering, the women walked dazed and bewildered, in Vienna they wept.

Irena, watching victorious London, could not help weeping herself.

There was a knock on her door. Hastily she banished her tears, dabbed her eyes and face.

"Come."

She thought it would be Harry but it was a pageboy in uniform and pillbox. He handed her a white oblong box. She thanked him. She could not tip him, she had no English money. Expressively, with her eyes and her smile, and a little shrug, she indicated her deep regret. The pageboy grinned and said, "Don't you worry, madam." He could smell generous tips when she had English coinage.

She closed the door and opened the box. It contained a dozen late autumn roses, perfectly budded and all a deep red. Their scent was a fragrant reminder of summer departed. There was a card.

"For bravery. Harry."

"Oh," she gasped and sat down in new emotion. With the box on her knees she gazed numbly at the blooms. *For bravery.* She wanted to cry again. She knew flowers from Harry really belonged to Elisabeth. She knew she was keeping him from his fiancée, that she was making a terrible mistake. He would think about it and begin to resent it. But for the moment he had thought to send her roses. She sat very quietly for a while, the tumult of London pounding in on her through the open window. She got up and closed it. She hesitated, then went along to room 27. She knocked. Harry answered in his shirt, tie and trousers. He looked a little sleepy.

"I had my feet up," he said.

"The roses," she said, trying to sound delighted but not intense, "oh, they are lovely. Thank you so much."

"Oh, yes. The roses." He smiled. "They were overdue."

He did not invite her in. She understood. They had to be very circumspect.

"No one has ever sent me flowers because of my bravery," she said.

"Well, I have," said Harry.

"They are nicer than a medal," she said, "thank you, Harry." And she hurried back to her room. He called to her and she turned in the corridor. He came up to her.

"Princess, will you dine with me at Romano's tonight? I've managed to get them to squeeze us in. I think you'll like it there."

"Oh, I am sure I will like it anywhere tonight," she said breathlessly.

"I'll call for you at eight and we'll look at London first," he said.

She was ready at eight. She looked beautiful. Harry had had his uniform pressed and she would have liked to have said how proud she was of him. When they walked through the lobby the pageboy bowed to her and outside the commissionaire saluted them. They were able to get a taxi and it took them around London. Harry said she must see the Palace, the residence of her distant relatives. The taxi skipped and flirted around revellers who claimed the roads as well as the pavements as their right this night. In front of the Palace the people thronged, the façade of lighted windows a magnet and a hopeful sign that the royal family would appear yet again. They drove down the Mall and into the heart of the West End. There traffic moved at a walking-pace, hemmed in by rivers of people. The lights were on, the theatres brilliant with flashing bulbs, and there was a special charity performance of *Chu Chin Chow,* the musical which had dominated London's entertainment throughout the war. Irena peered and looked, entranced and exhilarated, a gossamer scarf around her piled hair, a coat over her shoulders. Dearly she would have liked a stole, a rich, soft, warm fur stole. She had not thought of victory night in London when buying things in France.

The noise was of horns, bells, songs and cheers. And triumph. Peace would come later, a bewildering peace. Tonight they were still dancing, soldiers, sailors and girls. There were so many girls, so many women, scores of them, hundreds of them, haunted by the men who had gone, who lay in Flanders, in Mesopotamia, in Salonika, in Gallipoli and in drowned iron battleships. The British Empire had prevailed, but it had lost a million of its finest men and it had seen its most brilliant and exciting era during the Edwardian years. Edward and Alexandra had given it gaiety, color and an almost blinding splendor, had matched it with the magnificence of Ancient Rome, and few realized that the flame lit by

Victoria's gregarious son had burnt itself out in a consuming war only a few years after his death. Picadilly Circus, the hub of the Empire, did not cast any mantle of darkness, it was ablaze with its multitude of lights, and the men and women who had served the Empire and survived did not know they were dancing around a heart that was dying.

"Harry, I did not know it was like this," said Irena as the cab eased its way into the brilliance. The lights were like running, flashing fire. Hats waved, flags flew, and the girls were laughing at the moment and forgetting both the past and the future.

"What didn't you know was like this?" asked Harry.

"London," said Irena, "you never told me a thing about it, yet look how exciting it is."

"It'll be cold and cluttered at dawn," said Harry, "and probably foggy."

"Please don't be so gloomy. Harry, aren't you proud? Look at everything and everyone. Oh, I should be very proud."

"What of?" said Harry. He was aware of her warmth, her scent, her excitement.

"Of belonging here, of knowing I had done something to make London and the people proud of me."

"You're inebriated," said Harry.

"Inebriated?"

"Ah—drunk," said Harry.

"I am not!" She took his English very literally at times. "I have not had anything. Harry," she said, "can we go and see—what is it now?—a clock, yes? Big Benk, isn't it?"

"Big what?"

"Isn't that right, Big Benk?"

"Big Ben?"

"Yes, that is right," she said, pleased with herself.

"I'll see if the driver can get us there."

The driver said he'd do his best, but if they got squeezed flat, taxi and all, he wouldn't half have something to say about it. But he got there and they sat in the cab and looked up at the huge, shining face of the illuminated clock. They waited until it struck nine o'clock. The strokes boomed out over the inky Thames, darkly flowing, and the haunting, lingering echo of each stroke filled Irena with wonder. Westminster Bridge was a tideway of people, the Houses of Parliament and Westminster Abbey etched against the black sky, and Irena could not think why Harry was so quiet, why he was not stirred. She glanced at him. The lights reached into the cab. His eyes were still and reflective. And she knew he was not thinking of victory but of men he had known, men who had not been as lucky as he had.

Involuntarily she reached and pressed his hand. He squeezed her fingers.

"Let's go to Romano's now, shall we?" he said.

"Yes. But thank you for Big Ben. It was very stirring."

"Just an old clock," he said.

Romano's was beautifully warm and welcoming. Its plush red and gilt and its Edwardian opulence reminded her a little of Maxim's in Paris. The tables glittered with glasses and silvery buckets of crushed ice glittered with condensation. Miniature flags of the Allies formed the table decorations. There were Allied officers crowding in, French, British and a few American. The French seemed to arrive with a woman on each arm, the Americans came as a party and in uninhibited possession of a bevy of girls. The British officers, who were, of course, playing at home, seemed in a state of correct bonhomie with one lady apiece. Other men arrived in toppers, tails and cloaks, a splendid pre-war style.

Younger women, girls, came in modern 1918 style, in evening dresses whose lines were straight. A number of the maturer women arrived in striking defiance of straight lines and wartime austerity. They wore plunging, off-shoulder gowns bravely lifted from wardrobes they had put aside, and they looked as if they were Edwardian beauties brilliantly reborn. What other fashions could do justice to Armistice night? What was there of imaginative flair in November 1918 that matched even the most modest of Edwardian styles? As far as these women at Romano's were concerned there was nothing, and they left every trace of a tired 1918 at home. They declared for the sumptuous, exotic and banished Empire lines, they declared for Queen Alexandra, for Alexandra was the inspiration and arbiter of all Edwardian grace and style, and had refused to clothe herself like a shapeless neuter. They retraced their steps on Armistice night to bring back the recent, the glorious past, as if they knew that the present was synonymous with drabness and the future would offer them nothing memorable. They had been young when Edward was King and this was their final flamboyant salute to the world which, in retrospect, seemed hauntingly and excitingly beautiful. So they came to Romano's, these women of London, the society figures, the actresses and the paramours, and for one night they brought back the splendor of Edward and Alexandra and their mighty Empire. And they made anonymous figures of the girls and the women who declared for the shapelessness of 1918.

Irena did not disgrace their challenging appeal. She came in the beauty of the silk gown she had bought in Padua, so different with its long flowing sleeves and its studded collar. Preceding Harry she followed the head waiter to their table. Her gown shimmeringly clasped her body, her dark hair was piled high, her vivid beauty enriched by the lights and the luminous quality of her excited eyes. She wore no gloves and no jewellery, none at all, except for a plain gold wedding band, but in her dark hair was a single red rose. She turned heads, she drew eyes, and she walked, thought Harry, as he imagined all princesses did, in graceful, inherent obliviousness of everything but her own regality.

My God, he thought, what am I doing here with her? What the devil would Elisabeth say?

The plush red embraced her as she sat down.

Romano's crowded them with warm, vibrating excitement. Irena sparkled, adoring it all, the magnificent color to which every gown, every dress and every uniform contributed, and every white tie seemed like a neatly outlined shape on the glowing canvas. Harry avoided looking at her. She was a warm radiance. He felt extremely proud of her but he was very aware that to look at her was no help at all. So he kept his eyes elsewhere. She was sensitively quick to realize this. He did not even look at her when he spoke to her or when she spoke to him.

"There is something wrong with me? I have not powdered my nose?"

"Why do you ask that?"

"You're not looking at me. I mean, you are looking as if I am not here."

"I've got something in my eye," said Harry.

"Let me see."

"It's a mote."

"What is that, what is a mote? Isn't it water round a castle?"

He laughed. That made her happier. They ordered from a menu that seemed surprisingly varied considering the shortages. But considering also that the food was secondary to the privilege of being here on Armistice night, what they had was excellent. Tiny chicken vol-au-vent which melted in the mouth came crisp and hot. They followed with little strips of fish in sauce which were delicious, although Harry said they were dismembered pilchards.

Above the hubbub Irena said, "Pilchards? They are fish?"

"What do they sound like to you, Bulgarian policemen?"

"I hope I am not eating dismembered Bulgarian policemen," said Irena.

Harry, in the midst of swallowing a piece, put a hand up to his mouth.

"Oh, good God," he said muffledly.

"What is wrong?"

"Nothing. Just very funny."

"You are making a joke?" she said.

"You made the joke."

"Bulgarian policemen? That was a joke?"

"Wasn't it?"

"I was very serious. Would you like to be eating—"

"No, don't, not again, Princess."

Their eyes met. She colored. He smiled. She laughed nervously.

They drank champagne. The war had reduced supplies but not shut them off completely. It was prohibitively expensive but Harry had no intention of settling for less on such a night, with such a woman. And the champagne would do for him what his resolution could not, it would cast a glow over his problems. Irena loved the champagne and enjoyed the food. She ate the main course with relish. It was a roast. The English translation on the menu said rib of beef and indeed it had been carved for them in front of their eyes. Irena thought it delicious and said so.

"It's very eatable," said Harry, "but I'm not sure whether it's beef or horse."

"Horse?" She was beginning to have a warm, delightful evening. She knew he was not being serious. "Horse?" she said.

"Did you see the shape of that rib? Very round. Horse, I tell you."

"But beefs are round too."

He let her get away with beefs.

"Beefs are squarer," he said.

"We are eating horse? Because of the war? Well, horse is very nice," she said.

"No, it's my joke this time," he said, "I don't want you to have a dull evening."

"Dull? Dull? But, Harry, it's wonderful, isn't it? Everyone looking so grand."

She was looking so vivid, so alive. The champagne was casting its glow. Over both of them. Over others. A French officer at a nearby table raised his glass to Irena, winked at her and drank to her. Irena acknowledged the gesture with a smile. Corks popped, girls shrieked. The Frenchmen stood up and sang the Marseillaise. Everyone else stood up and joined in. That brought on the cabaret star, a flame-haired woman wearing a flag as a sash over her black satin dress. She began to sing the songs of war. She sang *Tipperary*, *Home Fires* and *Soldiers of the Queen*. She did not sing alone. They would not let her go, nor did she wish to with such an audience as this. She sang on.

Irena was watching Harry. He was sitting back, he was not singing. He was remembering the guns, the belching, recoiling guns, the limbered guns, the sweating horses, the mud of Flanders and the heat of Mesopotamia. And the German guns, the German shells, the savage, straining effort to bring the battery clear, the carnage when horses were blown to bits. Despite the golden aura of the champagne he did not find the singer uplifting. Her songs were not meant for cabaret, they were songs of the men of war, of men marching to entrain for leave, of recruits marching for the first time into the line. They were the songs of the infantry, and they belonged to these men.

"Harry?" whispered Irena.

"Send her home," he said.

What was he saying? She thought the songs so varied, some haunting and some heart-quickening, though she did not really know them too well. Harry was odd and had said odd things this evening.

Streamers ran through the air and balloons sailed like light colorful ships. And still they would not let the singer go. She was looking at Harry, the only man who had not been responsive to her rich voice. He sat there, not far from her, she bathed in the spotlight, he dark in the shadow. She saw Irena watching him. She turned to her pianist and spoke to him.

She sang *Greensleeves,* a ballad not about war but about a lady, attributed to Henry VIII. At which Harry smiled and the singer smiled back. And the women clothed in Edwardian splendor listened and they too had their memories.

People merged, tables merged, and Harry and Irena found themselves drawn into the midst of women who wanted to kiss Harry and men who could not take their eyes off Irena. She watched flamboyant women kiss his mouth and she fumed, although she laughed. To men who wanted to kiss her she offered her hand. The French, British and Americans drank and celebrated, the cosmopolitan factor adding its own international excitement to the atmosphere. Irena seemed to put aside all her pro-German sentiments and lose herself in the evocative exhilaration brought about by a long war grimly fought and well won.

Champagne bottles came and went.

"More, please, Harry." Irena held out her glass. She was flushed, excited, her eyes softly brilliant.

"You sure?" Harry looked into the lambent eyes. Her dreamy smile embraced him. "A victory's a victory, an intoxicated princess is a defeat."

"Oh, pooh," she said.

"Cheri?" A French officer gallantly filled her glass for her. She gave him her sweetest smile. He was on his feet, leaning over her shoulder. Just as gallantly he kissed her. She was too dreamy to escape that one.

"Hm," said Harry.

"Hm?" Irena, her flush deeper, turned to him. "What is hm for? Everyone is kissing, you are kissing, so I am kissing too."

"So there," said Harry and laughed. She was an irresistible princess.

It was late, so late, when they left Romano's. The Strand was quietening, although there were still some revellers about, still some soldiers and girls swinging along. The sky was black but clear, the Strand shining like a dark river.

"Shall we walk, Harry? I am not tired, are you?"

He gave her his arm. She was grateful for it, drawing close to him, for it was cold after the warmth. But she wanted to walk to feel the air on her face, and what was the cold of a London night after the bitter cold of Trieste? She was, despite the temperature, full of dreamy well-being. They did not have far to go, but the pavements were damp and she hitched her gown with her free hand.

"Are you cold?" His voice had well-being in it too.

"Oh, no. Harry, thank you for taking me there, I am still so excited. It was lovely, wasn't it?"

"Well, better than beans in Belgrade," he said, conscious of her warmth, her nearness. The gossamer scarf stirred around her head, caressing her hair and the red rose. "I'll take you round the shops tomorrow. I'd like to have you meet some lords and ladies, but I don't know any—"

"Why should I meet lords and ladies?"

"To make you feel more at home. Your Highness, I—"

"Oh!" That incensed her, she felt a deliberateness about it, as if the cold night had already swept away the lovely warm excitement they had just shared. "I am Sonya Irena, why don't you call me that, why don't you? I'm not too proud to call you Harry, you should not be too proud to call me Sonya Irena."

"I intend to behave with perfect decorum from start to finish," said Harry as they crossed the road in front of Charing Cross station.

"Perfect decorum?" Irena had her chin in the air. "What is that, some stupid English name for starch?"

"Starch?" He knew what was coming but he had to invite it.

"Yes, starch." She was almost disdainful. "That is what I've heard about the English, they are all stuff and starch. You are all stuff and starch."

"Well, my father's a bank manager," said Harry.

"How ridiculous." She was superbly lofty. "What is it to do with your father? He is probably a very nice man."

"Yes, quite so, but—"

"You are a snob. I have heard that about the English too."

"Haven't you heard anything nice?"

"No," she said and wondered if the tall slender pedestal on which Nelson stood was swaying in the night or whether she was not quite steady herself. "No, I have not."

"Then it's damn lucky for you I didn't turn out an absolute bounder and sell you to the highest bidder." He helped her avoid carousing sailors as they turned into Northumberland Avenue. "Now look here, Sonya Irena—"

"Oh, that is better. What do you mean, highest bidder?"

They were not really quarrelling. They were fencing, and a little recklessly because of the evening they had had. In an acutely sensitive relationship it is better to strike sparks than to show warmth.

"Some of the French have money," said Harry, "and a very fine appreciation of beautiful women."

"I am a beautiful woman?" said Irena lightly.

"I don't think I'd have had any problem selling you to a French millionaire."

"Now who is drunk?"

"I'm not."

"Then you are disgusting. Harry, isn't it a lovely night?"

"No, it's damp and cold. You should exile yourself to the South of France."

"Oh, there is no need to give me any pushes," said Irena, "you will be rid of me soon enough."

"Don't be silly," said Harry.

That hurt her. Her arm stiffened through his and her chin lifted high.

"You are forgetting yourself, Captain Phillips."

"I see. Very well, Your Highness."

"Oh!"

"I like to know where I stand."

"You are walking and being stuffy."

They laughed at each other then and at themselves. They entered the hotel. He said goodnight to her at the door to room 21. It was early morning. Her eyes were soft, dreamy, a message lurking.

Please kiss me. Just once, won't you?

"Goodnight," he said again and went on to room 27.

Thirteen

She slept very late. In the afternoon Harry took her out to the shops, which delighted her because she loved the shops of any capital city and the London shops were festooned with the flags and banners of victory. And because he took her to places like Bond Street, Oxford Street, Regent Street and Burlington Arcade.

But, "I have no money, I can't buy anything."

"Good," said Harry, which made her laugh. She had her arm through his, she was warmly wrapped up in coat and hat, and she falsified reality and let herself belong to him.

"Oh, I am quite happy just looking."

"You'll amaze me if you are. If there's anything you really want I'll pay for by check and we'll add them up and charge them to Major Carlsen as expenses. I presume we'll hear from him sometime."

"But I have my jewels," she said, "I can sell some."

She was earnest, soft, lovely. Oh, my God, he thought, oh my God. For all her moments of putting her nose in the air, for all the difference in their positions, they both knew that what counted most was the risks and the hazards they had shared. He knew she regarded him as a close friend, would always accept him as such, would speak of him as such. She walked on his ground now, as if there were no differences, but by doing so, by coming down from her castle, she was making things the more impossible for him. Better by far for her to be what she was. He was an idiot. He hadn't even told Elisabeth he was back.

"Well, look here—"

"You are so sweet, Harry. Each time you say look here I know you are going to be nice to me—" She stopped, realizing how she was talking. It was affectionately proprietary. But that was how it was, and getting worse each day, and not wanting to face the awful moment when he would have to go back to Elisabeth. "Oh, it doesn't matter, really. I don't want to buy anything, I will wait until I am more settled. I will buy all the wrong things if I shop now, yes?"

"All the same, you must have some money. Come on, we'll go and cash a check."

They went to a bank. He drew fifty pounds and gave her thirty. She looked at the crisp, white five-pound notes with their fine black script. It was not something to get emotional about. They knew each other now, trusted each other, and she would pay him back. The gesture was a practical one but she still felt emotional. He only had a captain's pay, that hardly made him rich.

"Harry—"

"It cost you pearls to get us out of Trieste, remember?" he said.

"Oh, that was nothing," she said and led the way out of the bank, wondering in distress how she was going to manage without him. Not because she was a useless or helpless person. She wasn't.

"Where the devil are you going?" Harry's hand took her by the arm, pulling her back from the curb. The street was a maelstrom of horse-drawn traffic and motor vehicles.

"I am all right."

"Yes, I daresay, but don't get carried away. Princesses crossing a London street incognita are in as much danger as ordinary people. If you want to stop the traffic wear your tiara."

"Oh, you are so ridiculous," she said but she was laughing.

They went on with their window-shopping, their walking, their strolling, their peering. Irena rubbed shoulders with the people, except that she hung on to Harry's arm and wondered desperately from time to time if any woman had more problems than she had. There was so much that separated her from Harry, and being arm-in-arm with him neither eased the problems nor made them go away.

The afternoon darkness of November decended. This brought on the shop and street lights, and after the dark years all over Europe, illuminated London seemed to glow with warm triumph. The people about were still in a mood of cheer and buoyancy. When, at closing time, some of the shops began to put shutters up Irena felt it to be an affront to the spirit of the Armistice. She did not want any of the lights to go out, any withdrawals from the bright arena of celebration or, for that matter, any suggestion that she and Harry should leave it. But they had to return to the hotel eventually.

They dined quietly in the hotel restaurant that evening. Irena had no objection. She thought it would be cosy and it was. They talked, and freely. They talked about their journey, about Michalides, and laughed. Irena was loquacious, reminiscent. Do you remember, do you remember? They both remembered. Her eyes shone. She felt she and Harry had shared dangers and adventures that set them apart, that whatever else happened they would remember each other very specially. She did not want to think about what was going to happen, for the future in all its facets compulsorily embraced Elisabeth.

Harry was such good company. They communicated so easily and they spent the whole evening being together, talking together and laughing together. The hours sped so swiftly, midnight rushed at them. He escorted her up to her room. At the door she said, "Oh, I have talked so much, I have not been boring, have I?"

"Quite the reverse," said Harry, "and it's a time for talking one's head off."

"Yes, the war is really over, isn't it?"

"And we can have some peace now."

"Yes," she said. They looked at each other and suddenly there were no more words except those which were easily spoken and did not mean anything.

"Goodnight, Sonya Irena."

"Goodnight, Harry."

Fourteen

At lunch next day Harry said, "I ought to go home now, you agree?"

Irena put her hands in her lap and looked at her plate.

"Yes," she said. "I don't wish you to worry about me any more, you have worried quite enough. I shall stay here for a little while and think about things. You must go home to Elisabeth."

It had gone, the two days' respite.

"Yes, I must," said Harry. The restaurant was almost full but they had both gone beyond using atmosphere to minimize their problems. "But I still don't think much of my idea of leaving you here. I think now Major Carlsen meant for me to look after you until the annulment or until he turns up, which I'm sure he will do. Will you come home with me?"

She kept her eyes on the plate, hiding the hope that was dormant and sometimes alive. It was alive now.

"No, it would not be fair to you," she said.

"But would you rather come than stay here? You must understand it's not a palace, it's very ordinary."

She knew she was fighting Elisabeth again. It did not make her feel very happy. But she could not bear the thought of being left. It would be like an abysmal plunge into nothingness.

"I'm such a problem, aren't I?" She tried to smile. "But may I come? And it would not be a bad thing, would it, if I met Elisabeth and told her everything myself? You see, some women— I mean she is going to look at you when you begin to tell her about our marriage, it might not be as easy as you think."

Her brown eyes were earnest. Harry knew that if he took her home he might be doing the worst possible thing for Elisabeth, for himself and even for Irena. She needed a week of quiet, gracious living in a first-class hotel, a week that would relax her, refresh her and bring her within the context of her own special kind of existence again. He had kept his distance as much as he could, he had given her the help he had bargained to give. But if she came to live under his roof, even for only a few days, he frankly did not know how he was going to trust himself. But he could not walk away from her, he could not leave her alone.

"We'll pack this afternoon," he said, "and

348

catch a train from Waterloo. We can explain together to Elisabeth. Yes, that might be the best thing. But," he said with a faint smile, "do you think you could try looking a little drab and dowdy when you meet her? It'll be difficult enough as it is, without you turning up looking like the awakened Sleeping Beauty."

Irena wondered how much it would matter if in middle of her lunch in this busy hotel restaurant she had a little cry.

Instead she said lightly, "Oh, it is quite easy for any Sleeping Beauty to make herself look dreadfully unappealing."

"I'll believe that in your case when I see it," said Harry.

They checked out of the hotel after lunch and went to Waterloo. There, because he remembered he ought to use the telephone, he left her to make her first astonished acquaintance with the oddities of an English railway buffet, where yellow wartime buns, with hardly a currant between a baker's dozen, were served from under a glass case. And tea was tapped from an urn into a cup containing a measure of milk so that what one received was not tea as she knew it but a *fait accompli* of an obstinately English kind. One hardly liked to complain when one was still a newcomer. All the same, she thought she would get Harry to write to someone about it. He would be very good at ordering someone in the railway hierarchy to do things properly.

Harry phoned his parents' home first, using a telephone in the public house. His mother was rapturous to hear him. He talked to her affectionately, but guardedly, saying nothing for the moment about Irena. She talked to him in exclamation marks. Then he telephoned Elisabeth. Her mother answered. She was delighted to know he was safe and actually in London. Elisabeth, unfortunately, wasn't in. She was working in the library at Portlington, she had taken the job three months ago and was quite in love with it. She adored books. Of course, now Harry was home he must not let that sort of thing go on. Harry said he would talk to Elisabeth about it. He said he would telephone again, he had a long story to tell. She said Elisabeth would be off her head with relief and happiness.

Harry, putting the phone down, thought Elisabeth would show her happiness with a warm, sweet kiss, not by turning cartwheels. Curiously he realized if anyone would jump over the moon in a moment of excessive happiness it would be a princess he happened to know.

He sighed a little. Thoughts and things kept coming back to Her Irrepressible Highness.

He found her looking quite incredulous at the vast amount of milky tea being drunk in the station buffet. She was happy he had returned and began to tell him that perhaps something could be done about people who gave you milk with your tea when you did not want it—

"I know how you feel," said Harry, "but do you mind terribly if we leave that for some other time?"

"No, not at all, I was only—"

"Come along," said Harry.

They caught a train which took them southwest into Hampshire. She was taut with nerves and he was quiet. The restraint imposed by the presence of other passengers was not unwelcome in its way. It was teatime and dark when they arrived at the village of Amblestoke. The station gas lamps flickered as old Bill Parkin took their tickets, recognized Harry, welcomed him home and blinked with candid interest at the woman he had brought home with him.

He looked, he blinked again, Irena smiled and he said, "Well, I'm blowed." And Harry knew it would be all over the village before lights went out that night.

"How are your chickens?" he asked.

Old Bill looked as if he wanted to know how Harry's were. Irena, coat tight around her, the cold a wintry embrace, smiled again and old Bill reckoned afterwards that she fairly lit the place up, fog and all. Harry enquired after the possibilities of a cab.

"Ain't been no cab for months," said Bill, "but lend you a handcart for them bags if you like."

"You're on," said Harry. Irena loved him for that. That was how he was, he never made a fuss about the unimportant things, he simply got on with them. He would make a fine farmer. She thought of warm, golden corn and of watching him reap it.

They piled the luggage, which had grown by two more cases, on the handcart outside the station, and Harry pushed it home. Irena walked by his side and reflected on what it was all about. It was all about simple living after a dreadful war.

They did not have far to go, no more than a mile, and the walk warmed her. They reached houses. Lights showed behind curtains. There were small houses and country cottages, some with low wooden fences, others with little hedges. She could smell the smoke of coal fires and wood fires. Harry trundled the cart up against a grass verge and stopped. She saw a little wooden gate about three feet high. There was a path leading up to a small house, which was in darkness.

"Stay there," said Harry, "while I get the key from Mrs. Sawyer. She's been keeping an eye on things for me. It's been lived in, a soldiers' billet, so it shouldn't be too damp."

She wanted to say something absurd, such as she wouldn't have minded if it had only been a tent in a wet field and that she wished her name was Elisabeth instead of Sonya Irena Helene Magda.

But all she said was, "After everything else, do you think I would care about a little damp?"

She waited at the little gate. He was longer than she expected, although Mrs. Sawyer was only in the next house about thirty yards away. But Mrs. Sawyer kept him gassing, he said. Mrs. Sawyer liked a good gas. Irena asked what a good gas was.

"A very long chat," said Harry and let her into the house. He applied a match to every mantle in the place until all was bathed in cheerful light. Mrs. Sawyer had been conscientious since the last soldiers left some months ago. The rooms looked clean and tidy and only the kitchen felt a little damp. Irena turned on the brass tap over the sink. Water gushed.

"Oh, that is good," she said, "in Rumanian villages houses have no running water."

"Here," said Harry, "we're full of civilized amenities. There's even a bathroom upstairs. Mrs. Sawyer brings her children in to use it on Fridays. She has six."

"Six children? How lovely," said Irena.

"Don't tell her that."

"But six is lovely," said Irena, forgetting that in Rumania she had always been able to recognize what was admirably practical about romance and what was cloud cuckooland. She was excited, intrigued, exploratory. He told her to look around if she wanted to and she did. It was only a small village house but it was Harry's, and she put her lovely nose into everything while he brought in the luggage and took it up to the bedrooms. Upstairs there were two bedrooms and the bathroom. The beds were not made, the linen and blankets were in the landing cupboard, which was heated by pipes running up from the kitchen range. The range was laid and he lit it. The balled paper flared. He also lit the fire in the sitting-room. The sitting-room was wallpapered and cosy. The fire, when it began to burn, made it cosier. Irena, still in her hat and coat, was wandering about. She roamed upstairs. She roamed down again. It was such a nice little house. It wasn't at all grand. It was just right for two people.

The fire in the kitchen range was crackling and leaping, already warming the room and the hot water pipes. Harry put his head round the door and said he was going down to the village store to try and get some food. If it was shut he

353

would knock them up. "You forage around," he smiled.

"Forage?" She puzzled over that. "Forage is for horses, isn't it?"

"Yes. But foraging around is for princesses who leave their castles and come down to look into the mysteries of rustic dwellings."

"You mean poking my nose in. That is right, isn't it?"

She went upstairs again when he had gone. The bedrooms had latticed gable windows and low ceilings. The brass of the bedsteads was polished and there were small bedside rugs on the linoleum-covered floors. She could smell the faint, clean tang of furniture polish. She went down to the sitting-room and sat in an armchair in front of the fire. The flames licked up from the glowing coal. It was quiet, so quiet. She felt sad, lonely. She was here but she did not really belong. She was in Elisabeth's chair. It was not right to have come, it made things so much more complicated for Harry. Perhaps when she had first seen him she should have said to Major Carlsen, "No, I do not want him, find me someone else."

Harry came back with food. He had half a loaf of bread, some cheese, margarine and pickled onions, the onions wrapped in stiff brown paper. He also had plum jam, two tomatoes, two pounds of potatoes, some greens, some milk and a bottle of Camp coffee. And a small lemon, which looked with its dry tough skin as if it had lain forgotten for a year. She could not quite relate each item to the next as far as a meal was concerned. Harry said he wasn't going to throw them all into a stew together. What was the lemon for?

"Ah, yes," he said. He fished out the last item. "That's a packet of tea. The lemon is for your tea. You'll have to make it last, I'm afraid."

"Oh," she said, and there was a dreadful lump in her throat all because of an old lemon.

Was she hungry? She was famished. He prepared a simple meal, cooking potatoes, mashing them and creaming them with margarine and milk. He sliced the tomatoes while the dish of creamed potato was browning under the grill of the gas stove. Then he put the sliced tomatoes on top of the creamed potato and when they were hot, covered them with grated cheese and grilled the whole dish some more. The cheese softened, spread and turned brown. The aroma was delicious. Irena looked on fascinated. The kitchen was beautifully warm, Harry so efficient. She told him how good he was.

"You should see Elisabeth at work," he said, "this is very rough and ready."

"Elisabeth is a fine woman, isn't she?"

Strangely, he did not answer that.

"I'm afraid it's not much of a meal," he said, removing the dish, "but it was impossible to get any meat. We'll see about ration cards tomorrow."

They ate in the small dining-room, off a small refectory table of mahogany, and when they had finished the hot vegetarian dish Harry made some toast, which they had with margarine and plum jam. They were still hungry. So they finished up what was left of the cheese and bread, except for what was required of the latter for tomorrow's breakfast. Irena watched Harry

crisply munch a pickled onion with his bread
and cheese. She distrusted them herself, but his
munching spoke of such enjoyment that she
asked if she might please try one. They had been
a little careful with each other, just a little con-
strained even, but when she attempted to cut
her round, slippery onion with a knife and fork
and it skidded off the plate and landed in her
lap, Harry made no bones about what he felt.
He roared with laughter. Irena flushed and put
her chin up a little.

"Oh, it's a stupid thing," she said, placing
the onion back on her plate.

"Pick it up and bite it," said Harry, "that'll
bring it to its senses."

She did so. Her white teeth crunched it. It
was juicy and delicious. She was so pleased at
having brought it to its senses and found it so
good that she laughed. It eased the constraint
and brought the little dining-room to life. Harry
made coffee and they had it in front of the sitting-
room fire. Harry was quiet, staring almost frowningly into the flames. She was keyed-up. She
should have stayed in London. In that hotel she
could have managed very well. It would not
have been like this, too intimate, too tense, too
uneasy. Elisabeth would not like her being here.
In Elisabeth's place she would not have liked it
at all and would have wanted to scratch.

"Are you warm enough?" asked Harry. She
was sitting with her arms embracing herself.

"Oh, yes, the fire is lovely."

"Would you like more coffee?"

"Thank you, no."

The constraint burdened the atmosphere.

"It's a little more humdrum here than it was on that train," said Harry.

"What is humdrum?"

"Dull," said Harry.

"No, that is not the word," she said, "it is peaceful. Oh, you are not thinking of palaces and servants because of me, are you?"

"That has crossed my mind," said Harry, "but just then I was thinking of the train ambush and how you shot those Croats to pieces."

"Oh, but I have been on hunting trips with my father, he taught me how to use a rifle."

"What, when you were a child?" said Harry.

"A child? Oh, yes," she said and blushed. "I was a very precocious child, you see."

"Were you?" He had discovered modesty in her and shyness, but she could also be a little spirited and haughty. He supposed that it was not uncommon for young princesses to be a bit wilful.

"Harry," she said quietly, "perhaps it would be better for me to be in London. I will go back tomorrow. I am sorry—oh—" She was horrified because tears were so close. He saw them in her eyes and wanted to kiss them away.

"I don't know whether you should be alone," he said. "It can't have been the easiest thing in the world for you to have left your country and everything that means so much to you. I'd suggest you return to London when you're feeling better about that. It doesn't matter to me that you have German sympathies. I suppose you could say we met some very likeable ones. You're very likeable yourself, quite the most likeable princess I expect to meet. It's a privilege to have you here. I'll nail a plaque to the front door when you've gone. You know, Princess Irena of Moldavia slept here."

Her eyes brimmed.

"Harry—oh, I am in such a mess," she said and bent her head and stared unseeingly and moistly at the fire.

"You do need more coffee," said Harry sympathetically, "I'll go and make some."

She had recovered by the time he brought the fresh coffee in. She wondered why, when he was so self-sufficient, he needed a wife.

"You are so good at everything that when you are married you will leave Elisabeth nothing to do," she said.

"I've only learned how to do a few things for myself during the war," he said, "I haven't learned how to do without marriage. Don't most people like to share their lives with others? To have families? Royalty must have its courts and its responsibilities, we must have apple trees in our gardens and kids to play in them."

"Yes, how wonderful," said Irena.

"But not six," said Harry, stirring his coffee.

"Four would be nice," said Irena.

"Not in this place, but on a farm, yes."

"Yes, how wonderful," said Irena again.

They sat before the fire until Harry said good God, the beds had to be made. She went up with him, insisting that she helped. The airing cupboard was hot as he took out the blankets and bed linen. Together they made the beds, and suddenly she seemed so competent and domesticated that it made him ask questions.

"Harry, I am not as hopeless as that!" She

was indignant. "When I was at school in Switzerland we all had to make our own beds and learn domestic science."

"Domestic science? You should be able to cook, then."

She blushed.

"Oh, a little, perhaps, but I am very modest about it."

"But in Belgrade," he said as they tucked blankets in, "you didn't even know what a green bean was."

"Yes, I did, I said it was for eating."

He shook his head at her. She blushed again.

"Your Highness," he said severely, "you can cook breakfast in the morning."

"Oh, may I?" It was said impulsively, happily.

"I wasn't serious, I can't have you—"

"Why can't you?" She had burned a boat and was willing to take the consequences. "I would like to, it's only fair."

He shook his head again, smiling. She was full of surprises.

"Just toast, then," he said, "and coffee or tea, whichever you prefer."

They said goodnight after that. She was quite tired. But she lay awake for a while, wanting what she knew she could not have. She had never realized love made one so terribly hungry emotionally and physically.

The sun was pale and wintry in the morning but the light was enough to let her see, as she stood at the bedroom window, that the village was in the heart of green farmland. Everything looked quiet, peaceful, and moist with November damp. But it would be lovely in the spring and rich in the summer.

Harry slept even later than she did. When he came down to the kitchen she was making toast, the slices of bread sitting neatly under the gas grill. The kitchen table with its covering of green and white oilcloth was laid. She had put out the margarine and plum jam. She had stirred the embers of the range fire and it was glowing. She was slightly flushed. And very nervous.

"Good morning," she said. She was in a neat cream blouse and dark skirt. Her hair was soft and loose, the slide holding it only at the back of her neck. Harry felt strange twinges. She looked as if the bright, warm kitchen was hers.

"You're managing?" he said.

"Yes, except where is the coffee?"

He showed her the bottle of dark chicory and told her she needed a spoonful in each cup with hot water.

"That is English coffee?" she said.

"Not very good?"

"It was what we had last night? It was better than some we have had, wasn't it?"

"There's a brave girl," he said. "No, I'm sorry, that was—"

"Harry, that was very nice," she said, turning the toast. "I would rather be called a brave girl than Your Highness, although I am not a girl, you know."

"Yes, I do know," said Harry.

They breakfasted on the toast and coffee. He said he would try and get some marmalade and eggs. They became careful and polite with each other again because of the intimacy of breakfasting together with Elisabeth in the near

360

background. He complimented her on the excellence of the toast. Afterwards he told her he was going to the library at Portlington.

"Elisabeth works there. I must see her."

"Yes, of course," she said, "I shall be quite all right. You must see her and explain. I will also see her if you wish me to. Tell her we will arrange the annulment quickly."

"I'll see a solicitor," said Harry.

Her heart plummeted.

When he had gone she tidied up. It was quiet and she felt so alone. She was so used to having him around. She bit her lip because she did not like being without him and because there was nothing to take the place of his companionship. Someone knocked at the front door. It confused her. She stood for a moment and composed herself, then answered the knock. A young woman in a dark blue coat and matching hat stared in amazement at her. And Irena knew that this was Elisabeth.

Elisabeth, grey-eyed, slim and very fair, said, "Oh."

Irena braced herself.

"You are looking for Captain Phillips?" she said. Her accent was a further mystery to the bemused caller.

"Yes, I thought he was back—oh, are you renting the house?"

"Please, will you come in?"

Elisabeth entered in something of a trance. Irena drew on more reserves. It was going to be terrible. She smiled.

"Captain Phillips is out," she said, "he has gone to Portlington. I think that was the name of the place he said. It was to see you, I think. You are Elisabeth, yes?"

"Portlington? Oh." It was a soft little exclamation of disappointment. "But when he telephoned my mother yesterday he said nothing about—" Elisabeth broke off, not disposed to launch into a trying conversation with someone who was not only a stranger and foreign, but whose presence in the house was highly suspect. "I'm sorry," she said, "but I'm completely at a loss. May I know who I'm talking to?"

"I am someone from Rumania," said Irena. "I met Captain Phillips in Bucharest. He has spoken so much about you. Please, won't you sit down?"

"I think I must," confessed Elisabeth, "my head is suddenly spinning."

They sat down. Irena was at the crossroads. Harry's fiancée was quietly formidable under her bewilderment. Some women would have been inclined to scream and some to faint at the appearance of another woman in a fiancé's bachelor establishment. Elisabeth, however, was perceptibly pulling herself together. Irena admired that. It would make things easier because Elisabeth would listen. She would not have tantrums and stamp about. She looked very English. Fair and clear-eyed and dreadfully lovely. Dreadfully. Irena knew she had to talk to her. It could not be avoided. But perhaps it would help Harry. He would then only have to add his own words, the reassuring ones, the affectionate ones.

"There are things I must tell you," said Irena.

"Obviously," said Elisabeth.

At which Irena took a deep breath and told

the story from the beginning, leaving out only the incidents which might make Elisabeth draw the wrong inferences. She said nothing, for instance, about how she and Harry had shared the tiny apartment in Belgrade or the hotel suite in Padua or how they had stayed in London to celebrate. She spoke of Harry as impersonally as she could, referring to him always as Captain Phillips, although she could not hide the fact that she considered him a quite exceptional man. She could not make light of all he had done.

Elisabeth, listening with a stunned expression, did manage to find her voice at one point.

"He actually drove that train?"

"We both did," said Irena a little proudly, "but without either of us having any real idea of how we were managing it."

At the end Elisabeth came out of her trance to say, "You'll forgive me, but am I to believe all this?"

"It is all true," said Irena.

There was a long silence, with Elisabeth deep in thought. Consciously, the implications and impossibilities were staggering.

"You're saying you are Princess Irena of Moldavia?" she said at last.

"That isn't easy to believe, is it?" Irena smiled. Elisabeth regarded her in wonder and curiosity. She was not angry, she was not shocked. She was intelligently aware of one obvious fact, that few men could have refused to help a woman as vividly attractive as this one.

"It's not too difficult, either," she said. The compliment surprised Irena. "What is difficult," Elisabeth went on, "is trying to take it all in. It's so incredible. I had no idea Harry was such a

363

Don Quixote. He has really been quite mad. He's actually married to you?"

"Oh, you must believe what I told you," said Irena, "it was arranged only to get me into England."

"Was it?" Elisabeth was not sarcastic, she was calmly enquiring, although underlying incredulity was still there. She looked around the sitting-room. She even smiled. She is telling me, thought Irena, that a marriage of convenience could easily become a lot more than that under the roof of this small house.

"Believe me," said Irena.

"Do you mind if I take my coat off?" said Elisabeth. "It's warm in here with the fire."

"Please do," said Irena. She had flutters under her friendly smile, for Elisabeth was beginning to be quite dangerously calm, divesting herself unhurriedly of her coat and laying it over the back of a chair. Her dress was royal blue, with white collar and cuffs. It was most suitable for a librarian, it was charming, it was right. She would be at home amongst literature, thought Irena, she is probably much more intelligent and well-read than I am.

"Let's have some tea," said Elisabeth.

"Tea?" Irena was slightly taken aback by that piece of coolness.

"If it's not too much trouble. I think I need a stimulant."

Not at all confident that she could prepare tea satisfying to the highly critical taste of this poised Englishwoman, Irena said, "There is coffee, if you prefer." She patted her hair, striving for a naturalness.

"Coffee? Ground coffee? No, it can't be."

Elisabeth was definite. "I'm certain it could only be chicory. It's not what you like, is it?"

"It is better than what we had to drink in most places."

"Then let's have some," said Elisabeth, "I don't mind chicory in the least. Shall I make it or will you?"

"Perhaps you would like to?" said Irena, conceding Elisabeth's prior moral right.

They were both so polite that they both suddenly smiled.

"It's no use pretending the situation isn't very odd," said Elisabeth as they went into the kitchen, "but there are worse things to have come out of the war."

She made the coffee. It gave her time to think. Irena stirred the range fire which did not need stirring.

"I'm not sure," said Elisabeth as they sat drinking the coffee at the kitchen table, "what am I to call you?"

She really was quite the calmest person, thought Irena, she would fight all her battles without ever raising her voice. She would tranquilize a marriage.

"I am Sonya Irena and so on," she said, "please call me Sonya. I should like us to be friends, I should not simply want to go away and forget all Captain Phillips has done for me." She drew patterns on the green and white oilcloth with her finger. "I could not forget how correct he has been."

"Correct?" Elisabeth smiled. "Well, he has principles but I've found him rather devilish at times. I'm not a princess, however. When is the marriage to be annulled?"

"When we are sure nobody knows I am here and it can be done quietly."

"Nobody does know, do they? Except me," said Elisabeth.

"Then it can be very soon," said Irena. She got up and looked at the range fire again and poked it again, then flushed because her action was that of a woman in possession. Elisabeth, indeed, was regarding her very curiously.

"I really must go." Elisabeth consulted her watch. "I arranged to take the morning off to come and see Harry, I must catch the next train to Portlington. I live fifteen miles from here, near his parents. I hope he'll wait in the library and not go to my home, otherwise we'll be running around in circles. If I miss him perhaps he'll call on me this evening. I wonder," she said with a smile, "what he'll say to me? Extraordinary man."

"You must believe," said Irena, "that there's nothing he has done to affect your relationship with him."

"Except that he's married to you," said Elisabeth. "The cool cheek of the man. I didn't realize he was as adventurous as this. I mean, it was rather more quixotic than climbing a mountain. And one can climb a mountain without having to marry it. Goodbye. It's been a little head-spinning but I think we'll all calm down in the end."

When she had gone Irena wondered how it was possible to fight someone who neither cried nor screamed, neither kicked nor scratched.

She had lost the fight before she had ever begun it.

Fifteen

Elisabeth arrived at the Portlington library just before twelve-thirty. Two minutes later she was at her desk. Ten minutes later Harry came in. She looked up from her careful cataloguing work and there he was, uniformed and healthy, but with the air of a man on tenterhooks. She was sweetly happy to have the advantage.

"Harry? Why, how lovely." She stood up. They were unable to embrace because of people around. The most intimate gesture he could make was to lightly brush her lips with his finger. "I thought you might have called to see me last night. I was in a state of very happy anticipation."

"I couldn't, so I came here this morning." His smile was wry. "I was told you'd taken the morning off. If I'd known I'd have called at your home. I've just come back from seeing my parents. Your colleagues told me you'd be here about now. Is there somewhere we can talk?"

She spoke to the chief librarian, then retired with Harry to the little staff room. She turned to him as he closed the door, her action deliberate, intrigued. He hesitated. She noticed it. Then he kissed her. She let him. Her mouth was soft and warm, his firmly affectionate. Hm, she thought.

"My dearest Elisabeth," he said.

"My dear Harry," she said. They had always been good friends, always understood each other. She knew they could have a good marriage. "I'm so glad the war is over, so glad for you and all the other men who have managed to survive."

"You look just the same," he said.

"I hope you can do better than that."

"Do I have to? I like you looking the same."

"But my dress is new." She was lightly teasing. "Tell me about yourself now that you've won the war and the right to a future."

"Elisabeth—"

"Oh, I'm very proud of you," she smiled, and she was, "you're an exceptional man, aren't you?"

"You won't think so when I tell you what's been happening."

She could have punished him a little, let him tackle the awkward problem of finding the right way to tell his story, but she was not like that. She said, "I know what's been happening. I called on you this morning. My state of happy anticipation wouldn't let me wait for you to call on me later. You weren't home. But Princess Irena of Moldavia was. Harry, a princess. You did fly high, didn't you?"

"Damn," said Harry.

"Damn?" said Elisabeth.

"What else? That was the one thing you should have been protected against, seeing her there before you knew anything about her. I wanted you to know all there was to know before you met her. Damn it. But it means nothing, nothing at all, the fact that she's there."

"It means you're married to her." Elisabeth seemed more curious than anything else. "Harry, my dear sweet man, what on earth possessed you to become involved in an escapade as mad as that?"

"She's told you about it?" said Harry.

"I've had the most extraordinary story from her," said Elisabeth, "but naturally I don't know if she's left anything out. Anything important, that is."

"Important to you and me? There was nothing," said Harry.

"Harry, what made you do it?"

"In simple terms, pressure of circumstances, I suppose," said Harry. "I was in German hands at the time and she was being harassed by gangs of bearded Bolsheviks who wanted to cut her throat."

"Yes, I think I've heard all that," said Elisabeth, as smooth as her neatly-parted hair. "What I'd like to know is this—was the prospect of adventure too irresistible or was she?"

"Now wait a moment," said Harry. "Let's make it clear, shall we, that that aspect never entered into it."

"Which aspect?" asked Elisabeth sweetly. "The prospect of adventure or beauty in distress?"

"Elisabeth, look here, it's not been a picnic,

it's been damn trying." That was true, by God. "So stop making me jump through hoops."

"Harry dear, you have no idea how intrigued I am." Elisabeth brushed a fleck from his jacket. "You simply could not resist the challenge of it all, could you? I'm quite bowled over by your dashing gallantry. No praise is too high for you. And princesses are no more immune to valor than ordinary women. You realize what has happened, don't you?"

"What?" said Harry, feeling her cool good humor was a little suspect. He had known she would not have hysterics, he had not expected her to take it as calmly as this.

"She's fallen hopelessly in love with you."

"What?" He was shaken by that and by the placid way it was said.

"I think you heard me, Harry."

"Are you out of your mind?"

"Now, Harry." She was sweet reason personified.

"Look here," he said grimly, "you're too cool by half. Damn it, you're having me on."

"Indeed I'm not, that's not my style at all. You, my Don Quixote, must take the consequences of your romantic tilt at the windmills of adventure. If a man did for me what you've done for her, he'd be my lifelong Galahad. Oh, feckless Harry." Elisabeth wagged her finger at him. "Why didn't you think of that? She may be a princess but you've spoiled her for any other man. That was very unfair of you, since in me you already had your Guinevere. You should have let that German officer carry the responsibility—"

"That German officer, if you must know, is the man she's sweet on."

"Oh, my poor pet, you are confused, aren't you?" Elisabeth thought back over the years. She had known him as a devilish boy, as a comforting man. She had never known him confused. "But you have the coolest cheek, you know, coming home to me with a wife on your arm. Wait till the newspapers find out who she is."

"That mustn't happen," said Harry, "it'll cause havoc. The marriage is due for annulment. The radical politicians will crucify her, they'll shout their heads off that she used me merely to get into the country."

"Which is true, isn't it? Well, that's what she told me."

"I know, damn it, but she was running for her life, and even here she could be in danger if there's too much publicity. Elisabeth, keep it under your hat, there's a sweet."

"You propose to be her shining knight for ever?" said Elisabeth with accrued interest.

"No, of course not," he said decisively, "I've got you to think about."

"And her. She loves you, Harry."

"Don't be silly."

"And far more than I do, I think. Do you mind me saying that?"

"I mind you talking nonsense."

Elisabeth put cool fingers over his lips to stop his muttering.

"It isn't nonsense, my sweet," she said. "You weren't there listening to her, watching her as she talked about you. I thought her very natural and calm at first, then I began to realize she was quite emotional underneath. Her hands were never still. She's all nerves, and desperate about something. About you and me, I think, and our engagement. Harry, my dear, we've been such good friends, you and I, we've liked each other tremendously, and we've grown up thinking we should marry eventually, probably as much to please our parents as each other. But is there a grand passion? Oh, I'd be quite happy to marry you, but listening to your Princess Irena this morning I knew I wouldn't feel desolate if your marriage to her weren't annulled. She's hoping, you know, that you'll go to her and tell her it won't be. I suppose she can have a commoner for a husband. She's not in line for a crown, is she? Harry, do you love her?"

"This is madness," said Harry, guilt discomfiting him, "and I'm not going to continue with it. This is the right place to thump you with a good book, if that's the only way to make you see sense."

"Here is a very good book," said Elisabeth, picking one up from the table. "*The History of Mr. Polly* by H. G. Wells. Thump me with and I shall know you love me very much. I might be cross at first, as I don't like violence, but later I shall feel thrilled—"

"You're off your head."

"No, not a bit."

"We're talking ourselves into a crazy condition," said Harry firmly, "and it's got to stop. We'll all sit down when we're clearheaded and discuss it rationally."

"Rationally?" Elisabeth laughed softly. "Do you expect a woman madly in love to be rational?"

"Well, you tell me," said Harry, walking

about, "what's more irrational than a rich princess thinking of herself as a farmer's wife, if she's thinking of that at all? Can you see Her Serene Highness in a farmhouse? I'd have to hang it with chandeliers and hire a butler."

"Harry," she said gently, "you aren't very convincing."

"The right kind of love is what you and I have," said Harry.

"I must say," said Elisabeth, "you're doing your very best for me and you're doing your very best by all your principles." She smiled affectionately. "That's sweet, but I don't know whether it's right or even sensible. It depends, doesn't it, on whether you love her. Do you?"

"Elisabeth," he said, "have you met someone else?"

Elisabeth looked a little shocked.

"I've met other men, yes, a lot of them during my charity work at the military hospital. But I haven't fallen in love with any of them. However, if you've fallen in love yourself, with your house-guest, I shan't stand in your way, I'd be happy for you to tell her so. I think her reaction will surprise you. I think she'll cry."

"Madness," said Harry again, and walked around and muttered.

"Go and talk to her," said Elisabeth, "you owe her an awful lot of your time and understanding for making her fall in love with you. I don't think you can send her away, my sweet. Rumanians aren't noted for being stoical, for stiff upper lips. If you make her terribly unhappy she's quite likely to jump out of a high window. So go and talk to her. You're not to think of our parents, you're to think of her. And me."

"Damn it, I am thinking of you," said Harry, convinced that he had let her down and she was making the grand gesture.

"I know, but I'd not want to marry you if you were more in love with someone else. Why did you bring her to your house?"

"Elisabeth, I couldn't leave her alone in London."

"There, you see?" said Elisabeth coolly.

"Oh, women," said Harry raggedly.

"We are God's sweeter creatures," said Elisabeth with her most tranquil smile.

"Look here," said Harry, "I'll do this much, I'll think things over. But I know you haven't considered the impossibility of it all and I have."

"Have you, sweet? Then you've considered the possibility as well, haven't you?" Elisabeth's laugh was soft, forgiving and very affectionate. "You know, it's all so terribly intriguing and quite splendid in its way, and I think your Princess very likeable. Harry, we'll say nothing to our parents for a while. You and I, we are the best of friends, aren't we? I've always known that. So have you."

"I think you still need thumping," said Harry.

"What on earth did you say to Elisabeth?" They were his first words to Irena when he got back.

Irena rose up from her chair by the fire. The fire was glowing brightly. A little pulse beat in her throat.

"Oh, have you seen her? She thought she might miss you. Harry, I only told her what you would have told her yourself."

"Oh, the Lord help the unanointed," said Harry helplessly. He knew how expressive she was, how she would have embellished the part he had played. He ran his hand through his hair and looked at her with some of Elisabeth's words drumming in his mind. She had changed into a soft green dress, something else she had bought in France, and he wished that sometimes she would put on rusty old black and not look so lovely. "She's got some bee in her bonnet that there's more to it than there is."

"What is a bee in her bonnet?" she asked, and he thought the whole endearing quality of her appeal was in the way she put that question.

"An odd idea."

"She is suspicious, she is cross?"

"No. As calm as you like."

"Oh. That isn't an awfully good sign." She took up the poker and moved a piece of hot coal. "Oh, she will come round, you will see."

He noticed the coal bucket was full.

"Who filled that?" he asked, pointing.

"I did," she said, "I found where it was kept in the little shed in the garden. And there were some old gloves—"

"My God," said Harry, "you don't have to carry coal in."

"Why not? I am to let the fires go out?" She was quick, nervous, putting the poker back on its stand and straightening the cushion on a chair. "Harry, come and see what I've done in the kitchen, I've polished everything twice over and you have never seen such a shine."

"What the devil have you been doing?" He was brusque.

"I am here, so I've been helping. I am not

going to just sit and do nothing. Harry, you aren't cross, are you?" She glanced anxiously at him. He wasn't dark or scowling, he had the oddest look on his face. "I told Elisabeth everything so that you would not have to explain it all yourself. I was very nice about you, wanting her to be proud of you."

"Oh, she's very proud of me." He sat down. He picked up the poker and jabbed the coals. "My God," he muttered, "I'm at it now."

"Harry? Elisabeth is not very happy?" Irena was tentatively enquiring. "Well, how could she be at first? You did not expect her to laugh about it, did you?"

"No," said Harry, "but she did."

"She laughed?" The little pulse fluttered again. "Harry, she laughed?"

"Yes," said Harry ironically, "I think you can say that."

"How very odd," said Irena.

"You think so, do you?" he said.

He sounded, she thought, as if he intended to provoke a quarrel. That was unfair.

"Yes, I think it very odd," she said. "In her place I would have kicked and scratched."

"Kicked and scratched?" He was mildly amazed.

"But yes. If I were your—if we were—well, I mean, yes, I would pull another woman's hair out."

"Good grief, is that how the Rumanians bring all their princesses up?"

"It's nothing to do with being a princess," said Irena. "Harry, I had to explain to her when she came, I could not simply say nothing. But I should not have thought it would have made her laugh."

"Well, it did. What did you tell her about me?"

Irena managed to re-orientate herself and sit down. Her slim, silk-clad ankles peeped, her pointed black button-up shoes toed into the fireside rug. She smoothed her dress, then clasped her hands in her lap.

"Harry, I told her you had been quite marvellous—"

"Marvellous? Didn't you mention that I'd been bumptious, that I'd ordered you about and bullied you?"

"No, of course not." A little heatedly she said, "She probably knew, there was no need to tell her what she would be aware of. I expect you have bullied her at times."

"I haven't had to. She's never been as obstinate as Your Highness."

"Oh, that is not fair."

"I apologize. Did you tell her we spent two days in London together?"

"No. That would have been silly."

"I appreciate that," said Harry. "You know, to do the right thing by Elisabeth I think we should arrange an immediate annulment."

"Oh." She swallowed. She smoothed her dress again. "Yes, of course," she said with an effort.

"We have to convince her that ours is a relationship due to circumstances, not emotions," he said woodenly, "or she'll insist on making sacrifices."

"Sacrifices?" Her knuckles whitened, her heart began to pump. "What do you mean?"

"Did I say sacrifices? Perhaps that's the wrong word. I mean she'll make gestures, and she'll begin by breaking the engagement."

"What are you saying?" She could not keep emotion out of her voice. "Does she think that we—that you and I—"

"Yes," said Harry, "she does."

She looked up. Their eyes met. Color rushed into her face.

"That is silly," she breathed, "we have done nothing. It isn't as if we have those kind of feelings for each other, as if there was anything that mattered in our marriage."

"Yes, what could be more impossible between us than a real marriage?"

She winced and said, "Mostly you don't even like me."

"What rubbish," said Harry.

"It's true—"

"It's rubbish." Abruptly he got up and went into the kitchen. She was not equipped at that moment to react philosophically to such cursory behavior and she knew she was either going to cry or kick. Pride and spirit triumphed and she stood up, threw her armchair cushion to the floor, hitched her dress and kicked. The cushion flew. Its short flight coincided with a thudding crash from the kitchen. She jumped, then stood transfixed by the awful silence. Oh! The polished kitchen floor, the floor that shone, the blue linoleum that gleamed. Oh, no! She rushed from the room. In the kitchen Harry was lying on his back, his head close to the kitchen range, and he was quite still.

"Harry! Oh, my darling!"

She was down on her knees, distraught, and Harry was opening his eyes. Her color became fiery red. He had heard her anguished endearment, he must have, for he was looking at her so strangely.

Lightly, courageously, covering her mistake, she said, "Oh, you silly darling man, there's no need to throw yourself about, Elisabeth will feel better about it tomorrow." He lay there saying nothing, just looking up at her. Anxiety returned and she said, "Harry, you aren't hurt, are you? Please?"

He smiled in a rueful way.

"You silly darling Princess," he said in reciprocal lightness, "you waxed it."

"Waxed it?" Everything was thumping at her.

"The floor." He got up. He helped her to her feet. He rubbed his head. He winced. She was in such a sensitive state that she felt the hurt herself.

"Please let me see," she said. She did not know what to make of what he had called her, except that it did not seem right for him to have said it without then kissing her.

"It's nothing, just a slight knock," he said.

"I'm so sorry, I polished it too much."

"Never mind," he said. "I'd better go down to the shops."

"I will come with you," she said.

"No, I think not, if you don't mind," said Harry.

She knew he meant that it would not do for them to walk out together, but she was here, and people in the village were aware that she was, so it could hardly matter if she went shopping with him. His attitude dismayed her.

It was no better during the next day or two. There was so much constraint, tension and terrible politeness, a politeness so civilized and English that at times she had a wildly primitive desire to shock him out of it. She knew they could not go on like this. He caught a train to Portlington immediately after breakfast on their fourth morning together, saying he was going to see Elisabeth again and also a solicitor. The annulment had to be taken in hand. Elisabeth could not be left to face the curious questions and pitying glances of friends, neighbors and relatives.

He left her in a state she had never experienced before. She recognized the stranger as sheer misery.

"What have I done?" she asked herself. "What have I done to make him like this? It isn't just Elisabeth. I should never have come, I am in the way and he's beginning to hate me."

Harry returned ninety minutes later. He had got off the train midway to Portlington and waited thirty minutes to catch one back. He walked or, rather, stalked into the sitting-room like a dark, athletic priest who had come to conduct a dialogue with a graceless heretic. The room was empty. The kitchen was empty. The silence was empty. He went to the foot of the stairs.

"Your Highness?" he called, his voice biting.

There was no reply. He climbed to the landing. The bedrooms and the bathroom were unresponsive. The room she had used was neat and tidy, but her clothes were gone, her cases gone.

She was gone.

"Oh, my God," he said.

He would never find her. He thought of a high window. He must go back to the station and find out if she had taken a train to London.

He heard the back door open and close. Swiftly he descended the stairs. She came through the kitchen and into the sitting-room. She was wearing the black coat with a white fur collar and the matching hat, bought in Trieste, and she looked just as she had when she first tried them on. Like a winter princess. Sub-consciously he admitted himself prejudiced because of his feelings for her.

Irena, not expecting to see him, stiffened. And his grim, unsmiling look made her shiver a little.

"What d'you think you're doing?" he asked.

"I am going," she said.

"I think not," said Harry, "at least not yet." The front door shook to a loud knocking.

"There is a trap outside which has taken me trouble to find," said Irena, "and that is the driver to collect my things."

"Is it? Is it indeed," said Harry and went to the door. He saw the trap waiting. He paid the man off for his time and his lost fare. He returned to the sitting-room. Irena stood in proud aloofness but trembling perceptibly.

"What have you done?" she asked.

"Sent him away."

"How dared you? You cannot keep me here. If I wish to go, I will go."

"Incidentally, where are your things?" asked Harry.

"In the dining-room. I am quite packed up, thank you, and I intend to go." She was at her proudest. It cut no ice with Harry.

"I didn't look in the dining-room," he said, "but never mind that for the moment."

"I do mind. I am going." She attempted to sweep past him. He put himself in her way. "Captain Phillips, you are forgetting yourself."

He returned her proud look with one of uncompromising grimness. It sent new shivers down her back. What terrible thing had she done now?

"Until I find out whether you're an out-of-work Rumanian actress or Mata Hari's most promising pupil, you're staying here," he said.

And suddenly Irena had a dreadful feeling that an earthquake was about to engulf her.

"Oh, no," she said faintly, "oh, no."

"Oh, yes," he said, "I've something here I want you to see." He produced a newspaper he had bought on his way to the station. "I was reading this on the train. It made me get out before I'd reached Portlington. I caught the next train back. Would you care to glance at it?" He showed her a small paragraph on the second page. She saw the headline.

"ROYAL EXILE LEAVES FOR AMERICA."

There was a photograph, a portrait of a young woman not unlike herself, a formal portrait similar to the one Major Carlsen had shown Harry, although it had lost something in its coarse-screened newsprint reproduction. The paragraph under the headline referred to the departure of Princess Irena of Moldavia from Cherbourg to New York, the Princess stating that certain circumstances were forcing her into exile in the United States.

Irena prayed desperately for an earthquake to happen. She read the item twice, taking time to adjust herself to the tearing, shattering quarrel that was utterly inevitable. She prayed again, for salvation.

"I am ill," she gasped and sat heavily down.

"Ill?" Harry's eyes glinted. "No tricks, madam. Stand up and look me in the face."

"Oh, how can I?" She was in despair. "You will strike me."

"Fortunately for you I've gone past that. Did you and Major Carlsen enjoy making a fool out of me?"

Indescribably wounded by that she gave a tragic moan. Harry sensed her performance was going to be rivetting.

"Oh, God forgive you for even thinking that," she gasped.

Harry responded with a look which to Irena was doomladen. She shuddered.

"You witch," he said.

"Harry!"

"You've had me on the end of your string since we first met. By God, the nerve of your Major. What a cool pair of lovebirds the two of you are."

"Oh, how can you say such things! You are making me die!"

"I'm sure you'll expire very realistically," said Harry. She moaned again. "Why not tell me who you really are, why not be sincere with me for a change and tell me your story? Are you an actress?"

Irena, pale with guilt and despair, was not

sure just how hard he was going to be on her, but to be called an actress!

"How dare you think that!" Her spirit flashed.

"Madam," said Harry, sitting down opposite her and tapping her knees with the rolled-up newspaper, "kindly realize calamity has struck and that you're poised over a yawning gap. No more lines from your field of drama, if you please. Just the truth."

"Oh, Harry, this is awful, awful," she gasped, "I've been dreading it. Oh, please don't look so angry. I would have told you, I wanted to so much, but I promised Major Carlsen never to breathe a word to anyone until it was known that Princess Irena was safe. And at least I really *am* Sonya Irena Helene Magda Ananescu."

"How touching," said Harry. "I count myself fortunate in nipping your sly little getaway in the bud. I ought to get some satisfaction from cornering you, my flash young flyaway."

"Oh, that's a dreadful thing to say, and I was not going because of this but because you dislike me so."

"Really?"

"Yes." She was in sheer unhappiness. Never had she seen him so cold. She prayed again. "Harry, I will tell you."

"Proceed, madam."

"I am Sonya Irena, truly," she said earnestly. "I was at school in Switzerland when I was seventeen and I met Princess Irena there. We are the same age. My father is a Rumanian banker. Irena and I became friends. She is a brave person, very outspoken, never afraid to say what she thinks, and if she was mistaken about some things, well, we all are at times, aren't we? She truly believed the defeat of Germany and Austria would be the worst possible thing for Europe, and she said so. I think I believe that too. She has not been a traitor to Rumania but she has been made to look so, to sound so."

"Go on," said Harry impassively.

"Yes, I will." She cast him a quick, nervous glance, her long lashes agitatedly fluttering. "Oh, you are believing me, aren't you?"

"You haven't said anything yet," observed Harry.

"In Bucharest she and I met Major Carlsen. He admired her at once and she admired him. He was sure she would lose her life unless she got away, far away, and so he thought up the idea of having me pose as the Princess and going off with you, and having her enemies chase after us. Because her enemies said she loved the Germans they would think it natural for her to run from Bucharest with a man they thought was a German colonel. They watched Irena night and day and were suspicious of Major Carlsen, thinking he would be the one most likely to get her away. So you see, he had this idea of making Michalides and others think it was the Princess who left the house with you that night. I was afraid it had gone wrong the moment Michalides spoke to us, but you see, he was so sure I was Irena that he did not bother to pull me out of the cab and take a good look at me. It was very dark, you remember, yes? In the cab even darker, yes? And I am quite like Irena in appearance."

"I see," said Harry, "you were the decoy very neatly paired off with the dupe."

"That is unkind." She was more controlled

now and just a little proud even. She was sure she was going to sink without trace, but she was not going to go down crying her eyes out. And it was a relief to confess it all at last. "Yes, I was the decoy. But no, never once did I think of you as the dupe. And Major Carlsen may have deceived you but he admired you very much in the end."

"Impressed by my simple charm, no doubt."

"Harry, I am so unhappy, please don't make it worse for me."

"Forgive me if I sound unreasonable. But please go on."

"Major Carlsen did admire you, believe me," she insisted. "But he did not completely know you, he would not risk telling you everything. He made me promise to say nothing about the real Irena. I kept that promise. After you and I had taken that cab to Chitila, he got away in his civilian clothes with her. By then Michalides and his men were running about looking for you and me. When Major Carlsen met me in that cafe in Belgrade—"

"By arrangement?"

"Yes. He told me then that he had Princess Irena safely out of sight for the moment, and he wanted you and me to stay in Belgrade long enough to keep Michalides occupied until he received orders which would enable him to take Irena out of the city. He received them quite soon. She was on that train to Zagreb, disguised as one of the peasant women. Those poor women did not know what it was all about. He did not risk getting on the train at Belgrade but at that little station. He had seen those women on his way there and had simply placed them under arrest, telling them they were to go to Zagreb. But, of course, it was so that he could hide Princess Irena among them, and when we reached Vrycho he put them off there. The ambush was a dreadful shock and worry to him, and you can imagine how he admired you for getting the train through. He got off at Vrycho too, with Princess Irena."

"No wonder he didn't appear when we reached Zagreb," said Harry. He pondered while Irena's heart went up and down. "Yes, it's making sense," he said, "I felt there was something too obvious about that flashing torch and standing cab. He wanted Michalides to suspect that something was up. He had to take the risk that you'd be found out. That would have been a disappointment, but nothing would have been lost and he'd have tried again with another scheme, or a different version of this one."

"Yes, that is right," she said, "but Michalides was taken in and began to chase us. And, you see, when you knocked him out in the cab that was the best thing you could have done to convince him I was the Princess, especially after making him think it was something to do with your secret service. You were very good, Harry."

"I'd been sucked in myself by that time. Carry on."

"Well, you see," she said, flushed and still earnest, "it left Major Carlsen free to go off with Irena, except that he disliked it when he found us on that train to Zagreb. It put us too close to him and Irena, and it was close, wasn't it, because Michalides had that awful girl Nadia watching us. Major Carlsen got over the danger of that by slipping away at Vrycho, though he did not know about Nadia. He only suspected someone might be on board, keeping an eye on us. He was right."

"What a Prussian fox," said Harry. "Now I understand why you were never recognized. You weren't the Princess. No wonder you didn't bother to hide your face at times, and why you were never in a hurry. You knew I was the man Michalides had marked as the Princess's escort, and while I was around the comrades were around too, and Major Carlsen was getting farther away with the prize."

"You are terribly angry?" she said unhappily.

"I'm sick," said Harry, "that neither of you confided in me."

Her flush deepened.

"Oh, I am sorry—"

"Go on, you haven't finished yet."

"At least you do not have to be angry with yourself," she said. "You see, you did help Princess Irena, even if not in quite the way you thought. Yes?" She tried a desperate little smile. It evoked a look of dark suspicion, as if he thought she was about to be devious. It made her heart feel painfully squeezed. "Oh, the woman who saw me in the shop at Trieste, she knew who I really was, of course. So did Count Alberto in Padua. I had such awful moments then, not because of the plan but because of what you would think and say if either of them had made you realize I wasn't Princess Irena, just Sonya Irena. And you would not have taken me to England."

"Would that have mattered?"

Her mouth trembled and her unhappy eyes dropped.

"Harry, I have had terrible times wondering what you would think. I—"

"Would it have mattered, my not taking you to England?"

"Oh, please, I can't answer that," she said.

"Continue," he said.

"You saw Irena once, though you did not know. She was the housemaid who let you in that night and witnessed the wedding. When Michalides at last realized I was not her, he must have guessed Major Carlsen had tricked him."

"Yes," said Harry, "his friends in Zagreb found you out and would have informed him. That was why they were shouting at you. Damn it, of course. They knew you weren't the Princess, they wanted you to tell them where she was. Is that right?"

"Oh, yes. You have been right so many times. You are maddeningly clever, Harry."

He received that little piece of soft soap without comment. He was damned, all the same, by the hold she had on him. Elisabeth was right. Affectionate friendship was satisfying, but it was not enough.

"What am I going to do with you?" he said.

She perceived a little ray of hope.

"Oh, please forgive me, won't you?" Her brown eyes begged him. "I told you the other evening I was in a mess. I knew you would find out in the end and I was praying to hear that Irena was all right so that I could confess to you first."

"Wait a moment." Harry had a new dark

thought. "There's something not quite right. Damn it, yes. Once they'd found you out in Zagreb what was the point of you running any farther? They weren't going to be after you any more. You could have remained there."

"No," she said emotionally.

"Why not?"

She searched desperately for words.

"You see," she said, having found some, "they would have wanted to get hold of me again and made me tell them things."

"In Padua, then? You could have stayed in Padua."

She had to engage in another search.

"Oh, it was lovely in Padua, wasn't it?" she said with tremulous irrelevance.

"So why didn't you stay there instead of coming to England? Damn it," said Harry, "we didn't even have to get married."

"But we did," she gasped, "how could I have got into England except as your wife?"

"Look at me," said Harry. She lifted downcast lashes and looked at him. He had never seen such guilt. "Shall we have all the truth? We might as well, don't you think?"

"Oh, please, I can't," she said.

"You can and you will," said Harry.

"But you will never forgive me," she breathed.

"I'll try to be Christianlike," said Harry.

"Oh, you are going to be so angry and I am going to be so miserable." She took a deep breath. "You see, Harry, you see, Major Carlsen said that once we reached Trieste—he was sure you would go there—I did not need to go any farther. He said you would be able to make the rest of your escape easily from there, and that by then he should have had Irena well on the way to safety. All the real danger for me was between Bucharest and Trieste. He said that from Trieste—oh, Harry, please don't make me say any more."

"Tell me," said Harry mercilessly.

"No," she gasped.

"Tell me."

"Oh, you are giving me a dreadful time. Harry, Major Carlsen said I would be able to get back to Rumania from Trieste without too much difficulty if I wanted to. I did not have to be an exile myself."

"So?"

With an effort she whispered, "I was to leave you in Trieste."

"I see. To slip away? No goodbyes?" He was smiling at last, but it was a smile that made her shudder. "You'd have left a note, I suppose?"

"Oh, please don't look at me like that, I am enduring an awful time, and you are hating me for deceiving you."

"Why didn't you slip away, may I ask?"

The crimson suffused her face.

"Oh, how can I tell you that? You must know why." She put her gloved hands to her hot face. "I could not help myself, I had to come with you, even though there was Elisabeth."

"Why?"

"Oh," She shook her head, then plunged into admission. "Did you think that after being with you on that train, after that wonderful moment in Zagreb and after being with you in

Padua, I could simply turn round and go back to Rumania? Oh, Harry, please be kind, I am so in love."

"You're grateful, I expect—"

"Grateful? No!"

"—and we both have Elisabeth to think about."

"Yes. Yes, I know. But you see," she said in her desperation, "I thought when she knew how we had been together, all the way from Bucharest, and that we were married—Harry, I thought she would kick and scream and have nothing more to do with you."

"Good God," said Harry and wondered if this was the way the minds of all Balkan people worked. If so, that would account for their fractious politics and irrational behaviour.

"But she isn't like that, is she?" Irena's clasped hands were trembling in her lap. He felt completely and incurably in love with her, he felt pangs for her. He had given her a hard time. "Harry, does it take very long to fall out of love?"

"I don't know," said Harry, "but my parents are still known to hold hands occasionally." He wondered if he had had all the story. He felt something still had to fall into place. Something that nagged at him but which he could not put his finger on. "Whose jewels have you been carrying?"

"Irena's truly. Except the pearls. They are mine. You see, if they had caught her they would have taken everything from her. Major Carlsen knew that if they caught me they would only be angry, they would not have suspected I had her jewellry. I'm to keep it until I hear from her. She will get in touch with my parents in Bucharest."

"Why your parents?"

"But you see it was supposed I would return to Rumania from Trieste sooner or later but not go to Bucharest until it had all died down and her enemies did not wish to bother with me any more. I was to go to our country house in Moldavia and keep in touch with my parents from there."

Harry's dark look finally faded. She was a remarkable young woman. She had taken tremendous risks in helping Princess Irena. It had put her on the wrong side with the extremists. They would have put her name on their lists.

"You've been carrying more than those diamonds for her?"

"Yes, much more," she said, turning her eyes on the fire and seeing only miserable pictures in the flames.

"You lost two of your pearls to Captain Sabata."

"Yes," she said, "but I would have given him all of them as long as it meant I could still be with you. I am sorry, I know I must not be in love with you. But I am."

"There's something still not quite right," said Harry, "I still can't see why we had to get married. Sonya Irena, are you sure you've told me everything?"

She kept her eyes on the fire as she said, "I have tried to. It was Major Carlsen's idea that we must be married. He was sure it would convince you of the desperate danger Irena was in, that it would make you commit yourself like a true officer and gentleman."

Harry hid a smile.

"Heavens," he said, "mine is only a wartime

commission. There's a difference, as any regular officer will tell you."

"Major Carlsen did not seem to think so. And the marriage really was necessary if things went terribly wrong and I did have to continue on to England with you. He said there was always the risk the extremists would still come after me. Oh, Harry, it is right, isn't it, I am in such a mess. It is awful to be so much in love."

"I've found it very trying," said Harry. "Tomorrow I'm going to look over a farm I'm interested in. It shouldn't be too long before I'm out of the Army. Would you like to come and look it over with me? Perhaps, if you don't mind being a farmer's wife, you'd better come. I wouldn't want to make an offer for it unless we both liked it."

Irena lifted her eyes. They were huge in their disbelief. Harry was smiling.

"Harry?" she said faintly.

"You were beautiful at Romano's, Sonya Irena, did you know that?"

"Oh, something is happening, isn't it?" Her heart was hammering. "Something wonderful? Oh, I could not bear it if you were joking. You are saying you love me, aren't you?"

"I think the happening occurred when I saw you through all that soot."

"Oh, say it, Harry, please say it," she begged.

"That I love you? Well, I love you, don't you know that? Why do you think I brought you here? I couldn't part with you, but I didn't know what the devil I was going to do with you. Good God, I thought, what can any ordinary man do with a princess except keep her in a glass case?"

"Oh, Harry!" She was rapturously emotional.

"You aren't joking? I am really to be your wife?"

"You are my wife, and as Elisabeth and I have discovered we're just very good friends, it sounds serious to me. A princess would have been impossible, you'll be lovely."

He stood up, took her hands and brought her to her feet. Her brown eyes were swimming. She fell into his arms. Her hat lost its bearings and the kisses were very erratic until the communication of warm love prevailed.

"I am being kissed?" she gasped, pausing for breath.

"I think so," said Harry.

"It is not before time. Oh, it's lovely, isn't it?" She was richly alive in her delight. "I mean, after being so dreadful to me, now you are being wonderful. I am losing my head."

"That's your hat," he said. She laughed, flung her hat off and hugged him. "Now," he said, "if you're really sure you've told me everything—?"

"Oh, yes," she said with feeling, "except have I told you I love you? Oh, you have no idea, I—"

"Hold on," said Harry. The nebulous, nagging something had suddenly crystallized into being. He held her at arm's length and looked into her shining eyes. "There is something else, isn't there? Tell me, young lady, if you had decided to slip away at Trieste, what was going to happen to the annulment? I'd have been left in a fine fix trying to get myself unmarried to you and married to Elisabeth. And just how would you have got on if you'd met someone else?"

Lashes swept down to cover the last guilty secret, but the telltale flush was all too visible. She pressed herself back into his arms and hid her face in his shoulder. She took her deepest breath and rushed muffledly into ingenious confession. "Darling, I was just going to say I should be so glad if we could be married soon. Do you think tomorrow?"

"Oh, my God," said Harry.

"Harry." She pressed closer, as desperate now as she had ever been. "Oh, you must be forgiving, darling, this is my most terrible moment of all. You see, we aren't really married. It was all done to impress you and to make us look married if I had to go to England with you, and I did have to, I could not bear you leaving me. But I would not have risked marrying a man I did not really know, not even for Princess Irena. So they faked the ceremony and the certificate. But wasn't it wonderful that they did? I should not have got into England otherwise—" She stopped, not because she had no more words but because Harry seemed so frigidly unreceptive. She held on frantically to him, certain that if she let him push her away she would never get close to him again.

"I'm speechless," said Harry.

She shivered. She said, "Harry, it was all for Princess Irena, and Major Carlsen said there would be times when it would be easier if I were your wife."

"But you never were."

"No, oh, I know, but I was supposed to be. We had the marriage certificate and your people passed it when we landed. So we were almost nearly married. Harry? Oh, please don't be angry, please don't send me away."

Suddenly he was laughing. She unwound

herself and looked at him. And she knew he was not going to send her away. The blissful relief drowned her.

"I'm damned if this doesn't beat everything," he said. "You witch, you'll get me hanged."

"Hanged?" she gasped, but he was still laughing. "Oh, how was I to know what would happen, that you would make me fall in love with you?"

"Make you?" Harry was beginning to realize she had her own sense of logic.

"Yes," she said. "Well, you should not have been so gallant, so masterful." Her return to rapture made her teasingly imaginative. "You should not have bundled me about. It is dangerous to bundle any woman about, it makes her feel she is the object of special care and devotion, and she simply will not let you go. When it happened to me—"

"Just a moment," said Harry. He could not let her ride on clouds, she must be brought down to earth. "Sonya Irena, do you want to be a farmer's wife?"

"Oh, more than anything, as long as the farmer is you."

"Then I should tell you it's not going to be like dancing at Padua or Romano's. It's going to be very hard work. For both of us. I'd like to have you with me because I love you in a way I don't think I could love another woman, but I wonder if I'm asking too much of you."

She became intense in her reaction to that.

"You think I have never really known hard work?"

"Have you?"

397

"No. My father is rich, you see. But then I have never really known life, either. I did not begin to live until I promised to help Princess Irena and met you. You are not going to ask me to stop living because you feel it would be nicer for me in a glass case, are you? Or because you feel I could not work hard? You know I could, you are just trying to say to me, 'Sonya Irena, take care, think seriously if this is what you want.' Well, it is. It is. Oh, perhaps I will kick and scream sometimes, but please please don't have doubts about what I want. I want you."

He remembered her courage, her resourcefulness. He smiled.

"I think you'll do very well," he said, "I think we'll both do very well, but you won't have time to kick and scream."

"Harry, of course we will do well, we shall be together." She looked very intently at the top button of his jacket. A little breathlessly she said, "And we can't farm night and day, darling, there has to be time for some other things."

"Ah," said Harry. "I'll do my best," he added.

"You had better if we are going to have four children. And we have time now to kiss again, yes?"

"I think so," said Harry, "I think there should always be time for that, Sonya Irena."

"Oh, it's wonderful, isn't it?" said Sonya Irena after only a short time.

It was emotional as well. So much so that she was crying her eyes out, as Elisabeth had known she would.

OUTSTANDING READING
FROM WARNER BOOKS

PASSION STAR
by Julia Grice
(91-498, $2.50)

The sapphire was called the Passion Star. It was stone-mined by men and polished to brilliance—but to Adrienne McGill the six-spurred Passion Star was both magic charm and mystic curse. It transported her out of the slums of Glasgow to training and stardom on the stage. But the girl with the radiantly pale blonde hair had stolen the treasure in the throes of rape. Now she must pay for her deed with her heart...

AMERICAN ROYAL
by Anne Rudeen
(81-827, $2.50)

They had loved each other once . . . but with a youthful passion that consumed them; now Selena, more beautiful than ever, was a rich widow whose husband nearly had become President of the United States. And Hank was now a racing car magnate who had agreed, without knowing his parentage, to let Selena's son Blair race for him. For a race that may be the beginning or the end.

THE BEACH CLUB
by Claire Howard
(91-616, $2.50)

Have fun in the sun with . . . Laurie: a smouldering redhead whose husband, down from the city only on weekends, brings along a teenage babysitter bursting out of her bikini and out of bounds; B. J.: sharp-tongued rich girl who trapped her husband into marriage and herself into a swinging scene; Sandy: the loving wife whose husband has so much love in him it just overflows—to other women; and Jan: the plain girl whose husband lost interest in her as soon as her father took him into the business. It's hot in the sun and getting hotter for the four couples exposing bodies, secrets and passions under the umbrellas at THE BEACH CLUB.

CARVER'S KINGDOM
by Frederick Nolan
(81-201, $2.50)

Sarah Hutchinson, married to an irresponsible wanderer when Theo Carver, the merchant adventurer, first met her, loved her and lost her. Sarah Hutchinson, who irrevocably changed the lives of the ruthless brothers who had wrestled riches and power from expanding America . . . the men of CARVER'S KINGDOM.

PULSE-RACING, PASSIONATE, ADVENTURE-FILLED FICTION

CASABLANCA INTRIGUE
by Clarissa Ross   (91-027, $2.50)

Morocco, 1890. Beautiful Gale Cormier is on her honeymoon. Her husband is talking to a dark man in a red fez . . . at least, he was a moment ago. Now she is alone as a curious crowd moves in upon her . . . examining . . . begging . . . menacing . . .

CARESS AND CONQUER
by Donna Comeaux Zide   (82-949, $2.25)

She was Cat Devlan, a violet-eyed, copper-haired beauty bent on vengeance. She was a living challenge to Ryan Nicholls, but was she the mistress of a pirate as she claimed when they first met? Or the favorite of the King of France? . . . and a Murderess?

LIBERTY TAVERN
by Thomas Fleming   (91-220, $2.50)

The American Revolution is love and hate, a beautiful woman, flogged for loving a Royalist. It is a young idealist who murders in the cause of liberty. "A big historical novel with a bracing climate of political sophistication."

—*New York Times Book Review*

The world has changed and so has Bond, James Bond.
#1 international and *New York Times* bestselling author

Jeffery Deaver

brings 007, the greatest spy of all time,
into the twenty-first century with
this page-turning global suspense blockbuster

CARTE BLANCHE

"Ian Fleming was a master of succinct plotting and deft characterization. . . . Deaver too is a genius and this publishing marriage was truly made in heaven. Bond fans will enjoy Deaver's slightly mischievous take on Ian Fleming."

—*The Sunday Express* (London)

"A magnificently manic, impeccably researched and at times gory plot, with Deaver's trademark misdirection and twists flying."

—*The Washington Post*

"Fantastic. . . . Deaver knows psychology and it shines here. Moreover, he knows human relationships . . . Jeffery Deaver truly *got it*."

—*Ann Arbor News* (MI)

This title is also available as an eBook

"Bond fans should be satisfied with the rollicking pace of 007's new adventure. Deaver is a master of the twist in the tale and he deploys it here with cinematic verve, keeping the reader biting their nails until the last minute. . . . Deaver's Bond is quite recognizably Bond, but a new, streamlined incarnation for a new generation of global fears."

—*The Guardian* (UK)

More international acclaim for *Carte Blanche*

"A master of misdirection . . . Deaver has clearly done his homework. . . . The most impressive feature of *Carte Blanche* is the ingenuity of the breathless, bloodthirsty plot. . . . Kingsley Amis, John Gardner, and Sebastian Faulks are among those who have tried to bring Bond back to life. Deaver, though, is in a class of his own: nobody's done it better."

—*The Evening Standard* (London)

"Could Deaver assume Fleming's identity rather than write another Jeffery Deaver novel only with a hero called Bond? And could he resist [the] current obsession with relentless action inspired by the success of the Bourne movie franchise—and indeed *Quantum of Solace*? The answers are emphatically 'Yes.' Deaver preserves his book's timeless feel . . . [and] adds a series of twists that reveal a Bond with more Sherlockian intelligence than Fleming's."

—*The Telegraph* (London)

"Ian Fleming's estate tapped Deaver, and the pairing is as smooth as vodka and vermouth. Yes, the villains are creepy and the women brainy and beautiful, but in a clever reboot, this 007 (who served in Afghanistan) comes armed with a tricked-out cell phone and an appealing sense of empathy."

—*Parade*

"His creator may be long gone, but James Bond (with his gadgets, women, and suave lines) lives on in the skillful hands of a suspense superstar."

—Malcolm Jones, *Newsweek*

"Crucially, the novel proves itself worthy of the 007 logo by presenting us with one of the most bone-chillingly creepy bad guys in history. . . . Deaver's immaculate sense of pace comes into its own. While giving Bond fans enough of the trinkets they deserve, he also keeps the narrative pacey throughout and still allows our hero a few crucial moments of modern self-reflection. . . . It's hard to imagine anyone not being impressed by this novel."

—*The Independent* (UK)

"It's a tightrope walk, balancing the tradition with the requirements of contemporary life, and Deaver handles it with panache. . . . But what the Fleming aficionado will inevitably notice here are the differences, which turn this latest escapade into what feels, and should feel, like one of those things that are very popular these days: a reboot."

—Olen Steinhauer, author of *The Tourist, The Nearest Exit, The Bridge of Sighs,* and *Victory Square*

"The story's a corker. . . . Deaver never tries to imitate the style used by Bond creator Ian Fleming, but despite the book's modern setting and paraphernalia (Bond still carries a Walther pistol, but he also carries a cell phone), it feels just right."

—*The Chronicle Herald* (Canada)

CARTE BLANCHE

THE NEW JAMES BOND NOVEL
JEFFERY DEAVER

POCKET STAR BOOKS

New York   London   Toronto   Sydney   New Delhi

Pocket Star Books
A Division of Simon & Schuster, Inc.
1230 Avenue of the Americas
New York, NY 10020

This book is a work of fiction. Names, characters, places, and incidents either are products of the author's imagination or are used fictitiously. Any resemblance to actual events or locales or persons, living or dead, is entirely coincidental.

This Pocket Star Books export edition February 2012

James Bond and 007 are registered trademarks of Danjaq LLC used under license by Ian Fleming Publications Ltd.

POCKET STAR BOOKS and colophon are registered trademarks of Simon & Schuster, Inc.

For information about special discounts for bulk purchases, please contact Simon & Schuster Special Sales at 1-866-506-1949 or business@simonandschuster.com.

The Simon & Schuster Speakers Bureau can bring authors to your live event. For more information or to book an event, contact the Simon & Schuster Speakers Bureau at 1-866-248-3049 or visit our website at www.simonspeakers.com.

Manufactured in the United States of America

10 9 8 7 6 5 4 3 2 1

ISBN 978-1-4516-6424-9
ISBN 978-1-4516-2167-9 (ebook)

*To the man who taught us we could still
believe in heroes, Ian Fleming*

Author's Note

This is a work of fiction, although for authenticity I have referred to real places, a few famous historical figures, and some well-known brands, such as Audi, Bentley, InterContinental, iPhone, Mercedes, Maserati, and Oakley. Also, with a few exceptions, the intelligence organizations referred to are real. By contrast, all of the characters, their companies, and their actions in the book are entirely fictional, and any similarity to any real company or living person is purely coincidental.

The world of intelligence, counterintelligence, and espionage is one of acronyms and shorthand. Since the alphabet soup of security agencies can be a bit daunting, I thought a glossary might prove helpful. It appears at the end of the book.

J.D.

"What is needed is a new organization to coordinate, inspire, control, and assist the nationals of the oppressed countries. . . . We need absolute secrecy, a certain fanatical enthusiasm, willingness to work with people of different nationalities, and complete political reliability. The organization should, in my view, be entirely independent of the War Office machinery."

—Hugh Dalton, Minister of Economic Warfare, describing the formation of Britain's Special Operations Executive espionage and sabotage group at the outbreak of the Second World War

Sunday

The Red Danube

Chapter 1

His hand on the dead-man throttle, the driver of the Serbian Rail diesel felt the thrill he always did on this particular stretch of railway, heading north from Belgrade and approaching Novi Sad.

This was the route of the famed Arlberg Orient Express, which ran from Greece through Belgrade and points north from the 1930s until the 1960s. Of course, he was not piloting a glistening Pacific 231 steam locomotive towing elegant mahogany-and-brass dining cars, suites and sleepers, where passengers floated upon vapors of luxury and anticipation. He commanded a battered old thing from America that tugged behind it a string of more or less dependable rolling stock packed snugly with mundane cargo.

But still he felt the thrill of history in every vista that the journey offered, especially as they approached the river, *his* river.

And yet he was ill at ease.

Among the wagons bound for Budapest, containing coal, scrap metal, consumer products and timber, there was one that worried him greatly. It was loaded with drums of MIC—methyl isocyanate—to be used in Hungary in the manufacture of rubber.

The driver—a round, balding man in a well-worn cap and stained overalls—had been briefed at length about this deadly chemical by his supervisor and some idiot from the Serbian Safety and Well-being Transportation Oversight Ministry. Some years ago this substance had killed eight thousand people in Bhopal, India, within a few days of leaking from a manufacturing plant there.

He'd acknowledged the danger his cargo presented but, a veteran railway man and union member, he'd asked, "What does that mean for the journey to Budapest . . . specifically?"

The boss and the bureaucrat had regarded each other with the eyes of officialdom and, after a pause, settled for "Just be very careful."

The lights of Novi Sad, Serbia's second-largest city, began to coalesce in the distance, and ahead in the encroaching evening the Danube appeared as a pale stripe. In history and in music the river was celebrated. In reality it was brown, undramatic and home to barges and tankers, not candlelit vessels filled with lovers and Viennese orchestras—or not here, at least. Still, it *was* the Danube, an icon of Balkan pride, and the railway man's chest always swelled as he took his train over the bridge.

His river . . .

He peered through the speckled windscreen and inspected the track before him in the headlight of the General Electric diesel. Nothing to be concerned about.

There were eight notch positions on the throttle, number one being the lowest. He was presently at five and he eased back to three to slow the train as it entered a series of turns. The 4,000-horsepower engine grew softer as it cut back the voltage to the traction motors.

As the cars entered the straight section to the

bridge the driver shifted up to notch five again and then six. The engine pulsed louder and faster and there came a series of sharp clangs from behind. The sound was, the driver knew, simply the couplings between wagons protesting at the change in speed, a minor cacophony he'd heard a thousand times in his job. But his imagination told him the noise was the metal containers of the deadly chemical in car number three, jostling against one another, at risk of spewing forth their poison.

Nonsense, he told himself and concentrated on keeping the speed steady. Then, for no reason at all, except that it made him feel better, he tugged at the air horn.

Chapter 2

Lying at the top of a hill, surrounded by obscuring grass, a man of serious face and hunter's demeanor heard the wail of a horn in the distance, miles away. A glance told him that the sound had come from the train approaching from the south. It would arrive here in ten or fifteen minutes. He wondered how it might affect the precarious operation that was about to unfurl.

Shifting position slightly, he studied the diesel locomotive and the lengthy string of wagons behind it through his night-vision monocular.

Judging that the train was of no consequence to himself and his plans, James Bond turned the scope back to the restaurant of the spa and hotel and once again regarded his target through the window. The weathered building was large, yellow stucco with brown trim. Apparently it was a favorite with the locals, from the number of Zastava and Fiat saloons in the car park.

It was eight forty and the Sunday evening was clear here, near Novi Sad, where the Pannonian Plain rose to a landscape that the Serbs called "mountainous," though Bond guessed the adjective must have been chosen to attract tourists; the rises were mere hills to him, an avid skier. The May air was dry and cool, the surroundings as quiet as an undertaker's chapel of rest. Bond shifted position again. In his thirties, he was six feet tall and weighed

170 pounds. His black hair was parted on one side and a comma of loose strands fell over one eye. A three-inch scar ran down his right cheek.

This evening he'd taken some care with his outfit. He was wearing a dark green jacket and rainproof trousers from the American company 5.11, which made the best tactical clothing on the market. On his feet were well-worn leather boots that had been made for pursuit and sure footing in a fight.

As night descended, the lights to the north glowed more intensely: the old city of Novi Sad. As lively and charming as it was now, Bond knew the place had a dark past. After the Hungarians had slaughtered thousands of its citizens in January 1942 and flung the bodies into the icy Danube, Novi Sad had become a crucible for partisan resistance. Bond was here tonight to prevent another horror, different in nature but of equal or worse magnitude.

Yesterday, Saturday, an alert had rippled through the British intelligence community. GCHQ, in Cheltenham, had decrypted an electronic whisper about an attack later in the week.

> meeting at noah's office, confirm
> incident friday night, 20th, estimated
> initial casualties in the thousands, british
> interests adversely affected, funds
> transfers as discussed.

Not long after, the government eavesdroppers had also cracked part of a second text message, sent from the same phone, same encryption algorithm, but to a different number.

meet me sunday at restaurant rostilj
outside novi sad, 20:00. i am 6+ feet tall,
irish accent.

Then the Irishman—who'd courteously, if inad-
vertently, supplied his own nickname—had destroyed
the phone or flicked out the batteries, as had the other
text recipients.

In London the Joint Intelligence Committee and
members of COBRA, the crisis management body,
met into the night to assess the risk of Incident 20, so
called because of Friday's date.

There was no solid information on the origin or
nature of the threat but MI6 was of the opinion that
it was coming out of the tribal regions in Afghanistan,
where al-Qaeda and its affiliates had taken to hir-
ing Western operatives in European countries. Six's
agents in Kabul began a major effort to learn more.
The Serbian connection had to be pursued, too. And
so at ten o'clock last night the rangy tentacles of these
events had reached out and clutched Bond, who'd
been sitting in an exclusive restaurant off Charing
Cross Road with a beautiful woman, whose lengthy
description of her life as an underappreciated painter
had grown tiresome. The message on Bond's mobile
had read, NIACT, Call COS.

The Night Action alert meant an immediate response was required, at whatever time it was received.
The call to his chief of staff had blessedly cut the date
short and soon he had been en route to Serbia, under
a Level 2 project order, authorizing him to identify the
Irishman, plant trackers and other surveillance devices
and follow him. If that proved impossible, the order

authorized Bond to conduct an extraordinary rendition of the Irishman and spirit him back to England or to a black site on the Continent for interrogation.

So now Bond lay among white narcissi, taking care to avoid the leaves of that beautiful but poisonous spring flower. He concentrated on peering through the Restoran Roštilj's front window, on the other side of which the Irishman was sitting over an almost untouched plate and talking to his partner, as yet unidentified but Slavic in appearance. Perhaps because he was nervous, the local contact had parked elsewhere and walked here, providing no number-plate to scan.

The Irishman had not been so timid. His low-end Mercedes had arrived forty minutes ago. Its plate had revealed that the vehicle had been hired today for cash under a false name, with a fake British driving license and passport. The man was about Bond's age, perhaps a bit older, six foot two and lean. He'd walked into the restaurant in an ungainly way, his feet turned out. An odd line of blond fringe dipped over a high forehead and his cheekbones angled down to a square-cut chin.

Bond was satisfied that this man was the target. Two hours ago he had gone into the restaurant for a cup of coffee and stuck a listening device inside the front door. A man had arrived at the appointed time and spoken to the headwaiter in English—slowly and loudly, as foreigners often do when talking to locals. To Bond, listening through an app on his phone from thirty yards away, the accent was clearly mid-Ulster—most likely Belfast or the surrounding area. Unfortunately the meeting between the Irishman and his local contact was taking place out of the bug's range.

Through the tunnel of his monocular, Bond now studied his adversary, taking note of every detail— "Small clues save you. Small errors kill," as the instructors at Fort Monckton were wont to remind. He noted that the Irishman's manner was precise and that he made no unnecessary gestures. When the partner drew a diagram the Irishman moved it closer with the rubber of a propelling pencil so that he left no fingerprints. He sat with his back to the window and in front of his partner; the surveillance apps on Bond's mobile could not read either set of lips. Once, the Irishman turned quickly, looking outside, as if triggered by a sixth sense. The pale eyes were devoid of expression. After some time he turned back to the food that apparently didn't interest him.

The meal now seemed to be winding down. Bond eased off the hillock and made his way through widely spaced spruce and pine trees and anemic undergrowth, with clusters of the ubiquitous white flowers. He passed a faded sign in Serbian, French and English that had amused him when he'd arrived:

SPA AND RESTAURANT ROŠTILJ

LOCATED IN A DECLARED THERAPEUTIC
REGION, AND IS RECOMMENDED BY
ALL FOR CONVALESCENCES AFTER
SURGERIES, ESPECIALLY HELPING FOR
ACUTE AND CHRONIC DISEASES OF
RESPIRATION ORGANS, AND ANEMIA.
FULL BAR.

He returned to the staging area, behind a decrepit garden shed that smelled of engine oil, petrol and piss, near the driveway to the restaurant. His two "comrades," as he thought of them, were waiting here.

James Bond preferred to operate alone but the plan he'd devised required two local agents. They were with the BIA, the Serbian Security Information Agency, as benign a name for a spy outfit as one could imagine. The men, however, were undercover in the uniform of local police from Novi Sad, sporting the golden badge of the Ministry of Internal Affairs.

Faces squat, heads round, perpetually unsmiling, they wore their hair close-cropped beneath navy-blue brimmed caps. Their woolen uniforms were the same shade. One was around forty, the other twenty-five. Despite their cover roles as rural officers, they'd come girded for battle. They carried heavy Beretta pistols and swaths of ammunition. In the backseat of their borrowed police car, a Volkswagen Jetta, there were two green-camouflaged Kalashnikov machine guns, an Uzi and a canvas bag of fragmentation hand grenades—serious ones, Swiss HG 85s.

Bond turned to the older agent but before he spoke he heard a fierce slapping from behind. His hand moving to his Walther PPS, he whirled round—to see the younger Serb ramming a pack of cigarettes into his palm, a ritual that Bond, a former smoker, had always found absurdly self-conscious and unnecessary.

What was the man *thinking*?

"Quiet," he whispered coldly. "And put those away. No smoking."

Perplexity sidled into the dark eyes. "My brother, he smokes all time he is out on operations. Looks more normal than *not* smoking in Serbia." On the drive here the young man had prattled on and on about his brother, a senior agent with the infamous JSO, technically a unit of the state secret service, though Bond knew it was really a black-ops paramilitary group. The young agent had let slip—probably intentionally, for he had said it with pride—that big brother had fought with Arkan's Tigers, a ruthless gang that had committed some of the worst atrocities in the fighting in Croatia, Bosnia and Kosovo.

"Maybe on the streets of Belgrade a cigarette won't be noticed," Bond muttered, "but this is a tactical operation. Put them away."

The agent slowly complied. He seemed about to say something to his partner, then thought better of it, perhaps recalling that Bond had a working knowledge of Serbo-Croatian.

Bond looked again into the restaurant and saw that the Irishman was laying some dinars on the metal tray—no traceable credit card, of course. The partner was pulling on a jacket.

"All right. It's time." Bond reiterated the plan. In the police car they would follow the Irishman's Mercedes out of the drive and along the road until he was a mile or so from the restaurant. The Serbian agents would then pull the car over, telling him it matched a vehicle used in a drug crime in Novi Sad. The Irishman would be asked politely to get out and would be handcuffed. His mobile phone, wallet and identity papers would be placed on the boot of the Mercedes and he'd be led aside and made to sit facing away from the car.

Meanwhile Bond would slip out of the backseat, photograph the documents, download what he could from the phone, look through laptops and luggage, then plant tracking devices.

By then the Irishman would have caught on that this was a shakedown and offered a suitable bribe. He'd be freed to go on his way.

If the local partner left the restaurant with him, they'd execute essentially the same plan with both men.

"Now, I'm ninety percent sure he'll believe you," Bond said. "But if not, and he engages, remember that under no circumstances is he to be killed. I need him alive. Aim to wound in the arm he favors, near the elbow, not the shoulder." Despite what one saw in the movies, a shoulder wound was usually as fatal as one to the abdomen or chest.

The Irishman now stepped outside, feet splayed. He looked around, pausing to study the area. Was anything different? he'd be thinking. New cars had arrived since they'd entered; was there anything significant about them? He apparently decided there was no threat and both men climbed into the Mercedes.

"It's the pair of them," Bond said. "Same plan."

"*Da.*"

The Irishman started the engine. The lights flashed on.

Bond oriented his hand on his Walther, snug in the D. M. Bullard leather pancake holster, and climbed into the backseat of the police car, noticing an empty tin on the floor. One of his comrades had enjoyed a Jelen Pivo, a Deer Beer, while Bond had been conducting surveillance. The insubordination bothered him less than the carelessness. The Irishman might grow suspicious when stopped by a cop with beer on his breath. Another man's ego and greed can be helpful, Bond believed, but incompetence is simply a useless and inexcusable danger.

The Serbs got into the front. The engine hummed to life. Bond tapped the earpiece of his SRAC, the short-range agent communication device used for cloaked radio transmissions on tactical operations. "Channel two," he reminded them.

"*Da, da.*" The older man sounded bored. They both plugged in earpieces.

And James Bond asked himself yet again: Had he planned this properly? Despite the speed with which the operation had been put together, he'd spent hours formulating the tactics. He believed he'd anticipated every possible variation.

Except one, it appeared.

The Irishman did not do what he absolutely had to. He didn't leave.

The Mercedes turned *away* from the drive and rolled out of the car park on to the lawn beside the restaurant, on the other side of a tall hedge, unseen by the staff and diners. It was heading for a weed-riddled field to the east.

The younger agent snapped, "*Govno!* What he is doing?" The three men stepped out to get a better view. The older one drew his gun and started after the car.

Bond waved him to a halt. "No! Wait."

"He's escaping. He knows about us!"

"No—it's something else." The Irishman wasn't driving as if he were being pursued. He was moving slowly, the Mercedes easing forward, like a boat in a gentle morning swell. Besides, there was no place to escape *to*. He was hemmed in by cliffs overlooking the Danube, the railway embankment and the forest on the Fruška Gora rise.

Bond watched as the Mercedes arrived at the rail track, a hundred yards from where they stood. It slowed, made a U-turn and parked, the bonnet facing back toward the restaurant. It was close to a railway work shed and switch rails, where a second track peeled off from the main line. Both men climbed out and the Irishman collected something from the boot.

Your enemy's purpose will dictate your response—Bond silently recited another maxim from the lectures at Fort Monckton's Specialist Training Center in Gosport. You must find the adversary's intention.

But what *was* his purpose?

Bond pulled out the monocular again, clicked on the night vision and focused. The partner opened a panel mounted on a signal beside the switch rails and began fiddling with the components inside. Bond saw that the second track, leading off to the right, was a rusting, disused spur, ending in a barrier at the top of a hill.

So it was sabotage. They were going to derail the train by shunting it on to the spur. The cars would tumble down the hill into a stream that flowed into the Danube.

But why?

Bond turned the monocular toward the diesel engine and the wagons behind it and saw the answer. The first two cars contained only scrap metal, but behind them a canvas-covered flatbed was marked OPASNOST–DANGER! He saw, too, a hazardous-materials diamond, the universal warning sign that told emergency rescuers the risks of a particular shipment. Alarmingly, this diamond had high numbers for all three categories: health, instability and inflammability. The *W* at the bottom meant that the substance would react dangerously with water. Whatever was being carried in that car was in the deadliest category, short of nuclear materials.

The train was now three-quarters of a mile away from the switch rails, picking up speed to make the gradient to the bridge.

Your enemy's purpose will dictate your response. . . .

He didn't know how the sabotage related to Incident 20, if at all, but their immediate goal was clear—as was the response Bond now instinctively formulated. He said to the comrades, "If they try to leave, block them at the drive and take them. No lethal force."

He leaped into the driver's seat of the Jetta. He pointed the car toward the fields where he'd been conducting surveillance and jammed down the accelerator as he released the clutch. The light car shot forward, engine and gearbox crying out at the rough treatment, as it crashed over brush, saplings, narcissi and the raspberry bushes that grew everywhere in Serbia. Dogs fled and lights in the tiny cottages nearby flicked on. Residents in their gardens waved their arms angrily in protest.

Bond ignored them and concentrated on maintaining his speed as he drove toward his destination, guided only by scant illumination: a partial moon above and the doomed train's headlight, far brighter and rounder than the lamp of heaven.

Chapter 3

The impending death weighed on him.

Niall Dunne crouched among weeds, thirty feet from the switch rails. He squinted through the fading light of early evening at the Serbian Rail driver's cab of the freight train as it approached and he again thought: a tragedy.

For one thing, death was usually a waste and Dunne was, first and foremost, a man who disliked waste—it was almost sinful. Diesel engines, hydraulic pumps, drawbridges, electric motors, computers, assembly lines . . . all machines were meant to perform their tasks with as little waste as possible.

Death was efficiency squandered.

Yet there seemed to be no way around it tonight.

He looked south, at the glistening needles of white illumination on the rails from the train's headlight. He glanced round. The Mercedes was out of sight of the train, parked at just the right angle to keep it hidden from the cab. It was yet another of the precise calculations he had incorporated into his blueprint for the evening. He heard, in memory, his boss's voice.

This is Niall. He's brilliant. He's my draftsman . . .

Dunne believed he could see the shadow of the driver's head in the cab of the diesel. Death . . . He tried to shrug away the thought.

The train was now four or five hundred yards away. Aldo Karic joined him.

"The speed?" Dunne asked the middle-aged Serb. "Is it all right? He seems slow."

In syrupy English the Serbian said, "No, is good. Accelerating now—look. You can see. Is good." Karic, a bearish man, sucked air through his teeth. He'd seemed nervous throughout dinner—not, he'd confessed, because he might be arrested or fired but because of the difficulty in keeping the ten thousand euros secret from everyone, including his wife and two children.

Dunne regarded the train again. He calculated speed, mass, incline. Yes, it *was* good. At this point even if someone tried to wave the train down, even if a Belgrade supervisor happened to notice something was amiss, phoned the driver and ordered him to apply full brakes, it would be physically impossible to stop the train before it hit the switch rails, now configured to betray.

And he reminded himself: Sometimes death is necessary.

The train was now three hundred yards away.

It would all be over in ninety seconds. And then—

But what was this? Dunne was suddenly aware of movement in a field nearby, an indistinct shape pounding over the uneven ground making directly for the track. "Do you see that?" he asked Karic.

The Serbian gasped. "Yes, I am seeing— It's a car! What is happening?"

It was indeed. In the faint moonlight Dunne could see the small, light-colored saloon, assaulting hillocks and swerving around trees and fragments of fences. How could the driver keep his high speed on such a course? It seemed impossible.

Teenagers, perhaps, playing one of their stupid games. As he stared at the mad transit, he judged velocity, he judged angles. If the car didn't slow it would cross the track with some seconds to spare . . . but the driver would have to vault over the tracks themselves; there was no crossing here. If it were stuck on the rail, the diesel would crush it like a tin of vegetables. Still, that wouldn't affect Dunne's mission here. The tiny car would be pitched aside and the train would continue to the deadly spur.

Now—wait—what was *this*? Dunne realized it was a police car. But why no lights or siren? It must have been stolen. A suicide?

But the police car's driver had no intention of stopping on the rail or crossing to the other side. With a final leap into the air from the crest of hill, the saloon crashed to earth and skidded to a stop, just short of the roadbed, around fifty yards in front of the train. The driver jumped out—a man. He was wearing dark clothing. Dunne couldn't see him clearly but he appeared not to be a policeman. Neither was he trying to flag down the engine driver. He ran into the middle of the track itself and crouched calmly, directly in front of the locomotive, which bore down upon him at fifty or sixty miles an hour.

The frantic blare of the train's horn filled the night and orange streaks of sparks shot from the locked wheels.

With the train feet away from him, the man launched himself from the track and vanished into the ditch.

"What is happening?" Karic whispered.

Just then a yellow-white flash burst from the tracks

in front of the diesel and a moment later Dunne heard
a crack he recognized: the explosion of a small IED or
grenade. A similar blast followed seconds later.

The driver of the police car, it seemed, had a blueprint of his own.

One that trumped Dunne's.

No, he wasn't a policeman or a suicide. He was an
operative of some sort, with experience in demolition
work. The first explosion had blown out the spikes fixing the rail to the wooden ties, the second had pushed
the unsecured track to the side slightly so that the diesel's front left wheels would slip off.

Karic muttered something in Serbian. Dunne ignored him and watched the disc of the diesel's headlight waver. Then, with a rumble and a terrible squeal,
the engine and the massive wagons it tugged behind
sidled off the track and, spewing a world of dust,
pushed forward through the soil and chipped rock of
the rail bed.

Chapter 4

From the ditch, James Bond watched the locomotive and the cars continue their passage, slowing as they dug into the soft earth, peeling up rails and flinging sand, dirt and stones everywhere. Finally he climbed out and assessed the situation. He'd had only minutes to work out how to avert the calamity that would send the deadly substance into the Danube. After braking to a stop, he'd grabbed two of the grenades the Serbians had brought with them, then leaped onto the tracks to plant the devices.

As he had calculated, the locomotive and wagons had stayed upright and hadn't toppled into the stream. He'd orchestrated *his* derailment where the ground was still flat, unlike the intended setting of the Irishman's sabotage. Finally, hissing, groaning and creaking, the train came to a standstill not far from the Irishman and his partner, though Bond could not see them through the dust and smoke.

He spoke into the SRAC radio. "This is Leader One. Are you there?" Silence. "Are you there?" he growled. "Respond." Bond massaged his shoulder, where a piece of whistling shrapnel had torn through his jacket and sliced skin.

A crackle. Finally: "The train is derailed!" It was the older Serbian's voice. "Did you see? Where are you?"

"Listen to me carefully."

"What has happened?"

"Listen! We don't have much time. I think they'll try to blow up or shoot the hazmat containers. It's their only way to spill the contents. I'm going to fire toward them and drive them back to their car. Wait till the Mercedes is in that muddy area near the restaurant, then shoot out the tires and keep them inside it."

"We should take them now!"

"No. Don't do anything until they're beside the restaurant. They'll have no defensive position inside the Mercedes. They'll have to surrender. Do you understand me?"

The SRAC went dead.

Damn. Bond started forward through the dust toward the place where the third railcar, the one containing the hazardous material, waited to be ripped open.

Niall Dunne tried to reconstruct what had happened. He'd known he might have to improvise but this was one thing he had not considered: a preemptive strike by an unknown enemy.

He looked out carefully from his vantage point, a stand of bushes near where the locomotive sat, smoking, clicking and hissing. The assailant was invisible, hidden by the darkness of night, the dust and fumes. Maybe the man had been crushed to death. Or fled. Dunne lifted the rucksack over his shoulder and made his way round the diesel to the far side, where the derailed wagons would give him cover from the intruder—if he was still alive and present.

In a curious way, Dunne found himself relieved of his nagging anxiety. The death had been averted.

He'd been fully prepared for it, had steeled himself—anything for his boss, of course—but the other man's intervention had settled the matter.

As he approached the diesel he couldn't help but admire the massive machine. It was an American General Electric Dash 8–40B, old and battered, as you usually saw in the Balkans, but a classic beauty, 4,000 horsepower. He noted the sheets of steel, the wheels, vents, bearings and valves, the springs, hoses and pipes . . . all so beautiful, elegant in simple functionality. Yes, it was such a relief that—

He was startled by a man staggering toward him, begging for help. It was the train driver. Dunne shot him twice in the head.

It was such a relief that he hadn't been forced to cause the death of this wonderful machine, as he'd been dreading. He ran his hand along the side of the locomotive, as a father would stroke the hair of a sick child whose fever had just broken. The diesel would be back in service in a few months' time.

Niall Dunne hitched the rucksack higher on his shoulder and slipped between the wagons to get to work.

Chapter 5

The two shots James Bond had heard had not hit the hazardous-materials car—he was covering that from thirty yards away. He guessed the engine driver and perhaps his mate had been the victims.

Then, through the dust, he saw the Irishman. Gripping a black pistol, he stood between the two jackknifed wagons filled with scrap metal directly behind the engine. A rucksack hung from his shoulder. It seemed to be full, which meant that if he intended to blow up the hazardous-material containers, he hadn't set the charges yet.

Bond aimed his pistol and fired two shots close to the Irishman, to drive him back to the Mercedes. The man crouched, startled, then vanished fast.

Bond looked toward the restaurant side of the track, where the Mercedes was parked. His mouth tightened. The Serbian agents hadn't followed his orders. They were now flanking the work shed, having pulled the Irishman's Slavic associate to the ground and slipped nylon restraints around his wrists. The two were now moving closer to the train.

Incompetence . . .

Bond scrabbled to his feet and, keeping low, ran toward them.

The Serbs were pointing at the tracks. The rucksack now sat on the ground, among some tall plants near the engine, obscuring a man. Crouching, the agents moved forward cautiously.

The bag was the Irishman's . . . but, of course, the man behind it was not. The driver's body, probably.

"No," Bond whispered into the SRAC. "It's a trick! . . . Are you there?"

But the older agent wasn't listening. He stepped forward, shouting, "*Ne mrdaj!* Do not move!"

At that moment the Irishman leaned out of the engine's cab and fired a burst from his pistol, hitting him in the head. He dropped hard.

His younger colleague assumed that the man on the ground was firing and emptied his automatic weapon into the dead body of the driver.

Bond shouted, "*Opasnost!*"

But it was too late. The Irishman now shot the younger agent in the right arm, near the elbow. He dropped his gun and cried out, falling backward.

As the Irishman leaped from the train, he let go half a dozen rounds toward Bond, who returned fire, aiming for the feet and ankles. But the haze and vapors were thick; he missed. The Irishman holstered his gun, shouldered the rucksack and dragged the younger agent toward the Mercedes. They disappeared.

Bond sprinted back to the Jetta, jumped in and sped off. Five minutes later he soared over a hillock and landed, skidding, in the field behind Restoran Roštilj. The scene was one of complete chaos as diners and staff fled in panic. The Mercedes was gone. Glancing at the derailed train, he could see that the Irishman had killed not only the older agent but his own associate—the Serbian he'd dined with. He'd shot him as he'd lain on his belly, hands bound.

Bond got out of the Jetta and frisked the body for pocket litter but the Irishman had stripped the man of his wallet and any other material. Bond pulled out his own Oakley sunglasses, wiped them clean, then pressed the dead man's thumb and index finger against the lens. He ran back to the Jetta and sped after the Mercedes, urging the car to seventy miles an hour despite the meandering road and potholes pitting the tarmac.

A few minutes later he glimpsed something light-colored in a lay-by ahead. He braked hard, barely controlling the fishtailing skid, and stopped, the car engulfed in smoke from its tires, a few yards from the younger agent. He got out and bent over the man, who was shivering, crying. The wound in his arm was bad and he'd lost a great deal of blood. One shoe was off and a toenail was gone. The Irishman had tortured him.

Bond opened his folding knife, cut the man's shirt with the razor-sharp blade and bound a wool strip round his arm. With a stick he found just off the lay-by he made a tourniquet and applied it. He leaned down and wiped sweat from the man's face. "Where is he going?"

Gasping, his face a mask of agony, he rambled in Serbo-Croatian. Then, realizing who Bond was, he said, "You will call my brother. . . . You must take me to the hospital. I will tell you a place to go."

"I need to know where he went."

"I didn't say nothing. He tried. But I didn't tell nothing about you."

The boy had spilt out everything he knew about the operation, of course, but that wasn't the issue now. Bond said, "Where did he go?"

"The hospital . . . Take me and I will tell you."

"Tell me or you'll die in five minutes," Bond said evenly, loosening the tourniquet on his right arm. Blood cascaded.

The young man blinked away tears. "All right! You bastard! He ask how to get to E Seven-five, the fast road from Highway Twenty-one. That will take him to Hungary. He is going north. Please!"

Bond tightened the tourniquet again. He knew, of course, that the Irishman wasn't going north: The man was a cruel and clever tactician. He didn't need directions. Bond saw his own devotion to tradecraft in the Irishman. Even before he had arrived in Serbia the man would have memorized the geography around Novi Sad. He'd go *south* on Highway 21, the only major road nearby. He'd be making for Belgrade or an evacuation site in the area.

Bond patted the young agent's pockets and pulled out his mobile. He hit the emergency call number, 112. When he heard a woman's voice answer, he propped the phone beside the man's mouth, then ran back to the Jetta. He concentrated on driving as fast as he could over the uneven road surface, losing himself in the choreography of braking and steering.

He took a turn fast and the car skidded, crossing the white line. An oncoming lorry loomed, a big one, with a Cyrillic logo. It veered away and the driver hit the horn angrily. Bond swerved back into his lane, missing a collision by inches, and continued in pursuit of the only lead they had to Noah and the thousands of deaths on Friday.

Five minutes later, approaching Highway 21, Bond slowed. Ahead he saw a flicker of orange and, in the sky, roiling smoke, obscuring the moon and stars. He soon arrived at the accident site. The Irishman had missed a sharp bend and sought refuge in what seemed to be a wide grass shoulder but in fact was not. A line of brush masked a steep drop. The car had gone over and was now upside down. The engine was on fire.

Bond pulled up, killed the Jetta's motor and got out. Then, drawing the Walther, he half ran, half slid down the hill to where the vehicle lay, scanning for threats and seeing none. As he closed on it he stopped. The Irishman was dead. Still strapped into the seat, he was inverted, arms dangling over his shoulders. Blood covered his face and neck and pooled on the car's ceiling.

Squinting against the fumes, Bond kicked in the driver's window to drag the body out. He would salvage the man's mobile and what pocket litter he could, then wrench open the boot to collect luggage and laptops.

He opened his knife again to cut the seat belt. In the distance: the urgent *wah-ha* of sirens, growing louder. He looked back up the road. The fire engines were still a few miles away but they'd be here soon. Get on with it! The flames from the engine were increasingly energetic. The smoke was vile.

As he began to saw away at the belt, though, he thought suddenly: Firefighters? Already?

That made no sense. Police, yes. But not the fire brigade. He gripped the driver's bloodied hair and turned the head.

It was not the Irishman. Bond gazed at the man's jacket: The Cyrillic lettering was the same as on the lorry he'd nearly hit. The Irishman had forced the vehicle to stop. He'd cut the driver's throat, strapped him into the Mercedes and sent it over the cliff here, then called the local fire service in order to slow the traffic and prevent Bond pursuing him.

The Irishman would have taken the rucksack and everything else from the boot, of course. Inside the car, though, on the inverted ceiling, toward the back-seat, there were a few scraps of paper. Bond jammed them into his pockets before the flames forced him away. He ran back to the Jetta and sped off toward Highway 21, away from the approaching flashing lights.

He fished out his mobile. It resembled an iPhone but was a bit larger and featured special optics, audio systems and other hardware. The unit contained multiple phones—one that could be registered to an agent's official or nonofficial cover identity, then a hidden unit, with hundreds of operational apps and encryption packages. (Because the device had been de-veloped by Q Branch it had taken all of a day for some wit in the office to dub them "iQPhones.")

He opened an app that gave him a priority link to a GCHQ tracking center. He recited into the voice-recognition system a description of the yellow Zastava Eurozeta lorry the Irishman was driving. The com-puter in Cheltenham would automatically recognize Bond's location and determine projected routes for the truck, then train the satellite to look for any nearby vehicle of this sort and track it.

Five minutes later he heard his phone buzz. Excel-lent. He glanced at the screen.

But the message was not from the snoops; it was from Bill Tanner, chief of staff at Bond's outfit. The subject heading said:

CRASH DIVE.

Shorthand for Emergency. Eyes flipping from the road to the phone, Bond read on.

> GCHQ intercept: Serbian security agent
> assigned to you in Incident 20 operation
> died on way to hospital. Reported you
> abandoned him. Serbs have priority order
> for your arrest. Evacuate immediately.

Monday

The
Rag-and-Bone Man

Chapter 6

After three and a half hours' sleep James Bond was woken at 7 A.M. in his Chelsea flat by the electronic tone of his mobile phone's alarm clock. His eyes focused on the white ceiling of the small bedroom. He blinked twice and, ignoring the pain in his shoulder, head and knees, rolled out of the double bed, prodded by the urge to get on the trail of the Irishman and Noah.

His clothes from the mission to Novi Sad lay on the hardwood floor. He tossed the tactical outfit into a training kit bag, gathered up the rest of his clothes and dropped them into the laundry bin, a courtesy to May, his treasure of a Scottish housekeeper who came three times a week to sort out his domestic life. He would not think of having her pick up his clutter.

Naked, Bond walked into the bathroom, turned on the shower as hot as he could stand it and scrubbed himself hard with unscented soap. Then he turned the temperature down, stood under freezing water until he could tolerate *that* no longer, stepped out and dried himself. He examined his wounds from last night: two large, aubergine-colored bruises on his leg, some scrapes and the slice on his shoulder from the grenade shrapnel. Nothing serious.

He shaved with a heavy, double-bladed safety razor, its handle of light buffalo horn. He used this fine accessory not because it was greener to the envi-

ronment than the plastic disposables that most men
employed but simply because it gave a better shave—
and required some skill to wield; James Bond found
comfort even in small challenges.

By seven fifteen he was dressed: a navy-blue
Canali suit, a white sea island shirt and a burgundy
grenadine tie, the latter items from Turnbull &
Asser. He donned black shoes, slip-ons; he never
wore laces, except for combat footwear or when
tradecraft required him to send silent messages to a
fellow agent via prearranged loopings.

Onto his wrist he slipped his steel Rolex Oyster
Perpetual, the 34-mm model, date window its only
complication; Bond did not need to know the phases
of the moon or the exact moment of high tide at
Southampton. And he suspected very few people did.

Most days he had breakfast—his favorite meal of
the day—at a small hotel nearby in Pont Street. Occasionally he cooked for himself one of the few things he
was capable of whipping up in the kitchen: three eggs
softly scrambled with Irish butter. The steaming curds
were accompanied by bacon and crisp wholemeal toast,
with more Irish butter and marmalade.

Today, though, the urgency of Incident 20 was in
full bloom so there was no time for food. Instead he
brewed a cup of fiercely strong Jamaica Blue Mountain coffee, which he drank from a china mug as he
listened to Radio 4 to learn whether or not the train
incident and subsequent deaths had made the international news. They had not.

His wallet and cash were in his pocket, his car key,
too. He grabbed the plastic carrier bag of the items
he had collected in Serbia and the locked steel box

that contained his weapon and ammunition, which he could not carry legally within the UK.

He hurried down the stairs of his flat—formerly two spacious stables. He unlocked the door and stepped into the garage. The cramped space was large enough, just, for the two cars that were inside, plus a few extra tires and tools. He climbed into the newer of the vehicles, the latest-model Bentley Continental GT, its exterior the company's distinctive granite gray, with supple black hide inside.

The turbo W12 engine murmured to life. Tapping the downshift paddle into first gear, he eased into the road, leaving behind his other vehicle, less powerful and more temperamental but just as elegant: a 1960s E-type Jaguar, which had been his father's.

Driving north, Bond maneuvered through the traffic, with tens of thousands of others who were similarly making their way to offices throughout London at the start of yet another week—although, of course, in Bond's case this mundane image belied the truth.

Exactly the same could be said for his employer itself.

Three years ago, James Bond had been sitting at a gray desk in the monolithic gray Ministry of Defense building in Whitehall, the sky outside not gray at all but the blue of a Highland loch on a bright summer's day. After leaving the Royal Naval Reserve, he had had no desire for a job managing accounts at Saatchi & Saatchi or reviewing balance sheets for NatWest and had telephoned a former Fettes fencing teammate, who had suggested he try Defense Intelligence.

After a stint at DI, writing analyses that were described as both blunt and valuable, he had wondered to his supervisor if there might be a chance to see a little more action.

Not long after that conversation, he had received a mysterious missive, handwritten, not an e-mail, requesting his presence for lunch in Pall Mall, at the Travellers Club.

On the day in question, Bond had been led into the dining room and seated in a corner opposite a solid man in his midsixties, identified only as "the Admiral." He wore a gray suit that perfectly matched his eyes. His face was jowled and his head crowned with a sparse constellation of birthmarks, evident through the thinning, swept-back brown and gray hair. The Admiral had looked steadily at Bond without challenge or disdain or excessive analysis. Bond had no trouble returning the gaze—a man who has killed in battle and nearly died himself is not cowed by anyone's stare. He realized, however, that he had absolutely no idea what was going on in the man's mind.

They did not shake hands.

Menus descended. Bond ordered halibut on the bone, steamed, with hollandaise, boiled potatoes and grilled asparagus. The Admiral selected the grilled kidney and bacon, then asked Bond, "Wine?"

"Yes, please."

"You choose."

"Burgundy, I should think," Bond said. "Côte de Beaune? Or a Chablis?"

"The Alex Gambal Puligny, perhaps?" the waiter suggested.

"Perfect."

The bottle arrived a moment later. The waiter smoothly displayed the label and poured a little into

Bond's glass. The wine was the color of pale butter, earthy and excellent, and exactly the right temperature, not too chilled. Bond sipped, nodded his approval. The glasses were half filled.

When the waiter had departed, the older man said gruffly, "You're a veteran and so am I. Neither of us has any interest in small talk. I've asked you here to discuss a career opportunity."

"I thought as much, sir." Bond hadn't intended to add the final word but it had been impossible not to do so.

"You may be familiar with the rule at the Travellers about not exposing business documents. Afraid we'll have to break it." The older man withdrew from his breast pocket an envelope. He handed it over. "This is similar to the Official Secrets Act declaration."

"I've signed one—"

"Of course you have—for Defense Intelligence," the man said briskly, revealing an impatience at stating the obvious. "This has a few more teeth. Read it."

Bond did so. More teeth indeed, to put it mildly.

The Admiral said, "If you're not interested in signing we'll finish our lunch and discuss the recent election or trout fishing in the north or how those damn Kiwis beat us again last week and get back to our offices." He lifted a bushy eyebrow.

Bond hesitated only a moment, then scrawled his name across the line and handed it back. The document vanished.

A sip of wine. The Admiral asked, "Have you heard of the Special Operations Executive?"

"I have, yes." Bond had few idols, but high on the list was Winston Churchill. In his young days as a reporter and soldier in Cuba and Sudan, Churchill had formed a great respect for guerrilla operations and later, after the outbreak of the Second World War, he and the minister for economic warfare, Hugh Dalton, had created the SOE to arm partisans behind German lines and to parachute in British spies and saboteurs. Also called Churchill's Secret Army, it had caused immeasurable harm to the Nazis.

"Good outfit," the Admiral said, then grumbled, "They closed it down after the war. Interagency nonsense, organizational difficulties, infighting at MI6 and Whitehall." He took a sip of the fragrant wine and conversation slowed while they ate. The meal was superb. Bond said so. The Admiral rasped, "Chef knows what he's about. No aspirations to cook his way onto American television. Are you familiar with how Five and Six got going?"

"Yes, sir—I've read quite a lot about it."

In 1909, in response to concerns about a German invasion and spies within England (concerns that had been prompted, curiously, by popular thriller novels), the Admiralty and the War Office had formed the Secret Service Bureau. Not long after that, the SSB split into the Directorate of Military Intelligence Section 5, or MI5, to handle domestic security, and Section 6, or MI6, to handle foreign espionage. Six was the oldest continuously operating spy organization in the world, despite China's claim to the contrary.

The Admiral said, "What's the one element that stands out about them both?"

Bond couldn't begin to guess.

"Plausible deniability," the older man muttered. "Both Five and Six were created as cutouts so that the Crown, the prime minister, the Cabinet and the War Office didn't have to get their hands dirty with that nasty business of spying. Just as bad now. Lot of scrutiny of what Five and Six do. Sexed-up dossiers, invasion of privacy, political snooping, rumors of illegal targeted killings . . . Everybody's clamoring for *transparency.* Of course, no one seems to care that the face of war is changing, that the other side doesn't play by the rules much anymore." Another sip of wine. "There's thinking, in some circles, that *we* need to play by a different set of rules too. Especially after Nineeleven and Seven-seven."

Bond said, "So, if I understand correctly, you're talking about starting a new version of the SOE but one that isn't technically part of Six, Five or the MoD."

The Admiral held Bond's eye. "I read those reports of your performance in Afghanistan—Royal Naval Reserve, yet still you managed to get yourself attached to forward combat units on the ground. Took some doing." The cool eyes regarded him closely. "I understand you also managed some missions behind the lines that weren't quite so official. Thanks to you, some fellows who could have caused quite a lot of mischief never got the chance."

Bond was about to sip from his glass of Puligny Montrachet, the highest incarnation of the chardonnay grape. He set the glass down without doing so. How the devil had the old man learned about *those?*

In a low, even voice the man said, "There's no shortage of Special Air or Boat Service chaps about who know their way around a knife and sniper rifle. But they don't necessarily fit into other, shall we say, *subtler* situations. And then there are plenty of tal-

ented Five and Six fellows who know the difference
between"—he glanced at Bond's glass—"a Côte de
Beaune and a Côte de Nuits and can speak French
as fluently as they can Arabic—but who'd faint at the
sight of blood, theirs or anyone else's." The steel eyes
zeroed in. "You seem to be a rather rare combination
of the best of both."

The Admiral put down his knife and fork on the
bone china. "Your question."

"My . . . ?"

"About a new version of the Special Operations
Executive. The answer is yes. In fact, it already exists.
Would you be interested in joining?"

"I would," Bond said without hesitation. "Though
I should like to ask: What exactly does it do?"

The Admiral thought for a moment, as if polishing
burrs off his reply. "Our mission," he said, "is simple.
We protect the Realm . . . by any means necessary."

Chapter 7

In the sleek, purring Bentley, Bond now approached the headquarters of this very organization, near Regent's Park, after half an hour of the zigzagging that driving in central London necessitates.

The name of his employer was nearly as vague as that of the Special Operations Executive: the Overseas Development Group. The director-general was the Admiral, known only as M.

Officially the ODG assisted British-based companies in opening or expanding foreign operations and investing abroad. Bond's OC, or official cover, within it was as a security and integrity analyst. His job was to travel the world and assess business risks.

No matter that the moment he landed he assumed an NOC—a *nonofficial* cover—with a fictitious identity, tucked away the Excel spreadsheets, put on his 5.11 tactical outfit and armed himself with a .308 rifle with Nikon Buckmasters scope. Or perhaps he'd slip into a well-cut Savile Row suit to play poker with a Chechnyan arms dealer in a private Kiev club, for the chance to assess his security detail in a run-up to the evening's main event: the man's rendition to a black site in Poland.

Tucked away inconspicuously in the hierarchy of the Foreign and Commonwealth Office, the ODG was housed in a narrow, six-story Edwardian building on a quiet road, just off Devonshire Street. It was separated from bustling Marylebone Road by lackluster—but camouflaging—solicitors' quarters, NGO offices and doctors' surgeries.

Bond now motored to the entrance of the tunnel leading to the car park beneath the building. He glanced into the iris scanner, then was vetted again, this time by a human being. The barrier lowered and he eased the car forward in search of a parking bay.

The lift, too, checked Bond's blue eyes, then took him up to the ground floor. He stepped into the armorer's office, beside the pistol range, and handed the locked steel box to redheaded Freddy Menzies, a former corporal in the SAS and one of the finest firearms men in the business. He would make sure the Walther was cleaned, oiled and checked for damage, the magazines filled with Bond's preferred loads.

"She'll be ready in half an hour," Menzies said. "She behave herself, 007?"

Bond had professional affection for certain tools of his trade but he didn't personify them—and, if anything, a .40-caliber Walther, even the compact Police Pistol Short, would definitely be a "he." "Acquitted itself well," he replied.

He took the lift to the third floor, where he stepped out and turned left, walking down a bland, white-painted corridor, the walls a bit scuffed, their monotony broken by prints of London from the era of Cromwell through Victoria's reign and of battlefields aplenty. Someone had brightened up the windowsills with vases of greenery—fake, of course; the real thing would have meant employing external maintenance staff to water and prune.

Bond spotted a young woman in front of a desk at

the end of a large open area filled with workstations. Sublime, he had thought, upon meeting her a month ago. Her face was heart-shaped, with high cheekbones, and surrounded by Rossetti-red hair that cascaded from her marvelous temples to past her shoulders. A tiny off-center dimple, which he found completely charming, distressed her chin. Her hazel eyes, golden green, held yours intently, and to Bond, her figure was as a woman's should be: slim and elegant. Her un-painted nails were trimmed short. Today she was in a knee-length black skirt and an apricot shirt, high-necked, yet thin enough to hint at lace beneath, man-aging to be both tasteful and provocative. Her legs were embraced by nylon the color of café au lait.

Stockings or tights? Bond couldn't help but wonder.

Ophelia Maidenstone was an intelligence ana-lyst with MI6. She was stationed with the ODG as a liaison officer because the Group was not an in-telligence-gathering organization; it was operational, tactical, largely. Accordingly, like the Cabinet and the prime minister, it was a consumer of "product," as intelligence was called. And the ODG's main sup-plier was Six.

Admittedly, Philly's appearance and forthright manner were what had initially caught Bond's atten-tion, just as her tireless efforts and resourcefulness had held it. Equally alluring, though, was her love of driv-ing. Her favorite vehicle was a BSA 1966 Spitfire, the A65, one of the most beautiful motorcycles ever made. It wasn't the most powerful bike in the Birmingham Small Arms line but it was a true classic and, when properly tuned (which, God bless her, she did herself), it left a broad streak of rubber at the takeoff line. She'd told Bond she liked to drive in all weather and had bought an insulated leather jumpsuit that let her take to the roads whenever she fancied. He'd imagined it as an extremely tight-fitting garment and arched an eyebrow. He'd received in return a sardonic smile, which told him that his gesture had ricocheted like a badly placed bullet.

She was, it emerged, engaged to be married. The ring, which he'd noted immediately, was a deceptive ruby.

So, that settled that.

Philly now looked up with an infectious smile. "James, hello! . . . Why are you looking at me like that?"

"I need you."

She tucked back a loose strand of hair. "Delighted to help if I could but I've got something on for John. He's in Sudan. They're about to start shooting."

The Sudanese had been fighting the British, the Egyptians, other nearby African nations—and themselves—for more than a hundred years. The Eastern Alliance, several Sudanese states near the Red Sea, wanted to secede and form a moderate secular country. The regime in Khartoum, still buffeted by the recent independence movement in the south, was not pleased by this initiative.

Bond said, "I know. I was the one going originally. I drew Belgrade instead."

"The food's better," she said, with studied gravity. "If you like plums."

"It's just that I collected some things in Serbia that should be looked into."

"It's never 'just' with you, James."

Her mobile buzzed. She frowned, peering at the screen. As she took the call, her piercing hazel eyes swung his way and regarded him with some humor. She said, into the phone, "I see." When she had disconnected, she said, "You pulled in some favors. Or bullied someone."

"Me? Never."

"It seems that war in Africa will have to soldier on without me. So to speak." She went to another workstation and handed the Khartoum baton to a fellow spook.

Bond sat down. There seemed to be something different about her space but he couldn't work out what it was. Perhaps she'd tidied it or rearranged the furniture—as far as anyone could in the tiny area.

When she came back she focused her eyes on him. "Right, then. I'm all yours. What do we have?"

"Incident Twenty."

"Ah, that. I wasn't on the hot list so you'd better brief me."

Like Bond, Ophelia Maidenstone was Developed Vetting Cleared by the Defense Vetting Agency, the FCO and Scotland Yard, which permitted virtually unlimited access to top secret material, short of the most classified nuclear-arms data. He briefed her on Noah, the Irishman, the threat on Friday and the incident in Serbia. She took careful notes.

"I need you to play detective inspector. This is all we have to go on." He handed her the carrier bag containing the slips of paper he'd snatched from the burning car outside Novi Sad and his own sunglasses. "I'll need identification fast—very fast—and anything else you dig up."

She lifted her phone and requested collection of the materials for analysis at the MI6 laboratory or, if that proved insufficient, Scotland Yard's extensive forensic operation in Specialist Crimes. She rang off. "Runner's on his way." She found a pair of tweezers in her handbag and extracted the two slips of paper. One was a bill from a pub near Cambridge, the date recent. It had been settled in cash, unfortunately.

The other slip of paper read: *Boots—March. 17. No later than that.* Was it code or merely a reminder from two months ago to pick up something at the chemist?

"And the Oakleys?" She was gazing down into the bag.

"There's a fingerprint in the middle of the right lens. The Irishman's partner. There was no pocket litter."

She made copies of the two documents, handed him a set, kept one for herself and replaced the originals in the bag with the glasses.

Bond then explained about the hazardous material that the Irishman was trying to spill into the Danube. "I need to know what it was. And what kind of damage it could have caused. Afraid I've ruffled some feathers among the Serbs. They won't want to cooperate."

"We'll see about that."

Just then his mobile buzzed. He looked at the screen, though he knew this distinctive chirp quite well. He answered. "Moneypenny."

The woman's low voice said, "Hello, James. Welcome back."

"M?" he asked.

"M."

The cleverness and speed of her retort and the use
of his first name, along with her radiant smile, instantly
and immutably defined their relationship: She'd kept
him in his place but opened the avenue of friendship.
So it had remained ever since, caring and close but
always professional. (Still, he harbored the belief that
of all the 00 Section agents she liked him best.)

Moneypenny looked him over and frowned. "You
had quite a time of it over there, I heard."

"You could say so."

She glanced at M's closed door and said, "This Noah
situation's a tough one, James. Signals flying everywhere.
He left at nine last night, came in at five this morning."
She added, in a whisper, "He was worried about you.
There were some moments last night when you were in-
communicado. He was on the phone quite often then."

They saw a light on her phone extinguish. She hit a
button and spoke through a nearly invisible stalk mic.
"It's 007, sir."

She nodded at the door, toward which Bond now
walked, as the do-not-disturb light above it flashed
on. This occurred silently, of course, but Bond always
imagined the illumination was accompanied by the
sound of a deadbolt crashing open to admit a new prisoner to a medieval dungeon.

"Morning, sir."

M looked exactly the same as he had at the Travellers Club lunch when they'd met three years ago and
might have been wearing the same gray suit. He gestured to one of the two functional chairs facing the
large oak desk. Bond sat down.

The office was carpeted and the walls were lined

Chapter 8

The sign beside the top-floor office read DIRECTOR-GENERAL.

Bond stepped into the anteroom, where a woman in her midthirties sat at a tidy desk. She wore a pale cream camisole beneath a jacket that was nearly the same shade as Bond's. A long face, handsome and regal, eyes that could flick from stern to compassionate faster than a Formula One gearbox.

"Hello, Moneypenny."

"It'll just be a moment, James. He's on the line to Whitehall again."

Her posture was upright, her gestures economical. Not a hair was out of place. He reflected, as he often did, that her military background had left an indelible mark. She'd resigned her commission with the Royal Navy to take her present job with M as his personal assistant.

Just after he'd joined the ODG, Bond had dropped into her office chair and flashed a broad smile. "Rank of lieutenant, were you, Moneypenny?" he'd quipped. "I'd prefer to picture you *above* me." Bond had left the service as a commander.

He'd received in reply not the searing rejoinder he deserved but a smooth riposte: "Oh, but I've found in life, James, that all positions must be earned through experience. And I'm pleased to say I have little doubt that my level of such does not *begin* to approach yours."

with bookshelves. The building was at the fulcrum where old London became new and M's windows in the corner office bore witness to this. To the west Marylebone High Street's period buildings contrasted sharply with Euston Road's skyscrapers of glass and metal, sculptures of high concept and questionable aesthetics and lift systems cleverer than you were.

These scenes, however, remained dim, even on sunny days, since the window glass was both bomb- and bulletproof and mirrored to prevent spying by any ingenious enemy hanging from a hot-air balloon over Regent's Park.

M looked up from his notes and scanned Bond. "No medical report, I gather."

Nothing escaped him. Ever.

"A scratch or two. Not serious."

The man's desk held a yellow pad, a complicated console phone, his mobile, an Edwardian brass lamp and a humidor stocked with the narrow black cheroots M sometimes allowed himself on drives to and from Whitehall or during his brief walks through Regent's Park, when he was accompanied by his thoughts and two P Branch guards. Bond knew very little of M's personal life, only that he lived in a Regency manor house on the edge of Windsor Forest and was a bridge player, a fisherman and a rather accomplished watercolorist of flowers. A personable and talented navy corporal named Andy Smith drove him about in a well-polished ten-year-old Rolls-Royce.

"Give me your report, 007."

Bond organized his thoughts. M did not tolerate a muddled narrative or padding. "Ums" and "ers" were as unacceptable as stating the obvious. He reiterated what had happened in Novi Sad, then added, "I found a few things in Serbia that might give us some details. Philly's sorting them now and finding out about the hazmat on the train."

"Philly?"

Bond recalled that M disliked the use of nicknames, even though he was referred to exclusively by one throughout the organization. "Ophelia Maidenstone," he explained. "Our liaison from Six. If there's anything to be found, she'll sniff it out."

"Your cover in Serbia?"

"I was working false flag. The senior people at BIA in Belgrade know I'm with the ODG and what my mission was but we told their two field agents I was with a fictional UN peacekeeping outfit. I had to mention Noah and the incident on Friday in case the BIA agents stumbled across something referring to them. But whatever the Irishman got out of the younger man, it wasn't compromising."

"The Yard and Five are wondering—with the train in Novi Sad, do you think Incident Twenty's about sabotaging a railway line here? Serbia was a dry run?"

"I wondered that too, sir. But it wouldn't be the sort of operation that'd need much rehearsal. Besides, the Irishman's partner rigged the derailment in about three minutes. Our rail systems here must be more sophisticated than a freight line in rural Serbia."

A bushy eyebrow rose, perhaps disputing that assumption. But M said, "You're right. It doesn't seem like a prelude to Incident Twenty."

"Now." Bond sat forward. "What I'd like to do, sir, is get back to Station Y immediately. Enter through Hungary and set up a rendition op to track down the Irish-man. I'll take a couple of our double-one agents with me. We can trace the lorry he stole. It'll be tricky but—"

M was shaking his head, rocking back in his well-worn throne. "It seems there's a bit of a flap, 007. It involves you."

"Whatever Belgrade's saying, the young agent who died—"

M waved a hand impatiently. "Yes, yes, *of course* what happened was their fault. There was never any question about that. Explanation is a sign of weakness, 007. Don't know why you're doing it now."

"Sorry, sir."

"I'm speaking of something else. Last night, Chel-tenham managed to get a satellite image of the lorry the Irishman escaped in."

"Very good, sir." So, his tracking tactic had appar-ently succeeded.

But M's scowl suggested Bond's satisfaction was premature. "About fifteen miles south of Novi Sad the lorry pulled over and the Irishman got into a helicop-ter. No registration or ID but GCHQ got a MASINT profile of it."

Material and Signature Intelligence was the latest in high-tech espionage. If information came from elec-tronic sources like microwave transmissions or radio, it was ELINT; from photographs and satellite images, IMINT; from mobile phones and e-mails, SIGINT; and from human sources, HUMINT. With MASINT, instruments collected and profiled data such as ther-mal energy; sound waves; airflow disruption; propeller and helicopter rotor vibrations; exhaust from jet en-gines, trains and cars; velocity patterns, and more.

The director-general continued: "Last night Five registered a MASINT profile that matched the helicopter he escaped in."

Bloody hell. . . . If MI5 had found the chopper, that meant it was in England. The Irishman—the sole lead to Noah and Incident 20—was in the one place where James Bond had no authority to pursue him.

M added, "The helicopter landed northeast of London at about one A.M. and vanished. They lost all track." He shook his head. "I don't see why Whitehall didn't give us more latitude about operating at home when they chartered us. Would have been easy. Hell, what if you'd followed the Irishman to the London Eye or Madame Tussauds? What should you have done—rung nine-nine-nine? For God's sake, these are the days of globalization, of the Internet, the EU, yet we can't follow leads in our own country."

The rationale for this rule, however, was clear. MI5 conducted brilliant investigations. MI6 was a master at foreign-intelligence gathering and "disruptive action," such as destroying a terrorist cell from within by planting misinformation. The Overseas Development Group did rather more, including occasionally, if rarely, ordering its 00 Section agents to lie in wait for enemies of the state and shoot them dead. But to do so within the UK, however morally justifiable or tactically convenient, would play rather badly among bloggers and the Fleet Street scribblers.

Not to mention that the Crown's prosecutors might be counted on to have a say in the matter as well.

But, politics aside, Bond adamantly wanted to pursue Incident 20. He'd developed a particular dislike for the Irishman. His words to M were measured: "I think

I'm in the best position to find this man and Noah and to suss out what they're up to. I want to keep on it, sir."

"I thought as much. And I *want* you to pursue it, 007. I've been on the phone this morning with Five and Specialist Operations at the Yard. They're both willing to let you have a consulting role."

"Consulting?" Bond said sourly, then realized that M would have done some impressive negotiating to achieve that much. "Thank you, sir."

M deflected the words with a jerk of his head. "You'll be working with someone from Division Three, a fellow named Osborne-Smith."

Division Three . . . British security and police operations were like human beings: forever being born, marrying, producing progeny, dying and even, Bond had once joked, undergoing sex-change operations. Division Three was one of the more recent offspring. It had some loose affiliation with Five, in much the same way that the ODG had a gossamer-thin connection to Six.

Plausible deniability . . .

While Five had broad investigation and surveillance powers, it had no arrest authority or tactical officers. Division Three did. It was a secretive, reclusive group of high-tech wizards, bureaucrats and former SAS and SBS tough boys with serious firepower. Bond had been impressed with its recent successes in taking down terrorist cells in Oldham, Leeds and London.

M regarded him evenly. "I know you're used to having carte blanche to handle the mission as you see fit, 007. You have your independent streak and it's served you well in the past." A dark look. "*Most* of the time. But at home your authority's limited. Significantly. Do I make myself clear?"

"Yes, sir."

So, no longer carte blanche, Bond reflected angrily, more carte grise.

Another dour glance from M. "Now, a complication. That security conference."

"Security conference?"

"Haven't read your Whitehall briefing?" M asked petulantly.

These were administrative announcements about internal government matters and, accordingly, no, Bond did not read them. "Sorry, sir."

M's jowls tightened. "We have thirteen security agencies in the UK. Maybe more as of this morning. The heads of Five, Six, SOCA, JTAC, SO Thirteen, DI, the whole lot—myself included—will be holed up in Whitehall for three days later in the week. Oh, the CIA and some chaps from the Continent too. Briefings on Islamabad, Pyongyang, Venezuela, Beijing, Jakarta. And there'll probably be some young analyst in Harry Potter glasses touting his theory that the Chechnyan rebels are responsible for that damned volcano in Iceland. A bloody inconvenience, the whole thing." He sighed. "I'll be largely incommunicado. Chief of staff will be running the Incident Twenty operation for the Group."

"Yes, sir. I'll coordinate with him."

"Get onto it, 007. And remember: You're operating in the UK. Treat it like a country you've never been to. Which means, for God's sake, be diplomatic with the natives."

Chapter 9

"It's pretty bad, sir. Are you sure you want to see it?"

To the foreman, the man replied immediately. "Yes."

"Right, then. I'll drive you out."

"Who else knows?"

"Just the shift chief and the lad what found it." Casting a glance at his boss, the foreman added, "They'll keep quiet. If that's what you want."

Severan Hydt said nothing.

Under an overcast and dusty sky, the two men left the loading bay of the ancient headquarters building and walked to a nearby car park. They climbed into a people carrier emblazoned with the logo of Green Way International Disposal and Recycling; the company name was printed over a delicate drawing of a verdant leaf. Hydt didn't much care for the design, which struck him as mockingly trendy, but he'd been told that the image had scored well in focus groups and was good for public relations ("Ah, the *public*," he'd responded with veiled contempt and reluctantly approved it).

He was a tall man—six foot three—and broad-shouldered, his columnar torso encased in a bespoke suit of black wool. His massive head was covered with dense, curly hair, black streaked with white, and he wore a matching beard. His yellowing fingernails extended well past his fingertips but were carefully filed; they were long by design, not neglect.

Hydt's pallor accentuated his dark nostrils and darker eyes, framed by a long face that appeared younger than his fifty-six years. He was a strong man still, having retained much of his youthful muscularity.

The van started through his company's disheveled grounds, more than a hundred acres of low buildings, rubbish tips, skips, hovering seagulls, smoke, dust . . .

And decay . . .

As they drove over the rough roads, Hydt's attention momentarily slipped to a construction about half a mile away. A new building was nearing completion. It was identical to two that stood already in the grounds: five-story boxes from which chimneys rose, the sky above them rippling from the rising heat. The buildings were known as destructors, a Victorian word that Severan Hydt loved. England was the first country in the world to make energy from municipal refuse. In the 1870s the first power plant to do so was built in Nottingham and soon hundreds were operating throughout the country, producing steam to generate electricity.

The destructor now nearing completion in the middle of his disposal and recycling operation was no different in theory from its gloomy Dickensian forebears, save that it used scrubbers and filters to clean the dangerous exhaust and was far more efficient, burning RDF—refuse-derived fuel—as it produced energy that was pumped (for profit, of course) into the London and Home County power grids.

Indeed, Green Way International, plc, was simply the latest in a long British tradition of innovation in refuse disposal and reclamation. Henry IV had decreed that rubbish should be collected and removed from the streets of towns and cities on threat of forfeit. Mudlarks had kept the banks of the Thames clean— for entrepreneurial profit, not government wages— and rag pickers had sold scraps of wool to mills for the production of cheap cloth called shoddy. In London, as early as the nineteenth century, women and girls had been employed to sift through incoming refuse and sort it according to future usefulness. The British Paper Company had been founded to manufacture recycled paper—in 1890.

Green Way was located nearly twenty miles east of London, well past the boxed sets of office buildings on the Isle of Dogs and the sea mine of the O2, past the ramble of Canning Town and Silvertown, the Docklands. To reach it you turned southeast off the A13 and drove toward the Thames. Soon you were down to a narrow lane, unwelcoming, even forbidding, surrounded by nothing but brush and stalky plants, pale and translucent as a dying patient's skin. The tarmac strip seemed a road to nowhere . . . until it crested a low rise and ahead you could see Green Way's massive complex, forever muted through a haze.

In the middle of this wonderland of rubbish the van now stopped beside a battered skip, six feet high, twenty long. Two workers, somewhere in their forties, wearing tan Green Way overalls, stood uncomfortably beside it. They didn't look any less uneasy now that the owner of the company himself, no less, was present.

"Crikey," one whispered to the other.

Hydt knew they were also cowed by his black eyes, the tight mass of his beard and his towering frame.

And then there were those fingernails.

He asked, "In there?"

The workers remained speechless and the foreman, the name JACK DENNISON stitched on his overalls,
said, "That's right, sir." Then he snapped to one of the
workers, "Right, sunshine, don't keep Mr. Hydt waiting. He hasn't got all day, has he?"

The employee hurried to the side of the skip and,
with some effort, pulled the large door open, assisted
by a spring. Inside were the ubiquitous mounds of
green bin liners and loose junk—bottles, magazines
and newspapers—that people had been too lazy to
separate for recycling.

And there was another item of discard inside: a
human body.

A woman's or teenage boy's, to judge from the stature. There wasn't much else to go on, since, clearly,
death had occurred months ago. He bent down and
probed with his long fingernails.

This enjoyable examination confirmed the corpse
was a woman's.

Staring at the loosening skin, the protruding
bones, the insect and animal work on what was left of
the flesh, Hydt felt his heart quicken. He said to the
two workers, "You'll keep this to yourselves."

They'll keep quiet.

"Yes, sir."

"Of course, sir."

"Wait over there."

They trotted away. Hydt glanced at Dennison, who
nodded that they'd behave themselves. Hydt didn't
doubt it. He ran Green Way more like a military base
than a rubbish tip and recycling yard. Security was
tight—mobile phones were banned, all outgoing communications monitored—and discipline harsh. But, in

compensation, Severan Hydt paid his people very, very well. A lesson of history was that professional soldiers stuck around far longer than amateurs, provided you had the money. And that particular commodity was never in short supply at Green Way. Disposing of what people no longer wanted had always been, and would forever be, a profitable endeavor.

Alone now, Hydt crouched beside the body.

The discovery of human remains here happened with some frequency. Sometimes workers in the construction debris and reclamation division of Green Way would find Victorian bones or desiccated skeletons in building foundations. Or a corpse of a homeless person, dead from exposure to the elements, drink or drugs, hurled unceremoniously onto the bin liners. Sometimes it was a murder victim—in which case the killers were usually polite enough to bring the body here directly.

Hydt never reported the deaths. The presence of the police was the last thing he wanted.

Besides, why should he give up such a treasure?

He eased closer to the body, knees pressing against what was left of the woman's jeans. The smell of decay—like bitter, wet cardboard—would be unpleasant to most people but discard had been Hydt's lifelong profession and he was no more repulsed by it than a garage mechanic is troubled by the scent of grease or an abattoir worker the odor of blood and viscera.

Dennison, the foreman, however, stood back some distance from the perfume.

With one of his jaundiced fingernails, Hydt reached forward and stroked the top of the skull, from which most of the hair was missing, then the jaw, the finger bones, the first to be exposed. Her nails too were long, though not because they had grown after her death, which was a myth; they simply *appeared* longer because the flesh beneath them had shrunk.

He studied his new friend for a long moment, then reluctantly eased back. He looked at his watch. He pulled his iPhone from his pocket and took a dozen pictures of the corpse.

Then he glanced around him. He pointed to a deserted spot between two large mounds over landfills, like barrows holding phalanxes of fallen soldiers. "Tell the men to bury it there."

"Yes, sir," Dennison replied.

As he walked back to the people carrier, he said, "Not too deep. And leave a marker. So I'll be able to find it again."

Half an hour later Hydt was in his office, scrolling through the pictures he'd taken of the corpse, lost in the images, sitting at the three-hundred-year-old jail door mounted on legs that was his desk. Finally he slipped the phone away and turned his dark eyes to other matters. And there were many. Green Way was one of the world leaders in the disposal, reclamation and recycling of discard.

The office was spacious and dimly lit, located on the top story of Green Way's headquarters, an old meat-processing factory, dating to 1896, renovated and turned into what interior design magazines might call shabby chic.

On the walls were architectural relics from buildings his company had demolished: scabby painted frames around cracked stained glass, concrete gargoyles, wildlife, effigies, mosaics. St. George and the dragon were represented several times. St. Joan, too. On one large bas-relief Zeus, operating undercover as a swan, had his way with beautiful Leda.

Hydt's secretary came and went with letters for his signature, reports for him to read, memos to approve, financial statements to consider. Green Way was doing extremely well. At a recycling-industry conference Hydt had once joked that the adage about certainty in life should not be limited to the well-known two. People had to pay taxes, they had to die . . . and they had to have their discard collected and disposed of.

His computer chimed and he called up an en-crypted e-mail from a colleague out of the country. It was about an important meeting tomorrow, Tues-day, confirming times and locations. The last line stirred him:

> The number of dead tomorrow will be significant—close to 100. Hope that suits.

It did indeed. And the desire that had arisen within him when he'd first gazed at the body in the skip churned all the hotter.

He glanced up as a slim woman in her midsixties entered, wearing a dark trouser suit and black shirt. Her hair was white, cut in a businesswoman's bob. A large, unadorned diamond hung from a platinum chain around her narrow neck, and similar stones, though in more complex arrangements, graced her wrists and several fingers.

"I've approved the proofs." Jessica Barnes was an American. She'd come from a small town outside Boston; the regional lilt continued, charmingly, to tint her voice. A beauty queen years ago, she'd met Hydt when she was a hostess at a smart New York restaurant. They'd lived together for several years and—to keep her close—he'd hired her to review Green Way's advertisements, another endeavor Hydt had little respect for or interest in. He'd been told, however, that she'd made some good decisions from time to time with regard to the company's marketing efforts.

But as Hydt gazed at her, he saw that something about her was different today.

He found himself studying her face. That was it. His preference, *insistence,* was that she wear only black and white and keep her face free of makeup; today she had on some very faint blush and perhaps—he couldn't quite be certain—some lipstick. He didn't frown but she saw the direction of his eyes and shifted a bit, breathing a little differently. Her fingers started toward a cheek. She stopped her hand.

But the point had been made. She proffered the ads. "Do you want to look at them?"

"I'm sure they're fine," he said.

"I'll send them off." She left his office, her destination not the marketing department, Hydt knew, but the cloakroom, where she would wash her face.

Jessica was not a foolish woman; she'd learned her lesson.

Then she was gone from his thoughts. He stared out of the window at his new destructor. He was very aware of the event coming up on Friday but at the moment he couldn't get tomorrow out of his head.

The number of dead . . . close to 100.

His gut twisted pleasantly.

It was then that his secretary announced on the intercom, "Mr. Dunne's here, sir."

"Ah, good."

A moment later, Niall Dunne entered and swung the door shut so that the two were alone. The cumbersome man's trapezoid face had rarely flickered with emotion in the nine months they'd known each other. Severan Hydt had little use for most people and no interest in social niceties. But Dunne chilled even him.

"Now, what happened over there?" Hydt asked. After the incident in Serbia, Dunne had said they should keep their phone conversations to a minimum.

The man turned his pale blue eyes to Hydt and explained in his Belfast accent that he and Karic, the Serbian contact, had been surprised by several men—at least two BIA Serbian intelligence officers masquerading as police and a Westerner, who'd told the Serbian agent he was with the European Peacekeeping and Monitoring Group.

Hydt frowned. "It's—"

"There is no such group," Dunne said calmly. "It had to be a private operation. There was no backup, no central communications, no medics. The Westerner probably bribed the intelligence officers to help him. It *is* the Balkans, after all. May have been a competitor." He added, "Maybe one of your partners or a worker here let slip something about the plan."

He was referring to Gehenna, of course. They did everything they could to keep the project secret but a number of people around the world were involved; it wasn't impossible that there'd been a leak and some crime syndicate was interested in learning more about it.

Dunne continued: "I don't want to minimize the risk—they were pretty clever. But it wasn't a major co-ordinated effort. I'm confident we can go forward."

Dunne handed Hydt a mobile phone. "Use this one for our conversations. Better encryption."

Hydt examined it. "Did you get a look at the Westerner?"

"No. There was a lot of smoke."

"And Karic?"

"I killed him." The blank face registered the same emotion as if he'd said, "Yes, it's cool outside today."

Hydt considered what the man had told him. No one was more precise or cautious when it came to analysis than Niall Dunne. If he was convinced this was no problem, then Hydt would accept his judgment.

Dunne continued: "I'm going up to the facility now. Once I get the last materials up there the team say they can finish in a few hours."

A fire flared within Hydt, ignited by an image of the woman's body in the skip—and the thought of what awaited up north. "I'll come with you."

Dunne said nothing. Finally he asked in a monotone, "You think that's a good idea? Might be risky." He offered this as if he'd detected the eagerness in Hydt's voice—Dunne seemed to feel that nothing good could come out of a decision based on emotion.

"I'll chance it." Hydt tapped his pocket to make certain his phone was there. He hoped there'd be an opportunity to take some more photographs.

Chapter 10

After leaving M's lair, Bond walked up the corridor. He greeted a smartly dressed Asian woman keyboarding deftly at a large computer and stepped into the doorway behind her.

"You've bought the duty," he said to the man hunched over a desk as loaded with papers and files as M's was empty.

"I have indeed." Bill Tanner looked up. "I'm now grand overlord of Incident Twenty. Take a pew, James." He nodded to an empty chair—or, rather, *the* empty chair. The office boasted a number of seats but the rest were serving as outposts for more files. As Bond sat, the ODG's chief of staff asked, "So, most important, did you get some decent wine and a gourmet meal on SAS Air last night?"

An Apache helicopter, courtesy of the Special Air Service, had plucked Bond from a field south of the Danube and whisked him to a NATO base in Germany, where a Hercules loaded with van parts completed his journey to London. He said, "Apparently they forgot to stock the galley."

Tanner laughed. The retired army officer, a former lieutenant colonel, was a solid man in his fifties, ruddy of complexion and upright—in all senses of the word. He was in his usual uniform: dark trousers and light blue shirt with the sleeves rolled up. Tanner had a tough job, running the ODG's day-to-day operations, and by rights he should have had little sense of humor, though in fact, he had a fine one. He'd been Bond's mentor when the young agent had joined and was now his closest friend within the organization. Tanner was a devout golfer and every few weeks he and Bond would try to get out to one of the more challenging courses, like Royal Cinque Ports or Royal St George's or, if time was tight, Sunningdale, near Windsor.

Tanner was, of course, generally familiar with Incident Twenty and the hunt for Noah but Bond now updated him—and explained about his own downsized role in the UK operation.

The chief of staff gave a sympathetic laugh. "Carte grise, eh? Must say, you're taking it rather well."

"Hardly have much choice," Bond allowed. "Is Whitehall still convinced that the threat's out of Afghanistan?"

"Let's just say they *hope* it's based there," Tanner said, his voice low. "For several reasons. You can probably work them out for yourself."

He meant politics, of course.

Then he nodded toward M's office. "Did you catch his opinion on that security conference he's been shanghaied to attend this week?"

"Not much room for interpretation," Bond said.

Tanner chuckled.

Bond glanced at his watch and stood up. "I've got to meet a man from Division Three. Osborne-Smith. You know anything about him?"

"Ah, Percy." Bill Tanner raised a cryptic eyebrow and smiled. "Good luck, James," he said. "Perhaps it's best just to leave it at that."

O Branch took up nearly the entire fourth floor.

It was a large open area, ringed with agents' offices.

In the center were workstations for PAs and other support staff. It might have been the sales department of a major supermarket, if not for the fact that every office door had an iris scanner and keypad lock. There were many flat-screen computers in the center but none of the giant monitors that seemed de rigueur in spy outfits on TV and in movies.

Bond strode through this busy area and nodded a greeting to a blonde in her midtwenties, perched forward in her office chair, presiding over an ordered work space. Had Mary Goodnight worked for any other department, Bond might have invited her to dinner and seen where matters led from there. But she wasn't in any other department: She was fifteen feet from his office door and was his human diary, his portcullis and drawbridge, and was capable of repelling the unannounced firmly and, most important in government service, with unimprovable tact. Although none were on view, Goodnight occasionally received—from office mates, friends and dates—cards or souvenirs inspired by the film *Titanic,* so closely did she resemble Kate Winslet.

"Good morning, Goodnight."

That play on words, and others like it, had long ago moved from flirtatiousness to affection. They had become like an endearment between spouses, almost automatic and never tiresome.

Goodnight ran through his appointments for the day but Bond told her to cancel everything. He'd be meeting a man from Division Three, coming over from Thames House, and afterward he might have to be off at a minute's notice.

"Shall I hold the signals too?" she asked.

Bond considered this. "I suppose I'll plow through

them now. Should probably clear my desk anyway. If I have to be away, I don't want to come back to a week's worth of reading."

She handed him the top-secret green-striped folders. With approval from the keypad lock and iris scanner beside his door Bond entered his office and turned on the light. The space wasn't small by London office standards, about fifteen by fifteen, but was rather sterile. His government-issue desk was slightly larger than, but the same color as, his desk at Defense Intelligence. The four wooden bookshelves were filled with volumes and periodicals that had been, or might be, helpful to him and varied in subject from the latest hacking techniques used by the Bulgarians to Thai idioms to a guide for reloading Lapua .338 sniper rounds. There was little of a personal nature to brighten the room. The one object he might have had on display, his Conspicuous Gallantry Cross, awarded for his duty in Afghanistan, was in the bottom drawer of his desk. He'd accepted the honor with good grace but to Bond courage was simply another tool in a soldier's kit and he saw no more point in displaying indications of its past use than in hanging a spent cipher pad on the wall.

Bond now sat in his chair and began to read the signals—intelligence reports from Requirements at MI6, suitably buffed and packaged. The first was from the Russia Desk. Their Station R had managed to hack into a government server in Moscow and suck out some classified documents. Bond, who had a natural facility for language and had studied Russian at Fort Monckton, skipped the English synopsis and went to the raw intelligence.

He got one paragraph into the leaden prose when

two words stopped him in his tracks. The Russian words for "Steel Cartridge."

The phrase pinged deep inside him, just as sonar on a submarine notes a distant but definite target.

Steel Cartridge appeared to be a code name for an "active measure," the Soviet term describing a tactical operation. It had involved "some deaths."

But there was nothing specific on operational details.

Bond sat back, staring at the ceiling. He heard women's voices outside his door and looked up. Philly, holding several files, was chatting with Mary Goodnight. Bond nodded and the Six agent joined him, taking a wooden chair opposite his desk.

"What've you found, Philly?"

She sat forward, crossing her legs, and Bond believed he heard the appealing rustle of nylon. "First, your photo skills are fine, James, but the light was too low. I couldn't get high enough resolution of the Irishman's face for recognition. And there were no prints on the pub bill or the other note, except for a partial of yours."

So, the man would have to remain anonymous for the time being.

"But the prints on the glasses were good. The local was Aldo Karic, Serbian. He lived in Belgrade and worked for the national railway." She pursed her lips in frustration, which emphasized the charming dimple. "But it's going to take a little longer than I'd hoped to get more details. The same with the hazmat on the train. Nobody's saying anything. You were right—Belgrade's not in the mood to cooperate.

"Now for the slips of paper you found in the burning car. I got some possible locations."

Bond noted the printouts she was producing from a folder. They were of maps emblazoned with the cheerful logo of MapQuest, the online directions-finding service. "Are you having budget problems at Six? I'd be happy to ring the Treasury for you."

She laughed, a breathy sound. "I used proxies, of course. Just wanted an idea of where on the pitch we're playing." She tapped one. "The receipt? The pub is here." It was just off the motorway near Cambridge.

Bond stared at the map. Who had eaten there? The Irishman? Noah? Other associates? Or someone who'd hired the car last week and had no connection whatsoever with Incident Twenty?

"And the other piece of paper? With the writing on it?"

Boots—March. 17. No later than that.

She produced a lengthy list. "I tried to think of every possible combination of what it could mean. Dates, footwear, geographical locations, the chemist." Her mouth tightened again. She was displeased that her efforts had fallen short. "Nothing obvious, I'm afraid."

He rose and pulled down several Ordnance Survey maps from the shelf. He flipped through one, scanning carefully.

Mary Goodnight appeared in the doorway. "James, someone downstairs to see you. From Division Three, he says. Percy Osborne-Smith."

Philly must have caught the sea change in Bond's expression. "I'll make myself scarce now, James. I'll keep on at the Serbs. They'll crack. I guarantee it."

"Oh, one more thing, Philly." He handed her the signal he'd just been reading. "I need you to catch everything you can about a Soviet or Russian operation called Steel Cartridge. There's a little in here, not much."

She glanced down at the printout.

He said, "Sorry it's not translated but you can probably—"

"*Ya govoryu po russki.*"

Bond smiled weakly. "And with a far better accent than mine." He told himself never to sell her short again.

Philly examined the printout closely. "This was hacked from an online source. Who has the original data file?"

"One of your people would. It came out of Station R."

"I'll contact the Russia Desk," she said. "I'll want to look at the metadata coded in the file. That'll have the date it was created, who the author was, maybe cross-references to other sources." She slipped the Russian document into a manila folder and took a pen to tick off one of the boxes on the front. "How do you want it classified?"

He debated for a moment. "Our eyes only."

"'Our'?" she asked. That pronoun was not used in official document classification.

"Yours and mine," he said softly. "No one else."

A brief hesitation and then, in her delicate lettering, she penned at the top: *Eyes only. SIS Agent Maidenstone. ODG Agent James Bond.* "And priority?" she wondered aloud.

At this question Bond did not hesitate at all. "Urgent."

Chapter 11

Bond was sitting forward at his desk, doing some research of his own in government databases, when he
heard footsteps approaching, accompanied by a loud
voice.

"I'm fine, just great. You can peel off now, please
and thank you—I can do without the sat-nav."

With that, a man in a close-fitting striped suit
strode into Bond's office, having discarded the Section P security officer who'd accompanied him. He'd
also bypassed Mary Goodnight, who had risen with a
frown as the man stormed past, ignoring her.

He walked up to Bond's desk, thrusting out a fleshy
palm. Slim but flabby, unimposing, he nonetheless had
assertive eyes and large hands at the end of his long
arms. He seemed the sort to deliver a bone-crusher
so Bond, darkening his computer screen and standing
up, prepared to counter it, shooting his hand in close
to deny him leverage.

In fact, Percy Osborne-Smith's clasp was brief and
harmless, though unpleasantly damp.

"Bond. James Bond." He motioned the Division
Three officer to the chair Philly had just occupied and
reminded himself not to let the man's coiffure—dark
blond hair combed and apparently glued to the side of
his head—pouting lips and rubbery neck deceive. A
weak chin did not mean a weak man, as anyone familiar
with Field Marshal Montgomery's career could certify.

"So," Osborne-Smith said, "here we are. Excitement galore with Incident Twenty. Who thinks up these names, do you wonder? The Intelligence Committee, I suppose."

Bond tipped his head noncommittally.

The man's eyes swept around the office, alighted briefly on a plastic gun with an orange muzzle used in close-combat training, and returned to Bond. "Now, from what I hear, Defense and Six are firing up the boilers to steam down the Afghan route, looking for baddies in the hinterland. Makes you and me the awkward younger brothers, left behind, stuck with this Serbian connection. But sometimes it's the pawns that win the game, isn't it?"

He dabbed his nose and mouth with a handkerchief. Bond couldn't recall the last time he'd seen anyone under the age of seventy employ this combination of gesture and accessory. "Heard about you, Bond . . . James. Let's go with givens, shall we? My surname's a bit of a mouthful. Crosses to bear. Just like my title— deputy senior director of field operations."

Rather unskillfully inserted, Bond reflected.

"So, it's Percy and James. Sounds like a stand-up act at a Comic Relief show. Anyway, I've heard about you, James. Your reputation precedes you. Not 'exceeds,' of course. At least, not from what I hear."

Oh God, Bond thought, his patience already worn thin. He preempted a continuation of the monologue and explained in detail what had happened in Serbia.

Osborne-Smith took it all in, jotting notes. Then he described what had happened on the British side of the Channel, which wasn't particularly informative. Even enlisting the impressive surveillance skills of MI5's A Branch—known as the Watchers—no one had been able to confirm more than that the helicopter carrying the Irishman had landed somewhere northeast of London. No MASINT or other trace of the chopper had been found since.

"So, our strategy?" Osborne-Smith said, though not as a question. Rather, it was a preface to a directive: "While Defense and Six and everybody under the sun are prowling the desert looking for Afghans of mass destruction, I want to go all out here, find this Irishman and Noah, wrap them up in tidy ribbons and bring them in."

"Arrest them?"

"Well, *detain* might be the happier word."

"Actually, I'm not sure that's the best approach," Bond said delicately.

For God's sake, be diplomatic with the natives. . . .

"Why not? We don't have time for surveillance." Bond noticed a faint lisp. "Only to interrogate."

"If thousands of lives are at risk, the Irishman and Noah can't be operating alone. They might even be pretty low in the food chain. All we know for sure is that there was a meeting at Noah's office. Nothing ever suggested he was in charge of the whole operation. And the Irishman? He's a triggerman. Certainly knows his craft but basically he's muscle. I think we need to identify them and keep them in play until we get more answers."

Osborne-Smith was nodding agreeably. "Ah, but you're not familiar with my background, James, my curriculum vitae." The smile and the smarminess vanished. "I cut my teeth grilling prisoners. In Northern Ireland. And Belmarsh."

The infamous so-called Terrorists' Prison in London.

"I've sunned myself in Cuba, too," he continued. "Guantánamo. Yes, indeed. People end up talking to me, James. After I've been going at them for a few days, they'll hand me the address where their brother's hiding, won't they? Or their son. Or daughter. Oh, people talk when I ask them . . . ever so politely."

Bond wasn't giving up. "But if Noah has partners and they learn he's been picked up, they might accelerate whatever's planned for Friday. Or disappear—and we'll lose them until they strike again in six or eight months when all the leads've gone cold. This Irishman would have planned for a contingency like that, I'm sure of it."

The soft nose wrinkled with regret. "It's just that, well, if we were on the Continent somewhere or padding about in Red Square, I'd be de*lighted* to sit back and watch you bowl leg or off breaks, as you thought best, but, well, it *is* our cricket ground here."

The whip crack was, of course, inevitable. Bond decided there was no point in arguing. The dandified puppet had a steel spine. He also had ultimate authority and could shut out Bond entirely if he wished to. "It's your call, of course," Bond said pleasantly. "So I suppose the first step is to find them. Let me show you the leads." He passed over a copy of the pub receipt and the note: *Boots—March. 17. No later than that.*

Osborne-Smith was frowning as he examined the sheets. "What do you make of them?" he asked.

"Nothing very sexy," Bond said. "The pub's outside Cambridge. The note's a bit of a mystery."

"March the seventeenth? A reminder to drop in at the chemist?"

"Maybe," Bond said dubiously. "I was thinking it might be code." He pushed forward the MapQuest printout that Philly had provided. "If you ask me, the pub's probably nothing. I can't find anything distinctive about it—it's not near anywhere important. Off the M11, near Wimpole Road." He touched the sheet. "Probably a waste of time. But it ought to be looked at. Why don't I take that? I'll head up there and look around Cambridge. Maybe you could run the March note past the cryptanalysts at Five and see what their computers have to say. That holds the key, I think."

"I will do. But actually, if you don't mind, James, it's probably best if I handle the pub myself. I know the lie of the land. I was at Cambridge—Magdalene." The map and the pub receipt vanished into Osborne-Smith's briefcase, with a copy of the March note. Then he produced another sheet of paper. "Can you get that girl in?"

Bond lifted an eyebrow. "Which one?"

"The pretty young thing outside. Single, I see."

"You mean my PA," Bond said drily. He rose and went to the door. "Miss Goodnight, would you come in, please?"

She did so, frowning.

"Our friend Percy wants a word with you."

Osborne-Smith missed the irony in Bond's choice of names and handed the sheet of paper to her. "Make a copy of this, would you?"

With a glance toward Bond, who nodded, she took the document and went to the copier. Osborne-Smith called after her, "Double-sided, of course. Waste works to the enemy's advantage, doesn't it?"

Goodnight returned a moment later. Osborne-

Smith put the original in his briefcase and handed the copy to Bond. "You ever get out to the firearms range?"

"From time to time," Bond told him. He didn't add: six hours a week, religiously, indoor here with small arms, outdoor with full-bore at Bisley. And once a fortnight he trained at Scotland Yard's FATS range—the high-definition computerized firearms-training simulator, in which an electrode was mounted against your back; if the terrorist shot you before you shot him, you ended up on your knees in excruciating pain.

"We have to observe the formalities, don't we?" Osborne-Smith gestured at the sheet in Bond's hand. "Application to become a temporary AFO."

Only a very few law enforcers—authorized firearms officers—could carry weapons in the UK.

"It's probably not a good idea to use my name on that," Bond pointed out.

Osborne-Smith seemed not to have thought of this. "You may be right. Well, use a nonofficial cover, why don't you? John Smith'll do. Just fill it in and do the quiz on the back—gun safety and all that. If you hit a speed bump, give me a shout. I'll walk you through."

"I'll get right to it."

"Good man. Glad that's settled. We'll coordinate later—after our respective secret missions." He tapped his briefcase. "Off to Cambridge."

He pivoted and strode out as boisterously as he'd arrived.

"What a positively *wretched* man," Goodnight whispered.

Bond gave a brief laugh. He pulled his jacket off the back of his chair and tugged it on, picked up the Ordnance Survey. "I'm going down to the armory to collect my gun and after that I'll be out for three or four hours."

"What about the firearms form, James?"

"Ah." He picked it up, tore it into neat strips and slipped them into the map booklet to mark his places. "Why waste departmental Post-it notes? Works to the enemy's advantage, you know."

Chapter 12

An hour and a half later, James Bond was in his Bentley Continental GT, a gray streak speeding north.

He was reflecting on his deception of Percy Osborne-Smith. He'd decided that the lead to the Cambridge pub wasn't, in fact, very promising. Yes, possibly the Incident 20 principals had eaten there—the bill suggested a meal for two or three. But the date was more than a week ago, so it was unlikely that anyone on the staff would remember a man fitting the Irishman's description and his companions. And since the man had proved to be particularly clever, Bond suspected he rotated the places where he dined and shopped; he would not be a regular there.

The lead in Cambridge had to be followed up, of course, but—equally important—Bond needed to keep Osborne-Smith diverted. He could simply not allow the Irishman or Noah to be arrested and hauled into Belmarsh like a drug dealer or an Islamist who'd been buying excessive fertilizer. They needed to keep both suspects in play to discover the nature of Incident 20.

And so Bond, a keen poker player, had bluffed. He'd taken inordinate interest in the clue about the pub and had mentioned it was not far from Wimpole Road. To most people this would have meant nothing. But Bond guessed that Osborne-Smith would know that a secret government facility connected to Porton Down, the Ministry of Defense biological weapons research center in Wiltshire, happened also to be on Wimpole Road. True, it was eight miles to the east, on the other side of Cambridge and nowhere near the pub, but Bond believed that associating the two would encourage the Division Three man to descend on the idea like a seabird spotting a fish head.

This relegated Bond to the apparently fruitless task of wrestling with the cryptic note. *Boots—March. 17. No later than that.*

Which he believed he had deciphered.

Most of Philly's suggestions about its meaning had involved the chemist, Boots, which had shops in every town across the UK. She'd also offered suggestions about footwear and about events that had taken place on March 17.

But one suggestion, toward the end of her list, had intrigued Bond. She'd noted that "Boots" and "March" were linked with a dash and she had found that there was a Boots Road that ran near the town of March, a couple of hours' drive north of London. She had seen, too, the full stop between "March" and "17." Given that the last phrase, "no later than that," suggested a deadline, "17" made sense as a date but was possibly 17 *May,* tomorrow.

Clever of her, Bond had thought and in his office, waiting for Osborne-Smith, he had gone into the Golden Wire—a secure fiber-optic network tying together records of all major British security agencies—to learn what he could about March and Boots Road.

He had found some intriguing facts: traffic reports about road diversions because a large number of lorries were coming and going along Boots Road near an old army base, and public notices relating to heavy plant work. References suggested that it had to be completed by midnight on the seventeenth or fines would be levied. He had a hunch that this might be a solid lead to the Irishman and Noah.

And tradecraft dictated that you ignored such intuition at your peril.

So he was now en route to March, losing himself in the consuming pleasure of driving.

Which meant, of course, driving fast.

Bond had to exercise some restraint since he wasn't on the N-260 in the Pyrenees or off the beaten track in the Lake District but was traveling north along the A1 as it switched identities arbitrarily between motorway and trunk road. Still, the speedometer needle occasionally reached 100 mph and frequently he'd tap the paddle of the silken, millisecond-response Quickshift gearbox to overtake a slow-moving horsebox or Ford Mondeo. He stayed mostly in the right lane, although once or twice he took to the hard shoulder for some exhilarating, if illegal, passing. He enjoyed a few controlled skids on stretches of adverse camber.

The police were not a problem. While the jurisdiction of ODG was limited in the UK—carte grise, not blanche, Bond now joked to himself again—it was often necessary for O Branch agents to get around the country quickly. Bond had phoned in an NDR—a Null Detain Request—and his number-plate was ignored by cameras and constables with speed guns.

Ah, the Bentley Continental GT coupé . . . the finest off-the-peg vehicle in the world, Bond believed.

He had always loved the marque; his father had kept hundreds of old newspaper photos of the famed Bentley brothers and their creations leaving Bugattis and the rest of the field in the dust at Le Mans in the 1920s and 1930s. Bond himself had witnessed the astonishing Bentley Speed 8 take the checkered flag at the race in 2003, back in the game after three-quarters of a century. It had always been his goal to own one of the stately yet wickedly fast and clever vehicles. While the E-type Jaguar sitting below his flat had been a legacy from his father, the GT had been an indirect bequest. He'd bought his first Continental some years ago, depleting what remained of the life-insurance payment that had come his way upon his parents' deaths. He'd recently traded up to the new model.

He now came off the motorway and proceeded toward March, in the heart of the Fens. He knew little about the place. He'd heard of the "March March March," a walk by students from March to Cambridge in, of course, the third month of the year. There was Whitemoor prison. And tourists came to see St. Wendreda's Church—Bond would have to trust the tourist office's word that it was spectacular; he hadn't been inside a house of worship, other than for surveillance purposes, in years.

Ahead loomed the old British Army base. He continued in a broad circle to the back, which was surrounded by vicious barbed-wire fencing and signs warning against intrusion. He saw why: It was being demolished. So this was the work he'd learned of. Half a dozen buildings had already been razed. Only one remained, three stories high, old red brick. A faded sign announced: HOSPITAL.

Several large lorries were present, along with bulldozers, other earth-moving equipment and caravans, which sat on a hill a hundred yards from the building, probably the temporary headquarters for the demolition crew. A black car was parked near the largest caravan but no one was about. Bond wondered why; today was Monday and not a bank holiday.

He nosed the car into a small copse, where it could not be seen. Climbing out, he surveyed the terrain: complicated waterways, potato and sugar-beet fields and clusters of trees. Bond donned his 5.11 tactical outfit, with the shrapnel tear in the shoulder of the jacket and tainted from the smell of scorching—from rescuing the clue in Serbia that had led him here—then stepped out of his City shoes into low combat boots.

He clipped his Walther and two holsters of ammunition to a canvas web utility belt.

If you hit a speed bump, give me a shout.

He also pocketed his silencer, a torch, a tool kit and his folding knife.

Then Bond paused, going into that other place, where he went before any tactical operation: dead calm, eyes focused and taking in every detail—branches that might betray with a snap, bushes that could hide the muzzle of a sniper rifle, evidence of wires, sensors and cameras that might report his presence to an enemy.

And preparing to take a life, quickly and efficiently, if he had to. That was part of the other world too.

And he was all the more cautious because of the many questions this assignment had raised.

Fit your response to your enemy's purpose.

But what was Noah's purpose?

Indeed, who the hell was he?

Bond moved through the trees, then cut across the corner of a field dotted with an early growth of sugar beet. He diverted around a fragrant bog and moved carefully through a tangle of brambles, making his way toward the hospital. Finally he came to the barbed-wire perimeter, posted with warning signs. Eastern Demolition and Scrap was doing the work, they announced. He'd never heard of the company but thought he might have seen their lorries—there was something familiar about the distinctive green and yellow coloring.

He scanned the overgrown field in front of the building, the parade grounds behind. He saw nobody, then began to clip his way through the fence with wire cutters, thinking how clever it would be to use the building for secret meetings relevant to Incident 20; the place would be soon torn down, which would destroy any evidence of its use.

No workers were nearby but the presence of the black car suggested someone might be inside. He looked for a back door or other unobtrusive entrance. Five minutes later he found one: a depression in the earth, ten feet deep, caused by the collapse of what must have been an underground supply tunnel. He climbed down into the bowl and shone his torch inside. It seemed to lead into the basement of the hospital, about fifty yards away.

He started forward, noting the ancient cracked brick walls and ceiling—just as two bricks dislodged themselves and crashed to the floor. On the ground there were small-gauge rail tracks, rusting and in places covered with mud.

Halfway along the grim passage, pebbles and a stream of damp earth pelted his head. He glanced up and saw that, six feet above, the tunnel ceiling was scored like a cracked eggshell. It looked as if a handclap would bring the whole thing down on him.

Not a great place to be buried alive, Bond reflected.

Then he added wryly to himself, *And just where exactly* would *be?*

"Brilliant job," Severan Hydt told Niall Dunne.

They were alone in Hydt's site caravan, parked a hundred yards from the dark, brooding British Army hospital outside March. Since the Gehenna team had been under pressure to finish the job by tomorrow, Hydt and Dunne had halted demolition this morning and made sure that the crew stayed away—most of Hydt's employees knew nothing of Gehenna and he had to be very careful when the two operations overlapped.

"I was satisfied," Dunne said flatly—in the tone with which he responded to nearly everything, be it praise, criticism or dispassionate observation.

The team had left with the device half an hour ago, having assembled it with the materials Dunne had provided. It would be hidden in a safe house nearby until Friday.

Hydt had spent some time walking around the last building to be razed: the hospital, erected more than eighty years ago.

Demolition made Green Way a huge amount of money. The company profited from people paying to tear down what they no longer wanted . . . and it profited by extracting from the rubble what other people *did* want: wooden and steel beams, wire, aluminum and copper pipes—beautiful copper, a rag-and-bone man's dream. But Hydt's interest in demolition, of course, went beyond the financial. He now studied the ancient building in a state of tense rapture, as a hunter stares at an unsuspecting animal moments before he fires the fatal shot.

He couldn't help but think of the hospital's former occupants too—the dead and dying.

The image brought with it a shiver of pleasure.

Hydt had snapped dozens of pictures of the grand old lady as he'd strolled through the rotting halls, the moldy rooms—particularly the mortuary and autopsy areas—collecting images of decay and decline. His photographic archives included shots of old buildings as well as bodies. He had quite a number, some rather artistic, of places like Northumberland Terrace, Palmers Green on the North Circular Road, the now-vanished Pura oil works on Bow Creek in Canning Town and the Gothic Royal Arsenal and Royal Laboratory in Woolwich. His photos of Lovell's Wharf in Greenwich, a testament to what aggressive neglect could achieve, never failed to move him.

On his mobile, Niall Dunne was giving instructions to the driver of the lorry that had just left, explaining how best to hide the device. They were quite precise details, in accord with his nature and that of the horrific weapon.

Although the Irishman made him uneasy, Hydt was grateful their paths had intersected. He could not have proceeded as quickly, or as safely, with Gehenna without him. Hydt had come to refer to him as "the man who thinks of everything," and indeed he was. So Severan Hydt was happy to put up with the eerie silences, the cold stares, the awkward arrangement of robotic steel that was Niall Dunne. The two men made an efficient partnership, if an ironic one: an engineer whose nature was to build, a rag-and-bone man whose passion was destruction.

What a curious package we humans are. Predictable only in death. Faithful only then too, Hydt reflected, and then discarded that thought.

Just after Dunne disconnected, there was a knock on the door. It opened. Eric Janssen, a Green Way security man, who'd driven them up to March, stood in the doorway, his face troubled.

"Mr. Hydt, Mr. Dunne, someone's gone into the building."

"What?" Hydt barked, turning his huge, equine head the man's way.

"He went in through the tunnel."

Dunne rattled off a number of questions. Was he alone? Had there been any transmissions that Janssen had monitored? Was his car nearby? Had there been any unusual traffic in the area? Was the man armed?

The answers suggested that he was operating by himself and wasn't with Scotland Yard or the Security Service.

"Did you get a picture or a good look at him?" Dunne asked.

"No, sir."

Hydt clicked two long nails together. "The man with the Serbs? From last night?" he asked Dunne. "The private operator?"

"Not impossible but I don't know how he could have traced us here." Dunne gazed out of the caravan's dirt-spattered window as if he wasn't seeing the building. Hydt knew the Irishman was drafting a blueprint in his mind. Or perhaps examining one he'd already prepared in case of such a contingency. For a long moment he was motionless. Finally, drawing his gun, Dunne stepped out of the caravan, gesturing to Janssen to follow.

Chapter 13

The smells of mold, rot, chemicals, oil and petrol were overwhelming. Bond struggled not to cough and blinked tears from his stinging eyes. Could he detect smoke too?

The hospital's basement here was windowless. Only faint illumination filtered in from where he'd entered the tunnel. Bond splayed light from his torch around him. He was beside a railway turntable, designed to rotate small locomotives after they'd carted in supplies or patients.

His Walther in hand, Bond searched the area, listening for voices, footsteps, the click of a weapon chambering bullets or going off safety. But the place was deserted.

He'd entered through the tunnel at the south end. As he moved farther north and away from the turntable, he came to a sign that prompted a brief laugh: MORTUARY.

It consisted of three large windowless rooms that had clearly been occupied recently; the floors were dust-free and new cheap workbenches were arranged throughout. One of these rooms seemed to be the source of the smoke. Bond saw electricity cables secured to the wall and floor with duct tape, presumably providing power for lights and whatever work had been going on. Perhaps an electrical short had produced the fumes.

He left the mortuary and came to a large open

space, with a double door, to the right, east, opening to the parade ground. Light filtered through the
crack between the panels—a possible escape route, he
noted, and he memorized its location and the place-
ment of columns that might provide cover in the event
he had to make his way to it under fire.

Ancient steel tables, stained brown and black, were
bolted to the floor, each with its own drain. For post-
mortems, of course.

Bond continued to the north end of the building, which ended in a series of smaller rooms with
barred windows. A sign here suggested why: MENTAL
HEALTH WARD.

He tried the doors leading up to the ground floor,
found them locked and returned to the three rooms
next to the turntable. A systematic search finally revealed the source of the smoke. On the floor in the
corner of one room there was an improvised hearth.
He spotted large curls of ash, on which he could dis-
cern writing. The flakes were delicate; he tried to pick
one up but it dissolved between his fingers.

Careful, he told himself.

He walked over to one of the wires running up
the wall. He pulled off several pieces of the silver duct
tape securing the cords and sliced them into six-inch
lengths with his knife. He then carefully pressed them
onto the gray and black ash curls, slipped them into
his pocket and continued his search. In a second room
something silvery caught his eye. He hurried to the
corner and found tiny splinters of metal littering the
floor. He picked them up with another piece of tape,
which he also pocketed.

Then Bond froze. The building had begun to vibrate. A moment later the shaking increased considerably. He heard a diesel engine rattling, not far away. That explained why the demolition site had been deserted; the workers must have been at lunch and now they'd returned. He couldn't get to the ground or higher floors without going outside, where he'd surely be spotted. It was time to leave.

He stepped back into the turntable room to leave through the tunnel.

And was saved from a broken skull by a matter of a few decibels.

He didn't see the attacker or hear his breathing or the hiss of whatever he swung but Bond sensed a faint muting of the diesel's rattle, as the man's clothing absorbed the sound.

Instinctively he leaped back and the metal pipe missed him by inches.

Bond grabbed it firmly in his left hand and his attacker stumbled, off balance, too surprised to release his weapon. The young blond man wore a cheap dark suit and white shirt, a security man's uniform, Bond assessed. He had no tie; he'd probably removed it in anticipation of the assault. His eyes wide in dismay, he staggered again and nearly fell but righted himself fast and clumsily launched himself into Bond. Together they crashed to the filthy floor of the circular room. He was not, Bond noted, the Irishman.

Bond jumped up and stepped forward, clenching his hands into fists, but it was a feint—he intended to get the muscular fellow to step back and avoid a blow, which he accommodatingly did, giving Bond the chance to draw his weapon. He didn't, however, fire; he needed the man alive.

Covered by Bond's .40-caliber pistol, he froze, although his hand went inside his jacket.

"Leave it," Bond said coldly. "Lie down, arms spread."

Still, the man remained motionless, sweating with nerves, hand hovering over the butt of his gun. A Glock, Bond noted. The man's phone began to hum. He glanced at his jacket pocket.

"Get down now!"

If he drew, Bond would try to wound but he might end up killing the man.

The phone stopped ringing.

"Now." Bond lowered his aim, focusing on the attacker's right arm, near the elbow.

It appeared the blond man was going to comply. His shoulders drooped and in the shadowy light his eyes widened with fear and uncertainty.

At that moment, though, the bulldozer must have rolled over the ground nearby; bricks and earth rained down from the ceiling. Bond was struck by a large chunk of stone. He winced and stepped back, blinking dust out of his eyes. Had his assailant been more professional—or less panicked—he would have drawn his weapon and fired. But he didn't; he turned and ran down the tunnel.

Bond slipped into his preferred stance, a fencer's, left foot pointing forward and the right perpendicular and behind. Two-handed, he fired a single deafening shot that struck the man in the calf; screaming, he went down hard, about ten yards from the entrance to the tunnel.

Bond raced after him. As he did so, the shaking grew stronger, the rattle louder, and more bricks fell from the walls. Cascades of plaster and dust poured from the ceiling. A cricket ball of concrete landed directly on Bond's shoulder wound and he grunted at the burst of pain.

But he kept moving steadily along the tunnel. His assailant was on the ground, dragging himself toward the fissure where sunlight eased in.

The bulldozer seemed directly overhead now. Move, dammit, Bond told himself. They were probably about to knock the whole bloody place down. As he got closer to the wounded man, the *chug chug chug* of the diesel engine rose in volume. More bricks plummeted to the floor.

Not a great place to be buried alive . . .

Only ten yards to the wounded man. Get a tourniquet on him, get him out of the tunnel and under cover—and start asking questions.

But at a stunning crash, the soft illumination of the spring day at the end of the tunnel dimmed. It was replaced by two burning white eyes, glowing through the dust. They paused and then, as if they belonged to a lion spotting its prey, shifted slightly, turning directly toward Bond. With a fierce cough, the bulldozer plowed relentlessly forward, pushing a surge of mud and stone before it.

Bond aimed his gun but there was no target—the blade of the machine was high, protecting the operator's cab. The vehicle crawled steadily on, pushing before it a mass of earth, brick and other debris.

"No!" cried the wounded man, as the bulldozer pressed forward. The driver didn't see him. Or if he did, he couldn't have cared less about the man's death.

With a scream, Bond's assailant disappeared under

the rocky blanket. A moment later the rattling treads
rolled over the spot where he was buried.

Soon the headlights were gone, blocked by debris,
and then all was total darkness. Bond clicked his torch
on and sprinted back to the turntable room. At the
entrance he tripped and fell hard as earth and brick
piled up to his ankles, then calves.

A moment later his knees were held fast.

Behind him the bulldozer continued to ram forward, shoving the muddy detritus farther into the
room. Bond was now gripped to the waist. Another
thirty seconds and his face would be covered.

But the weight of the debris mountain proved too
much for the bulldozer, or perhaps the vehicle had hit
the building's foundation. The tide ceased to move
forward. Before the operator could maneuver for better purchase, Bond dug himself free and scrabbled out
of the room. His eyes stung; his lungs were in agony.
Spitting dust and grit, he shone the torch back up the
tunnel. It was completely plugged.

He hurried back through the three windowless
rooms where he'd collected the ash and the bits of
metal. He paused beside the door that led to the autopsy chamber; had they sealed the exit to force him
into a trap? Were the Irishman and other security
people waiting in ambush for him? He screwed the
silencer onto his Walther.

Inhaling deep breaths, he paused for a moment,
then pushed the door open fast, dropping into a defensive shooting position, torch pointing forward from
his left hand, on which rested his right, clutching the
pistol.

The massive empty hall yawned. But the double

doors he'd seen earlier, admitting a shaft of light, were sealed; the bulldozer had piled tons of dirt against them too.

Trapped . . .

He sprinted to the smaller rooms on the north side of the basement, the mental health ward. The largest of these—the office, he assumed—had a door but it was securely locked. Bond aimed the Walther and, standing at an oblique angle, fired four wheezing shots into the metal lock plate, then four into the hinges.

This had no effect. Lead, even half-jacketed lead, is no match for steel. He reloaded and slipped the spent magazine into his left pocket, where he always kept the empties.

He was regarding the barred windows when a loud voice made him jump.

"*Attention! Opgelet! Groźba! Nebzpečí!*"

Swinging around, Bond looked for a target.

But the voice came from a loudspeaker on the wall.

"*Attention! Opgelet! Groźba! Nebzpečí! This is the three-minute warning!*" The last sentence, a recording, was repeated in Dutch, Polish and Ukrainian.

Warning?

"*Evacuate immediately! Danger! Explosive charges have been set!*"

Bond shone the torch around the room.

The wires! They weren't to provide electricity for construction—they were attached to explosives. Bond hadn't seen them since the charges were taped to steel joists high in the ceiling. The entire building had been rigged for demolition.

Three minutes . . .

The torch revealed dozens of packets of explosive,

enough to turn the stone walls around him to dust—
and Bond into vapor. And all the exits had been sealed.
His heart rate ratcheting, sweat dotting his forehead,
Bond slipped the torch and pistol away and gripped
one of the iron bars over a window. He tugged hard
but it held.

In the hazy light trickling through the glass, he
looked about, then climbed a nearby girder. He ripped
one of the explosive packets down and leaped back
to the floor. The charges were an RDX composite, to
judge from the smell. With his knife he cut off a large
wad and jammed it against the knob and lock on the
door. That should be enough to blow the lock without
killing himself in the process.

Get on with it!

Bond stepped back about twenty feet, steadied his
aim and fired. He hit the explosive dead on.

But, as he'd feared, nothing happened—except that
the yellow-gray mass of deadly plastic fell undramati-
cally to the floor with a plop. Composites explode only
with a detonator, not with physical impact, even that of
a bullet traveling at two thousand feet per second. He'd
hoped this substance might prove the exception.

The two-minute warning resounded through the
room.

Bond looked up, to where the detonator he'd pulled
from the charge now dangled obscenely. But the only
way to set it off was with an electric current.

Electricity . . .

The loudspeakers? No, the voltage was far too low
to set off a blasting cap. So was the battery in his torch.

The voice rang out again, giving the one-minute
warning.

Bond wiped the sweat from his palms and worked the pistol's slide, ejecting a bullet. With his knife he pried out the lead slug and tossed it aside. He then pressed the cartridge, filled with gunpowder, into the wad of explosive, which he molded to the door.

He stepped back, aimed carefully at the tiny disc of his cartridge and squeezed off a round. The bullet hit the primer, which set off the powder and in turn the plastic. With a huge flare the explosion blew the lock to pieces.

It also knocked Bond to the floor, amid a shower of wood splinters and smoke. For a few seconds he lay stunned; then he struggled to his feet and staggered to the door, which was open, though jammed. The gap was only about eight inches wide. He grabbed the knob and began to wrest the heavy, stubborn panel open.

"Attention! Opgelet! Groźba! Nebzpečí!"

Chapter 14

In the site caravan, Severan Hydt and Niall Dunne stood beside each other, watching the old British Army hospital in tense anticipation. Everybody—even the gear-cold Dunne, Hydt speculated—enjoyed watching a controlled explosion bring down a building.

Since Janssen had not answered his phone and Dunne had heard a gunshot from inside, the Irishman had told Hydt he was sure the security man, Eric Janssen, had to be dead. He had sealed the hospital exits, then sprinted back to the caravan, running like an awkward animal, and had told Hydt that he was going to detonate the charges in the building. It was scheduled to come down tomorrow but there was no reason that the demolition couldn't be brought forward.

Dunne had activated the computerized system and pressed two red buttons simultaneously, starting the sequence. An insurance liability policy required that a 180-second recorded warning be broadcast throughout the building in languages representing those spoken by 90 percent of the workers. It would have taken longer to override the safety measure but if the intruder wasn't buried in the tunnel he was stuck in the mortuary. There was no way he could escape in time.

If, tomorrow or the next day, someone came asking about a missing person Hydt could reply, "Certainly, we'll check . . . What? Oh my God, we had no idea! We did all we were supposed to with the fence and the signs. And how could he have missed the recorded warnings? We're sorry—but we're hardly responsible."

"Fifteen seconds," Dunne said.

Silence as Hydt mouthed the countdown.

The timer on the wall now hit 0 and the computer sent its prearranged signal to the detonators.

They couldn't see the flash of the explosions at first—the initial ones were internal and low, to take out the main structural beams. But a few seconds later bursts of light flared like paparazzi cameras, followed by the sound of Christmas crackers, then deeper booms. The building seemed to shudder. Then, as if kneeling to offer its neck to an executioner's blade, the hospital slowly dipped and went down, a cloud of dust and smoke rolling outward fast.

After a few moments, Dunne said, "People will have heard it. We should go."

Hydt, though, was mesmerized by the pile of debris, so very different from the elegant if faded structure it had been a few moments ago. What had been something was now naught.

"Severan," Dunne persisted.

Hydt found himself aroused. He thought of Jessica Barnes, her white hair, her pale, textured skin. She knew nothing about Gehenna so he hadn't brought her today, but he was sorry she wasn't there. Well, he'd ask her to meet him at his office, then drive home.

His belly gave a pleasant tap. A sensation supercharged by the memory of the body he'd found at Green Way that morning . . . and in anticipation of what would happen tomorrow.

A *hundred deaths* . . .

"Yes, yes." Severan Hydt collected his briefcase and

stepped outside. He didn't climb into the Audi A8 immediately, though. He turned to study once more the dust and smoke hovering over the destroyed building. He noted that the explosive had been skillfully set. He reminded himself to thank the crew. Rigging charges is a true art. The trick is not to blow up the building but simply to eliminate what keeps it upright, allowing nature—gravity, in this case—to do the job.

Which was, Hydt now reflected, a metaphor for his own role on earth.

Chapter 15

Early-afternoon zebra bands of sun and shadow rolled over the low rows of sugar beets in the Fenland field.

James Bond lay on his back, arms and legs splayed, like a child who'd been making angels in snow and didn't want to go home. Surrounded by the sea of low green leaves, he was thirty yards from the pile of rubble that had been the old army hospital . . . the pile of rubble that had very nearly entombed him. He was—temporarily, he prayed—deprived of his hearing, thanks to the shock waves from the plastic explosive. He'd kept his eyes closed against the flash and shrapnel, but he'd had to use both hands to manage his escape, wrenching open the mental health ward's door, as the main charges detonated and the building came down behind him.

He now rose slightly—sugar beets in May provided scant cover—and gazed around for signs of a threat.

Nothing. Whoever had been behind the plan—the Irishman, Noah or an associate—wasn't searching for him; they were probably convinced he had died in the collapse.

Breathing hard to clear his lungs of dust and sour chemical smoke, he got to his feet and staggered from the field.

He returned to the car and dropped into the front seat. He fished a bottle of water from the back and drank some, then leaned outside and poured the rest into his eyes.

He fired up the massive engine, comforted that he could now hear the bubble of the exhaust, and took a different route out of March, heading east to avoid running into anyone connected with the demolition site, then circling back west. Soon he was on the A1, heading to London to decipher whatever cryptic messages about Incident 20 the scraps of ash he'd collected might hold.

At close to four that afternoon Bond pulled into the ODG car park beneath the building.

He thought of having a shower but decided he didn't have time. He washed his hands and face, stuck a plaster on a small gash, courtesy of a falling brick, and hurried to Philly. He handed her the pieces of duct tape. "Can you get these analyzed?"

"For God's sake, James, what happened?" She sounded alarmed. The tactical trousers and jacket had taken the bulk of the abuse but some new bruises were already showing in glorious violet.

"Little run-in with a bulldozer and some C4 or Semtex—I'm fine. Find out everything you can about Eastern Demolition and Scrap. And I'd like to know who owns the army base outside March. The MoD? Or have they sold it?"

"I'll get onto it."

Bond returned to his office and had just sat down when Mary Goodnight buzzed him. "James. That man is on line two." Her tone made clear who the caller was.

Bond stabbed the button. "Percy."

The slick voice: "James. Hello! I'm en route back

from Cambridge. Thought you and me should have a chin-wag. See if we've found any pieces to our puzzle."

You and *me* . . . Unfortunate pronoun from an Oxbridge man. "How about *your* excursion?"

"When I got up there, I did some looking around. Turns out the Porton Down folk have a little operation nearby. Stumbled across it. Quite by chance."

This amused Bond. "Well, that's interesting. And is there a connection between biochemicals and Noah or Incident Twenty?"

"Can't say. Their CCTVs and visitor logs didn't turn up anything that stood out. But I've got my assistant toiling away."

"And the pub?"

"Curry was all right. The waitress didn't remember who'd ordered the pie or the plowman's so long ago but we could hardly expect her to, could we? What about you? Did the mysterious note about the chemist and two days past the Ides of March pan out?"

Bond had prepared for this. "I tried a long shot. I went to March, Boots Road, and ran across an old military base."

A pause. "Ah." The Division Three man laughed, though the sound seemed devoid of humor. "So you'd misread the clue when we were chatting earlier. And was the infamous number seventeen *tomorrow*'s date, by any chance?"

Whatever else, Osborne-Smith was sharp. "Possibly. When I got up there, the place was being demolished." Bond added evasively, "It turned up more questions than anything else, I'm afraid. The techies are looking at some finds. A few small things. I'll send over their reports."

"Do, thanks. I'm peering into all things Islamic here, Afghan connection, spikes in SIGINT, the usual. Should keep me busy for a while."

Good. Bond couldn't have asked for a better approach to Deputy Senior Director of Field Operations Mr. Percy Osborne-Smith.

Keep him busy . . .

They rang off and Bond called Bill Tanner to brief him about what had happened in March. They agreed to do nothing for now about the body of the man who had attacked Bond at the hospital, preferring to keep his cover intact rather than learn anything about the corpse.

Mary Goodnight stuck her head through the doorway. "Philly called when you were on the phone. She's found a few things for you. I told her to come up." His PA was frowning, her eyes turned to one of Bond's dim windows. "A shame, isn't it? About Philly."

"What are you talking about?"

"I thought you'd heard? Tim broke it off. He sat her down a few days ago—they even had the church booked, and her hen do was planned. A girls' weekend in Spain. I was going."

How observant am I? Bond thought. *That's* what was missing from her desk on the third floor. The pictures of her fiancé. Probably the engagement ring had gone MIA too.

"What happened?" he asked.

"I suppose it's always more than one thing, isn't it? They hadn't been getting on well recently, more than a few bad patches—rows about her driving too fast and working all hours. She missed a big family reunion at his parents'. Then, out of the blue, he had the chance of a posting to Singapore or Malaysia. He took it. They'd been together for three years, hadn't they?"

"Sorry to hear that."

The discussion of the drama ended, though, with the arrival of the person in question.

Not noticing the still atmosphere into which she'd walked, Philly strode past Goodnight with a smile and into Bond's office, where she dropped breezily into a chair. Her sensuous face seemed to have narrowed and her hazel eyes shone with the intensity of a hunter picking up sure track. It made her even more beautiful. A hen party in Spain with the girls? God, he simply could *not* picture that, any more than he could see Philly lugging home two Waitrose carrier bags to assemble a hearty dinner for a man named Tim and their children Matilda and Archie.

Enough! he upbraided himself and concentrated on what she was telling him. "Our people could read one scrap of the ash. The words were 'the Gehenna plan.' And below that 'Friday, May 20.'"

"Gehenna? Familiar but I can't place it."

"There's a reference to it in the Bible. I'll find out more. I only ran 'Gehenna plan' through the security agencies and criminal databases. It returned negative."

"What's on the other piece of ash?"

"That was more badly damaged. Our lab could make out the words 'term' and 'five million pounds' but the rest was beyond them. They sent it to Specialist Crime at the Yard, under an eyes-only order. They'll get back to me by this evening."

"'Term' . . . terms of the deal, I'd guess. Payment or down payment of five million for the attack or whatever it's to be. That suggests Noah's doing it for money, not for the sake of politics or ideology."

She nodded. "About the Serbian connection: My Hungarian ploy didn't work. The folk in Belgrade are really quite cross with you, James. But I had your I Branch set me up as somebody from the EU—the head of the Directorate of Transportation Safety Investigations."

"What the hell's that?"

"I made it up. I did a pretty good Swiss-French accent, though I say it myself. The Serbs are dying to do anything they can to keep the European Union happy so they're scurrying to get back to me about hazmats on the train and more details about Karic."

Philly was truly golden.

"And Eastern Demolition have headquarters in Slough. They were low bidders for the demolition project at the British Army base in March."

"Is it a public limited company?"

"Private. And owned by a holding company, also private: Green Way International. It's quite big and operates in half a dozen countries. One man owns all the shares. Severan Hydt."

"That's really his name?"

She laughed. "At first I wondered what his parents were thinking. But it seems he changed it by deed poll when he was in his twenties."

"What was his birth name?"

"Maarten Holt."

"Holt to Hydt," Bond mused. "I don't see the point—though it's hardly remarkable—but Maarten to Severan? Why, in heaven's name?"

She shrugged. "Green Way is a huge rubbish-collection and recycling operation. You've seen their lorries but probably haven't thought much about them. I couldn't find a great deal because they're not public and Hydt stays clear of the press. Article in the *Times* dubbed him the world's richest rag-and-bone man. The *Guardian* ran a profile of him a few years ago and was fairly complimentary but he gave them only a few generic quotes and that was it. I found out he was Dutch-born, kept dual citizenship for a time and is now just British."

Philly's body language and the hunter's sheen in her eyes hinted that she hadn't revealed all.

"And?" Bond asked.

She smiled. "I found some online references to when he was a mature student at the University of Bristol, where he did rather well, by the way." She explained that Hydt had been active in the university's sailing club, captaining a boat in competitions. "He not only raced but built his own. It earned him a nickname."

"And what was it?" Bond asked, though he had a feeling he knew.

"Noah."

Chapter 16

The time was now half past five. Since it would be several hours before Philly received the intelligence she was waiting for, Bond suggested they meet for dinner.

She agreed and returned to her workstation, while Bond composed an encrypted e-mail to M, copying in Bill Tanner, saying that Noah was Severan Hydt and including a synopsis of his background and what had happened in March. He added that Hydt referred to the attack involved in Incident 20 as the "Gehenna plan." More would be forthcoming.

He received a terse reply:

> 007—
>
> Authorized to proceed. Appropriate liaison with domestic organizations expected.
>
> M

My carte grise. . . .

Bond left his office, took the lift to the second floor and entered a large room filled with more computers than an electronics shop. A few men and women labored at monitors or at the type of workstations to be found in a university chemistry laboratory. Bond walked to a small, glass-walled office at the far end and tapped on the window.

Sanu Hirani, head of the ODG's Q Branch, was a

slim man of forty or so. His complexion was sallow and his luxuriant black hair framed a face handsome enough to get him roles in Bollywood. A brilliant cricketer, known for his fast bowling, he had degrees in chemistry, electrical engineering and computer science from top universities in the UK and America (where he had been successful in everything except introducing his sport to the Yanks, who could neither grasp the game's subtleties, nor tolerate the length of a Test match).

Q Branch was the technical support enclave within the ODG, and Hirani oversaw all aspects of the gadgetry that has always been used in tradecraft. Wizards for departments like Q Branch and the CIA's Science and Technology Division spent their time coming up with hardware and software innovations like miniature cameras, improbable weapons, concealments, communications devices and surveillance equipment—such as Hirani's latest: a hypersensitive omnidirectional microphone mounted within a dead fly. ("A bug in a bug," Bond had commented wryly to its creator, who had replied that he was the eighteenth person to make the joke and, by the way, a fly was not, biologically speaking, a bug.)

Since the ODG's raison d'être was operational, much of Hirani's work lay in ensuring he had sufficient monoculars, binoculars, camouflage, communications devices, specialized weapons and countersurveillance gear to hand. In this regard he was like a librarian who made sure the books were checked out appropriately and returned on time.

But Hirani's particular genius was his ability to invent and improvise, coming up with devices like the iQPhone. The ODG was, of all things, the pat-

ent holder on dozens of his inventions. When Bond
or other O Branch agents were in the field and found
themselves in a tight spot, one call to Hirani, at any
time of day or night, and he would find a solution.
He or his people might put something together in the
office and pop it into the FCO diplomatic pouch for
overnight delivery. More often, though, time was critical and Hirani would enlist one of his many wily innovators and scroungers around the world to build, find
or modify a device in the field.

"James." The men shook hands. "You've bought Incident Twenty, I hear."

"Seems so."

Bond sat down, noticing a book on Hirani's desk:
The Secret War of Charles Fraser-Smith. It was one of his
own favorites on the history of gadgetry in espionage.

"How serious is it?"

"Rather," Bond said laconically, not sharing that
he'd nearly been killed twice already in pursuing the
assignment, which he'd had for less than forty-eight
hours.

Sitting beneath pictures of early IBM computers
and Indian cricketers, Hirani asked, "What do you
need?"

Bond lowered his voice so that the closest Q Branch
worker, a young woman raptly staring at her screen,
could not hear. "What kind of surveillance kits do you
have that one man could put in place? I can't get to the
subject's computer or phone but I may be able to plant
something in his office, vehicle or home. Disposable. I
probably can't retrieve it later."

"Ah, yes . . ." Hirani's luminescent eyes dimmed.

"Some problem, Sanu?"

"Well, I must tell you, James. Not ten minutes ago I had a call from upstairs."

"Bill Tanner?"

"No—farther upstairs."

M. Dammit, Bond thought. He could see where this was going.

Hirani went on: "And he said that if anyone from O Branch wished to check out a surveillance kit I was to let him know immediately. A touch coincidental."

"A touch," Bond said sourly.

"So," Hirani said, with a qualified smile, "shall I tell him that someone from O Branch wishes to check out a surveillance kit?"

"Perhaps you could hold off for a bit."

"Well, get it sorted," the man offered, the gleam in his face restored. "I have some *wonderful* packages for you to choose from." He sounded like a car salesman. "A microphone that's powered by induction. You only have to place it near a power cord, no battery needed. It'll pick up voices from fifty feet away and adjust the volume automatically so there's no distortion. Oh, and another thing we've been having great success with is a two-pound coin—the 'ninety-four tercentenary of the Bank of England commemorative. It's relatively rare, so a target tends to keep it for good luck, but not so rare that he would sell it. Battery lasts for four months."

Bond sighed. The off-limits devices sounded so damn perfect. He thanked the man and told him he'd be in touch. He returned to his office, where he found Mary Goodnight at her desk. He saw no reason for her to stay. "Scoot on home now. Good evening, Goodnight."

She glanced at his latest injuries and forwent the opportunity for mothering him, which from past experience she knew would be deflected. She settled for "See to those, James," then gathered up her handbag and coat.

Sitting back, Bond was suddenly aware of the stench of his sweat and the crescents of brick dust under his nails. He wanted to get home and shower. Have his first drink of the day. Yet there was something he had to sort out first.

He turned to his screen and entered the Golden Wire's general information database, from which he learned where Severan Hydt's business and home were located, the latter, curiously, in a low-income area of East London known as Canning Town. Green Way's main premises were on the Thames near Rainham, abutting the Wildspace Conservation Park.

Bond peered at satellite maps of Hydt's home and Green Way's operation. It was vitally important to set up surveillance on the man. But there was no legitimate way to conduct it without enlisting Osborne-Smith and the A Branch snoop teams from MI5—and the instant the Division Three man learned Hydt's identity he'd move in to "detain" him and the Irishman. Bond considered the risk again. How realistic was his concern that if the two were pulled in, other co-conspirators would accelerate the carnage or vanish until they struck again next month or next year?

Evil, James Bond had learned, can be tirelessly patient.

Surveillance or not?

He debated. After a moment's hesitation, he reluctantly picked up the phone.

Chapter 17

At half past six, Bond drove to his flat and, in the garage, reversed into the spot beside his racing-green Jaguar. He climbed the stairs to the first floor, unlocked the door, disarmed the alarm and confirmed with a separate security function—a fast-framed video—that only May, his housekeeper, had been there. (Feeling somewhat embarrassed, he'd told her when she'd started working for him that the security camera was a requirement of his government employer's; the flat had to be monitored when he was away, even if she was working there. "Considering what you must do for the country, being a patriot and all, it's no bother's," the staunch woman had said, using the fragment of "sir," a mark of respect reserved for him alone.)

He checked messages on his home phone. He had only one. It was from a friend who lived in Mayfair, Fouad Kharaz, a wily, larger-than-life Jordanian, who had all manner of business dealings, involving vehicles mostly: cars, planes and the most astonishing yachts Bond had ever seen. Kharaz and he were members of the same gaming club in Berkeley Square, the Commodore.

Unlike many such clubs in London, where membership could be had with twenty-four hours' notice and five hundred pounds, the Commodore was a proper establishment, requiring patience and considerable vetting to join. Once you were a member, you were expected to adhere strictly to a number of rules, such as the dress code, and behave impeccably at the tables. It also boasted a fine restaurant and cellar.

Kharaz had called to invite Bond to dine there tonight. "A problem, James. I have fallen heir to two beautiful women from Saint-Tropez—how it happened is too long and delicate a story to leave as a message. But I can't be charming enough for both of them. Will you help?"

Smiling, Bond rang him back and told him he had another engagement. A rain check was arranged.

Then he went through his shower ritual—steaming hot, then icy cold—and dried himself briskly. He ran his fingers over his cheeks and chin and decided to maintain a lifelong prejudice against shaving twice in one day. Then he chided himself: Why were you even thinking about it? Philly Maidenstone's pretty and clever and she rides a hell of a fine motorcycle—but she's a colleague. That's all.

The black leather jumpsuit, however, made an unbidden appearance in his mind.

In a toweling robe Bond stepped into the kitchen and poured two fingers of bourbon, Basil Hayden's, into a glass, dropped in one ice cube and drank half, enjoying the sharp, nutty flavor. The first sip of the day was invariably the best, especially coming as this one did—after a harrowing excursion against an enemy and ahead of an evening with a beautiful woman . . .

He caught himself again. Stop.

He sat in an old leather chair in the living room, which was sparsely furnished. The majority of the items in it had been his parents', inherited when they had died and kept in storage near his aunt's in Kent.

He'd bought a few things: some lamps, a desk and chairs, a Bose sound system he rarely had a chance to listen to.

On the mantelpiece there were silver-framed photos of his parents and grandparents—on his father's side in Scotland, his mother's in Switzerland. Several showed his aunt Charmian with the young Bond in Kent. On the walls were other photographs, taken by his mother, a freelance photojournalist. Mostly black-and-white, the photos depicted a variety of images: political gatherings, labor union events, sports competitions, panoramic scenes of exotic locations.

There was also a curious objet d'art in the mantelpiece's center: a bullet. It had nothing to do with Bond's role as an agent in the 00 Section of the ODG's O Branch. Its source was a very different time and place of Bond's life. He walked to the fireplace and turned over the solid piece of ammunition in his hand once or twice, finally replacing it and returning to his chair.

Then, despite his protest that he keep affairs with Philly—that he keep *matters* relating to *Agent Maidenstone* purely professional—he couldn't stop thinking of her as a woman.

And one no longer betrothed.

Bond had to admit that what he felt for Philly was more than pure physical lust. And he now asked himself a question that had arisen at other times, about other women, albeit rarely: Could something serious develop between them?

Bond's romantic life was more complicated than most. The barriers to his having a partner were to some degree his extensive traveling, the demands of his job and the constant danger that surrounded him.

But more fundamental was the tricky matter of admitting who he really was and, more tellingly, his duties within the 00 Section, which some, perhaps most, women would find distasteful, if not abhorrent.

He knew that at some point he would have to admit to at least part of it to any woman who became more than a casual lover. You can keep secrets from those you're close to for only so long. People are far more clever and observant than we think and, between romantic partners, one's fundamental secrets stay hidden only because the other chooses to let them remain so.

Plausible deniability might work in Whitehall but it didn't last between lovers.

Yet with Philly Maidenstone this was not a problem. There would be no confessions about his profession over dinner or amid tousled morning bedclothes; she knew his CV and his remit—knew them intimately.

And she'd suggested a restaurant near her flat.

What sort of message lay in that choice?

James Bond glanced at his watch. It was time to dress and attempt to decipher the code.

Chapter 18

At eight fifteen the taxi dropped Bond at Antoine's in Bloomsbury and he immediately approved of Philly's choice. He hated crowded, noisy restaurants and bars and on more than one occasion had walked out of upmarket establishments when the decibel level had proved to be too irritating. Upscale pubs were more "ghastly" than "gastro," he'd once quipped.

But Antoine's was quiet and dimly lit. An impressive wine selection was visible at the back of the room and the walls were filled with muted portraits from the nineteenth century. Bond asked for a small booth not far from the wall of bottles. He settled into the plush leather, facing the front, as always, and studied the place. Businesspeople and locals, he judged.

"Something to drink?" asked the waiter, a pleasant man in his late thirties, with a shaved head and pierced ears.

Bond decided on a cocktail. "Crown Royal, on ice, a double, please. Add a half-measure of triple sec, two dashes of bitters and a twist of orange peel."

"Yes, sir. Interesting drink."

"Based on an Old Fashioned. My own creation, actually."

"Does it have a name?"

"Not yet," he said. "I've been looking for the right one."

A few moments later it arrived and he took a sip—

it was constructed perfectly and Bond said so. He'd just set the glass down when he saw Philly coming through the door, radiant with a smile. It seemed that her pace quickened when she saw him.

She was in close-fitting black jeans, a brown leather jacket and, under it, a tight dark green sweater, the color of his Jaguar.

He half rose as she joined him, sitting to his side, rather than across. She was carrying a briefcase.

"You all right?" she said.

He'd half expected something a bit more personal than this rather casual greeting. But then he asked himself sternly, Why?

She had barely taken off her jacket before she'd caught the eye of the waiter, who greeted her with a smile. "Ophelia."

"Aaron. I'll have a glass of the Mosel Riesling."

"On its way."

Her wine arrived and Bond told Aaron they'd wait to order. Their glasses nodded at one another but did not clink.

"First," Bond murmured, edging a little closer, "Hydt. Tell me about him."

"I checked with Specialist Operations at the Yard, Six, Interpol, NCIC and the CIA in America and the AIVD in the Netherlands. I made some discreet enquiries at Five, too." She'd obviously deduced the tension between Bond and Osborne-Smith. "No criminal records. No watch lists. More Tory than Labour but doesn't have much interest in politics. Not a member of any church. Treats his people well—no labor unrest of any kind. No problems with the Inland Revenue or Health and Safety. He just seems to be a wealthy busi-

nessman. *Very* wealthy. All he's ever done professionally is rubbish collection and recycling."

The Rag-and-Bone Man . . .

"He's fifty-six, never married. Both parents—they
were Dutch—are dead now. His father had some
money and traveled a lot on business. Hydt was born
in Amsterdam, then came here with his mother to live
when he was twelve. She had a breakdown so he grew
up mostly under the care of the housekeeper, who'd
accompanied them from Holland. Then his father lost
most of his money and vanished from his son's life. Because she wasn't getting paid, the housekeeper called
in Social Services and vanished—after *eight* years of
looking after the boy." Philly shook her head in sympathy. "He was fourteen."

Philly continued, "He started working as a dust-
man at fifteen. Then he's off the radar until he's in his
twenties. He opened Green Way just as the recycling
trend caught on."

"What happened? Did he inherit some money?"

"No. It's a bit of a mystery. He started penniless,
as far as I can tell. When he was older he put himself through university. He read ancient history and
archaeology."

"And Green Way?"

"It handles general rubbish disposal, wheelie-bin
collection, removal of construction waste at building
sites, scrap metal, demolition, recycling, document
shredding, dangerous-materials reclamation and disposal. According to the business press, it's moving into
a dozen other countries to start up rubbish tips and
recycling centers." Philly displayed a printout of a company sales brochure.

Bond frowned at the logo. It looked like a green dagger, resting on its side.

"It's not a knife," Philly said, laughing. "I thought the same thing. It's a leaf. Global warming, pollution and energy are the sexiest subjects in the au courant environmental movement. But rising quickly are planet-friendly rubbish disposal and recycling. And Green Way's one of the big innovators."

"Any Serbian connection?"

"Through a subsidiary he owns part of a small operation in Belgrade. But, like everybody else in the organization, nobody there has any criminal past."

"I just can't work out his game," Bond said. "He's not political, has no terrorist leanings. It almost looks like he's been hired to arrange the attack, or whatever it's to be, on Friday. But he hardly needs money." He sipped his cocktail. "Right, then, Detective Inspector Maidenstone, tell me about the evidence—that other bit of ash from up in March. Six made out the 'Gehenna plan' and 'Friday, 20 May.' Did Forensics at the Yard find anything else?"

Her voice dropped, which necessitated his leaning closer. He smelled a sweet but undefined scent. Her sweater, cashmere, brushed the back of his hand. "They did. They think the rest of the words were 'Course is confirmed. Blast radius must be a hundred feet minimum. Ten thirty is the optimal time.'"

"So, an explosive device of some kind. Ten thirty Friday—P.M., according to the original intercept. And 'course'—a shipping route or plane, most likely."

"Now," she continued, "the metal you found? It's a titanium-steel laminate. Unique. Nobody in the lab has ever seen anything like it. The pieces were shavings. They'd been machined in the past day or so."

Was that what Hydt's people had been doing in the basement of the hospital? Were they building a weapon with this metal?

"And Defence still owned the facility but it hasn't been used for three years."

His eyes swept over her marvelous profile from forehead to breasts as she sipped her wine.

Philly continued, "As for the Serbs, I practically said I'd force them to take on the euro in place of the dinar if they didn't help me. But they came through. The man working with the Irishman, Aldo Karic, was a load scheduler with the railway."

"He'd have known exactly which train the hazmat was on."

"Yes." Then she frowned. "About that, though, James. It's odd. The material was pretty bad. Methyl isocyanate, MIC. It's the chemical that killed all those people in Bhopal."

"God."

"But, look, here's the inventory of everything on board the train." She showed him the list, translated into English. "The chemical containers are practically bulletproof. You can drop one from a plane and supposedly it won't break open."

Bond was confused by this. "So a train crash wouldn't have produced a spill."

"Very unlikely. And another thing: the wagon with the chemical contained only about three hundred kilos of MIC. It's really bad stuff, certainly, but at Bhopal, forty-two *thousand* kilos were released. Even if a few of the drums had broken open, the damage would have been negligible."

But what else would the Irishman have been interested in? Bond looked over the list. Aside from the chemicals, the cargo was harmless: boilers, vehicle parts, motor oil, scrap, girders, timber . . . No weapons, unstable substances, other risky materials.

Maybe the incident had been an elaborate scheme to kill the train driver or someone living at the bottom of the hill below the restaurant. Had the Irishman been going to stage the death to look like an accident? Until they could home in on Noah's purpose, there could be no effective response. Bond could only hope that the surveillance he'd reluctantly put into play earlier in the evening would pay off. He asked, "Any more on Gehenna?"

"Hell."

"I'm sorry?"

Her face broke into a smile. "Gehenna is where the Judeo-Christian concept of hell came from. The word's a derivation of Gehinnom, or the Valley of Hinnom—a valley in Jerusalem. Ages ago, some people think, it was used as a site to burn rubbish and there may have been natural gas deposits in the rocks that kept the fires going perpetually. In the Bible, Gehenna came to mean a place where sinners and unbelievers would be punished.

"The only recent significant reference—if you can call a hundred and fifty years ago recent—was in a Rudyard Kipling poem." She'd memorized the verse and recited, "'Down to Gehenna or up to the Throne, / He travels the fastest who travels alone.'"

He liked that and repeated it to himself.

She said, "Now, for my other assignment, Steel Cartridge."

Relax, Bond told himself. He raised an eyebrow nonchalantly.

Philly said, "I couldn't see any connection between the Gehenna plan and Steel Cartridge."

"No, I understand that. I don't think they're related. This is something else—from before I joined the ODG."

The hazel eyes scanned his face, pausing momentarily on the scar. "You were Defense Intelligence, weren't you? And before that you were in Afghanistan with the Naval Reserve."

"That's right."

"Afghanistan . . . The Russians were there, of course, before we and the Americans decided to pop in for tea. Does it have to do with your assignments there?"

"Could very well. I don't know."

Philly realized she was asking questions he might not want to answer. "I got the original Russian data file that our Station R hacked and I went through the metadata. It sent me to other sources and I found out that Steel Cartridge was a targeted killing operation, sanctioned at a high level. That's what the phrase 'some deaths' referred to. I can't find out whether it was KGB or SVR, so we don't know the date yet."

In 1991 the KGB, the infamous Soviet security and spy apparatus, was redesigned as Russia's FSB, with domestic jurisdiction, and the SVR, with foreign. The consensus among those following the espionage world was that the change was cosmetic only.

Bond considered this. "Targeted killing."

"That's right. And one of our clandestine operators—an agent with Six—was in some way involved but I don't know who or how yet. Maybe our man was tracking the Russian assassin. Maybe he wanted to turn him and run him as a double. Or our agent might even have been the target himself. I'm getting more soon—I've opened channels."

He noticed that he was staring at the tablecloth, brow furrowed. He gave her a fast smile. "Brilliant, Philly. Thanks."

On his mobile, Bond typed a synopsis of what Philly had told him about Hydt, Incident 20 and Green Way International, omitting the information on Operation Steel Cartridge. He sent the message to M and Bill Tanner. Then he said, "Right. Now it's time for sustenance, after all our hard work. First, wine. Red or white?"

"I'm a girl who doesn't play by the rules." Philly let that linger—teasingly, it seemed to Bond. Then she explained: "I'll do a big red—a Margaux or St. Julien—with a mild-mannered fish like sole. And I'll have a pinot gris or Albariño with a nice juicy steak." She relented. "I'm saying whatever you're in the mood for, James, is fine with me." She buttered a piece of her roll and ate it, with obvious pleasure, then snatched up the menu and examined the sheet like a little girl trying to decide which Christmas present to open first. Bond was charmed.

A moment later Aaron, the waiter, was beside them. Philly said to Bond, "You first. I need seven seconds more."

"I'll start with the *pâté*. Then I'll have the grilled turbot."

Philly ordered a rocket and Parmesan salad with pear and, to follow, the poached lobster, with *haricots verts* and new potatoes.

Bond picked a bottle of unoaked chardonnay from Napa, California.

"Good," she said. "The Americans have the best chardonnay grapes outside Burgundy but they really must have the courage to throw out some of their damned oak casks."

Bond's opinion exactly.

The wine arrived and then the food, which proved excellent. He complimented her on her choice of restaurant.

Casual conversation ensued. She asked about his life in London, recent travels, where he'd grown up. Instinctively, he gave her only the broad brush of information that was already in the public domain—his parents' death, his childhood with his aunt Charmian in idyllic Pett Bottom, Kent, his brief tenure at Eton and subsequent attendance at his father's old school in Edinburgh, Fettes.

"Yes, I heard that at Eton you got into a spot of bother—something about a maid?" She let those words linger a bit too. Then smiled. "I heard the official story—a touch scandalous. But there were other rumors too. That you'd been defending the girl's honor."

"I think my lips must remain sealed on that." He offered a smile. "I'll plead the Official Secrets Act. *Un*officially."

"Well, if it's true, you were quite young to play knight errant."

"I think I'd just read Tolkien's *Sir Gawain*," Bond told her. And he couldn't help but note that she'd certainly done her research on him.

He asked about her childhood. Philly told him about growing up in Devon, boarding school in Cambridgeshire—where, as a teenager, she'd distinguished

herself as a volunteer for human rights organizations—
then reading law at the LSE. She loved to travel and
talked at length about holidays. She was at her most
animated when it came to her BSA motorcycle and her
other passion, skiing.

Interesting, Bond thought. Something else in
common.

Their eyes met and held for an easy five seconds.

Bond felt the electric sensation with which he was
so familiar. His knee brushed against hers, partly by
accident, partly not. She ran a hand through her loose
red hair.

Philly rubbed her closed eyes with her fingertips.
Looking back to Bond, she said in a low voice, "I must
say, this was a brilliant idea. Dinner, I mean. I definitely needed to . . ." She trailed off, her eyes crinkling
with amusement as she couldn't, or didn't want to, explain further. "I'm not sure I'm ready for the night to
be over. Look, it's only half past ten."

Bond leaned forward. Their forearms touched—
and this time there was no regrouping.

Philly said, "I'd like an after-dinner drink. But I
don't know exactly what they have here."

Those were her words but what she was actually
telling him was a bit different: that she had some port
or brandy in her flat just over the road, a sofa and
music too. And very likely something more awaited.

Codes . . .

His next line was to have been: "I could use one
too. Though maybe not *here*."

But then Bond happened to notice something very
small, very subtle.

The index finger and the thumb of her right hand

were gently rubbing the ring finger of her left. He noted a faint pallor where the tan from a recent holiday was missing; it had been cloaked from the sun by Tim's crimson engagement ring, now absent.

Her radiant golden-green eyes were still fixed on Bond's, her smile intact. He knew that, yes, they could settle the bill and leave and she would take his arm as they walked to her flat. He knew the humorous repartee would continue. He knew the lovemaking would be consuming—he could tell that from the way her eyes and voice sparkled, from how she'd dived into her food, from the clothes she wore and how she wore them. From her laugh.

And yet he knew, too, that it wasn't right. Not now. When she'd slipped the ring off and handed it back, she'd also returned a piece of her heart. He didn't doubt she was well on the way to recovery—a woman who fishtails a BSA motorcycle at speed along Peak District byways wouldn't be down for long.

But, he decided, it was better to wait.

If Ophelia Maidenstone was a woman he might let into his life, she would continue to be so in a month or two.

He said, "I believe I saw an Armagnac on the after-dinner list that intrigued me. I'd like to sample some."

And Bond knew he'd done the right thing when her face softened, relief and gratitude outweighing the disappointment—though only by a nose. She squeezed his arm and sat back. "You order for me, James. I'm sure you know what I'd like."

Death in the Sand

Chapter 19

James Bond awoke from a dream he could not recall but that had him sweating fiercely, his heart pounding—and pounding all the faster from the braying of his phone.

His bedside clock told him it was 5:01 A.M. He grabbed the mobile and glanced at the screen, blinking sleep from his eyes. Bless him, he thought.

He hit answer. *"Bonjour, mon ami."*

"Et toi aussi!" said the rich, rasping voice. "We are encrypted, are we not?"

"Oui. Yes, of course."

"What did we do in the days before encryption?" asked René Mathis, presumably in his office on Boulevard Mortier, in Paris's 20th *arrondissement*.

"There were no days before encryption, René. There were only days before there was an app for it on a touch screen."

"Well said, James. You are waxing wise, *comme un philosophe*. And so early in the morning."

The thirty-five-year-old Mathis was an agent for the French secret service, the Direction Générale de la Sécurité Extérieure. He and Bond worked together occasionally, in joint ODG and DGSE operations, most recently wrapping up al-Qaeda and other criminal enterprises in Europe and North Africa. They had also drunk significant quantities of Lillet and Louis Roederer together and spent some rather . . . well, colorful nights in such cities as Bucharest, Tunis and Bari, that freewheeling gem on Italy's Adriatic coast.

It had been René Mathis whom Bond had called yesterday evening, not Osborne-Smith, to ask his friend to run surveillance on Severan Hydt. He had made the decision reluctantly but he had realized he had to take the politically risky step of circumventing not only Division Three but M himself. He needed surveillance but had to make sure that Hydt and the Irishman remained unaware that the British authorities were on to them.

France, of course, has its own snoop operation, like GCHQ in England, the NSA in America and any other country's intelligence agency with a flush budget. The DGSE was continually listening in to conversations and reading e-mails of the citizens of other countries, the United Kingdom's included. (Yes, the countries were allies at the moment but there *was* that little matter of the history between them.)

So Bond had called in a favor. He'd asked René Mathis to listen to the ELINT and SIGINT from London being hoovered up by the hundred-meter antenna of France's gravity gradient stabilized spy satellite, searching for relevant keywords.

Mathis now said, "I have something for you, James."

"I'm dressing. I'll put you on speaker." Bond hit the button and leaped out of bed.

"Does this mean that the beautiful redhead lying beside you will be listening as well?"

Bond chuckled, not least because the Frenchman had happened to pick that particular hair color. A brief image surfaced of pressing his cheek against Philly's last night on her doorstep as her vibrant hair caressed his shoulder before he returned to his flat.

"I searched for signals tagged 'Severan Hydt' or his nickname 'Noah.' And anything related to Green Way International, the Gehenna plan, Serbia train derailments or threat-oriented events this coming Friday, and all of those in proximity to any names sounding Irish. But it is very odd, James: The satellite vector was aimed right at Green Way's premises east of London but there was virtually no SIGINT coming out of the place. It's as if he forbids his workers to have mobiles. Very curious."

Yes, it was, Bond reflected. He continued dressing fast.

"But there are several things we were able to pick up. Hydt is presently at home and he's leaving the country this morning. Soon, I believe. Going where, I don't know. But he'll be flying. There was a reference to an airport and another to passports. And it will be in a private jet, since his people had spoken to the pilot directly. I'm afraid there was no clue as to which airport. I know there are many in London. We have them targeted . . . for surveillance only, I must add quickly!"

Bond couldn't help but laugh.

"Now, James, we found nothing about this Gehenna plan. But I have some disturbing information. We decrypted a brief call fifteen minutes ago to a location about ten miles west of Green Way, outside London."

"Probably Hydt's home."

Mathis continued, "A man's voice said, 'Severan, it's me.' Accented but our algorithms couldn't tell region of origin. There were some pleasantries, then

this: 'We're confirmed for seven P.M. today. The number of dead will be ninety or so. You must be there no
later than six forty-five.'"

So Hydt either was part of a plan to murder scores
of people or was going to do so himself. "Who are the
victims? And why are they going to die?"

"I don't know, James. But what I found just as
troubling was your Mr. Hydt's reaction. His voice was
like that of *un enfant* offered chocolate. He said, 'Oh,
such wonderful news! Thank you so much.'" His voice
dark, Mathis said, "I've never heard that kind of joy
at the prospect of killing. But, even stranger, he then
asked, 'How close can I get to the bodies?'"

"He said that?"

"Indeed. The man told him he could be very close.
And Hydt sounded very pleased at that too. Then the
phones went silent and haven't been used again."

"Seven P.M. Somewhere out of the country. Anything more?"

"I'm afraid not."

"Thank you for all this. I'd better get on with the
hunt."

"I wish I could keep our satellite online longer but
my superiors are already asking questions about why I
am so interested in that insignificant little place called
London."

"Next time the Dom is on me, René."

"But of course. *Au revoir.*"

"*À bientôt, et merci beaucoup.*" Bond hit disconnect.

In his years as a Royal Naval Reserve commander
and as an agent for ODG, he'd been up against some
very bad people: insurgents, terrorists, psychopathic
criminals, amoral traitors selling nuclear secrets to

men mad enough to use them. But what was Hydt's game?

Purpose . . . response.

Well, even if it wasn't clear what the man's twisted goal might be, at least there was one response Bond could initiate.

Ten minutes later he ran down the stairs, fishing the car key from his pocket. He didn't need to look up Severan Hydt's address. He'd memorized it last night.

Chapter 20

Thames House, the home of MI5, the Northern Ireland Office and some related security organizations, is less impressive than the residence of MI6, which happens to be nearby, across the river on the South Bank. Six's headquarters look rather like a futuristic enclave from a Ridley Scott film (the structure is often referred to as Babylon-upon-Thames, for its resemblance to a ziggurat, and, less kindly, as Legoland).

But if not as architecturally striking, Thames House is far more intimidating. The ninety-year-old gray stone monolith is the sort of place where, were it a police headquarters in Soviet Russia or East Germany, you would begin answering before questions were asked. On the other hand, the place *does* boast some rather impressive sculpture (Charles Sargeant Jagger's *Britannia* and *St. George*, for instance) and every few days tourists from Arkansas or Tokyo stroll up to the front door thinking it's Tate Britain, which is located a short distance away.

In the windowless bowels of Thames House were the offices of Division Three. The organization conscientiously—for the sake of deniability—rented space and equipment from Five (and nobody has better equipment than MI5), all at arm's length.

In the middle of this fiefdom was a large control room, rather frayed at the edges, the green walls battered and scuffed, the furniture dented, the carpet insulted by too many heels. The requisite government regulatory posters about suspicious parcels, fire drills, health and trade union matters were omnipresent, often tarted up by bureaucrats with nothing better to do.

WEA
R EYE PR
OTEC
TION WHE
N NECES
SARY

But the computers here were voracious and the dozens of flat-screen monitors big and bright. Deputy Senior Director of Field Operations Percy Osborne-Smith was standing, arms folded, in front of the biggest and brightest. In brown jacket and mismatched trousers—he'd woken at 4 A.M. and dressed by five past—Osborne-Smith was with two young men: his assistant and a rumpled technician hovering over a keyboard.

Osborne-Smith bent forward and pressed a button, listened again to the recording that had just been made by the surveillance he'd put in place after the pointless drive up to Cambridge for, as it had developed, the sole purpose of consuming a meal of chicken curry

that had turned on him in the night. The snooping
didn't involve the suspect in Incident 20, since no one
had been courteous enough to share the man's identity
but Osborne-Smith's boys and girls had managed to
arrange a productive listen-in. Without informing MI5
that they were doing so, the troops had slapped some
microphones on the windows of one of the anonymous
evildoer's co-conspirators: a lad named James Bond,
00 Section, O Branch, Overseas Development Group,
Foreign and Commonwealth Office.

And so Osborne-Smith had learned about Severan
Hydt, that he was Noah and that he ran Green Way
International. Bond seemed to have neglected to mention that his mission to Boots the road, not Boots the
chemist, thank you very much, had resulted in these
rather important discoveries.

"Bastard," said Osborne-Smith's adjutant, a lean
young man with an irritating mop of abundant brown
hair. "Bond's playing games with lives."

"Just calm it now, eh?" Osborne-Smith said to the
youngster, whom he referred to as "Deputy-Deputy,"
though not in presence.

"Well, he is. Bastard."

For his part, Osborne-Smith was rather impressed
that Bond had contacted the French secret service.
Otherwise, nobody would have learned that Hydt was
about to leave the country and kill ninety-odd people
later today or at least be present at their deaths. This
intelligence solidified Osborne-Smith's determination
to clap Severan "Noah" Hydt in irons, drag him into
Belmarsh or Division Three's own interrogation room,
which was not much more hospitable than the prison's, and bleed him dry.

He said to Deputy-Deputy, "Run the whole battery on Hydt. I want to know about his good and his bad, what medicine he takes, the *Independent* or the *Daily Sport*, Arsenal or Chelsea, his dietary preferences, movies that scare him or that make him cry, who he's dallying or who's dallying him. And how. And get an arrest team together. Say, we didn't get Bond's firearms authorization form, did we?"

"No, sir."

Now *this* piqued Osborne-Smith.

"Where's my eye in the sky?" he asked the young technician, sitting at his video-game console.

They had tried to find Hydt's destination the easy way. Since the *espion* in Paris had learned the man was departing in a private aircraft, they'd searched CAA records for planes registered to Severan Hydt, Green Way or any subsidiaries. But none could be found. So, it was to be old-fashioned snooping, if one could describe a £3 million drone thus.

"Hold on, hold on," the technician said, wasting breath. Finally: "Got Big Bird peeping now."

Osborne-Smith regarded the screen. The view from two miles overhead was remarkably clear. But then he took in the image and said, "Are you *sure* that's Hydt's house? Not part of his company?"

"Positive. Private residence."

The home occupied a full square block in Canning Town. It was separated, not surprisingly, from the neighbors in their council houses or dilapidated flats by an imposing wall, glistening at the crest with razor wire. Within the grounds there were neatly tended gardens, in May bloom. The place had apparently been a modest warehouse or factory around a century ago but had been done up recently, it seemed. Four out-buildings and a garage were clustered together.

What was this about? he wondered. Why did such a wealthy man live in Canning Town? It was poor, ethnically complex, prone to violent crime and gangs but with fiercely loyal residents and activist council-ors who worked very, very hard for their constituents. A massive amount of redevelopment was going on, apart from the Olympics construction, which some said was taking the heart out of the place. His father, Osborne-Smith recalled, had seen the Police, Jeff Beck and Depeche Mode perform at some legendary pub in Canning Town decades ago.

"Why does Hydt live there?" he mused aloud.

His assistant called, "Just had word that Bond left his flat, heading east. He lost our man, though. Bond drives like Michael Schumacher."

"We *know* where he's going," Osborne-Smith said. "Hydt's." He hated to have to explain the obvious.

As the minutes rolled by without any activity at Hydt's, Osborne-Smith's young assistant gave him up-dates: An arrest team had been assembled, firearms of-ficers included. "They want to know their orders, sir."

Osborne-Smith considered this. "Get them ready but let's wait and see if Hydt's meeting anybody. I want to scoop up the entire cast and crew."

The technician said, "Sir, we have movement."

Leaning closer to the screen, Osborne-Smith ob-served that a bulky man in a black suit—bodyguard, he assessed—was wheeling suitcases out of Hydt's house and into the detached garage.

"Sir, Bond's just arrived in Canning Town." The man teased a joystick and the field of view expanded.

"There." He pointed. "That's him. The Bentley." The subdued gray vehicle slowed and pulled to the curb.

The assistant whistled. "A Continental GT. Now, *that*'s a bloody fine automobile. I think they reviewed it on *Top Gear*. You ever watch the show, Percy?"

"Sadly, I'm usually working." Osborne-Smith cast a mournful gaze toward tousle-haired Deputy-Deputy and decided that if the youngster couldn't muster a bit more humility and respect, he probably wouldn't survive—careerwise—much beyond the end of the Incident 20 assignment.

Bond's car was parked discreetly—if the word could be used to describe a £125,000 car in Canning Town—about fifty yards from Hydt's house, hidden behind several skips.

The assistant: "The arrest team's on board the chopper."

Osborne-Smith said, "Put them in the air. Get them to hover somewhere near the Gherkin."

The forty-story Swiss Re office building rising above the City—it looked more like a 1950s spaceship than a pickled cucumber, in Osborne-Smith's view—was centrally located and thus a good place from which to begin the hunt. "Alert security at all the airports: Heathrow, Gatwick, Luton, Stansted, London City, Southend and Biggin Hill."

"Right, sir."

"More subjects," the technician said.

On the screen, three people were leaving the house. A tall man in a suit, with salt-and-pepper hair and beard, walked next to a gangly blond man whose feet pointed outward. A slight woman in a black suit, her hair white, followed.

"That's Hydt," the technician said. "The one with the beard."

"Any idea about the woman?"

"No, sir."

"And the giraffe?" Osborne-Smith asked with a snide inflection. He was really quite irritated that Bond had ignored his firearms form. "Is he the Irishman everyone's talking about? Get a picture and run with it. Hurry up."

The trio walked into the garage. A moment later a black Audi A8 sped out through the front gate and pulled into the road, accelerating fast.

"Head count—all three are in the car, along with the bodyguard," Deputy-Deputy called.

"Lock on it, MASINT. And paint it with a laser for good measure."

"I'll try," the technician said.

"You better had."

They watched Bond in his Bentley, pulling smoothly into traffic and speeding after the Audi.

"Pan out and stay on them," Osborne-Smith said, with the lisp he was forever trying to slice off, though the affliction had proved a hydra all his life.

The camera latched on to the German car. "There's a good lad," he said to the technician.

The Audi sped up. Bond was following discreetly but never missing a turn. As skillful as the driver of the German car was, Bond was better—anticipating when the chauffeur would try something clever, some aborted turn or unexpected lane change, and counter the measure. The cars zipped through green, amber and red alike.

"Going north. Prince Regent Lane."

"So London City Airport's out."

The Audi hit Newham Way.

"All right," Deputy-Deputy enthused, tugging at his eruption of hair. "It's either Stansted or Luton."

"Going north on the A406," another technician, a round blonde woman who had materialized from nowhere, called.

Then, after some impressive fox and hound driving, the competitors, Audi and Bentley, were on the M25 going anticlockwise.

"It's Luton!" the assistant cried.

More subdued, Osborne-Smith ordered, "Get the whirlybird moving."

"Will do."

In silence they followed the progress of the Audi. Finally it sped into the short-term car park at Luton Airport. Bond wasn't far behind. The car parked carefully out of view of Hydt's.

"Chopper's setting down on the antiterror pad at the airport. Our people'll deploy toward the car park."

No one got out of the Audi. Osborne-Smith smiled. "I knew it! Hydt's waiting to meet associates. We'll get them all. Tell our people to stay under cover until I give the word. And get all the eyes at Luton online."

He reflected that the CCTV cameras on the ground might make it possible for them to see Bond's shocked reaction when the Division Three teams descended like hawks and arrested Hydt and the Irishman. That hadn't been Osborne-Smith's goal in ordering the video, of course . . . but it would be a very nice bonus.

Chapter 21

Hans Groelle sat behind the wheel of Severan Hydt's sleek black Audi A8. The thickly built, blond Dutch Army veteran had done some motocross and other racing in his younger days and he was pleased Mr. Hydt had asked him to put his driving skills to use this morning. Relishing the memory of the frantic drive from Canning Town to Luton Airport, Groelle listened absently to the three-way conversation of the man and woman in the backseat and the passenger in the front.

They were laughing about the excitement of the race. The driver of the Bentley was extremely competent but, more important, intuitive. He couldn't have known where Groelle was going so he'd had to anticipate the turns, many of them utterly random. It was as if the pursuing driver had had some sixth sense that told him when Groelle was going to turn, to slow, to speed forward.

A natural driver.

But who was he?

Well, they'd soon find out. No one in the Audi had been able to get a description of the driver—he was that clever—but they'd pieced together the number-plate. Groelle had called an associate in the Green Way headquarters, who was using some contacts at the Driver and Vehicle Licensing Agency in Swansea to find out who owned the car.

But whatever the threat, Hans Groelle would be ready.

A Colt 1911 .45 sat snug and warm in his left armpit.

He glanced once more at the sliver of the Bentley's gray wing and said to the man in the backseat, "It worked, Harry. We tricked them. Call Mr. Hydt."

The two passengers in the back and the man sitting beside Groelle were Green Way workers involved in Gehenna. They resembled Mr. Hydt, Ms. Barnes and Niall Dunne, who were currently en route to an entirely different airport, Gatwick, where a private jet was waiting to fly them out of the country.

The deception had been Dunne's idea, of course. He was a cold fish but that didn't dull his brain. There'd been trouble up in March—somebody had killed Eric Janssen, one of Groelle's fellow security men. The killer was himself dead but Dunne had assumed there might be others, watching the factory or the house, perhaps both. So he had found three employees close enough in appearance to deceive watchers and had driven them to Canning Town very early that morning. Groelle had then carted suitcases out to the garage, followed by Mr. Hydt, Ms. Barnes and the Irishman. Groelle and the decoys, who'd been waiting in the Audi, then sped toward Luton. Ten minutes later the real entourage got into the back of an unmarked Green Way International lorry and drove to Gatwick.

Now the decoys would remain in the Audi as long as possible to keep whoever was in the Bentley occupied long enough for Mr. Hydt and the others to get out of UK airspace.

Groelle said, "We have a bit of a wait." He gestured at the entertainment console with a glance toward the Green Way workers. "What'll it be?"

They voted and Radio 2 took the majority.

*   *   *

"Ah, ah. It was a bloody decoy," Osborne-Smith said. His voice was as calm as always but the expletive, if that was what it was nowadays, indicated that he was livid.

A CCTV camera in the Luton car park was now beaming an image on to the big screen in Division Three and the reality show presently airing was not felicitous. The angular view into the Audi wasn't the best in the world but it was clear that the couple in the backseats were not Severan Hydt and his female companion. And the passenger in the front, whom he'd taken to be the Irishman, was not the gawky blond man he'd seen earlier, plodding to the garage.

Decoys.

"They have to be going to *some* London airport," Deputy-Deputy pointed out. "Let's split up the team."

"Unless they decided to cruise up to Manchester or Leeds-Bradford."

"Oh. Right."

"Send all the Watchers in A Branch Hydt's picture. Without delay."

"Yes, sir."

Osborne-Smith squinted as he looked at the image broadcast from the CCTV. He could see a bit of the wing of James Bond's Bentley parked twenty-five yards from the Audi.

If there was any consolation to the flap, it was that at least Bond had fallen for the ruse too. Combined with his lack of cooperation, his questionable use of the French secret service and his holier-than-thou attitude, the lapse might just signal a significant downsizing of his career.

Chapter 22

The fifteen-foot lorry, leased to Green Way International but unmarked, pulled up to the curb at the executive flight services terminal at Gatwick Airport. The door slid open and Severan Hydt, an older woman and the Irishman climbed out and collected their suitcases.

Thirty feet away, in the car park, sat a black and red Mini Cooper, whose interior décor included a yellow rose in a plastic vase wedged into the cup holder. Behind the wheel, James Bond was watching the trio of passengers deploy to the pavement. The Irishman, naturally, was looking around carefully. He never seemed to drop his guard.

"What do you think of it?" Bond asked, into the hands-free connected to his mobile.

"It?"

"The Bentley."

"'It'? Honestly, James, a car like this simply *demands* a name," Philly Maidenstone chided. She was sitting in his Bentley Continental GT, at Luton Airport, having chased Hydt's Audi all the way from Canning Town.

"I never got into the habit of naming my cars." Any more than I'd give my gun a gender, he reflected. And kept his eyes on the threesome not far away.

Bond had been convinced that after the incidents in Serbia and March, Hydt—or the Irishman, more likely—would suspect he might be tailed in London. He was also concerned that Osborne-Smith had arranged to follow Bond himself. So, after he had talked to René Mathis, he'd left his flat and sped to a covered car park in the City, where he'd met Philly to swap cars. She was to trail Hydt's Audi, which Bond was sure would be a decoy, in his Bentley, while he, in her Mini, would wait for the man's true departure, which came just ten minutes after the German car had sped away from Hydt's Canning Town home.

Bond now watched Hydt, head down, making a phone call. Beside him stood the woman. In her early to midsixties, Bond guessed, she had attractive features, though her face was pale and gaunt, an image accentuated by her black overcoat. Too little sleep, perhaps.

His lover? Bond wondered. Or a longtime assistant? From her expression as she looked at Hydt, he decided the former.

Also, the Irishman. Bond hadn't seen him clearly in Serbia but there was no doubt; the gawky stride, feet turned out, bad posture, the odd blond fringe.

Bond supposed he was the man at the controls of the bulldozer in March—who had so ruthlessly crushed his own security man to death. He also pictured the dead in Serbia—the agents, the train and lorry drivers, as well as the man's own associate—and he let the anger rising in him crest and dissolve.

Philly said, "In answer to your question, I liked it very much. A lot of engines have horses nowadays; you can get AMG Mercedes estate cars to take the kids to school, for God's sake—but how many pounds' torque does the Bentley have? I've never felt anything like it."

"A touch over five hundred."

"Oh my God," Philly whispered, either impressed or envious, perhaps both. "And I'm in love with the all-wheel drive. How's it distributed?"

"Sixty-forty rear to front."

"Brilliant."

"Yours isn't bad either," he told her, of the Mini. "You added a supercharger."

"I did indeed."

"Whose?"

"Autorotor. The Swedish outfit. Nearly doubled the horsepower. Close to three hundred now."

"I thought as much." Bond was himself impressed. "I must get the name of your mechanic. I have an old Jaguar that needs work."

"Oh, tell me it's an E-type. That's the sexiest car in the history of motoring."

Yet one more thing in common. Bond wrapped this thought up and put it quickly away. "I'll leave you in suspense. Hold on. Hydt's on the move." Bond climbed out of the Mini and hid Philly's key in the wheel arch. He grabbed his suitcase and laptop bag, slipped on a new pair of tortoiseshell sunglasses and eased into a crowd to follow Hydt, the Irishman and the woman to Gatwick's private jet terminal.

"You there?" he asked, into the hands-free.

"I am," Philly replied.

"What's happening with the decoys?"

"They're just sitting in the Audi."

"They'll be waiting until Hydt takes off and the plane's out of UK airspace. Then they'll turn round to lead you—and probably Mr. Osborne-Smith—back to London."

"You think Ozzy's watching?"

Bond had to smile. "You've got a drone hovering about ten thousand feet over you, I'm sure. They're walking into the terminal now. I should go, Philly."

"I don't get out of the office enough, James. Thanks for the chance to play Formula One."

Impulsively he said, "Here's an idea. Maybe we'll take it out into the country together, do some serious driving."

"James!" she said crossly. He wondered if he'd crossed a line. "You simply can't keep referring to this magnificent machine as 'it.' I shall rack my brains and think up a proper name for *her*. And, yes, a trip out to the country sounds divine, provided you let me drive for exactly half the time. And we put in a null-detain request. I already have a few points on my driving license."

They rang off and Bond discreetly followed his prey. The threesome paused at a gate in a chain-link fence and presented passports to the guard. Bond saw that the woman's was blue. American? The uniformed man jotted on a clipboard and gestured the three through. As Bond got to the fence he caught a glimpse of them climbing the stairs to a white private jet, a large one, seven round windows on each side of the fuselage, running lights already on. The door closed.

Bond hit speed dial.

"Flanagan. Hello, James."

"Maurice," he said to the head of T Branch, the group within the ODG that handled all things vehicular. "I need a destination for a private plane, departing just about now from Gatwick." He read off the five-letter registration painted on the engine.

"Give me a minute."

The aircraft moved forward. Dammit, he thought angrily. Slow down. He was all too aware that, if René Mathis's information was correct, Hydt was on his way to oversee the murder of at least ninety people that evening.

Maurice Flanagan said, "I have it. Nice bird, Grumman Five-fifty. State of the art and damned expensive. That one's owned by a Dutch company in the business of waste and recycling."

One of Hydt's, of course.

"The flight plan's filed for Dubai."

Dubai? Was that where the deaths were going to happen? "Where will it stop for refueling?"

Flanagan laughed. "James, the range is over six and a half thousand miles. Flies at Mach point eight eight."

Bond watched the plane taxiing to the runway. Dubai was about thirty-five hundred miles from London. With the time difference the Grumman would land at 3 or 4 P.M.

"I need to beat that plane to Dubai, Maurice. What can you cobble together for me? I have passports, credit cards and three grand in cash. Whatever you can do. Oh, I have my weapon—you'll need to take that into account."

Bond kept staring at the sleek white jet, wingtips turned up. It looked less like a bird than a dragon, though that might have been because he knew who the occupants were and what they had planned.

Ninety dead . . .

Several tense moments passed as Bond watched the jet edge closer to the runway.

Then Flanagan said, "Sorry, James. The best I can

do is get you on a commercial flight out of Heathrow in a few hours. Puts you in Dubai around six twenty."

"Won't do, Maurice. Military? Government?"

"Nothing available. Absolutely nothing."

Damn. At least he could have Philly or Bill Tanner arrange with someone at Six's UAE desk to have a watcher meet the flight at Dubai airport and tail Hydt and Dunne to their destination.

He sighed. "Put me on the commercial flight."

"Will do. Sorry."

Bond glanced at his watch.

Nine hours until the deaths . . .

He could always hope for a delay to Hydt's flight.

Just then he saw the Grumman turn on to the main runway and, without pause, accelerate fast, lifting effortlessly from the concrete, then shrinking to a dot as the dragon shot higher into the sky, speeding directly away from him.

Percy Osborne-Smith was leaning toward the large, flat-screen monitor, split into six rectangles. Twenty minutes ago, they'd had a CCTV hit on the number-plate of a lorry registered to Severan Hydt's company at the Redhill and Reigate exit from the A23, which led to Gatwick. He and his underlings were now scanning every camera in and around the airport for the vehicle.

The second technician to join them finished securing her blonde hair with an elastic band and pointed a pudgy finger to one of the screens. "There. That's it."

It seemed that fifteen minutes ago, according to the time stamp, the lorry had paused at the curb near the private aviation terminal and several people had got out. Yes, it was the trio.

"Why didn't Hydt's face get read when he arrived? We can find hooligans from Rio before they get into Old Trafford but we can't spot a mass murderer in broad daylight. My God, does that say something about Whitehall's priorities? Don't repeat that, anyone. Scan the tarmac."

The technician manipulated the controls. There was an image of Hydt and the others walking to a private jet.

"Bring up the registration number. Run it."

To his credit Deputy-Deputy already had. "Owned by a Dutch company that does recycling. Okay, got the flight plan. He's headed for Dubai. They've already taken off."

"Where are they now? *Where?*"

"Checking . . ." The assistant sighed. "Just passing out of UK airspace."

Teeth clenched, Osborne-Smith stared at the still video image of the plane. He mused, "Wonder what it would take to scramble some Harriers and force them down?" Then he looked up to note everyone staring at him. "I'm not serious, people."

Though he had been, just a little.

"Look at that," the male technician interrupted.

"Look at bloody *what*?"

Deputy-Deputy said, "Yes, somebody *else* is watching them."

The screen was showing the entrance to the private jet terminal at Gatwick. A man was standing at the wire fence, staring at Hydt's plane.

My God—it was *Bond*.

So, the bloody clever ODG agent, with a fancy car and without permission to carry a firearm in the UK, had tailed Hydt, after all. Osborne-Smith wondered briefly who'd been in the Bentley. The ruse, he knew, had been not only to fool Hydt but to fool Division Three.

With considerable contentment he watched Bond turn from the fence and head back to the car park, head down and speaking into his mobile, undoubtedly enduring a verbal lashing from his boss for having let the fox slip away.

Chapter 23

Usually we never hear the sound that wakes us. Perhaps we might, if it repeats: an alarm or an urgent voice. But a once-only noise rouses without registering in our consciousness.

James Bond didn't know what lifted him from his dreamless sleep. He glanced at his watch.

It was just after 1 P.M.

Then he smelled a delicious aroma: a combination of floral perfume—jasmine, he believed—and the ripe, rich scent of vintage champagne. Above him he saw the heavenly form of a beautiful Middle Eastern woman, wearing a sleek burgundy skirt and long-sleeved golden shirt over her voluptuous figure. Her collar was secured with a pearl, which was different from the lower buttons. He found the tiny cream dot particularly appealing. Her hair was as blue-black as crow feathers, pinned up, though a teasing strand fell loose, cupping one side of her face, which was subtly and meticulously made-up.

He said to her, "*Salam alaikum.*"

"*Wa alaikum salam,*" she replied. She set the crystal flute on the tray table in front of him, along with the elegant bottle of the king of Moëts, Dom Pérignon. "I'm sorry, Mr. Bond, I've woken you. I'm afraid the cork popped more loudly than I'd hoped. I was just going to leave the glass and not disturb you."

"*Shukran,*" he said, as he took the glass. "And don't

worry. My second favorite way to wake up is to the sound of champagne opening."

She responded to this with a subtle smile. "I can arrange some lunch for you too."

"That would be lovely, if it's not too much trouble."

She returned to the galley.

Bond sipped his champagne and looked out of the private jet's spacious window, the twin Rolls-Royce engines pulsing smoothly as it flew toward Dubai at 42,000 feet, doing more than 600 miles an hour. The aircraft was, Bond reflected with amusement, a Grumman, like Severan Hydt's, but Bond was in a newer, faster model, with a greater range than the Rag-and-Bone Man's.

Bond had started the chase four hours ago, with the modern equivalent of a scene from an old American police movie, in which the detective leaps into a taxi and orders, "Follow that car." He'd decided that the commercial flight would get him to Dubai too late to stop the killings, so he'd placed a call to his Commodore Club friend, Fouad Kharaz, who had instantly put a private jet at his disposal. "My friend, you know I owe you," the Arab assured him.

A year ago he had approached Bond awkwardly for help, suspecting he did something that involved government security. On his way home from school, Kharaz's teenage son had become the target of some thugs, nineteen or twenty years old, who flaunted their antisocial behavior orders like insignias of rank. The police were sympathetic but had little time for the drama. Worried sick about his son, Kharaz asked if there was anything Bond could recommend. In a moment of weakness, the knight errant within Bond had prevailed and he had trailed the boy home from school one day when nothing much was going on at the ODG. When the tormentors had moved in, so had Bond.

With a few effortless martial arts maneuvers he had gently laid two of them out on the pavement and pinned the third, the ringleader, to a wall. He had taken their names from their driving licenses and whispered coldly that if the Kharaz boy was ever troubled again, the hoods' next visit from Bond would not end so civilly. The boys had strode off defiantly but the son was never troubled again; his status at school had soared.

So Bond had become Fouad Kharaz's "best friend of all best friends." He'd decided to call in the favor and borrow one of the man's jets.

According to the digital map on the bulkhead, beneath the airspeed and altitude indicators, they were over Iran. Two hours to go until they touched down in Dubai.

Just after takeoff, Bond had called Bill Tanner and told him of his destination and about the ninety or so deaths planned for seven o'clock that evening, presumably in Dubai, but perhaps anywhere in the United Arab Emirates.

"Why's Hydt going to kill them?" the chief of staff had asked.

"I'm not sure he is but all those people are going to die and he'll be there."

"I'll go through diplomatic channels, tell the embassies there's some threat but we don't have anything concrete. They'll leak word to the Dubai security apparatus too, through back channels."

"Don't mention Hydt's name. He needs to get into the country undisturbed. He can't suspect anything. I have to find out what he's up to."

"I agree. We'll handle it on the sly."

He'd asked Tanner to check the Golden Wire about Hydt's affiliation with the Emirates, hoping there was a specific place he might be headed for. A moment later the chief of staff was back. "No offices, residences or business affiliations anywhere in the area. And I've just done a data-mining search. No hotel reservations in his name."

Bond wasn't pleased. As soon as Hydt landed, he would disappear into the sprawling emirate of two and a half million people. It would be impossible to find him before the attack.

Just as he disconnected, the flight attendant appeared. "We have many different dishes but I saw you look at the Dom with appreciation so I decided you would like the best we have aboard. Mr. Kharaz said you were to be treated like a king." She set the silver tray on the table beside his champagne flute, which she refilled for him. "I've brought you Iranian caviar—beluga, of course—with toast, not blinis, crème fraîche and capers." The capers were the large ones, so large she had sliced them. "The grated onions are Vidalia, from America, the sweetest in the world." She added, "They are kind to the breath too. We call them 'lovers' onions.' To follow, there is duck in aspic, with minted yogurt and dates. I can also cook you a steak."

He laughed. "No, no. This is more than enough."

She left him to eat. When he had finished, he had two small cups of cardamom-flavored Arabic coffee as he read the intelligence that Philly Maidenstone had provided about Hydt and Green Way. He was struck by two things: the man's care in steering clear of organized crime and his almost fanatical efforts to expand the company throughout the world. She had discovered recently filed applications to do business in South Korea, China, India, Argentina and half a dozen smaller countries. He was disappointed that he could find no clue in any of the material as to the Irishman's identity. Philly had run the man's picture, along with that of the older woman, through databases but found no matches. And Bill Tanner had reported that the MI5 agents and SOCA and Specialist Crime officers who'd descended on Gatwick had been told that, unfortunately, records about the passengers on the Grumman "seem to have vanished."

It was then that he received more troubling news. An encrypted e-mail from Philly. Someone, it seemed, had been unofficially checking with Six about Bond's whereabouts and planned itinerary.

The "someone," Bond supposed, had to be his dear friend Percy Osborne-Smith. Technically he'd be out of the Division Three man's jurisdiction, in Dubai, but that didn't mean the man couldn't make a great deal of trouble for him and even blow his cover.

Bond had no relation with Six's people in Dubai. He'd have to assume, though, that Osborne-Smith might. Which meant Bond couldn't have local ops or assets meet Hydt's flight, after all. Indeed, he decided he couldn't have anything to do with *any* of his countrymen—a particular shame, because the consul general in Dubai was clever and savvy . . . and a friend of Bond's. He texted Bill Tanner and told him to hold off setting up liaison with Six.

Bond called the pilot on the intercom to learn the status of the jet they were pursuing. It seemed that air-traffic control had slowed their own plane, though not

Hydt's, and they would not be able to overtake him. They would land half an hour, at least, after Hydt did.

Damn. That thirty minutes could mean the difference between life and death for at least ninety people. He stared out of the window at the Persian Gulf. Pulling out his mobile, he was thinking again of the great espionage balance sheet as he scrolled through his extensive phone book to find a number. I'm beginning to feel a bit like Lehman Brothers, he thought. My debts vastly outweigh my assets.

Bond placed a call.

Chapter 24

The limousine bearing Severan Hydt, Jessica Barnes and Niall Dunne pulled up at the Intercontinental Hotel, situated on broad, peaceful Dubai Creek. The solid, stern driver was a local man they'd used before. Like Hans Groelle in England, he doubled as a bodyguard (and did a bit more than that from time to time).

They remained in the car while Dunne read a text or an e-mail. He logged off his iPhone, looked up and said to Hydt, "Hans has found out about the driver of the Bentley. It's interesting."

Hydt tapped his long fingernails together.

Dunne avoided looking at them. He said, "And there's a connection to March."

"Is there?" Hydt tried to read Dunne's eyes. As usual, they remained utterly cryptic.

The Irishman said nothing more—not with Jessica present. Hydt nodded. "We'll check in now."

Hydt lifted the cuff of his elegant suit jacket and regarded his watch. Two and a half hours to go.

The number of dead will be ninety or so.

Dunne stepped out first; his keen eyes made their usual scan for threats. "All right," came the Irishman's slight brogue. "It's clear."

Hydt and Jessica climbed out into the astonishing heat and headed quickly into the chill of the Intercontinental lobby, which was dominated by a stunning ten-foot-high assembly of exotic flowers. On a nearby

wall hung portraits of the United Arab Emirates' rul-
ing families, gazing down sternly and confidently.

Jessica signed for the room, which they'd taken
in her name, another of Dunne's ideas. Though they
would not be staying long—their onward flight was
this evening—it was helpful to have somewhere to
leave the bags and get some rest. They handed the luggage to the bell captain to have it taken to the room.

Leaving Jessica beside the flowers, Hydt nodded
Dunne aside. "The Bentley? Who was it?"

"Registered to a company in Manchester—same
address as Midlands Disposal."

Midlands was connected to one of the bigger
organized-crime syndicates operating out of south
Manchester. In America the Mob had traditionally
been heavily involved in waste management, and in
Naples, where the Camorra crime syndicate ruled, refuse collection was known as *Il Re del Crimine*. In Britain organized crime was less interested in the business
but occasionally some local underworld boss tried to
bluster his way into the market, like a heavy in a Guy
Ritchie film.

"And this morning," Dunne continued, "the cop-
pers came round to the army base site, showing pictures of somebody who'd been spotted in the area
the day before. There's a warrant on him for grievous
bodily harm. He worked for Midlands. The police said
he's gone missing."

As will happen, Hydt reflected, when one's body
is commencing to rot beneath a thousand tons of
wrecked hospital. "What would he have been doing up
there?" Hydt asked.

Dunne considered this. "Probably planning to sabotage the demolition job. Something goes wrong, you get bad publicity and Midlands moves in to pick up some of your business."

"So whoever was in the Bentley only wanted to find out what happened to his mate yesterday."

"Right."

Hydt was vastly relieved. The incident had nothing to do with Gehenna. And, more important, the intruder wasn't the police or Security Service. Merely one more instance of the underbelly of the discard business. "Good. We'll deal with Midlands later."

Hydt and Dunne returned to Jessica. "Niall and I have some things to take care of. I'll be back for dinner."

"I think I'll go for a walk," she said.

Hydt frowned. "In this heat? It might not be good for you." He didn't like her to stray too far afield. He wasn't worried that she'd let slip anything she shouldn't—he had kept all aspects of Gehenna from her. And what she knew of the rest of his darker life, well, that was potentially embarrassing but not illegal. It was just that when he wanted her, he wanted her, and Severan Hydt was a man whose belief in the inevitable power of decay had taught him that life is far too short and precarious to deny yourself anything at any time.

"I can judge that," she said, but spoke timidly.

"Of course, of course. Only . . . a woman alone?" Hydt continued. "The men, you know how they can be."

"You mean Arab men?" Jessica asked. "It's not Tehran or Jeddah. They don't even leer. In Dubai they're more respectful than they are in Paris."

Hydt smiled his gentle smile. That was amusing. And true. "But still . . . don't you think it would be best just to be safe? Anyway, the hotel has a wonderful spa. It will be perfect for you. And the pool is partly Plexiglas. You can look down and see the ground forty feet below. The view of the Burj Khalifa is quite impressive."

"I suppose."

It was then that Hydt noticed a new configuration of wrinkles around her eyes, as she peered up at the towering floral arrangement.

He thought, too, of the body of the woman found in the Green Way skip yesterday, her grave now subtly marked, according to the foreman, Jack Dennison. And Hydt felt that subtle unraveling within him, a spring loosening.

"As long as you're happy," he said to her softly and brushed her face, near the wrinkles, with one of his long nails. She'd stopped recoiling long ago, not that her reactions had ever affected him one bit.

Hydt was suddenly aware of Dunne's crystalline blue eyes turning his way. The younger man stiffened, ever so slightly, then recovered and looked elsewhere. Hydt was irritated. What business was it of his what Hydt found alluring? He wondered, as he often had, if perhaps Dunne's distaste for his brands of lust stemmed not from the fact that they were unconventional but from his disdain for *any* sexuality. In the months he'd known him, the Irishman hadn't so much as glanced at a woman or man, with bedroom eyes.

Hydt lowered his hand and looked again at Jessica, at the lines radiating from her resigned eyes. He gauged the timing. They would fly out tonight and the plane boasted no private suites. He couldn't imagine making love to her when Dunne was nearby, even if the man was asleep.

He debated. Was there time now to get to the room, lay Jessica on the bed, pull the curtains wide so that the low sun streamed across the soft flesh, illuminating the topography of her body . . .

. . . and run his nails over her skin?

The way he felt at the moment, absorbed with her and thinking of the spectacle at seven o'clock tonight, the liaison wouldn't take long.

"Severan," Dunne said crisply. "We don't know what al-Fulan has for us. We probably should go."

Hydt appeared to ponder the words but it was not serious consideration. He said, "It's been a long flight. I feel like a change of clothes." He glanced down at Jessica's weary eyes. "And you might like a nap, my dear." He directed her firmly to the lift.

Chapter 25

At around four forty-five on Tuesday afternoon Fouad Kharaz's private jet eased to a stop. James Bond unbuckled his seat belt and collected his luggage. He thanked the pilots and the flight attendant, gripping her hand warmly and resisting the urge to kiss her cheek; they were now in the Middle East.

The immigration officer lethargically stamped his passport, slid it back and gestured him into the country. Bond strode through the "Nothing to Declare" lane at Customs with a suitcase containing its deadly contraband, and was soon outside in the piquant heat, feeling as if a huge burden had been lifted.

He was in his element once more, the mission his and his alone to pursue. He was on foreign soil, his carte blanche restored.

The short ride from the airport to his destination at Festival City took Bond through a nondescript part of the town—drives to and from airports were similar throughout the world and this route was little different from the A4 just west of London or the toll road to Dulles in Washington, D.C., although it was decorated with far more sand and dust. And, like most of the emirate, it was immaculately clean.

On the way Bond gazed out over the sprawling city, looking north toward the Persian Gulf. In the late-afternoon, heat-shimmering light, the glowing needle of the Burj Khalifa soared above the geometrically complex skyline of Sheikh Zayed Road. It was presently the tallest building on earth. That distinction seemed to change monthly but this tower would surely hold that honor for a long time to come.

He noted one other ubiquitous characteristic of the city—the construction cranes, white and yellow and orange. They were everywhere and busy once again. On his last trip there had been just as many of these looming stalks but most were sitting idle, like toys discarded by a child who'd lost interest in playing with them. The emirate had been hit hard in the recent economic downturn. For his official cover Bond had to keep up on world finance and he found himself impatient with the criticism ladled upon places like Dubai, which often originated in London or New York; yet weren't the City and Wall Street the more enthusiastic co-conspirators in causing the economic woe?

Yes, there had been excess here and many ambitious projects might never be finished—like the artificial archipelago in the shape of a map of the world, composed of small sand islands offshore (you could actually buy a "country" of your choosing, though the good ones had long ago been spoken for). Yet the reputation for swelling luxury was but a small aspect of Dubai—and, in truth, the emirate was no different from Singapore, California, Monaco and hundreds of other places where the wealthy worked and played. To Bond, in any event, Dubai was not about unfettered business or real estate but about its exotic ways, a place where new and old blended, where many cultures and religions coexisted respectfully. He particularly enjoyed the vast, empty landscape of red sand, populated by camels and Range Rovers, as different from his boyhood vistas of Kent as one could imagine. He wondered if his mission today would take him to the Empty Quarter.

They drove on, past small brown, white and yellow one-story buildings whose names and services were disclosed in modest green Arabic lettering. No gaudy billboards, no neon lights, except for a few announcements of forthcoming events. The minarets of mosques rose above the low residences and businesses, persistent spikes of faith throughout the hazy distance. The intrusion of the ubiquitous desert was everywhere and date palm, neem and eucalyptus trees formed gallant outposts against the encroaching, endless sand.

The taxi driver dropped Bond, as directed, at a shopping center. He handed over some ten-dirham notes and climbed out. The mall was packed with locals—it was between *Asir* and *Maghrib* prayer times—as well as many foreigners, all carting carrier bags and crowding the shops, which were doing brisk business. The country was often referred to as "Do buy," he recalled.

Bond lost himself in the crowd, looking around, as if he were trying to find a companion he'd agreed to meet. In fact, he was searching for someone else: the man who'd been following him from the airport, probably with hostile intent. Twice now he'd seen someone in sunglasses and a blue shirt or jacket: at the airport and then in a dusty black Toyota behind Bond's taxi. For the drive he had donned a plain black cap but, from the set of his head and shoulders and the shape of his glasses, Bond knew he was the man he'd seen at the airport. The same Toyota had just now eased past the shopping center—driving slowly for no apparent reason—and vanished behind a nearby hotel.

This was no coincidence.

Bond had considered sending the taxi on a diversionary route but, in truth, he wasn't sure he wanted to lose the tail. More often than not it's better to trap your pursuer and see what he has to say for himself.

Who was he? Had he been waiting in Dubai for Bond? Or somehow followed him from London? Or did he not even know who Bond was but had chosen merely to keep an eye on a stranger in town?

Bond bought a newspaper. Today it was hot, searingly so, but he shunned the air-conditioned interior of the café he had selected and sat outside where he could observe all the entrances and exits to and from the area. He looked around occasionally for the tail but saw nothing specific.

As he sent and received several text messages, a waiter came to him. Bond glanced at the faded menu on the table and ordered Turkish coffee and sparkling water. As the man walked away, Bond looked at his watch: 5 P.M.

Only two hours until more than ninety people died somewhere in this elegant city of sand and heat.

Half a block away from the shopping center, a solidly built man in a blue jacket slipped a Dubai traffic warden several hundred dirhams and told him in English that he'd only be a short while. He'd certainly be gone before the crowds returned following sunset prayer.

The warden wandered off as if the conversation about the dusty black Toyota, parked illegally at the curb, had never occurred.

The man, who went by the name Nick, lit a cigarette and lifted his backpack over his shoulder. He eased into the shadows of the shopping center where his target was nonchalantly sipping espresso or Turkish coffee and reading the paper as if he hadn't a care in the world.

That was how he thought of the man: target. Not bastard, not enemy. Nick knew that in an operation like this you had to be utterly dispassionate, as difficult as that might be. This man was no more of a person than the black dot of a bull's-eye.

A target.

He supposed the man was talented but he'd been pretty damn careless leaving the airport. Nick had easily followed him. This gave him confidence in what he was about to do.

Face obscured by a baseball cap with a long brim and sunglasses, Nick moved closer to his target, dodging from shadow to shadow. Unlike in other places, the disguise did not draw attention to him; in Dubai everyone wore head coverings and sunglasses.

One thing that was a bit different was the long-sleeved jacket, which few local people wore, given the heat. But there was no other way to hide the pistol that was tucked into his waistband.

Nick's gold earring, too, might have earned him some curious glances but this area of Dubai Creek, with its shopping malls and amusement park, was filled with tourists and as long as people didn't drink alcohol or kiss one another in public, the locals forgave unusual dress.

He inhaled deeply on his cigarette, then dropped and crushed it, easing closer to his target.

A hawker appeared suddenly and asked, in English,

if he wanted to buy rugs. "Very cheap, very cheap. Many knots! Thousands upon thousands of knots!" One look from Nick shut his mouth and he vanished.

Nick considered his plan. There would be some logistical problems, of course—in this country everyone watched everyone else. He would have to get his target out of sight, into the car park or, better, the basement of the shopping center, perhaps during prayer time, when the crowds thinned. Probably the simplest approach was the best. Nick could slip up behind him, shove the gun into his back and "escort" him downstairs.

Then the knife work would begin.

Oh, the target—All right, maybe I *will* think of him as a bastard—would have many things to say when the blade began its leisurely journey across his skin.

Nick reached under his jacket and pushed up the safety lever of his pistol, as he began moving smoothly from shadow to shadow.

Chapter 26

James Bond had his coffee and water in front of him as he sat with the *National* newspaper, published out of Abu Dhabi. He considered it the best newspaper in the Middle East. You could find every sort of story imaginable, from a scandal about Mumbai firemen's inefficient uniforms to pieces about women's rights in the Arab world to a half-page exposé on a Cypriot gangster stealing the body of the island's former president from his grave.

Excellent Formula One coverage too—important to Bond.

Now, however, he was paying no attention to the paper but was using it as a prop . . . though not with the cliché of an eyehole torn from the gutter between ads for Dubai's Lulu Hypermarkets and the local news. The paper sat flat in front of him and his head was down. His eyes, however, were up, scanning.

It was at that moment that he heard a brief rasp of shoe leather behind him and was aware of someone moving quickly toward his table.

Bond remained completely still.

Then a large hand—pale and freckled—gripped the chair beside him and yanked it back.

A man dropped heavily into it.

"Howdy, James." The voice was thick with a Texas accent. "Welcome to Dubai."

Du-bah . . .

Bond turned to his friend with a grin. They shook hands warmly.

A few years older than Bond, Felix Leiter was tall and had a lanky frame, on which his suit hung loose. The pale complexion and mop of straw-colored hair largely precluded most undercover work in the Middle East unless he was playing exactly who he was: a brash, savvy *guy* from the American South, who'd ridden into town for business, with no small amount of pleasure thrown in. His slow manners and easygoing speech were deceptive; he could react like a spring knife when the occasion demanded . . . as Bond had seen firsthand.

When the pilot of Fouad Kharaz's Grumman had reported that they weren't going to beat Hydt's to Dubai, it was Felix Leiter whom Bond had rung, calling in his Lehman Brothers favor. While Bond was uneasy using the MI6 connections here, because of Osborne-Smith's inquiries earlier, he had no such reservations about enlisting the CIA, which had an extensive operation throughout the United Arab Emirates. Asking Leiter, a senior agent in the agency's National Clandestine Service, to help out was risky politically. Using a sister agency without clearance from the top might result in serious diplomatic repercussions and Bond had already done so once with René Mathis. He was certainly putting his newly reinstated carte blanche to the test.

Felix Leiter was more than willing to meet Hydt's plane and follow the trio to their destination, which had turned out to be the Intercontinental Hotel—it was connected to the shopping center where the two men now sat.

Bond had briefed him about Hydt, the Irishman and, ten minutes ago via text, about the man in the Toyota. Leiter had remained in surveillance positions at the shopping center for a time to—literally—watch Bond's back.

"So, do I have a friend hanging about?"

"Spotted him moving in, about forty yards to the south," said Leiter, smiling as if countersurveillance was the last thing on his mind. "He was by the entrance, thataway. But the son of a bitch vanished."

"Whoever he is, he's good."

"You got that right." Gazing around, Leiter now asked, "You believe the shopping here?" He gestured at the patrons. "You have malls in England, James?"

"Yes indeed. Televisions too. And running water. We're hoping to get computers someday."

"Ha. I'll come visit sometime. Soon as you learn how to refrigerate beer."

Leiter flagged down the waiter and ordered coffee. He whispered to Bond, "I'd say 'Americano,' but then people might guess my nationality, which'd blow my cover all to hell."

He tugged at his ear—a signal, it seemed, for a slightly built Arab man, dressed like a local, appeared quickly. Bond had no idea where he'd been stationed. The man looked as if he might have been piloting one of the *abra* boat taxis that plied Dubai Creek.

"Yusuf Nasad," Leiter introduced him. "This is Mr. Smith."

Bond assumed that Nasad was not the Arab's real name either. He would be a local asset and, because Leiter was running him, he'd be a damn good one too. Felix Leiter was a master handler. It was Nasad who'd helped him track Hydt from the airport, the American explained.

Nasad sat down. Leiter asked, "Our friend?"

"Gone. He saw you, I am thinking."

"I stand out too damn much." Leiter laughed. "Don't know why Langley sent me here. If I was undercover in Alabama, nobody'd notice me."

Bond said, "I didn't get much of a view. Dark hair, blue shirt."

"A tough boy," Nasad said, in what Bond thought of as American TV English. "Athletic. Hair's cut very short. And he has a gold earring. No beard. I tried to get a picture. But he was gone too fast."

"Besides," Leiter filled in, "all we've got is crap to take pictures with. You still have that fellow giving you folks neat toys? What's his name again—Q Somebody? Quentin? Quigley?"

"Q's the branch, not a person. Stands for Quartermaster."

"And it was a jacket he was wearing," Nasad added, "not a shirt. Like a windbreaker."

"In this heat?" Bond asked. "So he was carrying. You see what type of weapon?"

"No."

"Any idea who he might be?"

Nasad offered, "Definitely not Arab. Could have been a *katsa.*"

"Why the hell would a Mossad field officer be interested in me?"

Leiter said, "Only you can answer that, boy."

Bond shook his head. "Maybe somebody recruited by the secret police here?"

"Naw, doubt it. The Amn al-Dawla don't tail you.

They just invite you to their four-star accommodations in the Deira, where you spill everything they want to know. And I mean everything."

Nasad's quick eyes took in the café and surrounding area and apparently noted no threats. Bond had observed him doing this since his arrival.

Leiter asked Bond, "You think it was somebody working for Hydt?"

"Possibly. But if so I doubt they know who I am." Bond explained that before he'd left London he'd been concerned that Hydt and the Irishman would get too suspicious that he was on their trail, especially after the flap in Serbia. He'd had T Branch adjust the records of his Bentley to link the number plate to a disposal company in Manchester with possible underworld ties. Then Bill Tanner had sent agents posing as Scotland Yard officers to the March demolition site with a story about a Midland Disposal security man going missing in the area.

"It'll put Hydt and the Irishman off the scent at least for a few days," Bond said. "Now, have you heard any chatter here?"

The American's otherwise cheerful face tightened. "No relevant ELINT or SIGINT. Not that I care much about eavesdropping."

Felix Leiter, a former marine whom Bond had met in the service, was a HUMINT spy. He vastly preferred the role of handler—running local assets, like Yusuf Nasad. "I pulled in a lot of favors and talked to all my key assets. Whatever Hydt and his local contacts're up to, they're keeping the lid on really tight. I can't find any leads. Nobody's been moving any mysterious shipments of nasty stuff into Dubai. Nobody's been telling friends and family to avoid this mosque or that shopping center around seven tonight. No bad actors're slipping in from across the Gulf."

"That's the Irishman's doing—keeping the wraps on everything. I don't know exactly what he does for Hydt but he's bloody clever, always thinking about security. It's as if he can anticipate whatever we're going to do and think up a way to counter it."

They fell silent as they casually surveyed the shopping center. No sign of the blue-jacketed tail. No sign of Hydt or the Irishman.

Bond asked Leiter, "You still a scribbler?"

"Sure am," the Texan confirmed.

Leiter's cover was as a freelance journalist and blogger, specializing in music, particularly the blues, R&B and Afro-Caribbean. Journalism is a commonly used cover for intelligence agents; it gives credence to their frequent traveling, often to hot spots and the less-savory places of the world. Leiter was fortunate in that the best covers are those that mirror an agent's actual interests, since an assignment may require the operative to be undercover for weeks or months at a time. The filmmaker Alexander Korda—recruited by the famed British spymaster Sir Claude Dansey—reportedly used location-scouting expeditions as a cover to photograph off-limits areas in the run-up to the Second World War. Bond's bland official cover, a security and integrity analyst for the Overseas Development Group, subjected him to excruciatingly boring stints when he was on assignment. On a particularly bad day he would long for an official cover as a skiing or scuba instructor.

Bond sat forward and Leiter followed his gaze.

They watched two men come out of the front door of the Intercontinental and walk toward a black Lincoln Town Car.

"It's Hydt. And the Irishman."

Leiter sent Nasad to fetch his vehicle, then pointed to a dusty old Alfa Romeo in a nearby car park, whispering to Bond, "Over there. My wheels. Let's go."

Chapter 27

The Lincoln carrying Severan Hydt and Niall Dunne eased east through the haze and heat, paralleling the massive power lines conducting electricity to the outer regions of the city-state. Nearby was the Persian Gulf, the rich blue muted nearly to beige by the dust in the air and the glare of the low but unrelenting sun.

They were taking a convoluted route through Dubai, cruising past the indoor ski complex, the striking Burj Al-Arab hotel, which resembled a sail and was nearly as tall as the Eiffel Tower, and the luxurious Palm Jumeirah—the sculpted development of shops, homes and hotels extending far into the Gulf and fashioned, as the name suggested, in the likeness of an indigenous tree. These areas of glistening beauty upset Severan Hydt: the new, the unblemished. He felt much more comfortable when the vehicle slipped into the older Satwa neighborhood, densely populated by thousands upon thousands of working-class folk—mostly immigrants.

The time was nearly five thirty. An hour and a half before the event. It was also, Hydt had noted, with irony, an hour and a half until sunset.

Curious coincidence, he reflected. A good sign. His ancestors—his spiritual, if not necessarily genetic forebears—had believed in omens and portents and he allowed himself to do so as well; yes, he was a practical, hardheaded businessman . . . but he had his *other* side.

He thought again about tonight.

They continued to cruise along the roads in a complicated fashion. The purpose of this dizzying tour wasn't to sightsee. No, taking the roundabout route to get to a spot merely five miles from the Intercontinental had been Dunne's idea of security.

But the driver—a mercenary with experience in Afghanistan and Syria—reported, "I thought we were being followed, an Alfa and possibly a Ford. But if so, we've lost them, I'm sure."

Dunne looked back, then said, "Good. Go to the works."

They circled back to the city. In ten minutes they were at an industrial complex in the Deira, the cluttered and colorful area in the center of town nestled along Dubai Creek and the Gulf. This was another place in which Hydt felt immediately comfortable. To enter the neighborhood was to take a step back in time: its uneven houses, traditional markets and the rustic port along the Creek, whose docks teemed with dhows and other small vessels, might have been the backdrop to a 1930s adventure film. The ships were piled impossibly high with stacks of cargo lashed into place. The driver found the destination, a good-size factory and warehouse, with attached offices, one story, the shabby beige paint peeling. Razor wire, rare in low-crime Dubai, topped the chain-link fence surrounding the place. The driver pulled up to an intercom and spoke in Arabic. The gate slowly swung open. The Town Car eased into the car park and stopped.

The two men climbed out. With an hour and fifteen minutes to sunset, the air was cooling, even as the ground radiated heat banked during the day.

Hydt heard a voice, carried on the dusty wind. "Please! My friend, please come in!" The man waving his hand was in a white *dishdasha* robe—in the uniquely Emirates style—and had no head covering. He was in his midfifties, Hydt knew, although, like many Arab men, he looked younger. A studious face, smart glasses, Western shoes. His longish hair was swept back. A black beard framed his smile. Hydt had been amused to learn that, while hair coloring was not a good product to market in a land where both male and female heads were usually covered, beard dye was a best seller.

Mahdi al-Fulan strode over sprays of red sand, which drifted along the tarmac and sloped against the curb, the walkways and the sides of buildings. The Arab's eyes were bright, as if he were a schoolboy about to show off a treasured project. Which wasn't far from the truth, Hydt reflected.

Hands were gripped. "My friend." Hydt didn't try to offer an Arabic greeting. He had no talent for languages and believed it a weakness to attempt anything you were not skilled at.

Niall Dunne stepped forward, his shoulders bouncing as they always did in his gangling walk, and also greeted the man but the pale eyes were gazing past the Arab. For once, they were not searching for threats. He was staring raptly at the bounty that the warehouse held, which could be seen through the open door: perhaps fifty or so machines, in every shape a geometrician could name, made of raw and painted steel, iron, aluminum, carbon fiber . . . who knew what else? Pipes protruded, wires, control panels, lights, switches, chutes and belts. If robots had pleasant dreams, they would be set in this room.

They entered the warehouse, which was devoid of workers. Dunne paused to study and occasionally even caress some device or other.

Mahdi al-Fulan was an industrial product designer, MIT educated. He shunned the kind of high-profile entrepreneurship that gets you on the cover of business magazines—and often into the bankruptcy court—and specialized instead in designing functional industrial equipment and control systems for which there was a consistent market. He was one of Severan Hydt's main suppliers. Hydt had met him at a recycling-equipment conference. Once he'd learned about certain trips the Arab took abroad and about the dangerous men to whom he sold his wares, they'd become partners. Al-Fulan was a clever scientist, an innovative engineer, a man with ideas and inventions important to Gehenna.

And with other connections too.

Ninety dead . . .

At that thought, Hydt involuntarily consulted his watch. Nearly six.

"Follow me, please, Severan, Niall." Al-Fulan had caught Hydt's glance. The Arab led them through the various rooms, dim and still. Dunne again slowed his step to examine some machinery or a control panel. He'd nod approvingly or frown, perhaps trying to understand how a system worked.

Leaving behind the machines with their scent of oil, paint and the unique metallic, almost bloodlike odor of high-powered electrical systems, they entered the offices. At the end of a dim corridor, al-Fulan used a computer key to open an unmarked door and they stepped into a work area, which was large and cluttered with thousands of sheets of paper, blueprints and other documents on which were words, graphs and diagrams, many of them incomprehensible to Hydt.

The atmosphere was eerie, to say the least, both because of the dimness and the clutter . . . and because of what decorated the walls.

Images of eyes.

Eyes of all sorts—human, fish, canine, feline and insect—photos, computerized three-dimensional renderings, medical drawings from the 1800s. Particularly unsettling was a fanciful, detailed blueprint of a human eye, as if a modern-day Dr. Frankenstein had used current engineering techniques to construct his monster.

In front of one of the dozens of large computer monitors sat an attractive woman, a brunette, in her late twenties. She stood up, strode to Hydt and shook his hand vigorously. "Stella Kirkpatrick. I'm Mahdi's research assistant." She greeted Dunne too.

Hydt had been to Dubai several times but had not met her before. The woman's accent was American. Hydt supposed she was clever, hardheaded and typical of a common phenomenon in this part of the world, one that went back hundreds of years: the Westerner in love with Arab culture.

Al-Fulan said, "Stella worked up most of the algorithms."

"Did you now?" Hydt asked, with a smile.

She blushed, the ruddy color stemming from her affection for her mentor, whom she glanced at quickly, a supplication for approval, which al-Fulan provided in the form of a seductive smile; Hydt was not a participant in this exchange.

As the decorations on the walls suggested, al-

Fulan's specialty was optics. His goal in life was to invent an artificial eye for the blind that would work as well as those "Allah—praise be to Him—created for us." But until that happened he would make a great deal of money designing industrial machinery. He had come up with most of the specialized safety, control and inspection systems for Green Way's sorters and document-destruction devices.

Hydt had recently commissioned him to create yet another device for the company and had come here today with Dunne to see the prototype.

"A demonstration?" the Arab said.

"Please," Hydt replied.

They all walked back into the garden of machines. Al-Fulan led them to a complicated device, weighing several tons, sitting in the loading bay beside two large industrial refuse compactors.

The Arab hit some buttons and, with a growl, the machine slowly warmed up. It was about twenty feet long, six high and five wide. At the front end a metal conveyor belt led into a mouth about a yard square. Inside, all was blackness, although Hydt could just make out horizontal cylinders, covered with spikes, like a combine harvester. At the rear, half a dozen chutes led to bins, each containing a thick gray plastic liner, open at the top to catch whatever the machine disgorged.

Hydt studied it carefully. He and Green Way made a lot of money from destroying documents securely but the world was changing. Most data resided on computer and flash drives nowadays and this would be increasingly the case in the future. Hydt had decided to expand his empire by offering a new approach to destroying computer data storage devices.

A number of companies did this, as did Green Way, but the new approach would be different, thanks to al-Fulan's invention. At the moment, to destroy data effectively, computers had to be dismantled by hand and hard drives had to be wiped of data with magnetic degaussing units, then crushed. Other steps were required to separate the other components of the old computer—many of them dangerous e-waste.

This machine, however, did everything automatically. You simply tossed the old computer onto the belt and the device did the rest, breaking it apart while al-Fulan's optical systems identified the components and sent them to appropriate bins. Hydt's salespeople could assure his customers that this machine would make certain not only that the sensitive information on the hard drive was destroyed but that all the other components were identified and disposed of according to local environmental regulations.

At a nod from her boss, Stella picked up an old laptop and set it on the ribbed conveyor belt. It vanished into the dim recesses of the device.

They heard a series of sharp cracks and thuds and finally a loud grinding noise. Al-Fulan directed his guests to the rear, where, after five or so minutes, they watched the machine spit the various sorted bits of scrap into different bins—metal, plastic, circuit boards and the like. In the bin liner marked "Media Storage" they saw a fine metal and silicon dust, all that was left of the hard drive. The dangerous e-waste, like the batteries and heavy metals, was deposited in a receptacle marked with warning labels and the benign components were dropped into recycling bins.

Al-Fulan then directed Hydt and Dunne to a computer monitor, on which a report about the machine's efforts scrolled efficiently past.

Dunne's icy façade had slipped. He seemed almost excited.

Hydt, too, was pleased, very pleased. He began to ask a question. But then he looked at a clock on the wall. It was six thirty. He could concentrate on the machinery no longer.

Chapter 28

James Bond, Felix Leiter and Yusuf Nasad were fifty feet from the factory, crouching beside a large skip, observing Hydt, the Irishman, an Arab in a traditional white robe and an attractive dark-haired woman through a loading-bay window.

With Bond and Leiter in the American's Alfa and Nasad in his Ford bringing up the rear, they'd started to follow the Lincoln Town Car from the Intercontinental but both agents immediately recognized that the Arab driver was starting evasion techniques. Worried that they'd be spotted, Bond used an app in his mobile to paint the car with a MASINT profile and took its coordinates with a laser, then uploaded the data to the GCHQ tracking center. Leiter eased off the accelerator and let the satellites follow the vehicle, beaming the results to Bond's mobile.

"Damn," Leiter had drawled, looking at the phone in Bond's hand. "I want one of them."

Bond had followed the Town Car's progress on his map and directed Leiter, with Nasad following, in the general direction that Hydt was going, which was proving to be a very circuitous route. Finally the Lincoln headed back to the Deira, the old part of town. A few minutes later Bond, Leiter and his asset arrived, left the cars in an alleyway between two dusty warehouses and sliced their way through the chain-link for a closer view of what Hydt and the Irishman were up to. The driver of the Lincoln had remained in the car and could not observe the intruders.

Bond plugged in an earpiece and trained his phone's camera eye on the foursome, eavesdropping with an app that Sanu Hirani had developed. The Vibra-Mike reconstructed conversation observed through windows or transparent doors by reading vibrations on glass or other nearby smooth surfaces. It combined what it detected sonically with visual input of lip and cheek movement, eye expression and body language. In circumstances like this it could reconstruct conversations with about 85 percent accuracy.

After listening to the conversation, Bond told the others, "They're talking about equipment for the Green Way facilities, his legitimate company. Dammit."

"Look at the bastard," the American whispered. "He knows that around ninety people are going to die in a half hour and it's like he's talking to a store clerk about pixels on big-screen TVs."

Nasad's phone buzzed. He took the call, speaking in staccato Arabic, some of which Bond could decipher. He was getting information about the factory. He disconnected and explained to the agents that the place was owned by a Dubai citizen, Mahdi al-Fulan. A picture confirmed he was the man Hydt and the Irishman were with. He was not suspected of having any terrorist ties, had never been to Afghanistan and seemed to be merely an engineer and businessman. He did, however, design and sell his products to, among others, warlords and arms dealers. He had recently developed an optical scanner on a land mine that could differentiate between enemies' and friendlies' uniforms or badges.

Bond recalled the notes he'd found up in March: *blast radius* . . .

As conversation in the warehouse resumed, Bond cocked his head and listened once more. Hydt was saying to the Irishman, "I want to leave for the . . . event. Mahdi and I will go there now." He turned to his Arab associate with eerie, almost hungry, eyes. "It's not far, is it?"

"No, we can walk."

Hydt said to his Irish partner, "Maybe you and Stella could work out some of the technical details."

The Irishman turned to the woman as Hydt and the Arab vanished into the warehouse.

Bond closed down the app and glanced at Leiter. "Hydt and al-Fulan are going to the site where the attack is to take place. They're walking. I'll follow them. See if you can find out anything more here. The woman and the Irishman are going to stay. Get closer if you can. I'll call you when I find out what's going on."

"You bet," the Texan said.

Bay-at . . .

Nasad nodded.

Bond checked his Walther and slipped it back into the holster.

"Wait, James," Leiter said. "You know, saving these people, the ninety or whatever, well, it could tip your hand. If he thinks you're on to him, Hydt could rabbit—he'll disappear—and you'll never find him, until he comes up with a new Incident Twenty. And he'll be a lot more careful about keeping it secret then. If you let him go ahead with whatever he's about to do here, he'll stay in the dark about you."

"Sacrifice them, you mean?"

The American held Bond's eyes. "It's a tough call. I don't know that I could do it. But it's something to think about."

"I already have. And no, they're not dying."

He spotted the two men making their way out of the compound.

Crouching, Leiter ran to the building and hauled himself through a small window, disappearing silently on the other side. He reappeared and gestured. Nasad joined him.

Bond slipped back through the breach in the fence and made his way after his two targets. After several blocks of meandering through industrial alleys, Hydt and al-Fulan entered the Deira Covered Souk: hundreds of outdoor stalls, as well as more conventional shops, where you could buy gold, spices, shoes, TV sets, CDs, videos, Mars bars, souvenirs, toys, Middle Eastern and Western clothing . . . virtually anything imaginable. Only a portion of the population here seemed to be Emirates-born; Bond heard bits of conversation in Tamil, Malayalam, Urdu and Tagalog but relatively little Arabic. Shoppers were everywhere, hundreds of them. Intense negotiations were going on at every stall and in every shop, hands gesticulating feverishly, brows furrowed, clipped words flying back and forth.

Do buy . . .

Bond was following at a discreet distance, looking for any sign of their target: the people who were going to die in twenty-five minutes.

What could the Rag-and-Bone Man possibly have in mind? A trial run in anticipation of the carnage on Friday, which would be ten or twenty times as bad? Or was this unrelated? Perhaps Hydt was using his role as an international businessman as a cover. Were he and the Irishman just hired killers? State-of-the-art hitmen?

Bond dodged through the logjam of merchants, shoppers, tourists and dock workers loading the dhows with cargo. It was very crowded now, just before *Maghrib,* the sunset prayer. Were the markets to be the site of the attack?

Then Hydt and al-Fulan left the souk and continued to walk for half a block. They stopped and gazed up at a modern structure, three stories high, with large glass windows, overlooking Dubai Creek. It was a public building, filled with men, women and children. Bond moved closer and saw a sign in Arabic and English. THE MUSEUM OF THE EMIRATES.

So this was the target. And it was a damn good one. Bond scanned it. At least a hundred people meandered through the ground floor alone and there would surely be many more on the floors above. The building was close to the creek, with only a narrow road in front, which meant that emergency vehicles would have a difficult time getting close to the scene of the carnage.

Al-Fulan looked around uneasily but Hydt pushed through the front door. They vanished into the crowd.

I'm not letting those people die. Bond plugged his earpiece in and called up the eavesdropping app on his phone. He followed the two men inside, paid a small admission fee and eased closer to his targets, blending with a group of Western tourists.

He couldn't help but think about what Felix Leiter had said. Saving these people might indeed alert Hydt that someone was on to him.

What would M do under these circumstances?

He supposed the old man would sacrifice the ninety to save thousands. He'd been an active-duty admiral in the Royal Navy. Officers at that level had to make hard decisions like this all the time.

But, dammit, Bond thought, I have to do something. He saw children scampering around, saw men and women gazing at and talking animatedly about the exhibits, people laughing, people nodding with rapt interest as a tour guide lectured.

Hydt and al-Fulan moved farther into the building. What were they doing? Had they planned to leave an explosive device? Perhaps it was what had been constructed in the hospital basement in March.

Or perhaps the industrial designer al-Fulan himself had made a weapon for Hydt.

Bond circled through the large marble lobby, filled with Arabic art and antiquities. A massive chandelier, in gold, dominated the room. Bond casually pointed the microphone toward the men. He caught dozens of scraps of conversation from others but none between Hydt and al-Fulan. Angry with himself, he adjusted his aim more carefully and finally heard Hydt's voice: "I've been looking forward to this for a long time. I must thank you again for making it happen."

Al-Fulan: "I am pleased to do what I can. It is good we are in business together."

Distracted, Hydt whispered, "I would like to take pictures of the bodies."

"Yes, yes, of course. Anything you want, Severan."

How close can I get to the bodies?

Hydt then said, "It's almost seven. Are we ready?"

What should I do? Bond thought desperately. People are about to die.

Your enemy's purpose will dictate your response . . .

On the wall, he noted a fire alarm. He could pull it, evacuate the building. But he also saw CCTVs and security guards. He'd be identified immediately as the man who'd pulled the lever and, though he'd try to flee, the guards and police might stop him, find his weapon. Hydt might see him. He'd easily deduce what had happened. The mission would collapse.

Was there any better response?

He couldn't think of one and edged close to the fire-alarm panel.

Six fifty-five.

Hydt and al-Fulan were walking quickly to a door at the rear of the lobby. Bond was at the alarm now. He was in full view of three security cameras.

And a guard was no more than twenty feet away. He had noticed Bond now and perhaps registered that his behavior wasn't quite what you'd expect of a casual Western tourist in an arcane museum of this sort. The man bent his head and spoke into a microphone attached to his shoulder.

In front of Bond a family stood before a diorama of a camel race. The little boy and his father were laughing at the comical models.

Six fifty-six.

The squat guard turned toward Bond. He wore a pistol. And the protective flap covering it had been unsnapped.

Six fifty-seven.

The guard started forward, his hand near his gun.

Still, with Hydt and al-Fulan merely twenty feet away, Bond reached for the fire-alarm lever.

Chapter 29

At that moment an announcement in Arabic came over the public-address system.

Bond paused to listen. He understood most of it. The English translation a moment later confirmed his take on the words.

"Gentlemen. Will ticket holders for the seven o'clock show now proceed through the North Wing door."

That was the entrance Hydt and al-Fulan were now approaching, at the back of the main hall. They weren't leaving the museum; if this was the location where the people would die, why weren't the two men fleeing?

Bond left the alarm panel and stepped to the door. The guard eyed him once more, then turned away, fixing his holster flap.

Hydt and his colleague stood at the entrance to a special show the museum was hosting. Bond exhaled slowly as he understood at last. The title of the exhibition was "Death in the Sand." A notice at the entrance explained that last autumn archaeologists had discovered a mass grave dating back a thousand years, located near Abu Dhabi's Liwa Oasis, about a hundred kilometers inland from the Persian Gulf. An entire nomadic Arab tribe, ninety-two people, had been attacked and slaughtered. Just after the battle, a sandstorm had buried the bodies. When the village had been discovered last year the remains were found perfectly preserved in the hot dry sands.

The exhibition was of the desiccated bodies laid out exactly as they were found, in a re-creation of the village. For the general public, it seemed, the bodies were modestly covered. The special exhibition tonight, at seven—which included only men—was for scientists, doctors and professors. The corpses were not covered. Al-Fulan had apparently managed to get Hydt a ticket.

Bond nearly laughed out loud and relief flooded through him. Misunderstandings—and even outright errors—are not uncommon in the nuanced business of espionage, where operatives have to make plans and execute them with only fragments of information at hand. Often the results of such mistakes are disastrous; Bond couldn't recall an instance in which the opposite was true, as here, when a looming tragedy turned into an evening's innocuous cultural excursion. His first thought was that he'd enjoy telling Philly Maidenstone the story.

His amusement dimmed, however, as he reflected soberly that he'd almost destroyed the mission for the sake of ninety people who'd been dead for nearly a millennium.

His mood grew more somber yet as he looked into the large exhibition room and caught glimpses of the panorama of death: the bodies, some retaining much of the skin, like leather. Others were mostly skeletons. Hands reaching out, perhaps in the last plea for mercy. Emaciated forms of mothers cradling their children. Eye sockets empty, fingers mere twigs and more than a few mouths twisted into horrific smiles by the ravages of time and decay.

Bond looked at Hydt's face as the Rag-and-Bone

Man stared down at the victims. He was enraptured; an almost sexual lust glowed in his eyes. Even al-Fulan seemed troubled at the pleasure his business associate was displaying.

I've never heard that kind of joy at the prospect of killing . . .

Hydt was taking picture after picture, the repeated flash from his mobile bathing the corpses in brilliant light and making them all the more supernatural and horrific.

What a bloody waste of time, Bond reflected. All he'd learned from the trip was that Hydt had some fancy new machinery for his recycling operations and that he got a sick high from images of dead bodies. Was Incident 20, whatever it might be, a similar misreading of the intercept? He thought back to the phrasing of the original message and concluded that whatever was planned for Friday was a real threat.

> . . . estimated initial casualties in the thousands, british interests adversely affected, funds transfers as discussed.

That clearly described an attack.

Hydt and al-Fulan were moving deeper into the exhibition hall and, without a special ticket, Bond couldn't pursue them further. But Hydt was speaking again. Bond lifted the phone.

"I do hope you understand about that girl of yours. What's her name again?"

"Stella," al-Fulan said. "No, we don't have any choice. When she finds out I'm not leaving my wife she'll be a risk. She knows too much. And, frankly," he added, "she's been quite a nuisance lately."

Hydt continued, "My associate's handling everything. He'll take her out to the desert, make her disappear. Whatever he does, though, will be efficient. He's
quite amazing at planning . . . well, everything."

That was why the Irishman had remained at the
warehouse.

If he was going to kill Stella, there *was* something
more to this trip than legitimate business. He'd have
to assume it involved Incident 20. Bond hurried from
the museum, calling Felix Leiter. They had to save the
woman and learn what she knew.

Leiter's mobile, however, rang four times, then
stepped into voice mail. Bond tried again. Why the
hell wasn't the American picking up? Were he and
Nasad trying to save Stella at this moment, perhaps
fighting with the Irishman or the chauffeur? Or both
of them?

Another call. Voice mail again. Bond broke into
a run, weaving through the souks as haunting voices
calling the faithful to prayer filled the sunset sky.

Sweating hard, gasping, he arrived at al-Fulan's
warehouse five minutes later. Hydt's Town Car was
gone. Bond slipped through the hole they'd cut earlier
in the fence. The window Leiter had climbed through
was now closed. Bond ran to the warehouse and used a
lock pick to open a side door. He slipped inside, drawing the Walther.

The place seemed to be deserted, though he could
hear the loud whining of machinery from somewhere
nearby.

No sign of the girl.

And where were Leiter and Nasad?

Just a few seconds later Bond learned the answer to

that question—part of it, at least. In the room Leiter had entered, he found bloodstains on the floor, fresh. There were signs of a struggle, with several tools lying nearby . . . along with Leiter's pistol and phone.

Bond summoned a scenario of what might have happened. Leiter and Nasad had separated, with the American hiding here. He must have been watching the Irishman and Stella when the Arab chauffeur had slipped up behind and hit him with a spanner or pipe. Had Leiter been dragged off, thrown into the boot of the Town Car and taken to the desert with the girl?

Gun in hand, Bond headed for the doorway where he heard the sound of the machine.

He froze at what he saw ahead of him.

The man in the blue jacket—his tail from earlier—was rolling the barely conscious Felix Leiter into one of the massive rubbish-compacting machines. The CIA agent lay sprawled, feetfirst, on the conveyor belt, which wasn't moving, though the machine itself was running; in the center two huge metal plates on either side of the belt pressed forward, nearly meeting, then withdrawing to accept a new batch of junk.

Leiter's legs were a mere two yards from them.

The assailant glanced up and, scowling, stared at the intruder.

Bond steadied his weapon's sights on the man and shouted, "Hands out to your sides!"

The man did so but suddenly lunged to his right and slapped a button on the machine, then sprinted away, vanishing from sight.

The conveyor belt began rolling steadily forward, with Leiter easing toward the thick steel plates, which came within six inches of each other, then shot back to allow more refuse into their path.

Bond sped to the unit and slapped the red off button, then started after the attacker. But the heavy-duty motor didn't stop immediately; the belt continued to carry his friend toward the deadly plates, pulsing relentlessly back and forth.

Oh God! . . . Bond holstered his Walther and turned back. He grabbed Leiter and struggled to pull him out of the machinery. But the conveyor belt was dotted with pointed teeth, to improve its grip, and Leiter's clothing was caught.

Head lolling, blood streaming into his eyes, he continued to be drawn toward the compactor mechanism.

Eighteen inches away, sixteen . . . twelve.

Bond leaped on to the belt and jammed a foot against the frame, then wound Leiter's jacket around his hands and gripped furiously hard. The momentum slowed but the massive motor continued to drive the belt relentlessly under the faces of the plates shooting back and forth.

Leiter was eight inches, then six, from the plates that would turn his feet and ankles to pulp.

His arm and leg muscles in fiery agony, Bond tugged harder, groaning at the effort.

Three inches . . .

Finally the belt stopped and, with a hydraulic gasp, so did the plates.

Struggling for breath, Bond reached in and untangled the American's trousers from the teeth on the belt and pulled him out, easing him to the floor. He ran to the loading bay, drawing his weapon, but there was no sign of the man in blue. Then, scanning for other threats, Bond returned to the CIA agent, who was coming round. He sat up slowly, Bond helping, and oriented himself.

"Can't leave you alone for five minutes, can I?" Bond asked, masking the horror he'd felt at his friend's near fate, as he examined the wound in the man's head and mopped it with a rag he'd found nearby.

Leiter gazed at the machine. Shook his head. Then his familiar grin spread across his lean face. "You Brits're always barging in at the wrong time. I had him just where I wanted him."

"Hospital?" Bond asked. His heart pounded from the effort of the rescue and relief at the outcome.

"Naw." The American examined the rag. It was bloody but Leiter seemed more angry than injured. "Hell, James, we're past the deadline! The ninety people?"

Bond explained about the exhibition.

Leiter barked a harsh laugh. "What a screwup! Brother, did we misread that one. So Hydt gets off on dead bodies. And he wanted *pictures* of them? Man's got a whole new idea of porn."

Bond collected Leiter's phone and weapon and returned them to him. "What happened, Felix?"

Leiter's eyes stilled. "The driver of the Town Car came into the warehouse right after you left. I could see him and that Irishman talking, looking at the girl. I knew something was going down and that meant she'd know something. I was going to finesse it somehow and save her. Claim we were safety inspectors or something. Before I could move, they grabbed the girl and taped her up, dragged her toward the office. I sent Yusuf around to the other side and started toward them but that bastard nailed me before I got ten feet—the guy from the shopping center, your tail."

"I know. I spotted him."

"Man, the SOB knows some martial arts crap, I'll tell you that. He clocked me good and I was down for the count."

"Did he say anything?"

"Grunted a lot. When he hit me."

"Was he working with the Irishman or al-Fulan?"

"Couldn't tell. I didn't see them together."

"And the girl? We've got to find her if we can."

"They're probably on their way out to the desert. If we're lucky, Yusuf's following them. Probably tried to call when I was out." With Bond helping, the agent struggled to his feet. He took his phone and hit speed dial.

And from nearby came the chirp of a ringtone, a cheerful electronic tune. But muted.

Both men looked around.

Then Leiter turned to Bond. "Oh no," the American whispered, closing his eyes briefly. They hurried to the back of the compactor. The sound was coming from inside a large, filled bin liner, which the machine had automatically sealed with wire and then disgorged on to the loading-bay platform to be carted off for disposal.

Bond, too, had realized what had happened. "I'll look," he said.

"No," Leiter said firmly. "It's my job." He unwound the wire, took a deep breath and looked inside the bag. Bond joined him.

The dense jigsaw of sharp metal pieces, wires and nuts, bolts and screws were entwined with a mass of gore and bloody cloth, bits of human organs, bone.

The glazed eyes in Yusuf Nasad's crushed, distorted face stared directly between the two men.

Without a word, they returned to the Alfa and checked the satellite tracking system, which reported that Hydt's limo had returned to the Intercontinental. It had made two brief stops on the way—presumably to transfer the girl to another car, for her last trip out to the desert, and to collect Hydt from the museum.

Fifteen minutes later Bond piloted the Alfa past the hotel and into the car park.

"Do you want to get a room?" Bond asked. "Take care of that?" He gestured at Leiter's head.

"Naw, I need a goddamn drink. I'll just wash up. Meet you in the bar."

They parked and Bond opened the boot. He collected his laptop bag, leaving the suitcase inside. Leiter pulled his own small bag over his shoulder and found a cap—branded, so to speak, with the logo of the University of Texas Longhorns gridiron team. He pulled it gingerly over his wound and stuffed his straw-colored hair underneath. They took the side entrance into the hotel.

Inside, Leiter went to wash and Bond, making sure none of the Hydt entourage was in the lobby, passed through it and stepped outside. He assessed a group of limo drivers standing in a cluster and talking busily. Bond saw that none of them was Hydt's driver. He gestured to the smallest of the lot and the man walked over eagerly.

"You have a card?" Bond asked.

"Indeed, yes, I do, sir." And offered one. Bond glanced at and pocketed it. "What would like, sir? A dune-bashing trip? No, I know, the gold souk! For your lady. You will bring her something from Dubai and be her hero."

"The man who hired that limo?" Bond's gaze swept quickly over Hydt's Lincoln.

The driver's eyes went still. Bond wasn't worried; he knew when somebody was for sale. He tried once more. "You know him, don't you?"

"Not especially, sir."

"But you drivers always talk among yourselves. You know everything that goes on here. Especially regarding a curious fellow like Mr. Hydt."

He slipped the man five hundred dirhams.

"Yes, sir, yes, sir. I may have heard something. . . . Let me think. Yes, perhaps."

"And what might that have been?"

"I believe he and his friends have gone to the restaurant. They will be there for two hours or so. It's a very good restaurant. Meals are leisurely."

"Any idea where they're going from here?"

A nod. But no accompanying words.

Another five hundred dirhams joined their friends.

The man laughed softly and cynically. "People are careless around us. We are simply people to shepherd folks around. We are camels. Beasts of burden. I'm referring to the fact that people think we don't exist. Therefore whatever they say in front of us they believe we do not hear, however sensitive it might be. However *valuable*."

Bond held up more cash, then returned it to his pocket.

The driver glanced about briefly, then said, "He's flying to Cape Town tonight. A private jet, leaving in about three hours. As I told you, the restaurant downstairs is known for its sumptuous and leisurely dining experience." A fake pout. "But your questions tell me you probably do not want me to have an associate book a table. I understand. Perhaps on your next trip to Dubai."

Now Bond handed over the rest of the money. He then withdrew the man's business card and, flicking it with his thumb, asked, "My associate? The man who came in with me? Did you see him?"

"The tough one. He looked . . . tough."

"Very tough. Now, I will be leaving Dubai soon but he will be staying. He most sincerely hopes your information about Mr. Hydt is accurate."

The smile blew away like sand. "Yes, yes, sir, it is completely accurate, I swear to Allah. Praise be to Him."

Chapter 30

Bond went into the bar and took a table on the outdoor terrace overlooking Dubai Creek, a peaceful mirror dotted with swaying reflections of colored light, which utterly belied the horror he had witnessed at al-Fulan's works.

The waiter approached and asked what he would like. American bourbon was Bond's favorite spirit but he believed vodka was medicinal, if not curative, when served bitingly cold. He now ordered a double Stolichnaya martini, medium dry, and asked that it be shaken very well, which not only chilled the vodka better than stirring but bruised—aerated—it as well, improving the flavor considerably.

"Lemon peel only."

When the drink arrived, suitably opaque—evidence of a proper shaking—he drank half immediately and felt the oxymoronic burning chill flow from throat to face. It helped dull the frustration that he hadn't been able to save either the young woman or Yusuf Nasad.

It did nothing, however, to mitigate the memory of Hydt's eerie expression as he gazed, lusting, at the petrified bodies.

He sipped again, staring absently at the television above the bar, on whose screen the beautiful Bahraini singer Ahlam was swirling through a video edited in the jerky style fashionable on Arab and Indian TV. Her infectious, trilling voice floated from the speakers.

He drained the glass, then called Bill Tanner. He

explained about the false alarm at the history museum
and the deaths and added that Hydt would head for
Cape Town that night. Could T Branch arrange a ride
for Bond? He could no longer hitchhike on his friend's
Grumman, which had gone back to London.

"I'll see what I can do, James. Probably have to be
commercial. I don't know if I can get you there ahead
of Hydt, though."

"I just need a watcher to meet the flight and see
where he goes. What's the Six situation down there?"

"Station Z's got a covert operator on the Cape. Gregory Lamb. Let me check his status." Bond heard typing.
"He's up in Eritrea at the moment—that saber-rattling
on the Sudanese border's gotten worse. But, James, we
don't want to get Lamb involved if we can avoid it. He
doesn't have an entirely irreproachable record. He went
native, like some character out of a Graham Greene
novel. I think Six have been meaning to hand him a
redundancy package but haven't got round to it. I'll find
somebody local for you. I'd recommend the SAPS, the
police service, rather than National Intelligence—NIA's
been in the news lately and not in a good way. I'll make
some calls and let you know."

"Thanks, Bill. Can you patch me to Q?"

"Will do. Good luck."

A thoughtful voice was soon on the line: "Q
Branch. Hirani."

"It's 007, Sanu. I'm in Dubai. I need something fast."

After Bond had explained, Hirani seemed disappointed at the simplicity of the assignment. "Where
are you?" he asked.

"Intercontinental, Festival City."

Bond heard typing.

"All right. Thirty minutes. Just remember: flowers."

They rang off, just as Leiter arrived, sat down and ordered a Jim Beam, neat. "That means no ice, no water, no fruit salad, no nothing. But it does mean a double. And I could live with a triple."

Bond ordered another martini. When the waiter left he asked, "How's the head?"

"It's nothing," Leiter murmured. He didn't seem badly injured and Bond knew that his subdued mood was due to the loss of Nasad. "You find out anything about Hydt?"

"They're leaving tonight. A couple of hours. Going to Cape Town."

"What's down there?"

"No idea. That's what I have to find out."

And find out within three days, Bond reminded himself, if he wanted to save those thousands of people.

They fell silent as the waiter brought their drinks. Both agents scanned the large room as they sipped. There was no sign of the dark-haired man with the earring or of watchers paying too much attention—or not enough—to the men in the corner.

Neither man raised a toast to the memory of the asset who'd just died. As tempted as you were, you never did that.

"Nasad?" Bond asked. "His body?" The thought of an ally going to such an ignominious grave was hard.

Leiter's lips tightened. "If Hydt and the Irishman were involved and I called in a team, they'd know we were on to them. I'm not risking our cover at this point. Yusuf knew what he was getting into."

Bond nodded. It was the right way to handle it, though that didn't make the decision any easier.

Leiter inhaled the fumes of his whiskey, then drank again. "You know, in this business, it's choices like that that're the hard ones—not pulling out your six-shooter and playing Butch Cassidy. That, you just do without thinking."

Bond's mobile buzzed. T Branch had booked him an overnight flight on Emirates to Cape Town. It left in three hours. Bond was pleased with the choice of carrier. The airline had studiously avoided becoming just another mass market operation and treated its passengers to what he guessed was the quality service that typified the golden age of air travel fifty or sixty years ago. He told Leiter of his departure arrangements. He added, "Let's get some food."

The American waved over a waiter and asked for a *mezze* platter. "And then bring us a grilled hammour. Bone it, if y'all'd be so kind."

"Yes, şir."

Bond ordered a bottle of a good *premier cru* Chablis, which arrived a moment later. They sipped from the chilled glasses silently until the first course arrived: *kofta,* olives, hummus, cheese, aubergine, nuts and the best flatbread Bond had ever had. Both men began to eat. After the waiter had cleared away the remnants, he brought the main course. The simple white fish lay steaming on a bed of green lentils. It was very good, delicate, yet with a faint meatiness. Bond had eaten only a few mouthfuls when his phone hummed again. Caller ID showed only the code for a British government number. Thinking Philly might be ringing from a different office, Bond answered.

He immediately regretted doing so.

Chapter 31

"James! James! James! Guess who? Percy here. Long time no speak!"

Bond's heart sank.

Leiter frowned, at the glower on Bond's face.

"Percy . . . yes."

Division Three's Osborne-Smith inquired, "You well? No altercations requiring anything more than a plaster, I trust."

"I'm fine."

"Delighted to hear it. Now, things are proceeding apace here. Your boss has briefed everyone about the Gehenna plan. You were perhaps too busy fleeing the jurisdiction to be in touch." He let that hang for a moment, then said, "Aha. Just winding you up, James. Fact is, I'm calling for several reasons and the first is to apologize."

"Really?" Bond asked, suspicious.

The Division Three man's voice grew serious. "In London this morning, I'll admit I had a tac team ready to grab Hydt at the airport, bring him in for some tea and conversation. But it turns out you were right. The Watchers picked up a scrap and managed to decrypt it. Hold on—I quote from the record. Here we go: something garbled, then 'Severan has three main partners . . . any one of them can push the button if he's not available.' So you see, James, arresting him *would* have been a disaster, just as you said. The others would have scurried down the rabbit hole and we'd've lost any chance to find out what Gehenna was about and stop it." He paused for breath. "I was a touch whingey when we met and I'm sorry about that too. I want to work with you on this, James. Apologies accepted? Bygones turned to bygones with a swipe of Hermione's magic wand?"

In the intelligence world, Bond had learned, your allies sought forgiveness for their transgressions against you about as often as your enemies did. He supposed that some of Osborne-Smith's contrition was based on staying in the game for part of the glory but that was all right with Bond. All he cared about was learning what the Gehenna plan was and preventing thousands· of deaths.

"I suppose."

"Good. Now, your boss sent us a signal about what you found up in March and I'm following it up. The 'blast radius' is pretty obvious—an IED—so we're tracking down any reports of stray explosives. And we know that one of the 'terms' of the deal involves five million quid. I've called in some favors at the Bank of England to check SFT activity."

Bond, too, had thought of calling the bank with a request to flag suspect financial transactions. But nowadays five million pounds was such small change that he'd believed there would be far too many responses to plow through. Still, it couldn't hurt for Osborne-Smith to go ahead.

The Division Three man added, "As for the reference to the 'course' being confirmed, well, until we know more, there're no aircraft or ships to monitor. But I've put the aviation and port chaps on alert to move fast if we need to."

"Good," Bond said, without adding that he'd asked Bill Tanner to do much the same. "I've just found out that Hydt, his lady friend and the Irishman are on their way to Cape Town."

"Cape Town? Now that's worth chewing over. I've been peering into Hydt's recesses, so to speak."

This was, Bond supposed, what passed for a comradely joke with Percy Osborne-Smith.

"South Africa is one of Green Way's biggest operations. His home from home. I bet Gehenna must have some connection with it—Lord knows there're plenty of British interests there."

Bond told him about al-Fulan and the girl's death. "All we learned specifically is that Hydt gets a kick out of pictures of dead bodies. And the Arab's company probably has something to do with Gehenna. He's supplied equipment to arms dealers and warlords in the past."

"Really? Interesting. Which reminds me. Take a look at the photo I'm uploading. You should have it now."

Bond minimized the active-call screen on his mobile and opened a secure attachment. The picture was of the Irishman. "That's him," he told Osborne-Smith.

"Thought it might be. His name's Niall Dunne." He spelt it out.

"How did you find him?"

"Footage from the CCTVs at Gatwick. He's not in the databases but I had my indefatigable staff compare the pic with street cameras in London. There were some close hits of a man with that weird fringe inspecting tunnels that Green Way is building near the Victoria Embankment. It's the latest thing—underground rubbish transfer and collection. Keeps the roads clear and the tourists happy. A few of our boys pretended they were from Public Works, flashed his picture and got his real name. I've sent his file to Five, the Yard and your chief of staff."

"What's Dunne's story?" Bond asked. In front of him the fish cooled but he'd lost interest in it.

"It's curious. He was born in Belfast, studied architecture and engineering, came top of his year. Then he became a sapper in the army."

Sappers were combat engineers, the soldiers who built bridges, airports and bomb shelters for the troops, as well as laid and cleared minefields. They were known for their improvisational skills, building defensive or offensive machinery and bulwarks with whatever supplies were available and under less-than-ideal conditions.

The ODG's Lieutenant Colonel Bill Tanner had been a sapper and the soft-spoken, golf-loving chief of staff was one of the cleverest and most dangerous men Bond had ever met.

Osborne-Smith continued: "After he left the service he became a freelance engineering inspector. I didn't know that any such line of work existed but it turns out that in constructing a building, ship or plane, the project has to be inspected at hundreds of stages. Dunne would look over the work and say yea or nay. He was apparently at the top of his game—he could find flaws that nobody else could. But suddenly he quit and became a consultant, according to Inland Revenue records. He's a damn good one, too—he makes about two hundred grand a year . . . and doesn't have a company logo or cute mascots like Wenlock and Mandeville."

Bond found that, since the apology, he felt less impatient with Osborne-Smith's wit, such as it was. "That's probably how they met. Dunne inspected something for Green Way and Hydt hired him."

Osborne-Smith continued: "Data mining's placed Dunne going to and from Cape Town over the past four years. He's got a flat there and one in London, which we've been through, by the way, and found nothing of interest. The travel records also show he's been in India, Indonesia, the Caribbean and a few other places where trouble's brewing. Working on new outposts for his boss, I'd guess." He added, "Whitehall's still looking at Afghanistan but I don't give a toss about their theories. I'm sure you're on the money, James."

"Thanks, Percy. You've been very helpful."

"Delighted to be of service." The words that Bond would have found condescending yesterday now sounded sincere.

They rang off and Bond told Felix Leiter what Osborne-Smith had turned up.

"So that scarecrow Dunne's an engineer? We call 'em geeks in the States."

A hawker had entered the restaurant and was moving from table to table selling roses.

Leiter saw the direction of Bond's gaze. "Listen up, James, I've had a wonderful dinner but if you're thinking of sealing the deal with a bouquet, it ain't gonna happen."

Bond smiled.

The hawker stepped up to the table next to Bond's and extended a flower to a young couple seated there. "Please," he said to the wife, "the lovely lady will have this for free, with my compliments." He moved on.

After a moment Bond lifted his napkin and opened the envelope he'd casually removed from the man's pocket in a perfect brush pass.

Remember: flowers . . .

Discreetly he examined the forgery of a South African firearms permit, suitably franked and signed. "We should go," he said, noting the time. He didn't want to run into Hydt, Dunne and the woman on the way out of the hotel.

"We'll put this on Uncle Sam," Leiter said and settled the bill. They left the bar and slipped out by a side door, heading for the car park.

Within half an hour they were at the airport.

The men gripped hands and Leiter offered in a low voice, "Yusuf was a great asset, sure. But more than that, he was a friend. You run across that son of a bitch in the blue jacket again and you have a shot, James, take it."

Wednesday

Killing Fields

Chapter 32

As the Emirates Boeing taxied smoothly over the tarmac toward the gate in Cape Town, James Bond stretched, then slipped his shoes back on. He felt refreshed. Soon after takeoff in Dubai he'd administered to himself two Jim Beams with a little water. The nightcap had done the trick famously and he'd had nearly seven hours of blessedly uninterrupted sleep. He was now reviewing texts from Bill Tanner.

> Contact: Capt. Jordaan, Crime Combating
> & Investigation, SA Police Service.
> Jordaan to meet you landside @ airport.
> Surveillance active on Hydt.

A second followed.

> MI6's Gregory Lamb reportedly still in
> Eritrea. Opinion here all around, avoid him
> if possible.

There was a final one.

> Happy to hear you and Osborne-Smith
> have kissed and made up. When's the
> stag do?

Bond had to smile.

The plane eased to a stop at the gate and the purser

ran through the liturgy of landing with which Bond was all too familiar. "Cabin crew, doors to manual and cross-check. Ladies and gentlemen, please take care when opening the overhead lockers; the contents may have shifted during the flight."

Bless you, my child, for Fate has decided to bring you safely back to earth . . . at least for a little longer.

Bond pulled down his laptop bag—he'd checked in his suitcase, which contained his weapon—and proceeded to Immigration in the busy hall. He received a pro forma stamp in his passport. Then he went into the Customs hall. To a stocky, unsmiling officer he displayed the firearms permit so he could collect his suitcase. The man stared at him intently. Bond tensed and wondered if there was going to be a problem.

"Okay, okay," the man said, his broad, glistening face inflated with the power of small officialdom. "Now you will tell me the truth."

"The truth?" Bond asked calmly.

"Yes. . . . How do you get close enough to a kudu or springbok to use a handgun when you hunt?"

"That's the challenge," Bond replied.

"I must say it would be."

Then Bond frowned. "But I never hunt springbok."

"No? It makes the best biltong."

"Perhaps so but shooting a springbok would be very bad luck for England on the rugby pitch."

The Customs agent laughed hard, shook Bond's hand and nodded him to the exit.

The arrivals hall was packed. Most people were in Western clothing, though some wore traditional African garb: men's dashikis and brocade sets and, for the women, kente kaftans and head wraps, all brightly colored. Muslim robes and scarves were present as well and a few saris.

As Bond made his way through the passenger meeting point he detected several distinct languages and many more dialects. He had always been fascinated by the clicking in African languages; in some words, the mouth and tongue create that very sound for consonants. Khoisan—spoken by the original inhabitants of this part of Africa—made the most use of it, although Zulus and Xhosas also clicked. Bond had tried and found the sound impossible to replicate.

When his contact, Captain Jordaan, did not immediately appear he went into a café, dropped onto a stool at the counter and ordered a double espresso. He drank it down, paid and stepped outside, eyeing a beautiful businesswoman. She was in her midthirties, he guessed, with exotically high cheekbones. Her thick, wavy black hair contained a few strands of premature gray, which added to her sensuality. Her dark red suit, over a black shirt, was cut close and revealed a figure that was full yet tautly athletic.

I believe I shall enjoy South Africa, he thought, and smiled as he let her pass in front of him on her way to the exit. Like most attractive women in transitory worlds like airports, she ignored him.

He stood for several moments in the center of Arrivals, then decided that perhaps Jordaan was waiting for him to approach. He texted Tanner to ask for a photograph. But just after he hit send he spotted the police officer: A large, bearded redhead in a light brown suit—a bear of a man—glanced at Bond once, with a hint of reaction, but he turned away rather quickly and went to a kiosk to buy cigarettes.

Tradecraft is all about subtext: cover identities masking who you really are, dull conversations filled with code words to convey shocking facts, innocent objects used for concealment or as weapons.

Jordaan's sudden diversion to buy cigarettes was a message. He hadn't approached Bond because hostiles were present.

Glancing behind him, he saw no immediate sign of a threat. But instinctively he followed well-established procedures. When an agent waves you off, you circle casually out of the immediate area as inconspicuously as possible and contact a third-party intermediary who coordinates a new rendezvous in a safer location. Bill Tanner would be the cutout.

Bond started to move toward an exit.

Too late.

As he saw Jordaan slipping into the Gents, pocketing cigarettes he would probably never smoke, he heard an ominous voice close to his ear: "Do not turn around." The English was coated with a smooth layer of a native accent. He sensed that the man was lean and tall. From the corner of his eye, Bond was aware of at least one partner, shorter but stockier. This man moved in quickly and relieved him of his laptop bag and the suitcase containing his useless Walther.

The first assailant said, "Walk straight out of the hall—now."

There was nothing for it but to comply. He turned and went where the man had told him, down a deserted corridor.

Bond assessed the situation. From the echo of the footsteps he knew the tall man's partner was far enough away that his initial move could only neutralize one of them instantly. The shorter man would have to shed Bond's suitcase and laptop bag, which would give Bond a few seconds to get to him but he would still have a chance to draw his weapon. The man could be taken down but not before shots were fired.

No, Bond reflected, too many innocents. It was best to wait until they were outside.

"Through the door on your left. I said you are not to look back."

They walked out into stark sunlight. Here it was autumn, the temperature crisp, the sky a stunning azure. As they approached the curb in a deserted construction site, a battered black Range Rover sped forward and squealed to a stop.

More hostiles but no one as yet was getting out of the vehicle.

Purpose . . . response.

Their purpose was to kidnap him. His response would be the textbook protocol in an attempted rendition: disorient and then attack. Casually working his Rolex over his fingers to act as a knuckle-duster, he turned abruptly to confront the pair with a disdainful smile. They were young, deadly serious men, their skin contrasting sharply with the brilliant white of their starched shirts. They wore suits—one brown, the other navy—and narrow dark ties. They were probably armed but overconfidence, perhaps, had led them to keep their weapons holstered.

As the Range Rover door swung open behind him, Bond stepped aside so that he couldn't be attacked from behind and judged angles. He decided to break the jaw of the tallest first and use his body as a shield as he pushed forward toward the shorter man.

He looked calmly into the man's eyes and laughed. "I think I'll report you to the tourist bureau. I've heard a lot about the friendliness of South Africans. I was expecting rather more in the way of hospitality."

Just before he lunged, he heard from behind him, inside the vehicle, a woman's flinty voice: "And we would have offered some if you hadn't made yourself so obvious a target by enjoying a leisurely coffee in plain view with a hostile loose in the airport."

Bond relaxed his fist and turned. He looked into the vehicle and tried unsuccessfully to mask his surprise. The beautiful woman he'd seen just moments ago in Arrivals was sitting in the backseat.

"I'm Captain Bheka Jordaan, SAPS, Crime Combating and Investigation Division."

"Ah." Bond looked at her full lips, untouched by cosmetics, and her dark eyes. She wasn't smiling.

His mobile buzzed. The screen showed he had a message from Bill Tanner, along with, of course, an MMS picture of the woman in front of him.

The tall abductor said, "Commander Bond, I am SAPS Warrant Officer Kwalene Nkosi." He reached out his hand and their palms met in the traditional South African way—an initial grip, as in the West, followed by a vertical clasp and back to the original. Bond knew it was considered impolite to let go too quickly. Apparently he timed the gesture right; Nkosi grinned warmly, then nodded to the shorter man, who was taking Bond's suitcase and laptop bag to the rear of the Range Rover. "And that is Sergeant Mbalula."

The stocky man nodded unsmilingly and, after stowing Bond's belongings, vanished fast, presumably to his own vehicle.

"You will please forgive our brusqueness, Commander," Nkosi said. "We thought it best to get you out of the airport as quickly as possible, rather than spend the time to explain."

"We should not waste more time on pleasantries, Warrant Officer," Bheka Jordaan muttered impatiently.

Bond eased himself into the back beside her. Nkosi got into the passenger seat in the front. A moment later Sergeant Mbalula's black saloon, also unmarked, pulled up behind them.

"Let's go," Jordaan barked. "Quickly."

The Range Rover peeled away from the curb and skidded brazenly into the traffic, earning the driver a series of energetic hoots and lethargic curses, and accelerated to more than ninety kph in a zone marked forty.

Bond pulled his mobile off his belt. He typed into the keyboard, read the responses.

"Warrant Officer?" Jordaan asked Nkosi. "Anything?"

He had been staring into the wing mirror and answered in what seemed to be Zulu or Xhosa. Bond did not speak either language but it was clear from the tone of the answer, and the woman's reaction, that there was no tail. When they were outside the airport grounds and making their way toward a cluster of low but impressive mountains in the distance, the vehicle slowed somewhat.

Jordaan thrust her hand forward. Bond reached out to shake it, smiling, then stopped. She was holding a mobile phone. "If you don't mind," she said sternly, "you will touch the screen here."

So much for warming international relations.

He took the phone, pressed his thumb into the center of the screen and handed it back. She read the message that appeared. "James Bond. Overseas Development Group, Foreign and Commonwealth Office. Now, you'll want to confirm my identity." She held out her hand, fingers splayed. "You have an app that can take my prints too, I assume."

"There's no need."

"Why?" she asked coolly. "Because I'm what passes for a beautiful woman in your mind and you have no need to check further? I could be an assassin. I could be an al-Qaeda terrorist wearing a bomb vest."

He decided not to mention that his earlier perusal of her figure had revealed no evidence of explosives. He answered, perhaps a bit glibly, "I don't need your prints because, in addition to the photo of you that my office just sent me, my mobile read your iris a few minutes ago and confirmed to me that you are indeed Captain Bheka Jordaan, Crime Combating and Investigation Division, South African Police Service. You've worked for them for eight years. You live in Leeuwen Street in Cape Town. Last year you received a Gold Cross for Bravery. Congratulations."

He had also learned her age—thirty-two—her salary and that she was divorced.

Warrant Officer Nkosi twisted round in his seat, glanced at the mobile and said, with a broad smile, "Commander Bond, that is a nice toy. Without doubt."

Jordaan snapped, "Kwalene!"

The young man's smile vanished. He turned back to his wing mirror sentry duty.

She glanced with disdain at Bond's phone. "We

will go to my headquarters and consider how to approach the situation with Severan Hydt. I worked with your Lieutenant Colonel Tanner when he was with MI6 so I agreed to help you. He is intelligent and very devoted to his job. Quite a gentleman too."

The implication being that Bond himself probably was not. He was irritated that she'd taken such umbrage at what had been an innocent—*relatively* innocent—smile in the Arrivals hall. She was attractive and he couldn't have been the first man to lob a flirt her way. "Is Hydt in his office?" he asked.

"That's correct," Nkosi said. "He and Niall Dunne are both in Cape Town. Sergeant Mbalula and I followed them from the airport. There was a woman with them too."

"You have surveillance on them?"

"That's right," the lean man said. "We based our CCTV plan on London's so there are cameras everywhere downtown. He is in his office and being monitored from a central location. We can track him anywhere if he leaves. We ourselves are not completely free of toys, Commander."

Bond smiled at him, then said to Jordaan, "You mentioned a hostile at the airport."

"We learned from Immigration that a man arrived from Abu Dhabi around the time you did. He was traveling on a fake British passport. We discovered this only after he cleared Customs and disappeared."

The bearish man he'd mistaken for Jordaan? Or the man in the blue jacket at the shopping center on Dubai Creek? He described them.

"I don't know," Jordaan offered curtly. "As I said, our only information was documentary. Because he was unaccounted for, I thought it best not to meet you in person in the arrivals hall. I sent my officers instead." She leaned forward suddenly and asked Nkosi, "Anyone now?"

"No, Captain. We are not being followed."

Bond said to her, "You seem concerned about surveillance."

"South Africa is like Russia," she said. "The old regime has fallen and it is a whole new world here. This draws people who wish to make money and involve themselves in politics and all manner of affairs. Sometimes legally, sometimes not."

Nkosi said, "We have a saying. 'With many opportunities come many operatives.' We keep that always in mind at the SAPS and look over our shoulder often. You would be wise to do the same, Commander Bond. Without doubt."

Chapter 33

The central police station in Buitenkant Street, central Cape Town, resembled a pleasant hotel more than a government building. Two stories high, with walls of scrubbed red brick and a red-tiled roof, it overlooked the wide, clean avenue, which was dotted with palms and jacaranda.

The driver paused at the front to let them out. Jordaan and Nkosi stepped onto the pavement and looked around. When they saw no signs of surveillance or threat the warrant officer gestured Bond out. He went to the back for his laptop bag and suitcase, then followed the officers inside.

As they entered the building Bond blinked in surprise at what he saw. There was a plaque that read SERVAMUS ET SERVIMUS—the motto of the SAPS, he assumed. "We protect and we serve."

What gave him pause, though, was that the two principal words were eerie echoes of Severan Hydt's first name.

Without waiting for the lift, Jordaan climbed the stairs to the first floor. Her modest office was lined with books and professional journals, present-day maps of Cape Town and the Western Cape and a framed 120-year-old map of the eastern coast of South Africa, showing the region of Natal, with the port of D'Urban and the town of Ladysmith mysteriously circled in ancient fading ink. Zululand and Swaziland were depicted to the north.

There were framed photographs on Jordaan's desk. A blond man and a dark-skinned woman held hands in one—they appeared in several others. The woman bore a vague resemblance to Jordaan, and Bond assumed they were her parents. Prominent also were pictures of an elderly woman in traditional African clothing and several featuring children. Bond decided that they weren't Jordaan's. There were no shots of her with a partner.

Divorced, he recalled.

Her desktop was graced with fifty or so case folders. The world of policing, like that of espionage, involves far more paperwork than firearms and gadgets.

Despite the late autumn season in South Africa, the weather was temperate and her office warm. After a moment of debate, Jordaan removed her red jacket and hung it up. Her black blouse was short sleeved and he saw a large swath of makeup along the inside of her right forearm. She didn't seem like the tattoo sort but perhaps she was concealing one. Then he decided that, no, the cream covered a lengthy and wide scar.

Gold Cross for Bravery . . .

Bond sat across from her, beside Nkosi, who unbuttoned his jacket and remained stiffly upright. Bond asked them both, "Did Colonel Tanner tell you about my mission here?"

"Just that you were investigating Severan Hydt on a matter of national security."

Bond ran through what they knew of Incident 20—aka Gehenna—and the impending deaths on Friday.

Nkosi frowned ridges into his high forehead. Jordaan took in the information with still eyes. She pressed her hands together—modest rings encircled the middle fingers of both hands. "I see. And the evidence is credible?"

"It is. Does that surprise you?"

She said evenly, "Severan Hydt is an unlikely evil. We are aware of him, of course. He opened Green Way International here two years ago and has contracts for much of the refuse collection and recycling in the major cities in South Africa—Pretoria, Durban, Port Elizabeth, Joburg and, of course, throughout the west here. He's done many good things for our nation. Ours is a country in transition, as you know, and our past has led to problems with the environment. Gold and diamond mining, poverty and lack of infrastructure have taken their toll. Refuse collection was a serious problem in the townships and squatters' settlements. To make up for the displacement caused by the Group Areas Act under apartheid, the government built residences—*lokasies,* or locations, they are called—for the people to live in instead of shacks. But even there the population was so high that refuse collection could not be performed efficiently or sometimes at all. Disease was a problem. Severan Hydt has reversed much of that. He also donates to AIDS and hunger-relief charities."

Most serious criminal enterprises have public-relations specialists on board, Bond reflected; being an "unlikely evil" did not exempt you from diligent investigation.

Jordaan seemed to note his skepticism. She continued, "I'm simply saying that he does not much fit the profile of a terrorist or master criminal. But if he is, my department stands ready to do all it can to help."

"Thank you. Now, do you know anything about his associate, Niall Dunne?"

She said, "I had never heard the name until this morning. I've looked into him. He comes and goes here on a legitimate British passport and has been doing so for several years. We've never had any problem with him. He's not on any watch lists."

"What do you know of the woman with them?"

Nkosi consulted a file. "American passport. Jessica Barnes. She's a cipher to us, I'd say. No police record. No criminal activity. Nothing. We have some photos."

"That's not her," Bond said, looking at the images of a young, truly beautiful blonde.

"Ah, I am sorry, I should have said. These are old shots. I got them off the Internet." Nkosi turned the picture over. "This was from 1970. She was Miss Massachusetts and competed in the Miss America contest. She is now sixty-four years old."

Bond could see the resemblance, now that he knew the truth. Then he asked, "Where is the Green Way office?"

"There are two," Nkosi said. "One nearby and one about twenty miles north of here—Hydt's major refuse disposal and recycling plant."

"I need to get inside them, find out what he's up to."

"Of course," Bheka Jordaan said. There came a lengthy pause. "But you are speaking of legal means, correct?"

"'Legal means'?"

"You can follow him on the street, you can observe him in public. But I cannot get a warrant for you to place a bug in his home or office. As I said, Severan Hydt has done nothing wrong here."

Bond nearly smiled. "In my job I don't generally ask for warrants."

"Well, I do. Of course."

"Captain, this man has twice tried to kill me, in Serbia and the UK, and yesterday he engineered the death of a young woman and possibly a CIA asset in Dubai."

She frowned, sympathy evident in her face. "That's very unfortunate. But those crimes did not happen on South African soil. If I'm presented with extradition orders from those jurisdictions, approved by a magistrate here, I will be happy to execute them. But barring that . . ." She lifted her palms.

"We don't want him arrested," Bond said, with exasperation. "We don't want evidence for trial. The point of my coming here is to find out what he has planned for Friday and stop it. I intend to do that."

"And you may, provided you do so legally. If you're thinking of breaking into his home or office, that would be trespass, subjecting *you* to a criminal complaint." She turned her eyes, like black granite, toward him, and Bond had absolutely no doubt that she would enjoy ratcheting the shackles onto his wrists.

Chapter 34

"He has to die."

Sitting in his office at the Green Way International building in the center of Cape Town, Severan Hydt was holding his phone tightly as he listened to Niall Dunne's chilly words. No, he reflected, that wasn't accurate. There was neither chill nor heat. His comment had been completely neutral.

Which was chilling in its own way.

"Explain," Hydt said, absently tracing a triangle on the desktop with a long, yellowing fingernail.

Dunne told him that a Green Way worker had very likely learned something about Gehenna. He was one of the legitimate workers in the Cape Town disposal plant to the north of the city, who had known nothing of Hydt's clandestine activities. He'd accidentally got into a restricted area in the main building and might have seen some e-mails about the project. "He wouldn't know what they meant at this point but when the incident makes the news later in the week—which it's going to, of course—he might realize we were behind it and tell the police."

"So what do you suggest?"

"I'm looking into it now."

"But if you kill him, won't the police ask questions? Since he's an employee?"

"I'll take care of him where he lives—a squatters' camp. There won't be many police, probably none at all. The taxis'll look into it, most likely, and they won't cause us any problems."

In the townships, squatters' settlements and even the new *lokasies,* the minibus companies were more than just transport providers. They had taken on the role of vigilante judge and jury, hearing cases and tracking down and punishing criminals.

"All right. Let's move fast, though."

"Tonight, after he gets home."

Dunne disconnected and Hydt returned to his work. He'd spent all morning since their arrival making arrangements for the manufacture of Mahdi al-Fulan's new hard-drive destruction machines and for Green Way's salespeople to start hawking them to clients.

But his mind wandered and he kept imagining the body of the young woman, Stella, now in a grave somewhere beneath the restless sands of the Empty Quarter south of Dubai. While her beauty in life hadn't aroused him, the picture in his mind's eye of her in a few months or years certainly did. And in a thousand, she'd be just like the bodies he'd viewed at the museum last night.

He rose, slipped his suit jacket onto a hanger and returned to his desk. He took and placed a string of phone calls, all relating to Green Way's legitimate business. None was particularly engaging . . . until the company's head of sales for South Africa, who was on the floor just below Hydt's, called.

"Severan, I've got some Afrikaner from Durban on the line. He wants to talk to you about a disposal project."

"Send him a brochure and tell him I'll be tied up

till next week." Gehenna was the priority and Hydt had
no interest in taking on new accounts at the moment.

"He doesn't want to hire us. He's talking about some
arrangement between Green Way and his company."

"Joint venture?" Hydt asked cynically. Entrepre-
neurs always emerged when you started to enjoy success, and got publicity, in your chosen field. "Too much
going on now. I'm not interested. Thank him, though."

"All right. Oh, but I was supposed to mention one
thing. Something odd. He said to tell you that the
problem he's got is the same as at Isandlwana in the
eighteen seventies."

Hydt looked away from the documents on his desk.
A moment later he realized he was gripping the phone
hard once again. "You're sure that's what he said?"

"Yes. 'The same as at Isandlwana.' No idea what
he meant."

"He's in Durban?"

"His company's headquarters are there. He's at his
Cape Town office for the day."

"See if he's free to come in."

"When?" the sales manager asked.

A fractional pause, then Hydt said, "Now."

In January 1879, the war between Great Britain
and the Zulu Kingdom kicked off in earnest with
a stunning defeat for the British. At Isandlwana,
overwhelming forces (twenty thousand Zulus versus
fewer than two thousand British and colonial troops)
and some bad tactical decisions resulted in a complete
rout. It was there that the Zulus broke the British
Square, the famous defensive formation in which one
line of soldiers fired while another, directly behind,

reloaded, offering the enemy a nearly unremitting volley of bullets—in that instance, with the deadly Martini-Henry breech-loading rifles.

But the tactic hadn't worked; thirteen hundred British soldiers and allied forces died.

The "disposal" problem that the Afrikaner had referred to could mean only one thing. The battle had occurred in January, the fiercely hot dog days of summer in the region of what was now KwaZulu-Natal; removing the bodies quickly was a necessity . . . and a major logistical issue.

The disposal of remains was also one of the major problems that Gehenna would present in future projects and Hydt and Dunne had been discussing it over the past month.

Why on earth would a businessman from Durban have a problem along these lines that required Hydt's assistance?

Ten lengthy minutes later his secretary stepped into his doorway. "A Mr. Theron is here, sir. From Durban."

"Good, good. Show him in. Please."

She vanished and returned a moment later with a tough-looking, edgy man, who glanced around Hydt's office cautiously, yet with an air of challenge. He was dressed in the business outfit common to South Africa: a suit and smart shirt but no tie. Whatever his line he must have been successful; a heavy gold bracelet encircled his right wrist and his watch was a flashy Breitling. A gold initial ring too, which was a touch brash, Hydt thought.

"Morning." The man shook Hydt's hand. He noticed the long yellowing fingernails but did not recoil, as had happened on more than one occasion. "Gene Theron," he said.

"Severan Hydt."

They exchanged business cards.

EUGENE J. THERON
PRESIDENT, EJT SERVICES LTD.
DURBAN, CAPE TOWN, AND KINSHASA

Hydt reflected: an office in the capital of Congo, one of the most dangerous cities in Africa. This was interesting.

The man glanced at the door, which was open. Hydt rose and closed it, returned to his desk. "You're from Durban, Mr. Theron?"

"Yes, and my main office is there. But I travel a lot. And you?" The faint accent was melodious.

"London, Holland and here. I get to the Far East and India too. Wherever business takes me. Now, 'Theron.' The name's Huguenot, isn't it?"

"Yes."

"We forget Afrikaners are not always Dutch."

Theron lifted an eyebrow as if he'd heard such comments since he was a child and was tired of them.

Hydt's phone trilled. He looked at the screen. It was Niall Dunne. "Excuse me a moment," he said to Theron, who nodded. Then: "Yes?" Hydt asked, pressing the phone close to his ear.

"Theron's legit. South African passport. Lives in Durban and has a security company with headquarters there, with branches here and in Kinshasa. Father's Afrikaner, mother's British. Grew up mostly in Kenya."

Dunne continued: "He's been suspected of supplying troops and arms to conflict regions in Africa, Southeast Asia and Pakistan. No active investigations. The Cambodians detained him in a human trafficking and mercenary investigation because of what he'd been up to in Shan, Myanmar, but let him go. Nothing in Interpol. And he's pretty successful, from what I can tell."

Hydt had deduced that himself; the man's Breitling was worth around five thousand pounds.

"I just texted a picture to you," Dunne added.

It appeared on Hydt's screen and showed the man in front of him. Dunne went on, "But . . . whatever he's proposing, are you sure you want to think about it now?"

Hydt thought he sounded jealous—perhaps that the mercenary might have a project that would deflect attention from Dunne's plans for Gehenna. He said, "Those sales figures are better than I thought. Thank you." He disconnected. Then he asked Theron, "How did you hear about me?"

Although they were alone, Theron lowered his voice as he turned hard, knowing eyes on Hydt: "Cambodia. I was doing some work there. Some people told me of you."

Ah. Hydt understood now and the realization gave him a thrill. Last year on business in the Far East he'd stopped to visit several gravesites of the infamous Killing Fields, where the Khmer Rouge had slaughtered millions of Cambodians in the 1970s. At the memorial at Choeung Ek, where nearly nine thousand bodies had been buried in mass graves, Hydt had spoken to several veterans about the slaughter and taken hundreds of pictures for his collection. One of the locals must have mentioned his name to Theron.

"You had business there, you say?" Hydt asked, thinking of what Dunne had learned.

"Nearby," Theron replied with a suitable brush of evasion.

Hydt was intensely curious but, a businessman first and foremost, he tried not to appear too enthusiastic. "And what do Isandlwana and Cambodia have to do with me?"

"They are places where there was a great loss of life. Many bodies were interred where they fell in battle."

Choeung Ek was genocide, not a battle, but Hydt did not correct him.

"They've become sacred areas. And that's good, I suppose. Except . . ." The Afrikaner paused. "I'll tell you about a problem I have become aware of and about a solution that has occurred to me. Then you can tell me if that solution is possible and if you have an interest in helping me achieve it."

"Go on."

Theron said, "I have many connections to governments and companies in various parts of Africa." He paused. "Darfur, Congo, Central African Republic, Mozambique, Zimbabwe, a few others."

Conflict regions, Hydt observed.

"And these groups are concerned about the consequences that arise after, say, a terrible natural disaster—like drought or famine or storms—or, frankly, anywhere that a major loss of life has occurred and bodies have been buried. As in Cambodia or Isandlwana."

Hydt said innocently, "Such cases have serious

health implications. Water supply contamination, disease."

"No," Theron said bluntly. "I mean something else. Superstition."

"Superstition?"

"Say, for instance, because of a lack of money or resources, bodies have been left in mass graves. A shame but it happens."

"Indeed it does."

"Now, if a government or a charity wishes to build something for the good of the people—a hospital, a housing development or a road in that area—they would be reluctant to do so. The land is perfectly good, there is money to build and workers who wish to be employed, but many people would fear ghosts or spirits and be afraid to go to that hospital or move into those houses. It's absurd to me and to you too, I'm sure. But that's how many people feel." Theron shrugged. "How sad for the citizens of those areas if their health and safety were to suffer because of such foolish ideas."

Hydt was riveted. He was tapping his nails on the desk. He forced himself to stop.

"So. Here is my idea: I am thinking of offering a service to, well, those government agencies to remove the human remains." His face brightened. "This will allow more building of factories, hospitals, roads, farms, schools and it will help the poor, the unfortunate."

"Yes," Hydt said. "Rebury the bodies somewhere else."

Theron laid his hands on the desk. The gold initial ring glittered in a shaft of sunlight. "That's one possibility. But it would be very expensive. And the problem might arise later at the new location."

"True. But are there other alternatives?" Hydt asked.

"Your specialty."

"Which is?"

In a whisper Theron said, "Perhaps . . . recycling."

Hydt saw the scenario clearly. Gene Theron, a mercenary and obviously a very successful one, had supplied troops and weapons to various armies and warlords throughout Africa, men who'd secretly massacred hundreds or thousands of people and hidden the bodies in mass graves. Now they were growing worried that legitimate governments, peacekeeping forces, the press or human-rights groups would discover the corpses.

Theron had made money by providing the means of destruction. Now he wanted to make money by removing the evidence of their use.

"It seemed to me an interesting solution," Theron continued. "But I wouldn't know how to go about it. Your . . . interests in Cambodia and your recycling business here told me that perhaps this is something you had thought of, too. Or would be willing to consider." His cold eyes regarded Hydt. "I was thinking maybe concrete or plaster. Or fertilizer?"

Turning the bodies into products that ensured they couldn't be recognized as human remains! Hydt could hardly contain himself. Utterly brilliant. Why, there must be hundreds of opportunities like this throughout the world—Somalia, the former Yugoslavia, Latin America . . . and there were killing fields aplenty in Africa. Thousands. His chest pounded.

"So, that's my idea. A fifty-fifty partnership. I provide the refuse and you recycle it." Theron seemed to find this rather amusing.

"I think we may be able to do business." Hydt offered his hand to the Afrikaner.

Chapter 35

The worst risk of James Bond assuming the NOC—nonofficial cover—of Gene Theron was that Niall Dunne had perhaps got a look at him in Serbia or the Fens or had been given his description in Dubai—if the blue-jacketed man who'd been tailing him was in fact working for Hydt.

In which case when Bond walked brazenly into the Green Way office in Cape Town and sought to hire Hydt to dispose of bodies hidden in secret graves throughout Africa, Dunne would either kill him on the spot or spirit him to their own personal killing field, where the job would be done with cold efficiency.

But now, having shaken hands with an intrigued Severan Hydt, Bond believed his cover was holding. So far. Hydt had been suspicious at first, of course, but he had been willing to give Theron the benefit of the doubt. Why? Because Bond had tempted him with a dangle, a lure he couldn't resist: death and decay.

That morning, at SAPS headquarters, Bond had contacted Philly Maidenstone and Osborne-Smith—his new ally—and they had data-mined Hydt's and Green Way's credit cards. They'd learned that he'd not only traveled to the Killing Fields in Cambodia but to Krakow, Poland, where he'd taken several tours of Auschwitz. Among his purchases at the time were double-A batteries and a second flash chip for a camera.

Man's got a whole new idea about porn . . .

Bond decided that to work his way into Hydt's life he would offer a chance to satisfy that lust: access to secret killing fields throughout Africa and a proposal to recycle human remains.

For the past three hours Bond had struggled, under the tutelage of Bheka Jordaan, to become an Afrikaner mercenary from Durban. Gene Theron would have a slightly unusual background: He'd had Huguenot rather than Dutch forebears and his parents favored English and French in the household of his youth, which explained why he didn't speak much Afrikaans. A British education in Kenya would cover his accent. She had, however, made Bond learn something of the dialect; if Leonardo DiCaprio and Matt Damon had mastered the subtle intonation for recent films—and they were American, for heaven's sake—he could do so too.

While she'd coached him on facts that a South African mercenary might know, Sergeant Mbalula had gone to the evidence locker and found an incarcerated drug dealer's gaudy Breitling watch, to replace Bond's tasteful Rolex, and gold bracelet for the successful mercenary to wear. He'd then sped to a jeweler in the Gardens Shopping Center in Mill Street, where he'd bought a gold signet ring and had it engraved with the initials *EJT.*

Meanwhile, Warrant Officer Kwalene Nkosi had worked feverishly with the ODG's I Branch in London to create the fictional Gene Theron, uploading to the Internet biographical information about the hardboiled mercenary, with Photoshopped pictures and details about his fictional company.

A series of lectures on cover identities at Fort Monckton could be summarized in the instructor's introductory sentence: "If you don't have a Web presence, you're not real."

Nkosi had also printed business cards for EJT Services Ltd, and MI6 in Pretoria pulled in some favors to get the company registered in record time, the documents backdated. Jordaan was not happy about this—it was, to her, a breach of the sacred rule of law—but since she and the SAPS were not involved, she let it go. I Branch also created a fake criminal investigation in Cambodia about Theron's questionable behavior in Myanmar, which mentioned shady activities in other countries too.

The faux Afrikaner was over the first hurdle. The second—and most dangerous—was close. Hydt was on the phone summoning Niall Dunne to meet "a businessman from Durban."

After he'd hung up, Hydt said casually, "One question. Would you happen to have pictures of the fields? The graves?"

"That can be arranged," Bond said.

"Good." Hydt smiled like a schoolboy. He rubbed the back of his hand on his beard.

Bond heard the door behind him open. "Ah, here is my associate, Niall Dunne . . . Niall, this is Gene Theron. From Durban."

Now for it. Was he about to be shot? Bond rose, turned and went up to the Irishman, looking straight into his eyes and offering the stiff smile of one businessman meeting another for the first time. As they shook hands, Dunne stared at him, a knife slash from the chill blue eyes.

There was, however, no suspicion in the gaze; Bond was confident he had not been recognized.

Closing the door behind him, the Irishman shot a quizzical glance at his boss, who handed him the EJT Services business card. The men sat down. "Mr. Theron has a proposition," Hydt said enthusiastically. He ran through the plan in general terms.

Bond could see that Dunne, too, was intrigued. "Yes," he said. "This could be good. Some logistics to consider, of course."

Hydt continued, "Mr. Theron's going to arrange for us to see pictures of the locations. Give us a better idea of what would be involved."

Dunne shot him a troubled glance—the Irishman wasn't suspicious but seemed put off by this. He reminded Hydt, "We have to be at the plant by fifteen thirty. That meeting?" He turned his eyes on Bond again. "Your office is just round the corner." He'd memorized the address at a glance, Bond noted. "Why don't you get them now? Those photos?"

"Well . . . I suppose I could," Bond said, stalling.

Dunne eyed him levelly. "Good." As he opened the door for Bond, his jacket swung open, revealing the Beretta pistol on his belt, probably the one he'd used to murder the men in Serbia.

Was it a message? A warning?

Bond pretended not to see it. He nodded to both men. "I'll be back in thirty minutes."

But Gene Theron had been gone only five when Dunne said, "Let's go."

"Where to?" Hydt frowned.

"To Theron's office. Now."

Hydt noted that the gangly man had one of *those* expressions on his face, challenging, petulant.

That bizarre jealousy again. What went on in Dunne's soul?

"Why, don't you trust him?"

"It's not a bad idea, mind," Dunne said offhandedly. "We've been talking about disposal of bodies. But it doesn't matter for Friday. It just seems a bit dodgy to me that he shows up out of the blue. Makes me nervous."

As if such an emotion would ever register with the icy sapper.

Hydt relented. He needed somebody to keep his feet on the ground and it was true that he'd been seduced by Theron's proposition. "You're right, of course."

They picked up their jackets and left the office. Dunne directed them up the street, to the address printed on the man's business card.

The Irishman *was* right but Severan Hydt prayed that Theron was legitimate. The bodies, the acres of bones. He wanted to see them so badly, to breathe in the air surrounding them. And he wanted the pictures too.

They came to the office building where Theron's Cape Town branch was located. It was typical of the city's business district, functional metal and stone. This particular structure seemed half deserted. There was no guard in the lobby, which was curious. The men took the lift to the fourth floor and found the office door, number 403.

"There's no company name," Hydt observed. "Just the number. That's odd."

"This doesn't look right," Dunne said. He listened. "I don't hear anything."

"Try it."

He did so. "Locked."

Hydt was fiercely disappointed, wondering if he'd given anything away to Theron, anything incriminating. He didn't think so.

Dunne said, "We should get some of our security people together. When Theron comes back, if he does, we'll take him down to the basement. I'll find out what he's about."

They were about to leave when Hydt, desperate to believe Theron was legitimate, said, "Knock—see if anybody's in there."

Dunne hesitated, then drew aside his jacket, exposing the Beretta's grip. The man's large knuckles rapped on the wooden door.

Nothing.

They turned to the lift.

Just then the door swung open.

Gene Theron blinked in surprise. "Hydt . . . Dunne. What are you doing here?"

Chapter 36

The Afrikaner hesitated for a moment then bluntly gestured the two men inside. They entered. There had been no sign outside but here on the wall was a modest plaque: EJT SERVICES LTD., DURBAN, CAPE TOWN, KINSHASA.

The office was small and staffed with only three employees, their desks covered with files and the paperwork that is the mainstay of such entrepreneurial dens throughout the world, however noble or dark their products or services.

Dunne said, "We thought we'd save you the trouble."

"Did you now?" Theron responded.

Hydt knew that the mercenary understood that they had made their surprise visit because they didn't trust him completely. On the other hand, Theron was in a line of work where trust was as dangerous as unstable explosives, so his displeasure was minimal. After all, Theron must have done much the same, checking out Hydt's credentials with the Cambodians and elsewhere before coming to him with his proposal. That was how business worked.

Scuffed walls and windows offering a bleak view of a courtyard reminded Hydt that even illegal activity such as Theron plied was not necessarily as lucrative as the movies and news portrayed it. The biggest office, at the back, was Theron's but even that was modest.

One employee, a tall young African, was scrolling

through an online catalogue of automatic weapons. Some were flagged with bold stars, indicating a 10 percent discount. Another employee was typing urgently on a computer keyboard, using only his index fingers. Both men were in white shirts and narrow ties.

A secretary sat at a desk outside Theron's office. Hydt saw she was attractive but she was young and therefore of no interest to him.

Theron glanced at her. "My secretary was just printing out some of the files we were talking about." A moment later pictures of mass graves began easing from the color printer.

Yes, these are good, Hydt thought, staring down at them. Very good indeed. The first images had been taken not long after the killings. Men, women and children had been gunned down or hacked to death. Some had suffered earlier amputations—hands or arms above the elbow—a popular technique used by warlords and dictators in Africa to punish and control the people. About forty or so lay in a ditch. The setting was sub-Saharan but it was impossible to say exactly where. Sierra Leone, Liberia, Ivory Coast, Central African Republic—there were so many possibilities on this troubled continent.

Other pictures followed, showing different stages of decay. Hydt lingered on those particularly.

"LRA?" Dunne asked, looking them over clinically.

It was the tall, skinny employee who answered. "Mr. Theron does *not* work with the Lord's Resistance Army."

The rebel group, operating out of Uganda, the Central African Republic and parts of Congo and Sudan, had as its philosophy, if you could call it that, religious and mystical extremism—a violent Christian militia of sorts. It had committed untallied atrocities and was known, among other things, for employing child soldiers.

"There's plenty of other work," Theron said.

Hydt was amused by his sense of morality.

Another half-dozen pictures rolled from the printer. The last few showed a large field from which protruded bones and partial bodies with desiccated skin.

Hydt showed the pictures to Dunne. "What do you think?" He turned to Theron. "Niall is an engineer."

The Irishman studied them for a few minutes. "The graves look shallow. It's easy to get the bodies out. The trick is to cover up the fact that they were there in the first place. Depending on how long they've been in the ground, once we remove them there'd be measurable differences in the soil temperature. That lasts for many months. It's detectable with the right equipment."

"Months?" Theron asked, frowning. "I had no idea." He glanced at Dunne, then said to Hydt, "He's good."

"I call him the man who thinks of everything."

Dunne said thoughtfully, "Fast-growing vegetation could work. And there are some sprays that will eliminate DNA residue too. There's a lot to consider but nothing seems impossible."

The technical issues fell away and Hydt focused again on the images. "May I keep these?"

"Of course. Do you want digital copies too? They'd be sharper."

Hydt gave him a smile. "Thank you."

Theron put them on a flash drive and handed it to Hydt, who looked at his watch. "I'd like to discuss this further. Are you free later?"

"I can be."

But Dunne was frowning. "You're at the meeting this afternoon and there's the fund-raiser tonight."

Hydt scowled. "One of the charities I donate to is having an event. I have to be present. But . . . if you're free why don't you meet me there?"

"Do I have to give money?" Theron asked.

Hydt couldn't tell if he was joking. "Not necessarily. You'll have to listen to a few speeches and drink some wine."

"All right. Where is it?"

Hydt looked at Dunne, who said, "At the Lodge Club. Nineteen hundred hours."

Hydt added, "You should wear a jacket but don't bother with a tie."

"See you then." Theron shook their hands.

They left his offices and made their way outside.

"He's legitimate," Hydt said, half to himself.

They were en route to the Green Way office when Dunne took a phone call. After a few minutes he rang off and said, "That was about Stephan Dlamini."

"Who?"

"The worker we need to eliminate in the maintenance department. He's the one who might've seen the e-mails about Friday."

"Oh. Right."

"Our people found his shanty in Primrose Gardens, east of town."

"How are you going to handle it?"

"It seems that his teenage daughter complained

about a local drug dealer. He threatened to kill her. We'll set it up to make it seem that he's behind Dlamini's death. He's firebombed people before."

"So Dlamini has a family."

"A wife and five children," Dunne explained. "We'll have to kill them too. He could have told his wife what he saw. And if he's in a shantytown, the family will live in only one or two rooms, so anybody could have heard. We'll use grenades before the firebomb. I think suppertime is best—everybody will be in one room together." Dunne shot a glance toward the tall man. "They'll die fast."

Hydt replied, "I wasn't worried about them suffering."

"I wasn't either. I just meant that it'll be a pretty easy way to kill them all quickly. So there is no chance of survivors. Convenient, you know."

After the men had left, Warrant Officer Kwalene Nkosi rose from the desk where he'd been scrolling through price lists for automatic weapons and nodded at the screen. "It is truly amazing what you can buy online, isn't it, Commander Bond?"

"I suppose so."

"If we buy nine machine guns, we can get one for free," he joked to Sergeant Mbalula, the relentless two-finger typist.

"Thanks for that fast thinking about the LRA, Warrant Officer," Bond said. He hadn't recognized the abbreviation for the Lord's Resistance Army—a group that any mercenary in Africa would have been familiar with. The operation might have ended there and then in disaster.

Bond's "secretary," Bheka Jordaan, peered out of

the window. "They're heading away. I don't see any other security people."

"We fooled them, I think," said Sergeant Mbalula.

The trick indeed seemed to have been successful. Bond had been convinced that one of the men—the quick-minded Dunne, most likely—would want to see his branch in Cape Town. He believed that a good, solid set—a cover location—would be critical in seducing Hydt into believing he was an Afrikaner troubleshooter with a great many bodies to dispose of.

While Bond had telephoned Hydt to talk his way into Green Way, Jordaan had found a small government office leased by the Ministry of Culture but presently unused. Nkosi had printed some business cards with the address and before Bond had gone to meet Hydt and Dunne, the SAPS officers had moved in.

"You'll be my partner," Bond had told Jordaan, with a smile. "It'll be a good cover for me to have a clever—and attractive—associate."

She had bristled. "To be credible, an office like this needs a secretary and she must be a woman."

"If you like."

"I don't," she had said stiffly. "But that's how it must be."

Bond had anticipated the men's visit but not that Hydt would want to see pictures of the killing fields, though he supposed he should have. The minute he'd left Hydt's office, he'd called Jordaan and told her to find photos of mass graves in Africa from military and law enforcement archives. Sadly, it had been all too easy and she'd downloaded a dozen by the time he'd returned from Hydt's office.

"Can you keep some people here for a day or two?" Bond asked. "In case Dunne comes back."

"I can spare one officer," she said. "Sergeant Mbalula, you will stay for the time being."

"Yes, Captain."

"I'll brief a patrolman on the situation and he will replace you." She turned back to Bond. "Do you think Dunne will return?"

"No, but it's possible. Hydt's the boss but he gets distracted. Dunne is more focused and suspicious. To my mind, that makes him more dangerous."

"Commander." Nkosi opened a battered briefcase. "This came for you at Headquarters." He produced a thick envelope. Bond ripped it open. Inside he found ten thousand rand in used banknotes, a fake South African passport, credit cards and a debit card, all in the name of Eugene J. Theron. I Branch had worked its magic once more.

There was also a note: *Reservation for open stay at Table Mountain Hotel, waterfront room.*

Bond pocketed everything. "Now, the Lodge Club, where I'm meeting Hydt tonight. What's it like?"

"Too expensive for me," Nkosi said.

"It's a restaurant and venue for events," Jordaan told him. "I've never been either. It used to be a private hunting club. White men only. Then after the elections in 'ninety-four, when the ANC came to power, the owners chose to dissolve the club and sell the building rather than open up membership. The board wasn't concerned about admitting black or colored men but they didn't want women. I'm sure you have no clubs like that at home, James, do you?"

He didn't admit that there were indeed such establishments in the UK. "At my favorite club in London, you'll see pure democracy at work. Anyone at all is free to join . . . and lose money at the gaming tables. Just like I do. With some frequency, I might add."

Nkosi laughed.

"If you're ever in London, I'd be delighted to show it to you," he added to Jordaan.

She seemed to view this as yet more shameless flirting because she icily ignored him.

"I will drive you to your hotel." The tall police officer's face wore a serious look. "I think I shall quit the SAPS and see if you can get me a job in England, Commander."

To work for the ODG or MI6, you had to be a British citizen and the child of at least one citizen or someone with substantial ties to the UK. There was also a residency requirement.

"After my great undercover work"—Nkosi's arm swept around the room—"I now know I am quite the actor. I will come to London and work in the West End. That's where the famous theaters are—correct?"

"Well, yes." Though Bond had not been to one voluntarily in years.

The young man said, "I'm sure I will be quite successful. I'm partial to Shakespeare. David Mamet is quite good too. Without doubt."

Bond supposed that, working for a boss like Bheka Jordaan, Nkosi did not get much of a chance to exercise his sense of humor.

Chapter 37

The hotel was near Table Bay in the fashionable Green Point area of Cape Town. It was an older building, six stories, in classic Cape style, and could not quite disguise its colonial roots—though it didn't try very hard; you could see them clearly in the meticulous landscaping presently being tended by a number of diligent workers, the delicate but firm reminder on placards about the dining-room dress code, the spotless white uniforms of the demure, ever-present staff, the rattan furniture on the sweeping veranda overlooking the bay.

Another clue was the enquiry as to whether Mr. Theron would like a personal butler for his stay. He politely declined.

The Table Mountain Hotel—referred to everywhere as "TM" in scrolling letters, from the marble floor to embossed napkins—was just the place where a well-heeled Afrikaner businessman from Durban would stay, whether he was a legitimate computer salesman or a mercenary with ten thousand bodies to dispose of.

After checking in, Bond started toward the lift but something outside caught his eye. He popped into the gift shop for shaving foam he didn't need. Then he circled back to Reception to help himself to some complimentary fruit juice from a large glass tank surrounded by an arrangement of purple jacaranda and red and white roses.

He wasn't certain but someone might have been conducting surveillance. When he'd turned abruptly to get the juice, a shadow had vanished equally abruptly.

With many opportunities come many operatives . . .

Bond waited for a moment but the apparition didn't reappear.

Of course, operational life sows the seeds of paranoia and sometimes a passerby is just a passerby, a curious gaze signifies nothing more than a curious mind. Besides, you can't protect yourself from every risk in this business; if somebody wants you dead badly enough, they'll get their wish. Mentally Bond shrugged off the tail and took the lift to the first floor, where the rooms were accessed from an open balcony that overlooked the lobby. He stepped inside, closed and chained the door.

He tossed the suitcase on to one of the beds, strode to the window and closed the curtains. He slipped everything that identified him as James Bond into a large carbon-fiber envelope with an electronic lock on the flap and sealed it. With his shoulder he tipped a chest of drawers and pushed the pouch underneath. It might be found and stolen, of course, but any attempt to open it without his thumbprint on the lock would send an encrypted message to the ODG's C Branch, and Bill Tanner would send a *Crash Dive* text to alert him that his cover had been compromised.

He rang room service and ordered a club sandwich and a Gilroy's dark ale. Then he showered. By the time he'd dressed in a pair of battleship gray trousers and a black polo shirt, the food was at the door. He ran a comb through his damp hair, checked the peephole and let the waiter in.

The tray was placed on the small table, the bill signed as E. J. Theron—in Bond's own handwriting; that was one thing you never tried to fake, however deep your cover. The waiter pocketed his tip with overt gratitude. When Bond stepped back to the door to see the young man out and refix the chain, he automatically scanned the balcony and the lobby below.

He squinted, gazing down, then shut the door fast. Damn.

Glancing with regret at the sandwich—and even more regretfully at the beer—he stepped into his shoes and flung open his suitcase. He screwed the Gemtech silencer on to the muzzle of his Walther and, although he'd done so recently at SAPS headquarters, eased the slide of the pistol back a few millimeters to verify that a round was in the chamber.

The gun went into the folds of today's edition of the *Cape Times*, which Bond then set on the tray between his sandwich and the beer. He lifted it one-handed over his shoulder and left the room, the tray obscuring his face. He was not dressed in a waiter's uniform but he moved briskly, head down, and might have been mistaken by a casual observer for a harried member of staff.

At the end of the corridor, he went through the fire doors of the stairwell, put the tray down and picked up the newspaper with its deadly contents. Then he descended a flight of stairs, quietly, to the ground floor.

Looking out through a porthole in the swing door, he spotted his target, sitting in an armchair in the shadows of a far corner of the lobby, nearly invisible. Facing away from Bond, he was scanning from his newspaper to the lobby to the first-floor balcony. Apparently he had missed Bond's escape.

Bond gauged distances and angles, the location and number of guests, staff and security guards. He waited while a porter wheeled a cart of suitcases past, a waiter carried a tray bearing a silver coffee pot to another guest at the far end of the lobby, and a cluster of Japanese tourists moved *en masse* out of the door, taking with them his target's attention.

Bond thought clinically: Now.

He pushed out of the stairwell and walked fast toward the back of an armchair over which the crown of his target's head could just be seen. He circled around it and dropped into the chair just opposite, smiling as if he'd run into an old friend. He kept his finger off the trigger of the Walther, which Corporal Menzies had fine-tuned to a feather-light pull.

The freckled ruddy face glanced up. The man's eyes flashed wide in surprise that he'd been duped. In recognition too. The look said, no, it wasn't a coincidence. He *had* been conducting surveillance on Bond.

He was the man Bond had seen at the airport that morning, whom he'd originally taken for Captain Jordaan.

"Fancy seeing you here!" Bond said cheerfully, to allay the suspicions of anybody witnessing the rendezvous. He lifted the curled newspaper so that the muzzle of the silencer was focused on the bulky chest.

But, curiously, the surprise in the milky green eyes was replaced not by fear or desperation but amusement. "Ah, Mr. . . . Theron, is it? Is that who we are at the moment?" The accent was Mancunian. His pudgy hands swung up, palms out.

Bond cocked his head to one side. "These rounds

are nearly subsonic. With this suppressor, you'll be dead and I'll be gone long before anybody notices."

"Oh, but you don't want to kill me. That would go down rather badly."

Bond had heard plenty of monologues at moments like this when he'd got the draw on an opponent. Usually the bons mots were to buy time or for distraction as the target prepared himself for a desperate assault. Bond knew to ignore what the man was saying and watch his hands and body language.

Still, he could hardly dismiss the next lines issuing from the flabby lips. "After all, what would M say if he heard you'd gunned down one of the Crown's star agents? And in *such* a beautiful setting."

Chapter 38

His name was Gregory Lamb, confirmed by the iris and fingerprint scan app—MI6's man on the ground in Cape Town. The agent Bill Tanner had told him to avoid.

They were in Bond's room, sans beer and sandwich; to his consternation, the tray containing his lunch had been whisked out of the stairwell by an efficient hotel employee by the time he and Lamb had returned to the first floor.

"You could've got yourself killed," Bond muttered.

"I wasn't in any real danger. Your outfit doesn't give out those double oughts to trigger-happy fools . . . Now, now, my friend, don't get all ruffled. Some of us know what your Overseas Development outfit *really* does."

"How did you know I was in town?"

"Put it together, didn't I? Heard about some goings-on and got in touch with friends at Lambeth."

One of the disadvantages in having to use Six or DI for intelligence was that more people knew about your affairs than you might prefer. "Why didn't you just contact me through secure channels?" Bond snapped.

"I was going to but just as I got here I saw somebody playing shadow."

Now Bond paid attention. "Male, slim, blue jacket? Gold earring?"

"Well, now, didn't see the earring, did I? Eyes

aren't what they used to be. But you've got the general kit right. Hovered about for a while, then vanished like the Tablecloth when the sun comes out. You know what I mean: the fog on Table Mountain."

Bond was in no mood for travelogues. Dammit, the man who killed Yusuf Nasad and who had nearly done the same to Felix Leiter had learned he was here. He was probably the man Jordaan had told him about, the one who'd slipped into the country that morning from Abu Dhabi on a fake British passport.

Who the hell was he?

"Did you get a picture?" Bond asked.

"Drat no. The man was fast as a water bug."

"Spot anything else about him, type of mobile, possible weapons, vehicle?"

"None. Gone. Water bug." A shrug of the broad shoulders, which Bond supposed were as freckled and red as the face.

Bond said, "You were at the airport when I landed. Why did you turn away?"

"I saw Captain Jordaan. She never took to me, for some reason. Maybe she thinks I'm the great white hunter colonist here to steal back her country. She gave me a bloody tongue-lashing a few months ago, didn't she?"

"My chief of staff said you were in Eritrea," Bond said.

"I was indeed—there and across the border in Sudan for the past week. Looks like their hearts're set on war so I tooled on up to make sure my covers would survive the gunplay. I got that sorted and heard about an ODG operation." His eyes dimmed. "Surprised nobody gave me a bell about it."

"The thinking was that you were involved in a rather serious op. Delicate," Bond said judiciously.

"Ah." Lamb seemed to believe this. "Well, anyway, I thought I'd better race here to help out. You see, the Cape's tricky. It looks neat and clean and touristy but there's a lot more to it. I hate to blow my own trumpet, my friend, but you need somebody like me to weasel under the surface, tell you what's really going on. I'm *connected*. You know any other Six agent who's finagled local-government-development-fund money to finance his covers? I made the Crown a tidy profit last year."

"All went to Treasury coffers, did it?"

Lamb shrugged. "I've got a role to play, haven't I? To the world I'm a successful businessman. If you don't live your cover for all it's worth, well, a bit of sand gets into the works and the next thing you know there's a big pearl yelling, 'I'm a spy!' . . . Say, you mind if we hit that minibar of yours?"

Bond waved at it. "Go ahead." Lamb helped himself to a miniature of Bombay Sapphire gin, then another. He poured them into a glass. "No ice? Pity. Well, never mind." He sloshed in a bit of tonic.

"What *is* your cover?"

"Mostly I arrange cargo ship charters. Brilliant idea, if I say so myself. Gives me a chance to hobnob with the bad boys on the docks. I also do a spot of gold and aluminum exploration and road and infrastructure construction."

"And you still have time to spy?"

"Good one, my friend!" For some reason Lamb started telling Bond his life story. He was a British citizen, as was his mother, and his father was South African. He'd come down here with his parents and

decided he liked it better than life in Manchester. After
training at Fort Monckton he'd asked to be sent back.
Station Z was the only one he'd ever worked for . . .
and the only one he'd ever cared to. He spent most of
his time in the Western Cape but traveled frequently
around Africa, attending to his NOC operations.

When he noticed Bond was not listening, he
swigged at his drink and said, "So what exactly are
you working on? Something about this Severan Hydt?
Now there's a name to conjure with. And Incident
Twenty. Love it. Sounds rather like something from
DI Fifty-five—you know, the characters looking into
UFOs over the Midlands."

Exasperated, Bond said, "I was attached to Defense Intelligence. Division Fifty-five was about mis-
siles or planes breaching British airspace, not UFOs."

"Ah, yes, yes, I'm sure it was . . . Of course, that
would be the line they'd give the public, wouldn't it?"

Bond was close to throwing him out. Still, it might
just be worth picking his brain. "You heard about Incident Twenty, then. Any thoughts on how it could relate to South Africa?"

"I did get the signals," Lamb conceded, "but I
didn't pay much attention since the intercept said the
attack was going to be on British soil."

Bond reminded him of the exact wording, which
gave no location but said merely that British interests
would be "adversely affected."

"Could be anywhere, then. I didn't think of that."

Or you didn't read it very carefully.

"And now the cyclone has touched down on my
pitch. Odd how fate can strike, isn't it?"

The app on Bond's mobile that had verified

Lamb's identity had also indicated his security clearance, which was higher than Bond would have guessed. Now he felt more or less comfortable in talking about the Gehenna plan, Hydt and Dunne. He asked again, "So, have you any thoughts on a connection here? Thousands of people at risk, British interests threatened, the plan hatched in Severan Hydt's office."

Eyes on his glass, Lamb said thoughtfully, "The fact is, I don't know what kind of attack here would fit the bill. We've got plenty of British expats and tourists and a lot of business interests with connections to London. But killing that many people in one fell swoop? Sounds like it'd have to be civil unrest. And I don't see that happening in South Africa. We've got our troubles here, there's no denying it—Zimbabwe asylum seekers, trade union unrest, corruption, AIDS . . . but we're still the most stable country on the continent."

For once, the man had provided Bond with some real insight, slight though it was. This reinforced his idea that, while buttons might be pushed in South Africa, Friday's deaths could likely occur elsewhere.

The man had finished most of his gin. "You're not drinking?" When Bond didn't answer, he added, "We miss the old days, don't we, my friend?"

Bond didn't know what the old days were and decided it was unlikely he would miss them, whatever they had been. He also decided too that he quite disliked the phrase "my friend." "You said you didn't get on with Bheka Jordaan."

Lamb grunted.

"What do you know about her?"

"She's damn good at her job, I'll give her that. She was the officer who ran that investigation of the NIA— the South African National Intelligence Agency—for conducting illegal surveillance on politicians here." Lamb chuckled darkly. "Not that that'd ever happen in *our* country, would it?"

Bond recalled that Bill Tanner had chosen to use an SAPS liaison rather than National Intelligence.

Lamb continued, "They gave her the job hoping she'd fumble. But not Captain Jordaan. Oh, no. That would *never* do." His eyes gleamed perversely. "She started to make headway in the case and everybody at the top got scared. Her boss at the SAPS told her to lose the evidence against the NIA agents."

"So she arrested him?"

"And *his* boss too!" Lamb roared with laughter and knocked back the last of his drink. "She earned herself a big commendation."

The Gold Cross for Bravery? "Did she get roughed up in the investigation?"

"Roughed up?"

He mentioned her scarred arm.

"In a way. Afterward she was promoted. Had to happen—politically, you know how *that* works. Well, some of the SAPS men who were passed over didn't take too kindly to it. She got threats—women shouldn't be taking men's jobs, that sort of thing. Somebody chucked a Molotov cocktail under her squad car. She'd gone into the station but there was a prisoner in the backseat, drunk and sleeping it off. None of the attackers saw him. She ran outside and saved him but got burned in the process. They never found out who did it—the perpetrators were masked. But everybody knows it was people she was working with. Maybe still is."

"God." Now Bond believed he understood Jordaan's attitude toward him—perhaps she'd thought his flirtatious glance at the airport had meant he, too, didn't take a woman seriously as a police officer.

He explained to Lamb his next step: meeting Hydt tonight.

"Oh, the Lodge Club. It's all right. Used to be exclusive but now they let in everybody . . . Hey, I saw that look. I didn't mean what you think. I just have a low opinion of the general public. I do more business with blacks and coloreds than whites . . . There's that look again!"

"'Coloreds'?" Bond said sourly.

"It just means mixed-race and it's perfectly acceptable here. No one would take offense."

Bond's experience, however, was that people using such terms weren't the ones likely to be offended by them. But he wasn't going to debate politics with Gregory Lamb. Bond looked at the Breitling. "Thanks for your thoughts," he said, without much enthusiasm. "Now, I've got work to do before my meeting with Hydt." Jordaan had sent him some material on Afrikaners, South African culture and conflict regions that Gene Theron might have been active in.

Lamb rose and hovered awkwardly. "Well, I stand ready to assist. I'm at your service. Really, anything you need." He seemed painfully sincere.

"Thanks." Bond felt the urge, absurdly, to slip him twenty rand.

Before he left, Lamb returned to the minibar and relieved it of two miniatures of vodka. "You don't mind, do you? M's got a positively massive budget; everyone knows that."

Bond saw him out.

Good riddance, he thought, as the door closed. Percy Osborne-Smith was a charmer by comparison with this fellow.

Chapter 39

Bond sat at the expansive desk in the hotel suite, booted up his computer, logged on via his iris and fingerprint and scrolled through the information Bheka Jordaan had uploaded. He was plowing through it when an encrypted e-mail arrived.

James:

For your eyes only.
Have confirmed Steel Cartridge was a major active measure by KGB/SVR to assassinate clandestine MI6 and CIA agents and local assets, so that the extent of Russian infiltration would not be learned, in attempt to promote détente during fall of Soviet Union and improve relations with the West.
The last Steel Cartridge targeted killings occurred late '80s or early '90s. Found only one incident so far: the victim was a private contractor working for MI6. Deep cover. No other details, except that the active measures agent made the death appear to be an accident. Actual steel cartridges were sometimes left at the scenes of the deaths as warning to other agents to keep quiet.

Am continuing investigation.
Your other eyes,

Philly

Bond slouched back in the chair, staring at the ceiling. Well, what do I do with *this*? he asked himself.

He read the message again, then sent a brief e-mail thanking Philly. He rocked back and, in the mirror across the room, caught a glimpse of his eyes, hard and set like a predator's.

He reflected: So, the KGB active measures agent killed the MI6 contract op in the late '80s, early '90s.

James Bond's father had died during that period.

It had happened in December, not long after his eleventh birthday. Andrew and Monique Bond had dropped young James off with his aunt Charmian in Pett Bottom, Kent, leaving behind the promise that they would return in plenty of time for Christmas festivities. They had then flown to Switzerland and driven to Mont Blanc for five days of skiing and rock and ice climbing.

His parents' assurance, however, had been hollow. Two days later they were dead, having fallen from one of the astonishingly beautiful cliff faces of the Aiguilles Rouges, near Chamonix.

Beautiful cliffs, yes, impressive . . . but not excessively dangerous, not where they had been climbing. As an adult, Bond had looked into the circumstances of the accident. He'd learned that the slope they'd fallen from did not require advanced climbing techniques; indeed, no one had ever been injured, let alone died, there. But, of course, mountains are notoriously fickle and Bond had taken at face value the story the gendarme had told his aunt: that his parents had fallen because a rope frayed at the same time as a large boulder had given way.

"Mademoiselle, je suis désolé de vous dire . . ."

When he was young, James Bond had enjoyed traveling with his parents to the foreign countries where Andrew Bond's company sent him. He'd enjoyed living in hotel suites. He'd enjoyed the local cuisines, very different from that served in the pubs and restaurants in England and Scotland. He'd been captivated with the exotic cultures—the dress, the music, the language.

He also enjoyed spending time with his father. His mother would hand James over to carers and friends when one of her freelance photojournalism assignments arose but his father would occasionally take him to business meetings in restaurants or hotel lobbies. The boy would perch nearby, with a volume of Tolkien or an American detective novel, while his father talked to unsmiling men named Sam or Micah or Juan.

James was happy to be included—what son doesn't like to tag along with his dad? He had always been curious, though, as to why sometimes Andrew insisted that he join him while at others he said no quite firmly.

Bond had thought nothing more of this . . . until the training sessions at Fort Monckton.

It was there, in the lessons on clandestine operations, that one instructor had said something that caught his attention. The round, bespectacled man from MI6's tradecraft training section had told the group, "In most clandestine situations, it's not advisable for an agent or an asset to be married or have children. If they happen to, it's best to make sure the family is kept far removed from the agent's operational life. However, there's one instance in which it's advantageous to have a quote 'typical' life. These agents will be operating in deepest cover and handling the most critical assignments, where the intelligence to be gathered is vital. In these cases a family life is important to remove the enemy's suspicions that they're operatives. Typically their official cover will be working for a company or organization that interests enemy agents: infrastructure, information, armaments, aerospace or government. They will be posted to different locations every few years and take their families with them."

James Bond's father had worked for a major British armaments company. He had been posted to a number of international capitals. His wife and son had accompanied him.

The instructor had continued, "And in certain circumstances, on the most critical assignments—whether a brush pass or a face-to-face meeting—it's useful for the operative to take his child with him. Nothing proclaims innocence more than having a youngster with you. Seeing this, the enemy will almost always believe that you're the real deal—no parent would want to endanger his or her child." He regarded the agents sitting before him in the classroom, their faces registering varying reactions at his passionless message. "Combating evil sometimes requires a suspension of accepted values."

Bond had thought: His father a spy? Impossible. Absurd.

Still, after he had left Fort Monckton he spent some time looking into his father's past but found no evidence of a clandestine life. The only evidence was a series of payments made to his aunt for her and James's benefit, over and above the proceeds from his parents' insurance policy. These were made annually until James had turned eighteen by a company that must have had some affiliation with Andrew's employer, though he could never find out exactly where it was based or what the nature of the payments had been.

Eventually he convinced himself that whole idea was mad and forgot about it.

Until the Russian signal about Steel Cartridge.

Because one other aspect of his parents' death had been largely overlooked.

In the accident report that the gendarmes had prepared, it was mentioned that a steel rifle cartridge, 7.62mm, had been found near his father's body.

Young James had received it among his parents' effects and, since Andrew had been an executive with an arms company, it was assumed that the bullet had been a sample of his wares to show to customers.

On Monday, two days ago, after he had read the Russian report, Bond had gone into the online archives of his father's company. He'd learned that it did not manufacture ammunition. Neither had it ever sold any weapons that fired a 7.62mm round.

This was the bullet that sat now in a conspicuous place on the mantelpiece of his London flat.

Had it been dropped accidentally by a hunter? Or left intentionally as a warning?

The KGB's reference to Operation Steel Cartridge had solidified within Bond the desire to learn whether or not his father had been a secret agent. He had to.

He did not need to reconcile himself to the possibility that his father had lied to him. All parents deceive
their children. In most cases, though, it's for the sake
of expedience or through laziness or thoughtlessness;
if *his* father had lied it was because the Official Secrets
Act had compelled him to.

Neither did he need to know the truth so that he
could—as a TV psychiatrist might suggest—revisit his
youthful loss and mourn somehow more authentically.
What nonsense.

No, he wanted to know the truth for a much
simpler reason, one that fitted him like a Savile Row
bespoke suit: The person who had killed his parents
might still be at large in the world, enjoying the sun,
sitting down to a pleasant meal or even conspiring to
take other lives. If such were the case, Bond knew he
would make certain that his parents' assassin met the
same fate as they had, and he would do so efficiently
and in accordance with his official remit: by any means
necessary.

Chapter 40

At close to 5 P.M. on Wednesday, Bond's mobile emitted the ringtone reserved for emergency messages. He hurried from the bathroom, where he'd just showered, and read the encrypted e-mail. It was from GCHQ, reporting that Bond's attempt to bug Severan Hydt had been somewhat successful. Unknown to Captain Bheka Jordaan, the flash drive that Bond had given Hydt, holding digital pictures of the killing fields in Africa, also contained a small microphone and transmitter. What it lacked in audio resolution and battery life, it made up for in range. The signal was picked up by a satellite, amplified and beamed down to one of the massive receiving antennae at Menwith Hill in the beautiful Yorkshire countryside.

The device had transmitted fragments of a conversation Hydt and Dunne had had just after they'd left the fictional EJT Services office in downtown Cape Town. The jumbled words had finally made their way through the decryption queue and been read by an analyst, who had flagged them as critical and shot the missive to Bond.

He now read the CX—the raw intelligence—and the analyzed product. It seemed that Dunne was planning to kill one of Hydt's workers, Stephan Dlamini, and his family, because the employee had seen something in a secure part of Green Way that he shouldn't have, perhaps information that related to Gehenna. Bond's goal was clear: Save him at all costs.

Purpose . . . response.

The man lived outside Cape Town. The death would be made to look like a gang attack. Grenades and firebombs would be used. And the attack would occur at suppertime.

After that, though, the battery died and the device had stopped transmitting.

At suppertime. Perhaps any moment now.

Bond hadn't managed to rescue the woman in Dubai. He wasn't going to let this family die now. He needed to find out what Dlamini had learned.

But he could hardly contact Bheka Jordaan and tell her what he'd found out via illegal surveillance. He picked up the phone and called the concierge.

"Yes, sir?"

"I have a question for you," Bond said casually. "I had a problem with my car today and a local fellow helped me out. I didn't have much cash with me and I wanted to give him something for his trouble. How would I go about finding his address? I have his name and the town he lives in but nothing more."

"What's the town?"

"Primrose Gardens."

There was silence. Then the concierge said, "It's a township."

A squatters' camp, Bond recalled, from the briefing material Bheka Jordaan had given him. The shacks rarely had standard postal addresses. "Well, could I go there, ask if anyone knew him?"

Another pause. "Well, sir, it might not be very safe."

"I'm not too worried about that."

"I think it would not be practical, either."

"Why is that?"

"The population of Primrose Gardens is around fifty thousand."

At 17:30 hours, as autumn dusk descended, Niall Dunne watched Severan Hydt leave the Green Way office in Cape Town, striding tall and with a certain elegance to his limousine.

Hydt's feet didn't splay, *his* posture wasn't hunched, *his* arms didn't swing from side to side. ("Oi, lookit the tosser! Niall's a bleedin' giraffe!")

Hydt was on his way home, where he would change, then take Jessica to the fund-raiser at the Lodge Club.

Dunne was standing in the Green Way lobby, staring out of the window. His eyes lingered on Hydt as he vanished down the street, accompanied by one of his Green Way guards.

Watching him leave, en route to his home and his companion, Dunne felt a pang.

Don't be so bloody ridiculous, he told himself. Concentrate on the job. All hell's going to break loose on Friday and it'll be your fault if a single cog or gear malfunctions.

Concentrate.

So he did.

Dunne left Green Way, collected his car and drove out of Cape Town toward Primrose Gardens. He would meet up with a security man from the company and proceed with the plan, which he now ran through his mind: the timing, the approach, the number of grenades, the firebomb, the escape.

He reviewed the blueprint with precision and patience. The way he did everything.

This is Niall. He's brilliant. He's my draftsman. . . .

But other thoughts intruded and his sloping shoulders drooped even more as he pictured his boss at the fund-raising gala later that night. The pang stabbed him again.

Dunne supposed people wondered why he was alone, why he didn't have a partner. They assumed the answer was that he lacked the ability to feel. That he was a machine. They didn't understand that, according to the concept of classical mechanics, there were *simple* machines—like screws and levers and pulleys— and *complex* machines, like engines, which by definition transferred energy into motion.

Well, he reasoned logically, calories were turned into energy, which moved the human body. So, yes, he *was* a machine. But so were we all, every creature on earth. That didn't preclude the capacity for love.

No, the explanation of his solitude was simply that the object of his desire didn't, in turn, desire him.

How embarrassingly mundane, how common.

And bloody unfair, of course. God, it was unfair. No draftsman would design a machine in which the two parts necessary to create harmonious movement didn't work perfectly, each needing the other and in turn satisfying the reciprocal need. But that was exactly the situation in which he found himself: He and his boss were mismatched parts.

Besides, he thought bitterly, the laws of attraction were far riskier than the laws of mechanics. Relationships were messy, dangerous and plagued with waste, and while you could keep an engine humming for hundreds of thousands of hours, love between human beings often sputtered and seized just after it caught.

It betrayed you too, far more often than machinery did.

Bollocks, he told himself with what passed for anger within Niall Dunne. Forget all this. You have a job to do tonight. He ran through his blueprint again and then once more.

As the traffic thinned he drove quickly east of the city, heading toward the township along dark roads gritty and damp as a riverside dock.

He pulled into a shopping-center car park and killed the engine. A moment later a battered van stopped behind him. Dunne climbed from his car and got into the other vehicle, nodding to the security man, very large, wearing military fatigues. Without saying a word, they set off at once and, in ten minutes, were driving through the unmarked streets of Primrose Gardens. Dunne climbed into the back of the van, where there were no windows. He was, of course, distinctive here, with his height, his hair. More significant, he was white and would be extremely conspicuous in a South African township after dark. It was possible that the drug dealer who was threatening Dlamini's daughter was white or had whites who worked for him. But Dunne decided it was better to stay hidden—at least until the time to throw the grenades and firebombs through the windows of the shanty.

They drove along the endless paths that served as roads in the shantytown, past packs of running children, skinny dogs, men sitting on doorsteps.

"No GPS," the huge security man said, his first words. He wasn't smiling and Dunne didn't know if he was making a joke. The man had spent two hours that afternoon tracking down Dlamini's shack. "There it is."

They parked across the road. The place was tiny, one story, as were all the shacks in Primrose Gardens, and the walls were constructed of mismatched panels of plywood and corrugated metal, painted bold red, blue, yellow, as if in defiance of the squalor. A clothes-line hung in the yard to the side, festooned with laundry for a family ranging in age, it seemed, from five or six to adulthood.

This was an efficient location for a kill. The shack was opposite a patch of empty ground, so there would be few witnesses. Not that it mattered—the van had no number-plate, and white vehicles of this sort were as common in the Western Cape as seagulls at Green Way.

They sat in silence for ten minutes, just on the verge of attracting attention. Then the security man said, "There he is."

Stephan Dlamini was walking down the dusty road, a tall, thin man with graying hair, wearing a faded jacket, orange T-shirt and brown jeans. Beside him was one of his sons. The boy, who was about eleven, carried a mud-streaked football and wore a Springboks rugby shirt, without a jacket, despite the autumn chill.

Dlamini and the boy paused outside to kick the ball back and forth for a moment or two. Then they entered their home. Dunne nodded to the security man. They pulled on ski masks. Dunne surveyed the shanty. It was larger than most but the explosive and incendiary were sufficient. The curtains were drawn across the windows, the cheap fabric glowing with light from inside.

For some reason Dunne found himself thinking again about his boss, at the event that night. He put the image away.

He gave it five minutes more, to make sure that Dlamini had used the toilet—if there was one in the shack—and that the family was seated at the dinner table.

"Let's go," Dunne said. The security guard nodded. They stepped out of the van, each holding a powerful grenade, filled with deadly copper shot. The street was largely deserted.

Seven family members, Dunne reflected. "Now," he whispered. They pulled the pins on the grenades and flung them through each of the two windows. In the five seconds of silence that followed, Dunne grabbed the firebomb—a petrol can with a small detonator—and readied it. When stunning explosions shook the ground and blew out the remaining glass, he threw the incendiary through the window and the two men leaped into the van. The security man started the engine and they sped off.

Exactly five seconds later, flames erupted from the windows and, spectacularly, a stream of fire from the cooking stove chimney rose straight into the air twenty feet, reminding Dunne of the fireworks displays he'd so enjoyed as a boy in Belfast.

Chapter 41

"*Hayi! Hayi!*"

The woman's wail filled the night as she stared at the fiery shack, her home, tears lensing her eyes.

She and her five children were clustered behind the inferno. The back door was open, providing a wrenching view of the rampaging flames destroying all of the family's possessions. She struggled to run inside and rescue what she could but her husband, Stephan Dlamini, gripped her hard. He spoke to her in a language James Bond took to be Xhosa.

A large crowd was gathering and an informal fire brigade had assembled, passing buckets of water in a futile attempt to extinguish the raging flames.

"We have to leave," Bond said to the tall man standing beside him, next to an unmarked SAPS van.

"Without doubt," said Kwalene Nkosi.

Bond meant that they should get the family out of the township before Dunne realized they were still alive.

Nkosi, though, had a different concern. The warrant officer had been eyeing the growing crowd, who were staring at the white man; the collective gaze was not friendly.

"Display your badge," Bond told him.

Nkosi's eyes widened. "No, no, Commander, that is not a wise idea. Let us leave. Now."

They shepherded Stephan Dlamini and his family

into the van. Bond got in as well and Nkosi climbed behind the wheel, gunned the engine and steered them away into the night.

They left behind the angry, confused crowd and the tumultuous flames . . . but not a single injury.

It had been a true race to the finish line to save the family.

After he'd learned that Dlamini was going to be targeted by Dunne and that he lived virtually anonymously in a huge township, Bond had struggled to come up with a way to locate him. GCHQ and MI6 could find no mobile in his name or any personal information in South African census or trade-union records. He had taken a chance and called Kwalene Nkosi. "I'm going to tell you something, Warrant Officer, and I hope I can rely on you to keep it to yourself. From *everyone*."

There'd been a pause and the young man had said cautiously, "Go on."

Bond had laid out the problem, including the fact that the surveillance had been illegal.

"Your signal is breaking up, Commander. I missed that last part."

Bond had laughed. "But we have to find where this Stephan Dlamini lives. Now."

Nkosi had sighed. "It is going to be difficult. Primrose Gardens is huge. But I have an idea." The minibus taxi operations, it seemed, knew far more about the shantytowns and *lokasies* than the local government did. The warrant officer would begin calling them. He and Bond had met, then driven fast to Primrose Gardens, Nkosi continuing his search for the family's shack via his mobile. At close to 6 P.M. they'd been cruising through the township when a taxi driver had reported that he knew where Dlamini lived. He'd directed Bond and Nkosi there.

As they'd approached, they'd seen another van at the front, a white face glancing out.

"Dunne," Nkosi had said.

He and Bond had veered away and parked behind the shanty. They'd pushed through the back door and the family had panicked, but Nkosi had told them, in their own language, that the men had come to save them. They had to get out immediately. Stephan Dlamini was not at home yet but soon would be.

A few minutes later he'd come through the door with his young son, and Bond, knowing the attack was imminent, had had no choice but to draw his gun and force them out of the back door. Nkosi had just finished explaining Bond's purpose and the danger, when the grenades went off, followed by the petrol bomb.

Now they were on the N1, cruising west. Dlamini gripped Bond's hand and shook it. Then he leaned forward to the front passenger seat and hugged him. Tears stood in his eyes. His wife huddled in the back with her children, studying Bond suspiciously as the agent told him who'd been behind the attack.

Finally, after hearing the story, Dlamini asked in dismay, "Mr. Hydt? But how can that be? He is best boss. He treat all of us good. Very good. I am not understanding this."

Bond explained. It seemed that Dlamini had learned something about illegal activities Hydt and Dunne were engaged in.

His eyes flashed. "I know what you are speaking of." His head bobbed up and down. He told Bond that he was a maintenance man at the Green Way plant north of town. That morning he'd found the door to the company's Research and Development office left open for deliveries. The two employees inside were at the back of the room. Dlamini had seen an overflowing bin inside. The rubbish there was supposed to be handled by somebody else but he decided to empty it anyway. "I just was trying to do good job. That's all." He shook his head. "I go inside and start to empty this bin when one of the workers sees me and starts screaming at me. What did I see? What was I looking at? I said, 'Nothing.' He ordered me out."

"And *did* you see anything that might've upset them?"

"I don't think so. On the computer beside the bin there was a message, an e-mail, I think. I saw 'Serbia' in English. But I paid no more attention."

"Anything else?"

"No, sir."

Serbia . . .

So some of the secrets to Gehenna lay beyond the door to Research and Development.

Bond said to Nkosi, "We have to get the family away. If I give them money, is there a hotel where they can stay until the weekend?"

"I can find some rooms for them."

Bond gave them fifteen hundred rand. The man blinked as he stared at the sum. Nkosi explained to Dlamini that he would have to stay in hiding for a short while.

"And have him call other family members and close friends. He should tell them that he and his family are all right but that they have to play dead for a few days. Can you plant a story in the media about their deaths?"

"I think so." The warrant officer was hesitating. "But I'm wondering if . . ." His voice faded.

"We'll keep this between ourselves. Captain Jordaan does not need to know."

"Without doubt," the man whispered, "that is best."

As the glorious vista of Cape Town rose before them, Bond glanced at his watch. It was time for the second assignment of the night—one that would require him to enlist a very different set of tradecraft skills from dodging grenades and firebombs, though he suspected that this job would be no less challenging.

Chapter 42

Bond wasn't impressed by the Lodge Club.

Perhaps back in the day, when it was the enclave of hunters in jodhpurs and jackets embellished with loops to hold ammunition for their big-five game rifles, it had been more posh, but the atmosphere now was that of a suburban banquet hall hosting simultaneous marriage fetes. Bond wasn't even sure if the Cape buffalo head, staring down at him with a studious glare from near the front door, was real or had been manufactured in China.

He gave the name Gene Theron to one of the attractive young women at the door. She happened to be blonde and voluptuous and wearing a tight-fitting crimson dress with a lazy neckline. The other hostess was of Zulu or Xhosa ancestry but equally built and clad. Bond suspected that whoever ran the fundraising organization knew how to tactically appeal to what was, of whatever race, predominantly a male donor pool. He added, "Guest of Mr. Hydt."

"Ah, yes," the golden-haired woman said and let him into the low-lit room where fifty or so people milled about. Still wine, champagne and soft drinks were on offer and Bond went for the sparkling.

Bond had followed Hydt's suggestions on dress and the Durban mercenary was in light gray trousers, a black sports jacket and a light blue shirt, no tie.

Holding his champagne flute, Bond looked around

the plush hall. The group behind the event was the International Organization Against Hunger, based in Cape Town. Pictures on easels showed workers handing out large sacks to happy recipients—women, mostly—Hercules planes being unloaded and boats laden with sacks of rice or wheat. There were no pictures of starving emaciated children. A tasteful compromise all around. You wanted donors to feel slightly, but not too, uneasy. Bond guessed that the world of altruism had to be as carefully navigated as that of Whitehall politics.

From speakers in the ceiling, the harmonies of Ladysmith Black Mambazo and the inspirational songs of the Cape Town singer Verity provided an appealing sound track to the evening.

The event was a silent auction—tables were filled with all sorts of items donated by supporters of the group: a football signed by players from Bafana Bafana, the South African national football team, a whale-watching cruise, a weekend getaway in Stellenbosch, a Zulu sculpture, a pair of diamond earrings and much more. The guests would circulate and write their bids for each item on a sheet of paper; the one who'd put down the highest amount when the auction closed would win the article. Severan Hydt had donated a dinner for four, worth eight thousand rand—about seven hundred pounds, Bond calculated—at a first-class restaurant.

The wine flowed generously and waiters circulated with silver trays of elaborate canapés.

Ten minutes after Bond had arrived, Severan Hydt appeared with his female companion on his arm. Niall Dunne was nowhere to be seen. He nodded to Hydt, who was in a nicely cut navy blue suit, probably American, if he read the sloping shoulders right. The woman—her name, he recalled, was Jessica Barnes—was in a simple black dress and heavily bejeweled, all diamonds and platinum. Her stockings were pure white. Not a hint of color was to be found on her; she didn't even wear a touch of lipstick. His earlier impression held: how gaunt she was, despite her attractive figure and face. Her austerity aged her considerably, giving her a ghostly look. Bond was curious; every other woman here of Jessica's age had clearly spent hours dolling herself up.

"Ah, Theron," Hydt boomed and marched forward, detaching himself from Jessica, who followed. As Bond shook his hand, the woman regarded him with a noncommittal smile. He turned to her. Tradecraft requires constant, often exhausting effort. You must maintain an expression of faint curiosity when meeting a person you're familiar with only through surveillance. Lives have been lost because of a simple slip: "Ah, good to see you again," when in fact you've never met face to face.

Bond kept his eyes neutral as Hydt introduced her. "This is Jessica." He turned to her. "Gene Theron. We're doing business together."

The woman nodded and, though she held his eye, took his hand tentatively. It was a sign of insecurity, Bond concluded. Another indication of this was her handbag, which she kept over her shoulder and pinned tight beneath arm and rib cage.

Small talk ensued, Bond reciting snippets from Jordaan's lessons about the country, taking care to be accurate, assuming that Jessica might report their conversation to Hydt. In a low voice he offered that the South African government should busy itself with more important things than renaming Pretoria Tshwane. He was glad the trade union situation was calming. Yes, he enjoyed life on the east coast. The beaches near his home in Durban were particularly nice, especially now that the shark nets were up, though he'd never had any problems with the Great Whites, which occasionally took bites out of people. They talked then about wildlife. Jessica had visited the famed Kruger game reserve again recently and had seen two adolescent elephants tear up trees and bushes. It had reminded her of the gangs in Somerville, Massachusetts, just north of Boston—teenagers vandalizing public parks. Oh, yes, he'd thought her accent was American.

"Have you ever been there, Mr. Theron?"

"Call me Gene, please," Bond said, scrolling mentally through the biography written by Bheka Jordaan and I Branch. "No," he said. "But I hope to someday."

Bond looked at Hydt. His body language had shifted; he was giving out signs of impatience. A glance at Jessica suggested he wished her to leave them. Bond thought of the abuse Bheka Jordaan had endured at the hands of her coworkers. This was different only in degree. A moment later the woman excused herself to "powder her nose," an expression Bond had not heard in years. He thought it ironic that she used the term, considering that she probably wouldn't be doing so.

When they were alone, Hydt said to him, "I've thought more about your proposal and I'd like to move forward."

"Good." They took refills of champagne from an attractive young Afrikaner woman. Bond said, "*Dankie*," and reminded himself not to overdo his act.

He and Hydt retired to a corner of the room, the older man waving to and shaking hands with people on the way. When the men were alone, beneath the mounted head of a gazelle or antelope, Hydt peppered Bond with questions about the number of graves, the acreage, the countries they were in and how close the authorities were to discovering some of the killing fields. As Bond ad-libbed the answers, he couldn't help but be impressed with the man's thoroughness. It seemed he'd spent all afternoon thinking about the project. He was careful to remember what he told Hydt and made a mental note to write it down later so that he would be consistent in the future.

After fifteen minutes Bond said, "Now, there are things I would like to know. First, your operation here. I'd like to see it."

"I think you should."

When he didn't suggest a time, Bond said, "How about tomorrow?"

"That might be difficult, with my big project on Friday."

Bond nodded. "Some of my clients are eager to move forward. You are my first choice but if there'll be delays I'll have to—"

"No, no. Please. Tomorrow will be fine."

Bond began to probe more but just then the lights dimmed and a woman ascended the raised platform near where Hydt and Bond were standing. "Good evening," she called out, her low voice glazed with a South African accent. "Welcome, everyone. Thank you for coming to our event."

She was the managing director of the organization and Bond was amused by her name: Felicity Willing.

She wasn't, to Bond's eye, cover-girl beautiful, as was Philly Maidenstone. However, her face was intense, striking. Expertly made up, it exuded a feline quality. Her eyes were a deep green, like late-summer leaves caught in the sun, and her hair dark blonde, pulled back severely and pinned up, accentuating the determined angles of her nose and chin. She wore a close-fitting navy-blue cocktail dress that was cut low at the front and lower still at the back. Her silver shoes sported thin straps and precarious heels. Faintly pink pearls shone at her throat and she wore one ring, also a pearl, on her right index finger. Her nails were short and uncolored.

She scanned the audience with a penetrating, almost challenging gaze and said, "I must warn you all. . . ." Tension swelled. "At university I was known as Felicity *Willful*—an appropriate name, as you'll find out later when I make the rounds. I advise you all, for your own safety, to keep your checkbooks at the ready." A smile replaced the fierce visage.

As the laughter died down, Felicity began to talk about the problems of hunger. "Africa must import twenty-five percent of its food. . . . While the population has soared, crop yields today are no higher than they were in 1980. . . . In places like the Central African Republic, nearly a third of all households are food insecure. . . . In Africa iodine deficiency is the number one cause of brain damage, vitamin A deficiency is the number one cause of blindness. . . . Nearly three hundred million people in Africa do not have enough to eat—that number equals the entire population of the United States. . . ."

Africa, of course, was not alone in the need for food aid, she continued, and her organization was attacking the plague on all fronts. Thanks to the generosity of donors, including many here, the group had recently expanded its charter from being a purely South African charity to an international one, opening offices in Jakarta, Port-au-Prince and Mumbai, with others planned.

And, she added, the biggest shipment of maize, sorghum, milk powder and other high-nutrient staples ever to arrive in Africa was soon to be delivered in Cape Town for distribution across the continent.

Felicity acknowledged the applause. Then her smile vanished and she gazed at the crowd with piercing eyes once more, speaking in a low, even menacing, voice about the need to make poorer countries independent of Western "agropolies." She railed against the prevailing approach of America and Europe to end hunger: foreign-owned megafarms forcing their way into third-world nations and squeezing out the local farmers—the people who knew how to get the best yield from the land. Those enterprises were using Africa and other nations as laboratories to test untried methods and products, like synthetic fertilizers and genetically engineered seeds.

"The vast majority of international agribusiness cares only about profit, not about relieving the suffering of the people. And this is simply not acceptable."

Finally, having delivered her assault, she grew more relaxed, smiled and singled out the donors, Hydt among them. He responded to the applause with a wave. He was smiling, too, but his whisper to Bond told a different story: "If you want adulation, just give away money. The more desperate they are, the more they love you." He clearly didn't want to be here.

Felicity stepped off the platform to circulate as the guests continued their silent bidding.

Bond said to Hydt, "I don't know if you have plans but I was thinking we could go for some dinner. On me?"

"I'm sorry, Theron, but I have to meet an associate who's just arrived in town for that project I mentioned."

Gehenna. . . . Bond certainly wanted to meet whoever this man was. "I'd be happy to take everyone out, your associate too."

"Tonight's no good, I'm afraid," Hydt said absently, pulling his iPhone out and scrolling through messages or missed calls. He glanced up and spotted Jessica standing by herself awkwardly in front of a table on which items were being offered for auction. When she looked at him he beckoned her over impatiently.

Bond tried to think of some other way to conjure an invitation but decided to back off before Hydt became suspicious. Seduction in tradecraft is like seduction in love; it works best if you make the object of your desire come to you. Nothing ruins your efforts faster than desperate pursuit.

"Tomorrow then," Bond said, seemingly distracted and glancing at his own phone.

"Yes—good." Hydt looked up. "Felicity!"

With a smile, the charity's managing director detached herself from a fat, balding man in a dusty dinner jacket. He'd been gripping her hand for far longer than courtesy dictated. She joined Hydt, Jessica and Bond.

"Severan. Jessica." They brushed cheeks.

"And an associate, Gene Theron. He's from Durban, in town for a few days."

Felicity gripped Bond's hand. He asked obvious questions about her organization and the shipments of food arriving soon, hoping Hydt would change his mind about dinner.

But the man's large head turned once more at his iPhone and said, "I'm afraid we have to be going."

"Severan," Felicity said, "I don't think my remarks really conveyed our gratitude. You've introduced some important donors to us. I really can't thank you enough."

Bond took note of this. So she knew the names of some of Hydt's associates. He wondered how best to exploit this connection.

Hydt said, "I'm delighted to help. I've been lucky in life. I want to share that good fortune." He turned to Bond. "See you tomorrow, Theron. Around noon, if that's convenient. Wear old clothes and shoes." He brushed his curly beard with an index finger whose nail reflected a streak of jaundiced light. "You'll be taking a tour of hell."

After Hydt and Jessica had left, Bond turned to Felicity Willing. "Those statistics were disturbing. I might be interested in helping." Standing close, he was aware of her perfume, a musky scent.

"Might be interested?" she asked.

He nodded.

Felicity kept a smile on her face but it didn't reach her eyes. "Well, Mr. Theron, for every donor who actually writes a check, two others say they're 'interested' but I never see a rand. I'd rather somebody told me up front they don't want to give anything. Then I can get on with my business. Forgive me if I'm blunt but I'm fighting a war here."

"And you don't take prisoners."

"No," she said, smiling sincerely now. "I don't."

Felicity Willful . . .

"Then I'll most certainly help," Bond said, wondering what A Branch would say when they encountered a donation on his expense account back in London. "I'm not sure I'm able to rise to Severan's level of generosity."

"One rand donated is one rand closer to solving the problem," she said.

He paused a judicious moment, then said, "Just had a thought: Severan and Jessica couldn't make it for dinner and I'm alone in town. Would you care to join me after the auction?"

Felicity considered this. "I don't see why not. You look reasonably fit." And turned away, a lioness preparing to descend on a herd of gazelles.

Chapter 43

At the conclusion of the event, which raised the equivalent of thirty thousand pounds—including a modest donation on the credit card of Gene Theron—Bond and Felicity Willing walked to the car park behind the Lodge Club.

They approached a large van, beside which were dozens of large cardboard cartons. She tugged up her hem, bent down, like a stevedore on a dock, and muscled a heavy box through the open side door of the vehicle.

The reference to his physical well-being was suddenly clear. "Let me," he said.

"We'll both do it."

Together they began to transfer the cartons, which smelled of food. "Leftovers," he said.

"Didn't you think it was rather ironic that we were serving gourmet finger food at a campaign to raise money for the hungry?" Felicity asked.

"I did, yes."

"If I'd offered tinned biscuits and processed cheese, they'd have devoured the lot. But with fancier stuff—I extorted some three-star restaurants to donate it—they didn't dare take more than a bite or two. I wanted to make sure there was plenty left over."

"Where are we delivering the excess?"

"A food bank not far away. It's one of the outlets my organization works with."

When they had finished loading, they got into the van. Felicity climbed into the driver's seat and slipped off her shoes to drive barefoot. Then they sped into the night, bounding assertively over the uneven tarmac as she tormented the clutch and gearbox.

In fifteen minutes they were at the Cape Town Interdenominational Food Bank Center. Her shoes back on, Felicity opened the side door and together they offloaded the scampi, crab cakes and Jamaican chicken, which the staff carried inside the shelter.

When the van was empty, Felicity gestured to a large man in khaki slacks and T-shirt. He seemed impervious to the May chill. He hesitated, then joined them, eyeing Bond curiously. Then he said, "Yes, Miss Willing? Thank you, Miss Willing. Lot of good food for everyone tonight. Did you see inside the shelter? It's crowded."

She ignored his questions, which to Bond had sounded like diversionary chatter. "Joso, last week a shipment disappeared. Fifty kilos. Who took it?"

"I didn't hear anything—"

"I didn't ask whether you heard anything. I asked who took it."

His face was a mask but then it sagged. "Why you asking me, Miss Willing? I didn't do nothing."

"Joso, do you know how many people fifty kilos of rice will feed?"

"I—"

"Tell me. How many people." He towered over her but Felicity held her ground. Bond wondered if *this* was what she had meant with her assessment of his fitness—she had wanted someone to back her up. But her eyes revealed that, to her, Bond wasn't even present. This was between Felicity and a transgressor who'd stolen food from those she'd pledged to protect, and she was entirely capable of taking him on alone.

Her eyes reminded Bond of his own, when confronting an enemy.

"How many people?" she repeated.

Miserably, he lapsed into Zulu or Xhosa.

"No," she corrected. "It will feed more than that, many more."

"It was an accident," he protested. "I forgot to close the door. It was late. I was working—"

"It was no accident. Someone saw you unlock the door before you left. Who has the rice?"

"No, no you must believe me."

"Who?" she persisted coolly.

He was defeated. "A man from the Flats. In a gang. Oh, please, Miss Willing, if you tell the SAPS, he'll find out it was me. He'll know I told you. He will come for me and he will come for my family."

Her jaw tightened and Bond couldn't dislodge the impression he'd had earlier, of a feline—now about to strike. There was no sympathy in her voice as she said, "I won't go to the police. Not this time. But you'll tell the director what you did. And he'll decide whether to keep you on or not."

"This is my only job," he protested. "I have a family. My only job."

"Which you were happy to endanger," she responded. "Now, go and tell Reverend van Groot. And if he keeps you on and another theft occurs, I *will* tell the police."

"It will not happen again, Miss Willing." He turned and vanished inside.

Bond couldn't help but be impressed with her cool, efficient handling of the incident. He noted too that it made her all the more attractive.

She caught Bond's eye and her face softened. "The war I'm fighting? Sometimes you're never quite sure who the enemy is. They might even be on your side."

How well do I know that? thought Bond.

They returned to the van. Felicity bent down to remove her shoes again but Bond said quickly, "I'll drive. Save you unstrapping."

She laughed. They got in and set off. "Dinner?" she asked.

He almost felt guilty, after all he'd heard about hunger. "If you're still up for it."

"Oh, I most certainly am."

As they drove, Bond asked, "Would he really have been killed if you'd gone to the police?"

"Ah, the SAPS would have laughed at the idea of investigating fifty kilos of stolen rice. But the Cape Flats *are* dangerous, that's true, and if anyone there thought Joso betrayed them, he very likely would be killed. Let's hope he's learned his lesson." Her voice grew cool again as she added, "Leniency can win you allies. It can also be a cobra."

Felicity guided him back to Green Point. Since the restaurant she'd suggested was near the Table Mountain Hotel, he left the van there and they walked on. Several times, Bond noted, Felicity glanced behind her, her face alert, shoulders tensed. The road was deserted. What did she feel threatened by?

She relaxed once they were in the front lobby of the restaurant, which was decorated with tapestry, the fixtures dark wood and brass. The large windows overlooked the water, which danced with lights. Much of the illumination inside came from hundreds of cream-colored candles. As they were escorted to the table, Bond noticed that her clinging dress glistened in the light and seemed to change color with every step, from navy to azure to cerulean. Her skin glowed.

The waiter greeted her by name, then smiled at Bond. She ordered a Cosmopolitan, and Bond, in the mood for a cocktail, ordered the drink he had had with Philly Maidenstone. "Crown Royal whisky, a double, on ice. Half a measure of triple sec, two dashes of Angostura. Twist of orange peel, not a slice."

When the waiter left, Felicity said, "I've never heard of that before."

"My own invention."

"Have you named it?"

Bond smiled to himself, recalling that the waiter at Antoine's in London had wondered about the drink too. "Not yet." He had a flash of inspiration from his conversation with M several days earlier. "Though I think I will now. I'll call it the Carte Blanche. In your honor."

"Why?" she asked, her narrow brow furrowed.

"Because if your donors drink enough of them, they'll give you complete freedom to take their money."

She laughed and squeezed his arm, then picked up the menu.

Sitting closer to her now, Bond could see how expertly she'd applied her makeup, accentuating the feline eyes and the thrust of her cheeks and jaw. A thought came to him. Philly Maidenstone was classically attractive but hers was a passive beauty. Felicity's was far more assertive, forceful.

He upbraided himself for dwelling on the comparison, reached for the menu and began to study it. Scanning the extensive card he learned that the restaurant, Celsius, was famed for its special grill, which reached 950 degrees centigrade.

Felicity said, "You order for us. Anything to start but I must have a steak for my main course. There's nothing like the grilled meat at Celsius. My God, Gene, you're not a vegan, are you?"

"Hardly."

When the waiter arrived, Bond ordered fresh grilled sardines, to be followed by a large rib-eye steak for two. He asked if the chef could grill it with the bone in—known in America as the "cowboy cut."

The waiter mentioned that the steaks were typically served with exotic sauces: Argentinian *chimichurri,* Indonesian coffee, Madagascan peppercorn, Spanish Madeira or Peruvian *anticuchos.* But Bond declined them all. He believed that steaks had flavor enough of their own and should be eaten with only salt and pepper.

Felicity nodded that she was in agreement.

Bond then selected a bottle of South African red wine, the Rustenberg Peter Barlow cabernet 2005.

The wine came and was as good as he'd expected. They clinked glasses again and sipped.

The waiter brought the first course and they ate. Bond, deprived of his lunch by Gregory Lamb, was starving.

"What do you do for a living, Gene? Severan didn't say."

"Security work."

"Ah." A faint chill descended. Felicity was obviously a tough, worldly businesswoman and recognized the euphemism. She would guess he was in some way involved with the many conflicts in Africa. War, she'd said during her speech, was one of the main causes for the plague of hunger.

He said, "I have companies that install security systems and provide guards."

She seemed to believe this was at least partly true. "I was born in South Africa and have been living here now for four or five years. I've seen it change. Crime is less of a problem than it used to be but security staff are still needed. We have a number of them at the organization. We must. Charitable work doesn't exempt us from risk." She added darkly, "I'm happy to give food away. I won't have it stolen from me."

To divert her from asking more questions about him Bond inquired about her life.

She'd grown up in the bush, in the Western Cape, the only child of English parents, her father a mining company executive. The family had moved back to London when she was thirteen. She was an outsider at boarding school, she confessed. "I might have fitted in a bit better if I'd kept my mouth shut about how to field-dress gazelles—especially in the dining hall."

Then it had been the London Business School and a stint at a major City investment bank, where she'd done "all right"; her dismissive modesty suggested she'd done extremely well.

But the work had proved ultimately unsatisfying. "It was too easy for me, Gene. There was no challenge. I needed a steeper mountain. Four or five years ago I decided to reassess my life. I took a month off and spent some time back here. I saw how pervasive hunger was. And I decided to do something about it. Everybody told me not to bother. It was impossible to make a difference. Well, that was like waving a red flag at a bull."

"Felicity Willful."

She smiled. "So, here I am, bullying donors to give us money and taking on the American and European megafarms."

"'Agropoly.' Clever term."

"I coined it," she said, then burst out, "They're destroying the continent. I'm not going to let them get away with it."

The serious discussion was cut short when the waiter appeared with the steak sizzling on an iron platter. It was charred on the outside and succulent within. They ate in silence for a time. At one point he sliced off a crusty piece of meat, but took a sip of wine before he put it into his mouth. When he returned to his plate the morsel was gone and Felicity was chewing mischievously. "Sorry. I tend to go after things that appeal to me."

Bond laughed. "Very clever, stealing from under the nose of a security expert." He waved to the sommelier, and a second bottle of the cabernet appeared. Bond steered the conversation to Severan Hydt.

He was disappointed to find that she didn't seem to know much about the man that might be helpful to his mission. She mentioned the names of several of his partners who'd donated money to her group and he memorized them. She had not met Niall Dunne but she knew Hydt had some brilliant assistant who performed all sorts of technical wizardry. She lifted an eyebrow and said, "I just realized—you're the one he uses."

"Sorry?"

"For his security at the Green Way operation north of town. I've never been but one of my assistants collected a donation from him. All those metal detectors and scanners. You can't get inside the place with a paper clip, let alone a mobile phone. You have to check everything at the door. Like in those old American westerns—you leave your guns outside when you go into the bar."

"He awarded that contract to somebody else. I do other jobs." This intelligence worried Bond; he'd intended to get into the Green Way building with far more than a paper clip and a mobile phone, despite Bheka Jordaan's disdain for illegal surveillance. He'd have to consider the implications.

The meal wound down and they finished the wine. They were the last patrons in the restaurant. Bond called for the bill and settled it. "The second of my donations," he said.

They returned to the entrance, where he collected her black cashmere coat and draped it over her shoulders. They started down the pavement, the narrow heels of her shoes tapping on the concrete. Again she surveyed the streets. Then, relaxing, she took his arm and held it tightly. He was keenly aware of her perfume and of the occasional pressure of her breast against his arm.

They approached his hotel, Bond fishing the van key from his pocket. Felicity slowed. The night sky was clear above them, encrusted with a plenitude of stars.

"A very nice evening," Felicity said. "And thank you for your help in delivering the leftovers. You're even fitter than I thought."

Bond found himself asking, "Another glass of wine?"

The green eyes were looking up and into his own. "Would *you* like one?"

"Yes," he said firmly.

In ten minutes they were in his room in the Table Mountain Hotel sitting on the sofa, which they had turned and slid close to the window. Glasses of a Stellenbosch pinotage were in their hands.

They looked out over the flickering lights in the bay, muted yellow and white, like benign insects hovering in anticipation.

Felicity turned to him, perhaps to say something, perhaps not, and he bent forward and pressed his lips gently to hers. Then he eased back a little, gauging her reaction, and moved forward and kissed her again, harder, losing himself in the contact, the taste, the heat. Her breath on his cheek, Felicity's arms snaked around his shoulders as her mouth held his. Then she kissed his neck and teasingly bit the base where it met his firm shoulder. Her tongue slid along a scar that arced down to his upper arm.

Bond's fingers slipped up her neck into her hair and pulled her closer. He was lost in the pungent musk of her perfume.

A parallel to this moment occurs in skiing, when you pause on the ridge atop a beautiful but perilous downhill run. You have a choice to go or not. You can always snap free the bindings and walk down the mountain. But in fact, for Bond, there never was such a choice; once on the edge, it was impossible not to give in to the seduction of gravity and speed. The only true choice left was how to control the accelerating descent.

The same now, here.

Bond whisked her dress off, the insubstantial blue cloth spilling leisurely to the floor. Felicity then eased back, pulling him with her, until they were lying on the couch, she beneath him, tugging at his lower lip with her teeth. He cupped her neck again and pulled her face to his, while her hands rested on the small of his back, kneading hard. Felicity shuddered and inhaled sharply and he understood that, for whatever reason, she liked touching him there. He knew too that she wanted his hands to curl firmly behind her waist. Such is the way in which lovers communicate, and he would remember that place, the delicate bones of her spine.

For his part, Bond found rapture throughout her body, all its aspects: her hungry lips, her strong, flawless thighs, breasts encased in taut black silk, her delicate neck and throat, from which a whispered moan issued, the dense hair framing her face, the softer strands elsewhere.

They kissed endlessly and then she broke away and locked onto his fierce eyes with her own, whose lids, dusted with faint green luminescence, halfway lowered. Mutual surrender, mutual victory.

Bond lifted her easily. Their lips met once more, briefly, and he carried her to the bed.

Thursday

Disappearance Row

Chapter 44

He awoke with a start from a nightmare he could not remember. Curiously James Bond's first thought was of Philly Maidenstone. He felt—absurdly—that he'd been unfaithful, yet his most intimate contact with her had been a brief brush of cheeks that had lasted half a second.

He rolled over. The other side of the bed was empty. He looked at the clock. It was half past seven. He could smell Felicity's perfume on the sheets and pillows.

The previous evening had begun as an exercise in learning more about his enemy and his enemy's purpose but had become something more. He had felt a strong empathy with Felicity Willing, a tough woman who'd conquered the City and was now turning her resources to a nobler battle. He reflected that, in their own ways, they were both knights errant.

And he wanted to see her again.

But first things first. He got out of bed and pulled on a toweling dressing gown. He hesitated for a moment then told himself: Has to be done.

He went to his laptop in the suite's living area. The device had been modified by Q Branch to incorporate a motion-activated, low-light camera. Bond booted up the machine and looked over the replay. It had been pointed only at the front door and the chair, where Bond had tossed his jacket and trousers, containing his wallet, passport and mobile. At around 5:30 A.M., according to the time stamp, Felicity, dressed, had walked past his clothing, showing no interest in his phone, pockets or the laptop. She paused and looked back toward the bed. With a smile? He believed so but couldn't be sure. She put something on the table by the door and let herself out.

He stood up and strode to the table. Her business card lay next to a lamp. She had penned a mobile number underneath her organization's main phone line. He slipped the card into his wallet.

He cleaned his teeth, showered and shaved, then dressed in blue jeans and a loose black Lacoste shirt, chosen to conceal his Walther. Laughing to himself, he donned the gaudy bracelet and watch and slipped on his finger the initial ring, *EJT.*

Checking his texts and e-mails, he found one from Percy Osborne-Smith. The man was staying true to his reformed ways and gave a succinct update on the investigation in Britain, though little headway had been made. He concluded:

> Our friends in Whitehall are positively
> obsessed with Afghanistan. I say, all the
> better for us, James. Looking forward to
> sharing a George Cross with you when we
> see Hydt in shackles.

While he had breakfast in his room, he considered his impending trip to Hydt's Green Way plant, thinking back to last night, to all he'd seen and heard, especially about the supertight security. When he finished, he called Q Branch and got through to Sanu Hirani. He could hear children's voices in the background and supposed he had been patched through to the branch director's mobile at home. Hirani had six children. They all played cricket, and his eldest daughter was a star batswoman.

Bond told him of his communications and weapons needs. Hirani had some ideas but was uncertain that he could come up quickly with a solution. "What's your time frame, James?"

"Two hours."

There followed a thoughtful exhalation from down the line seven thousand miles away. Then: "I'll need a cutout in Cape Town. Somebody with knowledge of the area and top clearance. Oh, and a solid NOC. Do you know anybody who fits the bill?"

"I'm afraid I do."

At 10:30 A.M. Bond, in a gray windbreaker, made his way to the central police station and was escorted to the Crime Combating and Investigation Division office.

"Morning, Commander," Kwalene Nkosi said, smiling.

"Warrant Officer." Bond nodded. Their eyes met conspiratorially.

"You see the news this morning?" Nkosi asked, tapping the *Cape Times*. "Tragic story. A family was killed in a firebombing in Primrose Gardens township last night." He frowned rather obviously.

"How terrible," Bond said, reflecting that, despite his West End ambitions, Nkosi was not a very good actor.

"Without doubt."

He glanced into Bheka Jordaan's office and she

waved him inside. "Morning," he said, spotting a pair of well-worn trainers in the corner of the office. He hadn't noticed them yesterday. "You run much?"

"Now and then. It's important to stay in shape for my job."

When he was in London, Bond spent at least an hour a day exercising and running, using the ODG's gym and jogging along the paths in Regent's Park. "I enjoy it too. Maybe if time permits you could show me some running trails. There must be some beautiful ones in town."

"I'm sure the hotel will have a map," she said dismissively. "Was your meeting at the Lodge Club successful?"

Bond gave her a rundown of what had happened at the fund-raiser.

Jordaan then asked, "And afterward? Ms. Willing proved . . . useful to you?"

Bond lifted an eyebrow. "I thought you didn't believe in unlawful surveillance."

"Making certain someone is safe on the public sidewalks and streets is hardly illegal. Warrant Officer Nkosi told you of our CCTV cameras in the center of town."

"Well, in answer to your question, yes, she *was* helpful. She gave me some information about the enhanced security at Green Way." He added stiffly, "I was lucky she did. No one else seemed to be aware of it. Otherwise my trip there today might have been disastrous."

"That's fortunate, then," Jordaan said.

Bond told her the names of the three donors Felicity had mentioned last night—the men Hydt had introduced her to.

Jordaan knew of two as successful legitimate businessmen. Nkosi conducted a search and learned that neither they nor the third had any criminal record. In any event, all three were out of town. Bond decided they would not be of any immediate help.

Bond was looking at the policewoman. "You don't like Felicity Willing?"

"You think I'm jealous?" Her face said: Just what a man would believe.

Nkosi turned away. Bond glanced toward him but he was offering no allegiance to Britain in this international dispute.

"That idea couldn't have been further from my mind. Your eyes told me you don't like her. Why?"

"I've never met her. She's probably a perfectly nice woman—I don't like what she represents."

"Which is?"

"A foreigner who comes here to pat us on the head and dispense alms. It's twenty-first-century imperialism. People used to exploit Africa for diamonds and slaves. Now it's exploited for its ability to purge the guilt of wealthy Westerners."

"It seems to me," Bond said evenly, "that no one can progress when they're hungry. It doesn't matter where the food comes from, does it?"

"Charity undermines. You need to fight your way out of oppression and deprivation. We can do it ourselves. Perhaps more slowly but we will do it."

"You have no problem when Britain or America imposes arms embargoes on warlords. Hunger's as dangerous as rocket-propelled grenades and land mines. Why shouldn't we help stop that too?"

"It's different. Obviously."

"I don't see how," he said coolly. "Besides, Felicity might be more on your side than you give her credit for. She's made some enemies among the big corporations in Europe, America and Asia. She thinks they're meddling in African affairs and that more should be left to the people here." He remembered her ill ease on the short walk to the restaurant last night. "My take is that she's put herself at quite some risk saying so. If you're interested."

But Jordaan clearly wasn't. How *completely* irritating this woman was.

Bond looked at his huge Breitling watch. "I should leave for Green Way soon. I need a car. Can someone arrange a hire in Theron's name?"

Nkosi nodded enthusiastically. "Without doubt. You like to drive, Commander."

"I do," Bond said. "How did you know?"

"On the way from the airport yesterday you looked with some interest at a Maserati, a Moto Guzzi and a left-hand-drive Mustang from America."

"You notice things, Warrant Officer."

"I try to. That Ford—it was a very nice set of wheels. Someday I will own a Jaguar. It is my goal."

Then a loud voice was calling a greeting from the corridor. "Hallo, hallo!"

Bond wasn't surprised it belonged to Gregory Lamb. The MI6 agent strode into the office, waving broadly to everyone. It was obvious that Bheka Jordaan didn't care for him, as Lamb had admitted yesterday, though he and Nkosi seemed to get on well. They had a brief conversation about a recent football match.

Casting a cautious glance at Jordaan, the big, ruddy man turned to Bond. "Came through for you, my friend. Got a signal from Vauxhall Cross to help you out."

Lamb was the cutout whom Bond had reluctantly mentioned to Hirani earlier that morning. He couldn't think of anybody else to use on such short notice and at least the man had been vetted.

"Leaped into the fray, even missed breakfast, my friend, I'll have you know. Talked to that chap in your office's Q Branch. Is he always so bloody cheerful that early in the morning?"

"Actually, he is," said Bond.

"Got talking to him. I'm having some navigation problems on my ship charters. Pirates've been jamming signals. Whatever happened to the eye patches and peg legs, hmm? Well, this Hirani says there are devices that will jam the jammers. He wouldn't ship me any, though. Any chance you could put in a word?"

"You know our outfit doesn't officially exist, Lamb."

"We're all part of the same team," he said huffily. "I've got a huge charter coming up in a day or so. Massive."

Helping Lamb's lucrative cover career was the last thing on Bond's mind at the moment. He asked sternly, "And your assignment today?"

"Ah, yes." Lamb handed Bond the black satchel he was carrying as if it contained the crown jewels. "Must say, in all modesty, the morning's been a smashing success. Positively brilliant. I've been running hither and yon. Had to tip rather heavily. You'll reimburse me, of course?"

"I'm sure it'll get sorted." Bond opened the satchel and regarded the contents. He examined one item closely. It was a small plastic tube labeled *Re-Leef. For Congestion Problems Caused by Asthma.*

Hirani was a genius.

"An inhaler. You have lung problems?" Nkosi asked. "My brother too. He is a gold miner."

"Not really." Bond pocketed it, along with the other items Lamb had delivered.

Nkosi took a call. When he hung up he said, "I have a nice car for you, Commander. Subaru. All-wheel drive."

A Subaru, thought Bond, skeptical. A suburban estate wagon. But Nkosi was beaming so he said graciously, "Thank you, Warrant Officer. I'll look forward to driving it."

"The petrol mileage is very good," Nkosi said enthusiastically.

"I'm sure it is." He started out of the door.

Gregory Lamb stopped him. "Bond," he said softly. "Sometimes I'm not sure the powers that be in London take me all that seriously. I was exaggerating a bit yesterday—about the Cape, I mean. Fact is, the worst that happens down here is a warlord coming in from Congo to take the waters. Or a Hamas chap in transit at the airport. Just want to thank you for including me, my friend. I—"

Bond interrupted, "You're welcome, Lamb, but how's this: Let's just assume I'm your friend. Then you won't have to keep repeating it. How's that?"

"Fair enough, my . . . fair enough." A grin spread over the fat face.

Then Bond was out the door, thinking: Next stop, hell.

Chapter 45

James Bond enjoyed Kwalene Nkosi's little joke.

Yes, the car he'd procured for the agent's use was a small Japanese import. It wasn't, however, a staid family saloon but a metallic blue Subaru Impreza WRX, the STI model, which boasted a turbocharged 305-horsepower engine, six gears and a high spoiler. The jaunty little vehicle would be far more at home on rally courses than in some Asda car park and, settling into the driver's seat, Bond couldn't restrain himself. He laid twin streaks of rubber as he sped up Buitenkant Street, heading for the motorway.

For the next half hour he made his way north of Cape Town proper, guided by sat-nav, and finally skidded the taut little Subaru off the N7 and proceeded east along an increasingly deserted road, past a vast bottomless quarry and then into a grubby landscape of low hills, some green, some brown with autumn tint. Sporadic stands of trees broke the monotony.

The May sky was overcast and the air was humid but dust rose from the road, churned up by the Green Way lorries carting their refuse in the direction Bond was going. In addition to the typical dust carts, there were much larger ones, painted with the Green Way name and distinctive green leaf—or dagger—logo. Signs on the sides indicated that they came from company operations throughout South Africa. Bond was surprised to see that one lorry was from a branch in

Pretoria, the administrative capital of the country, many miles away—why would Hydt go to the expense of bringing rubbish to Cape Town when he could open a recycling depot where it was needed?

Bond changed down and blew past a series of the lorries at speed. He was enjoying this sprightly vehicle very much. He'd have to tell Philly Maidenstone about it.

A large road sign, stark in black and white, flashed past.

GEVAAR!!!
DANGER!!!
PRIVAAT-EIENDOM
PRIVATE PROPERTY

He'd been off the N7 for several miles when the road divided, with the lorries going to the right. Bond steered down the left fork, with an arrowed sign:

HOOF KANTOOR
MAIN OFFICE

Motoring fast through a dense grove of trees—they were tall but looked recently planted—he came to a rise and shot over it, ignoring the posted limit of forty kph, and braked hard as Green Way International loomed. The rapid stop wasn't because of obstruction or a sharp curve but the unnerving sight that greeted him.

An endless expanse of the waste facility filled his view and disappeared into a smoky, dusty haze in the distance. The orange fires of some burn-off operation could be seen from at least a mile away.

Hell indeed.

In front of him, beyond a crowded car park, was the headquarters building. It was eerie, too, in its own way. Though not large, the structure was stark and bleakly imposing. The unpainted concrete bunker, one story high, had only a few windows, small ones— sealed, it seemed. The entire grounds were enclosed by two ten-foot metal fences, both topped with wicked razor wire, which glinted even in the muted light. The barriers were thirty feet apart, reminding Bond of a similar perimeter: the shoot-to-kill zone surrounding the North Korean prison from which he'd successfully rescued a local MI6 asset last year.

Bond scowled at the fences. One of his plans was ruined. He knew from what Felicity had told him that there'd be metal detectors and scanners and, most likely, an imposing security fence. But he'd assumed a single barrier. He'd planned to slip some of the equipment Hirani had provided—a weatherproof miniature communications device and weapon—through the fence into grass or bushes on the other side for him to retrieve once he had entered. That wasn't going to work with two fences and a great distance between them.

As he drove forward again, he saw that the entrance was barred by a thick steel gate, on top of which was a sign.

REDUCE, REUSE, RECYCLE

The Green Way anthem chilled Bond. Not the words themselves but the configuration: a crescent of stark black metal letters. It reminded him of the sign over the entrance to the Nazi death camp Auschwitz, the horrifically ironic assurance that work would set the prisoners free: ARBEIT MACHT FREI.

Bond parked. He climbed out, keeping his Walther and mobile with him so that he could find out how effective the security really was. He also had in his pocket the asthma inhaler Hirani had provided; he had hidden under the front seat the other items Lamb had delivered that morning—the weapon and com device.

He approached the first guardhouse at the outer fence. A large man in uniform greeted him with a reserved nod. Bond gave his cover name. The man made a call and a moment later an equally large, equally stern fellow in a dark business suit came up and said, "Mr. Theron, this way, please."

Bond followed him through the no man's land between the two fences. They entered a room where three armed guards sat about, watching a football match. They stood up immediately.

The security man turned to Bond. "Now, Mr. Theron, we have very strict rules here. Mr. Hydt and his associates do most of the research and development work for his companies on these premises. We must guard our trade secrets carefully. We don't allow any mobiles or radios of any kind in with you. No cameras or pagers either. You'll have to hand them in."

Bond was looking at a large rack, like the cubbyholes for keys behind the front desk in old-fashioned hotels. There were hundreds and most of them had phones in them. The guard noticed. "The rule applies to all our employees too."

Bond recalled that René Mathis had told him the same thing about Hydt's London operation—that there was virtually no SIGINT going into or coming out of the company. "Well, you have landlines I can use, I assume. I'll have to check my messages."

"There are some but all the lines go through a central switchboard in the security department. A guard could make the call for you but you wouldn't have any privacy. Most visitors wait until after they leave. The same is true for e-mail and Internet access. If you wish to keep anything metal on you, we'll have to X-ray it."

"I should tell you I'm armed."

"Yes." As if many people coming to visit Green Way were. "Of course—"

"I'll have to hand in my weapon too?"

"That's right."

Bond silently thanked Felicity Willing for filling him in on Hydt's security. Otherwise he would have been caught with one of Q Branch's standard-issue video or still surveillance cameras in a pen or jacket button, which would have shattered his credibility . . . and probably led to a full-on fight.

Playing the tough mercenary, he scoffed at the inconvenience but handed over his gun and phone, programmed to reveal only information about his Gene Theron cover identity, should anyone try to crack it. Then he stripped off his belt and watch, placed them and his keys in a tray for the X-ray.

He strode through quickly and was reunited with his possessions—after the guard had checked that the watch, keys and belt held no cameras, weapons or recording devices.

"Wait here, please, sir," the security man said. Bond sat where indicated.

The inhaler was still in his pocket. If they had

frisked him, found and dismantled the device, they would have discovered it was in fact a sensitive camera, constructed without a single metal part. One of Sanu Hirani's contacts in Cape Town had managed to find or assemble the device that morning. The shutter was carbon fiber, as were the springs operating it.

The image-storage medium was quite interesting—unique nowadays: old-fashioned microfilm, the sort spies had used during the Cold War. The camera had a fixed-focus lens and Bond could snap a picture by pressing the base, then twisting it to advance the film. It could take thirty pictures. In this digital age, the cobwebbed past occasionally offered an advantage.

Bond looked for a sign to Research and Development, which he knew from Stephan Dlamini contained at least some information about Gehenna, but there was none. He sat for five minutes before Severan Hydt appeared, in silhouette but unmistakable: the tall stature, the massive, regal head framed with curly hair and beard, the well-tailored suit. He paused, looming, in the doorway. "Theron." His black eyes bored into Bond's.

They shook hands and Bond tried to ignore the grotesque sensation he experienced as Hydt's long nails slid across his palm and wrist.

"Come with me," Hydt said and led him into the main office building, which was much less austere than the outside suggested. Indeed, the place was rather nicely appointed, with expensive furniture, art, antiques and comfortable work spaces for the staff. It seemed like a typical medium-size company. The front lobby was furnished with the obligatory sofa and chairs, a table with trade magazines and a Cape Town newspaper. On the walls there were pictures of forests, rolling fields of grain and flowers, streams and oceans.

And everywhere, that eerie logo—the leaf that looked like a knife.

As they walked along the corridors, Bond kept an eye open for the Research and Development department. Finally, toward the rear of the building, he saw a sign pointing to it. He memorized the location, noting landmarks nearby.

But Hydt turned the other way. "Come along. We're going for the fifty-rand tour."

At the back of the building Bond was handed a dark green hard hat. Hydt donned one too. They walked to a rear door, where Bond was surprised to see a second security post. Curiously, workers coming *into* the building from the rubbish yard were checked. Hydt and he stepped outside on to a patio overlooking scores of low buildings. Lorries and forklift trucks moved in and out of each one, like bees at a hive. Workers in hard hats and uniforms were everywhere.

The sheds, in neat rows like barracks, reminded Bond again of a prison or concentration camp.

ARBEIT MACHT FREI . . .

"This way," Hydt called loudly, striding through a landscape cluttered with earth-moving equipment, skips, oil drums, pallets holding bales of paper and cardboard. Low rumblings filled the air, and the ground seemed to quiver, as if huge underground furnaces or machines were at work, a counterpoint to the high-pitched shrieks of the seagulls that swooped in to pick up scraps in the wake of the lorries entering through a gate a quarter-mile to the east. "I'll give you a brief lesson in the business," he offered.

Bond nodded. "Please."

"There are four ways to rid ourselves of discard. Dump it somewhere out of the way—in tips or landfill now mostly but the ocean's still popular. Did you know that the Pacific has four times as much plastic in it as zooplankton? The biggest rubbish tip in the world is the Great Pacific Garbage Patch, circulating between Japan and North America. It's at least twice the size of Texas and could be as big as the entire United States. Nobody actually knows. But one thing *is* certain: It's getting bigger.

"The second way is to burn discard, which is very expensive and can produce dangerous ash. Third, you can recycle it—that's Green Way's area of expertise. Finally, there's minimizing, which means making sure that fewer disposable materials are created and sold. You're familiar with plastic water bottles?"

"Of course."

"They're a lot thinner now than they used to be."

Bond took his word for it.

"It's called 'lightweighting.' Much easier to compact. You see, generally the products themselves aren't the problem when it comes to discard. It's *packaging* that causes most of the volume. Discard was easily handled until we shifted to a consumer manufacturing society and started to mass-produce goods. How to get the products into the hands of the people? Encase it in polystyrene foam, put that in a cardboard box and then, for God's sake, put *that* in a plastic carrier bag to take home with you. Ah, and if it's a present, let's wrap it up in colored paper and ribbon! Christmas is an absolute hurricane of discard."

Standing tall, looking over his empire, Hydt continued: "Most waste plants extend over fifty to seventy-five acres. Ours here is a hundred. I have three others in South Africa and dozens of transfer stations, where the carters—the lorries you see on the streets—take all the discard for compacting and shipment to treatment depots. I was the first to set up transfer stations in the South African squatters' camps. In six months the countryside was sixty to seventy percent cleaner. Plastic carrier bags used to be called 'South Africa's national flower.' Not anymore. I've dealt with that."

"I saw the lorries bringing rubbish from Pretoria and Port Elizabeth to the yard here. Why from so far away?"

"Specialized material," Hydt said dismissively.

Were those substances particularly dangerous? Bond wondered.

His host continued, "But you must get your vocabulary right, Theron. We call wet discard 'garbage'—leftover food, for instance. 'Trash' means dry materials, like cardboard and dust and tins. What the bin collectors pick up from in front of homes and offices is 'municipal solid waste,' or 'MSW.' That's also called 'refuse' or 'rubbish.' 'C and D' is construction and demolition debris. Institutional, commercial and industrial waste is 'ICI.' The most inclusive term is 'waste' but I prefer 'discard.'"

He pointed east to the rear of the plant. "Everything that's not recyclable goes there, to the working face of the landfill, where it's buried in layers of plastic lining to keep bacteria and pollution from leaching into the ground. You can spot it by looking for the birds."

Bond followed his gaze toward the swooping gulls.

"We call the landfill 'Disappearance Row.'"

Hydt led Bond to the doorway of a long building. Unlike the other work sheds here, this one had imposing doors, which were sealed. Bond peered through the windows. Workers were disassembling computers, hard drives, TVs, radios, pagers, mobile phones and printers. There were bins overflowing with batteries, lightbulbs, computer hard drives, printed circuit boards, wires and chips. The staff were wearing more protective clothing than any other employees—respirators, heavy gloves and goggles or full face masks.

"Our e-waste department. We call this area 'Silicon Row.' E-waste accounts for more than ten percent of the deadly substances on earth. Heavy metals, lithium from batteries. Take computers and mobiles. They have a life expectancy of two or three years at most, so people just throw them out. Have you ever read the warning booklet that comes with your laptop or phone, 'Dispose of properly'?" He smiled.

"Not really."

"Of course not. No one does. But pound for pound computers and phones are the most deadly waste on earth. In China, they just bury or burn them. They're killing their population by doing that. I'm starting a new operation to address this situation—separating the components of computers at my clients' companies and then disposing of them properly."

Bond recalled the device he'd seen demonstrated at al-Fulan's, the one near to the compactor that had taken Yusuf Nasad's life.

"In a few years that will be my most lucrative operation." Hydt then pointed, with a long yellow fingernail. "And at the back of this building there is the

Dangerous-Materials Recovery department. One of our biggest moneymaking services. We handle everything from paint to motor oil to arsenic to polonium."

"Polonium?" Bond gave a cool laugh. This was the radioactive material that had been used to kill the Russian spy Alexander Litvinenko, an expatriate in London, a few years ago. It was one of the most toxic substances on earth. "It's just thrown out? That has to be illegal."

"Ah, but that's the thing about discard, Theron. People throw away an innocent-looking antistatic machine . . . that just happens to contain polonium. But nobody knows that."

He led Bond past a car park where several lorries stood, each about twenty feet long. On the side was the company name and logo, along with the words SECURE DOCUMENT DESTRUCTION SERVICES.

Hydt followed Bond's gaze and said, "Another of our specialties. We lease shredders to companies and government offices but smaller outfits would rather hire us to do it for them. Did you know that when the Iranian students took over the American embassy in the nineteen seventies, they were able to reassemble classified CIA documents that had been shredded? They learned the identities of most of the covert agents there. Local weavers did the work."

Everyone in the intelligence community knew this but Bond feigned surprise.

"At Green Way we perform DIN industrial standard level-six shredding. Basically, our machines turn the documents to dust. Even the most secret government installations hire us."

He then led Bond to the largest building on the

plant, three stories high and two hundred yards long. A continuous string of lorries rolled in through one door and came out through another. "The main recycling facility. We call *this* area 'Resurrection Row.'"

They stepped inside. Three huge devices were being fed an endless stream of paper, cardboard, plastic bottles, polystyrene, scrap metal, wood and hundreds of other items. "The sorters," Hydt shouted. The noise was deafening. At the far end, the separated materials were being packed into lorries for onward shipment—tins, glass, plastic, paper.

"Recycling's a curious business," Hydt yelled. "Only a few products—metals and glass, mostly—can be recycled indefinitely. Everything else breaks down after a while and has to be burned or go to landfill. Aluminum's the only consistently profitable recyclable. Most products are far cheaper, cleaner and easier to make from raw materials than recycled ones. The extra lorries for transporting recycling materials and the recycling process itself add to fossil fuel pollution. And remanufacturing uses *more* power than the initial production, which is a drain on resources."

He laughed. "But it's politically correct to recycle . . . so people come to me."

Bond followed his tour guide outside and noticed Niall Dunne approaching on his long legs, his gait clumsy and feet turned outward. The fringe of blond hair hung down above his blue eyes, which were as still as pebbles. Putting aside the memory of Dunne's cruel treatment of the men in Serbia and his murder of al-Fulan's assistant in Dubai, Bond smiled amiably and shook his wide hand.

"Theron." Dunne nodded, his own visage not particularly welcoming. He looked at Hydt. "We should go." He seemed impatient.

Hydt motioned for Bond to get into a nearby Range Rover. He did so, sitting in the front passenger seat. He was aware of a sense of anticipation in the two men, as if some plan had been made and was now about to unfurl. His sixth sense told him something had perhaps gone awry. Had they discovered his identity? Had he given something away?

As the other men climbed in, with the unsmiling Dunne taking the wheel, Bond reflected that if ever there was a place to dispose of a body clandestinely, this was it.

Disappearance Row . . .

Chapter 46

The Range Rover bounded east along a wide dirt road, passing squat lorries with massive ribbed wheels, carrying bales or containers of refuse. It passed a wide chasm, at least eighty feet deep.

Bond looked down. The lorries were dropping their loads, and bulldozers were compacting them against the face of the landfill site. The bottom of the pit was lined with thick dark sheets. Hydt had been right about the seagulls. They were everywhere, thousands of them. The sheer number, the screams, the frenzy, were unsettling and Bond felt a shiver trickle up his spine.

As they drove on, Hydt pointed to the flames Bond had seen earlier. Here, much closer, they were giant spheres of fire—he could feel their heat. "The landfill produces methane," Hydt said. "We drill down and extract it to power the generators, though there's usually too much gas and we have to burn some off. If we didn't, the entire landfill site could blow up. That happened in America not too long ago. Hundreds of people were injured."

After fifteen minutes, they passed through a dense row of trees and a gate. Bond barked an involuntary laugh. The wasteland of the rubbish tips had vanished. Surrounding them now was an astonishingly beautiful scene: trees, flowers, rock formations, paths, ponds, forest. The meticulously landscaped grounds extended for several miles.

"We call it Elysian Fields. Paradise . . . after our time in hell. And yet it's a landfill too. Underneath us there is nearly a hundred feet of discard. We've reclaimed the land. In a year or so I'll open it to the public. My gift to South Africa. Decay resurrected into beauty."

Bond was not an aficionado of botany—his customary reaction to the Chelsea Flower Show was irritation at the traffic problems it caused around his home—but he had to admit that these gardens were impressive. He found himself squinting at some tree roots.

Hydt noticed. "Do they seem a little odd?"

They were metal tubes, painted to look like roots.

"Those pipes transport the methane generated under here to be burned off or to the power plants."

He supposed this detail had been thought up by Hydt's star engineer.

They drove on into a grove of trees and parked. A blue crane, the South African national bird, stood regally in a pond nearby, perfectly balanced on one leg.

"Come on, Theron. Let's talk business."

Why here? Bond wondered, as he followed Hydt down a path, along which small signs identified the plants. Again he wondered if the men had plans for him and he looked, futilely, for possible weapons and escape routes.

Hydt stopped and looked back. Bond did too—and felt a jolt of alarm. Dunne was approaching, carrying a rifle.

Outwardly Bond remained calm. ("You wear your

cover to the grave," the lecturers at Fort Monckton would tell their students.)

"You shoot long guns?" Dunne displayed the hunting rifle, with its black plastic or carbon-fiber stock, brushed steel receiver and barrel.

"I do, yes." Bond had been captain of the shooting team at Fettes and had won competitions in both small and full bore. He'd also won the Queen's Medal for Shooting Excellence when in the Royal Naval Reserve—the only shooting medal that can be worn in uniform. He glanced down at what Dunne held. "Winchester two-seventy."

"Good gun, wouldn't you agree?"

"It is. I prefer that caliber to the thirty ought-six. Flatter trajectory."

Hydt asked, "Do you shoot game, Theron?"

"Never had much opportunity."

Hydt laughed. "I don't hunt either . . . except for one species." The smile faded. "Niall and I have been discussing you."

"Have you now?" Bond asked, his tone blasé.

"We've decided you might be a valuable addition to certain *other* projects we're working on now. But we need a show of faith."

"Money?" Bond was stalling; he believed he understood his enemy's purpose here and needed a response. Fast.

"No," Hydt said softly, the huge head turning Bond's way. "That's not what I mean."

Dunne stepped forward, the Winchester on his hip, muzzle skyward. "All right. Bring him out."

Two workers in security uniforms led a skinny man

in a T-shirt and shabby khaki trousers from behind a thick stand of jacaranda. The man's face was a mask of terror.

Hydt regarded him with contempt. He said to Bond, "This man broke into our property and was trying to steal mobile phones from the e-waste operation. When he was approached he pulled a gun and shot at a guard. He missed and was overpowered. I've checked his records and he's an escaped convict. In prison for rape and murder. I could turn him over to the authorities but his appearance here today has given me—and you—an opportunity."

"What are you talking about?"

"You are being given a chance to make your first kill as a hunter. If you shoot this man—"

"No!" the captive cried.

"If you kill him, that's all the down payment I need. We'll proceed with your project and I'll hire you to help me with others. If you choose not to kill him, which I would certainly understand, Niall will drive you back to the front gate and we will part ways. As tempting as your offer is, to cleanse the killing fields, I'll have to decline."

"Shoot a man in cold blood?"

Dunne said, "The decision's yours. Don't shoot him. Leave." The brogue seemed harsher.

But what a chance this was to get into the inner sanctum of Severan Hydt! Bond could learn everything about Gehenna. One life versus thousands.

And how many more would die if, as seemed likely, the event on Friday was only the first of other such projects?

He stared at the criminal's dark face, eyes wide, hands shaking at his sides.

Bond glanced at Dunne. He strode forward and took the rifle.

"No, please!" the man cried.

The guards shoved him on to his knees and stepped away. The man stared at Bond, who realized for the first time that, in firing squads, the blindfold wasn't for the condemned's benefit; it was for the *executioners,* so they didn't have to look into the prisoner's eyes.

"Please, no, sir!" the man cried.

"There's a round in the chamber," Dunne called. "Safety's on."

Had they slipped a blank in to test him? Or had Dunne not loaded the rifle at all? The thief clearly wasn't wearing a bulletproof vest under the thin T-shirt. Bond hefted the gun, which had open sights only, not telescopic. He assessed the thief, forty feet away, and aimed at him. The man raised his hands to cover his face. "No! Please!"

"You want to move closer?" Hydt asked.

"No. But I don't want him to suffer," Bond said matter-of-factly. "Does the rifle shoot high or low at this range?"

"I couldn't tell you," Dunne said.

Bond aimed toward the right, at a leaf that was about the same distance as the captive. He squeezed the trigger. There was a sharp crack and a hole appeared in the center of the leaf, just where he was aiming. Bond worked the bolt, ejecting the spent shell and chambering another. Still, he hesitated.

"What's it to be, Theron?" Hydt whispered.

Bond lifted the gun, aiming steadily at the victim once again.

There was a moment's pause. He pulled the trigger. Another stunning crack and a red dot blossomed in the middle of the man's T-shirt as he fell backward into the dust.

Chapter 47

"So," Bond snapped, opening the rifle's bolt and tossing the weapon to Dunne. "Are you satisfied?"

The Irishman easily caught the weapon in his large hands. He remained as impassive as ever. He said nothing.

Hydt, however, seemed pleased.

He said, "Good. Now let us go to the office and have a drink to celebrate our partnership . . . and to allow me to apologize to you."

"For forcing me to kill a man."

"No, for forcing you to *believe* you were killing a man."

"What?"

"William!"

The man Bond had shot leaped to his feet with a big grin on his face.

Bond spun toward Hydt. "I—"

"Wax bullets," Dunne called. "Police use them in training, filmmakers use them in action scenes."

"It was a goddamn test?"

"Which our friend Niall here devised. It was a good one and you passed."

"You think I'm a schoolboy? Go to hell." Bond turned and stormed toward the garden's gate.

"Wait—wait." Hydt was walking after him, frowning. "We're businesspeople. This is what we do. We must make certain."

Bond spat an obscenity and continued down the path, his fists clenching and unclenching.

Urgently Hydt said, "You can keep going. But please know, Theron, you're walking away not only from me but from one million dollars, which will be yours tomorrow if you stay. And there will be much more."

Bond stopped. He turned.

"Let us go back to the office and talk. Let us be professional."

Bond looked at the man he'd shot, who was still grinning happily. He asked Hydt, "A million?"

Hydt nodded. "Yours tomorrow."

Bond remained where he was for a moment, staring across the gardens, which were truly magnificent. Then he walked back to Hydt, casting a cool glance at Niall Dunne, who was unloading the rifle and cleaning it carefully, caressing the metal parts.

Bond tried to keep an indignant look on his face, playing the role of offended party.

And fiction it was, for he'd figured out about the wax bullets. Nobody who's fired a gun with a normal load of gunpowder and a lead bullet would be fooled by a wax round, which produces far less recoil than a real slug (giving a blank round to a soldier in a firing squad is absurd; he clearly knows his bullet is not real the minute he shoots). A few moments ago Bond had been given the clue when the "thief" covered his eyes. People about to be shot don't shield anything with their hands. So, Bond had reflected, he's afraid of being blinded, not killed. That suggested that the bullets were blank or wax.

He'd fired into the foliage to judge the recoil and

learned from the very light kick that these were non-lethal rounds.

He guessed that the man would earn hazard pay for his efforts. Hydt seemed to take care of his employees, whatever else one could say about him. This was confirmed now. Hydt peeled off some rand and gave them to the man, who walked up to Bond and pumped his hand. "Hey, mister, sir! You a good shot. You got me in a blessed spot. Look, right here!" He tapped his chest. "One man shot me down below, you know where. He was bastard. Oh, that hurt and hurt for days. An' my lady, she complain much."

In the Range Rover once more, the three men drove in silence back to the plant, the beautiful gardens giving way to harrowing Disappearance Row, the cacophony of the gulls, the fumes.

Gehenna . . .

Dunne parked at the main building, nodded to Bond and told Hydt, "Our associates? I'll meet the flights. They're arriving around nineteen hundred hours. I'll get them settled and then come back."

So, Dunne and Hydt would be working into the night. Did that bode well or badly for any future reconnaissance at Green Way? One thing was clear: Bond had to get inside Research and Development now.

Dunne strode away, while Hydt and Bond continued to the building. "You going to give me a tour here?" Bond asked Hydt. "It's warmer . . . and there aren't as many seagulls."

Hydt laughed. "There isn't much to see. We'll just go to my office." He didn't, however, spare his new partner the procedures at the backdoor security post—though the guards missed the inhaler again. As they stepped into the main corridor, Bond noted again the sign to Research and Development. He lowered his voice. "Well, I wouldn't mind a tour of the toilet."

"That way." Hydt pointed, then pulled out his mobile to make a call. Bond walked quickly down the corridor. He entered the empty men's room, grabbed a large handful of paper towels and tossed them into one of the toilets. When he flushed, the paper jammed in the drain. He went to the door and looked toward where Hydt was waiting. The man's head was down and he was concentrating on his call. There was no CCTV, Bond saw, so he walked away from Hydt, planning his cover story.

Oh, one cubicle was occupied and the other was jammed so I went for another one. Didn't want to bother you when you were on the phone.

Plausible deniability . . .

Bond remembered where he'd seen the sign when he'd entered. He now hurried down a deserted hallway.

RESEARCH AND DEVELOPMENT.
RESTRICTED

The metal security door was operated by a number pad, in conjunction with a key-card reader. Bond palmed the inhaler and took several pictures, including close-ups of the pad.

Come on, he urged an unsuspecting confederate inside the room—someone must be thinking about a visit to the loo or fetching some coffee from the canteen.

But no one cooperated. The door remained shut

and Bond decided he had to get back to Hydt. He turned on his heel and hurried down the corridor again. Thank God, Hydt was still on his mobile. He looked up when Bond was past the bathroom door; to Hydt's mind he had just exited.

He disconnected. "Come this way, Theron."

He led Bond down a corridor and into a large room that seemed to serve as both an office and living quarters. A huge desk faced a picture window, with a view of Hydt's wasteland empire. A bedroom, curiously, was off to the side. Bond noticed that the bed was unmade. Hydt diverted him away from it and closed the door. He gestured Bond to a sofa and coffee table in a corner.

"Drink?"

"Whisky. Scotch. Not a blend."

"Auchentoshan?"

Bond knew the distillery, outside Glasgow. "Good. A splash of water."

Hydt tipped a generous quantity into a glass, added the water and handed it to him. He poured himself a glass of South African Constantia. Bond knew the honey-sweet wine, a recently revived version of Napoleon's favorite drink. The deposed emperor had had hundreds of gallons shipped to St. Helena, where he spent his last years in exile. He had sipped it on his deathbed.

The gloomy room was filled with antiques. Mary Goodnight was forever reporting excitedly on bargains she'd found in London's Portobello Road market but none of the items in Hydt's office looked as if they'd fetch much money there; they were scuffed, battered, lopsided. Old photographs, paintings and bas-reliefs hung on the walls. Slabs of stone showed fading images of Greek and Roman gods and goddesses, though Bond couldn't tell who they were supposed to be.

Hydt sat and they tipped their glasses toward one another. Hydt gazed affectionately at the walls. "Most of these have come from buildings my companies demolished. To me, they're like relics from the bodies of saints. Which also interest me, by the way. I own several—though that is a fact that no one in Rome is aware of." He caressed his wine glass. "Whatever is old or discarded gives me comfort. I couldn't tell you why. Nor do I care to know. I think, Theron, most people waste far too much time wondering why they are as they are. Accept your nature and satisfy it. I love decay, decline . . . the things others shun." He paused, then asked, "Would you like to know how I got started in this business? It's an informative story."

"Yes, please."

"I had some difficult times in my youth. Ah, who didn't, of course? But I was forced to start work young. It happened to be at a rubbish collection company. I was a London binman. One day my mates and I were having tea, taking a break, when the driver pointed to a flat over the road. He said, 'That's where one of those blokes with the Clerkenwell crowd lives.'"

Clerkenwell: perhaps the biggest and most successful organized-crime syndicate in British history. It was now largely dismantled but for twenty years its members had brutally ruled their turf around Islington. They were reportedly responsible for twenty-five murders.

Hydt continued, his dark eyes sparkling, "I was intrigued. After tea we continued on our rounds but without the others knowing I hid the rubbish from *that* flat nearby. I went back at night and collected the bag, brought it home and went through it. I did that for weeks. I examined every letter, every tin, every bill, every condom wrapper. Most of it was useless. But I found one thing that was interesting. A note with an address in East London. 'Here,' was all it said. But I had an idea what it meant. Now, in those days I was supplementing my income as a detectorist. You know about them? Those folks who walk along the beach at Brighton or Eastbourne and find coins and rings in the sand after the tourists have gone for the day. I had a good metal detector and so the next weekend I went to the property mentioned in the note. As I'd expected it was a vacant lot." Hydt was animated, enjoying himself. "It took me ten minutes to find the buried gun. I bought a fingerprint kit and, though I was no expert, it seemed that the prints on the gun and the note matched. I didn't know exactly what the gun had been used for but—"

"But why bury it if it hadn't been used to murder somebody?"

"Exactly. I went to see the Clerkenwell man. I told him that my solicitor had the gun and the note—there was no solicitor, of course, but I bluffed well. I said if I didn't call him in an hour he would send everything to Scotland Yard. Was it a gamble? Of course. But a calculated one. The man blanched and immediately asked me what I wanted. I named a figure. He paid in cash. I was on my way to opening a small collection company of my own. It eventually became Green Way."

"That gives a whole new meaning to the word 're-cycling,' doesn't it?"

"Indeed." Hydt seemed amused by the comment. He sipped his wine and gazed out at the grounds, the spheres of the burn-off flames glowing in the distance. "Did you know that there were three man-made phenomena you could see from outer space? The Great Wall of China, the Pyramids . . . and the old Fresh Kills landfill on Staten Island."

Bond did not.

"To me discard is more than a business," Hydt said. "It's a window onto our society . . . and into our souls." He sat forward. "You see, we may *acquire* something in life unintentionally—through a gift, neglect, inheritance, fate, error, greed, laziness—but when we discard something, it's almost always with cold intent."

He took a judicious sip of wine. "Theron, do you know what entropy is?"

"No, I don't."

"Entropy," said Hydt, clicking his long, yellow nails, "is the essential truth of nature. It's the tendency toward decay and disorder—in physics, in society, in art, in living creatures . . . in everything. It's the path to anarchy." He smiled. "That sounds pessimistic but it isn't. It's the most wonderful thing in the world. You can never go wrong by embracing the truth. And truth it is."

His eyes settled on a bas-relief. "I changed my name, you know."

"I didn't," Bond said, thinking: Maarten Holt.

"I changed it because my surname was my father's and my given name was selected by him. I wished to have no more connection with him." A cool smile.

"That lovely childhood I was mentioning. I chose 'Hydt' because it echoed the dark side of the protagonist in *Dr. Jekyll and Mr. Hyde,* which I'd read at school and enjoyed. You see, I believe we all have a public side and a dark side. The book confirmed that."

"And 'Severan'? It's unusual."

"You wouldn't think so if you'd lived in Rome in the second and third centuries A.D."

"No?"

"I read history and archaeology at university. Mention ancient Rome, Theron, and most people think of what? The Julio-Claudian line of emperors. Augustus, Tiberius, Caligula, Claudius and Nero. At least they think so if they read *I, Claudius* or saw Derek Jacobi in brilliant form on the BBC. But that whole line lasted a pathetically short time—slightly over a hundred years. Yes, yes, *mare nostrum,* Praetorian guards, films starring Russell Crowe . . . all very decadent and dramatic. 'My God, Caligula, that's your *sister!*' But for me, the truth of Rome was revealed much later in a different family line, the Severan emperors, founded by Septimius Severus many years after Nero killed himself. You see, they presided over the *decay* of the empire. Their reign culminated in what historians called the Period of Anarchy."

"Entropy," Bond said.

"*Exactly.*" Hydt beamed. "I'd seen a statue of Septimius Severus and I look a bit like him so I took his family name." He focused on Bond. "Are you feeling uneasy, Theron? Don't worry. You haven't signed on with Ahab. I'm not mad."

Bond laughed. "I wasn't thinking you were. Honestly. I was thinking about the million dollars you mentioned."

"Of course." He studied Bond closely. "Tomorrow the first of a number of projects I'm engaged in will come to fruition. My main partners will be here. You will come too. Then you'll see what we're about."

"For a million, what do you want me to do?" He frowned. "Shoot somebody with *real* bullets?"

Hydt fondled his beard again. He did indeed resemble a Roman emperor. "You don't need to do anything tomorrow. That project is finished. We'll just be watching the results. And celebrating, I hope. We'll call your million a signature bonus. After that, you'll be very busy."

Bond forced himself to smile. "I'm pleased to be included."

Just then Hydt's mobile rang. He looked at the screen, rose and turned away. Bond guessed there was some difficulty. Hydt didn't get angry but his stillness indicated he wasn't happy. He disconnected. "I'm sorry. A problem in Paris. Inspectors. Trade unions. It's a Green Way issue, nothing to do with tomorrow's project."

Bond didn't want to make the man suspicious so he backed off. "All right. What time do you want me?"

"Ten A.M."

Recalling the original intercept that GCHQ had decrypted and the clues he'd found up in March about the time the attack would take place, Bond understood he would have about twelve hours to find out what Gehenna was about and stop it.

A figure appeared in the doorway. It was Jessica Barnes, wearing what seemed to be her typical garb:

a black skirt and modest white shirt. Bond had never liked women to wear excessive makeup but he wondered again why she didn't use even the minimum.

"Jessica, this is Gene Theron," Hydt said absently. He'd forgotten they'd met last night.

The woman didn't remind him.

Bond took her hand. She returned a timid nod. Then she said to Hydt, "The ad proofs didn't come in. They won't be here till tomorrow."

"You can review them then, can't you?"

"Yes, but there's nothing more to do here. I was thinking I'd like to go back to Cape Town."

"Something's come up. I'll be a few hours, maybe more. You can wait. . . ." His eyes strayed to the door behind which Bond had seen the bed.

She hesitated. "All right." A sigh.

Bond said, "I'm going back into town. I can drive you if you like."

"Really? It's not too much trouble?" Her question, however, was not directed toward Bond but to Hydt.

The man was scrolling through his mobile. He looked up. "Good of you, Theron. I'll see you tomorrow."

They shook hands.

"*Totsiens*." Bond gave the Afrikaans farewell, which he knew courtesy of the Captain Bheka Jordaan School of Language.

"What time will you be home, Severan?" Jessica asked Hydt.

"When I get there," he responded absently, punching a number into his phone.

Five minutes later Jessica and Bond were at the front security post, where he again passed through the metal detector. But before he was reunited with his gun and mobile, a guard walked up and said, "What is that, sir? I see something in your pocket."

The inhaler. How the hell had he spotted the slight bulge in the windbreaker? "It's nothing."

"I'll see it, please."

"I'm not stealing anything from a junkyard," he snapped, "if that's what you're thinking."

Patiently the man said, "Our rules are very clear, sir. I'll see it or I have to call Mr. Dunne or Mr. Hydt."

Follow your cover to the grave. . . .

With a steady hand Bond withdrew the black plastic tube and displayed it. "It's medicine."

"Is it now?" The man took the device and examined it closely. The camera lens was recessed but, to Bond, seemed all too obvious. The guard was about to hand it back but then changed his mind. He lifted the hinged cap, exposed the plunger and put his thumb on it.

Bond eyed his Walther, sitting in one of the cubbyholes. It was ten feet away and separated from him by the two other guards, both armed.

The guard pressed the plunger . . . and released a fine mist of denatured alcohol into the air near his face.

Sanu Hirani, of course, had created the toy with typical forethought. The spray mechanism was real, even if the chemical inside was not; the camera was located in the *lower* part of the base. The smell of the alcohol was strong. The guard wrinkled his nose and his eyes were watering as he handed back the device. "Thank you, sir. I hope you need not take that medicine often. It seems quite unpleasant."

Without replying, Bond pocketed the inhaler and received his weapon and phone.

He headed toward the front door, which opened on to the no man's land between the two fences. He was almost outside when an alarm klaxon blared fiercely and lights began to flash.

Chapter 48

Bond was a split second away from spinning around, dropping into a combat shooting stance and drawing down on priority targets.

But instinct told him to hold back.

It was a good thing he did. The guards weren't even looking at him. They had gone back to watching the TV.

Bond glanced casually around. The alarm had gone off because Jessica, exempt from security procedures, had come through the metal detector with her handbag and jewelry. A guard casually flicked a switch to reset the unit.

His heartbeat returning to normal, Bond continued outside with Jessica, through the next security post and out into the car park, filled with curled brown leaves blowing in the light wind. Bond opened the passenger door of the Subaru for her, then got into the driver's seat and started the engine. They drove along the dusty road toward the N7, amid the ever-present Green Way lorries.

For a while Bond said nothing but then, subtly, he went to work. He started with innocuous questions, easing her into talking to him. Did she like to travel? Which were her favorite restaurants here? What was her job at Green Way?

Then he asked, "I'm curious—how did you two meet?"

"You really want to know?"

"Tell me."

"I was a beauty queen when I was young."

"Really? I've never met one before." He smiled.

"I didn't do too badly. I was in the Miss America Pageant once. But what really . . ." She blushed. "No, it's silly."

"Please. Go on."

"Well, once I was competing in New York, at the Waldorf-Astoria. It was before the pageant and a lot of us girls were in the lobby. Jackie Kennedy saw me and she came up to me and said how pretty she thought I was." She glowed with a pride he had not seen in her face. "That was one of the high points of my life. She was my idol when I was a little girl." The smile tempered. "You don't really want to know this, do you?"

"I asked."

"Well, you can only go on for so long, of course, in the pageant world. After I stopped the circuit, I did some commercials and then infomercials. Then, well, those jobs dried up too. A few years later my mother passed away—I was very close to her—and I went through a rough time. I got a job as a hostess in a restaurant in New York. Severan was doing some business nearby and he'd come in to meet clients. We got to talking. He was so fascinating. He loves history and he's traveled everywhere. We talked about a thousand different things.

"We had such a connection. It was very . . . refreshing. In the pageants, I used to joke that life isn't even skin-deep; it's *makeup*-deep. That's all people see. Makeup and clothes. Severan saw some depth in me,

I guess. We hit it off. He asked for my number and kept calling. Well, I wasn't a stupid woman. I was fifty-seven years old, no family, very little money. And here was a handsome man . . . a *vital* man."

Bond wondered if that meant what he suspected it might.

Sat-nav instructed him to leave the highway. He drove carefully along a congested road. The minibus taxis were everywhere. Tow trucks waited at intersections, apparently to be the first at the site of an accident. People sold drinks by the roadside; impromptu businesses operated from the backs of lorries and vans. Several were doing a booming trade selling batteries and performing alternator repairs. Why did that malady plague South African vehicles in particular?

Now that he had broken yet more ice, Bond asked casually about the meeting tomorrow but she said she knew nothing about it and he believed her. Frustratingly to Bond, it seemed that Hydt kept her in the dark about Gehenna and any other illegal activities he, Dunne or the company were involved in.

They were five minutes from their destination, the sat-nav reported, when Bond said, "I have to be honest. It's odd."

"What is?"

"Just how he surrounds himself with it all."

"All of what?" Jessica asked, her eyes on him closely.

"Decay, destruction."

"Well, it's his business."

"I don't mean his work with Green Way. That I understand. I'm speaking of his *personal* interest with the old, the used . . . the discarded."

Jessica said nothing for a moment. She pointed

ahead to a large wooden private residence, surrounded by an imposing stone fence. "That's it, the house. That's—"

Her voice choked and she began to cry.

Bond pulled to the curb. "Jessica, what's the matter?"

"I . . ." Her breathing was coming fast.

"Are you all right?" He reached down and pulled the adjustment lever, moving the seat back, so he could turn to face her.

"It's nothing, oh, nothing. How embarrassing is this?"

Bond took her handbag and dug around inside for a tissue. He found one and handed it to her.

"Thank you." She tried to speak, then surrendered to her sobs. When she had calmed, she tilted the rearview mirror toward herself. "He doesn't let me wear makeup—so at least my mascara hasn't run and turned me into a clown."

"Doesn't let you . . . What do you mean?"

The confession died on her lips. "Nothing," Jessica whispered.

"Was it something I said? I'm sorry if I've upset you. I was just making conversation."

"No, no, it's nothing you've done, Gene."

"Tell me what's wrong." His eyes locked with hers.

She debated a moment. "I wasn't being honest with you. I put on a good show but it's all a façade. We don't have a connection. We never have. He wants me . . ." She raised her hand. "Oh, you don't want to hear this."

Bond touched her arm. "Please, I'm responsible in some way. I was just blundering along. I feel the fool. Tell me."

"Yes, he loves the old . . . the used, the discarded. *Me*."

"My God, no. I didn't mean—"

"I know you didn't. But that *is* what Severan wants me for—because I'm part of the downward spiral too. I'm his laboratory for fading, for aging, for decay.

"That's all I mean to him. He hardly talks to me, ever. I've got almost no idea what goes on in that mind of his and he has no interest in finding out who I am. He gives me credit cards, takes me nice places, provides for me. In return he . . . well, he watches me age. I'll catch him staring at me, a new wrinkle here, an age spot there. That's why I can't wear makeup. He leaves the lights on when . . . you know what I mean. Do you know how humiliating that is for me? He knows it too. Because humiliation is another form of decay."

She laughed bitterly, dabbing her eyes with the tissue. "And the irony, Gene? The goddamn irony? When I was young I lived for beauty pageants. Nobody cared about who I was inside, the judges, my fellow contestants . . . even my mother. Now I'm old and Severan doesn't care about who I am inside either. There are times when I hate being with him. But what can I do? I'm powerless."

Bond applied a bit more pressure to her arm. "That's not true. You're not powerless at all. Being older is strength. It's experience, judgment, discernment, knowing your resources. Youth is mistake and impulse. Believe me, I know that quite well."

"But without him what could I do—where would I go?"

"Anywhere. You could do whatever you wanted. You're obviously clever. You must have some money."

"Some. But it's not about money. It's about finding someone at my age."

"Why do you need someone?"

"Spoken like a young man."

"And *that*'s spoken like someone who believes what she's been told, rather than thinking for herself."

Jessica gave a faint smile. "Touché, Gene." She patted his hand. "You've been very kind and I can't believe I had a meltdown with a total stranger. Please, I've got to get inside. He'll be calling to check up on me." She gestured at the house.

Bond drove forward and pulled up to the gate, under the watchful eye of a security guard—which put to rest his plan to get inside the house and see what secrets lay there. Jessica gripped his hand in both of hers, then climbed out.

"I will see you tomorrow?" he asked. "At the plant?"

A faint smile. "Yes, I'll be there. My leash is pretty short." She turned and walked quickly through the opening gate.

Then Bond shoved the car into first and skidded away, Jessica Barnes vanishing instantly from his thoughts. His attention was on his next destination and what would greet him there.

Friend or foe?

In his chosen profession, though, James Bond had learned that those two categories were not mutually exclusive.

Chapter 49

All Thursday morning, all afternoon there had been talk of threats.

Threats from the North Koreans, threats from the Taliban, threats from al-Qaeda, the Chechnyans, the Islamic Jihad Brotherhood, eastern Malaysia, Sudan, Indonesia. There'd been a brief discussion about the Iranians; despite the surreal rhetoric issuing from their presidential palace, nobody took them too seriously. M almost felt sorry for the poor regime in Tehran. Persia had once been such a great empire.

Threats . . .

But the actual assault, he thought wryly, was occurring only now, during a tea break at the security conference. M disconnected from Moneypenny and sat back stiffly in the well-worn gilt drawing room of a building in Richmond Terrace, between Whitehall and the Victoria Embankment. It was one of those utterly unremarkable fading structures of indeterminate age in which the sweat work of governing a country is done.

The impending assault involved two ministers who sat on the Joint Intelligence Committee. Their heads were now poking through the door, side by side, bespectacled faces scanning the room until they spotted their target. Once an image of television's Two Ronnies had sidled into his head, M could not dislodge it. As they strode forward, however, there was nothing comedic about their expressions.

"Miles," the older one greeted him. "Sir Andrew" prefaced the man's surname and those two words were in perfect harmony with his distinguished face and silver mane.

The other, Bixton, tipped his head, whose fleshy dome reflected light from the dusty chandelier. He was breathing hard. In fact, they both were.

M didn't invite them to sit but they did anyway, upon the Edwardian sofa across from the tea tray. He longed to remove a cheroot from his attaché case and chew on it but he decided against the prop.

"We'll come straight to the point," Sir Andrew said.

"We know you have to get back to the security conference," Bixton interjected.

"We've just been with the foreign secretary. He's in the chamber at the moment."

That explained their heaving chests. They couldn't have driven up from the House of Commons, since Whitehall, from Horse Guards Avenue to just past King Charles Street, had been sealed, like a submarine about to dive, so that the security conference might meet, well, securely.

"Incident Twenty?" M asked.

"Just so," Bixton said. "We're trying to track down the DG of Six, as well, but this bloody conference . . ." He was new to Joint Intelligence and appeared suddenly to realize perhaps he shouldn't be quite so bluntly birching the rears of those who paid him.

". . . is bloody disruptive," M grumbled, filling

in. He had no problem whipping anyone or anything when it was deserved.

Sir Andrew took over. He said, "Defense Intelligence and GCHQ are reporting a swell of SIGINT in Afghanistan over the past six hours."

"General consensus is that it's to do with Incident Twenty."

M asked, "Anything specific to Hydt—Noah—or thousands of deaths? Niall Dunne? Army bases in March? Improvised explosive devices? Engineers in Dubai? Rubbish and recycling facilities in Cape Town?" M read every signal that crossed his desk or arrived in his mobile phone.

"We can't tell, can we?" Bixton answered. "The Doughnut hasn't broken the codes yet." GCHQ's headquarters in Cheltenham was built in the shape of a fat ring. "The encryption packages are brand spanking new. Which has stymied everyone."

"SIGINT is cyclical over there," M muttered dismissively. He had been very, very senior at MI6 and had earned a reputation for unparalleled skill at mining intelligence and, more important, *refining* it into something useful.

"True," Sir Andrew agreed. "Rather too coincidental, though, that all these calls and e-mails have popped up just now, the day before Incident Twenty, wouldn't you think?"

Not necessarily.

He continued, "And nobody's turned up *anything* that specifically links Hydt to the threat."

"Nobody" translated to "007."

M looked at his wristwatch, which had belonged to his son, a soldier with the Royal Regiment of Fusiliers. The security meeting was set to resume in a half hour. He was exhausted, and Friday, tomorrow, would be an even longer session, culminating in a tiresome dinner followed by a speech by the home secretary.

Sir Andrew noted the less-than-subtle glance at the battered timepiece: "Long story short, Miles, the JIC is of the opinion that this Severan Hydt fellow in South Africa's a diversion. Maybe he's involved but he's not a key player in Incident Twenty. Five and Six's people think the real actors are in Afghanistan and that's where the attack will happen: military or aid workers, contractors."

Of course, that was what they would *say*—whatever they actually *thought*. The adventure in Kabul had cost billions of pounds and far too many lives; the more evil that could be found there to justify the incursion, the better. M had been aware of this from the beginning of the Incident 20 operation.

"Now, Bond—"

"He's good, we know that," Bixton interrupted, eyeing the chocolate biscuits M had asked not to be brought with the tea but had arrived anyway.

Sir Andrew frowned.

"It's just that he hasn't actually found much," Bixton went on. "Unless there've been details that haven't yet circulated."

M said nothing, merely regarded both men with equal frost.

Sir Andrew said, "Bond *is* a star, of course. So the thinking is that it would be good for everybody if he deployed to Kabul posthaste. Tonight, if you could make that work. Put him in a hot zone along with a couple of dozen of Six's premier-league lads. We'll tap the CIA too. We don't mind spreading the glory."

And the blame, thought M, if they get it wrong.

Bixton said, "Makes sense. Bond was stationed in Afghanistan."

M said, "Incident Twenty's supposed to happen tomorrow. It'll take him all night to get to Kabul. How can he stop anything happening?"

"The thinking is . . ." Sir Andrew fell silent, realizing, M supposed, that he'd repeated his own irritating verbal filler. "We aren't sure it *can* be stopped."

Silence washed in unpleasantly, like a tide polluted with hospital waste.

"Our approach would be for your man and the others to head up a postmortem analysis team. Try to find out for certain who was behind it. Put together a response proposal. Bond could even head it up."

M knew, of course, what was happening here: The Two Ronnies were offering the ODG a face-saving measure. Your organization could be a star 95 percent of the time but if you erred even once, with a big loss, you might appear at the office on Monday morning and find your whole outfit disbanded or, worse, turned into a vetting agency.

And the Overseas Development Group was on thin ice to start with, hosting as it did the 00 Section, to which many people objected. To stumble on Incident 20 would be a big stumble indeed. By getting Bond to Afghanistan forthwith, at least the ODG would have a player in the game, even if he arrived on the pitch a bit late.

M said evenly, "Your point is noted, gentlemen. Let me make some phone calls."

Bixton beamed. But Sir Andrew hadn't quite finished. His persistence, infused with shrewdness, was one of the reasons M believed that future audiences with him might take place at 10 Downing Street. "Bond will be all-hands-on-deck?"

The threat implicit in the question was that if 007 remained in South Africa in defiance of M's orders, Sir Andrew's protection of Bond, M and the ODG would cease.

The irony in giving an agent like 007 carte blanche was that he was *supposed* to exercise it and act as he saw fit—which sometimes meant he would *not* be on deck with all of the other hands. You can't have it both ways, M reflected. "As I said, I'll make some calls."

"Good. We'd better be off."

As they departed, M stood up and went through the French doors on to the balcony, where he noted a Metropolitan Police Specialist Protection officer, armed with a machine gun. After an examination of and a nod to the new arrival on his turf, the man returned to looking down over the street, thirty feet below. "All quiet?" M asked.

"Yes, sir."

M walked to the far end of the balcony and lit a cheroot, sucking the smoke in deep. The streets were eerily quiet. The barricades were not just the tubular metal fences you saw outside Parliament; they were cement blocks, four feet high, solid enough to stop a speeding car. The pavements were patrolled by armed guards and M noted several snipers on the roofs of nearby buildings. He gazed absently down Richmond Terrace toward Victoria Embankment.

He took out his mobile and called Moneypenny.

Only a single ring before she answered. "Yes, sir?"

"I need to talk to the chief of staff."

"He's popped down to the canteen. I'll connect you."

As he waited, M squinted and gave a gruff laugh. At the intersection, near the barricade, there was a large lorry and a few men were dragging bins to and from it. They were employees of Severan Hydt's company, Green Way International. He realized he'd been watching them for the past few minutes yet not actually noticing them. They'd been invisible.

"Tanner here, sir."

The dustmen vanished from M's thoughts. He plucked the cheroot from between his teeth and said evenly, "Bill, I need to talk to you about 007."

Chapter 50

Guided by sat-nav, Bond made his way through central Cape Town, past businesses and residences. He found himself in an area of small, brightly colored houses, blue, pink, red and yellow, tucked under Signal Hill. The narrow streets were largely cobbled. The area reminded him of villages in the Caribbean, with the difference that here careful Arabic designs patterned many homes. He passed a quiet mosque.

It was six thirty on this cool Thursday evening and he was en route to Bheka Jordaan's house.

Friend or foe . . .

He wound the car through the uneven streets and parked nearby. She met him at the door and greeted him with an unsmiling nod. She had shed her work clothing and wore blue jeans and a close-fitting dark red cardigan. Her shiny black hair hung loose and he was taken by the rich aura of lilac scent from a recent shampooing. "This is an interesting area," he said. "Nice."

"It's called Bo-Kaap. It used to be very poor, mostly Muslim, immigrants from Malaysia. I moved here with . . . well, with someone years ago. It was poorer then. Now the place is becoming very chic. There used to be only bicycles parked outside. Now it's Toyotas but soon it'll be Mercedes. I don't like that. I'd rather it was as it used to be. But it's my home. Besides, my sisters and I take turns to have Ugogo living with us and they're close so it's convenient."

"Ugogo?" Bond asked.

"It means 'grandmother.' Our mother's mother. My parents live in Pietermaritzburg, in KwaZulu-Natal, some way east of here."

Bond recalled the antique map in her office.

"So we look after Ugogo. That's the Zulu way."

She didn't invite him in, so, on the porch, Bond gave her an account of his trip to Green Way. "I need the film in this developed." He handed her the inhaler. "It's eight-millimeter, ISO is twelve hundred. Can you sort it?"

"Me? Not your MI6 associate?" she asked acerbically.

Bond felt no need to defend Gregory Lamb. "I trust him but he raided my minibar of two hundred rands' worth of drink. I'd like somebody with a clear head to handle it. Developing film can be tricky."

"I'll take care of it."

"Now, Hydt has some associates coming into town tonight. There's a meeting at the Green Way plant tomorrow morning." He thought back to what Dunne had said. "They're arriving at about seven. Can you find out their names?"

"Do you know the airlines?"

"No, but Dunne's meeting them."

"We'll put a stakeout in place. Kwalene is good at that. He jokes but he's very good."

He certainly is. Discreet, too, Bond reflected.

A woman's voice called from inside.

Jordaan turned her head. "*Ize balulekile.*"

Some more Zulu words were exchanged.

Jordaan's face was still. "Will you come in? So Ugogo can see you're not someone in a gang? I've told her it's no one. But she worries."

No one?

Bond followed her into the small flat, which was tidy and nicely furnished. Prints, hangings and photos decorated the walls.

The elderly woman who'd spoken to Jordaan was sitting at a large dining table set with two places. The meal had largely concluded. The woman was very frail. Bond recognized her as the woman in many of the pictures in Jordaan's office. She wore a loose orange and brown frock and slippers. Her gray hair was short. She started to rise.

"No, please," Bond said.

She stood anyway and, hunched, shuffled forward to shake his hand with a firm, dry grip.

"You are the Englishman Bheka spoke of. You don't look so bad to me."

Jordaan glared at her.

The older woman introduced herself: "I'm Mbali."

"James."

"I am going to rest. Bheka, give him some food. He's too thin."

"No, I must be going."

"You are hungry. I saw how you looked at the *bobotie*. It tastes even better than it looks."

Bond smiled. He *had* been looking at the pot on the stove.

"My granddaughter is a very good cook. You will like it. And you will have some Zulu beer. Have you ever had any?"

"I've had Birkenhead and Gilroy."

"No, Zulu beer is the best." Mbali shot a look at her granddaughter. "Give him some beer and he will have some food too. Bring him a plate of *bobotie*. And *sambal* sauce." She looked critically at Bond. "You like spice?"

"I do, yes."

"Good."

Exasperated, Jordaan said, "Ugogo, he said he has to be going."

"He said that because of you. Give him some beer and some food. Look how thin he is!"

"Honestly, Ugogo."

"That's my granddaughter. A mind of her own."

The old woman picked up a ceramic crock of beer and walked into a bedroom. The door closed.

"Is she well?" Bond asked.

"Cancer."

"I'm sorry."

"She's doing better than expected. She's ninety-seven."

Bond was surprised. "I would have thought she was in her seventies."

As if afraid of the silence that might engender the need for conversation, Jordaan strode to a battered CD player and loaded a disc. A woman's low voice, buoyed by hip-hop rhythms, burst from the speakers. Bond saw the CD cover: Thandiswa Mazwai.

"Sit down," Jordaan said, gesturing at the table.

"No, it's all right."

"What do you mean, no, it's all right?"

"You don't have to feed me."

Jordaan said shortly, "If Ugogo learns I haven't of-fered you any beer or *bobotie,* she won't be happy." She produced a clay pot with a rattan lid and poured some frothy pinkish liquid into a glass.

"So that's Zulu beer?"

"Yes."

"Homemade?"

"Zulu beer is always homemade. It takes three days to brew and you drink it while it's still fermenting."

Bond sipped. It was sour yet sweet and seemed low in alcohol.

Jordaan then served him a plate of *bobotie* and spooned on some reddish sauce. It was a bit like shepherd's pie, with egg instead of potato on top, but better than any pie Bond had ever had in England. The thick sauce was well flavored and indeed spicy.

"You're not joining me?" Bond nodded toward an empty chair. Jordaan was standing, leaning against the sink, arms folded across her voluptuous chest.

"I'm through eating," she said, the words clipped. She remained where she was.

Friend or foe . . .

He finished the food. "I must say, you're quite talented—a clever policewoman who also makes marvelous beer and"—a nod at the cooking pot—"*bobotie*. If I'm pronouncing that right."

He received no response. Did he insult her with every remark he made?

Bond tamped down his irritation and found himself regarding the many photographs of the family on the walls and mantelpiece. "Your grandmother must have seen a great deal of history in the making."

Glancing affectionately at the bedroom door, she said, "Ugogo *is* South Africa. Her uncle was wounded at the battle of Kambula, fighting the British—a few months after the battle I told you about, Isandlwana. She was born just a few years after the Union of South Africa was formed from the Cape and Natal provinces.

She was relocated under apartheid's Group Areas Act in the fifties. And she was wounded in a protest in nineteen sixty."

"What happened?"

"The Sharpeville Massacre. She was among those protesting against the *dompas*—the 'dumb pass,' it was called. Under apartheid people were legally classified as white, black, colored or Indian."

Bond recalled Gregory Lamb's comments.

"Blacks had to carry a passbook signed by their employer allowing them to be in a white area. It was humiliating, it was horrible. There was a peaceful protest but the police fired on the demonstrators. Nearly seventy people were killed. Ugogo was shot. Her leg. That's why she limps."

Jordaan hesitated and at last poured herself some beer, then sipped. "Ugogo gave me my name. That is, she told my parents what they would call me and they did. One usually does what Ugogo says."

"'Bheka,'" Bond said.

"In Zulu it means 'one who watches over people.'"

"A protector. So you were destined to become a policewoman." Bond was quite enjoying the music.

"Ugogo is the old South Africa. I'm the new. A mix of Zulu and Afrikaner. They call us a rainbow country, yes, but look at a rainbow and you still see different colors, all separate. We need to become like me, blended together. It will be a long time before that happens. But it will." She glanced coolly at Bond. "Then we'll be able to dislike people for who they really are. Not for the color of their skin."

Bond returned her gaze evenly and said, "Thank you for the food and the beer. I should be going."

She walked with him to the door. He stepped outside.

Which was when he caught his first clear glimpse of the man who'd pursued him from Dubai. The man in the blue jacket and the gold earring, the man who had killed Yusuf Nasad and had very nearly killed Felix Leiter.

He was standing across the road, in the shadows of an old building covered with Arabic scrolls and mosaics.

"What is it?" Jordaan asked.

"A hostile."

The man had a mobile but wasn't making a call; he was taking a picture of Bond with Jordaan—proof that Bond was working with the police.

Bond snapped, "Get your weapon and stay inside with your grandmother."

He sprinted hard across the street as the man fled up a narrow alley leading toward Signal Hill, through the deepening dusk.

Chapter 51

The man had a ten-yard lead but Bond began closing the distance as they pounded up the alley. Angry cats and scrawny dogs fled; a child with round Malaysian features stepped out of a door into Bond's path and was instantly jerked back by a parental hand.

He was nearly fifteen feet from the assailant when operational instinct kicked in. Bond realized that the man might have prepared a trap to aid his escape. He glanced down. Yes! The attacker had strung a piece of wire across the alley, a foot off the ground, nearly invisible in the darkness. The man himself had known where it was—a shard of broken crockery marked the spot—and had stepped over it smoothly. Bond wasn't able to stop in time but he could prepare himself for the fall.

He twisted his shoulder forward and when his own momentum swept his legs out from under him, he half somersaulted onto the ground. He landed hard and lay dazed for a moment, cursing himself for letting the man get away.

Except that he wasn't escaping.

The wire hadn't been intended to hinder pursuit but to render Bond vulnerable.

In an instant the man was on him, exuding the stench of beer, stale cigarette smoke and unwashed flesh, and ripped Bond's Walther from the holster.

Bond launched himself upward, gripping the man's right arm in a lock and twisting his wrist until the weapon fell to the ground. The attacker kicked the gun, which flew far from Bond's reach. Gasping, Bond kept hold of the man's right arm and dodged vicious blows from his other fist.

He glanced back, wondering if Bheka Jordaan had ignored his advice and come after him, armed with her own weapon. The empty alley gaped at him.

Now his assailant eased back to deliver a forehead blow. But, as Bond twisted to avoid it, the man rolled away, in a virtual backward somersault, like a gymnast. It was a brilliant feint. Bond recalled Felix Leiter's words.

Man, the SOB knows some martial arts crap . . .

Then Bond was on his feet, facing the man, who stood in a fighter's stance, a knife in his hand, blade protruding downward, sharp edge facing out. His left hand, open and palm down, floated distractingly, ready to grab Bond's clothing and pull him in to be stabbed to death.

On the balls of his feet, Bond circled.

Ever since his days at Fettes in Edinburgh, he had practiced various types of close combat but the ODG taught its agents a rare style of unarmed fighting, borrowed from a former (or not so former) enemy—the Russians. An ancient martial art of the Cossacks, *systema* had been updated by the Spetsnaz, the special forces branch of GRU military intelligence.

Systema practitioners rarely use their fists. Open palms, elbows and knees are the main weapons. The goal, though, is to strike as infrequently as possible.

Rather, you tire out your opponent, then catch him in a come-on or takedown hold on the shoulder, wrist, arm or ankle. The best *systema* fighters never come into contact with their adversary at all . . . until the final moment, when the exhausted attacker is largely defenseless. Then the victor takes him to the ground and drops a knee into his chest or throat.

Instinctively falling into *systema* choreography, Bond now dodged the man's assault.

Evade, evade, evade . . . Use his energy against him.

Bond was largely successful but twice the knife blade swept inches from his face.

The man moved in fast, swinging his massive hands, testing Bond, who stepped aside, sizing up his opponent's strengths (he was very muscular and experienced in hand-to-hand combat and was psychologically prepared to kill) and his weaknesses (alcohol and smoking seemed to be taking their toll).

The man grew frustrated at Bond's defense. Now he gripped the knife for thrusting and began to move in, almost desperate. He was grinning demonically, sweating despite the chill in the air.

Presenting a vulnerable target, his lower back, Bond stepped toward his Walther. But the move was a feint. And even before the man lunged, Bond reared back, pushed the knife blade away with his forearm and delivered a fierce open-palm slap to the man's left ear. He cupped his hand as he made contact and felt the pressure that would damage if not burst the attacker's eardrum. The man howled in pain, infuriated, and lunged carelessly. Bond easily lifted the knife arm away and up, then stepped in, gripping the wrist in both hands, a solid compliance hold, and bent it backward until the knife fell to the ground. He assessed the assailant's strength and his mad determination. He made a decision . . . and twisted further until the wrist cracked.

The man cried out and sank to his knees, then dropped into a sitting position, face pale. His head lolled to the side and Bond kicked the knife away. He frisked the man carefully and took a small automatic pistol from his pocket, along with a roll of duct tape. A pistol? Why didn't he just shoot me? Bond wondered.

He slipped the gun into his pocket and collected his Walther. He grabbed the man's phone—to whom had he texted the photo of him and Jordaan? If it had been to Dunne alone, could Bond find and incapacitate the Irishman before he reported to Hydt?

He scrolled through the call and text logs. Thank God, he had sent nothing. He'd simply been videoing Bond.

What was the point of that?

Then he had his answer.

"*Jebi ti!*" his attacker spat.

The Balkan obscenity explained everything.

Bond went through the man's papers and confirmed he was with the JSO, the Serbian paramilitary group. His name was Nicholas Rathko.

He was moaning now, cradling his arm. "You let my brother die! You abandoned him! He was your partner on that assignment. You *never* abandon your partner!"

Rathko's brother had been the younger of the BIA agents with Bond on that Sunday night near Novi Sad.

My brother, he smokes all time he is out on operations. Looks more normal than not smoking in Serbia . . .

Bond knew now how the man had found him in Dubai. To secure the BIA's cooperation in Serbia, the ODG and Six had given the senior security people in Belgrade Bond's real name and mission. After his brother had died, Rathko and his comrades at the JSO would have put together a full-scale operation to find Bond, using contacts through NATO and Six. They'd learned Bond was bound for Dubai. Of course, Bond now realized, it had been *Rathko,* not Osborne-Smith, who'd been making those subtle inquiries at MI6 about Bond's plans earlier in the week. Among Rathko's papers he now found authorization for a flight by military jet from Belgrade to Dubai. Which explained how he'd beaten Bond to the emirate. A local mercenary, the documents revealed, had put an untraceable car—the black Toyota—at the JSO agent's disposal.

And the purpose?

Probably not arrest and rendition. Rathko had most likely been planning to video Bond confessing or apologizing—or perhaps to record his torture and death.

"You call yourself Nicholas or Nick?" Bond asked, crouching.

"*Jebi ti,*" was the only response.

"Listen to me. I'm sorry your brother lost his life. But he had no business being in the BIA. He was careless and he wouldn't follow orders. He was the reason we lost the target."

"He was young."

"That's no excuse. It wouldn't be an excuse for me and it wasn't an excuse for you when you were with Arkan's Tigers."

"He was only a boy." Tears glistened in the man's eyes, whether from the pain of the broken wrist or the sorrow he felt for his dead brother, Bond couldn't tell.

Bond looked down the alleyway and saw Bheka Jordaan and some SAPS officers sprinting toward him. He bent down, picked up the man's knife and sliced through the trip wire.

He squatted beside the Serb. "We'll get you to a doctor."

Then he heard a woman's voice call sharply, "Stop!"

He glanced at Bheka Jordaan. "It's all right. I have his weapons."

But then he realized that her pistol was aimed at himself. He frowned and stood up.

"Leave him alone!" she snapped.

Two SAPS officers stepped between Bond and Rathko. One hesitated, then carefully took the knife from his hand.

"He's a Serbian intelligence agent. He was trying to kill me. He's the one who murdered that CIA asset in Dubai the other day."

"That doesn't mean you can cut his throat." Her dark eyes were narrow with anger.

"What are you talking about?"

"You are in my country. You will obey the law!"

The other officers were staring at him, Bond saw, some angrily. He glanced at Jordaan and stepped away, gesturing to her to follow.

Jordaan did so and when they were out of earshot, she continued harshly, "You won. He was down, he wasn't a threat. Why were you going to kill him?"

"I wasn't," he said.

"I don't believe you. You told me to stay in the

house with my grandmother. You didn't ask me to call my officers because you didn't want witnesses while you tortured and killed him."

"I assumed you'd call for backup. I didn't want you to leave your grandmother in case he wasn't working alone."

But Jordaan wasn't listening. She raged, "You come here, to our country, with that double-0 number of yours. Oh, I know all about what you do!"

Finally Bond understood the source of her anger with him. It had nothing to do with any attempted flirtation, nothing to do with the fact that he represented the oppressive male. She despised his shameless disregard for the law: his Level 1 missions—assassinations—for the ODG.

He stepped forward and said in a low murmur, barely able to control his anger, "In a few instances when there's been no other way to protect my country, yes, I've taken a life. And only if I've been ordered to. I don't do it because I want to. I don't enjoy it. I do it to save people who deserve to be saved. You may call it a sin—but it's a necessary sin."

"There was no need to kill him," she spat back.

"I wasn't going to."

"The knife . . . I saw—"

"He left a trap. The trip wire." He gestured. "I cut it so nobody would fall. As for him"—he nodded toward the Serb—"I was just telling him we'd get him to a doctor. Ask him. I rarely take someone to hospital when I'm about to murder them." He turned and pushed past the two police officers blocking his way. His eyes defied them to try and stop him. Without looking back, he called, "I'll need that film developed as soon as possible. And the IDs of everyone coming to Hydt's tomorrow." He strode away from them down the alley.

Soon he was in the Subaru, streaking past the colorful houses of Bo-Kaap, driving far faster than was safe through the winding, picturesque streets.

Chapter 52

A restaurant featuring local cuisine beckoned and James Bond, still angry from his run-in with Bheka Jordaan, decided he needed a strong drink.

He'd enjoyed the stew at Jordaan's house but the portion was rather small, as if doled out with the intent that the diner finish quickly and depart. Bond now ordered a hearty meal of *sosaties*—grilled meat skewers—with yellow rice and *marog* spinach (having politely declined an offer to try the house specialty of *mopane* worms). He downed two vodka martinis with the food, then returned to the Table Mountain Hotel.

Bond had a shower, dried himself and dressed. There was a knock on the door. A porter delivered a large envelope. Whatever else, Jordaan had not let her personal view that he was a cold-blooded serial killer interfere with the job. Inside he found black-and-white prints of the images he'd taken with the inhaler camera. Some were blurred and others had missed their mark but he had managed a clear series of what he was most interested in: the door to Research and Development at Green Way and its alarm and locking mechanisms. Jordaan had also been professional enough to provide a flash drive of the scanned pictures, and his anger diminished further. He loaded them on to his laptop, encrypted them and sent them to Sanu Hirani, with a set of instructions.

Thirty seconds after he'd hit send, he received a message back.

We never sleep.

He smiled and texted an acknowledgment.

A few minutes later he took a call from Bill Tanner in London.

"I was just about to ring you," Bond said.

"James . . ." Tanner sounded grave. There was a problem.

"Go ahead."

"There's a bit of a flap on here. Whitehall's come round to thinking that Incident Twenty doesn't have much of a connection with South Africa."

"What?"

"They think Hydt's a diversion. The killings in Incident Twenty are going to be in Afghanistan, aid workers or contractors, they reckon. The Intelligence Committee voted to pull you out and send you to Kabul—since, frankly, you haven't found much of anything concrete where you are."

Bond's heart was pounding. "Bill, I'm convinced the key—"

"Hold on," Tanner interrupted. "I'm just telling you what they wanted. But M dug his heels in and insisted you stay. It turned into Trafalgar, big and loud. We all went to the foreign secretary and pitched the case. There's some talk the PM was involved, though I can't confirm that. Anyway, M won. You're to stay in place. And you'll be interested to know there was a witness for the defense—in your support."

"Who?"

"Your new friend Percy."

"Osborne-Smith?" Bond nearly laughed.

"He said if you had a lead you ought to be allowed to follow it up."

"Did he now? I'll buy him a pint when all this is over. You too."

"Well, things aren't as rosy as they seem," Tanner said glumly. "The old man put the ODG's reputation on the line to keep you there. *Your* reputation too. If it turns out Hydt *is* a diversion, there'll be repercussions. Serious ones."

Was the very future of the ODG riding on his success?

Politics, Bond reflected cynically. He said, "I'm sure Hydt's behind it."

"And M's going with that judgment." Tanner asked what his next steps would be.

"I'll be at Hydt's plant tomorrow morning. Depending on what I find, I'm going to have to move fast and communications could be a problem. If I can't learn anything by late afternoon, I'll get Bheka Jordaan to raid the place, interrogate the hell out of Hydt and Dunne and find out what's planned for tomorrow night."

"All right, James. Keep me informed. I'll brief M. He'll be in that security meeting all day."

"'Night, Bill. And thank him for me."

After they had rung off, Bond poured a generous amount of Crown Royal into a crystal glass, added two ice cubes and turned off the lights. He flung wide the curtains, sat on the sofa and gazed out over the snow-flake lights on the harbor. A massive British-flag cruise ship was easing up to the dock. It seemed even larger than his hotel.

His phone trilled and he glanced at the screen.

"Philly." He took another sip of the fragrant whisky.

"Are you in the middle of dinner?"

"It's *après*-cocktail cocktail hour here."

"You *are* a man after my own heart." As she said this, Bond's eyes happened to be on the bed he'd shared last night with Felicity Willing. Philly continued, "I didn't know if you wanted more updates on the Steel Cartridge operation. . . ."

He sat forward. "Yes, please. What've you found?"

"Something interesting, I think. Seems the whole point of the operation wasn't to kill just *any* of our agents and contractors. The Russians were killing their moles within MI6 and the CIA."

Bond felt something detonate inside him. He put his glass down.

"With the fall of the Soviet Union, the Kremlin wanted to solidify ties with the West. It would've been awkward politically if their doubles were exposed. So active KGB agents killed the most successful moles in Six and the CIA and made the murders look like accidents—but left a steel cartridge at the scene as a warning to the others to keep quiet. That's all I know at this point."

My God, Bond thought. His father . . . his father had been a double—a *traitor*?

"Are you still there?"

"Yes—just a bit distracted by what's going on here. But that's good work, Philly. I'll be incommunicado for most of tomorrow but text me or e-mail what you find."

"I will. Take care of yourself, James. I worry."

They rang off.

Bond lifted the cold crystal glass, wet with condensation, and pressed it against his forehead. He now scrolled mentally through his family's past, trying to find clues about Andrew Bond that might shed light on this appalling theory. Bond had been quite fond of his father, who was a collector of stamps and photographs of cars. He'd owned several vehicles but took more pleasure in repairing and cleaning them than in fast driving. When older, Bond had asked his aunt about the man. Charmian had thought for a moment and said, "He was a good man, of course. Solid, dependable. A rock. But quiet. Andrew was never one to stand out."

Qualities of the best covert intelligence agents.

Could he have been a mole for the Russians?

Another jarring thought: His father's duplicity—if the story were true—had resulted in the death of his wife, Bond's mother, too.

Not just the Russians but his father's betrayal had orphaned young Bond.

He started as his phone buzzed with an incoming text.

> Late night getting ready for food
> shipments. Just left office. Interested in
> some company? Felicity.

James Bond hesitated a moment. Then he typed Yes.

Ten minutes later, after slipping his Walther under the bed beneath a towel, he heard a soft knock. He opened the door and let in Felicity Willing. Any doubt he might have had about whether or not they would pick up where they left off yesterday was dashed when she flung her arms around him and kissed him hard. He smelled her perfume, radiating from behind her ear, and she tasted of mint.

"I'm a mess," she said, laughing. She wore a blue cotton shirt, tucked into designer jeans, which were crumpled and dusty.

"I won't hear of it," he said, and kissed her again.

"You're sitting in the dark, Gene," she said. And for the first time in the operation he was jarred by the reminder of his Afrikaner cover.

"I like the view."

They stepped apart and in the dim light from outside Bond took in her face and thought it as intensely sensual as last night, but she was clearly tired. He supposed the logistics of marshaling the largest shipment of food ever to arrive on the African continent were daunting, to say the least.

"Here." A wine bottle appeared from her shoulder bag—vintage Three Cape Ladies, a red blend from Muldersvlei on the Cape. Bond knew its reputation. He took out the cork and poured. They sat on the sofa and sipped.

"Wonderful," he said.

She worked her boots off. Bond slipped his arm around her shoulders and struggled to put aside thoughts of his father.

Felicity slumped and rested her head against him. On the horizon there were even more ships than there had been last night. "Look at them all," she said. "Our food deliveries. You hear so many bad things about people but that's not the complete truth. There's a lot of good out there. You can't always count on it, it's never certain but at least—"

Bond interrupted, "At least someone's . . . *willing* to help."

She laughed. "You nearly made me spill my wine, Gene. I could've ruined my shirt."

"I have a solution."

"Stop drinking the wine?" She pouted playfully. "But it's so nice."

"Another solution, a better one." He kissed her and slowly began to unfix the buttons of the garment.

An hour later, they lay in bed, on their sides, Bond behind Felicity. His arm was curled around her and his hand cupped her breast. Her fingers were entwined in his.

Unlike last night, however, in the after-moment, Bond was wholly awake.

His mind was racing furiously, past all assortments of topics. Exactly how much was the future of the ODG resting on him? What secrets did the Research and Development department of Green Way hold? What precisely was Hydt's goal with Gehenna and how could Bond craft a suitable countermeasure?

Purpose . . . response.

And what of his father?

"You're thinking about something serious," Felicity said drowsily.

"What makes you say that?"

"Women know."

"I'm thinking how beautiful you are."

She lifted his hand to her face and gently bit his finger. "The first lie you've told me."

"My job," he said.

"Then I'll forgive you. It's the same with me. Coordinating the help on the docks, paying the pilots' fees, working on the ship charters and lorry leases, the trade unions." Her voice took on the edge he'd heard before, as she said, "And then *your* specialty. We've already had two attempted break-ins at the dock. And no food has even been offloaded yet. That was odd." Silence for a moment. Then: "Gene?"

Bond knew something significant was coming. He now grew alert and receptive. The intimacy of bodies comes prepackaged with an intimacy of mind and spirit, and you ought not to seek the first if you're unwilling to take delivery of the second. "Yes?"

She said evenly, "I have a feeling there's more to your work than you've told me. No, don't say anything. I don't know how you feel but if it turns out we can keep seeing each other, if . . ." She trailed off.

"Go on," he whispered.

"If it turns out we see each other again, do you think that maybe you could change just a bit? I mean, if you *do* go to some dark places, could you promise me not to go to the . . . worst?" When he said nothing he felt tension ripple through her. "Oh, I don't know what I'm saying. Ignore me, Gene."

Although she was speaking to a security expert–cum–mercenary soldier from Durban, in a way she was also talking to him, James Bond, a 00 Section agent.

And, ironically, he took her acknowledgment that she could live with a certain degree of darkness in Theron as indication that she might accept Bond as he was.

He whispered, "I think that's very possible."

She kissed his hand. "Don't say any more. That's all I wanted to hear. Now, I have an idea. I don't know what your plans are for this weekend . . ."

Neither do I, Bond thought sourly.

". . . but we'll have finished the food shipments tomorrow night. There's an inn I know in Franschhoek—have you been to that area?"

"No."

"It's the most beautiful spot on the Western Cape. A wine district. The restaurant has a Michelin star and the most romantic deck in the world, overlooking the hills. Come with me on Saturday?"

"I'd love to," he said and kissed her hair.

"You really mean that?" The tough warrior who seemed so at ease fighing the world's agropolies now sounded vulnerable and unsure.

"Yes," he whispered. "I do."

In five minutes she was asleep.

Bond, however, remained awake, staring out at the lights of the harbor. His thoughts were no longer on his father's possible betrayal, nor on his promise to Felicity Willing to consider changing his darkest nature, nor on the anticipation of the time they might spend together this weekend. No, James Bond was focusing on one thing only: the indistinct faces of those, somewhere in the world, whose lives—despite Whitehall's belief—he knew that he alone could save.

Friday

Down to Gehenna

Chapter 53

At 8:40 A.M. Bond steered his dusty, mud-spattered Subaru into the Cape Town SAPS headquarters car park. He killed the engine, climbed out and entered the building, where he found Bheka Jordaan, Gregory Lamb and Kwalene Nkosi in her office.

Bond greeted them with a nod. Lamb responded with a look that bespoke intrigue, Nkosi with an energetic smile.

Jordaan said, "Regarding Hydt's newly arrived associates, we've identified them." She spun her laptop and clicked on a slide show. The first photos depicted a large man with a round ebony face. He wore a brash gold and silver shirt, designer sunglasses and voluminous brown slacks.

"Charles Mathebula. He's a black diamond from Joburg."

Lamb explained: "From the new wealthy class in South Africa. Some of them become rich overnight in ways that aren't quite transparent, if you get my drift."

"And some," Jordaan added frostily, "became wealthy by hard work. Mathebula owns businesses that seem to be legitimate—shipping and transport. He was on the borderline with some arms deliveries a few years ago, true, but there was no evidence of wrongdoing." A tap of a key and another picture appeared. "Now, this is David Huang." He was slim and smiled at the camera. "His daughter posted the snapshot on her Facebook page. Stupid girl . . . though good for us."

"A known mobster?"

Nkosi qualified, "A *suspected* mobster. Singapore. Mostly money-laundering. Possibly human trafficking."

Another face appeared. Jordaan tapped her computer screen. "The German—Hans Eberhard. He came in on Wednesday. Mining interests, diamonds primarily. Industrial grade but some jewelry." A good-looking blond man was pictured leaving the airport. He was wearing a well-cut light suit, a shirt without a tie. "He's been suspected of various crimes but he's technically clean."

Bond studied the photos of the men.

Eberhard.

Huang.

Mathebula.

He memorized the names.

Frowning, Jordaan said, "I don't understand why Hydt needs partners, though. He's got money enough to fund Gehenna himself, I should think."

Bond had already considered this. "Two reasons, most likely. Gehenna must be expensive. He'd want outside money so that if he's ever audited he doesn't have to explain huge liabilities on the books. But, more important, he doesn't have a criminal background or network. Whatever Gehenna's about, he'll need the contacts that people like these three can offer."

"Yes," Jordaan allowed. "That makes sense."

Bond looked at Lamb. "Sanu Hirani in Q Branch texted me this morning. He said you had something for me."

"Ah, yes—sorry." The Six agent handed him an envelope.

Bond peered inside and then pocketed it. "I'm going out to the plant now. Once I'm inside I'll try to find out what Incident Twenty is, who's at risk and where. I'll get word out as soon as I can. But we need a fallback plan." If they hadn't heard from him by 4 P.M., Jordaan should order tactical officers to raid the plant, detain Hydt, Dunne and the partners and seize the contents of the Research and Development department. "This will give us—or you, if I'm no longer in the game—five or six hours to interrogate them and find out what Incident Twenty's all about."

"A raid?" Jordaan was frowning. "I can't do that."

"Why not?"

"I've told you. Unless I have reasonable belief that a crime is occurring at Green Way or a magistrate's order, there's nothing I can do."

Damn the woman. "This isn't about preserving his rights for a fair trial. This is about saving thousands of people—possibly many South Africans."

"I can do nothing without a warrant and there's no evidence to present to the court to get one. No justification to act."

"If I don't turn up by four, you can assume he's killed me."

"Obviously I hope that doesn't happen, Commander, but your absence doesn't equal cause."

"I've told you he's willing to dig up the graves of massacre victims and turn them into building materials. What more do you want?"

"Evidence of a crime somewhere in the plant." Her

jaw was set and her eyes black granite. It was clear she wouldn't yield.

Bond said sharply, "Then let's hope to God I can find the answer. For the sake of several thousand innocent people." He nodded to Nkosi and Lamb and, ignoring Jordaan, left the office. He strode downstairs to his car, dropped into the driver's seat and fired up the engine.

"James, wait!" Turning, he saw Bheka Jordaan walking toward him. "Please, wait."

Bond thought about speeding away but instead he rolled the window down.

"Yesterday," she said, bending down, close to him, "the Serbian?"

"Yes?"

"I spoke to him. He told me what you'd said—that you were going to get him to a doctor."

Bond nodded.

After a breath, the policewoman added, "I was making assumptions. I . . . sometimes I do that. I judge first. I try not to but it's hard for me to stop. I wanted to apologize."

"Accepted," he said.

"About a raid at Green Way, though? You must understand. Under apartheid the old police, the SAP and their Criminal Investigation Department, did terrible things. Now everyone watches *us,* the new police, to make sure we don't do the same. An illegal raid, arbitrary arrests and interrogations . . . that's what the old regime did. We cannot do the same. We must be *better* than the people who came before us." Her face taut with determination, she said, "I'll fight side by side with you if the law permits but without cause, without a warrant, there's nothing I can do. I'm sorry."

Much of the training of 00 Section agents in the Group was psychological and part of that arduous instruction was to instill within them the belief that they were different, that they were allowed to—no, *required* to—operate outside the law. A Level 1 project order, authorizing assassination, had to be, to James Bond, just another aspect of his job, no different from taking pictures of secret installations or planting misinformation in the press.

As M had put it, Bond had to have carte blanche to do whatever was required to fulfill his mission.

We protect the Realm . . . by any means necessary.

That attitude was part of Bond's fabric—indeed, he couldn't do his job without it—and he had to remind himself continually that Bheka Jordaan and the other hardworking law enforcers of the world were 100 percent right in respecting the rules. It was *he* who was the outlier.

He said, not unkindly, "I do understand, Captain. And whatever happens, it's been quite an experience working with you."

Her response was a smile, faint and fleeting but, Bond judged, honest—the first time that such an expression had warmed her beautiful face in his presence.

Chapter 54

Bond skidded the Subaru into the car park outside the fortress of Green Way International and braked to a stop.

Several limousines were lined up close to the gate.

REDUCE, REUSE, RECYCLE

A few people were milling about. Bond recognized the German businessman, Hans Eberhard, in a beige suit and white shoes. He was talking to Niall Dunne, who stood still as a Japanese fighting fish. The breeze ruffled his blond fringe. Eberhard was finishing a cigarette. Perhaps Hydt didn't allow anyone to smoke inside the plant, which seemed ironic; the outside air was bleached with haze and vapors from the power plant and the methane that was being burned.

Bond waved to Dunne, who acknowledged him with a blank nod and continued his conversation with the German. Then Dunne pulled his phone off his belt and read a text or e-mail. He whispered something to Eberhard, then stepped away to make a call. On the pretense of using his own phone, Bond loaded the eavesdropping app and lifted it to his ear, rolling down the passenger window of his car and aiming it in the direction of the Irishman. He stared ahead and mouthed to himself so that Dunne would not guess a microphone was pointed his way.

The Irishman's conversation was one-sided but Bond heard him say, ". . . outside with Hans. He wanted a smoke. . . . I know."

He was probably speaking to Hydt.

Dunne continued, "We're on schedule. I just had an e-mail. The lorry left March for York. Should be there any minute. The device is already armed."

So, this was Incident 20! The attack would take place in York.

"The target's confirmed. Detonation's still scheduled for ten thirty, their time."

Dismayed, Bond noted the time of the attack. They'd assumed ten thirty at night but every time Dunne had referred to a time he'd used the twenty-four-hour clock. Had it been half past ten in the evening he would have said, "Twenty-two thirty."

Dunne looked at Bond's car and said into the phone, "Theron's here . . . Right, then." He disconnected and called to Eberhard that the meeting would start soon. Then he turned to Bond. He seemed impatient.

Bond dialed a number. Please, he whispered silently. Answer.

Then: "Osborne-Smith."

Thank God. "Percy. It's James Bond. Listen carefully. I have about sixty seconds. I've got the answer to Incident Twenty. You'll have to move fast. Mobilize a team. SOCA, Five, local police. The bomb's in York."

"York?"

"Hydt's people're driving the device in a lorry from March to York. It's going to detonate later this morning. I don't know where they'll plant it. Maybe a sporting event—there was that reference to 'course,' so try the racecourse. Or somewhere there's a big crowd. Check all the CCTVs in and around March, get the number-plates of as many lorries as you can. Then compare them to the plates of any lorries arriving in York about now. You need to—"

"Hold on there, Bond," Osborne-Smith said coolly. "It has nothing to do with March or Yorkshire."

Bond noted the use of his last name and the imperious tone in Osborne-Smith's voice. "What are you talking about?"

Dunne gestured to him. Bond nodded, struggling to smile amiably.

"Did you know Hydt's companies reclaim dangerous materials?"

"Well, yes. But—"

"Remember I told you he was digging tunnels for some fancy new rubbish collection system under London, including around Whitehall?" Osborne-Smith sounded like a barrister before a witness.

Bond was sweating now. "But that's not what this is about."

Dunne was acting increasingly impatient, his eyes focusing on Bond.

"I beg to differ," Osborne-Smith said prissily. "One of the tunnels isn't far from the security meeting today in Richmond Terrace. Your boss, mine, senior CIA, Six, Joint Intelligence Committee—it's a veritable who's who of the security world. Hydt was going to release something nasty that his hazardous-materials operation had recovered. Kill everybody. His people have been hauling bins in and out of the tunnels and buildings near Whitehall for the past several days. Nobody's thought to check them out."

Bond said evenly, "Percy, that's not what's going on. He's not going to use Green Way people directly for the attack. It's too obvious. He'd be implicated himself."

"Then how do you explain our little find in the tunnels? Radiation."

"How much?" Bond asked bluntly.

A pause. Osborne-Smith replied in his petulant lisp, "About four millirems."

"That's *nothing*, Percy." All O Branch agents were well versed in nuclear exposure statistics. "Every human being on earth gets hit with sixty millirems from cosmic rays alone each year. Add an X-ray or two and you're up to two hundred. A dirty bomb's going to leave more trace than four."

Ignoring him, Osborne-Smith said brightly, "Now, about York, you misheard. It must be the Duke of York pub or the theater in London. Could be a staging area. We'll check it. In the event, I canceled the security meeting, moved everyone to secure locations. Bond, I've been thinking about what makes Hydt tick ever since I saw he was living in Canning Town and you told me all about his obsession with thousand-year-old dead bodies. He revels in decay, cities crumbling."

Dunne was now walking slowly forward, making directly for the Subaru.

Bond said, "I know, Percy, but—"

"What better way to promote social decay than to take down the security apparatus of half the Western powers?"

"Dammit, fine. Do what you want in London. But have SOCA or some teams from Five follow up in York."

"We don't have the manpower, do we? Can't spare a soul. Maybe this afternoon but for now, afraid not. Nothing's going to happen till tonight, anyway."

Bond explained that the time of the operation had been moved forward.

A chuckle. "Your Irishman prefers the twenty-four-hour clock, does he? . . . Bit fine-tuned, that. No, we'll stick with my plan."

This was why Osborne-Smith had backed M's stand to have Bond remain in South Africa; he hadn't in fact believed Bond was on to anything. He had simply wanted to steal the thunder. Bond disconnected and started to dial Bill Tanner.

But Dunne was at the door, yanking it open. "Come on, Theron. You're keeping your new boss waiting. You know the drill. Leave the phone and the gun in the car."

"I thought I'd check them in with your smiling concierge."

If it came down to a fight, he hoped to be able to pick up his weapon and to communicate with the outside world.

But Dunne said, "Not today."

Bond didn't argue. He secured his phone and the Walther in the car's glove box, joined Dunne and locked the car with the key fob.

As he once again endured the rituals at the security post, Bond happened to glance at a clock on the wall. It was nearly 8 A.M. in York. He had just over two and a half hours to find out where the bomb was planted.

Chapter 55

The Green Way lobby was deserted. Bond supposed Hydt—or, more likely, Dunne—had arranged for the staff to have the day off so that the meeting and the Gehenna plan's maiden voyage could go forward without interruption.

Severan Hydt strode up the hall, greeting Bond warmly. He was in good spirits, ebullient even. His dark eyes shone. "Theron!"

Bond shook his hand.

"I'll want you to make a presentation to my associates about the killing-fields project. It'll be their money too that'll fund it. Now, you don't need to do anything formal. Just outline on a map where the major graves are, how many corpses roughly are in each one, how long they've been in the ground and what you think your clients will be willing to pay. Oh, by the way, one or two of my partners are in lines of work similar to yours. You might know each other."

The alarming thought now occurred to Bond that these men might wonder the opposite: why they had *not* heard of the ruthless Durban-based mercenary Gene Theron, who'd seeded the African earth with so many bodies.

As they walked through the Green Way building, Bond asked where he could work, hoping that Hydt might take him to Research and Development, now that he was a trusted partner.

"We have an office for you." But the man led him past the R&D department to a large, windowless room. Inside were a few chairs, a worktable and a desk. He'd been provided with office supplies like yellow pads and pens, dozens of detailed maps of Africa and an intercom but no phone. Corkboards on the walls displayed copies of the pictures that Bond had delivered of the decaying bodies. He wondered where the originals were.

In Hydt's bedroom?

The Rag-and-Bone Man asked pleasantly, "Will this do?"

"Fine. A computer would be helpful."

"I could arrange that—for word processing and printing. No Internet access, of course."

"No?"

"We're concerned about hacking and security. But for now, don't worry about writing anything up formally. Handwritten notes are enough."

Bond maintained a calm façade as he noted the clock. It was now eight twenty in York. Just over two hours to go. "Well, I'd better get down to it."

"We'll be up the hall in the main conference room. Go to the end and turn left. Number nine hundred. Join us whenever you like but make sure you're there before half twelve. We'll have something on television I think you'll find interesting."

Ten thirty York time.

After Hydt had gone, Bond bent over the map and drew circles around some of the areas he'd arbitrarily picked as battle zones when he and Hydt had met at the Lodge Club. He jotted a few numbers—signifying the body counts—then bundled up the maps, a yellow pad and some pens. He stepped into the corridor, which was empty. Orienting himself, Bond went back to Research and Development.

Tradecraft dictated that simpler was usually the best approach, even in a black bag operation like this.

Accordingly Bond knocked on the door.

Mr. Hydt asked me to find some papers for him. . . . Sorry to bother you, I'll just be a moment . . .

He was prepared to rush the person who opened the door and use a takedown hold on wrist or arm to overpower them. Prepared for an armed guard too—indeed, hoping for one, so he could relieve the man of his weapon.

But there was no answer. These staff had apparently been given the day off too.

Bond fell back on plan two, which was somewhat less simple. Last night he had uploaded to Sanu Hirani the digital pictures he'd taken of the security door to Research and Development. The head of Q Branch had reported that the lock was virtually impregnable. It would take hours to hack. He and his team would try to think up another solution.

Shortly thereafter Bond had received word that Hirani had sent Gregory Lamb to scrounge another tool of the trade. He'd be delivering it that morning, along with written instructions on how to open the door. This was what the MI6 agent had handed to Bond in Bheka Jordaan's office.

Bond now checked behind him once more, then went to work. From his inside jacket pocket he took out what Lamb had provided: a length of two-hundred-pound-test fishing line, nylon that wouldn't be picked up by the Green Way metal detector. Bond now fed

one end through the small gap at the top of the door
and continued until it had reached the floor on the
other side. He ripped a strip of the cardboard backing
from the pad of yellow paper and tore it, fashioning a J
shape—a rudimentary hook. This he slipped through
the bottom gap until he managed to snag the fishing
line and pull it out.

He executed a triple surgeon's knot to fix the ends
together. He now had a loop that encircled the door
from top to bottom. Using a pen, he made this into a
huge tourniquet and began to tighten it.

The nylon strand grew increasingly taut . . . compressing the exit bar on the other side of the door. Finally, as Hirani had said would "most likely" happen,
the door clicked open, as if an employee on the inside
had pushed the bar to let himself out. For the sake of
fire safety, there could be no number pad lock release
on the inside.

Bond stepped into the dim room, unwound the
tourniquet and pocketed the evidence of his intrusion.
Closing the door till it latched, he swept the lights on
and glanced around the laboratory, looking for phones,
radios or weapons. None. There were a dozen computers, desk- and laptop models, but the three he booted
up were password protected. He didn't waste time on
the others.

Discouragingly, the desks and worktables were
covered with thousands of documents and file folders,
and none was conveniently labeled *Gehenna*.

He plowed through reams of blueprints, technical
diagrams, specification sheets, schematic drawings.
Some had to do with weapons and security systems,
others with vehicles. None answered the vital ques-

tions of who was in danger in York and where exactly was the bomb?

Then, at last, he found a folder marked *Serbia* and ripped it open, scanning the documents.

Bond froze, hardly able to believe what he was seeing.

In front of him there were photographs of the tables in the morgue at the old British Army hospital in March. Sitting on one was a weapon that theoretically didn't exist. The explosive device was unofficially dubbed the "Cutter." MI6 and the CIA suspected the Serbian government was developing it but local assets hadn't found any proof that it had actually been built. The Cutter was a hypervelocity antipersonnel weapon that used regular explosives enhanced with solid rocket fuel to fire hundreds of small titanium blades at close to three thousand miles an hour.

The Cutter was so horrific that, even though it was only rumored to be in development, it had already been condemned by the UN and human rights organizations. Serbia adamantly denied that it was building one and nobody—even the best-connected arms dealers—had ever seen such a device.

How the hell had Hydt come by it?

Bond continued through the files, finding elaborate engineering diagrams and blueprints, along with instructions on machining the blades that were the weapons' shrapnel and on programming the arming system, all written in Serbian, with English translations. This explained it: Hydt had *made* one. He had somehow come into possession of these plans and had ordered his engineers to build one of the damn things. The bits of titanium Bond had found in the Fens army base were shavings from the deadly blades.

And the train in Serbia—this explained the mystery of the dangerous chemical; it had had nothing to do with Dunne's mission there. He probably hadn't even known about the poison. The purpose of his trip to Novi Sad had been to steal some of the titanium on the train to use it in the device—there had been two wagons of scrap metal behind the locomotive. *Those* had been his target. Dunne's rucksack hadn't contained weapons or bombs to blow open the chemical drums on railcar three; the bag had been *empty* when Dunne arrived. He'd filled it with unique titanium scraps and taken them back to March to make the Cutter.

The Irishman had arranged the derailment to make it look like an accident so no one would realize the metal had been stolen.

But how had Dunne and Hydt got hold of the plans? The Serbs would have done all they could to keep the blueprints and specifications secret.

Bond found the answer a moment later in a memo from the Dubai engineer Mahdi al-Fulan, dated a year ago.

Severan:

I have looked into your request to see if it is possible to fabricate a system that will reconstruct shredded classified documents. I'm afraid with modern shredders the answer is no. But I would propose this: I can create an electric eye system that serves as a safety device to prevent injuries when someone tries to reach into a document shredder. In fact, though, it would double as a hyperspeed optical scanner. When the documents are fed into the system, the scanner reads all the information on them before they are shredded. The data can be stored on a 3- or 4-terabyte hard drive hidden somewhere in the shredder and uploaded via a secure mobile or satellite link, or even physically retrieved when your employees replace the blades or clean the units.

I further recommend that you make and offer to your clients shredders that are so efficient they literally turn their documents to dust, so that you will instill confidence in them to hire you to destroy even the most sensitive materials.

In addition, I have a plan for a similar device that would extract data from hard drives before they are destroyed. I believe it's possible to create a machine that would break apart laptop or desktop computers, optically identify the hard drive, and route it to a special station where the drive would be temporarily connected to a processor in the destruction machine. Classified information could be copied before the drives were wiped.

He recalled his tour of Green Way and Hydt's excitement about the automated computer destruction devices.

In a few years that will be my most lucrative operation. . . .

Bond read on. The document-shredder scanners were already in use in every city where Green Way had a base, including at top-secret Serbian military facilities and weapons contractors outside Belgrade.

Other memos detailed plans to capture less classified but still valuable documents, using special teams of Green Way refuse collectors to gather the rubbish of targeted individuals, bring it to special locations and sort through it for personal and sensitive information.

Bond noted the value of this: He found copies of credit-card receipts, some intact, others reconstructed from simple document shredders. One bill, for instance, was from a hotel outside Pretoria. The cardholder had the title "Right Honorable." Notes attached to it warned that the man's extramarital affair would be made public if he didn't agree to a list of demands an opposing politician was making. So, such items would be the "special materials" Bond had seen being shipped here in Green Way lorries.

There were also pages upon pages of what seemed to be phone numbers, along with many other digits, screen names, pass codes and excerpts of e-mails and text messages. E-waste. Of course, workers in Silicon Row were looking through phones and computers, extracting electronic serial numbers for mobiles, passwords, banking information, texts, records of instant messages and who knew what else?

But the immediate question, of course: Where exactly was the Cutter going to be detonated?

He flipped through the notes again. None of the information he'd found gave him a clue as to the location of the York bomb, which would explode in a little over an hour. His temples throbbed as he leaned forward over a worktable, staring at the diagram of the device.

Think, he told himself furiously.

Think . . .

For some minutes, nothing occurred to him. Then he had an idea. What was Severan Hydt doing? Assembling useful information from scraps and fragments.

Do the same, Bond told himself. Put the pieces of the puzzle together.

And what scraps do I have?

- The target is in York.
- One message contained the words "term" and "£5 million."
- Hydt is willing to cause mass destruction to divert attention from the real crime he intends to commit, as with the derailment in Serbia.
- The Cutter was hidden somewhere near March and has just been driven to York.
- He's being paid for the attack, not acting out of ideology.
- He could have used any explosive device but he's gone to great trouble to build a Cutter with actual Serbian military designations, a weapon not available on the general arms market.
- Thousands of people will die.
- The blast must have a radius of 100 feet minimum.
- The Cutter is to be detonated at a specific time, 10:30 A.M.
- The attack has something to do with a "course," a road or other route.

But rearrange these ragged bits as he might, Bond saw only unrelated scraps.

Well, keep at it, he raged. He focused again on each shred. He picked it up mentally and placed it somewhere else.

One possibility became clear: If Hydt and Dunne had re-created a Cutter, the forensic teams doing post-blast analysis would find the military designations and believe the Serbian government or army was behind it since the devices weren't yet available on the black market. Hydt had done this to shift attention away from the real perpetrators: himself and whoever had paid him millions of pounds. It would be a misdirection—just like the planned train crash.

That meant there were *two* targets: The apparent one would have some connection to Serbia and, to the public and police, would be the purpose of the attack. But the real victim would be someone else caught in the blast, an apparent bystander. No one would ever know that he or she was the person Hydt and his client really wanted to die . . . and *that* death would be the one that harmed British interests.

Who? A government official in York? A scientist? And, goddammit, where specifically would the attack take place?

Bond played with the confetti of information once more.

Nothing . . .

But then, in his mind, he heard a resounding tap. "Term" had ended up next to "course."

What if the former didn't refer to a clause in a contract but a period in the academic year? And "course" was just that—a course of study?

That made some sense. A large institution, thousands of students.

But where?

The best Bond could come up with was an institution at which there was a course, a lecture, a rally, a museum exhibit or the like involving Serbia, at half past ten this morning. This suggested a university.

Did his reassembled theory hold up?

There was no time left for speculation. He glanced at the digital clock on the wall, which advanced another minute.

In York it was nine forty.

Chapter 56

Carrying the killing-fields map, Bond walked casually down a corridor.

A guard with a massive bullet-shaped head eyed him suspiciously. The man was unarmed, Bond saw to his disappointment; neither did he have a radio. He asked the guard for directions to Hydt's conference room. The man pointed it out.

Bond started to walk away, then turned back as if he'd just remembered something. "Oh, I need to ask Ms. Barnes about lunch. Do you know where she is?"

The guard hesitated, then pointed to another corridor. "Her office is down there. The double doors on the left. Number one oh eight. You will knock first."

Bond moved off in the direction indicated. In a few minutes he arrived and glanced back. No one was in the corridor. He knocked on the door. "Jessica, it's Gene. I need to talk to you."

There was a pause. She'd said she'd be here but she might be ill or have felt too tired to come in, notwithstanding her "short leash."

Then, the click of a lock. The door opened and he stepped inside. Jessica Barnes, alone, blinked in surprise. "Gene. What's the matter?"

He swung the door shut and his eyes fell on her mobile phone, lying on her desk.

She sensed immediately what was happening. Her dark eyes wide, she went to the desk, grabbed the mobile and backed away from him. "You . . ." She shook her head. "You're a policeman. You're after him. I should've known."

"Listen to me."

"Oh, I get it now. Yesterday, in the car . . . you were, what do the Brits say? Chatting me up? To get on my good side."

Bond said, "In forty-five minutes Severan's going to kill a lot of people."

"Impossible."

"It's true. Thousands are at risk. He's going to blow up a university in England."

"I don't believe you! He'd never do that." But she hadn't sounded convinced. She'd probably seen too many of Hydt's pictures to deny her partner's obsession with death and decay.

Bond said, "He's selling secrets and blackmailing and killing people because of what he reconstructs from their rubbish." He stepped forward, his hand out for the phone. "Please."

She backed further away, shaking her head. Just outside the open window there was a puddle from a recent storm. She thrust her hand out and held the mobile over it. "Stop!"

Bond did. "I'm running out of time. Please help me."

Interminable seconds passed. Finally her narrow shoulders slumped. She said, "He has a dark side. I used to think it involved just pictures of . . . well, terrible pictures. His sick love of decay. But I've always suspected there was more. Something worse. In his heart he doesn't want to be just a witness to destruction. He wants to *cause* it." She stepped away from the window and handed him the phone.

He took it. "Thank you."

Just then the door flew open. The guard who'd given Bond directions stood there. "What is this? There are no phones for visitors here."

Bond said, "I have an emergency at home. There's an illness in my family. I wanted to see about it. I asked to borrow Ms. Barnes's mobile and she was kind enough to say yes."

"That's right," she confirmed.

"Well, I think I will take it."

"I think you won't," Bond replied.

There was a heavy pause. The man launched himself at Bond, who tossed the phone onto the desk and went into a *systema* defense position. The fight began.

The man had three or four stones on Bond and he was talented—very talented. He'd studied kickboxing and aikido. Bond could counter his moves but it took a lot of effort, and maneuvering was difficult because the office, though large, was cluttered with furniture. At one point the massive guard backed up fast, slamming into Jessica, who screamed and fell to the floor. She lay stunned.

For sixty seconds or so they sparred fiercely, Bond realizing that *systema*'s evasive moves would not be enough. His opponent was strong and showed no sign of tiring.

His eyes focused and fierce, the man judged angles and distances and came in with a kick—or so it seemed. The move was a feint. Bond had anticipated this, though, and when the huge man twisted away, Bond delivered a powerful thrust of his elbow into his kidney, a blow that would not only be excruciatingly painful but could permanently damage the organ.

But, Bond realized too late, the guard had feinted again; he'd taken the hit intentionally so that now he could do as he'd planned and launch himself sideways toward the table where the phone lay. He grabbed the Nokia, snapped it in half and flung the pieces out of the window. One skipped across the surface of the water before it sank.

By the time the man righted himself, however, Bond was on him. He dropped *systema* and went into a classic boxer's stance, swung a left fist into his opponent's solar plexus, doubling him over, then drew back his right and brought it arching down to a spot below and behind the man's ear. The strike was perfectly aimed. The guard shivered and went down, unconscious. He wouldn't be out for long, though, even with a solid hit like that. Bond quickly trussed him with lamp cord and gagged him with napkins from a breakfast tray.

As he did so he turned to Jessica, who was getting to her feet. "Are you all right?" he asked.

"Yes," she whispered breathlessly. She ran to the window. "The phone is gone. What are we going to do? There aren't any others. Only Severan and Niall have them. And he's closed the switchboard today because the employees are off."

Bond said, "Turn round. I'm going to tie you up. It'll be tight—we have to make them believe you didn't try to help me."

She held her hands behind her back and he bound her wrists. "I'm sorry. I tried."

"Sssh," Bond whispered. "I know you did. If someone comes in, tell them you don't know where I went. Just act scared."

"I won't have to act," she said. Then: "Gene . . ."

He glanced at her.

"My mother and I prayed before every one of my beauty contests. I won a lot. We must've prayed pretty well. I'll pray for you now."

Chapter 57

Bond was hurrying down the dim corridor, passing photographs of the reclaimed land that Hydt's workers had turned into Elysian Fields, the beautiful gardens covering Green Way's landfills to the east.

It was nine fifty-five in York. The detonation would take place in thirty-five minutes.

He had to get out of the plant immediately. He was sure there'd be an armory of some kind, probably near the front security post. That was where he was headed now, walking steadily, head down, carrying the maps and the yellow pad. He was about fifty yards from the entrance, thinking tactically. Three men at the security post in front. Was the rear door guarded too? Presumably it was; although there were no employees in the business office, Bond had seen workers throughout the grounds. Three guards had been there yesterday. How many other security personnel would be present? Had any of the visitors handed weapons in or had they all been told to leave them in their cars? Maybe—

"There you are, sir!"

The voice startled him. Two beefy guards appeared and walked in front of him, barring his way. Their faces revealed no emotion. Bond wondered if they'd discovered Jessica and the man he'd trussed up. Apparently not. "Mr. Theron, Mr. Hydt is looking for you. You were not in your office so he sent us to bring you to the conference room."

The smaller one regarded him with eyes as hard as a black beetle's carapace.

There was nothing for it but to go with them. They arrived at the conference room a few minutes later. The larger guard knocked on the door. Dunne opened it, examined Bond with a neutral face and beckoned the men inside. Hydt's three partners sat around a table. The huge, dark-suited security man who'd escorted Bond into the plant yesterday stood near the door, arms crossed.

Hydt called, with the excitement he'd exhibited earlier, "Theron! How have you been getting on?"

"Very well. But I've not quite finished. I'd say I need another fifteen or twenty minutes." He glanced at the door.

But Hydt was like a child. "Yes, yes, but first let me introduce you to the people you'll be working with. I've told them about you and they're eager to meet you. I have about ten investors altogether but these are the three main ones."

As introductions were made, Bond wondered if any one of the three would be suspicious that they had not heard of Mr. Theron. But Mathebula, Eberhard and Huang were distracted by the day's business and, contrary to Hydt's comment, apart from brief nods, they ignored him.

The clock read 12:05. It was 10:05 in York.

Bond tried to leave. But Hydt said, "No, stay." He nodded at the TV, which Dunne had turned on to Sky News in London. He lowered the volume.

"You'll want to see this, our first project. Let me tell you what's going on." Hydt sat down and explained to Bond what he already knew: that Gehenna was about the reconstruction or scanning of classified material, for sale, extortion and blackmail.

Bond lifted an eyebrow, pretending to be impressed. Another glance at the exits. He decided he could hardly bolt for the door; the huge security man in the black suit was inches from it.

"So you see, Theron, I was not quite honest with you the other day when I described the Green Way document-shredding operation. But that was before we had our little test with the Winchester rifle. I apologize."

Bond shrugged it off and measured distances and assessed the strength of his enemy. The conclusions were not encouraging.

With his long, yellowing nails, Hydt raked at his beard. "I'm sure you're curious about what's happening today. I started Gehenna merely to steal and sell classified information. But then I grasped there was a more lucrative . . . and, for me, more *satisfying* use for resurrected secrets. They could be used as weapons. To kill, to destroy.

"Some months ago I met with the head of a drug company I'd been selling reconstructed trade secrets to—outfit called R and K Pharmaceuticals in Apex, North Carolina. He was pleased with that but he had another proposition for me, something a bit more extreme. He told me of a brilliant researcher, a professor in York, who was developing a new cancer drug. When it came to market, my client's company would go out of business. He was willing to pay millions to make sure that the researcher died and his office was destroyed. That was when Gehenna truly blossomed."

Hydt then confirmed Bond's other deductions— about using a prototype of a Serbian bomb they'd

constructed from reassembled plans and blueprints
that people in Hydt's Belgrade subsidiary had managed to piece together. This would make it appear that
the intended target was another professor at the same
university in York—a man who'd testified at the International Criminal Tribunal for the former Yugoslavia. He was teaching a course in Balkan history in the
room next to the cancer researcher's. Everyone would
think that the Slav was the intended target.

Bond glanced at the time on the TV program
crawl. It was ten fifteen in England.

He had to get out now. "Brilliant, absolutely brilliant," he said. "But let me get my notes so I can tell
you all about my idea."

"Stay and watch the festivities." A nod toward the
television. Dunne turned the volume up. Hydt said to
Bond, "We were originally going to detonate the device at ten thirty in England but since we've got confir-
mation that both classes are in session, I think we can
do it now. Besides," Hydt confessed, "I'm rather eager
to see if our device works."

Before Bond could react, Hydt had dialed a number on his phone. He looked at the screen. "Well, the
signal's gone through. We shall see."

Silent, everyone turned to stare at the television. A
recorded item about the royal family was in progress. A
few minutes later the screen went blank, then flashed
to a stark red-and-black logo.

BREAKING NEWS

The screen went to a smartly dressed South Asian
woman sitting at a desk in the newsroom. Her voice

was shaking as she read the story. "We're interrupting this program to report that there has been an explosion in York. Apparently a car bomb . . . the authorities are saying a car bomb has detonated and destroyed a large part of a university building. . . . We're just learning . . . yes, the building is on the grounds of Yorkshire-Bradford University. . . . We have a report that lectures were in progress at the time of the explosion and the rooms nearest the bomb were thought to be full. . . . No one has yet claimed responsibility."

Bond's breath hissed through his set teeth as he stared at the screen. But Severan Hydt's eyes shone in triumph. And everyone else in the room applauded as heartily as if their favorite striker had just kicked a goal at the World Cup.

Chapter 58

Five minutes later, a local news crew had arrived and was beaming pictures of the tragedy to the world. The video footage showed a half-destroyed building, smoke, glass and wreckage covering the ground, rescue workers running, dozens of police cars and fire engines pulling up. The crawl said, *Massive explosion at university in York.*

In this era we've become inured to terrible images on television. Scenes appalling to an eyewitness are somehow tame when observed in two dimensions on the medium that brings us *Doctor Who* and advertisements for Ford Mondeos and M&S fashions.

But this picture of tragedy—a university building in ruins, enveloped by smoke and dust, and people standing about, confused, helpless—was gripping beyond words. It would have been impossible for anybody in the rooms closest to the bomb to survive.

Bond could only stare at the screen.

Hydt did, too, but he, of course, was enraptured. His three partners were chatting among themselves, boisterous, as one might expect of people who had made millions of pounds in a thousandth of a second.

The presenter now reported that the bomb had been loaded with metal shards, like razor blades, which had shot out at thousands of miles per hour. The explosive had ripped apart most of the lecture theaters and the teaching staff's offices on the ground and first floors.

The presenter reported that a newspaper in Hungary had just found a letter, left in its reception area, from a group of Serbian military officers claiming responsibility. The university, the note stated, was "harboring and giving succor" to a professor described as "a traitor to the Serbian people and his race."

Hydt said, "That was our doing too. We collected some Serbian army letterhead from a rubbish bin. That's what the statement's printed on." He glanced at Dunne, and Bond understood that the Irishman had incorporated this fillip into the master blueprint.

The man who thinks of everything . . .

Hydt said, "Now, we need to plan a celebratory lunch."

Bond glanced once more at the screen and started to make for the door.

Just then, though, the presenter cocked her head and said, "We have a new development in York." She sounded confused. She was touching her earpiece, listening. "Yorkshire Police Chief Superintendent Phil Pelham is about to make a statement. We'll go live to him now."

The camera showed a harried middle-aged man in police uniform but without hat or jacket standing in front of a fire engine. A dozen microphones were being thrust toward him. He cleared his throat. "At approximately ten fifteen A.M. today an explosive device detonated on the grounds of Yorkshire-Bradford University. Although property damage was extensive, it appears that there were no fatalities and only half a dozen minor injuries."

The three partners had fallen silent. Niall Dunne's blue eyes twitched with uncharacteristic emotion.

Frowning deeply, Hydt inhaled a rasping breath.

"About ten minutes before the explosion, authorities received word that a bomb had been planted in or around a university in York. Certain additional facts suggested that Yorkshire-Bradford might be the target but as a precaution all educational institutions in the city were evacuated, according to plans put into effect by officials after the Seven-seven attacks in London.

"The injuries—and again I stress they were minor—were sustained mostly by staff, who remained after the students had gone to make certain the evacuation was complete. In addition, one professor—a medical researcher who was lecturing in the hall nearest the bomb—was slightly injured retrieving files from his office just before the explosion.

"We are aware that a Serbian group is claiming credit for the attack and I can assure you that police here in Yorkshire, the Metropolitan Police in London and Security Service investigators are giving this attack the highest priority—"

With the silent tap of a button, Hydt blackened the screen.

"One of your people there?" Huang snapped. "He had a change of heart and warned them!"

"You said we could trust everyone!" the German observed coldly, glaring at Hydt.

The partnership was fraying.

Hydt's eyes slipped to Dunne, on whose face the fractional emotion was gone; the Irishman was concentrating—an engineer calmly analyzing a malfunction. As the partners argued heatedly among themselves Bond took the chance to move to the door.

He was halfway to freedom when it burst open. A

security guard squinted at him and pointed a finger. "Him. He's the one."

"What?" Hydt demanded.

"We found Chenzira and Miss Barnes tied up in her room. He'd been knocked unconscious but as he came to he saw that man reach into Miss Barnes's purse and take something out. A small radio, he thought. That man spoke to someone on it."

Hydt frowned, trying to make sense of this. Yet the look on Dunne's face revealed that he'd almost been expecting a betrayal from Gene Theron. At a glance from the engineer, the massive security man in the black suit drew his gun and pointed it directly at Bond's chest.

Chapter 59

So the guard in Jessica's office had woken sooner than Bond had anticipated . . . and had seen what had happened after he'd tied her up: He had retrieved from her handbag the other items Gregory Lamb had delivered, along with the inhaler, yesterday morning.

The reason Bond had asked Jessica such insensitive questions when they were parked near her house yesterday was to upset, distract and, ideally, to make her cry so that he could take her handbag to find a tissue . . . and to slip into a side pocket the items Sanu Hirani had provided yesterday via Lamb. Among them was the miniature satellite phone, the size of a thick pen. Since the double fence around Green Way made it impossible to hide the instrument in the grass or bushes just inside the perimeter and since Bond knew Jessica was coming back today, he'd decided to hide it in her bag, knowing she'd walk through the metal detector undisturbed.

"Give it to me," Hydt ordered.

Bond reached into his pocket and dug it out. Hydt examined it, then dropped and crushed it beneath his heel. "Who are you? Who are you working for?"

Bond shook his head.

No longer calm, Hydt gazed at the angry faces of his partners, who were asking furiously what steps had been taken to shield their identities. They wanted their mobile phones. Mathebula demanded his gun.

Dunne studied Bond in the way he might a misfiring engine. He spoke softly, as if to himself: "*You* had to be the one in Serbia. And at the army base in March." His brow beneath the blond fringe furrowed. "How did you escape? . . . *How?*" He didn't seem to want an answer; he wasn't speaking to anyone but himself. "And Midlands Disposal wasn't involved. That was a cover for your surveillance there. Then here, the killing fields . . ." His voice ebbed. A look approaching admiration tinted his face, as perhaps he decided Bond was an engineer in his own right, a man who also drafted clever blueprints.

He said to Hydt, "He has contacts in the UK—it's the only way they could have evacuated the university in time. He's with some British security agency. But he would've been working with somebody here. London will have to call Pretoria, though, and we've got enough people in our pocket to stall for a time." He said to one of the guards, "Get the remaining workers out of the plant. Keep only security. Hit the toxic-spill alarm. Marshal everyone into the car park. That'll jam things up nicely if the SAPS or NIA decides to pay us a visit."

The guard walked to an intercom and gave the instructions. An alarm blared and an announcement rattled from the public-address system in various languages.

"And him?" Huang asked, nodding to Bond.

"Oh," Dunne said matter-of-factly, as if it were understood. He looked at the security man. "Kill him and get the body into a furnace."

The huge man was equally blasé as he stepped forward, aiming his Glock pistol with care.

"Please, no!" Bond cried and lifted a hand imploringly.

A natural gesture under the circumstances.

So the guard was surprised by the swirling black razor knife that Bond had pitched toward his face. This was the final item in Hirani's CARE package, hidden in Jessica's bag.

Bond had not been able to adjust his distance for knife throwing, at which he was not particularly proficient anyway, but he'd flung it more as a distraction. The security man, though, swatted away the spiraling weapon and the honed edge cut his hand deeply. Before he recovered or anyone else could react, Bond moved in, twisted the man's wrist back and relieved him of his gun, which he fired into the man's fat leg, both to make sure that the weapon was ready to shoot and to disable the guard further. As Dunne and the other armed guard drew their weapons and began firing, Bond rolled through the door.

The corridor was empty. Slamming the door shut, he sprinted twenty yards and took cover behind, ironically, a green recycling bin.

The door to the conference room opened cautiously. The second armed guard eased out, narrow eyes scanning. Bond saw no reason to kill the young man so he shot him near the elbow. He dropped to the floor, screaming.

Bond knew they would have called for backup so he stood up and continued his flight. As he ran he dropped out the magazine and glanced at it. Ten rounds left. Nine-millimeter, 110-grain, full-metal jacket. Light rounds and with the copper jacketing they'd have less stopping power than a hollow point but they'd shoot flat and fast.

He shoved the magazine back in.

Ten rounds.

Always count . . .

But before he got far, there was a huge snap near his head and the nearly simultaneous boom of a rifle from a side corridor. He saw two men in security-guard khaki approaching, holding Bushmaster assault rifles. Bond fired twice, missing, but giving himself enough cover to kick in the door to the office beside him and run into the cluttered workspace. No one was inside. A fusillade from the .223 slugs tore up the jamb, wall and door.

Eight rounds left.

The two guards seemed to know what they were about—ex-army, he guessed. Deafened by the shots, he couldn't hear voices but from the shadows in the corridor he got the impression that the men had joined up with others, perhaps Dunne among them. He sensed, too, they were about to make a dynamic entry, all of them at once, fanning out, going high and low, right and left. Bond would have no chance against a formation like that.

The shadows moved closer.

Only one move was possible and not a very clever or subtle one. Bond flung a chair through the window and leaped after it, sprawling on the ground six feet below. He landed hard, but with nothing sprained or broken, and sprinted into the Green Way facility, now deserted of workers.

Again he turned toward his pursuers, dropped to the ground, under cover of a detached bulldozer blade sitting near Resurrection Row. He aimed back at the window and a nearby door.

Eight rounds left, eight rounds, eight . . .

He put a bit of pressure on the sensitive trigger, waiting, waiting. Controlling his breathing as best he could.

But the guards weren't going to fall for a trap. The shattered window remained empty. That meant they were heading outside by other exits. Their intention, of course, was to flank him. Which they now did—and very effectively, too. At the south end of the building Dunne and two Green Way guards sprinted to cover behind some lorries.

Instinctively Bond glanced the other way and saw the two guards who'd fired on him in the corridor. They were moving in from the north. They too went to cover, behind a yellow and green digger.

The bulldozer blade protected him from assault only from the west, and the hostiles weren't coming from that direction but from the poles. Bond rolled away just as one of the men started to fire out of the north—the Bushmaster was a short but frighteningly accurate weapon. The bullets thudded into the ground and clanged loudly against the bulldozer's yoke and Bond was pelted with searing shards of lead and copper from the fracturing slugs.

With Bond pinned down by the two in the north, the other team, Dunne leading, moved in closer from the opposite direction. Bond lifted his head slightly to scan for a target. But before he could paint one of his attackers, they moved on, finding cover among the many piles of rubbish, oil drums and equipment. Bond scanned again but couldn't spot them.

Suddenly earth exploded all around him as both groups caught him in a crossfire, the slugs finding homes closer and closer to where he huddled in a dip in the ground. The men to the north vanished behind a low hill, presumably intending to crest it, where they'd have a perfect vantage point from which to snipe at him.

Bond had to leave his position immediately. He turned and crawled as quickly as he could through grass and weeds, east, deeper into the grounds, feeling the chill of absolute vulnerability. The hill was behind him and to the left and he knew the two shooters would soon be at the top, targeting him.

He tried to picture their progress. Fifteen feet from the top, ten, five? Bond imagined them easing slowly up to the hillock, then aiming at him.

Now, he told himself.

But he waited five harrowing seconds more, just to be sure. It seemed like hours. He then rolled onto his back and lifted his pistol over his feet.

One guard was indeed standing on top of the rise, painting a target, his partner crouching beside him.

Bond squeezed the trigger once, then shifted his aim to the right and fired again.

The standing man gripped his chest and went down hard, tumbling to the base of the hill. The Bushmaster slid after him. The other guard had rolled away, unhurt.

Six rounds left. Six.

Four hostiles remaining.

As Dunne and the others peppered his location with rounds, Bond rolled between oil drums in a tall stand of grass, studying his surroundings. His only chance of escape was through the front entrance, a hundred feet away. The pedestrian walkway was open. But a lot of unprotected ground separated him from it. Dunne and his two guards would have a good shooting position, as would the remaining guard still at the top of the hill to the north. He could—

A barrage erupted. Bond kept his face pressed into the dusty ground until there was a pause. Surveying the scene and the positions of the shooters, he rose fast and started to sprint to an anemic tree—at its foot there was some decent cover: oil drums and the carcasses of engines and transmissions. He ran flat-out. But halfway to his destination he stopped abruptly and spun round. One of the guards with Dunne assumed he was going to continue running and had stood tall, leading with his rifle to fire in front of Bond so the bullets would meet him a few yards further on. It hadn't occurred to him that Bond was running solely to force a target to present; the double tap of Bond's 9-mm rounds took the guard down. As the others ducked, he kept running and made it to the tree, then beyond that to a small mound of rubbish. Fifty feet from the gate. A series of shots from Dunne's position forced him to roll into a patch of low vegetation.

Four rounds.

Three hostiles.

He could make it to the gate in ten seconds but that would mean five of full exposure.

He didn't have much choice, though. He would soon be flanked. But then, looking for the enemy, he saw movement through a gap in two tall piles of construction debris. Low on the ground, barely visible through stands of grass, three heads were close to-

gether. The surviving guard from the north had joined
Dunne and the man with him. They didn't notice they
were exposed to Bond and seemed to be whispering
urgently, as if planning their strategy.

All three men were in his field of fire.

It wasn't an impossible shot by any means, though
with the light rounds and an unfamiliar gun, Bond
was at a disadvantage.

Still, he couldn't let the opportunity pass. He had
to act now. At any moment they'd realize they were
vulnerable and go to cover.

Lying prone, Bond aimed the boxy pistol. In com-
petitive shooting, you're never conscious of pulling the
trigger. Accuracy is about controlling your breathing
and keeping your arm and body completely still, with
the sights of your weapon resting steadily on the target. Your trigger finger slowly tightens until the gun
discharges, seemingly of its own accord; the most talented shooters are always somewhat surprised when
their weapons fire.

Under these circumstances, the second and third
shots would have to come more quickly, of course. But
the first was meant for Dunne, and Bond was going to
be sure he didn't miss.

And he didn't.

One powerful crack, then two others in succession.

In shooting, as in golf, you usually know the instant the missile leaves your control whether you've
aimed well or badly. And the fast, shiny rounds struck
exactly where they were aimed, as Bond had known
they would.

Except, he now realized to his dismay, accuracy
wasn't the issue. He'd hit what he'd aimed at, which

turned out not to be his enemies at all but a large piece of shiny chrome that one of the men—the Irishman, of course—must have found in a nearby skip and set up at an angle to reflect their images and draw Bond's fire. The reflective metal tumbled to the ground.

Dammit . . .

The man who thinks of everything. . . .

Instantly the men split up, as Dunne would have instructed, and moved into position, now that Bond had helpfully revealed his exact location.

Two ran to Bond's right, to secure the gate, and Dunne to the left.

One round left. One round.

They didn't know he was nearly out of ammunition, though they soon would.

He was trapped, his only cover a low pile of cardboard and books. They were moving in a circle round him, Dunne in one direction, the other two guards together in another. Soon he'd be in a cross fire again, with no effective protection.

He decided his only chance was to give them a reason not to kill him. He'd tell them he had information to help them get away or offer them a huge sum of money. Anything to stall. He called, "I'm out!" then stood, flinging the gun away, lifting his hands.

The two guards to the right peered out. Seeing that he was unarmed, they cautiously came closer, crouching. "Don't move!" one called. "Keep your hands in the air." Their muzzles were aimed directly at him.

Then, from nearby, a voice said, "What the hell are you doing? We don't need a bloody prisoner. Kill him." The intonation was, of course, Irish.

Chapter 60

The guards looked at each other and apparently decided to share the glory of murdering the man who had brought down Gehenna and killed several of their fellow workers.

They both raised their black weapons to their shoulders.

But just as Bond was about to dive to the ground in a hopeless bid to avoid the slugs, there was a crash behind him. A white van had plowed through the gate, sending chain-link and razor wire flying. Now the vehicle skidded to a stop and the doors flew open. A tall man in a suit, wearing body armor under his jacket, leaped out and began firing at the two guards.

It was Kwalene Nkosi, nervous and tense, but standing his ground.

The guards returned fire, though only to cover their retreat east, deeper into the Green Way facility. They disappeared into the brush. Bond glimpsed Dunne, who was surveying the situation calmly. He turned and sprinted in the same direction as the guards.

Bond picked up the weapon he'd been using and ran to the police vehicle. Bheka Jordaan climbed out and stood beside Nkosi, who was looking around for more targets. Gregory Lamb peered out and stepped cautiously to the ground. He carried a large 1911 Colt .45.

"You decided to come to the party after all," Bond said to her.

"I thought it wouldn't hurt to drive here with some other officers. While we were waiting nearby up the road I heard gunshots. I suspected poaching, which is a crime. That was sufficient cause to enter the premises."

She didn't seem to be joking. He wondered if she had prepared the lines for her superiors. If so, she needed to work on her delivery, Bond decided.

Jordaan said, "I brought a small team with me. Sergeant Mbalula and some other officers are securing the main building."

Bond told her, "Hydt's in there—or was. His three partners too. I'd assume they're armed by now. There'll be other guards." He explained where the hostiles had been and gave a rough geography of the headquarters. Jessica's office, too. He added that the older woman had helped him; she would not be a threat.

At a nod from the captain, Nkosi, keeping low, started for the building.

Jordaan sighed. "We had trouble getting backup. Hydt's being protected by somebody in Pretoria. But I called a friend in the Recces—our special-forces brigade. A team is on its way. They aren't so much concerned about politics; they look for any excuse to fight. But it'll be twenty or thirty minutes before they arrive."

Suddenly Gregory Lamb stiffened. Crouching low, he lumbered south, toward a stand of trees. "I'll flank them."

Flank them? Flank *who*?

"Wait," Bond shouted. "There's nobody there. Go with Kwalene! Secure Hydt."

But the big man seemed not to have heard and

plodded over the ground like an elderly Cape buffalo, disappearing into the brush. What the hell was he doing?

Just then a few rounds peppered the ground near them. Bond and Jordaan dropped to the ground. He forgot about Lamb and looked for a target.

Several hundred yards away Dunne and the two men with him had regrouped and paused in their retreat, firing back at their pursuers. A dozen bullets hit near the van but caused no damage or injury. The three men vanished behind piles of rubbish on the edge of Disappearance Row, the seagull population thinning as the birds fled from the gunfire.

Bond jumped into the driver's seat of the van. In the back, he was pleased to see, were several large containers of ammunition. He started the engine. Jordaan ran to the passenger side. "I'm coming with you," she said.

"Better if I do this myself." He suddenly recalled Philly Maidenstone's recitation of Kipling's verse, which he'd decided was not a bad battle cry.

Down to Gehenna or up to the throne, / He travels the fastest who travels alone. . . .

But Jordaan jumped into the seat beside him and slammed the door. "I said I'd fight by your side if it was legal to do so. Now it is. So go! They're getting away."

Bond hesitated only a moment, then slammed the van into first and they bounded off down the dirt roads that gridded the huge complex, past Silicon Row, Resurrection Row, the power plants.

And rubbish, of course—millions of tons of it: paper, carrier bags, bits of dull and shiny metal, cans, broken furniture, fragments of ceramic and food scraps, over which the eerie canopy of frantic seagulls was reassembling.

It was hard driving as they swerved around earth-moving equipment, skips and bales of refuse awaiting burial, but at least the winding route gave Dunne and the two guards no easy target. The three men turned and fired sporadically but were concentrating mostly on escaping.

On her radio Jordaan called in and reported where they were and whom they were pursuing. The special-forces team would not arrive for at least another thirty minutes, Bond heard the dispatcher tell her.

Just as Dunne and the other men reached the fence separating the filthy sprawl of the plant from the reclaimed area, one guard spun around and fired an entire magazine their way. The rounds pounded the front grille and tires. The van jerked sideways, out of control, and plowed headfirst into a pile of paper bales. The air bags deployed and Bond and Jordaan sat stunned.

Seeing that their enemy was down, Dunne and the other guards began firing in earnest.

Amid the sound of bullets slamming into sheet metal, Bond and Jordaan rolled out of the shuddering vehicle and into a ditch. "You injured?" he asked.

"No. I . . . It's so loud!" Her voice quivered but her eyes told Bond she was successfully fighting down her fear.

From beneath the wing of the van, Bond had a good shot at one of their adversaries and, lying prone, he aimed with the automatic.

One round left.

He squeezed the trigger—but the instant the firing pin hit primer, the man ducked. He was gone when the bullet arrived.

Bond grabbed an ammunition box and ripped off the lid. It contained only .223 rounds, for rifles. The second held the same. In fact, they all did. There were. no 9-mm pistol rounds. He sighed and looked through the van. "Do you have anything that'll shoot these?" He gestured at the bullets, which were useless in his weapon.

"No assault rifles. All I have is this." She drew her own weapon. "Here, you take it."

The pistol was a Colt Python, a .357-caliber magnum—powerful and boasting a tight cylinder lockup and superb pull. A good weapon. But it was a revolver, holding only six rounds.

No, he corrected when he checked. Jordaan was a conservative gun owner and kept the chamber under the hammer empty. "Speedloader? Loose rounds?"

"No."

So they had five bullets against three adversaries with semiautomatic weapons. "You've never heard of Glocks?" he muttered, slipping the empty one into his back waistband and weighing the Colt in his palm.

"I investigate crimes," she replied coolly. "I don't have much occasion to shoot people."

Though when those rare instances *do* arise, he thought angrily, it would be helpful to have the right tool. He said, "You go back. Just keep to cover."

She was looking steadily into his eyes, sweat beading at her temples, where her luxurious black hair frothed. "If you're going after them I'm coming with you."

"Without a weapon, there's nothing you can do."

Jordaan glanced to where Dunne and the others had disappeared. "They have a number of guns and we only have one. That's not fair. We must take one away from them."

Well, maybe Captain Bheka Jordaan had a sense of humor after all.

They shared a smile and in her fierce eyes Bond saw the reflection of orange flames from the burning methane. It was a striking image.

Crouching, they slipped into Elysian Fields, using for cover a dense garden of fine-needled fynbos varieties, watsonias, grasses, jacaranda and king protea. There were kigelia trees too, and some young baobabs. Even in the late autumn, much of the foliage was in full color, thanks to the Western Cape climate. A brace of guinea fowl observed them with some irritation and continued on their awkward way. Their gait reminded Bond of Niall Dunne's.

He and Jordaan were seventy-five yards into the park when the assault began. The trio had been moving away but it seemed that they had done so merely to lure Bond and the SAPS officer further into the wilderness . . . and a trap. The men had split up. One of the guards dropped on to a hillock of soft green ground cover and laid down suppressing fire while the other—Dunne, too, possibly, though Bond couldn't see him—crashed through the tall grasses toward them.

Bond had a good shot and took it but the guard went to cover the instant Bond fired. He missed again. Slow down, he told himself.

Four rounds left. Four.

Jordaan and Bond scrabbled into a dip near a small

field filled with succulents and a pond that would probably be home to stately koi, come the spring. They looked up, over the grass veld, scanning for targets. Then what seemed to be a thousand shots, though it was probably more like forty or fifty, rained down on them, striking close, shattering rock and spraying water.

The two men in khaki, probably desperate and frustrated at their delayed escape, tried a bold assault, charging Bond and Jordaan from different directions. Bond fired twice at the man coming at them from the left, hitting the man's rifle and left arm. The guard cried out in pain and dropped the weapon, which tumbled to the bottom of the hill. Bond saw that, though the man's forearm was injured, he'd drawn a pistol with his right hand and was otherwise capable of fighting. The second guard made a run to cover and Bond fired fast, tapping him somewhere on his thigh, but that wound too seemed superficial. He vanished into the brush.

One round, one round.

Where was Dunne?

Sneaking up behind them?

Then silence again, though silence filled with ringing in their ears and the internal bass of heartbeats. Jordaan was shivering. Bond eyed the Bushmaster, the rifle that the injured guard had dropped. It lay around ten yards from them.

He studied the scene around them carefully, the landscape, the plants, the trees.

Then he noted tall grasses swaying fifty or sixty yards distant; the two guards, invisible in the thick foliage, were moving in, keeping some distance between them. In a minute or two they'd be on top of Bond and Jordaan. He might take one out with his last bullet but the other guard would be successful.

"James," Jordaan whispered, squeezing his arm. "I'll lead them off—I'll go that way." She pointed to a plain covered with low grass. "If you fire, you can hit one and the other may take cover. That'll give you a chance to get to the rifle."

"It's suicide," he whispered back. "You'd be completely exposed."

"You really *must* stop your incessant flirting, James."

He smiled. "Listen. If anybody's going to be a hero, it's me. I'm going to head toward them. When I tell you, go for the Bushmaster." He pointed to the black rifle lying in the dust. "You're qualified to use it?"

She nodded.

The guards moved closer. Thirty yards now.

Bond whispered, "Stay low until I tell you. Get ready."

The guards were making their way cautiously through the tall grass. Bond surveyed the landscape again, took a deep breath, then rose calmly and walked toward them, his pistol pointed down at his side. He raised his left hand.

"James, no!" Jordaan whispered.

Bond did not respond. He called to the men, "I want to talk to you. If you help me get the names of the other people involved, you'll receive a reward. There'll be no charges against you. You understand?"

The two guards, about ten paces apart, stopped. They were confused. They saw that he couldn't hit them both before the other shot him, yet he was walking slowly in their direction, calm, not lifting his pistol.

"Do you understand? The reward is fifty thousand rand."

They stared at each other, nodding a little too enthusiastically. Bond knew they were not seriously considering his offer; they were thinking they might draw him closer before they fired. They faced him.

And as they did so the powerful gun in Bond's hand barked once, still pointed downward, letting go its final bullet into the ground. As the guards crouched, startled, Bond sprinted to his left, putting a row of trees between him and the guards.

They glanced at each other, then grinned and ran forward to where they had a better view of Bond, who dived behind a hill as their Bushmasters began to clatter.

It was then that the entire world exploded.

The muzzle flashes from the men's rifles ignited the methane spewing from the fake tree root, transporting the gas from the landfill beneath them to Green Way's burn off facilities. Bond had ruptured it with his last bullet.

The men now vanished in a tidal wave of flame, a roiling thunderhead. The guards and the ground they'd stood on were simply gone, the fire widening as panicked birds fled into the air, the trees and brush bursting into flames as if they were soaked in incendiary accelerant.

Twenty feet away Jordaan rose unsteadily. She started toward the Bushmaster. But Bond ran to her, shouting, "Change of plan. Forget it!"

"What should we do?"

They were thrown to the ground as another mushroom cloud of flame erupted not far away. The roar was so loud Bond had to press his lips against her sumptuous hair to make himself heard. "Might be a good idea to leave."

Chapter 61

"You are making a terrible mistake!"

Severan Hydt's voice was low with threat but a very different state of mind was revealed in the expression on his long, bearded face: horror at the destruction of his empire, both physical, from the fires in the distance, and legal, from the special-forces troops and police descending on the grounds and office.

There was nothing imperious about him now.

Hydt, in handcuffs, and Jordaan, Nkosi and Bond were standing amid a cluster of bulldozers and lorries in the open area between the office and Resurrection Row. They were near the spot where Bond would have been killed . . . if not for Bheka Jordaan's dramatic arrival to arrest the "poachers."

Sergeant Mbalula handed Bond his Walther, extra clips and mobile phone from the Subaru.

"Thank you, Sergeant."

SAPS officers and South African Special Forces roamed through the facility, looking for more suspects and collecting evidence. In the distance, fire crews were struggling—and it was a struggle—to put out the methane fires, as the western edge of Elysian Fields became just another outpost of hell.

Apparently the corrupt politicians in Pretoria, the ones in Hydt's pocket, had not been so very high up, after all. Senior officials stepped in quickly and ordered their arrest and full backup for Jordaan's operation in Cape Town. Additional officers were sent to seize Green Way's offices in all South African cities.

Medics scurried about here too, attending to the wounded, which included only Hydt's security staff.

Hydt's three partners were in custody, Huang, Eberhard and Mathebula. It was not clear yet what their crimes were but that would be established soon. At the very least they had all smuggled firearms into the country, justifying their arrest.

Four of the surviving guards were in custody and most of the hundred or so Green Way employees who'd been milling about in the car park had been detained, pending questioning.

Dunne had escaped. Special-forces officers had found evidence of a motorcycle, which had apparently been hidden under a tarp covered with straw. Of course, the Irishman would have kept his lifeboat ready.

Severan Hydt persisted, "I'm innocent! You're persecuting me because I'm British. And white. You're prejudiced."

Jordaan could not ignore this. "Prejudiced? I've arrested six black men, four whites and an Asian. If that's not a rainbow, I don't know what is."

The reality of the disaster kept coming home to him. His eyes swiveled away from the fires and began taking in the rest of the grounds. He was probably looking for Dunne. He would be lost without his engineer.

He glanced at Bond, then said to Jordaan, his voice laced with desperation, "What sort of arrangement could we work out? I'm very wealthy."

"That's fortunate," she said. "Your legal bills will be quite high."

"I'm not trying to bribe you."

"I should hope not. That's a very serious offense." She then said matter-of-factly, "I want to know where Niall Dunne has gone. If you tell me, I'll let the prosecution know that you helped me find him."

"I can give you the address of his flat here—"

"I've already sent officers there. Tell me some other places he might go to."

"Yes . . . I'm sure I can think of something."

Bond noticed Gregory Lamb approaching from a deserted part of the grounds, carrying his large pistol as if he'd never fired a weapon. Bond left Jordaan and Hydt standing together between rows of pallets containing empty oil drums and joined Lamb near a battered skip.

"Ah, Bond," the Six agent said, breathing heavily and sweating despite the chilly autumn air. His face was streaked with dirt and there was a tear in the sleeve of his jacket.

"You catch one?" Bond nodded at the slash, caused, it seemed, by a bullet.

"Didn't do any damage, thankfully. Except to my favorite gabardine."

He was lucky. An inch to the left and the slug would have shattered his upper arm. The assailant had been close; powder burns surrounded the rent.

"What happened to the guys you went after?" Bond asked. "I never saw them."

"Got away, sorry to say. They split up. I knew they were trying to circle back on me but I went after one of them anyway. That's how I got my Lord Nelson here." He touched his sleeve. "But dammit, they knew the lie of the land and I didn't. I got a piece of one of them, though."

"Do you want to follow the blood trail?"

He blinked. "Oh. I did. But it vanished."

Bond lost interest in the adventurer's excursion into the bush and moved aside to call London. He was just punching in the number when, a few yards away, he heard a series of loud cracks he recognized instantly as powerful bullets finding a target, followed by the booms of a distant rifle's report.

Bond spun round, his hand going for his Walther as he scanned the grounds. But he saw no sign of the shooter—only his victim: Bheka Jordaan, her chest and face a mass of blood, clawed at the air as she stumbled backward and rolled into a muddy ditch.

Chapter 62

"No!" Bond cried.

His inclination was to run to her aid. But the amount of blood, bone, and and tissue he'd seen told him she could not have survived the devastating shots.

No . . .

Bond thought of Ugogo, of the fiery orange gleam in Jordaan's eye as they'd taken on the two guards in Elysian Fields, the faint smile.

They have a number of guns and we only have one. That's not fair. We must take one away from them. . . .

"Captain!" Nkosi cried, from his position behind a skip nearby. Other SAPS officers were firing randomly now.

"Hold your fire!" Bond shouted. "No blind shooting. Guard the visible perimeter, look for muzzle flashes."

The special forces were more restrained, watching for targets from good cover positions.

So the engineer *did* have an escape plan for his beloved boss. *That's what* Hydt had been looking for. Dunne would keep the officers pinned down while Hydt fled, probably to where the other security guards were waiting in the woods nearby with a car or perhaps even a helicopter hidden on the grounds. Hydt had not started his sprint to freedom yet, though; he'd still be hiding between the rows of pallets where Jordaan had been questioning him. He would be waiting for more covering fire.

Crouching, Bond began to make his way there. Any minute now, the man would make a run for the brush, protected by Dunne and perhaps other loyal guards.

And James Bond was not going to let that happen.

He heard Gregory Lamb whisper, "Is it safe?" but couldn't see him. He realized the man had dived into a full skip.

Bond had to move. Even if it meant exposing himself to Dunne's fine marksmanship, he wouldn't let Hydt escape. Bheka Jordaan would not have died in vain.

He sprinted into the shadowy space between the tall pallets of oil drums to secure Hydt, his gun raised to firing position.

And froze at what he saw before him. Severan Hydt was not about to escape anywhere. The Rag-and-Bone Man, the visionary king of decay, the lord of entropy, lay on his back, two bullet wounds in his chest, a third in his forehead. A significant part of the back of his skull was missing.

Bond slipped his gun away. Around him the tactical forces began to rise. One called that the sniper had left his shooting position and vanished into the bush.

Then a harsh sound behind him, a woman's voice: "*Sihlama!*"

Bond spun around to see Bheka Jordaan crawling from the ditch, wiping her face and spitting blood. She was unharmed.

Either Dunne had missed completely or his boss had been his intended target. The gore on Jordaan was Hydt's—it had spattered her as she stood beside him.

Bond pulled her to cover behind the oil drums,

smelling the sickly copper scent of blood. "Dunne's still out there somewhere."

Nkosi called, "You are okay, Captain?"

"Yes, yes," she said dismissively. "What about Hydt?"

"He's dead," Bond said.

"*Masende!*" she snapped.

This brought a smile to Nkosi's face.

Jordaan tugged her shirt off—underneath she wore body armor over a black cotton vest—and wiped her face, neck and hair with it.

A call came in from officers on the ridge that the perimeter was clear. Dunne, of course, would have had no interest in staying; he'd accomplished what he needed to.

Bond regarded the body once more. He decided that the tight grouping of the shots meant that Hydt had indeed been the intended target. Of course, this made sense; Dunne had had to kill the man to make sure he told the police nothing about him. Now he recalled several glances that Dunne had cast toward Hydt over the past few days, dark looks, hinting at . . . what? Irritation, resentment? Almost jealousy, it seemed. Perhaps there was something else behind the murder of the Rag-and-Bone Man. Something personal.

Whatever the reason, he'd certainly done a typically proficient job.

Jordaan hurried into the office building. Ten minutes later she emerged. She'd found a shower or tap somewhere; her face and hair were damp but more or less blood-free. She was furious with herself. "I lost my prisoner. I should have guarded him better. I never thought—"

A ghastly wail interrupted her. Someone was speeding forward, "No, no, no . . ."

Jessica Barnes was running toward Hydt's body. She flung herself to the ground, oblivious to the grotesque wounds, and cradled her dead lover.

Bond stepped forward, gripped her narrow, quivering shoulders and helped her up. "No, Jessica. Come over here with me." Bond led her to cover behind a bulldozer. Bheka Jordaan joined them.

"He's dead, he's dead. . . ." Jessica pressed her head against Bond's shoulder.

Bheka Jordaan lifted her handcuffs out of their holster.

"She tried to help me," Bond reminded her. "She didn't know what Hydt was doing. I'm sure of it."

Jordaan put the cuffs away. "We'll drive her down to the station, take a statement. I don't think we'll have to pursue it beyond that."

Bond detached himself from Jessica. He took her by the shoulders. "Thank you for helping me. I know it was hard."

She breathed in deeply. Then, calmer, she asked, "Who did it? Who shot him?"

"Dunne."

She didn't seem surprised. "I never liked him. Severan was passionate, impulsive. He never thought things through. Niall realized that and seduced him with all his planning and his intelligence. I didn't think he could be trusted. But I never had the courage to say anything." She closed her eyes momentarily.

"You did a good job with the praying," Bond told her.

"Too good," she whispered.

On Jessica's cheek and neck were stark patches of

Hydt's blood. It was the first time, Bond realized, that he'd seen any color on her.

He looked her in the eye. "I know some people who can help when you get back to London. They'll be in touch. I'll see to it."

"Thank you," Jessica murmured.

A policewoman led her away.

Bond was startled by a man's voice nearby: "Is it clear?"

He frowned, unable to see the speaker. Then he understood. Gregory Lamb was still in the skip. "It's clear."

The agent scrambled out of his hiding place.

"Mind the blood," Bond told Lamb, as he nearly stepped in some.

"Oh my God!" Lamb muttered and looked as if he was going to be sick.

Ignoring him, Bond said to Jordaan, "I need to know how extensive Gehenna is. Can you get your officers to collect all the files and computers in Research and Development? And I'll need your computer-crimes outfit to crack the passwords."

"Yes, of course. We'll have them brought to the SAPS office. You can review them there."

Nkosi said, "I'll do it, Commander."

Bond thanked him. The man's round face seemed less wry and irrepressible than earlier. Bond supposed this had been his first firefight. He'd be changed forever by the incident but, from what Bond was seeing, the change would not diminish but rather would enhance the young officer. Nkosi gestured toward some SAPS Forensic Science Service officers and led them inside the building.

Bond glanced at Jordaan. "Can I ask you a question?"

She turned to him.

"What did you say? After you climbed out of the ditch, you said something."

With her particular complexion, she might or might not have been blushing. "Don't tell Ugogo."

"I won't."

"The first was Zulu for . . . I guess you'd say, in English, 'crap.'"

"I have some variations on that myself. And the other word?"

She squinted. "That, I think, I will not tell you, James."

"Why not?"

"Because it refers to a certain part of the male anatomy . . . and I do not think it wise to encourage you in that regard."

Chapter 63

Late afternoon, the sun beginning to dip in the north-west, James Bond drove from the Table Mountain Hotel, where he'd showered and changed, to Cape Town's central police station.

As he entered and made for Jordaan's office he noticed several pairs of eyes staring at him. The expressions were no longer wary or curious, as had been the case upon his first visit here, several days ago; they were admiring. Perhaps the story of his role in foiling Severan Hydt's plan had circulated. Or the tale of how he'd taken out two adversaries and blown up a landfill with a single bullet, no mean accomplishment. (The fire, Bond had learned, was largely extinguished—to his immense relief. He would not have wanted to be known as the man who had burned a sizable area of Cape Town to its sandstone foundation.)

He was met by Bheka Jordaan in the hall. She'd taken another shower to clean off the remnants of Severan Hydt and had changed into dark trousers and a yellow shirt, bright and cheerful, perhaps an antidote to the horror of the events at Green Way.

She gestured him into her office. They sat together in chairs before her desk. "Dunne's managed to get to Mozambique. Government security spotted him there but he got lost in some unsavory part of Maputo—which, frankly, is most of the city. I called some colleagues in Pretoria, in Financial Intelligence, the Special Investigations Unit and the Banking Risk Information Center. They checked his accounts—under a warrant, of course. Yesterday afternoon two hundred thousand pounds were wired into a Swiss account of Dunne's. Half an hour ago he transferred it to dozens of anonymous online accounts. He can access it from anywhere, so we have no idea where he intends to go."

Bond's expression of disgust closely matched hers.

"If he surfaces or leaves Mozambique, their security people will let me know. But until then he's out of our reach."

It was then that Nkosi appeared, pushing a large cart filled with boxes—the documents and laptop computers from the Green Way Research and Development department.

The warrant officer and Bond followed Jordaan to an empty office where Nkosi put the boxes on the floor around the desk. Bond started to lift off a lid but Jordaan said quickly, "Put these on. I won't have you ruining evidence." She handed him blue latex gloves.

Bond gave a wry laugh but took them. Jordaan and Nkosi left him to the job. Before he opened the boxes, though, he placed a call to Bill Tanner.

"James," the chief of staff said. "We've got the signals. Sounds like all hell's broken loose down there."

Bond laughed at his choice of words and explained in detail about the shootout at Green Way, Hydt's fate and Dunne's escape. He explained too about the drug company president in North Carolina, the man who'd hired Hydt; Tanner would ask the FBI in Washington to open an investigation of their own and arrest the man.

Bond said, "I need a rendition team to capture Dunne—if we can find out where he is. Any of our double-one agents nearby?"

Tanner sighed. "I'll see what I can do, James, but I don't have a lot of people to spare, not with the situation in eastern Sudan. We're helping the FCO and the marines with security. I might be able to get you some special forces—SAS or SBS? Would that suit?"

"Fine. I'm going to look through everything we've collected from Hydt's headquarters. I'll call back when I've finished and brief M."

They rang off and Bond started to lay out the Gehenna documents on the large desk in the office Jordaan had provided. He hesitated. Then, feeling ridiculous, he slipped on the blue gloves, deciding that at least they would provide an amusing story for his friend Ronnie Vallance of the Yard. Vallance often said that Bond would make a terrible detective-inspector, given his preference for beating up or shooting perpetrators, rather than marshaling evidence to see them in the dock.

He leafed through the documents for almost an hour. Finally, when he felt well enough informed to discuss the situation, he telephoned London again.

M said gruffly, "It's a nightmare here, 007. That fool in Division Three pushed a very big button. Got all of Whitehall closed up. Downing Street, too. If there's anything that plays badly with the tabloids, it's an international security meeting being canceled because of a bloody security alert."

"Was it groundless?" Bond had been convinced

that York was the site of the attack but that didn't mean London wasn't at some risk, as he'd told Tanner during his satellite call from Jessica Barnes's office.

"Nothing. Green Way had its legitimate side, of course. The company's engineers were working with the police to make sure the refuse-removal tunnels around Whitehall were safe. No dangerous radiation, no explosives, no Guy Fawkes. And as for Afghanistan, yes, there was a spike in SIGINT traffic recently but that was because we and the CIA descended on the place like wolves last Monday. And everybody was wondering what the hell we were doing there."

"And Osborne-Smith?"

"Inconsequential."

Bond didn't know whether the word referred to the man himself or meant that his fate was not worth discussing.

"Now, what's been going on down there, 007? I want details."

Bond explained first about Hydt's death and the arrest of his three main partners. He also described Dunne's escape and Bond's plan to execute the Level 2 project order from Sunday, which was still valid, for the Irishman's rendition when they found him.

Then Bond detailed Gehenna—Hydt's stealing and assembling classified information—the blackmail and extortion, adding the cities where most of his efforts had taken place: "London, Moscow, Paris, Tokyo, New York and Mumbai, and there are smaller operations in Belgrade, Washington, Taipei and Sydney."

There was silence for a moment and Bond imagined M chomping his cheroot as he took it all in. The man said, "Damn clever, putting all that together from rubbish."

"Hydt said nobody ever sees dustmen and it's true. They're invisible. They're everywhere and yet you look right through them."

M gave a rare chuckle. "I happened to be thinking much the same myself yesterday." Then he grew serious. "What're your recommendations, 007?"

"I'd get our embassy people and Six to roll up all the Green Way operations as fast as they can before the actors start disappearing. Freeze their assets and trace all incoming monies. That'll lead us to the rest of the Gehenna clients."

"Hmm," M said, his voice uncharacteristically light. "I suppose we *could*."

What was the old man thinking?

"Though I'm not sure we should be too hasty. Let's arrest the principals in all the locations, yes. But what do you think about getting some double-one agents into their offices and keeping Gehenna going a bit longer in some places, 007? I'd love to see what GRS Aerospace outside Moscow throws away. And I wonder what the Pakistani consulate in Mumbai is shredding. Be interesting to find out. We'd have to pull in some favors with the press to stop them reporting what Hydt was really up to. I'll have the misinformation chaps at Six leak word that he was mixed up with organized crime or some such. We'll keep it vague. Word will get out at some point but by then we'll have scooped up some valuable finds."

The old fox. Bond laughed to himself. So the ODG was going into the recycling business. "Brilliant, sir."

"Get all the details to Bill Tanner and we'll go from there." M paused, then barked, "Osborne-bloody-Smith has brought traffic in London to a complete standstill. It'll take me ages to get home. I've *never* understood why they couldn't run the M4 all the way in to Earls Court."

The line went dead.

Chapter 64

James Bond found Felicity Willing's business card and called her at her office to break the news that one of her donors was a criminal . . . and had died in an operation to arrest him.

But she'd heard. Already reporters had been on to her and asked for a statement, in light of the fact that Green Way was heavily involved with the Mafia and the Camorra (Bond reflected that the grass did not grow beneath the feet of the "misinformation chaps at Six").

Felicity was furious that some journalists were suggesting she'd known there was something disreputable about him but that she'd been happy to take his donations anyway. "How the bloody hell could they ask that, Gene? For heaven's sake, Hydt gave us fifty or sixty thousand pounds a year, which was generous but nothing compared to what a lot of people donate. I'd drop anyone in an instant if I thought they were up to something illegal." Her voice softened. "But you're all right, aren't you?"

"I wasn't even there when they raided the place. The police rang me and asked a few questions. That's all. Hell of a shock, though."

"I'm sure it was."

Bond asked how the deliveries were going. She told him that the tonnage was even higher than had been pledged. Distribution was already under way to ten different countries in sub-Saharan Africa. There was enough food to keep hundreds of thousands of people fed for months.

Bond congratulated her, then said, "You're not too busy for Franschhoek?"

"If you think you're getting out of our weekend in the country, Gene, you'd better think again."

They made plans to meet in the morning. He reminded himself to find someone to wash and polish the Subaru, for which he'd formed some affection, despite the flashy color and the largely cosmetic spoiler on the boot.

After they'd disconnected, he sat back, relishing the cheer in her voice. Relishing, too, the memory of the time they'd spent together. And thinking of the future.

If you do go to some dark places, could you promise me not to go to the . . . worst?

Smiling, he flicked her card, then put it down and pulled on the gloves once more to continue plowing through the documents and computers, jotting notes about Green Way's offices and the Gehenna operation for M and Bill Tanner. He labored for an hour or so until he decided it was time for a drink.

He stretched luxuriously.

And paused, slowly lowering his arms. At that moment he had felt a jolt deep within him. He knew the sensation. It arose occasionally in the world of espionage, that great landscape of subtext where so little is as it seems. Often the source for such an unsettling stab was a suspicion that a basic assumption had been wrong, perhaps disastrously so.

Staring at his notes, he heard himself breathing fast, his lips dry. His heartbeat quickened.

Bond flipped through hundreds of documents again, then grabbed his mobile and e-mailed Philly Maidenstone a priority request. As he waited for her reply, he rose and paced in the small office, his mind inundated with thoughts, hovering and swooping like the frantic seagulls over Disappearance Row at Green Way.

When Philly responded he snatched up his mobile and read the message, sitting back slowly in the uncomfortable chair.

A shadow fell over him. He looked up and found Bheka Jordaan standing there. She was saying, "James, I brought you some coffee. In a proper mug." It was decorated with the smiling faces of the players from Bafana Bafana in all their football finest.

When he said nothing and didn't take it, she set it down. "James?"

Bond knew his face betrayed the alarm burning within him. After a moment he whispered, "I think I got it wrong."

"What do you mean?"

"Everything. About Gehenna, about Incident Twenty."

"Tell me."

Bond sat forward. "The original intelligence we had was that someone named Noah was involved in the event today—the event that would result in all those deaths."

"Yes." She sat next to him. "Severan Hydt."

Bond shook his head. He waved at the boxes of documents from Green Way. "But I've been through nearly every damn piece of paper and most of the mobiles and computers. There isn't a single reference to

Noah in any of it. And in all my meetings with Hydt and Dunne there was no reference to the name. If that *was* his nickname, why didn't it turn up in *something*? An idea occurred to me so I contacted an associate at MI6. She knows computers rather well. Are you familiar with metadata?"

Jordaan said, "Information embedded in computer files. We convicted a government minister of corruption because of it."

He nodded at his phone. "My colleague looked at the half-dozen Internet references we found that mentioned Hydt's nickname was Noah. The metadata in every one of them showed they were written and uploaded this week."

"Just like *we* uploaded data about Gene Theron to create your cover."

"Exactly. The real Noah did that to keep us focused on Hydt. Which means Incident Twenty—the thousands of deaths—*wasn't* the bombing in York. Gehenna and Incident Twenty are two entirely different plans. Something else is going to happen. And soon—tonight. That's what the original e-mail said. Those people, whoever they are, are still at risk."

Despite the success at Green Way, he was back to the vital questions once more: Who was his enemy and what was his purpose?

Until he answered those inquiries he couldn't form a response.

Yet he had to. There was little time left.

confirm incident friday night, 20th,
estimated initial casualties in the
thousands . . .

"James?"

Fragments of facts, memories and theories spiraled through his mind. Once again, as he'd done in the bowels of Green Way's research facility, he began to assemble all the bits of information he possessed, trying to put back together the shredded blueprint of Incident Twenty. He rose and, hands clasped behind his back, bent forward as he looked over the papers and notes covering the desk.

Jordaan had fallen silent.

Finally he whispered, "Gregory Lamb."

She frowned. "What about him?"

Bond didn't answer immediately. He sat down again. "I'll need your help."

"Of course."

Chapter 65

"What's the matter, Gene? You said it was urgent."

They were alone in Felicity Willing's office at the charity in downtown Cape Town, not far from the club where they'd met at the auction on Wednesday night. Bond had interrupted a meeting involving a dozen men and women, aid workers instrumental in the food deliveries, and asked to see her alone. He now swung her door closed. "I'm hoping you can help me. There aren't many people in Cape Town I can trust."

"Of course." They sat on her cheap sofa. In black jeans and a white shirt, Felicity moved closer to Bond. Their knees touched. She seemed even more tired than yesterday. He recalled she'd left his room before dawn.

"First, I have to confess something to you. And, well, it may affect our plans for Franschhoek—it may affect a lot of plans."

Frowning, she nodded.

"And I have to ask you to keep this to yourself. That's very important."

Her keen eyes probed his face. "Of course. But tell me, please. You're making me nervous."

"I'm not who I said I was. From time to time I do some work for the British government."

A whisper: "You're a . . . spy?"

He laughed. "No, nothing as grand as that. The

title is security and integrity analyst. Usually it's as boring as can be."

"But you're one of the good guys?"

"You could put it like that."

Felicity lowered her head to his shoulder. "When you said you were a security consultant, in Africa that usually means a mercenary. You said you weren't but I didn't quite believe it."

"It was a cover. I was investigating Hydt."

Her face flooded with relief. "And I was asking if you could change a little bit. And . . . now you've changed *completely* from who I thought you were. A hundred and eighty degrees."

Bond said wryly, "How often does a man do that?"

She smiled briefly. "That means . . . you're not Gene? And you're not from Durban?"

"No. I live in London." And discarding the faint Afrikaans accent, he extended his hand. "My name's James. It's good to meet you, Miss Willing. Are you going to throw me out?"

She hesitated only briefly, then flung her arms around him, laughing. She sat back. "But you said you needed my help."

"I wouldn't involve you if there was any other way but I've run out of time. Thousands of lives are at stake."

"My God! What can I do?"

"Do you know anything about Gregory Lamb?"

"Lamb?" Felicity's thin eyebrows drew together. "He comes over as a rather high roller so I've ap-proached him for donations several times. He always said he'd give us something but he never did. He's rather a queer man. A boor." She laughed. "B-O-O-R. Not Afrikaner."

"I have to tell you he's a bit more than that."

"We heard rumors that he was in the pay of somebody. Though I can't imagine anybody taking him seriously as a spy."

"I think that's an act. He plays the fool to put people at ease around him so they don't suspect he's up to some pretty rough business. Now, you've been down at the docks for the past few days, right?"

"Yes, quite a bit."

"Did you hear anything about a big ship charter that Lamb's putting together tonight?"

"I did, yes, but I don't know anything about it. I'm sorry."

Bond was silent for a moment. Then: "Have you ever heard anyone refer to Lamb as Noah?"

Felicity thought about it. "I can't say for certain but . . . wait, yes, I think so. A nickname somebody once used for him. Because of the shipping business. But what did you mean when you said, 'Thousands of lives are at stake'?"

"I'm not sure exactly what he has in mind. My guess is he's going to use the cargo ship to sink a cruise liner, a British one."

"My God, no! But why on earth would he do that?"

"With Lamb, it has to be money. Hired by Islamists, warlords or pirates. I'll know more soon. We've tapped his phone. He's meeting somebody in an hour or so at a deserted hotel south of town, the Sixth Apostle Inn. I'll be there to find out what he's up to."

Felicity said, "But . . . James, why do you have to go? Why not call the police and have him arrested?"

Bond hesitated. "I can't really use the police for this."

"Because of your job," she asked evenly, "as a 'security analyst'?"

He paused. "Yes."

"I see." Felicity Willing nodded. Then she leaned forward fast and kissed him full on the lips. "In answer to your question, whatever you do, James, whatever you're *going* to do, it won't affect our plans for Franschhoek one bit. Or our plans for anything else, as far as I'm concerned."

Chapter 66

In May the sun sets in Cape Town around half past five. As Bond sped south on Victoria Road, the scenery grew surreal, bathed in a glorious sunset. Then dusk descended, streaked by slashes of purple cloud over the turbulent Atlantic.

He'd left Table Mountain behind, Lion's Head too, and was now motoring parallel to the solemn craggy rock formations of the Twelve Apostles mountain chain to his left, dotted with grasses, fynbos and splashes of protea. Defiant cluster pines sprouted in incongruous places.

Half an hour after leaving Felicity Willing's office, he spotted the turning to the Sixth Apostle Inn, to the left, east. Two signs marked the drive: the name of the place in peeling, faded paint, and below that, brighter and newer, a warning about construction in progress, prohibiting trespass.

Bond skidded the Subaru into the entrance, doused the lights and proceeded slowly along a lengthy winding drive, gravel grinding under the tires. It led directly toward the imposing face of the Apostle ridge, which rose a hundred or more feet behind the building.

Before him was the inn, shabby and desperately in need of the promised reconstruction, though he supposed it had once been *the* place for a holiday or to romance your mistress from London or Hong Kong. The rambling one-story structure was set amid extensive gardens, now overgrown and gone to seed.

Bond drove round to the back and into the weed-filled car park. He hid the Subaru in a stand of brush and tall grass, climbed out and looked toward the darkened caravan used by the construction crews. He swept his torch over it. There were no signs of occupation. Then, drawing his Walther, he made his way silently to the inn.

The front door was unlocked and he walked inside, smelling mold, new concrete and paint. At the end of the lobby, the front desk had no counter. To the right he found sitting rooms and a library, to the left a large breakfast room and lounge, with French windows facing north, offering a view of the gardens and above them the Twelve Apostles, still faintly visible in the dusk. Inside this room the construction workers had left their drill presses, table saws and various other tools, all chained and padlocked. Behind that area there was a passage to the kitchen. Bond noticed switches for both work and overhead lights but he kept the place dark.

Tiny animal feet skittered beneath the floorboards and in the walls.

Bond sat down in a corner of the breakfast room, on a workman's tool kit. There was nothing to do but wait until the enemy appeared.

Bond thought of Lieutenant Colonel Bill Tanner, who had said to him not long after he joined ODG, "Listen, 007, most of your job is going to involve waiting. I hope you're a patient man."

He wasn't. But if his mission called for waiting, he waited.

Sooner than he had expected, a fragment of light hit the wall and he rose to look out of one of the front windows. A car bounded toward the inn, then stopped in the undergrowth near the front door.

Someone emerged from the vehicle. Bond's eyes narrowed. It was Felicity Willing. She was clutching her belly.

Holstering his gun, Bond pushed through the front door and ran toward her. "Felicity!"

She struggled forward but fell to the gravel. "James, help me! I'm . . . Help me! I'm hurt."

As he approached he saw a red stain on the front of her shirt. Her fingers, too, were bloodied. He dropped to his knees and cradled her. "What happened?"

"I went to . . . I went to check on a shipment at the docks. There was a man there," she gasped. "He pulled out a gun and shot me! He didn't say anything—just shot me and ran. I made it back into the car and drove here. You have to help me!"

"The police? Why didn't you—"

"He *was* a policeman, James."

"*What?*"

"I saw a badge on his belt."

Bond lifted her and carried her into the break-fast room, laying her gently on some dust sheets that were stacked against the wall. "I'll find a bandage," he murmured. Then he said angrily, "This is my fault. I should have worked it out! *You*'re the target of Incident Twenty. Lamb's not after a cruise liner; it's the food ships. He was hired by one of those agribusiness companies in America and Europe you were telling me about, to kill you and destroy the food. He must've paid someone in the police to help him."

"Don't let me die!"

"You'll be fine. I'll get some bandages and call Bheka. We can trust her."

He started toward the kitchen.

"No," Felicity said. Her voice was eerily calm and steady.

Bond stopped. He turned.

"Throw your mobile away, James."

He was staring at her sharp green eyes, focused on him like a predator's. In her hand was his own weapon, the Walther PPS.

He slapped his holster, from which she'd slipped the gun as he'd whisked her inside.

"The phone," she repeated. "Don't touch the screen. Just hold it by the side and toss it into the corner of the room."

He did as she instructed.

"I'm sorry," she said. "I'm so sorry."

And James Bond believed that, in some very tiny part of her heart, she was.

Chapter 67

"What's that?" James asked, gesturing at her blouse.

It was blood, of course. Real blood. Hers. Felicity still felt the sting in the back of her hand where she'd pricked a vein with a safety pin. It had bled sufficiently to stain her shirt and make a credible appearance of a bullet wound.

She didn't answer him. But the agent's eyes noted her bruised hand and revealed that he'd deduced what she'd done. "There was no cop on the dock."

"I lied, didn't I? Sit down. On the floor."

When he had done so, Felicity had worked the slide of the Walther, which ejected one round, but made sure one was in the chamber, ready to fire. "I know you're trained to disarm people. I've killed before and it has no effect on me. It's not essential that you stay alive, so I'm happy to shoot you now if you make any move."

Her voice, though, almost caught on "happy." *What the hell is the matter with you?* she asked herself angrily. "Put them on." She tossed handcuffs toward him.

He caught them. Good reflexes, she noted. She stepped back three feet or so.

Felicity smelled the pleasant scent from where he'd gripped her a moment ago. It would be soap or shampoo from the hotel. He was not an aftershave sort of man.

The anger again. Damn him!

"The cuffs," she repeated.

A hesitation, then he ratcheted them on to his wrists. "So? Explain."

"Tighter."

He squeezed the mechanism. She was satisfied.

"Who exactly do you work for?" she asked.

"An outfit in London. We'll have to leave it at that. So, you're working with Lamb?"

She gave a laugh. "With that fat sweaty fool? No. Whatever he's coming here for, it has nothing to do with my project tonight. It's probably some ridiculous business venture he has in mind. Maybe buying this place. I was lying when I told you I'd heard him referred to as Noah."

"Then what are you doing here?"

"I'm here because I'm sure you've briefed your bosses in London that Lamb's your main suspect."

A flicker in his eyes confirmed this.

"What Captain Jordaan and her moderately competent officers will find in the morning here is a fight to the death. You and the traitor who was going to bomb a cruise liner, Gregory Lamb, and anybody he was meeting here. You found them and there was a gunfight. Everybody died. There'll be loose ends but, on the whole, the matter will go away. Or at least go away from me."

"Leaving you free to do whatever it is you're doing. But I don't understand. Who the hell is Noah?"

"It's not a who, James, it's a what. N-O-A-H."

Confusion in his handsome face. Then understanding dawned. "My God . . . your group is the International Organization Against Hunger. IOAH.

At the fund-raiser you said you'd recently expanded to make it international in scope. Which meant that it used to be National Organization Against Hunger. NOAH."

She nodded.

Frowning, he mused, "In the text we intercepted last weekend, 'noah' was typed all lowercase. Everything else in the message was too. I just assumed it was a name."

"We were careless there. It hasn't been NOAH for a while but that was the original name and we still refer to it like that."

"We? Who sent that message?"

"Niall Dunne. He's *my* associate, not Hydt's. He's just on loan to Green Way."

"Yours?"

"Been working together for a few years now."

"And how did you get with Hydt?"

"Niall and I work with a lot of warlords and dictators in sub-Saharan Africa. Nine, ten months ago Niall heard about Hydt's plan, this Gehenna, through some of them. It was pretty far-fetched but there was a good chance of a decent return on investment. I gave Dunne ten million to put into the pot. He told Hydt it was from an anonymous businessman. A condition for the money was that Dunne himself worked with Hydt to oversee how it was spent."

"Yes," Bond said, "he mentioned other investors. So Hydt knew nothing about you?"

"Nothing at all. And it turned out that Severan was delighted to use Dunne as a tactical planner. Gehenna wouldn't have got nearly so far without him."

"The man who thinks of everything."

"Yes, he was rather proud that Hydt described him like that."

James said, "There was another reason Dunne stayed close to Hydt, though. Right? He was your escape plan, a possible diversion."

Felicity said, "If somebody got suspicious—just as you did—we'd sacrifice Hydt. Make him the fall guy so nobody would look any further. That was why Dunne convinced Hydt that the bombing in York should happen today."

"You'd just sacrifice ten million dollars?"

"Good insurance is expensive."

"I always wondered why Hydt kept going with his plan—after I turned up in Serbia and in March. I was careful to cover my tracks but he accepted me a lot more readily here, as Gene Theron, than I would have. That was because Dunne kept telling him I was safe."

She nodded. "Severan always listened to Niall Dunne."

"So it was Dunne who planted the reference on the Internet to Hydt's nickname being Noah. And that he used to build his own boats in Bristol."

"That's right." Her anger and disappointment blossomed again. "But dammit! Why didn't you let it go when you should have—after Hydt was dead?"

He was looking at her coldly. "And then what? You'd wait for me to fall asleep next to you . . . and cut my throat?"

She snapped, "I hoped you were who you claimed to be, a mercenary from Durban. That was why I kept on at you last night, asking if you could change—giving you the chance to confess you really were a killer.

I thought things might . . ." Her voice trickled to silence.

"Work out between us?" His lips tightened. "If it matters, I thought so too."

Ironic, Felicity thought. She was bitterly disappointed that he had turned out to be one of the good guys. He must be equally disappointed to discover that she was not at all what she'd seemed.

"So what are you doing tonight? What is the project we've been calling Incident Twenty?" he asked, shifting on the floor. The cuffs jingled.

Keeping the gun trained on him, she said, "You know about world conflict?"

"I listen to the BBC," he responded dryly.

"When I was a banker in the City my clients sometimes invested in companies in trouble spots of the world. I got to know those regions. The one thing I noticed was that in every single conflict zone, hunger was a critical factor. Those who were hungry were desperate. You could get them to do anything if you promised them food—switch political loyalties, fight, kill civilians, overthrow dictatorships or democracies. Anything. It occurred to me that hunger could be used as a weapon. So that's what I became—an arms dealer, you could say."

"You're a hunger broker."

Well put, Felicity thought.

Smiling coolly, she continued: "The IOAH controls thirty-two percent of the food aid coming into the country. We'll soon be doing the same in various Latin American countries, India, Southeast Asia. If, say, a warlord in the Central African Republic wants to get into power and he pays me what I ask, I'll make sure his soldiers and the people supporting him get all the food they need and his opponent's followers get nothing."

He blinked in surprise. "Sudan. *That's* what's happening tonight—war in Sudan."

"Exactly. I've been working with the central authority in Khartoum. The president doesn't want the Eastern Alliance to break away and form a secular state. The regime in the east plans to solidify their ties to the UK and shift their oil sales there rather than to China. But Khartoum's not strong enough to subdue the east without assistance. So it's paying me to supply food to Eritrea, Uganda and Ethiopia. Their troops will invade simultaneously with the central forces. The Eastern Alliance won't stand a chance."

"So the thousands of deaths in the message we intercepted—that's the body count of the initial invasion tonight."

"That's right. I had to guarantee a certain loss of life of Eastern Alliance troops. If the number is more than two thousand, I get a bonus."

"The adverse impact on Britain? That the oil's going to Beijing, not to us?"

A nod. "The Chinese helped Khartoum pay my bill."

"When does the fighting start?"

"In about an hour and a half. As soon as the food planes are in the air and the ships are in international waters, the invasion of eastern Sudan begins." Felicity looked at her demure Baume & Mercier watch. She supposed Gregory Lamb would arrive soon. "Now, I need to broker something else: your cooperation."

He laughed coldly.

"If you don't, your friend Bheka Jordaan will die. Simple as that. I have many friends throughout Africa who are quite skilled at killing and happy to put those talents to work."

She was pleased to see how this troubled him. Felicity Willing always enjoyed finding people's weaknesses.

"What do you want?" he asked.

"You send a message to your superiors that you've confirmed Gregory Lamb is behind an attempted cruise-ship bombing. You've managed to stop the plot and you'll be meeting with him soon."

"You know I can't do that."

"We're negotiating for the life of your friend. Come on, James, be a proper hero. You're going to die anyway."

He turned his eyes to her and repeated, "I really thought it might work out between us."

A shiver ran down Felicity Willing's spine.

But then Bond's eyes grew stony and he snapped, "Okay, that's enough. We have to move fast."

She frowned. What was he talking about?

He added, "Try to use nonlethal force on her . . . if you can."

"Oh, Christ, no," Felicity whispered.

A tidal wave of light—the overheads—came on and, as she started to turn toward the sound of running feet, the Walther was ripped out of her hand. She was slammed onto her belly by two people, one of whom knelt hard in the small of her back and secured her hands expertly behind her with handcuffs.

Felicity heard a crisp voice, a woman's: "In accordance with Section Thirty-five of the Constitution of South Africa, nineteen ninety-six, you have the right to remain silent and to be advised that any statements made to your arresting officers can be used as evidence in trial against you."

Chapter 68

"No!" Felicity Willing gasped, her face a mask of disbelief. Then the word was repeated in rage, nearly a scream.

James Bond looked down at the petite woman sitting on the floor in about the same place that he had been a moment before. She shouted, "You knew! You son of a bitch, you knew! You never suspected Lamb at all!"

"I lied, didn't I?" he said coldly, throwing the words back at her.

Bheka Jordaan was also gazing down at her, unemotionally, assessing her prisoner.

Bond was rubbing his wrists, from which the cuffs had been removed. Gregory Lamb was nearby, on his mobile.

Lamb and Jordaan had arrived before Bond to plant microphones and monitor the conversation, in case Felicity took the bait. They'd hidden in the workers' caravan; Bond's flash of the torch earlier had verified they were invisible and alerted them that he was going inside. He hadn't wanted to use radio transmissions.

Jordaan's phone rang and she answered it. She listened, jotting information in her notebook, then said, "My people have raided Ms. Willing's office. We've got the landing locations of all the planes and the routes of the ships delivering the food."

Gregory Lamb looked over her notes and relayed

the information into his phone. While the man did not instill confidence as an intelligence agent, apparently he indeed had his contacts on the continent and he was using them now.

"You can't do this!" Felicity wailed. "You don't understand!"

Bond and Jordaan ignored her and stared at Lamb. Finally he disconnected. "There's an American carrier off the coast. They've launched fighters to intercept the food planes. And RAF and South African attack helicopters are on their way to turn the ships."

Bond thanked the big, sweating man for his efforts. He'd never suspected Lamb, whose odd behavior stemmed from the fact that he was essentially a coward. He'd admitted that he'd disappeared during the action at the Green Way plant to avoid getting shot, though stopped short of confessing that he'd fired a bullet across his own sleeve. But Bond had thought him the perfect bait to lay before his suspect, Felicity Willing.

Bheka Jordaan took a call too. "Backup's going to be a little delayed—bad accident on Victoria Road. But Kwalene says they should be here in twenty or thirty minutes."

Bond looked down at Felicity. Even now, sitting on the filthy floor of this decrepit construction site, she radiated defiance, a caged, angry lioness.

"How . . . how did you know?" she asked.

They could hear the soothing yet powerful sound of the Atlantic crashing on the rocks, birds calling, a far-off car horn bleating. This place wasn't far from the center of Cape Town but the city seemed a universe away.

"A number of things made me wonder," Bond told her. "The first was Dunne himself. Why the mysterious funds transfer to his account yesterday—*before* Gehenna? That suggested Dunne had another partner. And so did another intercept we caught, mentioning that if Hydt was out of the picture, there were other partners who could proceed with the project. Who had that been sent to? One explanation was that it was somebody entirely independent of Gehenna.

"Then I remembered Dunne traveled to India, Indonesia and the Caribbean. At the fund-raiser you said your charity had opened offices in Mumbai, Jakarta and Port-au-Prince. Bit of a coincidence, that. Both you and Dunne had connections in London and Cape Town and you'd both had a presence in South Africa *before* Hydt opened the Green Way office here.

"And I made the NOAH connection on my own," Bond continued. When he was in SAPS headquarters he'd found himself staring at her card. IOAH. He'd suddenly realized there was merely one letter difference. "I checked company records in Pretoria and found the group's original name. So when you told me you'd heard Lamb referred to as Noah, I knew you were lying. That confirmed your guilt. But we still needed to trick you into telling us what you knew and what Incident Twenty was." He regarded her coldly. "I didn't have time for aggressive interrogation."

Purpose . . . response.

Not knowing Felicity's goal, this deception had been the best response he could put together.

Felicity eased herself toward the wall. The movement was accompanied by a glance out of the window.

Suddenly several thoughts coalesced in Bond's

mind: the shift of her eyes, the "accident" blocking Victoria Road, Dunne's genius for planning and the car horn, which had sounded about three minutes earlier. It had been a signal, of course, and Felicity had been counting down since it had blared in the distance.

"Incoming!" Bond cried and launched himself into Bheka Jordaan.

The two of them and Lamb tumbled to the floor as bullets crashed through the windows, filling the room with shards of glistening confetti.

Chapter 69

Bond, Lamb and Jordaan took cover as best they could, which wasn't easy because the entire north wall of the room was exposed. Table saws and the rest of the construction equipment provided some protection but they were still vulnerable, since the work lights and overheads gave the sniper a perfect view of the rooms.

Felicity hunkered down further.

"How many men does Dunne have with him?" Bond snapped to her.

She didn't answer.

He aimed close to her leg and fired a deafening shot, which spat splinters of wood into her face and chest. She screamed. "Just him for now," she whispered quickly. "He's got some other people on the way. Listen, just let me go and—"

"Shut up!"

So, Bond reflected, Dunne had used part of his money to bribe security forces in Mozambique to lie that he'd been spotted in the country while he had remained here to back up Felicity. And to hire mercenaries to extract them, if necessary.

Bond glanced round the breakfast room and the nearby lobby. There was simply no way to get to cover. Aiming carefully, he shot out the work lights but the overheads were still bright and too numerous to take out. They gave Dunne a perfect view of the interior. Bond rose but was rewarded with two close shots. He'd seen no target. There was some moonlight but the glare inside rendered outdoors black. He could tell Dunne was shooting from high ground, on the Apostles range. Yet the Irishman could be anywhere up there.

A moment or two passed, then more bullets crashed into the room, striking bags of plaster. The dust rose and Bond and Jordaan coughed. Bond noted that the angle of those shots had been different; Dunne was working his way into a position from which he could begin to pick them off.

"The lights," Lamb called. "We've got to get them out."

The switch, however, was in the passage to the kitchen and to get to it one of them would have to run past a series of glass doors and windows, presenting a perfect target to Dunne.

Bond tried but he was in the most vulnerable position and the instant he rose slugs slammed into a pillar and the tools beside him. He fell back to the floor.

"I'll go," said Bheka Jordaan. She was gauging distances to the light switch, Bond saw. "I'm closest. I think I can make it. Did I tell you, James, I was a star rugby player at university? I moved very quickly."

"No," Bond said firmly. "It's suicide. We'll wait for your officers."

"They won't be here in time. He'll be in position to kill us all in a few minutes. James, rugby is a wonderful game. Have you ever played?" She laughed. "No, of course not. I can't see you on a team."

His smile matched hers.

"You're better placed to give covering fire," Bond said. "That big Colt of yours'll scare the hell out of him. I'm going on three. One . . . two—"

Suddenly a voice called, "Oh, please!"

Bond looked toward Lamb, who continued, "Those countdown scenes in movies are such dreadful clichés. Nonsense. In real life nobody counts. You just stand up and go!"

Which was exactly what Lamb now did. He leaped to his meaty legs and lumbered toward the light switch. Bond and Jordaan both aimed into the blackness and fired covering rounds. They had no idea where Dunne was and it was unlikely that their slugs went anywhere near him. Yet whether they did or not, the rounds didn't deter the Irishman from firing a spot-on burst when Lamb was ten feet from the switch. The bullets shattered the windows beside him and found their target. A spray of the agent's blood painted the floor and wall and he lurched forward, collapsed and lay still.

"No," Jordaan cried. "Oh, no."

The casualty must have given Dunne some confidence, because the next shots were even closer to their mark. Finally Bond had to abandon his position. He crawled back to where Jordaan crouched behind a table saw, its blade dented by Dunne's .223 rounds.

Bond and the policewoman now pressed against each other. The black slits of windows glared at them. There was nowhere else to go. A bullet snapped over Bond's head—it broke the sound barrier inches from his ear.

He felt, but couldn't see, Dunne moving in for the kill.

Felicity said, "I can stop this. Just let me go. I'll call him. Give me a phone."

A muzzle flash, and Bond shoved Jordaan's head down as the wall beside them exploded. The slug actually tugged at the strands beside her ear. She gasped and pressed against him, shivering. The smell of burning hair wafted around them.

Felicity said, "Nobody'll know you let me escape. Give me a phone. I'll call Dunne."

"Oh, go to hell, bitch!" came a voice from across the room and, staggering to his feet, gripping his bloody chest, Lamb rose and charged to the far wall. He swept his hand down on the light switch as he dropped once more to the floor. The inn went dark.

Instantly Bond was on his feet, kicking out one of the side doors. He plunged into the brush to pursue his prey.

Thinking: Four rounds left, one more magazine.

Bond was sprinting through the brush that led to the base of the steep cliff, the Twelve Apostles ridge. He ran in an S pattern as Dunne fired toward him. The moon wasn't full but there was light to shoot by, yet none of the slugs hit closer than three or four feet from him.

Finally the Irishman stopped targeting Bond—he must have assumed he'd hit him or that he'd fled to find help. Dunne's goal, of course, wasn't necessarily to kill his victims but simply to keep them contained until his associates arrived. How soon would that be?

Bond huddled against a large rock. The night was now freezing cold and a wind had come up. Dunne would be about a hundred feet directly above him. His sniper's aerie was an outcrop of rock with a perfect view of the inn, the approaches to it . . . and of Bond himself in the moonlight, had Dunne simply leaned over and looked.

Then a powerful torch was signaling from the rocks above. Bond turned to where it was pointed. Offshore a boat churned toward the beach. The mercenaries, of course.

He wondered how many were on board and what they were armed with. In ten minutes the vessel would land and he and Bheka Jordaan would be overrun—Dunne would have made sure that Victoria Road remained impassable for longer than that. Still, he pulled out his phone and texted Kwalene Nkosi about the impending beach landing.

Bond looked back up the mountain face.

Only two approaches would lead him to Dunne. To the right, the south, there was a series of steep but smooth traverses—narrow footpaths for hikers—that led from the back of the Sixth Apostle Inn past the outcrop where Dunne lay. But if Bond went that way, he'd be exposed to Dunne's gunfire along much of the path; there was no cover.

The other option was to assault the castle directly: to climb straight up a craggy but steep rock face, one hundred vertical feet.

He studied this possible route.

Four years nearly to the day after his parents had died, fifteen-year-old James Bond had decided he'd had enough of the nightmares and fears that reared up when he looked at mountains or rock walls—even, say, the impressive but tame foundation of Edinburgh Castle as seen from the Castle Terrace car park. He'd talked a master at Fettes into setting up a climbing club, which made regular trips to the Highlands for the members to learn the sport.

It took two weeks but the dragon of fear had died

and Bond had added rock climbing to his repertoire of outdoor activities. He now holstered the Walther and looked up, reiterating to himself the basic rules: Use only enough strength for a sufficient grip, no more; use your legs to support your body, your arms for balance and shifting weight; keep your body close to the rock face; use momentum to peak at the dead point.

And so, with no ropes, no gloves, no chalk and in leather shoes—quite stylish but a fool's footwear on a damp face like this—Bond began his ascent.

Chapter 70

Niall Dunne was making his way down the face of the Twelve Apostles ridge, along the hiking trails that led to the inn. His Beretta pistol in hand, he carefully stayed out of sight of the man who'd masqueraded so cleverly as Gene Theron—the man Felicity had told him an hour or so ago was a British agent, first name James.

Although he couldn't see him any longer, Dunne had spotted the man a few minutes ago ascending the rock cliff. James had taken the bait and was assaulting the citadel—while Dunne had slipped out of the back door, so to speak, and was now moving carefully down the traverses. In five minutes he'd be at the inn, while the British agent would be fully occupied on the cliff face.

All according to the blueprint . . . well, the *revised* blueprint.

Now there was nothing for it but to get out of the country, fast and forever. Though not alone, of course. He would leave with the person he admired most in the world, the person he loved, the person who was the engine of all his fantasies.

His boss, Felicity Willing.

This is Niall. He's brilliant. He's my draftsman. . . .

She'd described him thus several years ago. His face had warmed with pleasure when he'd heard the words and now he carried them in his memory, like a lock of her hair, just as he carried the memory of their first job together, when she was a City investment banker and had hired him to inspect some works installations her client was lending money to complete. Dunne had rejected the shoddy job, saving her and the client millions. She'd taken him to dinner and he'd had too much wine and prattled on about how morality had no place in combat or business or, bloody hell, in *anything*. The beautiful woman had agreed. My God, he'd thought, here's somebody who doesn't care that my feet go in different directions, that I'm built out of spare parts, that I can't tell a joke or turn on the charm to save my life.

Felicity was his perfect match at detachment. Her passion for making money was identical to his for creating efficient machines.

They'd ended up in her luxurious flat in Knightsbridge and made love. It had been, without question, the best night of his life.

They had begun to work together more frequently, making the transition into jobs that were, well, not to put too fine a point on it, a bit more profitable and a lot less legitimate than taking a percentage of a revolving-credit construction loan.

The jobs had become bolder, darker and more lucrative, but the other thing—between them—well, that had changed . . . as he'd supposed all along it would. She didn't, she finally confessed, think of him in *that* way. The night they were together, yes, it had been wonderful and she was sorely tempted but she was worried that it would ruin their astonishing intellectual—no, *spiritual*—connection. Besides, she'd been hurt before, very badly. She was a bird with a broken wing that hadn't yet mended. Could they simply remain partners and friends, oh, please? You can be my draftsman. . . .

The story rang a bit hollow but he had chosen to believe her, as one will do when a lover spins a tale less painful than the truth.

But their business soared with success—an embezzlement here, some extortion there—and Dunne bided his time, because he believed that Felicity would come round. He made it seem that he, too, was over the romance. He managed to keep his obsession for her buried, as hidden and as explosive as a VS-50 land mine.

Now, though, everything had changed. They were soon to be together.

Niall Dunne believed this in his soul.

Because he was going to win her love by saving her. Against all the odds, he'd save her. He'd spirit her away to safety on Madagascar, where he'd created an enclave for them to live very comfortably.

As he approached the inn, Dunne was recalling that James had caught Hydt out with his comment about Isandlwana—the Zulu massacre in the 1800s. Now he was thinking of the *second* battle that day in January, the one at Rorke's Drift. There, a force of four thousand Zulus had attacked a small outpost and hospital manned by about 130 British soldiers. As impossible as it seemed, the British had successfully defended it, suffering minimal casualties.

What was significant about the battle to Niall Dunne, though, was the commander of the British troops, Lieutenant John Chard. He was with the Corps of Royal Engineers—a sapper, like Dunne. Chard had come up with a blueprint for the defense against overwhelming odds and executed it brilliantly. He'd earned the Victoria Cross. Niall Dunne was now about to win a decoration of his own—the heart of Felicity Willing.

Moving slowly through the autumn evening, he now arrived at the inn, staying well out of sight of the rock face and the British spy.

He considered his plan. He knew the fat agent was dead or dying. He remembered what he'd seen of the breakfast or dining room through the rifle scope before the man, irritatingly, had turned off the lights. The only other officer in the inn seemed to be the SAPS woman. He could easily take her—he would fling something through the window to distract her, then kill her and get Felicity out.

The two of them would sprint to the beach for the extraction, then speed to the helicopter that would take them to freedom in Madagascar.

Together . . .

He stepped silently to a window of the Sixth Apostle Inn. Looking in carefully, Dunne saw the British agent he'd shot, lying on the floor. His eyes were open, glazed in death.

Felicity sat on the floor nearby, her hands cuffed behind her, breathing hard.

Dunne was shaken by the sight of his love being so ill treated. More anger. This time it did not go away. Then he heard the policewoman, in the kitchen, make a call on her radio and ask about backup. "Well, how long is it going to be?" she snapped.

Probably some time, Dunne reflected. His associates had overturned a large lorry and set it on fire. Victoria Road was completely blocked.

Dunne slipped round the back of the hotel into the car park, overgrown and filled with weeds and rubbish, and went to the kitchen door. His gun before him, he eased it open without a sound. He heard the clatter of the radio, a transmission about a fire engine.

Good, he thought. The SAPS officer was concentrating on the radio call. He'd take her from behind.

He stepped further inside and moved down a narrow corridor to the kitchen. He could—

But the room was empty. On a counter sat the radio, the staticky voice rambling on and on. He realized that these were just random transmissions from the SAPS's central emergency dispatch, about fires, robberies, noise complaints.

The radio was set to scan mode, not communications.

Why had she done that?

This couldn't be a trap to lure him inside. James wouldn't possibly know that he'd left the sniper's nest and was here. He stepped to the window and gazed up at the rock face, where he could see the man climbing slowly.

His heart stuttered. No. . . . The vague form was exactly where it had been ten minutes ago. And Dunne realized that what he'd glanced at earlier on the rock face might not have been the spy at all but perhaps his jacket, draped over a rock and moving in the breeze.

No, no . . .

Then a man's voice said, in a smooth British accent, "Drop your weapon. Don't turn round or you'll be shot."

Dunne's shoulders slumped. He remained staring out at the Twelve Apostles ridge. He gave a brief laugh.

"Logic told me you'd climb to the sniper's nest. I was so certain."

The spy replied, "And logic told me you'd bluff and come here. I just climbed high enough to leave my jacket in case you looked."

Dunne glanced over his shoulder. The SAPS officer was standing beside the spy. Both were armed. Dunne could see the man's cold eyes. The South African officer was just as determined. Through the doorway, in the lobby, Dunne could also see Felicity Willing, his boss, his love, straining to look into the kitchen. Felicity called, "What's going on in there? Somebody answer me!"

My draftsman . . .

The British agent said harshly, "I won't tell you again. In five seconds I'll shoot into your arms."

There was no blueprint for this. And for once the inarguable logic of engineering and the science of mechanics failed Niall Dunne. He was suddenly amused, thinking that this would be perhaps the first wholly irrational decision he'd ever made. But did that mean it wouldn't succeed?

Faith, he'd been told, sometimes worked.

He leaped sideways on his long legs, dropping into a crouch, spinning about and aiming toward the woman officer first, his pistol rising.

Shattering the stillness, several guns sang, voices similar but differently pitched, in harmonies low and high.

Chapter 71

The ambulances and SAPS cars were arriving. A Recces special-forces helicopter was hovering over the vessel containing the mercenaries who'd come to collect Dunne and Felicity. Glaring spotlights pointed downward, as did the barrels of two 20-mm cannons. One short burst over the bow was enough to force the occupants to surrender.

An unmarked police car screeched up amid a cloud of dust, directly in front of the hotel. Kwalene Nkosi leaped out and nodded to Bond. Other officers joined them. Bond recognized some from the raid earlier today at the Green Way plant.

Bheka Jordaan assisted Felicity Willing to her feet. She asked, "Is Dunne dead?"

He was. Bond and Jordaan had fired simultaneously before the muzzle of his Beretta could rise to the threat position. He'd died a moment later, blue eyes as flat in death as they had been in life, though his last glance had been toward the room where Felicity sat, not at the pair who had shot him.

"Yes," Jordaan said. "I'm sorry." She spoke this with some sympathy, apparently having assumed a personal as well as professional connection between the two.

"*You're* sorry," Felicity responded cynically. "What good is he to me dead?"

Bond understood that she wasn't mourning the loss of a partner but of a bargaining chip.

Felicity Willful . . .

"Listen to me. You have no idea what you're up against," she muttered to Jordaan. "I'm the queen of food aid. I'm the one saving the starving babies. You may as well give up your badge right now if you try to arrest me. And if *that* doesn't impress you, remember my partners. You've cost some very dangerous people millions and millions of dollars today. Here's my offer. I'll close down my operation here. I'll move elsewhere. You'll be safe. I guarantee it.

"If you don't agree, you won't live out the month. Neither will your family. And don't think you're going to throw me into a secret prison somewhere. If there's even a hint that the SAPS treated a suspect illegally, the press and the courts'll crucify you."

"You're not going to be arrested," Bond told her.

"Good."

"The story everybody will hear is that you're fleeing the country after embezzling five million dollars from the IOAH treasury. Your partners aren't going to be interested in revenge on Captain Jordaan or anybody else. They'll be interested in finding you . . . and their money."

In reality, she'd be whisked off to a black site for extensive "discussions."

"You can't do that!" she raged, her green eyes fiery.

At that moment a black van pulled up. Two uniformed men got out and walked up to Bond. He recognized on their sleeves the chevron of the British Special Boat Service, depicting a sword over a motto Bond had always liked: "By Strength and Guile."

This was the rendition team Bill Tanner had arranged.

One saluted. "Commander."

The civilian Bond nodded. "Here's the package." A glance at Felicity Willing.

"What?" the lioness cried. "No!"

He said to the soldiers, "I'm authorizing you to execute an ODG Level Two project order dated Sunday last."

"Yes, sir. We have the paperwork. We'll handle it from here."

They led her away, struggling. She disappeared into their van, which sped down the gravel drive.

Bond turned back to Bheka Jordaan. But she was walking briskly to her car. Without looking back she climbed in, started the engine and drove away.

He walked up to Kwalene Nkosi and handed over Dunne's Beretta. "And there's a rifle up there, Warrant Officer. You'll want to get it down." He pointed out the general area where Dunne had been sniping.

"Yes indeed—my family and I hike here many weekends. I know the Apostles well. I'll collect it."

Bond's eyes were on Jordaan's car, the taillights receding. "She left rather quickly. She wasn't upset about the rendition, was she? Our embassy contacted your government. A magistrate in Bloemfontein approved the plan."

"No, no," the officer said. "Tonight Captain Jordaan has to take her *ugogo* to her sister's house. She is never late, not when it involves her grandmother."

Nkosi was watching closely as Bond stared after Jordaan's car. He laughed. "That woman is something, is she not?"

"She is indeed. Well, good night, Warrant Officer. You must get in touch if you're ever in London."

"I will do that, Commander Bond. I am not, I think, such a great actor, after all. But I do love my theater. Perhaps we could go to the West End and attend a play."

"Perhaps we could."

A traditional handshake followed, Bond pressing firmly, keeping the three-part rhythm smooth and, most important, making sure that he did not release his grip too soon.

Chapter 72

James Bond was sitting outside, in a corner of the terrace restaurant at the Table Mountain Hotel.

Calor gas heaters glowed overhead, sending down a cascade of warmth. The scent of propane was curiously appealing in the cool night air.

He held a heavy crystal glass containing Baker's bourbon, on ice. The spirit had the same DNA as the Basil Hayden's but was of higher proof; accordingly he swirled it to allow the cubes to mellow the impact, though he wasn't sure he wanted much mellowing, not after this evening.

Finally he took a long sip and glanced at the tables nearby, all of them occupied by couples. Hands caressed hands, knees pressed against knees, while secrets and promises were whispered on wine-scented breath. Veils of silky hair swirled as women tilted their heads to hear their companions' soft words.

Bond thought of Franschhoek and Felicity Willing.

What would Saturday's agenda have been? Was she planning to tell Gene Theron, ruthless mercenary, about her career as a hunger broker and recruit him to join her?

And, if she had been the woman *he* had at first believed, the savior of Africa, would he have confessed to her that he was an operational agent for the British government?

But speculation irritated James Bond—it was a waste of time—and he was relieved when his mobile buzzed.

"Bill."

"So here's the overall position, James," Tanner said. "The troops in the countries surrounding eastern Sudan have stood down. Khartoum issued a statement that the West has once again 'interfered with the democratic process of a sovereign nation, in an attempt to spread feudalism throughout the region.'"

"'Feudalism'?" Bond asked, chuckling.

"I suspect the writer meant to say 'imperialism' but got muddled. Don't see why Khartoum can't just use Google to find a decent press agent like everyone else."

"And the Chinese? They've been deprived of quite a lot of discount petrol."

"They're hardly in a position to complain since they were partly responsible for what would have been a very unpleasant war. But the regional government in the Eastern Alliance is over the moon. Their governor let slip to the PM that they're voting to separate from Khartoum next year and hold democratic elections. They want long-term economic connections with us and America."

"And they have a lot of oil."

Tanner said, "Gushers, James, positive gushers. Now, nearly all the food that Felicity Willing was doling out is on its way back to Cape Town. The World Food Program is going to oversee distribution. It's a good outfit. They'll send it to places that need it." He then said, "Sorry to hear about Lamb."

"Walked into the line of fire to save us. He ought to get a posthumous commendation for it."

"I'll give Vauxhall Cross a bell and let them know. Now, sorry, James, but I need you back by Monday. Something's heating up in Malaysia. There's a Tokyo connection."

"Odd combination."

"Indeed."

"I'll be in at nine."

"Ten'll do. You've had a rather busy week."

They rang off and Bond had enough time for one sip of whiskey before the phone vibrated once more. He peered at the screen.

On the third buzz he hit answer.

"Philly."

"James, I've been reading the signals. My God— are you all right?"

"Yes. A bit of a rough day but it looks like we got everything sorted."

"You *are* the master of the understatement. So Gehenna and Incident Twenty were entirely different? I wouldn't have thought it. How did you suss it all out?"

"Correlation of analysis and, of course, you need to think three-dimensionally," Bond said gravely.

A pause. Then Philly Maidenstone asked, "You're winding me up, aren't you, James?"

"I suppose I am."

A faint trickle of laughter. "Now, I'm sure you're knackered and need to get some rest but I found one more piece of the Steel Cartridge puzzle. If you're interested."

Relax, he told himself.

But he couldn't. Had his father been a traitor or not?

"I've got the identity of the KGB mole inside Six, the one who was murdered."

"I see." He inhaled slowly. "Who was he?"

"Hold on a second . . . where is it now? I *did* have it."

Agony. He struggled to stay calm.

Then she said, "Ah, here we go. His cover name was Robert Witherspoon. Recruited by a KGB handler when he was at Cambridge. He was shoved in front of a tube train at Piccadilly Circus by a KGB active-measures agent in nineteen eighty-eight."

Bond closed his eyes. Andrew Bond had not been at Cambridge. And he and his wife had died in 1990, on a mountain in France. His father had been no traitor. Neither had he been a spy.

Philly continued, "But I also found that *another* MI6 freelance operator was killed as part of Steel Cartridge, not a double—considered quite a superstar agent, apparently, working counterintelligence, tracking down moles in Six and the CIA."

Bond swirled this around in his mind, like the whiskey in his glass. He said, "Do you know anything about his death?"

"Pretty hush-hush. But I do know it occurred around nineteen ninety, somewhere in France or Italy. It was disguised as an accident, too, and a steel cartridge was left at the scene as a warning to other agents."

A wry smile crossed Bond's lips. So maybe his father *had* been a spy after all—though not a traitor. At least, not to his country. But, Bond reflected, had he been a traitor to his family and to his son? Hadn't

Andrew been foolhardy in taking young James along when he was meeting enemy agents he was trying to trick?

"But one thing, James. You said 'his death.'"

"How's that?"

"The Six counterintelligence op who was killed in nineteen ninety—you said 'his.' A signal in the archives suggested the agent was a woman."

My God, Bond thought. No. . . . His *mother* a spy? Monique Delacroix Bond? Impossible. But she *was* a freelance photojournalist, which was a frequently used nonofficial cover for agents. And she was by far the more adventurous of his parents; it was she who had encouraged her husband to take up rock climbing and skiing. Bond also recalled her polite but firm refusal to let young James accompany her on photographic assignments.

A mother, of course, would never endanger her child, whatever tradecraft recommended.

Bond didn't know the recruitment requirements back then but presumably the fact that she was Swiss-born would not have been an obstacle to her working as a contract op.

There was more research to do, of course, to confirm the suspicion. And, if it was true, he would find out who had ordered the killing and who had carried it out. But that was for Bond alone to pursue. He said, "Thanks, Philly. I think that's all I need. You've been a star. You deserve an OBE."

"A Selfridges gift voucher will do. . . . I'll stock up when they have Bollywood week in the food hall."

Ah, another instance of their similar interests. "In that case, better yet, I'll take you to a curry house I know in Brick Lane. The best in London. They're not fully licensed but we can bring a bottle of one of those Bordeaux you were talking about. A week on Saturday, how's that?"

She paused, consulting her calendar, Bond guessed. "Yes, James, that'll be great."

He imagined her again: the abundant red hair, the sparkling golden-green eyes, the rustling as she crossed her legs.

Then she added, "And you'll have to bring a date."

The whiskey stopped halfway to his lips. "Of course," Bond said automatically.

"You and yours, Tim and me. It'll be such great fun."

"Tim. Your fiancé."

"You might've heard—we went through a bad patch. But he turned down a chance of a big job overseas to stay in London."

"Good man. Came to his senses."

"It's hardly his fault for considering it. I'm not easy to live with. But we decided to see if we could make it work. We have history together. Oh, do let's try for Saturday. You and Tim can talk cars and motorbikes. He knows quite a lot about them. More than I do, even."

She was talking quickly—too quickly. Ophelia Maidenstone was savvy, in addition to being clever, of course, and she was fully aware of what had happened between them at the restaurant last Monday. She'd sensed the very real connection they'd had and would be thinking even now that something might have developed . . . had the past not intruded.

The past, Bond reflected wryly: Severan Hydt's passion.

And his nemesis.

He said sincerely, "I'm very glad for you, Philly."

"Thank you, James," she said, a dash of emotion in her voice.

"But listen, I won't have you spending your life wheeling babies around Clapham in a pram. You're the best liaison officer we've ever had and I'm insisting on using you on every assignment I possibly can."

"I'll be there for you, James. Whenever and wherever you want me."

Under the circumstances, probably not the best choice of words, he reflected, smiling to himself. "I have to go, Philly. I'll ring you next week for the post-mortem on Incident Twenty."

They disconnected.

Bond ordered another drink. When it arrived, he drank half as he looked out over the harbor, though he was not seeing much of its spectacular beauty. And his distraction had nothing—well, little—to do with Ophelia Maidenstone's repaired engagement.

No, his thoughts dealt with a more primal theme.

His mother, a spy . . .

Suddenly a voice intruded on his turbulent musings. "I'm late. I'm sorry."

James Bond turned to Bheka Jordaan, sitting down across from him. "She's well, Ugogo?"

"Oh, yes, but at my sister's she made us all watch a *'Sgudi 'Snaysi* rerun."

Bond lifted an eyebrow.

"A Zulu-language sitcom from some years ago."

It was warm under the terrace's heater and Jordaan slipped off her navy blue jacket. Her red shirt had short sleeves and he could see that she had not used makeup on her arm. The scar inflicted by her former coworkers was quite prominent. He wondered why she was not concealing it tonight.

Jordaan regarded him carefully. "I was surprised you accepted my invitation to dinner. I am paying, by the way."

"That's not necessary."

Frowning, she said briskly, "I didn't assume it was."

Bond said, "Thank you, then."

"I wasn't sure I'd ask you. I actually debated for some time. I'm not a person who debates much. I usually decide rather quickly, as I think I've told you." She paused and looked away. "I'm sorry your date in the wine country didn't work out."

"Well, all things considered, I'd rather be here with you than in Franschhoek."

"I should think so. I'm a difficult woman but not a mass murderer." She added ominously, "But you should not flirt with me . . . Ah, don't deny it! I remember very well your look in the airport the day you arrived."

"I flirt a lot less than you think I do. Psychologists have a term for that. It's called projecting. You project your feelings on to me."

"That remark in itself is flirtatious!"

Bond laughed and gestured the sommelier forward. He displayed the bottle of the South African sparkling wine Bond had ordered to be brought when his companion arrived. The man opened it.

Bond tasted it and nodded approval. Then he said to Jordaan, "You'll like this. A Graham Beck Cuvée Clive. Chardonnay and pinot noir. The 2003 vintage. It's from Robertson, the Western Cape."

Jordaan gave one of her rare laughs. "Here I've been lecturing you about South Africa but it seems you know a few things yourself."

"This wine's as good as anything you'll get in Reims."

"Where is that?"

"France—where champagne is made. East of Paris. A beautiful place. You'd enjoy it."

"I'm sure it's lovely but apparently there's no need to go there if our wine is as good as theirs."

Her logic was unassailable. They tilted their glasses toward each other. "*Khotso*," she said. "Peace."

"*Khotso*."

They sipped and sat for some moments in silence. He was surprisingly comfortable in the company of this "difficult woman."

She set her glass down. "May I ask?"

"Please," Bond responded.

"When Gregory Lamb and I were in the caravan at the Sixth Apostle, recording your conversation with Felicity Willing, you said to her that you'd hoped it might work out between you two. Was that true?"

"Yes."

"Then I'm sorry. I've had some bad luck too when it comes to relationships. I know what it's like when the heart turns against you. But we're resilient creatures."

"We are indeed. Against all odds."

Her eyes slipped away and she stared at the harbor for a time.

Bond said, "It was my bullet that killed him, you know—Niall Dunne, I mean."

Startled, she began, "How did you know I was . . . ?" Her voice faded.

"Was that the first time you'd shot someone?"

"Yes, it was. But how can you be sure it was your bullet?"

"I'd decided at that range to make my target vector a head shot. Dunne had one wound in his forehead and one in the torso. The head shot was mine. It was fatal. The lower wound, yours, was superficial."

"You're sure it was your shot in his head?"

"Yes."

"Why?"

"In that shooting scenario I wouldn't've missed," Bond said simply.

Jordaan was silent for a moment. Then she said, "I suppose I'll have to believe you. Anyone who uses the phrases 'target vector' and 'shooting scenario' surely would know where his bullets went."

Earlier, Bond thought, she might have said this with derision—a reference to his violent nature and flagrant disregard for the rule of law—but now she was simply making an observation.

They sat back and chatted for a time, about her family and his life in London, his travels.

Night was cloaking the city now, a kind autumn evening of the sort that graces this part of the Southern Hemisphere, and the vista sparkled with fixed lights on land and floating lights on vessels. Stars, too, except in the black voids nearby—where the king and prince of Cape Town's rock formations blocked out the sky: Table Mountain and Lion's Head.

The plaintive baritone call of a horn reached up to them from the harbor.

Bond wondered if its source was one of the ships delivering food.

Or perhaps it was from a tour boat bringing people back from the prison museum on nearby Robben Island, where people like Nelson Mandela, Kgalema Motlanthe and Jacob Zuma—all of whom had become presidents of South Africa—had been locked away for so many hard years during apartheid.

Or maybe the horn was from a cruise ship preparing to depart for other ports of call, summoning tired passengers, carrying bags of cling-film-wrapped *biltong*, pinotage wine and ANC black, green and yellow tea towels, along with their tourist impressions of this complicated country.

Bond gestured to the waiter, who proffered menus. As the policewoman took one, her wounded arm brushed his elbow briefly. And they shared a smile, which was slightly less brief.

Yet despite the personal truth-and-reconciliation occurring between them at the moment, Bond knew that, when dinner concluded, he would put her into a taxi that would take her to Bo-Kaap and return to his room to pack for his flight to London tomorrow morning.

He knew this, as Kwalene Nkosi would say, without doubt.

Oh, the idea of a woman who was perfectly attuned to him, with whom he could share all secrets—could share his life—appealed to James Bond and had proved comforting and sustaining in the past. But in the end, he now realized, such a woman, indeed *any* woman, could occupy but a small role in the peculiar reality in which he lived. After all, he was a man whose purpose found him constantly on the move, from place to place, and his survival and peace of mind required that this transit be fast, relentlessly fast, so that he might overtake prey and outpace pursuer.

And, if he correctly recalled the poem Philly Maidenstone had so elegantly quoted, traveling fast meant traveling forever alone.

Glossary

AIVD: Algemene Inlichtingen-en Veiligheidsdienst. The Netherlands security service, focusing on intelligence gathering and combating internal, nonmilitary threats.

BIA: Bezbednosno-informativna Agencija. The Serbian foreign intelligence and internal security agency.

CIA: Central Intelligence Agency. The main foreign intelligence-gathering and espionage organization of the United States. Ian Fleming reportedly played a role in the founding of the CIA. During the Second World War, he penned an extensive memo on creating and running an espionage operation for General William "Wild Bill" Donovan, head of America's Office of Strategic Services. Donovan was instrumental in the formation of OSS's successor, the CIA.

COBRA: Cabinet Office Briefing Room A. A senior-level crisis-response committee in the United Kingdom, usually headed by the prime minister or other high-ranking government official and composed of individuals whose jobs are relevant to a particular threat facing the nation. Although the name usually includes—in the media, at least—a reference to Conference Room A in the main Cabinet Office building in Whitehall, it could convene in any meeting room.

Crime Combating and Investigation Division of SAPS, the South African Police Service (see below): The major investigative unit. It specializes primarily in serious crimes, such as murder, rape and terrorism.

DI: Defense Intelligence. The British military's intelligence operation.

Division Three: A fictional security organ of the British government based in Thames House. Loosely affiliated with the Security Service (see below), Division Three engages in tactical and operational missions within the UK's borders to investigate and neutralize threats.

FBI: Federal Bureau of Investigation. The main domestic security agency in the United States, responsible for investigating criminal activities within the borders and certain threats to the United States and its citizens abroad.

Five: Informal reference to MI5, the Security Service (see below).

FO or FCO: The Foreign and Commonwealth Office. The main diplomatic and foreign policy agency of the United Kingdom, headed by the foreign secretary, who is a senior member of the cabinet.

FSB: Federal'naya Sluzhba Bezopasnosti Rossiyskoy Federatsii. The domestic security agency within Russia. Similar to the FBI (see above) and the Security Service (see below). Formerly the KGB (see below) performed this function.

GCHQ: Government Communications Headquarters. The government agency in the United Kingdom that collects and analyzes foreign signals intelligence. Similar to the NSA (see below) in America. Also referred to as the Doughnut, because of the shape of the main building, which is located in Cheltenham.

GRU: Glavnoye Razvedyvatel'noye Upravleniye. The Russian military intelligence organization.

KGB: Komitet Gosudarstvennoy Bezopasnosti. The Soviet foreign intelligence and domestic security organization until 1991, when it was replaced by the SVR (see below) for foreign intelligence and the FSB (see above) for internal intelligence and security.

Metropolitan Police Service: The police force whose jurisdiction is Greater London (excluding the City of London, which has its own police). Known informally as the Met, Scotland Yard, or the Yard.

MI5: The Security Service (see below).

MI6: The Secret Intelligence Service (see below).

MoD: Ministry of Defense. The organization within the United Kingdom overseeing the armed forces.

NIA: National Intelligence Agency. The domestic security agency of South Africa, like MI5 (see above) or the FBI (see above).

NSA: National Security Agency. The government agency in the United States that collects and analyzes foreign signals and related intelligence, from mobile phones, computers and the like. It is the American version of the UK's GCHQ (see above), with which it shares facilities both in England and the United States.

ODG: Overseas Development Group. A covert operational unit of British security operating largely independently but ultimately under the control of the UK's Foreign and Commonwealth Office (see above). Its purpose is to identify and eliminate threats to the country by extraordinary means. The fictional ODG operates from an office building near Regent's Park, London. James Bond is an agent with the 00 Section of O (Operations) Branch of the ODG. Its director-general is known as M.

SAPS: South African Police Service. The main domestic police operation serving South Africa. Its efforts range from street patrol to major crime.

SAS: Special Air Service. The British Army's special forces unit. It was formed during the Second World War.

SBS: Special Boat Service. The Royal Navy's special forces unit. It was formed during the Second World War.

Security Service: The domestic security agency in the United Kingdom, responsible for investigating both foreign threats and criminal activities within the borders. It corresponds to the FBI (see above) in the United States, though it is primarily an investigative and surveillance operation—unlike the FBI, it has no authority to make arrests. Known informally as MI5, or Five.

SIS: Secret Intelligence Service. The foreign-intelligence-gathering and espionage agency of the United Kingdom. It corresponds to the CIA in the United States. Known informally as MI6, or Six.

SOCA: Serious Organized Crime Agency. The law-enforcement organization within the United Kingdom responsible for investigating major criminal activity inside the borders. Its agents and officers have the power of arrest.

Spetznaz: Voyska Spetsialnogo Naznacheniya. A general reference to special forces in the Russian intelligence community and the military.

SVR: Sluzhba Vneshney Razvedk. The Russian foreign-intelligence-gathering and espionage agency. Formerly the KGB (see above) performed this function.

Acknowledgments

All novels are to some extent collaborative efforts, and this one more so than most. I wish to express my deep appreciation to the following for so tirelessly assisting to make sure this project got off the ground and that it grew into the best book it could be: Sophie Baker, Francesca Best, Felicity Blunt, Jessica Craig, Sarah Fairbairn, Cathy Gleason, Jonathan Karp, Sarah Knight, Victoria Marini, Carolyn Mays, Zoe Pagnamenta, Betsy Robbins, Deborah Schneider, Simon Trewin, Corinne Turner and my friends in the Fleming family. Special thanks go to the copyeditor of all copyeditors, Hazel Orme, as well as Vivienne Schuster, whose inspired title graces the novel.

Finally, thanks to the operatives of my own Overseas Development Group: Will and Tina Anderson, Jane Davis, Julie Deaver, Jenna Dolan and, of course, Madelyn Warcholik.

And for readers thinking that Cape Town's Table Mountain Hotel I mention in the book sounds familiar, that's because its inspiration is the Cape Grace, which is just as lovely but is not—to my knowledge—populated by any spies.

About Ian Fleming

Ian Fleming, creator of James Bond, was born in London on May 28, 1908. He was educated at Eton and later spent a formative period in Kitzbuhel, Austria, where he learned languages and made his first tentative forays into fiction writing. In the 1930s he worked for Reuters, where he honed his writing skills and, thanks to a Moscow posting, gained valuable insights into what would become his literary bête noire—the Soviet Union.

He spent the Second World War as Assistant to the Director of Naval Intelligence, where his fertile imagination spawned a variety of covert operations, all of them notable for their daring and ingenuity. The experience would provide a rich source of material in the future.

After the war he worked as foreign manager of the *Sunday Times,* a job that allowed him to spend two months each year in Jamaica. Here, in 1952, at his home Goldeneye, he wrote a book called *Casino Royale.* It was published a year later—and James Bond was born. For the next twelve years Fleming produced a novel a year featuring agent 007, the most famous spy of the century. His interest in cars, travel, good food and beautiful women, as well as his love of golf and gambling, was reflected in the books that were to sell in the millions, boosted by the vastly successful film franchise.

His literary career was not restricted to Bond.

Apart from being an accomplished journalist and travel writer he also wrote *Chitty Chitty Bang Bang*, a much-loved children's story about a car that flies, which has inspired both film and stage productions. He was a notable bibliophile, amassing a library of first editions which was considered so important that it was evacuated from London during the Blitz. And from 1952 he managed his own specialist publishing imprint, Queen Anne Press.

Fleming died of heart failure in 1964 at the age of fifty-six. He lived to see only the first two Bond films, *Dr. No* and *From Russia With Love*, and can scarcely have imagined what he had set in motion. Yet today, with a Bond film having been seen by an estimated one in five of the planet's population, James Bond has become not only a household name but a global phenomenon.

For further information about Ian Fleming and his books please visit www.ianfleming.com.

About Jeffery Deaver

A former attorney and the *New York Times* bestselling author hailed as "the best psychological thriller writer around" (*The Times,* London), Jeffery Deaver is the originator of the acclaimed detective hero Lincoln Rhyme, featured in nine hit novels, including *The Bone Collector*—which became a Universal Pictures feature film starring Denzel Washington and Angelina Jolie—and *The Cold Moon,* which won a Grand Prix from the Japanese Adventure Fiction Association and was named Book of the Year by the Mystery Writers Association of Japan.

A lifelong fan of Ian Fleming's James Bond novels, Deaver was honored to be handpicked by Fleming's estate to carry on the literary tradition, beginning with his #1 international and *New York Times* bestseller *Carte Blanche.*

His numerous stand-alone novels include *The Devil's Teardrop,* which became a Lifetime Television movie; and *The Bodies Left Behind,* winner of the 2009 Best Novel of the Year award from the International Thriller Writers organization.

He's been nominated for seven Edgar Awards from the Mystery Writers of America, an Anthony Award, and a Gumshoe Award, and was short-listed for the ITV3 Crime Thriller Award for Best International Author. He is a three-time recipient of the Ellery Queen

Readers Award for Best Short Story of the Year, and a winner of the British Thumping Good Read Award. He has also won a Steel Dagger for best thriller of the year for *Garden of Beasts* and a Short Story Dagger from the British Crime Writers' Association.

Visit www.jefferydeaver.com.